Avatars of the Pantheon
Book 1

Jackson Owens

Dedication

I would like to thank my loving wife Christina for putting up with me during the process of writing this book, and for being a supportive beta reader. My friend Will for being my second beta reader and providing quality feedback on the story and the book. I would like to thank the avatars who would not let me take the easy route on their stories and refused to leave me alone until I had their voice down pact. To the chaos that sparks big creation, the force of change that molded impromptu scenes into the larger narrative like they were always part of the plan, the war of good ideas that lead to turbulent battles until the best ideas stand tall the only survivors and the unity that keeps everything weaved together. And finally, I want to thank you the reader, I hope you have the same thrill reading this story that I had writing it.

Table of Contents

Introduction

From the author:

Welcome to the world of the Seven Kingdoms—an earth both familiar and foreign, shaped by ancient legacies, unbreakable alliances, and hidden conflicts. Here, seven great realms carve their place upon the land, each a pillar of power and influence. From the bustling trade routes of Opulentia to the shadowed halls of Umbrathorn, every kingdom thrives on its own unique strengths, yet none can stand alone. Beyond their borders, the ever-watchful Order of Saint Lorraine chronicles the world's history and guides the chosen avatars of the Twelve Goddesses, while the formidable Aurorium Clan, born from the ashes of slavery, upholds law and order with unshakable resolve. In this land of grand ambitions and whispered secrets, pirates and privateers sail the high seas, chasing fortune and freedom. The Seven Kingdoms are a realm of both opportunity and peril, where every choice shapes the fate of nations.

Opulentia, renowned as the kingdom of horse traders and master merchants, stands as the beating heart of commerce in the Seven Kingdoms. Trade is the lifeblood of this prosperous realm, where every deal is an opportunity and wealth flows like a mighty river. Its merchants are known for their cunning and resourcefulness, acquiring raw materials from one kingdom, commissioning artisans from another, and transforming their investments into coveted goods sold worldwide. Whether brokering deals in bustling markets or negotiating contracts in grand halls, the people of Opulentia master the art of trade, shaping economies and influencing the course of nations.

Laminae, the revered land of libraries, is a kingdom built upon the belief that knowledge is the greatest power of all. Its people are relentless in their pursuit of wisdom, devoting their lives to acquiring, preserving, and sharing knowledge in all its forms. Towering libraries brim with ancient tomes and cutting-edge discoveries they are monuments to their unyielding quest for understanding. Scholars, scribes, and seekers journey from every kingdom to Laminae, hoping to unearth lost secrets or contribute their insights to its ever-growing archives. In Laminae, every question is worth asking, and every answer holds the power to shape the future.

Verdantia, known far and wide as the Sacred Acres, is a kingdom where the land is revered and agriculture elevated to an art. Rolling fields, lush orchards, and fertile plains yield harvests unmatched across the world, sustaining not just their own people, but the entire Seven Kingdoms. Verdantia's farmers possess a near-mystical connection to the earth, blending ancient techniques with innovative cultivation to ensure abundance in every season. Humble in their craft yet proud of their legacy, they often say with quiet confidence, "The fields of Verdantia feed the world." Here, every seed is a promise— and every harvest, a testament to their devotion.

Stoneridge, a land of unforgiving terrain and unyielding spirit, stands as a testament to the resilience of its people. Harsh, rocky landscapes that would break lesser souls are shaped and tamed by the grit of Stonebridge's inhabitants. Here, hardship is not a burden but a forge, tempering people into warriors and artisans of unmatched skill. Masters of metallurgy, they craft weapons and armor of legendary quality, coveted by kings and feared by foes. Stonebridge's armies are a force to be reckoned with: hardened by their environment, sharpened by generations of conflict. They do not merely endure—they conquer, bending steel and stone to their will with disciplined might and peerless craftsmanship.

Magitekopolis, the radiant beacon of innovation, is a kingdom where magic and technology converge to shape the future. Its people are tireless visionaries, pushing the limits of possibility with wondrous machines and arcane devices that transform life across the Seven Kingdoms. Towering automata assist in daily labor, while intricate enchantments power entire cities—each invention a tribute to their brilliance and ambition. In the glowing workshops and gleaming laboratories of Magitekopolis, scholars and artificers labor with relentless drive, fueled by curiosity and an unshakable belief that progress is the key to a better world. To them, innovation is not just a pursuit, but their very way of life.

Islewind, the cradle of modern sailing, is a kingdom bound to the rhythm of the tides and the whisper of the wind. With an inseparable bond to the sea, its people are the finest sailors, fishermen, and shipwrights in all the Seven Kingdoms. Every vessel, from nimble fishing boats to towering warships, stands as proof of their craftsmanship and deep maritime heritage. The people of Islewind are born with salt in their veins and adventure in their hearts, charting bold courses into the unknown. Whether harvesting the ocean's bounty or navigating treacherous waters, they embody the spirit of mastery and exploration on the ever-changing seas.

The Umbrathorn Empire, a kingdom draped in secrecy and steeped in tradition, is a place where whispers wield power and beauty are woven into every thread of life. Renowned for exquisite textiles that rival the world's finest art, Umbrathorn's artisans craft fabrics of breathtaking intricacy and value. Yet behind the shimmering silks and opulent tapestries lies a culture veiled in mystery—a society bound by ancient oaths and silent understandings. Its people move with quiet elegance; their loyalties forged in shadow and tradition. To outsiders, Umbrathorn is an enigma: a place of veiled intentions and untold stories, where the past lingers like a shadow and nothing is ever quite as it seems.

Beyond the borders of the Seven Kingdoms lies the revered **Order of Saint Lorraine**—a neutral and ancient institution dedicated to the pursuit of knowledge and diplomacy. Bound by a sacred mission, the Order's scholars and emissaries journey across the known world, meticulously chronicling the histories, cultures, and magics that shape the Seven Kingdoms. Their vast archives preserve the wisdom of ages, safeguarding the triumphs and tragedies of nations alike. Yet their most unyielding tenet remains clear: they do not intervene in worldly affairs—they merely observe and record. Even in times of war and upheaval, the Order stands as impartial witnesses to history's unfolding. Still, one solemn duty transcends neutrality: guiding the avatars of the Twelve Goddesses and ensuring they fulfill their divine destinies. As silent observers and trusted advisors, the Order walks a delicate line between impartiality and influence; ever watchful, ever present.

Born from the chains of oppression, the **Aurorium Clan** now stands as the unwavering guardians of the Seven Kingdoms, enforcing law and protecting the people with steadfast resolve. Once the children of slaves, they have carved out their destiny, rising from bondage to become a force feared by the wicked and revered by the just. Bound by duty and discipline, the Aurorium serve as both shield and sword—preserving order, delivering justice, and ensuring that the hard-won freedoms of the past are never forgotten. Their presence is a living reminder that vigilance is the price of liberty, and through their sacrifice, the Seven Kingdoms remain secure. To the world, they are guardians; to those who break the law, they are an inescapable reckoning.

On the boundless high seas, where winds whisper promises of fortune and freedom, sails the infamous **Pirate Nation**—home to those who defy the kingdoms and live by their own code. For some, the lure of coin and sanctioned chaos draws them to a life of privateering, sailing and providing services under a royal decree. For others, the thrill of lawlessness births true piracy, where every raid is for self and no allegiance binds. Yet both pirates and privateers share a culture forged on salt, steel, and survival—marked by loyalty, rivalry, and an unshakable belief in freedom. In the Pirate Nation, allegiances shift like tides, and fortunes rise or fall with a single roll of the dice. To sail these waters is to dance with danger, for the sea belongs to no one—except those bold enough to seize it.

Chapter 1

Fourteen-year-old Sophie Griffin, ranked Sentinel in the Aurorium Clan, stepped into the office of Viceroy Kevin Longrin, the local representative of King Archimedes. She wore her standard plain clothes uniform: a purple suit, a long-billed purple fedora to match, and a crisp white shirt. The outfit might have seemed out of place, if not for her striking purple hair and eyes, which complemented her rich chocolate skin, pulling the whole look together effortlessly.

With a practiced ease, she set her backpack, stuffed with training clothes, equipment, and a snack lovingly packed by her momma down beside the coat rack. She placed her fedora on a hook, revealing two neatly styled afro-puffs perched atop her head. Turning with purpose, she straightened her posture in front of the secretary's desk, standing tall and composed just as she'd been trained to do countless times.

"Sentinel Griffin reporting for bodyguard duty," she announced, her voice steady and confident.

The secretary, a woman with short, curly brown hair and a warm, familiar smile, replied in an official yet playful tone, "Welcome, Sentinel Griffin. The Viceroy is away at a meeting, but he should return shortly. You're welcome to wait for him in his office."

Sophie grinned, and the two shared a soft giggle.

"Sophie, you're *still* a Sentinel?" the secretary asked, tilting her head with curiosity.

"The Shadow exam is next month. I just need to finish my application," Sophie said, pouring herself a cup of tea from the pot on the secretary's desk. She took a careful sip, letting the warmth settle her nerves. "How's Michael been?"

"Oh, he's doing great! His trade union master says he's a natural," Connie replied, her eyes twinkling with mischief. "Funny enough, he was asking about you too." A knowing smile played on her lips, hinting at her not-so-secret desire to play matchmaker between Sophie and her younger cousin.

Sophie felt a flush rise to her cheeks, a mixture of embarrassment and pride bubbling within her. She tried to play it cool, hiding behind her cup as she took another sip. "Oh, he was?" she said, her voice laced with forced nonchalance. "That's... nice."

Connie leaned in slightly, her voice adopting the affectionate tone that only an honorary aunt could pull off. "Sophie, this is your *Auntie Connie* you're talking to. You don't have to hide from me," she teased, her eyes sparkling with gentle mischief. "What should I tell him?"

Sophie shifted her stance but couldn't help the shy smile tugging at her lips. *Connie, is at it again*, but she did see right through her.

"Hmm," Connie mused, taking a sip of her own tea and giving Sophie a moment to squirm. "You're fourteen now, Miss Sentinel Sophie Griffin. You can't wait too long, you know."

Sophie rolled her eyes but couldn't suppress a grin. Setting her cup down, she carefully considered her words. "Tell him... I asked about him," she said slowly, then hesitated before adding, "And... that I was wondering if he'd be interested in taking a tour of the Frankstetter Complex."

Connie's grin widened. "I'll make sure he gets the message," she said, her tone dripping with amusement.

The door behind them creaked open, and Viceroy Longrin strode into the room, a briefcase in hand. His brows lifted in surprise at the sight of Sophie. "Sentinel Griffin, you're here already?"

Sophie set down her teacup with a quiet clink. "I came straight from morning training, Viceroy," she replied with practiced composure. "I didn't want to risk being late."

A small smile tugged at Longrin's lips as he passed Connie's desk and made his way to his office. "That's what I like about you, Sentinel Griffin. Always thinking ahead." He adjusted his grip on the briefcase. "Give me a few minutes, and I'll be ready."

"Of course, sir. I'll be here," Sophie said with a respectful nod.

The Viceroy disappeared into his office, and almost immediately, the soft rustle of papers and the opening and closing of drawers filled the air.

Sophie and Connie exchanged a glance; a silent understanding passing between them. Connie mouthed, *I'll tell him*, before returning to her paperwork with a small, amused smile.

Sophie took the moment to finish her tea, placing the empty cup carefully in the water basin. She put her hat back on her head with practiced ease, checking herself in the nearby mirror, then performed a quick check of her pistol. With a practiced flick, she spun the cylinder, confirming her usual loadout: four regular rounds and two fire shots. Satisfied, she holstered the weapon at her hip with a quiet click.

The office door swung open again, and Viceroy Longrin stepped out, now clad In a crisp white suit and black tie. A leather-bound book rested in his hand, an ink pen secured in a slot on the cover. He glanced at Connie.

"Miss Constance, I'll be making my rounds, followed by a meeting with the trade unions."

Connie nodded, already jotting down a note. "Understood, Viceroy. Should I expect you back before six?"

"Sometime after," he replied, shifting his gaze to Sophie. "Shall we, Miss Griffin?" He gestured toward the door.

"We shall," Sophie answered, adjusting her hat with a smooth, practiced touch before stepping out of the office. She led the way down the staircase to the street, her movements precise and deliberate. They exited through a side door, and once they reached the bustling road, the Viceroy naturally took the lead, their routine seamless.

As they walked, Sophie spoke in a calm, conversational tone. "Apex Molina asked me to congratulate you and your wife on the birth of your son." To any casual observer, the words might have seemed like polite small talk, but beneath them lay a carefully crafted smokescreen. Their steady conversation made it nearly impossible to notice Sophie subtly scanning the surroundings, her gaze sweeping for potential threats.

Viceroy Longrin played his role with practiced ease, a warm smile spreading across his face. "Please extend my thanks to Apex Molina," he responded smoothly. Without missing a beat, he added, "Has there been any word from Aurorium regarding the upcoming festival on the sea?" His tone remained casual, but both knew the performance was for protection; appearances had to be maintained at all times.

Sophie's eyes flicked briefly toward the crowd, her expression steady. "The only concern I've heard about is a rainstorm," she said evenly, her words carrying deeper meaning.

Rainstorm.

One of the three coded signals they had established. **Rain** meant all was clear—no threats detected. The other two were far more serious: **Taxes** signaled a potential threat requiring evaluation, while **Muffin** meant imminent danger and an immediate need to retreat.

Hearing the all-clear, the Viceroy gave a casual nod, adjusting his grip on his book as if their exchange were nothing more than idle conversation.

They stopped at a bustling vendor's booth overflowing with colorful dresses and finely crafted garments. The vendor, a large olive-skinned man, spread his arms wide in welcome. "Viceroy Longrin, you honor me today!" His voice boomed with warmth, and his attire, loose pants, a flowing shirt, and a sash belt, marked him as a native of the Islewind Kingdom. "I heard your wife has blessed you with a strong son."

The Viceroy chuckled, placing a hand over his chest. "Well, his lungs are certainly strong," he replied, implying his newborn had quite the powerful cry. "Tell me, Asad, how are things in Islewind?" As he spoke, his gaze flicked momentarily to Sophie, who was already scanning the crowd with quiet precision.

Her sharp eyes swept across the market, taking in the vibrant scene. Booths and tables spilled over with goods from across the Seven Kingdoms—clothes, trinkets, and sizzling fried foods rich with the spices of distant lands. But Sophie isn't here to browse. Her focus is trained on anyone paying too much attention to them.

With her purple suit and striking features, she knew she stood out. But noticing her was one thing, staring too long was another. Her gaze moved with efficient calm, cataloging faces. A woman herded children with practiced grace, keeping them out of trouble. An elderly man in a black hat scanned the wares, his interest squarely on merchandise. Harmless. Probably looking for something specific to buy.

A cluster of boys from her school strolled past, laughing and chatting, each holding a sausage roll from a nearby stand. Sophie glanced at the food with mild curiosity. **Verdantian sausage rolls**, she'd never tried one, but they looked delicious.

Behind her, Asad continued his enthusiastic pitch. "This would be the perfect outfit for your son!" he said, holding up a miniature version of his own clothing. The one-piece featured short sleeves, an open skirted bottom, and a red baby chick embroidered on the chest, its tiny wings outstretched.

The Viceroy stroked his chin thoughtfully. "That is nice. How much?"

Asad grinned broadly. "For you, Mr. Longrin, a special price. Only five coin."

Sophie nearly did a double take. That was barely the cost of a bread roll and a slice of meat. A bargain, she thought, keeping her expression neutral while her eyes remained vigilant.

Satisfied that no threats lurked nearby, Sophie allowed herself to tune back into the conversation—just in time to see the Viceroy hand Asad a small handful of gold coins in exchange for the outfit, now neatly tucked into a bag.

"You are too kind, Asad," the Viceroy said with a gracious nod.

3

"The pleasure is all mine," Asad replied, tucking the coins into a nearly invisible box on a shelf behind him. His smile remained warm as he offered a parting phrase in the Islewind tradition: "Have a great and prosperous day."

With a polite nod, the Viceroy responded in kind, and Sophie took one last sweeping glance around the market before falling back into step beside him.

Taking Sophie's subtle cue, the Viceroy resumed walking, glancing at her with an easy smile. "Miss Griffin, what do you know of Islewind?" he asked, his tone conversational yet purposeful.

Sophie kept her pace steady, eyes still scanning the bustling market as she answered. "From what I understand, the kingdom of Islewind is an archipelago surrounding a large peninsula, with the capital city of Aquaverna located on the peninsula's coast, central to the kingdom." She paused before continuing, "Aquaverna is ruled by King Marious, known for his fair governance. The kingdom thrives on textile production, sailing expertise, and fish exports."

She caught herself before delving too far into a textbook-style report and pivoted to a more strategic tone. "Islewind also experiences a rainy season that lasts for three months each year, which unfortunately impacts their tourism industry."

The Viceroy gave an approving nod at the coded all-clear. "Very good, Miss Griffin. You're well-informed." His words held a double meaning, acknowledging both her knowledge and her vigilance.

As they continued through the market square, the Viceroy waved to passing vendors with his signature charm, while Sophie remained sharp-eyed and composed, scanning the crowd for anything out of place. Around them, the vibrant marketplace buzzed merchants haggling, shoppers laughing, the rich aromas of spices and grilled meats hanging in the air.

Soon, they approached a food vendor's booth where a striking woman with flowing blonde hair stood behind a grill sizzling with various cuts of meat. She wore a blue tunic over a flowing dress, and shelves on either side of the booth displayed rows of exotic spices. Fresh loaves and smaller rolls were arranged neatly at the front, golden and warm in the late-morning light.

As soon as she spotted the Viceroy, the woman's face lit up with a broad smile, and she hurried to the front of the booth. "Mr. Longrin!" she beamed.

The Viceroy's face broke into a matching grin. "Ilsa! How are you?"

"Me? I'm doing so good," Ilsa said, smoothing the front of her dress with both hands. "I hear you have a son."

"I do," the Viceroy replied proudly. "Carter. He's a beautiful boy."

Ilsa's smile softened with warmth. "Your wife has truly blessed you," she said sincerely.

Sophie scanned the crowd once more as the Viceroy and Ilsa continued their easy banter, their conversation flowing between business and friendly familiarity. The market square had grown even busier; shoppers mingled between colorful booths, voices overlapping in a chorus of trade and laughter. A group of girls around Sophie's age clustered near a clothing stall run by a merchant from Verdantia, commonly known as the "Sacred Acres." Sophie didn't know much about the enchanted kingdom beyond what was taught in school, since there wasn't an Aurorium village stationed there.

Nearby, a man and woman examined plates and dishware at a Stoneridge booth. They looked like a couple considering upgrades to their kitchen. Sophie's eyes drifted again, and there he was. The old man in the leather hat she'd noticed earlier. He was still scanning the market, his gaze moving carefully over the booths.

But this time, he noticed her watching him.

His reaction was immediate; he quickly turned toward the vendor's table, pretending to examine the wares.

Hiding something?

Sophie's instincts flared.

Not wanting to take any chances, she turned smoothly toward the Viceroy and Ilsa, who were now engrossed in a discussion over a jar of spices.

"My apologies," Sophie interjected politely, keeping her tone light. "I hate to intrude, but... what are the taxes like in Stoneridge?" She flashed an innocent smile at Ilsa. "I'm working on a school report and couldn't find anything about them in my books."

The Viceroy didn't miss a beat. His expression remained neutral, but Sophie knew he understood the message:

Taxes: *possible threat detected.*

Ilsa blinked, momentarily caught off guard. "Taxes?" she repeated, stumbling for a beat before recovering. "Well, we pay taxes to the miner's guild, and then to the local governments; they guarantee our safety, of course. Vendors like me also pay taxes to the Ministry of Foreigners for trade access, which is how I'm able to be here in Opulentia now." She gestured around the market proudly. "The Ministry handles travel and security until I return home. Was that what you were looking for?"

"Yes, thank you," Sophie replied smoothly, exchanging a brief glance with the Viceroy to confirm the message was received.

The Viceroy offered Ilsa an apologetic smile. "I'm sorry, Ilsa, I'm running a little late. How much for the speckled pepper?" He gestured to the spice jar she'd been showing him, his casual demeanor intact.

Sophie turned back to the crowd, steadying her breath. *Calm down,* she reminded herself. *Take your time.*

He doesn't know you've spotted him.

She forced herself to observe with precision—not panic.

But the man in the leather hat was gone.

Her heart skipped a beat, but she stayed composed, scanning the square again. A group of girls giggled as they tested beauty creams at a nearby booth. An older couple browsed spellbooks at a Laminae vendor, their brows furrowed in deep discussion. A cluster of children played near the fountain, their babysitter already moving to prevent the inevitable splash.

Focus. Details matter.

"Shall we?" the Viceroy asked, slipping the jar of spice into his bag beside the baby outfit.

Sophie nodded, falling into step beside him, her senses sharp and alert.

"Of course," she replied almost absently, her eyes still scanning the crowd. "The taxes in Stoneridge seem very simple." Her words carried the renewed warning—subtly urging the Viceroy to shorten his visit without drawing attention.

The Viceroy responded smoothly, his tone light beneath the conversational smokescreen. "The thing about taxes is that they're deceptively simple. Ilsa never mentioned how much of her income she actually pays to each organization." A subtle way of letting Sophie know he'd received the message.

Sophie's training echoed in her mind: *When a threat is uncertain, do not overreact.* Running could mean falling straight into a trap. The priority was to remain calm, gather intel, and extract the protected without causing panic. Move with purpose, as if they were simply late, not in danger.

"Please slow down," Sophie said evenly, her tone measured but firm.

The Viceroy glanced at her, confusion flickering across his face as if to say, *What are you talking about?*

"Taxes are important to a country," Sophie added, slipping in another coded phrase, "but they aren't as important as baked goods." She deliberately avoided the keyword *muffin*, knowing the Viceroy would grasp the underlying urgency.

"You have a point, Miss Griffin," the Viceroy replied, his tone touched with mild irritation. "But I don't want to keep the Trade Unions waiting." Sophie could tell he wasn't sure how to respond, but he trusted her judgment.

"Of course, sir," she said calmly, her gaze sweeping the market again.

The man in the leather hat was still nowhere in sight.

Did I imagine it? Doubt crept in, sharp and unwelcome, but Sophie couldn't afford uncertainty.

Against her better judgment, she turned to check behind them; something Eclipse Baker had always warned against during protection drills.

Never take your eyes off your protected.

But then she saw **him**.

The man now stood behind the large fountain in the middle of the square, watching her with an unwavering intensity. His focus wasn't on the market anymore—it was fixed on Sophie, and by extension, the Viceroy. His hands were moving, doing something she couldn't quite see, but his intent was clear.

He's not hiding anymore.

Eclipse Baker's words from training rang in her memory: *You don't need to know everything about a threat, only that there is one.*

"Viceroy Longrin," Sophie said steadily, "I'd like to try those strawberry muffins you told me about earlier."

The Viceroy hesitated only a fraction of a second before catching on. He met her gaze and replied smoothly, "The shop's right around the corner, but we'll have to hurry. I think it's closing soon." His voice held a faint strain, skepticism flickering, but Sophie knew he trusted her.

Keeping her steps measured, she fell into place beside him, every muscle taut with controlled tension.

Before she could respond, a trio of men in black crashed into the market, sending crates and vibrant fabrics flying as they tore through a booth. Their suits pulsed with glowing blue lines from head to toe, intricate sigils forming at their elbows and knees. The moment Sophie saw the eerie light, her instincts flared.

No time to waste.

She placed a firm hand on the Viceroy's shoulder and shoved him forward. "The guards can handle them; we need to move. Now!" Her voice was low and sharp. Her right hand hovered over her pistol, fingers twitching, but she held off. *Not yet.*

Chaos exploded around them. Shoppers screamed and scattered, trampling goods in their panic. The glowing men locked onto Sophie and the Viceroy, breaking into a run.

From the corner of her eye, Sophie caught sight of the leather-hatted man. He was running away from the fountain, disappearing into the whirlwind of people and goods. But not before locking eyes with her one last time.

Is he with them? She asked herself, building a profile for later.

Her gaze snapped to the main road, the one leading to the Trade Union Hall. The safe zone. Reinforced. Guarded.

The problem?

A straight, three-hundred-step shot. Perfect kill zone.

Without hesitation, Sophie veered right, guiding the Viceroy into a narrow alleyway between two buildings.

He followed without protest, breath coming in ragged gasps as they ran. "Why aren't we heading straight to the meeting hall?" he demanded, voice strained.

Sophie tightened her grip on his arm, pulling him left into another alley without slowing. "Because it's a straight shot," she said, clipped and focused. "Anyone with a crossbow or gun would kill you in on our two shots."

A smirk ghosted across her lips despite the adrenaline. "I like you, Viceroy Longrin. I don't want to see you shot."

He let out a breathless chuckle but didn't argue.

Footsteps thundered on the cobblestones behind them. The chase was still on.

They tore through the narrow alley, gaining ground; until a figure emerged at the far end. His suit glowed with that same electric blue, washing the walls in sick light. In his hand gleamed an axe, wicked and heavy.

Sophie halted on instinct, yanking the Viceroy to a stop.

"They got in front of us," the Viceroy said, breathless, frustration seeping into his tone.

Sophie's eyes narrowed. "Doubt it. We were too fast. Too unpredictable."

Without hesitation, Sophie drew her pistol and fired two clean shots into the glowing man's chest. The gunfire cracked through the alley, echoing off the stone walls. The figure collapsed, the axe slipping from his grip and clattering against the cobblestones.

She and the Viceroy panted, trying to catch their breath; but Sophie knew they couldn't linger. "We need to move," she said, eyes scanning the alley. "Gunshots will bring the others right on top of us."

A low, metallic scrape sent a chill down her spine.

Her gaze snapped back to the fallen attacker, just in time to see him rising from the ground.

Two gaping holes still marred his chest, faint blue light pulsing from beneath the torn fabric of his suit. He reached down, dragging the axe across the stones with a screech that scraped against her nerves.

Sophie blinked, stunned; but only for a heartbeat. She grabbed the Viceroy and yanked him backward. "Move!" she barked, retreating down the alley they'd just come from.

The Viceroy's voice cracked with disbelief. "He got up after being shot? In the chest?! How... how is that possible?"

Sophie didn't slow. "After I get you to safety, I'll ask him," she shot back, voice steady as they twisted through the maze of alleys.

But their path was cut off again, another figure emerged ahead of them, suit glowing with that same pulsing blue.

No time to think. Just time to act.

Sophie pivoted sharply, dragging the Viceroy with her. In one fluid motion, she raised her pistol and fired two precise shots past him. The bullets struck the figure's knee with a loud crack. The man dropped instantly; and this time, the glow in his suit flickered and went out.

Noted.

Pushing the Viceroy forward, Sophie silently urged him past the fallen figure. They darted through another tight passage, veering right, then left, the labyrinth of alleys twisting around them. Her heart pounded like a war drum, but she forced herself to stay sharp, calculating, not panicking.

Ahead, a bright shaft of daylight spilled into the alley—the main street.

Sophie grabbed the Viceroy's shoulder and yanked him to a sudden stop. Her breathing stayed steady, her eyes sharp and searching.

"What's going on?" the Viceroy panted, glancing nervously over his shoulder.

"I have a plan." Sophie let go of him and reached into her suit jacket, pulling out a concussion tripwire with a length of wire attached. "We have to cross the street, but I'm sure more of them are behind us."

She unraveled the wire quickly, securing one end to the alley wall and pressing the adhesive-backed base to the opposite side. A firm tug confirmed it was tight.

"Wait...a grenade?" the Viceroy asked, alarm rising in his voice.

"A concussion tripwire," Sophie corrected. "It'll knock down whoever hits it...maybe even knock them out. But it won't kill them." She popped out the spent rounds from her pistol and loaded two fresh fire shots with smooth efficiency.

"We're about halfway to the meeting hall. When we hit the street, we turn right and run. It's one hundred and fifty king's steps..."

She didn't get to finish.

The man in the leather hat appeared at the mouth of the alley, flanked by four of the glowing-suited attackers.

"There she is! Take her!" he barked, lifting something in his hand.

Sophie moved instantly. "Move!" she snapped, grabbing the Viceroy's shoulder and propelling him forward.

They burst into the street, veering hard to the right.

BOOM.

The tripwire detonated behind them, sending a shockwave down the alley. Sophie didn't look back.

"She's there! Take her before she gets to the building!" the old man's voice rang out above the chaos.

Sophie's heart lurched. *He said 'her'... not 'them.' Not 'him.'*

The realization hit like a slap to the face.

They're after me.

"Keep running! Don't stop until you are inside!" Sophie shouted, giving the Viceroy one last shove forward.

Then she turned to face the oncoming danger.

Four glowing attackers barreled toward her. Two clutched farming pitchforks, the other two wielded axes...tools, not weapons. Marketplace grabs, Sophie noted.

They couldn't bring their own weapons in.

Testing her theory, she sprinted straight into the open.

The attackers followed; ignoring the Viceroy completely.

Confirmed.

Without hesitation, Sophie drew her pistol and fired.

The first shot struck the pitchfork-wielding man dead center. He collapsed instantly...flames erupting and consuming him where he fell.

Sophie's eyes widened in shock. The man didn't scream. He didn't move. He just... burned.

The remaining three pressed forward, completely unfazed by their comrade's immolation.

Sophie clenched her jaw and fired again. One by one, they dropped...each swallowed by fire the moment they hit the ground.

Cautiously, she approached the nearest smoldering body and knelt beside it. Gripping the hood, she yanked it back.

Straw.

"What...? But... how?" she whispered, staring at the stuffing beneath the fabric.

In the distance, the leather-hatted man's furious voice cut through the air.

"Dammit, get up! **they're all worthless!**"

Realizing too late that he'd exposed too much, he turned and disappeared into the alleyways.

Sophie tensed, every instinct screaming at her to give chase; but she exhaled slowly and clenched her fists.

Protect the Viceroy first.

She emptied one of the suits, rolled up the straw-stuffed husk, and slung it over her shoulder. As she walked briskly toward the meeting hall, her fingers traced the strange material of the attacker's suit, it is unlike anything she'd ever seen.

Near the building's entrance, a group of city guards stepped into her path, eyes narrowing.

"Halt! You there in the purple," the lead guard barked pointing his finger.

Sophie stopped and turned calmly, her stance steady. "Can I help you?"

The lead guard, a broad-chested man with a thick mustache, marched toward her. "Why are you carrying a weapon inside the market area?"

Sophie tapped the silver badge pinned to her lapel. "Sentinel Griffin of the Aurorium Clan. I'm on official protection duty."

He raised a skeptical eyebrow, glancing at the rolled-up suit on her shoulder. Behind him, his four fellow guards chuckled quietly.

"In protection of who, exactly?" he asked, the doubt thick in his tone, Sophie notices something about his accent is different just a bit off of what she was used to.

"Viceroy Longrin. He's inside the meeting hall." Sophie nodded toward the doors behind her. "I sent him there for safety. These *men* weren't after him, they were after me."

Her eyes narrowed slightly. "You didn't happen to pass an old man about two king's steps tall wearing a leather hat, did you?"

The guard scratched his head. "No... can't say I did."

Before Sophie could respond, a familiar voice called out behind her.

"Sentinel Griffin! Are you all right?"

She turned to see Viceroy Longrin jogging toward her, concern etched across his face.

"I'm fine, sir," Sophie replied, standing straighter. "I'm glad to see you made it."

The Viceroy offered a relieved smile. "Only because of you." He slowed to a stop, his gaze shifting to the surrounding guards. His expression darkened. "Is there a problem here?"

The mustached guard snapped to attention, arrogance draining from his face. "No problem at all, sir. Just... verifying the situation."

Sophie took the opportunity to press further. "If your patrol spots that old man in the leather hat, please take him into custody immediately. I have need to question him."

The guard gave a sharp nod. "Understood, ma'am." With a flick of his wrist, he and his team dispersed into the crowd, scanning the perimeter.

Sophie finally exhaled, the weight of the moment pressing down on her chest.

"Are you sure you're okay?" the Viceroy asked, his voice gentler now.

A faint flush warmed Sophie's cheeks, but she didn't let it shake her. "I'm Aurorium, sir. We train for these kinds of things so I'm just fine." Then, with the smallest smirk, she added, "Besides, my job was to keep *you* safe."

The Viceroy chuckled, shaking his head. "Well, if you say so, Miss Griffin. I have meetings to attend." He turned toward the hall, offering a wave over his shoulder. "Take care of yourself!"

"You too, Viceroy," Sophie replied, watching him disappear into the meeting hall before turning on her heel. She made her way back to his office, her mind racing.

Since she was the real target, there was no longer any need to guard him. But why was she the target? The question gnawed at her as she replayed the events in her mind.

The old man must have followed me to the Viceroy's office, waiting for the right moment to strike. Those glowing-suited men—were they trying to capture me, or kill me?

Sophie clenched her jaw. Considering what could have happened to her. *If I hadn't been on a bodyguard mission, I might've missed him entirely. When we locked eyes, it must have spooked him—and he just reacted.*

But the bigger question lingered—*why?* What was so important that he was willing to attack her in broad daylight? And what those suits...

Her thoughts drifted to the first man she shot in the chest—the bullets had passed clean through him, yet he stood up as if nothing had happened. He didn't teleport away. But the second man, the one she shot in the knee—he stayed down.

The mystery only deepened.

I'll need to go over this with Eclipse Baker when I get home, she resolved. He might have insights—maybe even answers.

By the time Sophie reached the Viceroy's office, dusk had settled over the city, casting long shadows across the streets. She climbed the stairs, expecting the usual warmth of Connie's presence. But the office was empty, eerily quiet.

Her backpack sat on the desk. On top of it rested a folded letter, her name "**Sen. Sophie Griffin**" written in an unfamiliar hand.

"What is this?" she asked the air, glancing around for any evidence of who left it.

Connie was gone for the day—her desk tidy, the lamps extinguished.

Sophie unfolded the letter and read silently:

"I hope this letter reaches you in time. Sentinel Griffin, you are in danger. Please—when you can—meet me at West's Tavern. I'll be in the back.
—Brother Albert The order of Saint Lorraine"

Sophie exhaled sharply and folded the letter. "Didn't reach me in time," she muttered under her breath.

Who is Brother Albert? And what does he know about all this?

Wasting no time, she stuffed the rolled-up black suit into her backpack and slung it over her shoulder. Moving cautiously, she descended the stairs and paused at the door, scanning the street. The day's events had left her wary, and she wasn't about to take any chances.

West's Tavern... that's by the pier, she thought as she stepped into the street. The scent of saltwater and the distant chatter from the docks drifted to her as she turned left, heading away from her village and deeper into the city.

As she walked, one thought lingered:

Just what have I gotten myself into?

Chapter 2

Annabelle Salazar, fourteen-year-old operations officer of the good ship *Stormfang*, strode down the gangplank, her unruly hair a mix of long braids and dread locks bouncing with each step. Today was supposed to be a day of fun; but first, she had a debt to collect.

Clad in a dark blue jacket over a crisp white button-up and an eye-catching orange skirt, Annabelle stood out against the muted tones of Granmark's bustling port. A bandana held most of her wild hair in place, though a few rebellious strands still escaped. As her boots clicked onto the wooden pier, she cast a glance back at her ship the *Stormfang*, nestled among the forest of masts and smokestacks in the harbor.

Her destination? The market district, where she planned to have a chat *all nice and friendly-like* with Mr. Aaron, a shopkeeper who owed the *Stormfang* payment for a recent job: *transporting* a small group and their cargo from Opulentia to Stoneridge, neatly bypassing both kingdoms' strict immigration and customs checks.

Just as she stepped off the pier and onto the cobblestone streets, a group of uniformed guards blocked her path. Their navy-blue jackets, brass buttons gleaming in the sunlight, and stiff peaked caps gave them an air of rigid authority. The head guard raised a gloved hand.

"Hey, girl!" His voice was firm. "No weapons in the market district. You'll have to leave that here." He gestured to the cutlass at her hip, his mustache twitching in disapproval.

Annabelle scoffed, resting a hand on the hilt. "This?" She unsheathed it just enough to reveal the weathered, nicked blade. "Tis just a ceremonial thing, I assure ye. Probably couldn't even cut butter."

The guard's eyes narrowed behind wire-rimmed glasses. "No exceptions," he said, extending his hand.

With a huff, Annabelle surrendered the sword. "Bah, fine." She watched him hand her a wooden chip stamped with the number 16. "And how do I get this back?"

"Hand the token to the guards on duty," he replied smoothly. "They'll return your... *ceremonial* sword."

Annabelle twirled the chip between her fingers and tucked it into her pocket. "Aye, isn't that nice." She flashed a sly grin. "And what if I lose it?"

The guard's smirk oozed condescending malice. "Then we keep your *ceremonial* sword."

Before she could step past, the officer squinted at her waist. "Why are you wearing an anchor around your waist?"

"'Tis me belt," Annabelle said casually, brushing past him and heading up the crowded street toward the marketplace.

By noon, the market was alive with motion, merchants shouting their wares, children weaving through the crowd, and the distant clang of a blacksmith's hammer. Annabelle loved it. The constant movement, the chatter, the raw energy could carry her away if she let it.

But first: *business.*

She made her way to a quaint storefront with a sign above the door that read *Aaron's Emporium*, the windows cluttered with an odd mix of dresses and food displays.

Inside, the store was crowded but quiet, shoppers browsing with little intent to buy. Annabelle strode to the counter, where an older man in a smock stood behind the register. She leaned in with a sly grin.

"Hello, Mr. Aaron," she said, keeping her voice low. "Yer friends John, Serif, and Malila wanted me to send their regards from Stoneridge."

Aaron looked up from the counter, his expression unreadable. "Ah, that's nice of them," he replied absently.

Before Annabelle could press further, a woman approached with two dresses: one blue with white trim, the other red with a white pattern.

Aaron turned to her with a polite nod. "One moment, miss." He wrapped the dresses in brown paper with practiced hands, tucked them into a cardboard box, then slipped it into a cloth bag. "That'll be thirty coin, ma'am."

The woman fished in her pocket, carefully counting out thirty gold coins and sliding them across the counter.

"Thank you kindly. Please come again." Aaron's smile was polite, but his eyes flicked back toward Annabelle as the woman exited the store.

Annabelle cleared her throat. "About the payment for carrying those folks to Stoneridge..." she said softly, leaning in again.

Aaron's brows knit. "Payment? Malila was supposed to settle that when they arrived," he said, feigning confusion.

Annabelle kept her tone calm, but there was a sharpness beneath it. "That wasn't the deal, Mr. Aaron. Me crew carried yer people and cargo safely to Stoneridge. We need to be paid."

Aaron's lips pressed into a thin line. "I don't know what to tell you, girl. You should've gotten your money from the passengers." His voice remained low, but there was iron in it.

Annabelle sighed. Her fingers drifted to the amulet around her neck: a skull-and-crossbones coin inset with tiny, glittering jewels. She traced its edge thoughtfully.

"Mr. Aaron," she said, voice still casual but heavy with meaning, "me crew won't be too happy about getting stiffed."

Aaron's eyes widened slightly, the bravado slipping. "Oh … the Stoneridge delivery. Right. I must've gotten things mixed up," he stammered. He ducked behind the counter, rummaging around before producing a small, jingling pouch. He set it down with an uneasy smile. "Here's your payment."

Annabelle took the bag and gave it a weighty shake before slipping it into her pocket. "Glad we could clear that up." She tilted her head. "Should I count it before I go?"

"No, no, it's all there," Aaron said quickly, his smile tight.

Annabelle flashed a grin. "Aye thanks, Mr. Aaron."

As she turned and exited the store, her gaze swept over the mismatched items on display. Once outside, she shook her head with a smirk. "Shopkeepers are the real crooks," she muttered. "Those Aurorium coppers ought to be arresting them instead harassin' good privateer folk like meself."

She glanced up at the sky, the sunlight warming her face. Deciding to enjoy the market a bit longer before heading back to the *Stormfang*, Annabelle set off down the lively street, blending effortlessly into the bustling crowd.

As she strolled through the square, her keen eyes scanned the rows of stalls and storefronts, weighing whether any goods might prove useful aboard ship.

One booth caught her attention, a cramped stall nearly swallowed by the sheer size of the man behind it. Towering and broad-shouldered with a shock of blond hair, he seemed to shrink the space around him. Hammers, chisels, and other sturdy tools lined the walls and display table in orderly rows. She didn't need to ask where he was from. *Stoneridge man. No doubt about it.* Hard people from a harder land of snow and mountains, where the weak didn't last too long.

Captain James "Kidd" Lowe always said Stoneridgers were locked in an endless battle with their land; constantly working to tame it, while the land fought back just as fiercely. Annabelle didn't doubt it. The tools looked like they'd survive storms, mutinies, and possibly time itself. But quality like that came at a cost, and she wasn't ready to part with the coin it would take. One look at the shopkeeper told her the five-finger discount would buy her a trip through the veil, sure he would not need a weapon.

Moving on, her gaze landed on another stall, this one run by a striking woman surrounded by stacks of pots, pans, plates, and flatware. Every inch of space was used with care and precision.

The vendor's olive skin, dark hair, and flowing brown sundress told Annabelle all she needed to know, a beautiful Islewind native. Annabelle had always loved porting in Islewind. Breathtaking views, people who minded their own business, and a healthy lack of nosy Aurorium coppers. A far cry from Opulentia, where staying off the radar was a full-time job.

Her eyes fell on something curious: a spoon, fork, and knife combo that folded into a sleek, compact rectangle. Space was always tight aboard a ship, especially one with *Stormfang's* line of "services" and anything that cut down on clutter was worth its weight in gold.

"Do you like it?" The woman's voice was smooth, her smile warm and disarming.

Annabelle blinked, realizing how long she'd been staring. "Aye, it's nice," she said, glancing at the woman's face. "How much?"

"Seven coin," the woman replied, her smile somehow even more dazzling. "Or two for ten."

Annabelle hesitated, pulling out her pouch. *Never spend ship coin on yerself,* Kidd's voice echoed in her mind. Her pouch felt painfully light. This had to count.

She glanced at the vendor and rehearsed her refusal. *Sorry, not today.* But what came out was, "I can only get one."

Where had that come from?

The woman accepted the coins with a graceful nod, her touch gentle but practiced. Humming softly, she wrapped the utensil in a delicate decorative bag with the care of an artist.

Annabelle thought she shouldn't stare, but something about the woman's movements was hypnotic. Fluid. Intentional.

Well, I paid for it, she thought. *Might as well enjoy the show.*

When the woman handed over the bag, Annabelle accepted it with a smile. "Have a great and prosperous day," she said, her tone effortless, polished, she is well-practiced in Islewind customs.

She turned away, resisting the urge to glance back... until curiosity got the better of her. A quick glance over her shoulder revealed the woman sneaking a second look.

Annabelle grinned. *A small victory.*

But with her pouch feeling much lighter, it was time to move on.

"Maybe it's time to head back to the *Fang*," she murmured, weaving through the crowded market.

Her musings ended abruptly as she walked straight into a street performance. A dozen dancers spun and stepped in perfect synchrony, sweeping across the square. Behind them, a band played an energetic tune that filled the air with rhythm and heat. The crowd clapped along, cheering as the dancers dipped and twirled.

Annabelle folded her arms, unimpressed. *Clapping's not really me ting, especially if I'm not getting a cut of the coin.*

Still, she couldn't help but admire their style. Judging by the music and attire, they had to be from Magitekopolis, maybe even the capital, Aetheria. The women wore flowing silk-like dresses in vibrant colors, while the men sported dark trousers, pale shirts, and matching vests. The coordination was striking, almost uniform-like, and Annabelle couldn't help but compare them to a seasoned ship's crew, each dancer a cog in a well-oiled machine.

Just then, someone bumped into her from behind, jolting her forward.

"Oi!" she snapped, spinning around. "Watch where yer going!"

The culprit was a short, grizzled old man with a leather cap and a pair of goggles strapped to it. Light stubble dusted his weathered white face, and he clutched a heavy bag tightly to his chest.

The man blinked, as if just noticing her. "Sorry, miss," he rasped. "Didn't see you." His gaze lingered way too long. "Truly, my apologies." He adjusted the bag awkwardly.

Annabelle shifted, unease crawling over her skin like a thousand tiny legs. She forced a tight smile. "It's alright. Just be careful."

The old man grinned, flashing yellowed, gold-speckled teeth, and gave a little wave before disappearing into the crowd.

"Something about that guy..." Annabelle muttered, brushing off the discomfort.

She turned back to the dancers. Their effortless rhythm and graceful movements reminded her of a well-run ship, each crew member in perfect sync, keeping the whole operation afloat.

She lingered longer than intended, captivated. Eventually, she flipped a pair of coins into a dish near the musicians, a rare moment of generosity, and walked away, still thinking about where they might have trained. Aetheria? Or had they traveled there to join a troupe?

Back when the *Stormfang* docked in Magitekopolis' port city of Harmonia's Reach, she didn't recall seeing anything like this. Sure, there were tavern dances and even that wild bonfire party with high-borns prancing barefoot. But nothing like this: so polished, so rehearsed.

In a quieter corner, Annabelle pulled out her coin purse and counted what was left. Ten universal coins... and twenty of those blasted "Crop Crowns" from the Sacred Acres.

She scowled.

The problem with Sacred Acres currency was simple; they refused to use universal coin. Instead, they minted their own, and most kingdoms wouldn't take it without a fuss. Captain Kidd's voice echoed in her head, clear as ever:

"These things are a leash!" he'd barked during a game of crew, after she'd won a handful from him. *"Ain't no freedom in currency ye can't spend wherever ye damn well please!"*

"Blasted things," she muttered, stuffing the coins away.

Looking up, she noticed the sun dipping low, dusk was setting in. Her day off was nearly over. Time to find food before heading back to the *Fang*.

As she walked toward the pier, food stalls lined the streets, their prices stabbing at her hope like tiny daggers. Looks like dinner would come from the galley after all, not terrible, but far from glamorous.

"Excuse me, miss," a voice called from a small stall.

Annabelle turned to see a woman standing behind a spread of round meat wrapped in golden-brown bread. She smiled warmly.

"Could I interest you in trying a new sandwich?"

Annabelle blinked. "Me?", She eyed the food. "How much?"

"Seven coin." The woman replied, still smiling.

Annabelle smirked, ready to decline, but then caught a detail: the vendor's high-quality apron bore the flag of the Sacred Acres. Below it, the word *Verdantia* was stitched in elegant script.

Her smirk sharpened. "Do ye take Crop Crowns?" she asked, deliberately playfully misnaming the currency.

The woman gave a tight laugh but quickly recovered, flashing her seller's grin. "Of course. As a Verdantian citizen I accept *Harvest Crowns*."

Annabelle shrugged, pulled out the coins, and dropped them onto the counter. She wasn't sure if she'd overpaid or underpaid, but the vendor accepted the lot without hesitation.

With practiced ease, the woman opened a small oven and retrieved a fresh roll. The bread was hot, the sausage sticking out on both ends. The aroma hit Annabelle like a broadside: spicy, savory, irresistible.

"I call this a meat roll," the woman said, wrapping it in paper. "Careful—it's hot."

Annabelle took a bite, and nearly choked. The spices exploded across her tongue like cannon fire. She coughed, eyes wide. "More like a powder keg," she wheezed, mouth still on fire.

The vendor laughed, delighted.

"This is really good," Annabelle admitted, fanning her mouth. "But I'm going to need a drink!"

The woman poured a cup of tea into a small tin cup and handed it over. "On the house," she said, still smiling.

Annabelle grinned. "Free is good to me," she quipped, echoing one of Captain Kidd's favorite sayings. She downed the tea gratefully, the cool liquid soothing the burn as she worked through the rest of the meat roll.

By the time she was halfway through, the tea was gone, and she let out a satisfied sigh… A sudden eruption of screams tore through the marketplace behind her.

Annabelle spun around, eyes wide as people scattered in all directions, some running straight toward her.

Not me problem, she thought, her hand instinctively going to the ship's coin in her pocket. She didn't need to get tangled in someone else's nonsense. Without hesitation, she joined the fleeing crowd, slipping into a narrow alley.

Once safely tucked away, she patted her pocket. The coin was still there. Satisfied, she wove through the winding alleys, taking sharp lefts and rights to avoid the rising commotion in the streets. But as she rounded one final corner, she was swallowed by complete darkness.

"What in the name of the sea...?" she muttered, slowing to a stop.

A cold voice echoed through the void, distant, yet piercing. "Your time has come, orange pirate."

Her gaze snapped toward a pair of glowing red eyes hovering in the dark.

Annabelle's hand flew to her cutlass, then cursed under her breath. *No weapons in the market... dammit!*

"What do ye want?" she called, forcing her voice steady. "I ain't gots no coin on me."

A figure stepped into the faint light arms raised, shadows trailing off her like living smoke.

"I am a loyal servant of the Great One. Mistress of the Shadows... Mage."

Annabelle rolled her eyes. "More like the loud-mouthed Queen of Talk," she muttered, reaching for her backup weapon.

With a flick of her wrist, she swung her miniature anchor—missed completely.

Mage sneered. "So much for that one."

With a dramatic gesture, she waved her hand and from the shadows emerged two enormous wolf-like beasts, their eyes glowing like coals, jaws low to the ground.

Annabelle's stomach tightened. *What the hell is this dark magic?*

She reached into her coat and pulled out a small metal cylinder packed with glowing stones. A sharp shake lit them up, casting a greenish glow down the alley.

And what the light revealed was far worse than she'd feared.

Mage's body was wrapped in living shadow, like a second skin. Only her hands, feet, and face remained exposed. The wolves, forged from that same dark essence, stalked forward, too quiet, eyes locked on Annabelle looking for a meal.

Annabelle had seen strange things in her travels. Smugglers from Stoneridge, thieves from Aetheria, spice merchants from the Coral Archipelago. But nothing like this. Her mind raced for a plan, a story, *anything* to help.

Nothing came.

Better to live another day, she thought, yanking her anchor back and running in the opposite direction as fast as she can.

Mage's laughter echoed through the alley, and the wolves leapt after her.

Annabelle cursed, heart pounding. The alley was too dark. She couldn't see a damn thing. Only the sound of paws pounding behind her, faster than any dog she'd ever known.

A low growl behind her, *all too close.*

Instinct kicked in. She dropped flat, skidding on her palms as one wolf soared over her head and landed hard in front of her with a snarl.

She rolled to her knees just in time to spot the second set of glowing eyes charging.

"Are they thinking for themselves, or is she pulling the strings?" she muttered to herself.

She didn't wait for an answer. Swinging her anchor on its chain, she aimed for the charging beast. The wolf dodged, but she yanked the chain mid-air, redirecting the arc. The anchor smashed into its flank, sending it skidding across the cobblestones.

"Independent?" Annabelle concluded *How can she create beasts?*

She didn't get time to finish the thought.

The other wolf lunged, faster this time.

Annabelle reached for her anchor, but it wouldn't make it back in time. Thinking fast, she grabbed the slack chain, looping it like a whip and lashing it toward the beast. The metal links hit their mark but barely slowed it down.

With no time left, she raised her arm and the wolf's jaws clamped down.

The impact drove her into the ground with a scream. Pain tore through her arm as the beast thrashed, its teeth trying to rip through flesh and bone.

Desperate, she fumbled for her amulet. "I need yer help!" she cried.

Nothing.

Was she too far from the sea?

Gritting her teeth, she balled her fist and punched the wolf again and again in its neck—but it was like hitting stone.

"Ye go down fighting," her father's voice rang in her head.

Annabelle groped blindly along the ground; her fingers brushed something sharp. A broken bottle.

Without hesitation, she grabbed the jagged glass and stabbed it into the beast's side, once, twice, again and again, kneeing its body as it writhed.

With a silent snarl, the creature finally collapsed into a pool of shadow.

She didn't stop to think.

The second wolf lunged again. She grabbed her anchor in her good hand and swung with everything she had, striking it again and again until it, too, dissolved into thick black mist, the darkness slithering back to Mage's outstretched fingers.

Annabelle staggered to her feet, panting. "I don't hear ye laughing now, ye ugly wench!" she snarled, glaring at the silhouette behind her dimming glow rod.

Mage's red eyes flared. "Oh, you will," she whispered, raising her hands.

Annabelle's stomach dropped as more shadow wolves slinked from the dark, their glowing eyes multiplying in the gloom. She couldn't count them all, but she knew there were more than two this time. With a wry smile, she flexed her bleeding arm and tightened her grip on the anchor. "Make sure to bring enough this time," she said, forcing bravado into her voice. "I needs me a challenge."

But inside, doubt gnawed at her. Her right arm was almost useless, her cutlass was out of reach, and her crew was nowhere nearby.

She was out of options. *So this is it*, she thought, swallowing hard.

"Zyl'ethis lumindralis, cindraera dremisso."

A voice rang out behind Mage, followed by a brilliant blast of sunlight. The alley exploded in golden radiance, vaporizing the shadow wolves instantly and sending Mage sprawling with a piercing scream. **"Annabelle Salazar, is that you?"**

Annabelle squinted toward the voice, panting. "Depends on who's asking?" she called back, gripping her injured arm.

"My name's Regina Fournier, and someone sent me a letter to save you!" the voice…Regina…shouted. "This spell won't hold long, and I don't know how long she'll stay   down!"

Annabelle glanced at Mage, now writhing on the ground, her shadowy body flickering like a dying candle as she clawed at the alley walls, desperate to escape the light.

Weighing her options, Annabelle ran toward Regina with all her speed. "How far is the street behind ye?"

Regina hesitated. "A few steps, I think? It got dark real fast when I turned into the alley."

"Good enough," Annabelle muttered, sprinting forward with the anchor swinging in her good hand. But as she passed Mage, she slowed and looked down at the trembling figure. Her lips curled into a smirk. She kicked Mage square in the stomach. "That's for me arm!"

Mage gasped, her body recoiling. Annabelle drew back for another strike...

"Please! We have to go, the spell's already fading!" Regina's voice cut through.

Annabelle looked up. Darkness was creeping back, little by little. With a huff, she turned and ran.

Regina pivoted and sprinted for the street, her long gray curly hair streaming behind her.

In a single step, the pair burst through the veil of shadow and into the bustling street. The glow of streetlamps and hum of conversation wrapped around them like a warm blanket. The earlier panic had passed; the market had settled into its evening rhythm, people drifting toward inns, homes, and the docks.

Annabelle paused, staring in awe at the wall of darkness behind them. "Never have I ever," she muttered, shaking her head.

Then she realized she was still holding Regina's hand. She let go quickly and turned to the girl...gray hair, round glasses, and an air of bookish precision. "Thanks for the help. Regina, right?"

Regina quickly withdrew her hand, noticing Annabelle's blood on her palm. "Yes. Regina Fournier," she said, fumbling for a handkerchief. Her eyes widened. "You're hurt, we need to get you to a doctor."

Annabelle glanced at her bleeding forearm and waved it off. "Nah, I just gotta get back to me ship." She wrapped the anchor around her waist like a belt again, wincing slightly as she did. "But... why'd ye save a lass back there?"

Regina adjusted her glasses, looking uncertain. "I... I got a letter last week. It told me I had to come save you, tonight, around nightfall."

Annabelle frowned. "A letter?"

Regina nodded and reached into her pocket, pulling out a crisp envelope. "It came with one for you too."

Annabelle took it, eyeing the elegant cursive that spelled out her full name: **Annabelle Salazar**. The handwriting was too perfect, too formal for the riffraff she usually dealt with. She flipped it over and examined the wax seal. The symbol pressed into it tugged at something in her memory, familiar maybe. "Hope it ain't a bill," she said with a smirk, breaking the seal and unfolding the letter.

The handwriting was clean and measured, the message short and to the point:

To Miss Annabelle Salazar,

You are in danger...as you've likely just discovered. I'm here to help.

Come to West's Tavern. I'll be waiting for you and Regina in the back room.

I also have a good paying job for the Stormfang.

Please come quickly.

—Brother Albert Thompson, The Order of Saint Lorraine

Annabelle let out a low whistle and slid the letter back into its envelope. "Well, that was straight to the point." She looked over at Regina. "Can I read yer letter?"

Regina hesitated for a moment, then shrugged. "I don't see why not." She pulled a nearly identical envelope from her pocket and handed it over. Annabelle immediately noticed the same broken wax seal.

Tucking her own letter into her jacket, she opened Regina's.

To Miss Regina Fournier,

A great danger threatens the Seven Kingdoms, and I require your help to stop it.

On the 23rd of February, travel to the port city of Granmark, in the country of Opulentia. At dusk, you will encounter a privateer girl with orange hair, she will be in grave danger. Please aid her if you can. I recommend bringing that sunlight spell of yours.

Once you have delivered the enclosed letter, meet me at West's Tavern. I will be waiting in the back.

—Brother Albert Thompson, The Order of Saint Lorraine

Annabelle handed the letter back, arching an eyebrow. "Looks like ye got pulled into this mess same as me."

Regina nodded and tucked the letter away.

Annabelle grinned. "Well, thanks for the assist, missy. I guess we're off to West's."

She knew West's Tavern all too well; whenever the *Stormfang* needed work, that's where they found the right kind of customers. Shady deals, strong drink, and even stronger opportunities. Whether it was a trap or not, she couldn't say, but coin is coin.

"West's is this way," Annabelle said, motioning for Regina to follow as they set off toward the tavern, the city's lights flickering to life around them.

Chapter 3

Lisa Nozaki and her four friends from Valorcrest Academy, nestled in the Kingdom of Laminae, arrived at their usual stop on Jetty #3. Among the bustling crowd, Lisa stood out with her striking forest-green hair and matching eyes. She wore a flowing white sundress that fluttered in the ocean breeze, and over her shoulder hung a medium-sized white purse adorned with the Valorcrest insignia.

As they stepped off the boat, a porter greeted them with a courteous bow, holding a glass jar of water in one hand and a silver platter of empty glasses in the other.

"Welcome, ladies," he said with a warm smile. "May I offer you a drink?"

The girls exchanged polite smiles and waved him off with a chorus of, "No, thank you," before continuing down the pier, their laughter mingling with the cries of seagulls and the distant honks of passing ships.

"I can't wait to see what new dresses the shops have from Umbrathorn," Maggie said eagerly. She was the tallest of the group, her tanned skin glowing in the sun. Her blonde hair was pulled into a ponytail, and she wore a white sundress layered beneath a yellow tunic. A matching white-and-yellow purse was tucked neatly under her arm.

"Umbrathorn? Maggie, the last time they sent imports here must have been ages ago," Anna teased. She adjusted the blue sash on her dress and clutched her purse tighter. "Lisa, what were we supposed to be looking for again?"

Lisa, adjusting the green sash tied around her waist, reached into her purse and pulled out a neatly folded piece of paper. She glanced at it and read aloud with a thoughtful expression, "Jade tree root, chili pepper seeds, a daigurie tree branch, if possible, fresh ginsum spice, void root, emberleaf, a whole king's fist of dreamroot, and lunar rosemary."

When she finished, she carefully folded the list and slipped it back into her purse.

Anna let out an exaggerated groan. "What are we learning next year? How to summon demons?"

Lisa giggled, shaking her head. "Anna, you are too much."

As they made their way down the pier, Lisa's eyes drifted toward the lower docks, where the constant bustle of sailors played out in a barely organized chaos. Crates of goods were stacked precariously, and travelers from distant lands wove through the crowds, each moving toward their own unseen destination.

She wondered how any of them ever knew where they were going in that maze of motion.

At a checkpoint ahead, a group of guards stood in their standard uniforms, each bearing the flag of Opulentia. The head guard, a burly man with a friendly smirk, eyed the group with mock suspicion.

"Hello, ladies," he said, his voice tinged with humor. "Is anyone here a terrorist?"

The girls giggled, their voices blending into a cheerful, "No, sir," almost in perfect unison.

The guard crossed his arms and feigned a stern glare. "Alright then, which one of you is smuggling weapons?"

Lisa and the others exchanged amused glances before, without hesitation, they all pointed at Sarah, the quietest of the group.

Maggie grinned mischievously. "He's got you, Sarah."

Lisa chimed in with mock seriousness. "Time to confess."

The headguard chuckled and leaned in, still playing along. "Well, Miss Sarah, is it? If you confess now, I might be able to get you a good deal with the magistrate."

Sarah's face flushed a deep red, and she shook her head vigorously. "I—I don't have anything!" she stammered, flustered but trying to laugh it off. "I swear!"

With a chuckle, the guard stepped back and gave them a playful salute. "Alright, alright. Have a good visit, ladies. And be sure to keep your valuables safe; there've been reports of pickpockets lurking around." He turned to Sarah one last time, grinning. "And since your bodyguard here didn't bring any weapons, do us all a favor and report any trouble to the city guard."

More laughter bubbled from the group as they nodded. "Yes, sir! Thank you!" they said in cheerful unison before continuing past the checkpoint.

They descended the stone stairway from the slip to the bustling market floor below. The air was thick with the mingling scents of spices, fresh bread, and the tang of sea salt. Upon reaching the ground level, Maggie and Sarah spotted a large olive-skinned man in an Islewind tunic with a sash belt, standing behind a well-stocked booth.

Without hesitation, they hurried toward him, excitement evident in their quickened steps.

"Ladies, you all look stunning, but I bet none of you have a dress as beautiful, and functional, as this one," the man said, holding up an exquisite garment with a proud grin.

The dress had a square neckline and sheer, silk-like fabric that shimmered under the market sunlight. Its soft tan base was intricately embroidered with red and green vines and leaves that climbed from hem to neckline. A dark blue trim lined the edges, matching the sash cinched neatly at the waist, tying the entire design together.

Lisa couldn't help but admire it. She'd never seen a dress quite like it, elegant yet grounded with a charm that felt just right. "How much does it cost?" she asked before she could stop herself.

The vendor's eyes twinkled. "I couldn't part with such a fine piece for less than fifteen coins," he said with a knowing smile.

Lisa reached into her purse. "Do you accept Harvest Crowns?"

He shook his head apologetically. "Ohh, Crowns? Sorry, miss, I can't take those."

Lisa's face fell. "Oh no... I do not have any universal coin." She sighed, gazing at the dress longingly. "but it feels like it was made just for me."

The vendor chuckled warmly. "Tell you what, my dear. I'll hold it for you until the end of the day. If you can come back with fifteen coin, it's yours." He gestured to the crowd. "And if my daughter's here when you return, just tell her Asad promised it to you."

Lisa nodded gracefully. "Thank you very much. I will be back."

Her friends exchanged knowing glances but said nothing. *The list came first.* Lisa's dress dilemma would have to wait. Stepping aside from the stand, they gathered in a huddle to plot their plan of attack.

"We should split up the list," Sarah suggested, ever the practical one. "It'll be faster. Then we can shop for ourselves afterward."

Lisa nodded, already pulling the crumpled list from her purse. "Good idea."

Spotting an empty table in the food court, they made their way over and sat down, laying the list out in front of them.

"I'll take the chili pepper seeds and daigurie tree leaves," Maggie volunteered, jotting the items onto a scrap of paper before tucking it into her own purse. "I know exactly where to get them."

"I'll get the ginsum spice and jade tree root," Sarah added, writing neatly in her notepad before snapping it shut.

Anna leaned forward, tapping the list thoughtfully. "Void root and emberleaf... I know where they sell those. The shop with the frogs."

Maggie smirked. "Oh, you mean the shop with that cute boy? Are you sure you don't want to trade assignments?"

Anna rolled her eyes, but couldn't hide the blush creeping into her cheeks. "I will survive, Maggie." She tells her dropping her tone to brush off her accusation.

Lisa smiled, cutting through the teasing. "That leaves dreamroot and lunar rosemary for me." She stood, raising her fist high. "Alright, Hawks, let's do this!"

The girls shared excited glances and raised their fists together.

"Ready... break!" they cheered, clapping fists before scattering into the bustling market, each on her own mission.

Lisa walked briskly past a row of brick-and-mortar shops, her eyes flicking up to the colorful signs above each door. "**Elegant Dresses**," one read, not the one she wanted. She moved on. "**Familiar Training Goods**," caught her eye. "No," she muttered, pressing forward.

Finally, she spotted a sign that read **Exotic Plants** and allowed herself a small smile. "A good start," she murmured, stepping inside.

The air inside was thick with the scent of damp earth and herbs. Dim lighting made it hard to make out the shapes of the plants and supplies scattered across the shop. Behind a worn wooden counter sat the shopkeeper, idly toying with a small lizard perched on his hand.

Lisa approached with polite confidence. "Excuse me, do you have any dreamroot?" Her eyes scanned the shadowy shelves, trying to make sense of their contents.

The shopkeeper barely glanced up. "I dunno," he said with a shrug. "You can look around if you want." His attention stayed on the lizard.

Lisa frowned. "It is quite dark in here. Could you open a window? I am having trouble seeing anything."

The shopkeeper chuckled, not looking away from his pet. "I can see just fine."

Lisa exhaled softly, recalling her father's advice: *Sometimes you have to make them care.* Squaring her shoulders, she leaned in slightly. "What kind of lizard is that?" she asked, voice warm with curiosity.

The shopkeeper's gaze finally shifted to her. "He's not a lizard," he said proudly. "He's my familiar. His name's Emmanuel."

As if on cue, the tiny creature turned to Lisa and let out a sharp hiss.

Lisa smiled graciously. "Oh he is so adorable."

The shopkeeper grinned. "Aww, see? He likes you."

23

Lisa tilted her head. "Can he perform any magic yet?"

The man sighed. "Not yet. I just got him."

Lisa's lips curled in thought. "Did you know dreamroot leaves can be brewed into tea to strengthen the bond between a mage and their familiar?"

The shopkeeper blinked, intrigued. "Really? I didn't know that." He reached behind the counter, pulling out a thick book and flipping through it. "Ugh, I can't read in here. It's too dark."

Emmanuel hissed again, the sound sharp and insistent.

Lisa smiled inwardly. *Such is the nature of familiars.* She put on her most diplomatic expression. "What did he say?"

The man sighed. "He says he doesn't like sunlight." He stroked the lizard's head thoughtfully, then nodded. "Alright, alright. I'll put you in my pocket." Carefully, he scooped Emmanuel up and tucked him into his shirt pocket, whispering, "Don't worry, it's not forever."

With Emmanuel secure, the shopkeeper stepped out from behind the counter and used a long wooden pole to pull back the heavy curtains.

Sunlight poured into the shop, illuminating the once-hidden shelves.

Lisa let out a breath of relief. "There, isn't that better?" She nodded toward the book. "Does it say where the dreamroot is?"

He skimmed a few pages, then gestured toward a shelf. "Yeah. The owner makes us keep an inventory. Dreamroot should be right... here."

He stopped in front of a small potted tree with wilted, dull leaves.

Lisa's heart sank. "Poor thing," she murmured, brushing her fingers lightly over the drooping branches. "These trees need a lot of sunlight to thrive. How long have you had your familiar?"

The shopkeeper hesitated. "Why does that matter?" he asked, a little defensive. "About a month, I guess."

Lisa nodded thoughtfully. "That makes sense. Does your employer know you bring him to work?"

A guilty look crossed his face. "No... I hide him when the boss comes around."

Lisa glanced at the struggling plants and offered a gentle smile. "I think your familiar has been influencing you more than you realize." She paused, then added, "When you first received him, were you given a special cage to keep him out of the sunlight?"

He nodded slowly. "Yeah, but it's too big to bring to work."

Lisa's expression remained kind but firm. "My father always says a good mage must find balance with their familiar. Maybe it's best to leave him at home from now on."

The shopkeeper sighed, his gaze sweeping the room. Only now did he seem to notice how many of the plants were in a similarly wilted state. "Oh no... what am I going to do? These plants are ruined!"

Lisa pressed a finger to her lips in a soft shushing motion. "They just need some love and attention."

She knelt beside the small tree, gently pressing her fingertip into the soil. Drawing it back, she traced delicate patterns in the air, weaving a shimmering spell circle. A glowing green ring appeared, its edges etched with ancient symbols that rotated gently in time with her movements. As the circle spun, a fine mist of vibrant energy unfurled, filling the shop like a fresh breeze.

The transformation was instant. Leaves once dry and brown bloomed into vivid shades of green, crimson, and amber. Taller plants, previously slumped in exhaustion, rose with renewed strength. Lisa watched quietly as life returned to the store around her.

The shopkeeper stared, wide-eyed. "How... how are you doing this? What kind of magic is that?"

Lisa withdrew her hand, letting the spell continue its slow rotation. "It's called Earthbloom, the magic of mother earth," she replied calmly.

The shopkeeper whistled. "That's incredible. You just saved me. Is there anything I can do to repay you?"

Lisa folded her hands gracefully. "Three things." Her tone was polite, but firm. "First, get your watering can and tend to every plant in the store. Without hydration, they'll wilt again when the spell fades. Second, take Emmanuel home. He doesn't belong here during the day. And third, let me pay with Harvest Crowns."

The shopkeeper grimaced. "Crowns? I'm not sure I can..."

Lisa raised an eyebrow, poised, but clearly not asking. *Are you serious?*

He exhaled in defeat. "Alright, alright. I'll figure something out."

With a resigned shrug, he trudged to the back of the store, grabbed a watering can, and stepped outside to fill it.

While he was gone, Lisa retrieved a small cloth sack from her purse. She carefully plucked fresh dreamroot leaves from the revitalized tree, measuring out roughly a king's fist's worth. Her practiced fingers worked quickly, but she made a mental note to weigh it later. Tying the sack shut, she moved down the aisles in search of Lunar rosemary.

After circling the shop twice with no luck, she returned to the counter. The shopkeeper was watering a small tree with oval-shaped leaves speckled in purple.

When he noticed her approach, he looked up. "About that tea..."

Lisa nodded. "Dry two leaves and steep them in a pot of water," she instructed. "Drink no more than two cups before bed."

The shopkeeper raised an eyebrow. "How much does Emmanuel drink?"

Lisa's expression turned serious. "You must ensure he doesn't consume any. It would put him into a deep sleep; one he might never wake from."

The shopkeeper gulped and nodded quickly. "Got it." He placed the sack on the scale and watched the needle sway. "This is just a hair over a king's fist." He checked his ledger. "That'll be fifty-eight Harvest Crowns."

Lisa's eyes widened. "Fifty-eight?" She could hardly believe it. Back in Verdantia, that amount could buy a full dinner for two.

The shopkeeper shrugged, a little sheepish. "Sorry, I have to follow the bank rates."

With a quiet sigh, Lisa reached into her purse and pulled out the circular coins, each stamped with the Harvest Tree on one side and the Great Flag of Verdantia on the other. She carefully stacked five ten-piece coins and eight ones, arranging them neatly on the counter. It looked like far too much for a simple pouch of leaves.

The shopkeeper counted the coins, then slid them into a separate box. "Alright, all set." He gave his pocket a small pat, checking on Emmanuel. "If you're still looking for Lunar Rosemary, try Scent of the Isle. They usually carry it."

Lisa's eyes lit up with hope. "Truly? Why do you not stock it here?"

The shopkeeper rubbed the back of his neck. "Let's just say Lunar Rosemary and emberleaf don't play nice. We had... incidents. So we stopped carrying it."

Lisa nodded, slipping the sack of dreamroot into her purse. "Where can I find this shop?"

"Across the market square, on Arcanus Street," he said, pointing toward the far side of the plaza.

"Thank you for your help," she said with a graceful nod, then turned and walked to the door.

25

"Thank you," Lisa added again, offering a gentle wave as she stepped back out into the sunlit street. She turned right, heading toward the square, where the bright hum of the crowd seemed even more vibrant than before.

As she walked, Lisa reached into her purse and counted her remaining coins: three five-piece coins and one ten-piece. Twenty-five in total. If she could pay with a combination of gold and Harvest Crowns, she might still afford the Lunar Rosemary—and maybe even the dress.

She passed a group of boys kicking a ball in a lively game she didn't recognize. Their laughter rang through the air, unbothered by the busy market around them. "Must be a local game," Lisa murmured to herself, smiling.

Just as she moved past them, she felt a gentle tug on her sundress. Turning, she found a small boy with brown skin and bright, curious eyes, grinning up at her. In his hands, he held an intricately crafted mechanical flower. Its petals glowed softly with a pulsing blue light.

"This is for you," he said, holding it out with both hands, beaming.

Lisa blinked. "For me? Aww…"

"An angel told me to give it to the pretty girl with green hair," the boy said, matter-of-factly.

A warm blush rose in her cheeks. She smiled, touched by the unexpected sweetness. "Well, thank you very much." Leaning down, she kissed his cheek lightly.

The boy's face turned bright pink. He giggled and ran back to his friends, disappearing into their game.

Lisa tucked the delicate flower into her purse, admiring its glow before continuing on. As she passed Asad's booth, her gaze lingered on the dress once more. Their eyes met briefly; he was busy chatting with a young woman who appeared to be shopping for her daughter.

Just you wait, Lisa thought, a flicker of determination blooming behind her calm smile, *I am coming back for you.*

Turning onto Arcanus Street, she stepped into a quieter lane where the energy of the market seemed to dim. The sounds faded, replaced by the hush of shaded storefronts and the scent of old wood and herbs. She passed a modest shop marked *Home for Familiars* and glanced at the small cages displayed in its window. A brief thought crossed her mind; *Maybe Emmanuel came from there.*

Then she remembered her father's words: *"A true mage does not purchase a familiar. They find one in the wild."*

Further down, she spotted a cozy eatery named *Potato Cakes*, its sign featuring an illustration of a smiling young girl joyfully eating a flat, brown cake. Lisa's stomach grumbled, but she sighed. "It looks delicious, but I do not have any extra coins."

She walked past another shop displaying a variety of enchanted toys, wooden carvings and small mechanical animals that moved on their own. *These must be from Magitekopolis,* Lisa thought, watching a tiny bear march in circles.

At the end of the street, she finally arrived at her destination. A large, well-maintained storefront stood before her, its sign reading *Scent of the Isle*, set against the backdrop of the Islewind flag.

Upon stepping inside, Lisa found herself bathed in an otherworldly purple glow. Crystals embedded in the ceiling pulsed gently, illuminating the store with soft, ethereal light. The nocturnal plants responded eagerly, their leaves and petals stretching toward the ceiling as if drawn to the enchanted illumination. Lisa couldn't help but admire the craftsmanship and the magic required to maintain such an effect throughout the day.

Approaching the counter, Lisa smiled at the shopkeeper, a young woman whose hair appeared either bright blue or blonde, difficult to discern in the purple glow.

"Hello," Lisa began politely, but before she could continue, the shopkeeper interrupted.

"Is your name Lisa Nuzaki?" she asked, mispronouncing it as Nuh-zaki instead of No-za-ki.

Lisa blinked. "Uh, yes… but it is No-za-ki," she corrected gently. "Why do you ask?"

With a knowing smile, the shopkeeper retrieved a letter from beneath the counter and held it up. Lisa's name shimmered under the soft light, with the subtitle beneath:

Lisa Nozaki

The girl with green hair and eyes.

Lisa grimaced slightly. *Must everyone comment on my hair?* she thought. She extended her hand. "May I have it?"

The shopkeeper handed over the letter with a cheerful, "Here you go!"

Lisa examined it closely, flipping it over to see a wax seal bearing the insignia of the Order of Saint Lorraine. A flicker of intrigue crossed her mind, she knew very little about the Order, but from her father's meetings, she understood they were people with wide spread diplomatic ties making them important.

Breaking the seal, Lisa opened the letter but quickly realized she couldn't read it in the dim purple glow of the crystals.

"I will have to read it later," she murmured, carefully tucking it into her purse.

Pushing aside her curiosity, she returned to the task at hand. "Do you have any lunar rosemary in stock?" she asked, offering a polite smile.

The shopkeeper leaned on the counter, grinning. "What, you're not going to tell us what was in the letter?"

Lisa smiled politely. "I cannot read it in here," she replied. "I will read it when I step outside, then I will tell you."

The shopkeeper laughed. "Fair enough. The lunar rosemary is on the side wall, back corner. We have ground and stalk."

Lisa thanked her and made her way to the shelf. She found the lunar rosemary easily; the stalks shimmered with a silver sheen, releasing a heavy mist that pooled on the floor, mingling with other fragrant vapors to create a mesmerizing rainbow haze.

Her heart sank when she read the price tags. "Lunar Rosemary, Ground – 25 coins per bottle. Lunar Rosemary Stalks – 10 coins each."

To meet her class requirements, she would need four stalks, but with her limited funds, the ground version was her only option.

Lisa sighed and recalled one of her business teacher's lessons: "Sometimes, you must create opportunities." She decided to try her luck.

Returning to the counter with the bottle in hand, she smiled sweetly. "Would you accept Harvest Crowns?" She tilted her head slightly, using her most innocent and vexing expression.

The shopkeeper flipped through a ledger, then shook her head. "Crowns?!? Sorry, I can't."

Lisa sighed inwardly. "How much was it again?" she asked, hoping she had misread the price.

"That will be twenty-five gold coins."

Lisa's shoulders slumped, but she kept her composure. She reached into her purse and carefully counted out the required amount, stacking the gold coins neatly on the counter. "Here you are," she said, forcing a polite smile despite the frustration bubbling inside her.

"Thank you, ma'am," the shopkeeper said cheerfully, sweeping the coins into a box beneath the counter.

Lisa sighed. "Thank you," she replied, dragging out the last syllable before turning to leave.

Halfway to the door, she heard the shopkeeper call out playfully, "Don't forget to tell us about the letter!"

Lisa chuckled lightly, shaking her head as she stepped outside into the bustling streets once more.

"Opportunity," Lisa whispered to herself, slipping the letter into her purse. "Will do," she called over her shoulder, stepping into the sunlit street.

Once in the daylight, she retrieved the letter and carefully unfolded it, the shimmering ink catching the sunlight.

To Miss Lisa Nozaki,

You are being followed, and I believe you are in grave danger. Please do not tell anyone about this letter. Come to West's Tavern—I will be waiting for you in the back.

Signed,

Brother Albert Thompson, The Order of Saint Lorraine

Lisa's eyes widened. "What?" she exclaimed, rereading the letter. "This makes no sense. Who would be after me?" She frowned, her grip tightening on the thick paper. "This cannot be right... it must be a mistake."

Turning on her heel, she strode back into Scent of the Isle, the letter still in hand. Approaching the counter, she held it up.

The shopkeeper perked up instantly. "Well? What does it say?"

Lisa narrowed her eyes. "How did you come to have this letter?"

The shopkeeper shrugged. "Some old man from the Order of Saint Lorraine dropped it off for you earlier this week." She leaned in with curiosity. "Why? What does it say?"

Lisa smiled playfully. "I am not supposed to tell you."

"You've got to be kidding me!" the shopkeeper groaned, throwing her hands up. "Come on, we've been wondering about it for days!"

Lisa tapped the letter thoughtfully against her chin. "What is it worth to you?" She smiled slyly. "Perhaps... five gold coins each?"

The three people in the store, two customers and the shopkeeper, exchanged glances, then stared at Lisa in disbelief.

"You can't be serious," the shopkeeper scoffed.

Lisa shrugged, placing the letter delicately on the counter. "You see, there's this dress I truly want in the square. It costs fifteen gold coins, and the shop owner refuses to accept Harvest Crowns, and I really want that dress."

The shopkeeper smirked. "For that much, we should be allowed to read the letter ourselves."

Lisa held up the letter teasingly. "I would need to see the coins first."

The trio exchanged a few hushed words before reluctantly producing three five-piece gold coins, setting them on the counter with a collective sigh.

Lisa smiled triumphantly. "Same time," she said, placing the letter down while sliding her hand protectively over the coins.

The shopkeeper placed a hand over the letter, and with a simultaneous nod, they exchanged their claims. Lisa scooped the coins into her purse while the trio eagerly crowded around the folded paper.

After a moment of silence, the shopkeeper looked back at Lisa, eyebrows raised. "So, what are you going to do?"

Lisa sighed, crossing her arms. "Honestly, I am going home. This cannot be real."

The shopkeeper groaned. "Really? But this Brother Albert knew you were going to be here."

Lisa shrugged. "I suppose, but he could have left letters all over town, hoping I'd come across one."

With a disappointed shake of her head, the shopkeeper handed the letter back. "Shame. It sounds interesting."

Lisa tucked the letter away, smiling to herself. "Perhaps. But I have better things to do."

She slipped the letter back into her purse and set off toward Asad's stand. As she made her way through the bustling street, she turned left at the corner, stepping back into the lively market square. The scent of spices and freshly baked bread filled the air as she spotted Asad standing behind his stall, arranging fabrics with his usual practiced efficiency.

"Mr. Asad I am back," Lisa announced, pulling the coins from her purse with a triumphant smile. "I am here for my dress."

Asad looked up with a raised brow. "Ah, welcome back. Do you have the coins?"

Lisa grinned and confidently placed the coins onto the wooden counter with a soft clink. "I have them right here."

Asad's eyes flicked to the coins, and for a moment, his expression darkened with doubt. "Only fifteen? I don't know…"

Lisa's heart skipped a beat. "What?" she exclaimed. "You promised me the dress if I brought fifteen gold coins!"

The merchant hesitated, looking at the dress thoughtfully before shrugging. "Well, if I said that…" He snatched up the coins quickly and retrieved the dress from the hanger, carefully placing it inside a decorative box.

Lisa let out a relieved breath, feeling the satisfaction of finally bringing that beautiful dress into her wardrobe. Glancing around the market, she spotted her friends seated at the same table from earlier, cool drinks in hand. Asad slid the box across the counter toward her.

"Thank you, miss. Have a great and prosperous day," he said, his tone businesslike and distant.

Lisa beamed at him. "Thank you," she replied brightly, picking up the box and making her way toward her friends.

Before she could reach them, a group of three guards surrounded the table, their leader speaking in a loud, commanding voice.

"Ladies, we're looking for your green-haired friend," he demanded.

Lisa froze, her heart pounding in her chest. Just as she was about to step forward, a hushed voice murmured urgently behind her.

"Don't let them catch you here."

She turned quickly and found herself face-to-face with an older man; his hair streaked with gray, his beard nearly fully silvered. He wore a crisp black-and-white uniform that looked official, yet unfamiliar.

"What?" Lisa asked, struggling to make sense of the situation.

The man gave a reassuring nod. "Did you receive my letter?"

Her eyes widened. "You are Brother Albert?"

He nodded once. "Yes. You must listen carefully. You are in danger."

Lisa's skepticism flared. "Who do you think is after me?" she demanded, her hand tightening around the box.

Albert glanced around warily. "Not here. Too many listening ears," he cautioned. "Your friends will be fine, but you need to disappear into the crowd."

Lisa frowned. "And what if I don't?"

Albert's expression grew grave. "If they get their hands on you, it will be the end of everything."

Lisa studied him, then arched an eyebrow. "So, you expect me to just go with you?" Her tone sharpened, skepticism swirling in her voice like the sash belt of her sundress caught in the wind.

Albert sighed. "I can't force you, and I don't want to fight with you." He leaned in slightly. "But tell me, if someone wanted to hurt your father, what do you think they'd do?"

Lisa glanced at the guards again, and suddenly the details stood out—subtle but wrong. Their uniforms were close, but not quite right. The armband color was off, and one had his insignia upside down.

Albert stepped away, blending into the crowd with a final word. "Keep yourself safe."

Lisa swallowed hard, realizing he was right.

"Where is she?" one of the guards barked.

"She's around here somewhere," Maggie's confident voice rang out. "We're just buying things for school."

Lisa took a careful step back, eyes scanning the market for an escape. Near her friends' table, she spotted a large potted plant. Taking a deep breath, she extended her right hand and traced a small spell circle in the air. Green energy crackled to life, forming a delicate glowing ring inscribed with six elegant glowing green runes that spun gently.

Suddenly, the market erupted into chaos.

A group of men dressed in black, with glowing blue ropes attached, stormed through the crowd, sending merchants and shoppers scrambling. Lisa seized the moment, ducking between two market stalls and pressing herself between their cloth walls, staying just within sight of her friends.

The false guards lunged for Maggie, Sarah, and Anna, but Lisa's spell took hold. The potted plant's vines shot upward, twisting around the impostors and yanking them away. The guards staggered back in shock, scanning the crowd for the source of the attack but unable to pinpoint Lisa's location.

Maggie and the others, now free, were swept up in the rush of panicked marketgoers.

From her hiding spot, Lisa peeked out and waved frantically. "Girls, over here!" she called, her voice barely cutting through the commotion.

Sarah spotted Lisa's frantic wave and immediately tapped Anna and Maggie. The three girls pushed through the fleeing crowd, dodging panicked shoppers and overturned stalls. At last, they reached Lisa, gathering in the narrow gap between the two booths.

"By The Harvest, are you all alright?" Lisa asked, scanning their faces with concern.

"What's going on?" Sarah demanded, wide-eyed as she took in the chaos.

"Lisa… what did you do?" Maggie asked, her brow furrowed in suspicion.

Lisa took a steadying breath. "I do not know what is happening, but I have to take care of something." She handed her bag, filled with Lunar Rosemary and Dreamroot leaves, to Maggie while clutching the dress box tightly against her chest. "Please take this. I will meet you all at the ship later."

"What?" Maggie's voice sharpened. "What do you mean, *you have something to do?* Lisa, this is insane!"

Lisa forced a reassuring smile. "I c…cannot explain right now, but I will be there. I promise."

Anna crossed her arms, her face full of doubt. "None of this makes sense. Why were those guards looking for you?"

Lisa hesitated before offering a careful reply. "I am not sure," she admitted, lowering her voice. "But I think someone is after us."

Maggie's eyes widened. "US?!?"

Lisa nodded, leaning in. "Yes. The only reason they didn't take you is because I was not with you. I have to meet someone who can help figure this out." Thinking of her father's teaching *You must make a person feel like they are important as long as they follow you.*

"Then we're coming with you," Anna insisted firmly.

Lisa shook her head. "No, that is too dangerous. If they see us together, they will take all of us. You must blend into the crowd while you still can. You do not stand out like I do." Motioning to her long green hair.

The three girls exchanged glances, suddenly aware of their hair, blonde, brown, and red, each blending seamlessly into the crowd, unlike Lisa's unmistakable forest-green locks.

Lisa softened her tone. "I swear I will meet you on the ship back to Laminae." Her eyes locked onto each of them, conveying quiet determination. "But for now, we must go our separate ways."

Reluctantly, Maggie nodded. "Alright, Lisa. But you better show up."

"I will," Lisa promised with a reassuring smile before slipping into the bustling marketplace, leaving her friends behind.

Lisa hurried through the market square, scanning the crowd for any sign of Brother Albert, but he was nowhere to be seen. Frustration crept into her chest as she pushed past vendors and shoppers, weaving through the labyrinth of stalls and carts.

Just as she was about to turn a corner, she collided with a solid figure. A strong hand caught her shoulder, steadying her.

"Oh! Excuse me," Lisa said breathlessly, looking up into the stern face of a uniformed city guard.

"Are you alright, miss?" the guard asked, his eyes searching her face with mild concern.

Lisa nodded quickly. "Yes, I am quite fine." Then, adopting a more timid demeanor, she added, "Do you know where I can find West's Tavern."

The guard's expression shifted to disapproval. "West's Tavern? Why would a young lady of your standing be looking for that place?"

Lisa straightened her posture, recalling her father's advice on persuasion. "The boat my family arrived on is docked nearby," she explained, her voice steady but with a carefully placed tremor. "I simply… I just want to go home." She widened her green eyes, letting a hint of distress slip through, playing the part of a lost girl perfectly.

The guard sighed, clearly falling for her act. "Alright, alright. Head down to the pier," he said, pointing. "Once you reach the pier, turn left and walk two blocks. You'll see West's Tavern on your left." He hesitated. "But don't go inside, young lady. That place is nothing but trouble."

Lisa put on her best expression of dismay, clutching the dress box tighter. "I most certainly will not," she said, her voice full of innocence.

The guard seemed satisfied and gave her a firm nod before continuing his patrol.

Once he was out of sight, Lisa exhaled, her resolve hardening. She turned toward the pier, the weight of the letter in her purse serving as a constant reminder that she was stepping into unknown territory.

Chapter 4

Albert Thompson, commonly known as "Brother Albert" among circles outside Order Island; is a dedicated member of the Order of Saint Lorraine, an esteemed society of men and women tasked with observing and recording the events that occur in the world of the Seven Kingdoms. Known simply as "The Order," their influence extends far beyond the kingdoms, fostering diplomatic ties with the secretive Aurorium Clan, the notorious Pirate Nation, and countless other enigmatic organizations scattered across the globe.

In his forty years, Albert has traversed vast distances in service of his duties. As an Order monk, observation is a sacred responsibility; one he has always undertaken to the best of his abilities. His peers often jest that he has filled an entire wing of journals on Order Island, chronicling his travels and duties. A decade into his service, Albert took on the role of investigator and soon realized the importance of cataloging information efficiently. His meticulous indexing transformed his wealth of knowledge into an indispensable resource, earning him quiet satisfaction whenever his brothers and sisters turned to his index books for guidance in their own investigations.

Now, Brother Albert faces his most critical and esteemed assignment, an honor bestowed upon only one member of each generation: *Guide to the Avatars*. His investigation led him to the discovery of four extraordinary girls, each born under a rare celestial alignment, their striking hair and eye colors marking them as chosen by the goddesses.

The violet-haired **Sophie Griffin**, born within the Aurorium Clan in Opulentia's grand capital, Granmark.

The fiery **Annabelle Salazar**, daughter of the infamous Pirate King, Javier Salazar, now in the care of Captain James "Kidd" Lowe aboard the good ship Stormfang.

The silver-eyed **Regina Fournier**, whose father Jules Fournier is a renowned ritualist, and her late mother Addison Fournier was a legendary Nexus Mage in the Kingdom of Laminae.

And the emerald-infused **Lisa Nozaki**, daughter of Governor Conrad Nozaki, ruler of Verdantia's sprawling Vendura Province.

Through the vast resources of the Order, Albert has kept a close watch over the girls for the past fourteen almost fifteen years, though Annabelle's unpredictable privateer lifestyle often proved a challenge. The Order holds a long-standing belief: *when girls are born under the same celestial sign with such unusual traits, it is a sign that the goddesses themselves have intervened, responding to an imminent threat looming over the world.*

As Albert continued his observations, a troubling pattern began to emerge. Isolated incidents, seemingly unconnected, revealed themselves as pieces of a far greater conspiracy: a young king of Stoneridge found dead, drained of all the blood inside him; an entire family of archaeologists slaughtered at a dig site, their notes and equipment mysteriously vanished; a pirate ship lost to the abyss, its lone survivor whispering tales of darkness rising to claim it. Together, these events painted a chilling picture.

On the girls' tenth birthday, Brother Marcus Igbinedion was appointed Albert's *First Assistant*, though the role remained largely inactive, as the Avatars had yet to awaken. However, recent developments left Albert with little doubt: *time was running out.*

A month ago, he made the decision: *he had to act today.*

Too many shadows had gathered, too many signs ignored. The conspiracy was moving against the girls, his girls, and Albert could not, would not, let them be caught unaware.

As Albert approached the front of West's Tavern, his eyes instinctively scanned the local security, a necessity in a place where the kingdom's guards rarely ventured. The leader of the security detail was a towering, broad-shouldered man clad in a vest adorned with an impressive collection of pins and medals received from the Stoneridge military. Albert recognized them instantly; these were no mere decorations. Unlike other kingdoms, the soldiers of Stoneridge served both in their formidable navy and their rugged mountain army, braving harsh, unforgiving terrain. The man's collection of honors testified to distinguished service in both arenas, an unmistakable mark of skill and resilience. His sheer bulk and the hard-earned weight of his reputation were more than enough to keep troublemakers in line. Anyone with a shred of sense knew better than to stir trouble inside West's.

As Albert neared, the four other guards seated at nearby tables cast quick, assessing glances at their leader, silently awaiting his judgment. The man raised a hand in a slow, dismissive wave, an unspoken signal that Albert posed no threat. Rising from his seat, he greeted him with a smile.

"Brother Albert," he said, his voice a deep rumble. "Back again, I see."

Albert returned the smile, his tone light. "Well, this is the best place in all the Seven Kingdoms to gather information."

He opened his jacket in a slow, deliberate motion, revealing nothing but a leather-bound book strapped securely to his lower back, alongside a pouch holding his writing utensils.

The guard raised a blond eyebrow, skepticism creeping into his expression. "Information, or ale?" he asked with a teasing edge, waving Albert inside.

Albert chuckled, fastening his jacket once more. "The best information is found with ale," he quipped, stepping past the man and pausing just long enough to add, "I'll be hosting four special visitors today. Can you let them through without too much hassle?"

The headguard crossed his arms, a smirk tugging at his lips. "Brother Albert, we don't hassle people," he replied, his voice carrying the weight of years spent enforcing order. "But everyone follows the laws of West's." He leaned in slightly. "How will we know your *special guests*?"

Albert grinned. "Easy, I gave them invitations," he said with a playful wink. "I'll be in the meeting room in the back."

"I'll let them know," the guard assured him with a nod.

Stepping inside, Albert took in the familiar scene. The first area of West's Tavern was a vast, bustling hall filled with long communal tables stretching lengthwise from the entrance, designed for patrons to settle in quickly. The walls were lined with a variety of tables, some circular, others rectangular, and even a few triangular. Albert knew firsthand the reason for the eclectic mix; the tavern's infamous brawls had a way of turning furniture into splinters, and the owner had long since given up on uniformity in favor of practicality.

The tavern's bar stretched across the entire far wall, directly opposite the communal tables. Strategically placed breaks in the counter allowed the waitstaff to weave in and out with remarkable speed, delivering food and drinks to eager patrons. Albert couldn't help but admire the seamless efficiency of the bartenders and servers. It was as if they had been born within these walls, each movement honed by years of experience, evolving to make the tavern operate like a well-oiled machine. Orders were taken, drinks mixed, plates delivered, payments collected, and change counted; all executed with practiced ease and, most impressively, with smiles that never faltered.

Albert challenged himself to find even a single bartender who wasn't smiling as they poured drinks or a waitress who wasn't beaming while darting between tables. After a full minute of silent observation, he sighed in surrender; his ever-watchful eye had failed him.

With a small smile of his own, he made his way to the private meeting room he had reserved the week prior. A tavern security guard stood at attention by the door, his posture as rigid as a statue. Albert gave him a respectful nod before stepping inside, shutting the door behind him.

The room was larger than he truly needed, but considering the personalities set to arrive today, the extra space might prove crucial. Sophie Griffin and Annabelle Salazar alone would need as much distance between them as possible if he wanted to avoid an early disaster.

A gentle knock at the door interrupted his thoughts. A cheerful waitress poked her head inside, offering him a bright smile.

"Anything I can get for you, Brother Albert?"

Albert reached into his pocket and retrieved a small pouch of tea leaves, handing it to her. "Could you brew me a pot with these?" He paused. "And a mug of ale, if you please." His own smile mirrored hers, warm and familiar.

"Right away," she replied, taking the leaves and disappearing through the door with practiced speed.

Left alone once more, Albert surveyed the room with a strategic eye, mentally placing each girl in a seat that would best minimize the inevitable tension. Satisfied with his arrangement, he finally selected his own spot at the head of the table; the ideal position to mediate and steer the conversation.

He walked over, unfastened the leather strap across his back, and carefully placed his journal on the table before settling into the chair. Taking a deep breath, he leaned back slightly, allowing a moment of stillness to settle over him.

"Any moment now," he whispered to himself, closing his eyes for just a second, steadying his thoughts for what was to come.

[----- 🛡 -----]

Being from Granmark and an Aurorium Sentinel, Sophie Griffin knew exactly where West's Tavern was and how to get there. Turn right past the gates, left at the docks, and walk straight. If you hit slip 79, you've gone too far. The route was etched into her mind like muscle memory.

As she walked, Sophie passed a row of bustling shops catering to sailors and merchants; places selling everything from rigging supplies to enchanted trinkets meant to ward off bad luck at sea. She recalled a lesson from Eclipse Baker during a previous tour of the area: "*These shops are goldmines for intel,*" he'd said, "*but they're also prime spots for pickpockets, so watch yourself.*" She took his advice to heart, walking with calculated caution while discreetly scanning her surroundings.

Arriving at the entrance of West's, Sophie spotted five men sitting together, West's security detail. At the center stood Dadid, the head of security, a seasoned veteran of the Stoneridge military. His vest bore the weight of his service, pins and medals marking his time in both the navy and the harsh mountain campaigns. To his left stood two men from Umbrathorn, their attire crafted from the same rugged blue fabric as Dadid's but lacking the distinctive pins of Stoneridge service. It made sense, they hadn't earned them. To his right were two more guards: one from Verdantia, sporting the region's signature farmer's hat, though stylized more commonly in Opulentia than in its homeland; and the other from Magitekopolis, his ears adorned with glowing earrings that pulsed in alternating hues of blue, yellow, and orange. Sophie did not know how they worked, but if she did, she'd have a pair of her own in purple, without the need for rotating colors.

Steeling herself, Sophie approached Dadid with confidence. "Hello, sir. I have an appointment here," she said, flashing her Aurorium badge for entry.

Dadid barely glanced at it before holding up a hand, palm out. "Nice try," he said with a smirk. "But we don't let Aurorium Sentinels in without a superior. Go find yourself a Shadow, an Eclipse, or an Apex if you want in."

Sophie groaned in frustration. "Seriously? I'm not trying to sneak in." She quickly pulled a folded letter from Brother Albert from her pocket and held it out.

Dadid took the letter, scanning it with a resigned shake of his head. "*Albert,*" he muttered. "Alright, alright. You can go in, but you'll need to check your weapons at the bar. No exceptions."

Sophie sighed, placing a hand on her hip. "I really don't want to give up my pistol."

Dadid crossed his arms. "Then come back with a Shadow or Eclipse," he said firmly. "Only Aurorium on active duty get to keep their weapons, and if you're here to see Brother Albert, I know you're not on duty."

Sophie instinctively glanced at her backpack, where the rolled-up jumpsuit inside seemed to weigh heavier on her shoulders. Her curiosity burned, and the need for answers outweighed her pride. With a resigned nod, she reached for the pistol holstered on her hip, but Dadid lifted a hand again, stopping her mid-motion.

"Inside," he instructed. "I got a guy who'll take it from you."

Sophie rolled her eyes but nodded, stepping inside the bustling tavern. The air was thick with the scent of ale, roasting meat, and the murmur of dozens of conversations. She scanned the room quickly and already spotted at least four criminal plots taking shape, two groups whispering over what were likely robbery plans, and a pirate crew sizing up their next mark with predatory grins.

A tap on her shoulder interrupted her thoughts.

"I'll take that from you," said a burly man clad in the same rugged vest as Dadid, his hand outstretched expectantly.

Sophie hesitated. "Are you sure I can't keep it?" she asked, her voice carrying a hint of hopeful persuasion.

The guard snorted, his fingers curling and uncurling in a silent demand. "Look, you're lucky to even be in here."

With a reluctant frown, Sophie unholstered her pistol and handed it over. "I'm going to need that back," she warned.

The man nodded, slipping the weapon into a lockbox behind the bar and handing her a tattered slip of paper. "No problem—just as soon as you leave," he promised.

Then, with a tilt of his head, he gestured toward a door at the back. "Brother Albert's waiting for you."

"Okay," Sophie muttered, heading toward the double doors the guard had pointed to. As she crossed the bustling tavern floor, a prickling sensation crept up her spine, too many eyes tracking her movements.

Great, she thought, resisting the urge to reach for the pistol no longer at her side. If things went south, she'd have to rely on her fists, and she wasn't thrilled by the odds.

As she navigated through the crowded room, a waitress suddenly stepped into her path, eyes wide with admiration.

"Oh my goodness, your hair is gorgeous!" the woman gushed. "How'd you dye it that shade of purple?"

Sophie blinked, momentarily thrown off by the question. "I didn't dye it. It's always been purple," she said flatly.

The waitress tilted her head, clearly skeptical. "Huh. Okay... I guess," she said, still eyeing Sophie's hair as she walked away.

Sophie shook off the odd encounter and pushed through the double doors, stepping into a quieter, more spacious room. At the center sat an older man, his head tilted back, eyes closed in apparent relaxation.

She hesitated. "Umm... are you Brother Albert?"

The man stirred at the sound of her voice, his eyes fluttering open as he straightened in his chair. "Oh! Yes, yes...that's me," he said quickly, his gaze sharpening as he took her in. "Miss Griffin. I'm glad you received my letter."

Sophie frowned, adjusting the strap of her backpack. "It was a bit late," she said, her voice edged with irritation. She motioned to the pack and the jumpsuit tucked inside. "I was attacked by strawmen in black suits that glowed blue...ropes. What do you know about that?"

Albert's brow furrowed in thought. "Strawmen... glowing blue, you say?" He shook his head. "I'm afraid that's not familiar to me. Perhaps one of the others will know."

Sophie's eyes narrowed. "Others?" she echoed, suspicion creeping into her tone. The size of the room suddenly made more sense. "How many?"

"Just three more," Albert said with a calming gesture. "They should be here shortly." He offered a small smile. "Please sit, and relax, I have tea on the way."

Sophie sighed and dropped into the chair Albert indicated, her backpack landing with a soft thud against the wall behind her. "Alright, but let's get to it why is the Order of Saint Lorraine interested in me?"

Albert's expression softened. "Tell me, Sophie... haven't you ever wondered why your hair is violet?" He leaned forward slightly. "No one else in your family has violet hair, or violet eyes, for that matter."

Sophie shifted uncomfortably. "It's... come up," she admitted. "Are you saying the Order did something to me?" Her voice hardened as unease tightened in her chest.

Albert raised a hand in reassurance. "Oh no, my dear. It wasn't the Order." His eyes twinkled with something deeper, something reverent. "It was one of the goddesses."

Before Sophie could respond, a soft knock at the door interrupted them. The waitress from earlier entered, balancing a tray laden with a steaming teapot, four cups, and a frothing glass of ale.

"Service as ordered," she chirped, placing the tray down with practiced grace.

Albert grinned. "Saved by the smile," he quipped. "Please, have a cup of tea, I think you'll like it."

Sophie eyed the shimmering surface of the tea as she poured it into a cup. The liquid glowed faintly under the dim lighting, its inviting aroma wafting up to her. She blew gently across the surface and took a cautious sip. Warmth flooded through her, and a surge of almost electric energy coursed through her veins.

"This... this is amazing," she said, genuinely surprised. "What is this?"

Albert took a sip of his ale and leaned back in his chair. "A special tea leaf that only grows on Order Island. We call it goddess tea."

Sophie eyed him over the rim of her cup. "You're not having any?"

Albert chuckled. "No, my dear," he said with an easy smile. "It's not to my taste."

[-----⦿-----]

Lisa Nozaki walked briskly toward the docks, following the guard's directions, past the gate, turn left at the fork. The deeper she ventured, the more she realized how different this area was from the bustling, well-patrolled port she had arrived at earlier. Here, the guards seemed to vanish after the entrance to the pier, leaving travelers to their own wits and instincts.

Sensing the shift in atmosphere, Lisa instinctively pulled her purse closer and tightened her grip on the bag holding her dress. Her eyes darted across the scene before her, shops and stalls lined the pier, each catering to the constant ebb and flow of sailors and dockworkers.

One storefront caught her attention: a cartoonish fish wearing a pirate hat, winking cheekily from the painted sign above the door. The shop's name, *Salmon's Selection*, was scrawled in bold, playful letters. Lisa chuckled to herself. *I have to check that place out later,* she thought, already picturing the fish mascot framed on her dorm room wall at the academy.

Continuing on, she passed a shadowy alley where a group of men sat huddled around a small fire, their clothes worn and tattered. Most were asleep, while the few awake whispered among themselves, their faces drawn and weary. Lisa's heart twinged with sympathy, but she didn't know what she could do, so she kept walking, trying not to stare.

As she approached a large tavern with a glowing sign that read *West's Tavern,* a wave of uncertainty washed over her. A group of rugged-looking men lounged outside, their eyes sweeping over newcomers with quiet assessment. Lisa swallowed hard, wondering if this was truly worth the risk.

I've come this far... she reminded herself, straightening her posture. Gathering her courage, she stepped toward the entrance, where a towering blond man stood guard. His tough blue vest sagged under the weight of service pins and medals, each one a testament to his time in the Stoneridge military.

Before she could speak, the man raised a large hand, palm out in a universal stop gesture.

"Oh no," he said, shaking his head. "Listen, miss, you've got to be in the wrong place. Why don't you..."

Then his eyes caught on her green hair, and his words faltered. He froze, his gaze lingering a moment too long.

Lisa, well accustomed to people staring at her hair, felt a familiar sting of annoyance. Some people commented; others whispered. But she couldn't remember the last time someone had actually frozen like this.

Offended, she crossed her arms. "You look as if you have seen a ghost," she said, her voice edged with impatience.

The blond man let out a sigh. "Let me guess," he muttered. "Brother Albert."

Lisa blinked, then quickly pulled the letter from her bag, realizing what he meant. She handed it over silently.

The Stoneridge guard glanced at the envelope, shaking his head in exasperation. "That old man…" he muttered, handing it back. Turning to one of his men, Jose, the Magitekopolis native with glowing, color-shifting earrings, he jerked his head toward Lisa. "Take this one to the back room."

Jose groaned. "Why me?"

The blond man didn't answer. He didn't need to. A single sharp look sent Jose scrambling to his feet. With a resigned sigh, he turned to Lisa and gestured toward the tavern's interior. "If you'll please follow me, ma'am," he said, tone polite but far from enthusiastic.

Lisa nodded. "Of course."

As they moved through the lively, crowded tavern, Lisa took in the boisterous atmosphere. The air buzzed with energy, laughter, shouting, and the clink of tankards blending into a constant hum. The place felt alive, brimming with stories and secrets waiting to be uncovered.

"This place looks like fun," she said aloud. "Is it always this lively?"

Jose didn't break stride. "Oh yeah," he replied without looking back. "Fun for everyone." His voice was flat, practiced, like someone who'd said the same thing too many times.

Lisa wasn't sure if that was meant to reassure her or warn her.

They reached a set of heavy double doors at the back. Without pause, Jose pushed them open, revealing a spacious room centered around a large square conference table. Sitting at its center, just as she remembered, was the older man, Brother Albert.

Jose held the door for her with a small nod. "Here you go."

Lisa stepped in, nerves tingling with anticipation. She offered Brother Albert a polite nod, then scanned the room. Her eyes landed on a girl dressed head to toe in purple, purple hair, purple eyes, and even a purple fedora resting casually on the table. Despite their striking differences, Lisa's pale complexion and the girl's dark, rich skin, something about her felt strangely familiar. As if they were connected in a way Lisa couldn't quite explain.

"Um… hi," Lisa said, unsure of what else to offer.

The girl looked up from her teacup. "Hello," she replied, taking another sip from a tea cup with calm detachment.

"Sentinel Sophie Griffin of the Aurorium Clan," Brother Albert said, gesturing toward the girl in purple. "Meet Lisa Nozaki of the great kingdom of Verdantia, a student at Valorcrest Academy." He turned to Lisa with a warm smile. "Please, Miss Nozaki, have a seat. The last two should arrive shortly." He took a sip from the mug in front of him.

Lisa moved to the indicated chair, setting her belongings neatly underneath the table. She slung her purse over the back of the chair and settled in. Offering a bright smile, she extended a hand to Sophie. "It is a pleasure to meet you."

Sophie hesitated briefly before setting down her cup and shaking Lisa's hand. "Pleasure," she replied, the word sounding unfamiliar on her tongue. After a beat, she asked, "You're from the Sacred Acres?"

Lisa's eyes lit up. "Yes! My father is the Governor of Vendura," she said proudly. "And you are from the Jiberau?"

Sophie's expression hardened instantly. Her gaze sharpened, the warmth in her face vanishing. "What?!" she snapped. "What did you just say?!"

Lisa flinched. "I—"

"Ladies, if I may," Albert said smoothly, raising a hand before Lisa could respond. His voice was calm, but firm. "Miss Sophie, as you know, Verdantia does not recognize the Aurorium Clan. It's understandable that Lisa may not realize using that term is... so inappropriate."

"You don't say," Sophie muttered, casting sharp glances between Albert and Lisa.

Lisa's confusion twisted into guilt. "I do apologize," she said carefully. "That is the name we have always used for your people."

Sophie's grip tightened around her teacup. "That name means *slave*. When you call someone that, you're calling them a **slave**." Her voice was steady, but full of quiet anger. "There's no existence worse than that, no hope, no home, not even a claim to your own body. Even the dead are free." She set her cup down gently, the porcelain clinking with finality. "So let me make this perfectly clear: I am *not* a Jiberau." The name came out like a curse, punctuated by a slight shake of her head. She leaned back, crossed her legs, and bounced one foot, her agitation barely contained.

Lisa swallowed, Sophie's words heavy in her chest. She took a breath and chose her words with care. "I am truly sorry," she said sincerely. "I promise I will never call you that again. I meant no disrespect."

Brother Albert gave a quiet nod of approval. "The correct name for her people is *Aurorium*," he said. "In the other six kingdoms, they serve as protectors and investigators, helping uphold justice and order." He glanced at Sophie with a small smile. "Miss Griffin is quite accomplished. With her record, I wouldn't be surprised if she earns a promotion within the year."

Sophie said nothing, only took another sip of tea—but the tension in her shoulders eased, if only slightly.

"How do you know that?" Sophie asked, her irritation still sharp as she leveled a cutting glance at Brother Albert.

Albert met her gaze with an easy smile, unfazed. "Miss Griffin, it's my duty to know these things about you," he said smoothly. "In fact, I make it my business to know everything about all of you." He leaned back slightly, steepling his fingers. "How do you think I got those letters to you?"

Lisa, relieved by the shift in attention away from her earlier misstep, quietly poured herself a cup of tea. She took a cautious sip, and the moment the warm liquid touched her tongue, she was wrapped in comfort, like slipping into soft pajamas beneath a heavy, cozy blanket on a cold night.

"Wow..." The word slipped out before she could stop it, cutting through the tension.

Albert pounced on the moment, his eyes twinkling with amusement. "I'm glad you like it," he said, using Lisa's reaction as a convenient diversion from Sophie's glare.

Sophie, however, wasn't so easily shaken. She crossed her arms, clearly still unsatisfied, but Lisa was too absorbed in the tea's warmth to notice.

[-----❀-----]

Just last week, Regina Fournier had been enjoying the quiet simplicity of life, helping her father tend the library, looking after her little brother Mattie, and studying for classes at Kingdom School Number Seventy-One. She was a star on the debate team, beloved by her teammates for her semi-photographic memory. Life had been predictable. Safe.

Now, she was hurrying through dimly lit streets toward a tavern, accompanied by a fierce-looking girl with wild orange hair and matching eyes. **Annabelle Salazar**, the girl had introduced herself earlier, a pirate or rather *privateer* through and through. Beautiful in a rough, untamed way that Regina found both intriguing and intimidating.

As they walked, Regina's mind buzzed with questions. Chief among them: *How had Brother Albert known where to find Annabelle?*

"I mean," Regina said aloud, glancing at her companion, "if you're a pirate and you got to port a day early, how would he know you'd even be here?"

Annabelle shrugged, cradling her arm where blood still trickled from fresh wounds. "I don't know," she muttered with a wince. "Magic? Spies? Who knows how these Order types operate." She shifted, visibly uncomfortable. "All I know is, that witch…uh, Mage, whoever she was didn't hold back a bit."

Regina winced. "I'd heal you if I could, but… I never learned healing magic." Her voice carried an edge of apology. "I know it exists; it just wasn't part of my studies."

Annabelle smirked despite the pain. "Figures," she said dryly. "Really a shame, could've used some right about now."

As they pressed on, they passed a group of ragged men huddled in an alley, some slumped in drunken sleep, others whispering around a shared bottle.

Regina hesitated. "Maybe they have something for your cuts," she offered, nodding toward the group.

Annabelle scoffed. "Better not," she warned. "Those guys? They'd cut your throat for a drink." Her voice was flat, matter-of-fact. "Most of 'em are Portside Petes, they used to crew ships, got booted at port when they couldn't keep up anymore."

Regina swallowed and quickened her pace. "Oh," she muttered. "Maybe someone at the tavern can help instead."

"That's the hope," Annabelle replied, her tone edged with frustration. She clenched her injured hand, clearly eager to get inside and end their search.

When they reached West's Tavern, they were met by the imposing sight of five men stationed outside. At the center stood a massive blond man from Stoneridge, his sturdy blue jacket decorated with twelve military pins and four gleaming medals, the highest honors of the Stoneridge military.

Regina's sharp eyes scanned them. Two pins for cold-weather training (levels one and two), three for distinguished naval service, another for commendable conduct. Four marked valor in land combat, one for defense of Stoneridge's shores, and the last, perhaps the most telling, denoted combat against pirates.

To his left stood a burly man from Islewind, wearing a beret in the flag's colors. Nearly as large as the Stoneridge veteran, he radiated the air of someone well-acquainted with rough seas—and rougher fights. On the opposite side, two smaller but no less intimidating men from Umbrathorn stood silently, their calculating stares making Regina uneasy.

Before they could take another step, the blond man raised a commanding hand. "What are you doing here?!?" he barked, eyes locking on Annabelle with a look of both authority and exasperation.

"Dadid," Annabelle said smoothly, slipping into charm despite the pain. "I have a meeting at yer establishment." She raised her injured arm with exaggerated innocence.

Dadid's expression didn't budge. His outstretched hand curled into a pointed finger. "What part of 'banned for a month' don't you understand?"

Annabelle's face contorted in protest. "What? That should be over by now! A lass was gone at least a month."

"You still have a week left," Dadid shot back. "So do yourself a favor and head back to your ship and send someone else to smash the place up."

Annabelle huffed and pulled out the letter Regina had given her. "I'll have you know I was invited," she said, holding it up triumphantly.

Dadid didn't hide his skepticism. "Who'd you steal this from?" he asked, eyeing the letter.

"Oi!" Annabelle snapped. "It's got me name on it, thank ye very much."

He snatched it, flipped it over, and inspected the seal. Then sighed. "By the spirit of the bear… that old man." Shaking his head, he finally turned to Regina.

"And who's this?" he asked, eyes scanning her with the same scrutiny he'd given Annabelle.

"Hello!" Regina said brightly, stepping forward. "I'm Regina Fournier, from the Kingdom of Laminae. My family's currently overseeing the main royal library there. I received a letter from the Order last week asking me to assist Ms. Salazar." She gestured toward Annabelle, who gave a half-hearted wave. "I arrived in Granmark today, had to save her with a sunlight spell… oh, and I gave her that letter. Her instructions said we were both supposed to meet Brother Albert here."

She paused, looking at Dadid with wide, hopeful eyes.
"I'm not sure how to find him, though, since I've never met him. This place is really busy. Do you know Brother Albert? Maybe he has a sign or something that says 'Brother Albert'?"

Regina pursed her lips in thought.

"I really should've studied locator magic. Or aura-sensing… Wait, no, that wouldn't help, I've never met him, so I wouldn't know his aura. Hmm. Maybe I should get a dog and make him my familiar. Then he could sniff out Brother Albert…"

Dadid stared at her, blinking slowly. Speechless. After a long moment, he dragged out a hesitant, "Okaaay."

Regina winced. "Sorry. My dad says I talk too fast when I'm excited." She took a calming breath, then smiled sheepishly. "It doesn't happen much when we're on caretaking service, so I was really happy to get the letters."
Her tone suddenly shifted.

"Anyway, do you have any medical supplies? Annabelle was bitten by some kind of shadow… or a dog… or something, and her arm's still bleeding."

Dadid, still mentally buffering from Regina's monologue, repeated dumbly, "Medical supplies?"

"Yes!" Regina said eagerly, ticking off items on her fingers. "Ember root, antiseptic tonic, or maybe some kintavae leaves to stop the bleeding? She says she's fine, but she's still holding her arm, and I'm really getting worried."

Dadid glanced at Annabelle, who gave him a knowing look.

"Yeah," she said, leaning against the wall with a smirk. "If ye don't say nothin', she'll just talk faster."

Shaking his head as if to clear it, Dadid refocused on the letter still in his hand. "Listen," he said at last, "Brother Albert's in the back. But you'll have to leave your weapons at the front." He looked straight at Annabelle. "**All** of your weapons."

Annabelle gasped, pressing her hand to her chest in mock offense. "Why are you looking at me? I'm an upstanding citizen!"

42

Before Dadid could respond, a towering man stepped out of the tavern. He wore a blue denim vest, and his glowing Sentavo earrings pulsed in rhythmic waves of blue, yellow, and green.

"Jose. Just in time," Dadid said, nodding toward Regina and Annabelle. "Take these two to Brother Albert's room."

He pointed again at Annabelle, his tone firm. "And make sure she's not carrying **anything** this time."

Jose grinned. "Sure thing, boss." He turned to them with a theatrical bow. "This way, ladies."

Regina and Annabelle followed him into the bustling tavern but stopped short just past the entrance.

A burly man wearing the same vest as the other guards, was perched on a stool, blocking the path. He extended a hand toward Annabelle. "You know the drill," he said gruffly.

Annabelle groaned, rolling her eyes. "Such a pain," she muttered, pulling the cutlass from her belt and handing it over. "I just got this back from the guards."

She tried to step past, but the guard's hand remained outstretched.

"The anchor too," he said, pointing at her waist.

Annabelle blinked innocently. "This? Tis me belt," she protested. "Ye want everyone to see me knickers fall down?"

The man didn't flinch. "We both know it isn't," he said, curling and uncurling his fingers in silent demand. "Cough it up."

Annabelle glanced toward the tavern door and huffed. "Ye people have no trust."

From outside, Dadid's voice thundered: "We know you're lying, girl. Just give up the anchor."

Annabelle let out a dramatic groan, then reluctantly unwrapped the heavy belt and handed it over. "I better get that back. It's got sentimental value."

"I bet it does," the guard said with a smirk, tucking the anchor and chain behind the bar.

Inside the meeting room, Regina and Annabelle were greeted by an unexpected sight. Sitting at the long table were two other girls; one with vibrant green hair and matching eyes, wearing a delicate white sundress, and the other dressed entirely in purple, right down to the fedora resting on the table before her. The girl in purple wore an Aurorium Sentinel badge pinned to her well-groomed suit, the insignia catching the light.

Regina's mind raced. *Who are they? And what's with their hair and eyes?* She could tell Annabelle was thrown too, though the pirate masked her surprise behind practiced nonchalance.

At the head of the table, Brother Albert watched the scene unfold with quiet fascination. The four girls: Salazar, Fournier, Griffin, and Nozaki, stood or sat in tense silence, sizing each other up. Despite their stark differences, there was an unmistakable thread between them.

Albert had no doubt what each of them was thinking. *Fournier's already analyzing the room. Griffin's gauging threats. Salazar's figuring how this benefits her. And Nozaki...* He glanced at Lisa. *She's probably planning how to make everyone friends.*

He cleared his throat before the silence took root.

"Ladies, welcome," he said warmly, spreading his arms. "Let me introduce you. Sophie Griffin of the Aurorium Clan, here in Granmark," he said, gesturing toward the girl in purple. "And Lisa Nozaki of the Kingdom of Verdantia, daughter of Governor

43

Nozaki of Vendura." He turned to the newcomers. "Please meet Regina Fournier of the Kingdom of Laminae, and Annabelle Salazar of the good ship *Stormfang*."

He gestured to the chairs. "Please, have a seat. Enjoy some tea, we have much to discuss."

As they settled in, Regina carefully placed her bag beneath the table, though her gaze kept drifting toward Sophie and Lisa. Annabelle flopped into a chair with a wince, drawing Brother Albert's attention to her arm.

"Annabelle, you're hurt," he noted, concern creeping into his voice. "What happened?"

Annabelle shrugged, brushing it off. "Got jumped by some dark shadow witch." She winced as Regina poured herself a cup of tea. "No idea why."

Albert sighed. "I think I might know. But first, Miss Nozaki, could you assist Miss Salazar with some healing?"

Lisa stood immediately. "I can try," she said, circling toward Annabelle.

Annabelle stiffened, lifting her good hand defensively. "I don't need no help. I ain't some helpless girlie."

Regina leaned in, speaking quickly. "I think you do. You've been holding your arm since we met, and it hasn't stopped bleeding. You could be in serious danger. It's better to deal with it now."

Albert, who had heard about Regina's fast-talking habits, found experiencing it in person something else entirely.

Lisa knelt beside Annabelle, her tone gentle. "Please let me take a look, okay?"

Annabelle glanced between her and Albert, then sighed. "How much is this gonna cost me?"

Albert smiled. "Don't worry…I'll cover it."

Reluctantly, Annabelle slid off her jacket, revealing the soaked fabric beneath. Lisa's eyes widened.

"Oh my," she breathed, frowning. "You must be in so much pain."

Annabelle shrugged. "Eh, I've had worse."

Lisa rolled up her sleeves past the elbows, and traced a glowing red spell circle with red runes surrounding it in the air. the circular healing sigil took form, pulsing with magic.

"This is going to sting a bit," she warned, as the spell began to flow.

Annabelle flinched, clenching her jaw. "A bit?" she hissed through her teeth.

"Sorry," Lisa said, keeping her focus on the spell. "That shadow thing bit into you very deep."

Regina, watching closely, couldn't hold back. "What kind of magic is that?" she asked, her words tumbling out in a rush. "It looks like earth magic or rune spells? No, maybe it's moon magic? But it could also be the sacred dance from Stoneridge—"

Annabelle groaned. "You better tell her, or she'll never stop."

Lisa chuckled softly. "It is called *Earthbloom*," she explained as she worked. "I can manipulate anything connected to the Earth."

Regina's eyes lit up. "Ohhh, Earthbloom! That makes sense mostly people from Verdantia can use that system. I'm a Nexus Mage," she added proudly. "I can use almost any magic system I just have to understand it first."

Sophie, who had been watching quietly, finally spoke. "How do you breathe?" she asked, tilting her head in mock curiosity.

Regina blinked, genuinely puzzled. "What do you mean?"

Before Sophie could answer, Lisa finished the spell with a gentle flourish. "All done," she announced. "It is still going to hurt for a while, but the wound's closed."

Annabelle flexed her arm, then gave a satisfied grin. "Aye, thanks," she said, nodding to Lisa. "I owe ye one missy."

Lisa returned to her seat beside Sophie, while Albert cleared his throat and took a deep breath.

"Ladies," he said, his voice firm but welcoming, "thank you all for coming. I am Brother Albert Thompson of the Order of Saint Lorraine." His gaze swept across the table, making sure each girl was paying attention. "I reached out to you because you are all so very special... and because you're in danger."

A hush fell over the room. The girls exchanged tense glances, their eyes flicking between one another, each noting the strange similarities they shared, yet unmistakably different.

Regina was the first to speak. "What do you mean, danger?" she asked, frowning.

"Aye," Annabelle added, leaning forward. "And how did ye even know I'd be here today?"

Sophie's tone was sharper. "How long have you been watching us?"

Lisa, ever composed, asked, "Why wouldn't you just contact our parents? Or the local guards?"

Albert raised a hand. "If I may continue," he said calmly. He waited until the room quieted. "Throughout history, young women like yourselves, touched by the twelve goddesses, have emerged. They each possessed distinctive traits, setting them apart."

He paused, his voice deepening. "When a goddess selects an avatar, it means she wants to bring change. But for four goddesses to choose avatars at once? That is... unprecedented." The room went still. Albert pressed on. "I have been chosen to serve as your guide."

Sophie crossed her arms. "Guide to what, exactly?"

"Aye," Annabelle said, eyes narrowing. "Where exactly are we going?"

Albert leaned in, his tone serious. "The goddesses gave you their power for a reason; and I am sure I know what that is." He looked at Annabelle. "There is a conspiracy moving through the Seven Kingdoms. The attack on you, Miss Salazar, is just part of it. They're targeting all of you."

Sophie's eyes narrowed. "That's not proof. Anyone could've attacked her, for a bounty, a grudge, an unpaid debt, or whatever."

Annabelle scowled. "Oi, I pay all me debts, thank ye very much, dumb grape copper."

Albert stepped in before the tension could boil over. "You could be right, Miss Griffin. But then how do you explain the attack on you? Do you have enemies?"

Sophie hesitated. "No... I don't know why they came after me."

Annabelle leaned back, smirking. "Maybe someone was settling a score. Coppers aren't exactly beloved, y'know."

Sophie sat straighter, her tone cold. "First of all, it's *Aurorium*, not copper. And second, we uphold justice in the Seven Kingdoms. Unlike criminal pirates like you."

Annabelle slammed her hand on the table. "You don't know a damn ting about us!" she snapped. "Without the Pirate Nation, the kingdoms would grind to a halt."

Sophie's gaze sharpened. "And without the Aurorium, they'd collapse into chaos."

Albert sighed, rubbing his temples. *I knew this would happen*, he admitted to himself. Then said in a loud voice: "Ladies, please. This isn't helping."

Annabelle wasn't done. "Criminals?" she repeated, glaring. "What do ye know? All ye coppers are go fer ..."

Lisa, who had been silent until now, slammed her hands on the table, startling everyone. "**Just stop it!!**" she snapped, glaring between Sophie and Annabelle. "Can you not even try to get along? He said we are in danger and you two are the ones who were actually attacked!"

Sophie exhaled sharply, clearly frustrated. She reached for her fedora and swept it off the table in a single motion. "You know what? This is a waste of my time." She stood abruptly, purple eyes flashing. "If there really is danger, then my clan, the Aurorium will handle it. Like we always do."

Albert stood too, urgency creeping into his voice. "Miss Griffin, please; hear me out. You and your clan could be in serious danger."

Sophie slung her bag over one shoulder and adjusted her hat. "Goodbye, Brother Albert." Her voice was clipped and dismissive. She walked to the door, paused, then glanced back. "Good day to you all."

And with that, she stepped out, the door slamming behind her.

"Good riddance," Annabelle called after her, loud enough for Sophie to hear. "We don't need any coppers mucking things up."

Albert sighed and rubbed his temple. "Way to go, Albert," he muttered admonishing himself, *first thing you do as their guide and I completely foul it all up.* He debated whether to follow her, But a glance at the three girls who remained, Lisa, Annabelle, and Regina, convinced him to stay. He lowered himself back into his seat with a weary smile.

"I apologize, ladies," he said, taking a slow sip from his mug. After a moment, he continued. "I believe the attacks on Salazar and Griffin confirm that all of you are targets. Thankfully, I was able to reach Miss Fournier in time to help Miss Salazar."

Regina frowned. "How did you even know where to find Annabelle? I just... stumbled into her."

"Aye," Annabelle added, her tone suspicious. "I came back to port a day early. How'd ye know I'd be here?"

Albert leaned back slightly, a knowing smile playing at his lips. "You made good time getting to Stoneridge to drop off that *cargo.* I bet Captain Kidd pushed hard to return to Granmark early and line up another job. That's how most privateer crews operate, *keep sailing while supplies are fresh.*"

He met Annabelle's gaze. "And after a hard sail like that, I figured you'd want at least a day to relax in port." His smile faded. "I also knew a Mage was tracking you after your last job. She couldn't strike aboard the *Stormfang,* so I assumed she'd wait until you got back to Granmark."

Annabelle folded her arms. "So ye *do* know that shadow witch."

Albert nodded. "Only by name and reputation" he replied coolly. "She's one of several I've tracked, members of this conspiracy. She's not the only one watching you."

The girls exchanged uneasy looks.

Albert turned to Regina. "Do you remember the man who trains birds outside the library?"

Regina tilted her head. "Yes... he's there every morning. But I only see him when we're staying at the library. When we're at home, I never see him."

Albert's expression sharpened. "When you're at home, he's walking dogs."

Regina's face drained of color.

Lisa spoke up, shaking her head. "I don't have anyone following me. My life is...*normal.*"

Albert flipped through his journal, his voice calm but firm. "Members of your household staff recently came into a surprising amount of money, one of your maids sent her son to a prestigious military school." He closed the book with a soft *thud.* "With a staff like yours, there's no need to plant someone close. They just need to listen. This trip to Granmark is the first thing you've done without them. That's why I had to wait until now to approach you."

His tone softened. "Your safety is of course my top priority."

Annabelle scoffed. "How could anyone be followin' me? I ain't got no servants or bird trainers. And I trust me crew to the ends of the sea."

Albert studied her. "Think about it, Ms. Salazar. How many shady passengers have you ferried across the seas? How many of them would sell your route for a pouch of coin?" He took a slow sip from his mug. "Or better yet... how many booked passage on the *Stormfang* just to keep an eye on *you*? you don't exactly do a background check on your passengers and crew."

Annabelle shifted, her confidence faltering.

Regina tapped her fingers on the table. "This could all be conjecture. Your *evidence* is all circumstantial. There are other explanations. How can you be sure?"

Albert smiled faintly. "Normally, you'd be right, Miss Fournier." He leaned forward, voice low and steady. "But I knew from the start that the four of you were touched by the goddesses. I was already watching. And when strangers start appearing... when small events line up just right... I don't believe in coincidence."

Annabelle raised her teacup, narrowing her eyes. "And how do ye know we're goddesses?"

Albert's smile widened slightly. "I never said you *were* goddesses." He let the silence hang. "You are their avatars, blessed with a fraction of their power."

He let that sink in, then added, "Tell me... haven't you wondered why *I'm* not drinking the tea?"

The room fell silent.

Regina froze mid-sip. Lisa blinked. Annabelle promptly spat her mouthful across the table.

"Oi!" she spluttered. "What did you do to the tea?!"

Albert raised his hands, amused. "Relax. The tea is harmless to you. It's brewed from leaves that only grow on Order Island. But if someone untouched by a goddess drinks it, it makes them violently ill within mere moments."

He glanced at their cups. "But I bet all of you feel fine. More than fine, right?"

The girls glanced at one another, unsettled.

"I have more answers," Albert went on. "But not here. I have everything you need in my workshop on Order Island."

He drained the last of his ale, then turned to Annabelle. "Ms. Salazar, I'd like to book passage aboard the *Stormfang*. Four passengers, to Order Island."

Annabelle wiped her mouth with her sleeve, eyeing him with renewed caution. "And what's in it fer me?"

Albert chuckled. "Besides avoiding another ambush from Mage?" He leaned back. "Let's just say the Order pays very well."

Annabelle's eyes lit up at that, but she didn't answer right away. Regina and Lisa exchanged wary glances, while Albert waited patiently.

"There's two problems with that," Annabelle said at last, reclining in her chair with a grin. "One—any ship that gets too close to Order Island gets sunk before it reaches the shore." She held up two fingers. "Two—the *Stormfang* don't move for free. We require at least a third upfront."

Albert didn't flinch. "Any vessel carrying a member of the Order may approach safely." He reached into his pouch and tossed a small bag across the table. "And this should cover the deposit."

Annabelle caught the bag, loosened the drawstring, and poured a few coins into her hand. Her eyes widened. "Bugger... this might actually be enough." She stuffed the bag into her jacket and stood. "I still need the captain's approval before I can promise passage."

Albert nodded. "Take your time. I've arranged rooms here for Miss Fournier and Miss Nozaki tonight. We'll be in town until morning. Speak to Captain Kidd. If he agrees, we will depart at dawn."

He gave her a meaningful look. "But if he says no... I will need that bag of coin back."

Annabelle grinned, patting her pocket. "Aye, see you when I get back." She waved over her shoulder and slipped into the tavern beyond.

The door clicked shut behind her, leaving the three remaining in quiet contemplation.

Regina finally spoke. "I have a question," she said thoughtfully. "How exactly does having grey hair mean I've been touched by a goddess?"

Albert raised an eyebrow. "Your hair isn't grey, Miss Fournier. It is silver." He stroked his beard, a smirk tugging at his lips. "This", he tapped a finger against his own "is grey." He let that hang a moment. "And let's not forget, silver hair and silver eyes. How often do you think that happens?"

Regina opened her mouth to reply but was cut off by Lisa, who suddenly sat up straighter, alarm flashing in her eyes.

"Wait a minute," Lisa said, voice sharp. "We're *going* to Order Island? My friends are waiting for me at the pier. Valorcrest expects me home tonight."

Albert sighed, as if he'd anticipated the pushback. "Your friends will have to leave without you," he said evenly. "The ship you arrived on only holds its dock for the day." He folded his hands on the table. "As for your parents, the Order will notify them of your whereabouts once we arrive."

Lisa's brow furrowed, worry creasing her forehead. Regina added softly, "Mine too? My dad's going to freak out. Ever since Mom died, he's been... overprotective."

Albert raised a hand to quiet them both. "Yes. All your parents will be informed, after we reach Order Island."

Lisa exhaled, still tense. "What's so important on Order Island anyway?"

Albert's faint smile held a trace of mystery. "For starters... all my notes." He gestured around him. "I have gathered vital knowledge over the last few years, knowledge that will help you stop what's coming."

Lisa exchanged a wary look with Regina, the weight of his words settling over the room like thick fog.

Chapter 5

Sophie hurried down the road leading to Aurorium Granmark, her home village, her backpack bouncing lightly against her shoulders. As she neared the village entrance, a small sigh of relief escaped her lips, *the torches weren't lit*. "Not too late," she thought, though the pitch-black sky above told a different story.

Stepping into the large open area known as the entrance zone, she glanced around. No guards. The sight tugged at old memories; long nights spent standing watch as an initiate, cold seeping into her bones as she forced herself to stay alert. Guard duty had been one of her least favorite tasks. Back then, she'd studied obsessively just to pass the Sentinel test on her first attempt.

But now, something felt... off.

The area was empty... too empty. There was always someone lingering here during the day, whether sneaking off to meet a secret lover or plotting mischief with friends. Even on the quietest days, the initiates would bring the flower displays inside to avoid public scrutiny if they wilted. Yet now, the decorations stood in the open, their colors muted under the night sky.

"Something isn't right."

Her fingers instinctively brushed the hilt of her pistol as she approached the small entry door. No need to open the towering main gates so close to nightfall. She reached for the handle and instantly recoiled.

It is ice-cold.

She frowned, flexing her fingers in surprise. It was spring; the air was cool but far from freezing. A chill prickled at the back of her neck as she scanned the area again, a growing sense of unease settling in her chest.

Dropping her backpack beside the door, she unholstered her pistol in one smooth motion. A quick check: standard load, four regular rounds and two flame shots.

With a deep breath, she tightened her grip and yanked the door open.

Gun raised, she stepped inside.

Then she saw it.

The gathering area where every major event was held, where the upcoming Shadow graduation was set to take place in just a month. The place where hopeful Sentinels would soon gather to begin the Shadow Exam, eager to advance. Sophie planned to be there she just had to finish her paperwork.

But now, it was a frozen graveyard.

Everything was encased in thick, blue-tinted ice, making the scene look surreal, like a nightmare sculpted in glass. Near the door where Sophie stood, Eclipse Burton was frozen mid-motion, sword raised in one hand, the other outstretched as if commanding his Sentinels and Shadows into position. She could almost hear him shouting orders, rallying them for a counterattack that would never come.

The firepit in the center, usually a place of camaraderie where guards waited for their shifts to begin, is frozen solid. Inside the central pit a metallic beast, its jaws locked onto a fallen Shadow clutching a shotgun, is frozen mid-bite.

The ground beneath Sophie is littered with familiar faces.

Sentinel Reeves. Mary.

Sophie's classmate, her friend, lies sprawled, frozen in place, pistol clutched in her hands. A mechanical creature has sunk its teeth into her back, and Sophie's breath catches. *Did she die screaming?*

Shadow Andrew Richards. Today was his turn on duty, organizing the initiates, making sure they showed up in uniform and ready for their shifts. His frozen body stands locked in place, pistol raised, the bullet trapped mid-air just inches from the barrel, never to find its mark. His face is frozen in focus and determination intent on a target long gone.

There are so many. Too many.

Each frozen figure locked in their final stand against monstrous metal invaders. Sophie treads carefully, weaving through the battlefield of her fallen clan, her tears falling freely.

With a loud sniff, she wipes her face and presses forward, but then—

Her stomach drops.

Panic sets in, and she abruptly changes course, running toward Living Area One— her home.

The doors leading into the housing section are frozen and shattered, shards of ice hanging from splintered wood. Sophie sprints to the third street, rushing past the frozen figures of Aurorium initiates. Some stand in battle formations, weapons raised, as if they never had the chance to strike. Others are frozen mid-flight, backs turned, fleeing from the unseen terror that claimed them. They never made it.

"Better to take a shot to the chest than to the back," Eclipse Baker always said.

Sophie never truly understood that lesson—until now.

She halts at the corner of her street and sees her.

Sentinel Irena Gomez.

Her best friend. Frozen solid in her favorite plain clothes uniform, blue trousers and a black vest—sword sheath strapped firmly to her back. Irena's body is locked mid-swing, her blade rising in an upward strike. She must have seen an opportunity, but whoever, or whatever, did this was faster. They froze her before she could finish her attack.

Sophie stares, her chest tightening.

Irena. Her friend. Her sister in arms. They had become Sentinels together. Trained together. Laughed together. They had gone to different schools in Granmark but always made time to talk about their classes, their training, the boys they liked.

And now, Sophie stands before her, Irena's beautiful face twisted in a frozen mask of rage and fear.

Tears stream down Sophie's face.

"I'm so sorry, Irena... I should have been here."

Her voice breaks, and the weight of everything crashes down on her.

She stands there, helpless, crying for a friend she can no longer save.

Sophie pushes forward, wiping the tears from her eyes with the back of her hand. She reaches her house, 185, the front door hanging open, creaking slightly in the still night air.

She takes a deep breath before stepping inside.

The sun porch, her momma's favorite spot, where Arisa used to sit for hours, gazing out at the street through the large windows. But now, the beloved chair is overturned, lying abandoned amid the chaos. The door to the living room stands ajar.

And as Sophie steps through it, she sees it.

The thing she feared the most.

Her momma.

Growing up, Arisa had always told Sophie and her little brother, Benjamin, that she was an Aurorium Shadow, just like their father. She was part of "The Pack," the Aurorium team from Magitekopolis, she'd say with pride. But Sophie had never truly believed it, brushing off the stories of heroic missions, capturing murderers, fighting kidnapping rings, and rogue pirates, as little more than boasting bedtime tales.

Until now.

Now, she believes every single word.

Her mother stands frozen in the middle of the living room, right in front of the door. Shield up, sword ready.

The triangular shield on her left arm bears the head of a lioness, her symbol from Magitekopolis. Her forward arm is angled slightly to cover her chest and vital organs, the sword in her right hand positioned beneath the shield, tip pointed forward. Sophie's eyes catch the dark crimson staining both, the sharp, triangular tip of the blade and the battered shield.

Sophie swallows hard. *She got them.*

Her mother had landed a hit. Maybe even two. A shield bash, followed by a precise strike with her sword, that's how the blood got there.

But she hadn't been fast enough.

Frozen mid-battle, Arisa's expression is fierce, her gaze locked on something just beyond Sophie's sight, the eyes of a lioness locked on its prey. Her mouth is open, frozen mid-cry whether a battle roar or a desperate warning, Sophie doesn't know.

Guilt crashes down on Sophie like a crushing weight.

"If I hadn't wasted time with those fools at West's... I should have been here."

She could have run interference. She could have backed her mother up, distracted the enemy, given her the opening she needed to finish them off.

"She was so close... so god damned close."

Sophie's pistol falls from her trembling hands, hitting the floor with a dull thud. "Momma..."

Her voice is barely a whisper, raw and choked with emotion.

"I'm so sorry, Momma," she sobs, the words spilling out as she crumples to her knees. The pain, sharp and relentless, flooding her heart and mind tears through her chest like an enraged beast, leaving her gasping.

She falls forward, her hands clutching at the frozen floor as gut-wrenching sobs wrack her body. Blame. Regret. Grief. They swirl inside her, suffocating her beneath their weight.

"I should have been here. I should have been here."

Her mother's frozen eyes bore into her soul, unyielding, forever locked in the moment of battle.

And then, a voice echoes from her memory.

"Your clan may be in danger," Brother Albert had warned.

"Please, I can help you."

But it's too late now.

Sophie can do nothing but kneel in front of her mother, crying, begging for forgiveness that will never come. "It is all my fault."

[----- ⚓ -----]

Annabelle Salazar arrived at Slip 17, where the *Stormfang* was docked—the same spot as always. It was their unofficial reservation, a tradition they never questioned. She strode up the gangplank, skipping every other step. No time to waste. Coin was waiting... good coin for once.

Reaching the deck, she came to a stop and called out, "OPSO requesting permission." A formality, yes, but one that mattered.

"Granted," came the gruff reply from Smithy, the first mate, who barely looked up from his work at the ship's wheel.

"Where's the Cap'n?" she asked, stepping closer.

Smithy, his hands busy tightening a bolt, jerked a thumb over his shoulder. "In his ops room."

"Aye, thanks, first mate" Annabelle said, already moving.

She hurried across the deck and took the stairs two at a time, knocking twice before pushing the door open. "Captain..." she started but froze mid-step.

Captain Kidd sat across from a woman in a flowing dress and a wide sun hat, both sharing a bottle of wine.

"Belle," the captain said, his easygoing charm unfaltering. "Give me a minute." He turned back to the woman, his blue eyes twinkling with interest. "You were saying, Miss Albethian?"

The woman swirled her wine, watching it with distant sadness. "I was looking for a ship to move some of my belongings to the city of Synotho, in the Umbrathorn Kingdom," she said with a weary sigh. "I'm... splitting from my husband, and I need to get home."

"That's truly a shame," Kidd said, shaking his head sympathetically. "Breakups are hard on everyone."

Annabelle fought the urge to roll her eyes. Classic Kidd. Being a captain meant being part salesman, and he was a master at making clients feel welcomed and understood.

"I'll be okay," Miss Albethian continued. "I just need to find a way through it all... but I don't know if I can pay your regular rates."

Captain Kidd leaned back, running a hand over his blonde hair. "We'd need to cover our expenses, you see. I couldn't take the job for less than three hundred coin."

"Oh! So steep," she gasped, shaking her head. "I couldn't possibly pay more than two hundred."

Annabelle smirked. *The dance had begun.* Always the same: offer, counteroffer, dramatic pause, repeat. She'd seen it almost every time.

But this time, there was no need for it. Brother Albert's job was different. No smarmy haggling, no games...just good coin.

"That's not enough," Annabelle cut in bluntly.

Captain Kidd shot her a look that screamed *shut up*, but she ignored it.

Miss Albethian clasped her hands together, her voice growing desperate. "That's really all I can afford, I swear. My husband took all our money, spent it on wenches, gambling, and booze." She paused, eyes pleading. "I'm sure there's some way we can work something out."

"I'm sure we can" Captain Kidd said smoothly, offering the woman his most reassuring smile, while simultaneously shooting daggers at Annabelle.

Annabelle folded her arms, unfazed. "Captain, if you recall, we have significant repairs to make on the ship, not to mention resupplying our stores, before we can even think about leaving port," she said firmly. "As Operations Officer, I have to insist we take full fare on this one."

It was her way of signaling, *this job isn't worth it.*

The woman shifted uncomfortably. "Oh..."

Captain Kidd didn't miss a beat. "Belle," he said, he is one of the few who called her by that name. "I think you need to check your records again." His tone was light but pointed. "After all, how could we abandon such a lovely woman in her time of need?"

He turned back to Miss Albethian with that same practiced charm. "I'm sure we can rearrange a few things to make it all work."

Annabelle clenched her jaw, frustration boiling beneath her skin. *Here we go again.*

She'd seen this act too many times before, a pretty face with a sob story always seemed to lure him in. This one had all the classic signs: the tragic tale of a husband lost to gambling, wenches, and drink. But somehow, despite being broke, she had a house full of fine furniture, expensive art, and linens too precious to part with. And, of course, she came straight to the captain wearing the most alluring dress in her possession.

Annabelle could practically recite the script by heart.

Then, like a lightning bolt, it hit her.

She reached into her pocket, pulled out the healthy pouch of coins Brother Albert had given her to secure passage, and without hesitation tossed it onto the table in front of Kidd.

The captain barely moved his wine glass out of the way in time, he sat blinking in surprise as the pudgy bag sat on the table it dominated his gaze for an extra moment.

"What the hell, Belle?" he said, narrowing his eyes at her.

Annabelle grinned, leaning against the doorframe. "Found a better job. No discounts."

Kidd picked up the pouch and peeked inside, his eyes widening slightly as he saw just how much coin they were talking about.

"Belle..." He trailed off, exhaling through his nose before glancing back at Miss Albethian.

"Miss Albethian," he said smoothly, setting the pouch aside, "do you happen to have a list of the items you need transported and their sizes?"

The woman blinked, caught off guard. "Oh, um... no, I didn't think to do that."

Captain Kidd's smile didn't waver. "No problem. Not a problem at all," he said with a reassuring nod. "Why don't you put one together and bring it back? That way, we can figure out what we can do for you."

"Oh... okay," she said uncertainly. "But if you're taking another job..."

Kidd chuckled, waving a dismissive hand. "Like my Ops O said, we've got a lot of repairs to handle first. But I'm sure we can find a way to help you." His voice was smooth as silk, effortlessly easing her worries. "Just head home, make your list, and bring it back. We'll be right here at Slip 17."

The woman hesitated for a moment, then nodded. "Alright, I'll do that right away." She gathered her things, slung her purse over her shoulder, and hurried out of the room.

As the door clicked shut behind her, Annabelle plastered on a fake smile and muttered, "Aye, we'll be here."

Once Miss Albethian was out of the ops room, Captain Kidd leaned back in his chair, his eyes flicking between Annabelle and the heavy pouch of coins on the table. Finally, he arched an eyebrow.

"Belle... did the shop owner give ye this?" he asked, gesturing toward the now-empty seat where Miss Albethian had been sitting.

Annabelle shook her head with a grin. "No, no, Cap'n." She reached into her pocket, pulling out another, noticeably smaller pouch and dropped it onto the table with a satisfying clink. "This one's from the shopkeeper."

Kidd's fingers drummed against the table as he glanced between the two bags. "So where in the hells did ye get that one?" he asked, pointing to the larger pouch. "And what's the job?"

Annabelle hesitated, realizing if she didn't tell the whole story, the captain wouldn't believe a word of it.

"Alright, Cap'n, get this," she said, leaning back in her chair with a smirk. "Turns out, I'm a goddess. One of four, actually."

Kidd stared at her, then took a long, deliberate sip of his wine. "Are ye serious?" he asked, his voice thick with skepticism. "I've spun better cons half-drunk in a back alley."

"No, no, listen." Annabelle held up her hands. "I was in town, right? Minding me own business when, **bam!** some ugly shadow witch attacks me, and I get bit by this wolf... or maybe it was a dog? Either way, this girl, Regina, shows up, saves me with a sunlight spell."

She paused, remembering the sheer speed at which Regina talked. "And man, she talks a lot, like a whole book's worth in a minute."

Kidd raised an unimpressed eyebrow. "Aye, and then what?"

"She takes me to this guy, Brother Al, Order of Saint Lorraine, all fancy-like and he explains everything."

"That ye're some kind of goddess?" Kidd said, swirling his wine.

"Aye." Annabelle nodded. "Born a goddess, apparently. That's where I gots me beautiful orange hair and eyes." She tossed her hair dramatically for effect. "Must be why me necklace works the way it does."

Kidd's expression darkened slightly. "Wait... he knew about yer necklace?"

Annabelle blinked, realizing she'd hit a nerve. "Well... no, he ain't said nothin' 'bout it." She could feel herself losing ground. "But wait! Look!"

She reached into her jacket and pulled out a folded letter, pressing it into the captain's hand. "Regina gave me this. It's got the same symbol that Brother Al had on his shirt."

Kidd took the letter, turning it over in his hands. His eyes lingered on the wax seal, he recognized the unmistakable symbol of the Order of Saint Lorraine.

He exhaled, shaking his head. "I don't know, Belle... this is a lot to swallow."

Suddenly, an overwhelming wave of sadness crashed over Annabelle, raw and unrelenting. She gripped the edge of the table, her chest tightening as tears spilled freely down her cheeks.

"Belle, what is it?!?" Kidd's voice was sharp with concern, his usual swagger replaced by the softer concern of an adoptive father.

Annabelle shook her head, wiping at her eyes, but the tears wouldn't stop. "I—I don't know, Cap'n," she stammered, choking on her breath. "It's like... I feel real sad all of a sudden. Like... like me momma just died or something."

Captain Kidd's brow furrowed, confusion flickering across his face. "But, Belle... your mama, Ada, she's been beyond the veil for almost a decade now." His tone was careful, watching her closely.

"I know, I know... I just..." She pressed the heels of her hands against her eyes, trying to shut out the storm inside her. "I don't understand." She took a shaky breath. "Just... give me a minute, yeah?"

Without hesitation, Kidd got up from his chair and moved behind her, wrapping his arms around her shoulders in a firm, grounding embrace.

"It's alright, Belle." His voice was steady, familiar. "I'm here for ye, we'll figure this out."

Annabelle's mind drifted back to that horrible day, the day she lost them all, the whole crew of the Espada Sovereign.

The Espada Sovereign, her father's proud ship, went down in flames, struck by the relentless force of the Stoneridge military. She could still see the flashes of cannon fire ripping through the hull, hear the mast snap, and the deafening roar as the sea swallowed it whole.

Her own mother, Ada, the ship's Operations Officer, had gone down with it.

Her father, Captain Javier Salazar, had known they were due for a shakedown. In preparation, he'd entrusted James "Kidd" Lowe, the man she now called captain, with two sacred tasks: keep Annabelle safe and protect the ship's chest full of coin from falling into the wrong hands.

Annabelle had made peace with that loss, she cried all those tears until there were none left. But this... this was different.

This grief felt fresh, raw, new. And it came with an unbearable weight of guilt, like she could have done something to stop it.

But just as suddenly as it came, the feeling lifted. The crushing sorrow evaporated, leaving her drained but oddly calm.

She blinked, sniffling, as the weight dissipated from her chest. "I ... I'm sorry, Cap'n," she whispered, leaning into his embrace for just a moment longer, letting it ground her like an anchor in the storm. "I think I'm good now."

Kidd's hands lingered gently on her shoulders. "Are ye sure, Belle?"

Annabelle took a deep breath, wiping the last remnants of tears from her face. "Yeah, I'm good. Sorry, Cap'n. I don't know what came over me..." She shook her head, forcing a smile. "But listen, about the job."

Captain Kidd let out a short chuckle, releasing his grip on her shoulders. "Always after the coin, just like yer papa?" he said, stepping back and leaning against the table. "Alright, start from the beginning. You left the ship, what happened next?"

Annabelle straightened in her chair. "I stopped by Aaron's to collect payment for the last job. He tried to short us, but I persuaded him to pay up." She smirked. "After that, I wandered around market square looking for an opportunity and, ye know, a bit of lunch."

Kidd nodded, listening.

"Next thing I know, there's a commotion, big enough to send everyone running." Annabelle frowned, replaying the moment in her mind. "So I ducked into an alley, I didn't want no guards or coppers sniffing around too close. But before I could make it back to the ship, this shadow witch jumped me."

Kidd's brows lifted. "And yer sure she was after ye? Not just some bad luck?" He returned to his seat, watching her closely.

Annabelle rolled up her sleeve, revealing bloodstains on her jacket. "Pretty sure. One of her shadow wolves got me, bit right into me arm."

Kidd's face darkened. "Show me."

She pulled off her coat and extended her arm. The skin was smooth, completely healed, but the shredded fabric of her shirt told a different story.

Kidd's eyes narrowed. "Whose blood is that?"

Annabelle shrugged. "Mine. It'll make sense in a minute."

Kidd exhaled through his nose. "Alright, so yer in the alley, bleeding from yer arm... then what?"

"Then Regina shows up, and uses some kinda sunlight magic to stop the witch and get rid of the wolves." Annabelle leaned forward. "I swear, Cap'n, I'd be done for if she hadn't shown up."

Kidd scratched his chin. "Regina? That girl you mentioned before?"

"Aye. After we got clear of the witch, she gave me that letter from Brother Al."

"Al? From the Order?"

Annabelle nodded. "Didn't know it at the time, but aye. We went to West's after that."

Kidd frowned. "West's?!? Belle, yer still banned from there for another week."

Annabelle rolled her eyes. "No, no, I had an invitation, so they let me in. That's where we met Brother Al, and that's where he told us the big secret."

Kidd raised a brow. "Big secret?"

Annabelle grinned her happy toothy grin. "Aye, I'm a goddess. One of four, actually."

Kidd let out a bark of laughter. "Yer a goddess? Belle, I've heard better tall tales from drunks lookin' fer a free ride at port."

Annabelle smirked. "I thought the same at first, Cap'n. But it wasn't just me. There's four of us; Regina, she's from the land of libraries; Eliza, from Sacred Acres; and some copper named Sophia. She's all purple...like, hair and eyes purple."

Kidd blinked. "Purple?"

"Aye. Like how me hair and eyes are orange."

"And the others?" Kidd asked, his curiosity piqued.

"Regina's gots silver hair, and Eliza's green top to bottom." Annabelle said with a grin. "Then Brother Al gave us some tea that proves we're goddesses. After that, he asked for the *Fang* to take us to Order Island."

"Order Island!" Kidd says in surprise his eyes locked on Annabelle "And yer sure about all this?"

Annabelle shrugged. "Well, I'm sure the grape copper ain't comin', she stormed off, but the rest of us? Aye."

Kidd sighed, rubbing his temples. "So, what's the plan?"

"If ye say yes, I'll round up Brother Al and the others from West's, and we set sail for Order Island." She hesitated. "Brother Al says if we've got him with us, the Order's cannons won't sink us."

Kidd snorted. "And if I say no?"

Annabelle tapped the bag of coins. "Then I gotta give this back."

Kidd eyed the coin, running his hand over his stubbled chin. "Belle, not all coin is good coin." His voice softened, thoughtful now. "But they did trust ye to bring it here, and they fixed ye up." He paused, weighing his options.

Finally, he leaned back in his chair. "Alright. We'll take the job. But if anything sketchy pops up, we toss 'em to the sea."

Annabelle grinned. "Aye, Cap'n." She grabbed her coat and slipped it back on.

"On your way out, tell the crew to get the ship ready for passengers. We shove off at first light." Kidd drained the rest of his wine.

"Aye, Cap'n." Annabelle headed for the door, but before she could step out, his voice stopped her.

"And Belle."

She paused, her hand on the door.

Kidd calls after her "Belle be careful. I've gots me a feeling 'bout this one."

She smirked over her shoulder. "Aye, Cap'n."

Once on deck, she cupped her hands and called out to the crew. "Listen up boyos! On the captain's orders, get the Stormfang ready fer passengers. We shove off at first light."

A chorus of "Aye!" rang back almost in unison.

Annabelle smiled to herself as she made her way down the gangplank and onto the pier. There was coin to make.

[-----🦜-----]

Brother Albert, Lisa, and Regina sat around the table in the warmly lit meeting room, speaking quietly among themselves. Brother Albert flipped through his well-worn journal, reviewing the information he had gathered about the girls.

Regina leaned forward, resting her elbows on the table. "So, do you know where I went to primary school?" she asked with a playful smirk.

Albert barely looked up, flipping a page with practiced ease. "Easy. The Academy of Saint Michaels," he said confidently. "And before you ask, the kids called it Red Michaels' Academy."

Regina raised her eyebrows, impressed. "Not bad."

Lisa, wearing a devious smile, chimed in, "What about my primary school?"

Albert flipped a few more pages, then stopped, tapping his forehead with an exaggerated motion. "Ah, yes! You were homeschooled by tutors until middle school." He glanced at Lisa with a knowing grin. "Sister Brunhilda always said you were a great student; so well-behaved."

Lisa's eyes widened, surprise flickering across her face. "You even know about her?" she asked softly. "How is Miss Brunhilda?"

Albert's face fell slightly, his tone turning somber. "She passed last year. She was on a ship bound for Magitekopolis, meant to teach the children there, but... it sank." His words were clinical, almost detached, but he quickly noticed the flicker of sadness in Lisa's green eyes and regretted his tone.

"I... I see," Lisa answered, blinking away the sudden sting of tears. "I always to tell her that I got into Valorcrest. We worked so hard on my essays and entrance exams."

Albert sighed, his voice softer this time. "I'm sorry, my dear. I didn't mean to be so blunt. It's a fault of mine."

Lisa forced a small smile and nodded. "No, it is fine." She wiped a tear from her cheek.

Before the silence could settle too deeply, a knock echoed from the double doors. A barmaid stepped in, balancing a tray expertly in one hand.

"Are you ready to order?" she asked, her voice cheerful. "Our specials today are ham sandwiches with toasted rolls, dill pickles, and potato chips; chicken noodle soup with garlic biscuits; or a large pretzel with melted cheddar cheese." She looked at them expectantly.

Brother Albert was the first to answer. "I'll have the ham sandwich, please." He glanced at his empty cup. "And another ale." Then, turning to the girls, he smiled. "Order whatever you like, ladies."

Lisa, contemplating her options, tilted her head. "Do you have any salads?"

Albert immediately shook his head. "Trust me, you don't want the salad."

Lisa glanced at the waitress, who quickly shook her head in agreement, her eyes wide in silent warning. *Why do I not want the salad?*

"Okay. I will have the pretzel, then. And a glass of water, please." Lisa sighed in defeat.

Meanwhile, Regina was lost in thought, her silver eyes darting between Albert and the barmaid. "The soup sounds good, but I wonder how big the sandwiches are. A pretzel might not be enough, but what's wrong with the salad anyway? My dad makes the best salad when it's his turn to cook. The soup does sound nice, though... but maybe I should get a sandwich instead. Ohhhh, I'm not sure." She finally turned to the waitress, eyes wide. "What do you think?"

The waitress blinked, clearly overwhelmed by Regina's rapid-fire indecision. She opened her mouth, but no words came out.

Brother Albert chuckled, stepping in to save the poor woman. "Let's go with the soup for her. Thank you."

The waitress let out a relieved sigh. "Fine orders. I'll be right back." She turned and hurried out of the room, no doubt grateful to escape.

Feeling self-conscious, Regina glanced at Albert. "Am I talking too much? I'm just trying to be open with everyone. I don't want to hold anything important back, my dad always tells me to slow down."

Albert gave her a warm smile. "You're quite... thorough. You provide more information than most people are used to, and it can be a bit overwhelming." He winked. "But I do appreciate that you leave nothing to chance."

Regina beamed. "Thank you."

Albert reached into his shirt pocket and pulled out a silver pocket watch, embossed with the symbol of the Order of Saint Lorraine. He pressed the latch, and the circular cap flipped open with a soft click. The hands pointed to nine o'clock.

"Ladies, we should turn in after dinner. It's getting late, and we have an early start tomorrow."

"We have a room here?" Lisa asked, tucking a strand of her green hair behind her ear. "Are we sharing a room?"

Albert smiled reassuringly. "No, ma'am. I figured you girls might want some time to yourselves. I'm sure all of this is a lot to take in."

Before he could say more, both Lisa and Regina suddenly burst into uncontrollable sobs.

Lisa buried her face in her hands, tears streaming down her cheeks. Regina yanked off her glasses, rubbing her eyes against the sleeve of her dress as sobs wracked her small frame.

Brother Albert blinked in shock. "By the goddesses, what's wrong?" he asked, flustered by the sudden flood of emotion. "You can share rooms if you like!"

Lisa's voice broke through her crying, words spilling out between hiccupped sobs. "I... I don't know why... but it feels like... like everyone I love is gone." She gasped for air. "They're all gone!"

Regina couldn't even form words, just ragged cries of pain. "Momma?!?" she choked out, sobbing into her sleeve.

58

Albert's brow furrowed. *Momma?* Her mother had passed away two years ago from illness, so why was she crying for her now?

A deep, sinking realization settled in Albert's chest.

They weren't crying for themselves.

The tea!

Their connection had strengthened. He'd suspected it would, but this reaction was far more intense than he expected. He should have explained it earlier, but how do you tell someone they might feel the pain of others as if it were their own? And now, the question gnawed at him, who was hurting this much?

His mind raced. Was it Salazar? Had Captain Kidd refused the job? No... that wouldn't cause such overwhelming grief.

Then it hit him.

Sophie Griffin

Something had happened to Sophie Griffin. Something very, very bad.

Albert's instinct was to rush out into the night, to her village and figure out what had gone so very wrong, but he couldn't leave Lisa and Regina here alone at West's. This place wasn't safe enough for that. Salazar, on the other hand, could handle herself. She'd know how to keep them safe.

He clenched his jaw and made the decision. *Stay put for now.* Once Annabelle returned from the Stormfang, he would leave them in her care and head to the Aurorium Granmark to find Sophie.

Is this what this assignment will be like? He wondered grimly. Endless impossible choices. He had looked forward to guiding the girls, but now, for the first time, a sense of overwhelming dread weighed down on him.

And just as suddenly as the episode had begun, it ended.

The sobs faded into quiet sniffles, leaving the girls shaken.

Lisa reached into her purse, pulling out a handkerchief to dab at her tear-streaked face. Regina wiped her eyes with her dress sleeve until Albert silently slid his own handkerchief across the table. She took it with a quiet "thanks" and blew her nose.

Lisa glanced up at him, her expression still confused and raw. "I... I do not know what came over me." Her voice wavered. "It just felt like I lost everyone I loved. It does not make any sense."

Albert exhaled and leaned back in his chair. "I think I know." He folded his hands on the table. "*The tea.* It's said to strengthen the bond between avatars. What you're feeling... it's not yours. It belongs to one of the others."

Regina sniffled, clutching the handkerchief tightly. "I felt like my mother died... but she passed almost three years ago. I have a new mommy now."

Albert rubbed his chin, eyeing the stained handkerchief as if it were a lost cause. He pieced together the information and finally solidified his theory.

It must be Sophie Griffin.

Annabelle had lost both her parents when she was so very young, after all. Her father's ship, the Espada Sovereign, sunk on the open sea. Annabelle made her way through life with James "Kidd" Lowe, who would later become Captain Kidd when he purchased the Stormfang.

But Annabelle must have long since made peace with that tragedy.

No, this pain belonged to Sophie Griffin.

When Annabelle returned, Albert planned to head to Aurorium Granmark himself and find out what happened. With any luck, Sophie might still make it aboard the Stormfang.

Pushing aside his thoughts for the moment, Albert pulled out his journal and began scribbling notes, recording every detail as any good investigator would.

The girls sat in silence, each lost in their thoughts, emotions still raw.

A soft knock interrupted the moment. The barmaid returned with their meals, placing the plates gently before them, offering a quick bow, and leaving the room.

"This looks tasty. Please, ladies, dig in," Brother Albert said, taking a hearty bite of his ham sandwich.

The trio ate in relative silence, Albert methodically working through his meal, occasionally crunching down on a pickle. Lisa leisurely enjoyed her pretzel, stretching the gooey cheese with each bite, while Regina slowly sipped her soup, nibbling on a biscuit between thoughtful glances at the others.

After a moment, Regina set down her spoon and looked at Albert. "Brother Albert, I've been thinking… where did you get this tea? And how do you know so much about it?"

Caught off guard, Albert finished his bite before replying. "That tea is grown on Order Island." He took a sip of ale, wiping his mouth with the back of his hand. "Legend has it, it was gifted to Saint Lorraine by a goddess herself." He leaned back slightly. "You must remember, my dears, the Order of Saint Lorraine is dedicated to studying and gathering knowledge about the world. It's our calling."

Lisa tapped her fingers thoughtfully against her glass. "You said before that you were our guide… what does that actually mean?"

Albert straightened in his chair, adjusting his shirt with a quiet sense of pride. "I've been tasked with guiding you in this world—watching over you, providing knowledge, counsel, and whatever assistance you may need." He looked between the two young women. "The goddesses have touched your lives for a reason, to accomplish something greater than yourselves. It's my duty to help you discover what that is."

He paused for a moment, softening his tone. "But it's important to understand… I am not your leader. You must find your own way on the path laid out for you. Think of me as a humble servant."

Regina grinned. "I've never had a servant before. Does that mean I can get you to do my homework?"

Albert chuckled. "Sadly, I'll have to respectfully decline that request."

"Servants are like that," Lisa added with a playful smirk. "But they are quite useful when you need them."

Albert bowed his head slightly, voice rich with amusement. "It would be my pleasure to be useful to you, ladies." He tapped the side of his journal. "I'll explain more when we reach my workshop on Order Island."

Noticing that both girls had nearly finished their meals, Albert leaned forward. "I think it's a good idea to turn in for the night. I'm sure you'll need the rest, trust me."

The girls exchanged glances and nodded in agreement, finishing the last bites of their food.

After gathering their things, Lisa slung her bag over her shoulder while Regina adjusted her glasses. Albert tucked his journal into its sling across his lower back after he stood, leading them out of the room. As they stepped into the hall, the barmaid entered behind them, clearing their plates with practiced efficiency.

The trio walked along the dimly lit corridor, their footsteps echoing softly against the aged wooden floors. A staircase at the far end led to the second level, and as they climbed, the wood creaked beneath their weight, whispering tales of years gone by.

At the top of the stairs, a bulky security guard sat behind a podium, clad in the same blue vest as the men at the entrance. His sharp eyes swept over them before he held up a hand to stop them.

"Do you have a room booked?" he asked, his voice gruff and expression unreadable.

Albert smiled politely. "Actually, I have four rooms booked under Albert Simmons."

The guard flipped through the ledger on his podium, running a finger down the list until he found the name. "Ah, here it is," he said, then motioned them forward.

Walking down the narrow hallway lined with numbered doors, the guard stopped at the first and unlocked it with a key. "Bathroom's down the hall. Keep your key with you, the door locks automatically. Check-out's at high noon." His tone was flat, almost mechanical, as if he had recited the same lines a thousand times.

Lisa stepped toward the door marked 5, turning to the others with a small smile. "Good night." Without another word, she disappeared inside, closing the door behind her.

The guard led Albert and Regina further down the hall, stopping at a door marked 16. He repeated the same line with the same monotone delivery, "Bathroom's down the hall. Keep your key with you, the door locks automatically. Check-out's at high noon."

Regina glanced at Albert. "Good night, Brother Albert." She smiled and waved before stepping inside her room and shutting the door softly behind her.

The guard lingered for a moment, eyeing Albert with mild curiosity.

Albert waved him off. "No room for me, thanks." He gestured back toward the staircase. "I'll be heading downstair to the meeting room if you need me."

Without waiting for a response, Albert turned and descended the stairs, his thoughts already on what lay ahead.

[----- 🕯 -----]

Later that night, Brother Albert sat alone at the table, waiting for Annabelle Salazar to return from the Stormfang with his answer.

He drummed his fingers lightly against the worn wood, his thoughts circling his plan, offer Annabelle a room, then head to Aurorium Granmark to find out what happened to Sophie Griffin.

With a weary sigh, he flipped through his journal, eyes scanning the notes he had taken earlier that day. The pages were filled with observations, theories, and lingering doubts.

He frowned. Losing Sophie had been a mistake. *I should have prepared better for her to clash with Annabelle Salazar; I will not make that mistake again.*

Despite his best efforts, he hadn't been able to convince her to stay, and now she was out there...alone. The weight of responsibility and failure weighed heavily on his chest.

Albert had read the stories, heard the warnings. Guides who lost their charges... it happened. Not often, but enough to serve as cautionary tales whispered among the ranks of the Order. He wouldn't be the first to fail...but he didn't want to join that unfortunate group either.

His fingers traced the edge of the open journal, lingering over Sophie's name.

"I hope she's okay..." he muttered under his breath. "I hope I can find her."

The flickering lanterns on the wall cast long shadows across the table, stretching over the pages like creeping doubts.

Albert leaned back in his chair and exhaled slowly. He had to find her.

And soon.

As Albert sat, mentally preparing for his next steps, a sharp series of four knocks echoed against the meeting room door.

He straightened, a flicker of hope crossing his face. *Annabelle Salazar, she must have returned from the Stormfang with good news.*

Rising from his seat, he walked to the door just as another set of four knocks rang out: louder this time, more urgent.

Albert opened the door, his usual greeting on the tip of his tongue, but the words died in his throat.

Standing before him was **Sophie Griffin**.

She wore her signature purple fedora and suit, the brim of her hat casting a shadow over her face. A heavy bag hung from her shoulders, but it was her eyes that caught Albert's attention, their once-sharp violet irises now adrift in a sea of red and white, evidence of endless tears.

Her voice was barely above a whisper. "I'm in."

Albert blinked, processing her words, but concern quickly overtook his surprise. "My dear," he said softly, worry threading his tone. "What happened?"

He stepped aside, silently inviting her in.

Sophie shuffled into the room, her movements slow, weighed down by exhaustion and grief. She barely made it past the threshold before the dam broke again. Her shoulders trembled, and fresh rivers of tears streamed down her face.

"My village... my family... they're all…" Sophie's voice cracked, and she collapsed inward, sobbing uncontrollably.

Albert stepped forward without hesitation, wrapping his arms around her in a firm, steady embrace. "I'm so sorry, my dear," he murmured, holding her tightly. "Come, sit. Tell me everything."

For a moment, Sophie leaned into the comfort, her breathing ragged and uneven. Then she gently pushed away, wiping at her eyes with trembling hands. She sank into the nearest chair—the same one Regina had occupied earlier.

With a shaky breath, she whispered, "When I got home... it was destroyed. Everyone was... was..." Her voice failed her, and she buried her face in her hands, the weight of grief too much to bear.

Albert sat beside her, his heart heavy with the knowledge that nothing he could say would ease her pain. He silently handed Sophie his spare handkerchief, making a mental note to stock up on more when they reached Order Island. He was going through them much faster than he expected.

Sophie took it with trembling hands, wiping her tear-streaked face before taking a shaky breath. "Everyone is dead," she said, her voice raw and hollow. "Frozen... torn apart by metal monsters."

Albert paused frozen and metal monsters…Gretta and Isabella.

Her grip on the handkerchief tightened. "I didn't know what to do, so I came back here... if the offer still stands?"

Albert's expression softened. "Of course it does, my dear." His voice was steady, filled with quiet reassurance. "I am so sorry for your loss. The Order will reach out to the Aurorium... let them know you're still alive."

Sophie's composure shattered again, fresh tears spilling over. Albert placed a comforting hand on her shoulder, kneeling beside her chair to meet her eyes. "Cry all you need, my dear. I'm here."

Without thinking, Sophie leaned forward and wrapped her arms tightly around him, sobbing into his shoulder. She clung to him as wave after wave of grief poured out…for her family, her friends, her home.

Albert held her patiently, letting her mourn, offering silent comfort.

Finally, the torrent of tears slowed, and Sophie pulled away, wiping her face with the now-ruined handkerchief. Her voice, though shaky, carried a desperate resolve. "So… what do we do now?"

Albert stood, resting a reassuring hand on her shoulder. "We will travel aboard Ms. Salazar's ship, the Stormfang, to Order Island. Once we arrive, I'll explain everything, and we can focus on our tasks."

Sophie blinked, hesitating. "A … pirate ship?" The thought seemed absurd, was she even allowed to board such a vessel? Oddly enough, nothing in her training had ever covered pirate travel.

Albert smiled, sensing her doubt. "Yes, but don't worry. I doubt the Stormfang will engage in high-seas piracy while we're aboard." He smiled gently, hoping to ease her concerns.

Sophie nodded slowly, but Albert could see the weariness clinging to her like a heavy cloak. He considered sending her to rest in one of the rooms he'd arranged, but a nagging thought held him back. *Could I really leave her alone right now?*

If only he had brought Brother Marcus with him—things would have been easier. He could have sent Sophie to rest under Marcus's watch while handling the growing list of concerns. But Albert had come alone, and now, he was here. So, he stayed.

The door to the meeting room burst open, and Annabelle Salazar strode in with her usual flair, her fiery orange hair practically glowing under the dim lighting. "Welcome to the Stormfang, ladies!" she declared, grinning—until she spotted Sophie Griffin sitting with Brother Albert.

Her grin faded into confusion. "What's going on here?" she asked, glancing around. No sign of the other two girls.

Albert looked up, ever composed. "Miss Salazar, right on cue." He closed his journal with a soft thud. "Miss Nozaki and Miss Fournier are upstairs, resting. As you can see, Miss Griffin has rejoined the group."

Annabelle folded her arms, eyeing Sophie with suspicion. "What's her problem? Someone take her badge?"

Sophie shot to her feet in a flash of anger, fists clenched, but Brother Albert's steady presence between them stopped her from lunging forward. "What?!" she snapped, seething.

Albert gave Annabelle a pointed look. "Miss Salazar, Sophie's village was attacked. Many—if not all—of her people are dead." His tone carried the weight of disapproval. "Please have some compassion."

Annabelle rolled her eyes, dragging out her response with a sigh. "Aye, sorry."

"Whatever," Sophie returned, the fury simmering just beneath the surface.

Albert cleared his throat, reclaiming control of the room. "Ladies, you're going to have to learn to get along." His gaze shifted between them, firm and unwavering. "There are bigger problems ahead, and you won't be able to face them if you're constantly at each   other's   throats."

Annabelle sighed dramatically and gave Albert a playful two-finger salute. "Aye, I apologize, governor."

Albert ignored the jab and focused on logistics. "Miss Salazar, when can we depart on the Stormfang?"

Annabelle's grin returned, her earlier irritation forgotten. "The Fang sets sail at first light."

Albert pulled out his pocket watch, pressing the latch to reveal the time—just past midnight. That left them about five hours.

"Very well." He turned to Sophie. "Miss Griffin, I suggest you get some rest. It will do you good."

Sophie gave a silent nod, slinging her bag over her shoulder and rising from her chair.

Albert then turned to Annabelle. "I've arranged a room for you as well. Given what happened to the Aurorium Clan, I don't think it's wise for you to return to the Stormfang until we leave."

Annabelle considered for a moment, then shrugged. "Aye, ye may be right, governor." Truth be told, the beds here were far more comfortable than her bunk on the ship.

As the trio stepped out into the main tavern area, a sudden commotion at the front entrance caught their attention.

An old man in a worn leather hat shoved his way through the door, flanked by a pack of armed thugs. The bar's security barely had time to react before he was knocked to the ground, groaning in pain.

Sophie's eyes narrowed, recognition sparking. "**Him.**"

The old man from earlier. Her fists clenched at her sides. *I'll beat some answers out of him!*

Before she could move, an explosion of splintered wood shattered the air. The wall to their right burst open, sending debris flying. From the gaping hole emerged a towering mechanical monster—a grotesque fusion of man and dinosaur, its joints humming with an eerie blue glow. Its metallic mouth hung open, rows of razor-sharp teeth gleaming, claws curled in anticipation of a kill.

From behind the beast, a cold, familiar monotone voice rang out. "Albert Thompson, you will surrender to me."

The voice belonged to a girl standing in the shadows, her piercing blue hair almost blending with the pulsing orb of blue spell energy she held in one hand. Her gaze locked onto Albert with chilling focus.

Albert's face paled as fear washed over him. He looked upon the emotionless, blue-eyed, blue-haired corrupted avatar of the goddess of Resilience. All he could manage was, "Oh no... Isabella."

Sophie, Annabelle, and Albert exchanged tense glances. They are trapped.

Chapter 6

Sophie Griffin surveyed West's Tavern with a sinking feeling. To her right, a towering mechanical monster loomed, its metal limbs moving with eerie precision under the control of a witch with striking blue hair. Directly in front of her, the thugs whose leader she'd escaped earlier, an older man in a weathered leather hat, blocked the entrance. This was the same man who had chased her with the straw-men in black suits. She'd have a long conversation with him, if she survived this mess.

Next to her stood Annabelle Salazar, a loud-mouthed pirate girl with a grin that suggested she relished the chaos. Behind her, Brother Albert Thompson, a monk from the Order, looked ready to faint at the sight of the unfolding disaster. Between the two, Sophie had no doubts: Annabelle could maybe fight. Brother Albert on the other hand could not fight a lick.

And a fight is definitely upon them.

"What's the plan?" Sophie asked, heart pounding as she realized her pistol and rifle were behind the bar, right where the tavern's security man was currently being flattened.

Annabelle's eyes darted between the threats, her expression darkening. "Aye, trouble from both sides, and me without me anchor belt or cutlass."

Taking command with the ease of someone used to barroom brawls, Annabelle turned to Albert. "Monk, upstairs. Get the other two girls and move fast, we might have to run away."

Albert hesitated, wide-eyed. "But…"

"Go!" Annabelle barked, and with a startled jump, Albert scurried up the stairs.

Turning back to Sophie, Annabelle's grin returned. "Copper, ye take care of that blue-haired biddy and her tin beast. I'll be fetching me tings."

Sophie nodded, slipping into the disciplined mindset drilled into her by years of Aurorium training. "I'll need my pistol and rifle from behind the bar." She surveyed the group of roughneck thugs advancing toward them and asked, "Are you sure you don't need any help?"

Annabelle glanced at the thugs and smirked. "Please, missy. If there's one thing I know, it's bar fights." She cracked her knuckles. "On three."

Sophie barely had time to nod before Annabelle took off at "two," charging straight into the gang with a reckless battle cry.

She watched Annabelle and Albert rush off and made a mental note, Annabelle was an "act on three" kind of girl.

With no time to dwell, Sophie turned to face the mechanical monster. The witch with blue hair stood behind it, her hand weaving in the air as the metal beast shifted with unnatural precision, squaring up to Sophie. *Great,* Sophie thought. *It's battle-ready.*

She sprinted toward it, swinging her bag with all her might. It thudded against the monster's metal skin with a dull clank…*absolutely useless.*

The creature retaliated, its heavy arm swinging in a wide arc. Sophie ducked beneath it, moving on instinct—just like her mother had taught her. In a single smooth motion, she reached into her jacket and pulled out a concussion trip wire.

Timing is everything.

She jammed the explosive device deep into the monster's exposed joints. As it wound up for another strike, Sophie darted behind it and yanked the wire with all her strength.

Boom!

The concussion charge detonated, blasting apart the creature's shoulder and neck. The blue aura flickered before the entire mass of metal collapsed to the floor with a loud crash, now just a heap of useless parts.

Sophie spun around to face the witch—and froze.

A cold realization settled over her. There was something different about the woman, an unsettling power radiating from her. Sophie recognized it instantly—a goddess touched the woman.

No time for hesitation. Sophie lunged forward, closing the distance and throwing a left-handed haymaker with everything she had.

But the witch moved in a quick flash.

With eerie calm, she caught Sophie's wrist mid-swing, stopping the punch dead in its tracks.

"Mistake," the witch explained in a monotone voice, her grip like an iron vice. Her eyes locked onto Sophie's with unsettling certainty. "You will also surrender to me, Sophie Griffin."

[-----  -----]

Annabelle charged toward the crowd, snatching up a chair with her left hand and hurling it at the nearest thug. The man barely had time to react before the wooden frame crashed into him, sending him stumbling backward with a grunt.

Wasting no time, Annabelle leapt forward, planting both feet squarely on his chest and springing off like a cat. She vaulted over another attacker wielding a wooden club, landing squarely on the back of an unfortunate man facing the bar. He barely had time to register her presence before she slammed into him, driving him face-first into the counter with a sickening thud. He crumpled to the floor, unconscious.

Now standing atop the bar, Annabelle grinned before hopping down behind it, moving swiftly to her goal. The security man was slumped on a stool, down and being pummeled by the group of thugs invading the bar.

Behind the bar lay a pile of large weapons, rifles and swords. She quickly searched through them before spotting her gear.

"Come to mama," she purred, snatching up her anchor belt. She fastened it around her waist with practiced ease, wrapping the thick chain securely before letting the hefty miniature anchor hang at her side.

Still grinning, she rifled through the pile once more until her fingers found the familiar hilt of her cutlass. Sliding it free, she tucked the sheath through her belt with a satisfied nod.

Right where it belongs, she thought, her fingers resting on the hilt.

With her weapons finally in place, Annabelle cracked her neck and peeked over the bar, ready to dive back into the fray for a bit of fun.

[----- ✚ -----]

Sophie couldn't believe the strength in the blue-haired woman's grip. No matter how hard she struggled, the woman effortlessly pried Sophie's hand away from her face, the ease almost casual.

Then Sophie caught a glimpse of her opponent's hand, metallic, intricate, moving with uncanny fluidity. *A machine?* Sophie's mind reeled. The precision, the strength... it didn't make sense. How did it work so smoothly?

"You should give up," the woman told her in the same monotone voice, flat, emotionless, as if giving directions rather than issuing a threat.

Sophie grit her teeth, fighting through the pain in her wrist. "Can't do that," she shot back.

Her mind snapped to training, her mother's voice clear as day.

Gather mana in your elbow, she recalled, clenching her free fist. *Form a spell circle at the back of the elbow and store the mana there. Then gather mana in your hand, create another spell circle at the tip of your fist, and store it.*

Release—first the elbow, then the fist.

She had trained for weeks, failing over and over until the day she shattered a tree trunk with one punch. That was the moment she understood why her mother drilled the technique so thoroughly.

Now it was second nature.

Sophie focused, feeling magic pulse through her body. Her elbow circle ignited first, unleashing a burst of force that propelled her fist forward at bullet speed. The second circle flared at her knuckles, forming a protective mana shield around her hand.

"Never forget the name," her mother had said. "Say it in your mind as you cast it."

HARDKNUCKLE!

The punch connected squarely with the blue-haired woman's face, sending her flying backward. Sophie felt the energy release reverberate through her bones as the grip on her wrist finally opened.

The woman hit the ground hard, lying motionless for a moment. Sophie exhaled, relief flooding through her...until she sat up, quickly.

She snapped upright in a single, fluid motion, like a door swinging open, and fixed her eerie gaze on Sophie. "You punch very hard," she said, completely unfazed.

Sophie's stomach dropped. That was a full-power HARDKNUCKLE. Yet this woman barely seemed rattled.

"What in the world..." Sophie muttered under her breath. She was out of options because hand-to-hand wasn't going to cut it.

Pivoting on her heel, she sprinted toward the entrance that led to the front of the tavern and shouted into the bar, "I need my pistol!!"

[----- ☕ -----]

Brother Albert reached the top of the stairs, his breath ragged. The security man sat on his stool, leaning over the railing, eyes squinting in confusion at the chaos below.

"What the hell's going on down there?!" the man barked, twisting to face Albert. "What's all that noise?"

Albert, still catching his breath, replied quickly, "The tavern is under attack. Ruffians stormed in and started smashing the place up, it is an all-out melee down there."

The man's eyes widened in alarm. "How'd they get past Dadid?" He stood abruptly, reaching into a hidden compartment in the podium and pulling out a heavy-looking bag.

"I wish I could tell you," Albert said, sidestepping him and hurrying toward the hallway. "I have to get the girls."

The security man muttered a curse under his breath as he shrugged off his vest. "I'll put down anyone who tries coming through here." Before handing Albert the keys, he paused briefly.

Albert glanced back, offering a quick, hopeful nod. "Good man." he said before pushing through the door.

As he crossed into the hallway, Albert caught a glimpse of the man fastening a necklace around his neck and clasping his hands together in what looked like a silent prayer—or preparation for something far less holy.

Albert pressed on, sprinting down the corridor until he reached door number five. He pounded on it with both fists, voice cracking with urgency. "Miss Lisa, please wake up! We need to go, now!"

[----- ⚓ -----]

Now armed and ready, Annabelle leapt onto the bar, her grin wide and wicked as she sized up the thugs. "I'll give ye all one chance to turn tail and run" she bellowed, raising her cutlass high. "If ye stay, yer wounds won't be me fault!"

The old man in the leather hat sneered, eyes narrowing as he jabbed a finger at her. "She's one of them! Take her too!"

The thugs snarled, shifting their focus as they surged forward.

Annabelle smirked. "Remember I gave ye a chance."

With a swift swing, she sliced her cutlass through the air and kicked the nearest man square in the face, sending him sprawling with a muffled yelp. Before she could savor the moment, another thug lunged, reaching for her ankles.

She saw it coming.

Springing into the air, Annabelle landed on the man's outstretched hands, driving her heels down hard enough to make him howl in pain.

"Ye—AAAHHHH!" he screamed, face twisted in agony as he glared up at her.

Without missing a beat, Annabelle backhanded him across the jaw with the flat of her blade. No need to kill, most of these poor sods were just hired muscle, in way over their heads.

She hopped up, planted her feet, and let the man's hands drop. He crumpled groaning to the floor.

"I need my pistol!" Sophie's voice cut through the chaos from the other side of the tavern.

Aye that's right! The copper needed her guns. Annabelle glanced toward the pile of weapons behind the bar but was stuck…no way to get there without leaving herself open.

A thug swung a heavy wooden club at her, but Annabelle reacted instantly, snapping her left foot up to avoid the blow. She stopped the club cold. With a sharp stomp, she trapped it under her boot, grinning wickedly at the thug's bewildered expression.

"Bad luck, mate," she said, then brought her cutlass down in a swift arc, slicing the club cleanly in half. The splintered wood clattered uselessly to the floor.

Thanks for that one, Smitty. She thought, recalling the first mate's advice on handling club-wielders.

With the crowd closing in, Annabelle steeled herself, gripping her cutlass tighter. "Who's next?" she taunted, ready for the next wave.

A deafening roar shattered the chaos, a sound somewhere between a bear's growl and thunderclap. Every head turned to the swinging doors as they burst apart. A massive man-bear hybrid crashed through, filling the entrance with hulking presence.

"**You are not welcome here!!**" the beast roared, voice thick with authority as he glared at the thugs crowding the bar. His gaze locked onto Annabelle, poised on the bar with cutlass ready. "Are they with you?" he rumbled.

"Nope," she answered quickly, raising a free hand in surrender. She had zero interest in getting on Bear Dadid's bad side, she'd seen him fight, and it wasn't pretty.

The old man in the leather hat scoffed. "It's just one bear! You can take him!" he barked, waving his hired goons forward.

Dadid responded with terrifying speed, charging into the crowd. His massive, clawed hands swept a thug off his feet, sending him crashing into a table with a pained oomph.

Annabelle seized the golden opportunity to leap behind the bar, eyes scanning the confiscated weapons.

"Let's see…" she muttered, fingers curling around a plain wooden-stock rifle, lever-action, a basic scope mounted on top. She'd half-expected something flashier, maybe purple like Sophie's suit. Nope, just an ordinary rifle.

She shrugged, slinging it over her back, the stock clattering against the anchor hanging at her waist. Turning to the pistols, she grimaced. Flintlocks, good ones, but Sophie wouldn't be caught dead with something so old-fashioned.

Feeling the pressure, Annabelle grabbed a rough, slapdash pistol that looked cobbled together from scrap. She studied it, rolling her eyes. This'll probably fire once before falling apart. She tossed it over her shoulder with a grunt. "No way *Princess Purple* carries this garbage."

She grabbed another pistol, sleek and shiny, with a polished brown wooden grip. It looked expensive, probably worth at least a hundred gold coins. *Now this*, Annabelle thought with a grin, *is her gun.*

Satisfied, she secured the pistol and rifle, then hopped over the bar once more. "Hang on, Copper, I'm coming." She muttered, cutting her way back to Sophie.

[-----⚓-----]

Sophie's mind raced through her options.

She had a few firebombs tucked inside her coat, a couple more concussion trip wires, and enough pistol and rifle reloads stashed in her inner pockets to put up a fight. But none of it seemed enough against her.

The blue-haired woman rose to her feet, her mechanical left-hand flexing with eerie precision. Sophie's sharp eyes caught another detail, a machine right leg moving with the same unnatural fluidity. There was no doubt now. This woman was touched by a goddess like Sophie was. She couldn't help but wonder what had happened to her.

Sophie backed away and considered using a firebomb, but the thought made her hesitate. The tavern was an enclosed wooden space, likely soaked with years' worth of spilled alcohol. A single spark could turn the whole place into an inferno.

69

Maybe something else.

The blue-haired woman didn't advance. Instead, she calmly raised her right hand. A ball of blue mana energy flickered to life in her palm, crackling with power. Sophie's heart sank as shimmering particles drifted from the orb to the heap of broken metal, the remnants of the mechanical monster she had just destroyed.

In a wave of glowing blue light, the wreckage twisted and reformed, metal gears, poles, and plates snapping into place with sickening grace.

Sophie's stomach tightened as the new creation emerged, an insect-like construct towering over her. Its sleek form resembled a mantis, standing on two segmented legs. Wicked pincer-like arms extended outward, their edges lined with small, menacing blades. Designed not to kill but maim and capture.

Sophie swallowed hard, backing away from is slowly.

Her gaze darted toward the bar, searching for Annabelle. The pirate had dived behind it with some ridiculous acrobatics, but there was no sign of her yet. "Come on, Annabelle," Sophie whispered, eyes flicking back to the mantis-monster advancing toward her. *I need that pistol.* The construct clicked and whirred, its bladed arms slicing through the air with chilling precision.

Sophie squared her stance, fingers inching toward her coat. If Annabelle didn't hurry, she'd have to face this thing head on without any weapons.

"Surrender, Sophie Griffin," the blue-haired woman said, her voice eerily monotone. She moved her hand, and the mechanical mantis lurched forward with precise, calculated steps. "I do not wish to harm you."

Sophie's grip tightened around a nearby chair, flipping it upside down in preparation. Her heart pounded, but her voice remained steady. "Why not? You already murdered my everyone else!"

"That was a mistake," the woman replied, as lifeless as before, offering no further explanation.

Sophie didn't wait for more empty words. As the mantis construct came within range, she swung the chair down with all her strength. The wood splintered on impact, shards flying in every direction, but the metal monster didn't even flinch.

With an unsettling click, its pincer arms unfolded in one swift motion, gleaming blades poised to snap shut around her.

Sophie's instincts kicked in. She planted her foot against the machine's midsection and shoved off, propelling herself away just in time to evade its grasp. She landed hard, skidding across the floor, her breath coming in ragged gasps.

I'm not equipped for this fight.

The mantis stalked forward, its arms folding back into a more compact form, moving with an eerie, deliberate grace. Sophie scrambled to her feet, eyes darting to the bar. Still no sign of Annabelle.

Think, Sophie.

Her fingers slid inside her jacket, feeling the familiar shape of a firebomb. It was risky, too risky but she was running out of other options. The heat might be enough to disable the thing… or it might turn the entire tavern into a death trap.

Before she could make a decision, a deafening roar shattered the air.

Sophie snapped her head toward the sound just in time to see a massive bear-man explode into the open bar area, barreling through the invading thugs like a force of nature.

No help there, she thought, grimacing.

Her hand closed around the firebomb in her coat. Time is running out, and unless a better plan reveals itself fast, she'd have no choice but to light this place up.

[----- 🍵 -----]

Albert rattled the handle of room number five, pounding on the door with growing desperation. "Lisa, you have to wake up!" he shouted, his voice cracking with urgency. "Hey!"

Albert turned to see the security man standing down the hallway, now covered head to toe in what looked like armor, except it wasn't metal. It was stone, jagged rocks clinging to his body like a second skin.

"Use these," the man called, tossing a ring of keys down the hall.

Albert caught them one-handed and immediately fumbled through the set, his fingers trembling. He tried the first key labeled 5. No luck. He cursed under his breath and jammed in the next one, marked with a faded 16. Nothing.

Frustration clawed at him. As he hurriedly tried another, he kicked the door in frustration. "Lisa, wake up!" he shouted again, his voice growing hoarse.

Just as he reached for the next key, the door cracked open. Lisa Nozaki peeked out, her long green hair pulled back in a messy ponytail, eyes half-lidded with sleep.

"What is it?!" she grumbled, blinking at Albert's panicked expression, clearly surprised she'd been woken up at all.

Albert exhaled in relief. "Lisa, we're under attack! You need to get ready... right now!" He moved to push past her, but Lisa pressed against the door, keeping it barely ajar.

"Whoa, hey—I'm not decent!" she protested, narrowing her eyes. "No night clothes, remember?"

Albert froze mid-step, his face heating up. "Oh... oh! I...uh...apologize." He stepped back awkwardly, rubbing the back of his neck. "Please, just... get ready as fast as you can. We're in real danger."

Lisa squinted at him, still half-asleep. "What? What is going on?" Before he could answer, a thunderous roar echoed from downstairs, followed by the unmistakable sound of furniture crashing and men screaming.

The two of them locked eyes, the weight of their predicament sinking in instantly.

Lisa's drowsiness vanished. She slammed the door shut with a loud thud. Albert flinched and knocked again, worried she had retreated back to sleep. "Lisa..."

"**I AM GETTING READY!**" she shouted from behind the door.

"Okay..." Albert answered, still surprised by Lisa's sudden cooperation. He could only hope the noise had roused Regina as well.

He hurried to the next door, slipping his journal into the strap across his lower back before pounding on it. "Regina! You have to wake up!"

Fumbling with the key labeled 16, he jammed it into the lock. To his surprise, it clicked open immediately.

"Finally, a stroke of good luck" Albert breathed, pushing the door open. Inside, Regina Fournier lay sprawled across the bed, completely undisturbed. Her curly silver hair was a tangled mess against the pillow, her glasses resting neatly on the table beside her folded clothes.

Albert blinked. *How in the world is she still asleep through all this?* Wasting no time, he rushed to her bedside and shook her gently, but firmly. "Regina, you need to wake up right now!"

In an instant, her eyes snapped open, and before Albert could react, she pointed her two fingers and cast a spell: "**Envoûtement des Cercles Éternels.**"

Glowing spell circles burst into existence around Albert, locking him in place mid-motion. His limbs froze, held by an invisible force that tightened around him.

"**WHAT IS THIS?!**" Albert shouted, eyes wide in awe. The fact that Regina could cast a spell in her sleep was equal parts impressive and unnerving.

Regina blinked blearily at him, finally registering his presence, and his predicament. "Oh," she said, rubbing her face as she looked around, realizing with a groggy frown that she wasn't in her bed at home.

With a casual flick of her wrist, the glowing circles vanished, and Albert stumbled forward, regaining control of his body.

"Sorry about that," Regina mumbled through a yawn. "My little brother Mattie likes to mess with me when I'm asleep."

Albert took a deep breath, forcing himself to focus. "Regina, this is important. We're under attack! You need to get ready right as fast as you can." His voice was firm, carrying all the persuasiveness he could muster.

Regina yawned again, rubbing her eyes as she climbed out of bed, wearing only an undershirt and panties.

Albert's face turned beet red. He spun around so fast he nearly tripped over himself. "P-please, let me know when you're ready," he stammered, staring intently at the door.

Behind him, Regina stretched lazily. "Okay."

Albert squeezed his eyes shut. "I'm just trying to survive the night, Regina. Please hurry."

[-----⊕-----]

The insect-like machine crept closer to Sophie, its steps slow and deliberate, each mechanical click sending a shiver down her spine. She pulled a firebomb from her jacket, eyes scanning the construct's sleek, armored frame, searching for a weak spot.

"Duck Copper!"

Annabelle's voice sliced through the chaos like a whipcrack.

Without hesitation, Sophie dropped to her knees just as Annabelle's anchor whipped past her head, latching onto the mantis's right pincer. With a fierce tug, Annabelle wrenched the limb aside, exposing a vulnerable joint beneath the reinforced plating.

Sophie didn't hesitate. She hurled the firebomb straight into the opening between the arm and chest.

BOOM!

The explosion rocked the mechanical insect. Flames burst from within as the force tore the arm clean off, sending the metal beast crashing to the floor, its blue aura fading while smoke poured from its side.

Annabelle jogged over, grinning as Sophie scrambled to her feet.

"That there was some damn fine teamwork," she said, unslinging the rifle from her back and handing it over. "I even got yer guns fer ye."

Sophie accepted the weapon with a relieved nod. "Just in time." She cocked the lever, chambering a round with a satisfying clack.

"Don't forget this," Annabelle said, holding up an ornate pistol with intricate engravings swirling along the barrel.

Sophie frowned, eyeing the weapon with suspicion. "That's not mine. It looks like a toy."

Annabelle shrugged. "Oi, it's not like I've ever seen it before," she teased, waving it playfully.

Before Sophie could argue, a low hum filled the air.

The blue-haired woman, calm as ever, raised her hands, summoning glowing blue particles once more. The mantis construct jerked violently, its remaining arm snapping back into place as it rose, still missing one pincer, so it is only a little less dangerous.

Sophie exhaled sharply, tightening her grip on the rifle. "Here we go again."

She raised the rifle, finger resting lightly on the trigger, and took careful aim at the mantis. A sudden realization struck her; she couldn't remember what kind of bullets she had loaded.

"You might want to get down," she warned Annabelle, bracing herself.

Annabelle barely had time to react before Sophie fired.

BANG!

The shot rang out. Sophie watched in mild disappointment as a regular bullet tore through the air and struck the mantis with a dull clank. No explosion. No special effects. Just a standard round.

"Aye, thanks for the warning, Copper." Annabelle quipped, grinning as she crouched slightly.

Sophie scowled but said nothing, a flicker of embarrassment prickling her chest. *I must've loaded regular bullets only.* Gritting her teeth, she fired again, and again. Each shot chipped away at the mantis's structure but failed to bring it down.

Then, on the sixth shot...

BOOM!

The round exploded in a fiery blast, obliterating the machine's chest pieces and sending it crashing to the floor in a smoking heap. Sophie exhaled sharply, realizing she had only one bullet left, and if she stayed to her normal pattern, it was another flame round.

Wasting no time, she snapped her rifle up, sights locked onto the blue-haired woman. This is it.

She pulled the trigger.

In a flash of blue energy, the woman raised a hand, manipulating the wreckage of the fallen mantis. Metal groaned as it surged upward between them, taking the brunt of Sophie's shot. The bullet exploded, blasting apart what remained of the machine's left leg.

"Damn," Sophie muttered, working the rifle's lever. The shallow click confirmed her worst fear, she is out of bullets.

The blue-haired woman's cold gaze settled on them. "Annabelle Salazar," she intoned, "Annabelle Salazar must be killed."

Annabelle didn't miss a beat. She flicked her wrist, her anchor snapping back into her grip with a smirk. "Sorry, hussy. Can't help ye."

Sophie and Annabelle tensed as the woman stretched out her hand. The remains of the mantis swirled into a whirlwind of glowing blue particles. With terrifying precision, the debris reassembled itself into a new creation, a two-legged beast with black, writhing tendrils protruding from its frame. Its mouth stretched unnaturally wide, filled with jagged metal teeth like an alligator's maw.

The monstrous machine hit the floor with a resounding clang and took a single step forward, releasing a high-pitched, tinny scream that sent a shiver down Sophie's spine.

[----- 🦅 -----]

"I'm ready now," Regina's voice came from behind Brother Albert—calm, though still groggy.

Albert turned to find her standing there, fully dressed and appearing somewhat composed. Though she looked ready, he wasn't convinced she was fully awake, but that would be a problem for later.

"Very well, Miss Fournier," he said. "Let's collect Lisa and assist Griffin and Salazar, posthaste."

With that, he led Regina into the hallway.

As they stepped out, Lisa emerged from her room wearing a brown and tan dress with an intricate pattern, a bag in hand stuffed with her earlier clothes. Her long green hair was pulled back in a hasty ponytail.

Albert blinked, puzzled. "Miss Lisa you... changed your clothes?"

Lisa raised an eyebrow. "Well, yeah," she said, as if it were the most obvious thing in the world. "My other clothes were dirty. Why would I put those back on?"

Albert opened his mouth to argue, then closed it, realizing he had no valid counterpoint. "Touché," he conceded with a sigh. "We have to go."

He led the two young women toward the top of the staircase, where the scene below was already a cacophony of chaos. But before they could descend, their attention was drawn to the security man standing guard.

Now fully encased in stone armor, he looked like a living statue, his expression as stoic as the rock covering his body.

"I have to stay here and protect the other guests," the guard rumbled, his voice gravelly beneath the thick layer of stone.

Albert nodded approvingly, placing a firm hand on the man's shoulder. "You're the best of us."

Then he turned back to Lisa and Regina, straightening his posture. "Ladies, be ready. I suspect it's a madhouse down there."

Lisa and Regina exchanged a glance, both steeling themselves.

Regina pulled a slender wand from the pocket of her dress, its tip glowing faintly as she twirled it with practiced ease.

Lisa clapped her hands together and rubbed them, a subtle shimmer forming between her palms as she focused her mana.

Albert exhaled, bracing himself. "Let's go."

[----- ⚓ -----]

Annabelle and Sophie stood side by side, facing off against the blue-haired woman and her monstrous tentacled alligator construct. Annabelle caught her anchor in her right hand with a satisfying clink and smoothly drew her cutlass with her left, the blade glinting under the tavern low lantern lights.

Sophie, meanwhile, held her rifle at a diagonal, muzzle pointed toward the floor, lever forward. She knew it was useless without more ammunition.

"What're ye thinkin', Copper?" Annabelle asked, eyeing her expectantly. If there was any kind of plan, she wanted it.

Sophie exhaled, frustration creeping into her voice. "I don't have enough time to reload." She glanced at the advancing machine and muttered, "Really wish I had my pistol." She was sure she could reload that faster than the tentacled monstrosity could reach them.

74

Annabelle rolled her eyes. "Yeah, yeah, yeah, I gave you a perfectly good gun," she said, switching into her *proper voice,* the one she'd learned from Captain Kidd to mock Sophie. "But it looks like a toy," she added with a smirk.

Sophie shot her a glare but didn't rise to the bait. Instead, she focused on the enemy. "The only advantage we have is that she doesn't seem able to fight and control that thing at the same time," she said, nodding toward the blue-haired woman. "But a direct attack on her isn't as easy as it looks. I hit her with a full-power HARDKNUCKLE, and she got right back up like it was nothing."

Annabelle cocked an eyebrow. "What's a hard knuckle? Some kinda Copper thing?"

Sophie's scowl deepened. "Yeah. Some kind of Copper thing," she muttered, shaking her head.

Annabelle grinned, twirling her cutlass. "Well, if brute force don't work, maybe we try somethin' else, aye?"

Sophie sighed, gripping her rifle tighter. "Let's hope we figure it out before that thing reaches us."

The machine took another ominous step forward, its tinny, shrieking whine filling the tavern like nails on a chalkboard. Its tentacles whipping around it creating a barrier around it.

The blue-haired woman moved her hand, and the mechanical alligator surged forward, black tendrils whipping toward Sophie and Annabelle with terrifying speed. Its mouth opened wide, releasing a tinny, artificial roar as it stomped closer, metal jaws clanking ominously.

Sophie raised her rifle, deflecting the flailing tentacles as best she could, while Annabelle parried with her cutlass. The strikes came faster, the tendrils lashing like whips and grazing their hands and arms. Sophie gritted her teeth against the stinging pain, until one tentacle caught her hard across the face.

With a sharp cry, she staggered. Her rifle slipped from her grasp and clattered to the floor.

Annabelle ducked the same strike and surged forward, her cutlass slashing at the monster's midsection. The blade bit into its metal hide but didn't cut through as expected. "Bollocks!" she cursed, tugging at the weapon. It remained lodged in the creature's body.

Before she could react, a tentacle slammed into her face, then her left arm, pain flaring through her body. She cried out but refused to drop her weapons. *I am not weak, not like the purple Copper.*

The mechanical beast reared back, jaws widening to snap down on her, a metallic screech filling the air.

Sophie, shaking off the pain, lunged forward. She rammed her shoulder into Annabelle's arm, driving the embedded cutlass deeper into the creature's core.

Shhhhk!

The blade sliced clean through, cutting the machine in half. With a final shudder, the construct collapsed in a sparking heap, its deadly bite halted just inches from Annabelle's head.

Sophie didn't hesitate. She yanked the so-called *toy* gun from Annabelle's waistband and spun on her heel. Without pause, she fired.

BANG!

The first shot struck the blue-haired woman square in the abdomen, making her stagger backwards. Sophie instinctively released the trigger, expecting the pistol to cycle the next round, just like her own pistol.

75

It didn't fire. Instead, the trigger remained locked in place.

"Damn it," Sophie muttered, quickly thumbing back the hammer and advancing the cylinder to the next shot.

Across the room, the blue-haired woman's expression finally shifted, her gaze dropping to the spreading stain of blood on her stomach. Her hand trembled slightly over the wound, surprise somehow flickering across her emotionless face.

Sophie leveled the pistol again, nudging aside the shattered remains of the mechanical monster with her boot. "Not so tough now, are you?" she said, steeling herself for whatever came next.

The woman looked up at Sophie, who now stood over her, pistol aimed squarely at her chest.

Sophie pulled the trigger.

Click.

Both women blinked in surprise.

Sophie frowned, flipped the gun in her hand, and inspected it with disgust. *Who the hell loads only one bullet?* She thought. Without hesitation, she hurled the weapon at the woman's head.

Thunk!

The pistol bounced off and skidded across the floor. The woman's head snapped back from the impact, but with eerie calm, she turned forward again, locking eyes with Sophie.

"That wasn't very effective," she said, her tone detached, almost clinical, like she was offering a critique.

Sophie's breath caught. Before she could react, the woman extended her metal hand toward her with chilling precision. Sophie's body tensed, but she didn't have time to move...

Suddenly, she was yanked backward.

A flash of orange streaked past. Annabelle. The pirate swung her anchor with brutal force, and it connected with the woman's face in a loud sickening crash, forcing her back a few steps.

Sophie stumbled, regaining her footing just as Annabelle planted herself between them, anchor raised and cutlass drawn.

"Git movin'!" Annabelle barked, her voice sharp with command. "Yer pistol's gotta be behind the bar!"

Sophie hesitated surprised for the assist, her eyes darting between the downed woman and Annabelle.

"I'll handle this!" Annabelle added, slamming her anchor into the floor. The impact rang through the tavern.

For the first time, Sophie saw something in Annabelle beyond reckless bravado, something unmistakably echoing camaraderie. The kind of presence she'd only seen in seasoned Shadows and Eclipses back in her clan. It startled her. Froze her.

Annabelle shot her a glare. "Move, Copper! I ain't gots time to babysit!"

Snapped from her trance, Sophie nodded and ran toward the bar, heart pounding.

Behind her, the woman's metal hand shot up, catching Annabelle's anchor mid-swing with an iron grip. Her cold gaze locked onto the pirate, and with a sudden tug, she tried to wrench the weapon free.

But Annabelle didn't resist.

She smirked and let go.

The anchor, still attached to the chain secured at her belt, flew past the woman. Without missing a beat, Annabelle wrapped the chain around her arm, braced herself, and dropped her full body weight to the floor.

THUD!

The sudden shift yanked the blue-haired woman forward, sending her tumbling like a barrel down a ramp. She hit the ground face-first with a satisfying crash, metal limbs scraping loudly against the tavern floor.

Annabelle rolled to her feet effortlessly, tugging the chain back with a practiced flick. The anchor snapped back into her hand.

[-----☕-----]

Albert led the way down the stairs, Lisa and Regina close behind. As they reached the tavern floor, chaos unfolded before them. Sophie Griffin was sprinting toward the bar—no doubt in search of her weapons.

But Albert's gaze locked onto something far more alarming.

Annabelle Salazar was locked in close combat with Isabella Morales, using her trick anchor belt to keep the blue-haired woman off balance.

Albert's heart seized with horror.

"**NO!**" he shouted, voice cracking with urgency. "Annabelle you cannot fight Isabella!"

Panic surged through him. Decades of training with the Order screamed for composure and restraint, to assess, to record, to think, but affection and instinct overrode it all. Before he realized it, he was charging forward, his body moving on its own.

"Get away from her!" he bellowed at Annabelle, his voice tight with desperation.

Regina blinked, startled by Albert's sudden shift. She didn't know who this Isabella was or why he was panicking, but she knew one thing:

Albert had been on her side. If he was charging someone like that, they had to be the problem.

"Right, then." she muttered, raising her wand and pointing it toward the blue-haired woman.

Drawing a steady breath, Regina focused her mana, compressing the air at the wand's tip. This spell—**Compression Space Cannon**—was a new personal favorite. Perfect for knocking someone off their feet. Or, in the case of that awful girl from Scholar Lucienne's gym class, for knocking her out after she kept stealing Regina's lunch money.

With a confident flick, Regina fired the spell.

A dense orb of compressed air hurtled toward the kneeling blue-haired woman.

This should knock her right to the ground, Regina thought smugly.

Except...

Regina hadn't accounted for the small fires scattered across the tavern floor. As the spell passed through the flames, it absorbed their heat, morphing into a fiery comet. Her eyes widened in horror. "Oh no. No, no, no, no..." There was no stopping it.

The burning projectile slammed into the blue-haired woman with a whoosh, sending her flying into the far wall with a deafening crash. Annabelle, caught in the blast, was hurled the opposite way, smashing into another wall with a grunt. Flames burst outward, licking at the nearby tables and chairs.

Albert stared at Regina, who still held out her wand, eyes wide with shock at the unintended explosion. In that brief moment, Albert realized he wasn't just surprised at her, he was shocked at himself.

77

What had I been thinking? Charging in like that, abandoning years of training, *letting my emotions take control of me like that?* And worse—*what would happen if Isabella got her hands on me... and my journal?*

Pushing those thoughts aside, he focused on Annabelle, sprawled on the floor, dazed but breathing. He dropped to one knee to meet her gaze. "Annabelle—Annabelle, are you okay?"

She blinked up at him, wincing. "Ow... What did ye tell her? 'Go ahead and kill 'em both'?" she whispered hoarsely, trying to gather herself.

Albert let out a relieved breath, a small smile tugging at his lips. "Thank the goddesses," he muttered. *If Annabelle was cracking jokes, she would live.*

Meanwhile, Lisa was less amused. "What in the name of the harvest are you doing?!" she shouted at Regina, eyes darting to the scorched debris and the smoldering remains of the mechanical creature.

"I—I'm sorry," Regina stammered, voice trembling. "I didn't..."

Lisa cut her off, exasperation clear in her tone. "That spell of yours almost killed them both!" Without another word, she rushed down the stairs to help Annabelle, leaving Regina frozen at the foot of the staircase, her face pale with guilt.

Regina's lower lip trembled as she looked around, mind racing for a way to fix this. *I didn't mean for that to happen,* she thought desperately.

Her gaze drifted to the blue-haired woman, now slumped against the wall, clearly wounded and unconscious. Something nagged at Regina about her blue hair. *When was the last time she'd seen someone with blue hair?*

"Wait a minute..." Regina's eyes widened with realization. She rushed toward Brother Albert, nearly tripping over her own feet in excitement. "Is she...she's touched by a goddess, isn't she?"

Albert, still kneeling beside Annabelle, looked up sharply and nodded, his expression hardening.

Regina swallowed, heart pounding in her chest. If she was right, this situation was about to get a lot more complicated.

[-----♆-----]

Sophie pushed through the chaos of the bar, now an all-out brawl. A bear-man roared, smashing his clawed hands into thugs' faces, sending them crashing into one another like rag dolls. Bar patrons scrambled for the nearest window, some fleeing, others throwing themselves into the fight with drunken enthusiasm.

She was halfway to the bar when she collided with the back of a burly man. He spun around, eyes lighting up with recognition.

"I got one of 'em!" he bellowed over his shoulder, his grip locking around Sophie's arm like a vice.

Damn it! Sophie thought, heart pounding. She'd almost forgotten, she was one of the targets.

Instinct took over.

She drove her knee into the man's leg, striking hard at the joint. As his grip loosened, she ripped her arm free and reeled back, fist tightening.

HARDKNUCKLE!

The spell activated instantly, mana surged through her arm, the first circle at her elbow releasing a burst of force that propelled her punch like a bullet. The second circle, wrapping her knuckles in raw energy, connected with the man's face with an explosive crack.

He flew backward, landing in a heap, motionless.

Sophie stood over him, exhaling hard. She flexed her fingers, feeling the lingering hum of magic in her fist. "I still got it," she acknowledged, allowing herself a brief moment of satisfaction. After her earlier encounter with the blue-haired woman, doubt had crept in making her wonder if she was really casting the spell correctly? But this... this was proof enough.

Shaking off the distraction, she refocused on the bar. Almost there.

The fight raged around her, but Sophie pressed on. She had to reach her pistol.

She pushed behind the bar, eyes locking on the far side where a stash of weapons was stored. To avoid drawing attention, she dropped to hands and knees, crawling along the bar's length.

The tavern's chaos raged on around her. A deafening **BOOM** shook the air, making her flinch. Somewhere above the din, she heard the green-haired girl, Lisa, if she remembered correctly, shouting frantically.

Curiosity got the better of her, and she popped up just enough to peek over the bar. Her stomach tightened; Brother Albert was down from the rooms, with the other two girls close behind him. Smoke and debris clouded the air near the far wall, where Annabelle was slumped against it, Albert rushing to her side.

"That explosion must've been right by them," Sophie muttered, clenching her fists and refocusing. "I really need my pistol."

Without wasting a second, she ducked back down and continued crawling, determination fueling her every move.

Finally reaching the shelf, she scanned the swords and clubs leaning haphazardly against the back wall. Beneath the bar was a large shelf packed with smaller hand weapons and pistols.

Come on, come on. Sophie thought, yanking open the first drawer.

Flintlock. Flintlock. Flintlock.

Her heart sank. An entire row of them.

Slamming it shut, she moved to the next drawer.

Flintlock. Flintlock. Flintlock. Still no luck. She bit her lip, feeling pressure mount in her chest. Flintlock. Flintlock. Empty. Flintlock.

"Damn it!" she yelled out, moving to the next row, desperation creeping into her fingers as she rifled through the contents.

Flintlock. Sophie swore under her breath. Flintlock. Revolver!

Her pulse spiked. Not her revolver, but progress. She closed the drawer and yanked open the next drawer.

And there she was.

Her baby, her pistol, inherited from her father *The Seeker.*

A sleek black revolver, runes delicately carved along the barrel, the Aurorium symbol proudly stamped into the grip.

Sophie exhaled in relief, gripping it tightly, feeling the familiar weight settle in her hand like the old friend she was. For the first time since this madness began, she felt like herself again.

"Finally," she whispered, lips curling into a small smile. It was like reuniting with a long-lost family member.

But there was no time to savor the moment. She snapped the revolver's chamber open, checking the rounds. Locked and loaded.

With renewed focus, she rose from behind the bar, ready to turn the tide.

Sophie stood tall, pistol firm in hand, and took in the escalating chaos. The brawl had only intensified, bar stools overturned, fists flying, tables reduced to wooden chunks and splinters.

The bear security man was a force of nature, knocking down hired thugs with heavy swings of his clawed hands. To his left, a man from Magitekopolis stood his ground, armor pulsing with rotating light across his arms and chest. Sophie's sharp eyes caught the we wasn't wearing his earrings his armor was somehow made of those earrings.

Interesting, she thought. But no time to dwell.

Without hesitation, Sophie raised her pistol high and fired.

BANG!

The sharp crack echoed through the tavern, freezing the chaos mid-motion. All eyes snapped to her, the weight of command settling into her stance.

"Listen up!" she shouted, voice cutting through the stunned silence. "It's time to leave. **EVERYONE, GET OUT—NOW!**"

She swept the pistol across the room, making sure the message landed.

A few patrons didn't need telling twice, scrambling out the window. Others, their drunken courage fading, hurried toward the front door.

But one voice, sharp and defiant, cut through the tension.

"You only got one gun girl." The old man in the leather hat sneered, pointing a crooked finger. "Six shots... and there's more than six of us." His voice dripped with smug satisfaction, as if he'd just uncovered some great secret.

Before Sophie could reply, the bear security man Dadid stepped forward, the crowd parting like waves.

Without hesitation, he swiped his massive paw across the old man's face with a thunderous slap, sending him crashing to the floor.

"I don't need a gun," the bear growled, his voice rumbling like distant thunder. **"GET OUT OF MY BAR!"**

The remaining stragglers took the hint, scattering out the door with renewed urgency.

With the immediate threat at the front bar handled, Sophie wasted no time. She pivoted and sprinted back toward Brother Albert and the others, there was still another problem to solve.

[----✪----]

Lisa reached Brother Albert and Annabelle, finding the older man kneeling beside the pirate girl, his brow furrowed in concentration as he gazed into her vivid orange eyes, trying to assess her condition. She tapped him gently on the shoulder. "I can help her," she   offered.

Albert blinked and quickly stepped aside. "Oh, yes—yes, that would be best," he said, relief evident in his voice as he gave Lisa space to work.

As Lisa knelt beside Annabelle, Albert's attention shifted to the blue-haired woman—Isabella Morales, who was already beginning to stir from the blast. A knot tightened in his stomach. She had been at the center of the explosion, yet she was still moving. This woman was truly the embodiment of the enduring.

His gaze then flicked toward Regina Fournier, who was cautiously approaching from the stairs, her wand still clutched tightly in her hand. Albert wasted no time. "Miss Fournier," he said, motioning toward Isabella. "Can you use that trap spell of yours on Isabella here?"

Regina hesitated for a moment, pointing at the blue-haired woman. "Her name is Isabella?" she asked, surprise lacing her voice.

Before Albert could respond, Regina straightened and flicked her wand forward. **"Envoûtement des Cercles Éternels!"** she declared confidently.

Golden magic flared to life around Isabella, swiftly shaping itself into four glowing rings. The first encircled her upper arms, pinning them tightly against her torso. Another constricted her human arm against her abdomen. The third snapped shut around her knees, locking them together, and the last bound her ankles, preventing any further movement.

Albert exhaled in relief. "Good work," he said, watching as Isabella sat lifeless against the glowing restraints. They held firm, for now.

Regina allowed herself a small, proud smile. "That should hold her." Albert nodded, though worry still lingered in his expression. "Let's hope you're right."

Albert watched as Regina's spell settled around Isabella Morales, the glowing circles locking her in place. A wave of relief washed over him, though he worried wouldn't hold for long.

Regina asked, "Is she touched by a goddess like us?"

His mind drifted back through the vast encyclopedia of knowledge he carried, recounting everything he knew about the young woman now trapped before him. "Yes," he said, half to himself, half to Regina, "her name is Isabella Morales. If you couldn't guess, she's from Magitekopolis—Alchemia's Reach, to be exact."

He shook his head, his expression darkening. "Her parents, Tomas and Maria... The Order didn't find out about her until after they died and by then, she had already disappeared." His voice grew heavier. "I've come across stories about a blue-haired witch creating mechanical monsters in the shadows. The Order failed her." He sighed heavily. "But seeing what she's become..."

Albert's thoughts trailed off, sorrow flickering behind his eyes.

Meanwhile, Lisa was fully focused on Annabelle. A red spell circle, inscribed with delicate red runes, pulsed gently just beyond her hands. She peered with her Earthbloom Sense, scanning Annabelle's body beyond the surface injuries. The burns and bruises were concerning, but the real problem was inside.

Lisa's stomach tightened. *A concussion.* The blast must have rattled Annabelle's brain inside her skull. Normally, a head injury like this would take days, maybe longer, to heal naturally. But they did not have days.

Taking a steadying breath, Lisa began her work.

She first focused on repairing the brain tissue itself, carefully knitting it back together with slow, deliberate precision. Too much movement, and Annabelle might lose control over basic motor functions or worse, her speech.

Once the tissue was stabilized, Lisa moved on to the next step: *unmixing the juices*, as her Earthbloom teachers used to say. Carefully, she worked to restore balance to the delicate fluids in Annabelle's skull. Even with magic, it wouldn't be perfect. Annabelle was going to wake up with a terrible headache.

But at least she'd wake up.

Sophie made her way toward the back of the tavern, her eyes lingering on the meeting room door she had walked through earlier.

That was before.

Before she learned she was touched by a goddess. Before she was given a destiny she never asked for. Before she found her home destroyed in an icy massacre.

Her gaze drifted down to the mangled remains of the mechanical monster in front of her, still glowing faintly with eerie blue energy. Machines just like this one had torn through her clan. Sophie clenched her jaw and quickly looked away, her chest tightening.

Instead, she turned her attention to the blue-haired woman trapped against the wall. The four golden circles encasing Isabella pulsed faintly, holding her in place.

Shaking off the memories clawing at the edges of her mind, Sophie bent down and retrieved her rifle. Holding the sling in her hand, she made her way to where she had dropped her pack near the meeting room door. Slinging the rifle over her shoulder, she grabbed the pack and looked back at the others.

"Looks like everything's sorted out here," she said, adjusting the straps.

Albert, who was already scanning the room, didn't look convinced. "Could be the calm before the storm," he replied, his eyes lingering on the flickering fires scattered across the tavern. "We should put these out while Miss Nozaki finishes treating Miss Salazar."

He started searching for something to carry water, then turned back to Sophie.

"Miss Griffin, please keep an eye on Miss Morales," Albert said, nodding toward Isabella. "You know how formidable she can be."

Sophie's grip tightened on her rifle as she turned toward Isabella, the blue-haired woman's cold gaze meeting hers. "I won't let her out of my sight," Sophie replied, jaw set. She was back in *Mission Mode* as Eclipse Baker would call it.

Sophie nodded and pulled her pistol from its holster, pointing it at the ground just in front of the blue-haired woman. "Morales?" she asked, puzzled. The thought hadn't even crossed her mind that the woman might have a name.

"Isabella Morales," Regina chimed in as she walked alongside Brother Albert, both carrying buckets of murky water. She tucked her wand back into the pocket of her dress. "She was touched by a goddess too."

Sophie's grip tightened slightly on her pistol as she kept her eyes locked on Isabella. The woman was slumped against the wall, motionless. Sophie studied the charred burns across her sleek blue-and-white form-fitting suit, the fabric singed and torn in places. *She must've been right next to that explosion*, Sophie thought.

Despite her appearance, something about Isabella made Sophie uneasy. She looked unconscious, but Sophie wasn't about to take any chances.

Her gaze flicked toward Lisa, who was kneeling beside Annabelle, focused intently on her healing magic. A soft red glow pulsed around and through the pirate girl's head, all of Lisa's efforts seemingly concentrated there. Sophie frowned, noticing the burns and scrapes on Annabelle's arms and legs were being completely ignored.

"Is she going to be okay?" Sophie asked, glancing between the unconscious Isabella and Lisa's unwavering concentration.

Lisa didn't look up. "Sure hope so," she said curtly, magic continuing to weave delicate patterns over Annabelle's forehead.

Albert and Regina returned, each holding a bucket of grimy water in both hands, their faces streaked with soot from digging through the wreckage. "How goes it, ladies?" Albert asked, his voice laced with forced cheerfulness, trying to inject some positivity into the tense atmosphere.

Lisa didn't even glance up. "**I am really trying to focus, so can everyone please be quiet!!**" she snapped, frustration bubbling over.

Albert blinked, momentarily taken aback, then gave a small, understanding nod. "Right. Quiet it is."

Sophie smirked faintly, turning back to Isabella and keeping her pistol steady.

The three of them exchanged silent glances, each wondering the same thing: *what is her problem?*

Without a word, Albert and Regina got to work, pouring water over the remaining small fires before they could spread further. The murky liquid hissed against the smoldering embers, sending brief wisps of steam into the air. Around them, a few people were still either out cold or more likely cowering behind overturned tables and broken furniture, too afraid to move after the chaos.

As Albert poured out the last of his bucket, his gaze drifted back to Isabella. A nagging thought gnawed at him. Annabelle had been conscious enough to speak cracking jokes even yet Isabella, who was undeniably tougher, remained completely motionless, slumped against the wall like a discarded puppet. Something didn't add up.

While dousing another small flame, he looked toward Regina and gave a subtle tilt of his head toward Isabella, silently asking if her binding spell was still intact.

Regina caught his signal, set her half-empty bucket down, and held up her hand, palm out. A soft glow flickered around her fingers as she checked the integrity of the spell. The four glowing circles surrounding Isabella remained perfectly in place, untouched and unbroken.

Regina glanced back at Albert, flashing a smile and giving him a confident thumbs-up. "Still good," she whispered.

Albert exhaled in relief and nodded.

Meanwhile, Lisa finished her work on Annabelle, at least all she could do. Healing brain injuries always made her uneasy; there were too many risks, too many things that could go wrong. One misstep, and she could do more harm than good.

With a sigh, Lisa closed the glowing red spell circle and sat back, studying Annabelle's face carefully.

Annabelle's eyes fluttered open, blinking a few times before she groaned and rubbed her temple. "Ahhh," she muttered, wincing. "Feels like someone beat me with a club." She cracked a half-smile, squinting at Lisa. "Did we win?"

Lisa let out a relieved breath and smirked. "You are alive, right?"

Albert, having watched the exchange from a distance, dropped his now-empty buckets and hurried to Annabelle's side, his heart lifting. He had feared he'd led this young woman to her death, and seeing her awake truly felt like a blessing.

Reaching her, he extended a hand to help her to her feet. "Miss Salazar," he said with a small, relieved smile, "I do believe you will owe Miss Nozaki a new dress by the time this is all over."

Annabelle took his hand, wincing as she stood. "Aye," she said, rolling her shoulders, "I guess that means I do owe her." She shot Lisa a playful grin. "Let's hope she doesn't want a fancy one."

Lisa snorted. "I think will."

Albert chuckled, tension finally easing from his shoulders, though he knew the fight wasn't over just yet.

Without warning, the now-repaired mechanical monster lunged forward, its massive jaws clamping down on Brother Albert's right arm and chest with terrifying force.

CRUNCH.

Albert barely had time to gasp before the creature swung him like a ragdoll, slamming him hard against the wall behind Annabelle. He hit with a sickening thud before being flung to the floor in front of Lisa.

Sophie's eyes darted to Isabella Morales, who, with a pulse of blue energy, shattered Regina's binding spell as if it were nothing more than paper chains.

Sophie didn't hesitate. She raised her pistol and fired a shot straight at Isabella's head.

BANG!

But Isabella was faster.

Her mechanical arm snapped up, intercepting the bullet with a sharp metallic clang. Then, with inhuman speed, she sprang to her feet, stepping toward Sophie with cold precision. Her expression remained emotionless as she pulled back her arm, preparing to deliver a brutal punch to Sophie's face.

Regina dropped her bucket, casting the binding spell again in desperation. **"Envoûtement des Cercles Éternels!"**

The glowing rings flared around Isabella, encircling her limbs once more, but she didn't even slow down. With a dismissive wave of her hand, blue energy crackled around her shattering the golden rings. "This spell is not powerful enough to stop anyone stronger than a child," Isabella said flatly.

Before Regina could react, Isabella seized Sophie's gun hand in a vice-like grip. The motion was so fast that Sophie's next shot discharged harmlessly into the ceiling.

"This fight is over," Isabella declared, her voice cold and final.

[----- 🐚 -----]

Meanwhile, the mechanical monster held its unrelenting grip on Albert, dragging him backward toward the jagged hole torn in the tavern's side wall leading to the alley. His body screamed in agony, and he let out an involuntary yell, legs kicking wildly as he struggled against the crushing force.

Albert had never been a warrior, never much of a fighter, his place was in study and investigation, not on the battlefield. But right now, none of that mattered.

This... this was the worst pain he had ever felt in his entire life.

Each jarring tug sent fresh waves of agony through him, and sheer panic took hold. He clawed desperately at the floor, kicking out in search of anything to grab onto. If the machine dragged him outside into the alley—

I'm as good as dead, Albert thought, terror gripping his chest tighter than the metal jaws.

[----- ⚓ -----]

Annabelle groggily pushed herself to her feet, her head swimming. She barely managed a step toward the metal beast dragging Albert before her legs gave out beneath her.

Damn it, not now!

She crashed to the floor with a grunt, her face pressed against the cool wood. Her body and mind was still recovering, she needed more time. But time was something they didn't have.

"Ahhhh!" Annabelle screamed in frustration, fists clenched uselessly against the floor.

[----- ☼ -----]

Lisa stumbled back, the chaos around her momentarily fading as she realized her hands and face were smeared with Brother Albert's blood. Her heart pounded as she looked up to see the mechanical beast dragging his struggling body toward the alley. Annabelle lay on the ground, too dizzy to move, and Sophie was locked in a losing battle with Isabella.

I must do something!!

Her eyes darted to Annabelle's pirate sword lying nearby, gleaming dully in the flickering firelight. Without hesitation, she scrambled forward, snatching up the sword and sprinting after the machine, sheer determination driving her forward.

[----- ⊕ -----]

Sophie couldn't believe it. Isabella Morales had completely overpowered her, holding Sophie's gun hand high like she was a misbehaving child at the shooting range. The crushing grip sent waves of pain through her fingers, making it impossible to break free.

She gritted her teeth. A HARDKNUCKLE attack would be useless, she'd only shatter her own hand. Desperate, she drove her knee hard into Isabella's bullet wound, but the woman barely reacted.

"That hurts," Isabella said in her usual cold monotone, pulling back her fist for a devastating punch.

Before the blow could land, a massive blur crashed into Isabella from the side. *Dadid.*

The bear-man roared as he barreled into Isabella, knocking her off balance before delivering a savage clawed swipe across her face, sending her sprawling to the floor.

"**No more fighting in my bar!**" Dadid bellowed, his voice like rolling thunder.

Isabella lost her grip on Sophie, and she snatched her hand back, shaking off the pain. Her pistol clattered to the ground, but she quickly grabbed it, eyes darting toward Brother Albert following Lisa, who was racing toward the machine outside.

Sophie dropped her rifle and bag without a second thought, raising her pistol and firing two precise shots at the mechanical beast's exposed joints. The bullets sparked on impact, causing minor damage, but she stopped when she remembered, the next rounds in her chamber were fire bullets.

Not yet.

Holding her pistol, she took off after Lisa.

[----- 🦅 -----]

In the alley, the mechanical monster dragged Albert mercilessly through debris. Lisa caught up, clutching Annabelle's sword tightly. As soon as she was within range, she jammed the blade into the damaged section Sophie had just shot, using it like a lever to pry the machine's jaws apart.

With a groaning screech of metal, the lower jaw snapped free. Albert fell to the ground with a sickening thud, blood pooling beneath him.

Before Lisa could react, the monster's tentacles lashed out in a frenzy, striking her face and arms with brutal force. She cried out, instinctively raising her arms to shield herself, curling into a defensive ball. The blows were relentless, each one sending jolts of pain through her body.

Sophie arrived just in time. She raised her pistol, taking careful aim she opened fire.

BANG! BANG! BANG!

The fire bullets ignited on impact, engulfing the machine in roaring flames. It screeched, halting its tentacle assault and turning toward Sophie.

Lisa, gasping and bruised, caught sight of the vines hanging from the rooftops of West's and the adjacent building. Gritting her teeth, she traced a green spell circle in the air, weaving her magic into the plants.

"Come on… work," she demanded.

The vines snapped to life, coiling around the machine's legs and yanking it from the ground. It let out a high-pitched whine as it was pulled high into the air, dangling precariously from the rooftop.

Sophie blinked in disbelief. "Well, that works."

Shaking herself out of it, she quickly flicked the release switch on her pistol, ejecting the spent cartridges with a metallic clink. Reaching into her coat pocket, she pulled out two regular rounds, and four fire rounds, loading them into the cylinder with practiced efficiency. With a final spin, she locked it back into place, scanning the alley for any more threats.

Nothing—just fleeing patrons and distant shouting.

[-----✿-----]

Lisa, her hands trembling, stumbled to Albert's side. His chest rose and fell in ragged, uneven gasps. Blood soaked his clothes, staining the stone path beneath him.

"Please hold on, Brother Albert," Lisa pleaded, tracing a red spell circle surrounded by six red runes over his battered body. Magic shimmered to life, pulsing over his wounds, but the damage was so severe: punctured lungs, broken ribs, internal bleeding.

Sweat dripped down Lisa's forehead as exhaustion crept in, each spell draining more of her mana. Healing this internal damage was like trudging through the dunes of Agrina without water slow, painful, and utterly draining.

Her vision blurred, tears welling up in her eyes, but she refused to stop.

With a shaky breath, she pressed on, willing the magic to do what her hands couldn't.

Just press on, she said to herself

[-----✿-----]

Regina stumbled forward, jolted from behind by the armored security man from Magitekopolis as he rushed past her to aid the bear-man. The impact knocked her off balance, but it also snapped her into action.

Shaking off the momentary shock, she hurried to Annabelle's side and helped her to her feet. Annabelle leaned heavily against her, still weak, but after a few steps, she straightened and shook her head, trying to clear the lingering dizziness.

"Girlie, yer spells pack a punch," Annabelle said with a weak but genuine grin, clear signs of recovery.

Regina returned a small smile as they made their way toward the alley, stepping carefully over the wreckage.

The sight that met her there hit like a punch to the gut.

Sophie stood guard, pistol in hand, watching over Lisa, who knelt beside Brother Albert. Red healing magic shimmered faintly around his bloodied body, but the energy was fading, barely holding together. Tears streamed down Lisa's face, her shoulders trembling from the effort of sustaining the spell.

Albert's eyes fluttered open. His vision swam as he took in the scene. Breathing was agony, every shallow inhale seared like fire through his chest. He couldn't move, but through the haze of pain, he heard Lisa's voice.

"Please do not try to move yet," she whispered, hands trembling as she poured everything she had left into him. The glow of the spell circle flickered weakly, her energy nearly spent.

86

Albert watched her struggle, watched her push through tears, her green hair clinging to her damp cheeks. The inferno in his chest dulled to embers, pain fading just enough for him to speak.

His hand, shaky and weak, reached out and touched Lisa's wrist.

"It's okay, Lisa," he croaked, his voice barely more than a whisper.

Lisa's head snapped up, eyes wide with desperation. "No, if I stop now…" she choked out, shaking her head violently as tears spilled down her cheeks. Strands of green hair clung to her face, but she did not care.

Albert forced a faint smile, touched by her unwavering devotion to a man she'd only known for hours. "I know, my dear… but you're almost out of mana." He coughed a dry, hacking sound that sent new spikes of pain through his ribs. "It's okay," he assured her gently.

The red glow of Lisa's spell flickered one last time before fading completely. She collapsed onto her knees, sobbing. "I am so sorry," she whispered, shoulders shaking.

Regina knelt beside her and placed a steady hand on her back. "I can do it," she said softly. "If I can understand how your magic works, I can cast your spell."

But Albert shook his head, inhaling a shallow, ragged breath. "There's no time," he rasped. "Her magic system… it's too complex." He winced, coughing again, the pain tearing through him like broken glass. "Please… just help me stand."

Without hesitation, Sophie holstered her pistol and knelt beside him, slipping his arm over her shoulder. "Up you go," she said firmly, lifting him with care.

Albert's entire body screamed in protest. Despite his best efforts, a ragged cry escaped him. His legs shook violently under his weight, and for a moment, the act of standing felt worse than the crushing bite of Isabella's mechanical monster.

As he struggled upright, the girls instinctively closed in, surrounding him with quiet solidarity.

The pain was unbearable, but Albert's mind drifted to a memory burned deep into him.

Years ago, as a young monk, he had once met a brother named Mathias who survived a bear attack, dragging himself for miles through the wilderness. Albert had asked him, "How did you do it?"

Mathias, scarred, one-armed, hollow-eyed, had said simply: "I got really angry." Angry at the bear. Angry at the goddesses for letting it happen. Angry at the parents who gave him to the Order.

And that anger had kept him alive.

Now, with the weight of his injuries and death pressing down on him, Albert felt that same fire ignite within. He was *angry, furious*, that he would not live to guide these four extraordinary young women. Angry that his predecessor, that lazy god damned brother Tony, had overlooked Isabella Morales. Angry at the goddesses for keeping their silence while danger bloomed in the shadows.

He had followed every rule he could, done everything he could correct, yet here he stood, broken and abandoned with his avatars, his girls on the verge of death.

No! I will not fail them!

"Listen, ladies," he said, voice frayed but resolute. Leaning heavily on Sophie, he met each of their eyes in turn. "This is important."

They tensed, sensing what was coming.

"You **must** get to the Stormfang and sail for Order Island."

A chorus of protests erupted, except from Lisa, who stayed silent, tears still falling. Annabelle scowled, Regina opened her mouth to argue, and Sophie's jaw clenched in resistance.

Albert lifted a trembling hand to silence them.

"Please, ladies," Albert rasped, his voice thin. "We don't have much time... and I'm sure we are all still in danger."

He reached into his coat and drew out a polished pocket watch. The silver gleamed under the dim alley light, the insignia of the Order of Saint Lorraine etched cleanly into its surface. With a trembling hand, he pressed it into Annabelle's palm.

"When you reach Order Island," he said, locking eyes with her, "show them this. Ask for Brother Marcus Igbinedion. He'll show you the way."

Annabelle stared at the watch, jaw clenched tight.

"Brother Albert, we can't just leave you," Sophie said, her voice low but burning with determination.

Annabelle gave a slow nod, her throat tight. "Aye... the *Fang* ain't that far. We might make it..."

Albert's gaze hardened, he could see where this was going, and he would not let that happen "**Stop it!** All of you."

The sharpness in his voice froze them in place.

He exhaled, weariness in every line of his body. "I'm so sorry, girls," he murmured, regret flickering behind his eyes. "I'm so sorry I won't be the one to guide you... to see who you'll become."

He coughed into his sleeve, a harsh sound that made him wince, but he pushed through. "But it's too late for me. **Now y̲o̲u̲ must go!**"

He reached beneath the leather strap across his back and pulled free his worn journal, its pages frayed and ink-stained from years of use.

"She's after me, after this." he said, his tone firm but not unkind. "If she takes me, she won't chase you. But you have to get running."

The girls shifted, protest already forming on their lips.

"**Listen to me!!**" Albert said, his voice suddenly sharper. "**You can't beat Isabella!** Not now. She'll kill you... or worse." His eyes darkened considering what *his girls* would be like if they were taken. "Don't waste your lives...your destinies ...on an old monk like me."

The words struck like iron.

Reluctantly, the girls exchanged quiet, pained glances. They knew he was right. And they hated it.

"**Promise me**." Albert demanded through shallow, rattling breaths. "Promise me you'll reach the *Stormfang*."

Annabelle's fists tightened. "I swear," she said, her voice shaking.

"I promise," Regina whispered, her glasses fogged with tears.

"Yes," Lisa choked, wiping her cheeks with the heel of her hand, "I promise". She vowed then and there: *I will never run out of mana again.*

"You have my word." Sophie said. Her voice was barely more than a whisper, her expression carved in grief, *I am losing someone else today.* The weight of her failure was pulling her heart down even more.

Albert nodded slowly, his face relaxing. Then his gaze flicked to Sophie. "Do you have any firebombs left?"

She hesitated, then opened her coat. "Two."

"I'll need both," he said with a small, bloody smile.

Sophie's hand lingered on the metal shells before she finally let go.

Albert took them, his arms trembling. He looked at each of them—*his girls*. And for a moment, the pain faded.

"You have to help each other," he explained. "Trust each other. The goddesses picked the four of you for a reason."

His breath hitched, but his words stayed strong. "One day, I hope you'll see each other the way I see you...*strong, dedicated, intelligent, principled...* and truly amazing. Every and every one of you."

A flicker of fire lit his eyes. A grin pulled at his bloodied lips.

"Ladies... I have a plan." His voice gathered strength. "Get your things. And when I say go...run."

[----- 🍎 -----]

A short time later, Brother Albert leaned against the alley wall opposite West's Tavern, his battered body barely holding him upright. His foot rested on his worn journal lying at his feet, a silent testament to everything he recent accomplishments.

From the gaping hole in the tavern wall, Isabella Morales emerged, moving with slow, deliberate steps. Her once-pristine blue and white overalls is now torn and scorched, and despite her usual composure, there was a stiffness to her movements, a sign even she wasn't invincible.

Trailing behind her, a smaller machine scuttled forward, its sharp limbs glinting in the dim alley light. Crude but deadly, it had been pieced together from the remains of the security man's arm and chest armor.

Isabella's cold eyes flicked upward, landing on her first construct, now tangled in vines and suspended at rooftop level. She tilted her head slightly.

"Unfortunate," she said flatly, emotionless.

Albert took a shallow breath, willing his voice to remain steady. He loudly called out to her "**Isabella.**"

He barely managed to get the word out before a violent coughing fit overtook him, his body trembling from the strain. Finally, he steadied himself and wiped his mouth on his sleeve. "**I'm over here,**" he rasped, giving it everything he had to draw her attention.

His eyes flickered toward the tavern's front, where Sophie and Lisa were slipping inside through the door, moving like shadows.

Isabella's gaze lingered on him, her expression impassive, emotionless. "Albert Thompson," she intoned. "You have no means to fight or escape. You have no choice but to surrender."

She approached slowly, almost cautiously, the weight of their earlier battles and injuries evident in every step.

Albert let out a tired chuckle, lips curling into a faint smile. "You may be right, Isabella," he admitted, his voice soft yet resolute.

He swallowed hard, gaze growing distant. "I'm so sorry, Isabella," he said, thick with regret. "I'm so sorry for what happened to you."

He met her eyes, and for the first time, there was no strategy or distraction, only raw, painful sincerity. "I'm sorry the Order failed you. I'm sorry Tomas and Maria never got to see you grow up."

Isabella blinked, the names foreign to her. "I don't know who those people are," she replied flatly.

Albert's throat tightened, and he felt a tear escape down his cheek.

"I know, my dear," he whispered, voice breaking. "I'm sorry that you don't."

One of the most important duties of a monk of the Order of Saint Lorraine was to keep his journal safe, at all costs. It must never fall into unwashed hands. Every monk tasked with observing the world beyond the Order's walls was taught a single spell: a small fire ritual designed to incinerate their journal should they face death or imprisonment.

Albert remembered how long it had taken him to master it, weeks of relentless practice drawing the intricate symbol, injecting his mana into it, and igniting the seal. As a young man, he'd burned off his eyebrows more than once, failing to channel his energy quickly enough.

Now, battered and bloodied at the alley's mouth, all that work is about to pay off.

Isabella approached, her mechanical arm extending. Behind her, the newly constructed machine, shaped like a small, sleek wildcat, stalked forward on metal paws. The eerie blue glow in its eyes sent a shiver down Albert's spine.

"Only your journal is required," Isabella stated, her monotone voice cutting through the tense silence.

Albert let out a weary chuckle. "Well yes... that does make sense."

Out of the corner of his eye, he saw them, Sophie and Lisa slipping out of West's Tavern, moving swiftly down the pier to join Annabelle and Regina.

Good, he thought, relief washing over him. *They are safe.*

Isabella stepped closer, towering over him now. Without hesitation, she grabbed him with her mechanical arm, her grip cold and unyielding. "You will come with me," she said, finality in her voice.

Albert coughed, wincing, but managed to smile. "No, my dear," he whispered, eyes gleaming with defiance. "*You will come with me.*"

With that, he shifted his foot, pressing firmly against the journal beneath him.

Mana surged through him, flowing into the carefully drawn symbol on the cover. The sigil flared to life, igniting instantly in a brilliant burst of flame.

The explosion engulfed them both in fire and smoke. On its own, the spell might have only slowed Isabella for but a moment, but Albert had prepared for this. Hidden in his pants pocket were Sophie's two firebombs, and as the initial flames licked at them, they detonated in a violent inferno.

BOOM!

The blast shook the alley, sending debris flying and swallowing Albert and Isabella in a roaring firestorm. Flames licked at the surrounding walls, illuminating the night with a hellish glow.

Albert closed his eyes, feeling the intense heat, hoping, praying, that it would be enough. Enough to stop Isabella. Enough to buy his girls the time they needed. Enough to ensure they had a future, even if he wouldn't be there to see it.

Please goddesses... please let this be enough.

Chapter 7

Sophie and Lisa made their way over to where Annabelle and Regina stood waiting. Lisa clutched her belongings tightly, while Sophie shifted the weight of her pack, the rifle strapped securely to her back. The four girls huddled together, speaking in low voices as they planned their next steps.

"All right," Annabelle began, pointing down the pier, "The *Fang* is docked at slip seventeen. We just head straight that way, and we'll be there in no time."

"Slip seventeen?" Sophie echoed, eyeing a nearby slip marked with the number: *73*. She scowled. "You might as well have said it's in Aurorium Granmark."

"Aye, it's not close," Annabelle admitted with a smirk. "But if we keep moving, we'll get there before ye know it."

Regina beamed, ever the optimist. "Yeah, how far can it be?"

Sophie sighed and rolled her eyes but didn't say anything.

A deafening explosion suddenly erupted behind them, shaking the pier. Screams tore through the air as people scattered, some rushing toward the blast, others fleeing to their ships. The girls exchanged panicked glances. The explosion confirmed what they had feared. Lisa's eyes welled with tears as the full weight of the situation settled over them.

Annabelle placed a comforting hand on Lisa's shoulder. "It'll be okay, missy," she said gently.

"We need to move," Sophie snapped, her voice cutting through the chaos. "Stick with the crowd for cover. If we get separated, stay in pairs." She pointed at Annabelle. "You stay with"

Annabelle didn't hesitate. She grabbed Lisa's hand tightly. "With her," she said firmly.

"Great." Sophie's jaw tightened. "Annabelle, you lead. Lisa and Regina, stay behind her. I'll cover our rear."

Regina tilted her head. "Why the back? What if we're attacked from the sides? Or above? I mean, if I were trying to…"

Sophie silenced her with a sharp look. "Exactly. The point of having a bodyguard is to deter attackers." She motioned them forward. "Let's go. It's a long walk."

Annabelle turned, her hand resting on the hilt of her cutlass as she led the way. Lisa followed close behind, clutching her shopping bag, white sundress tucked inside, tears threatening to spill. Regina trailed them, her sharp eyes scanning the crowd. Sophie brought up the rear, muscles taut, eyes flickering to their flanks and behind.

They pushed through the surging crowd, their pace quickening with each step toward slip seventeen.

As they walked, the tension thickened around them, pressing in like the salty harbor air. Regina, sensing it, glanced at Lisa and asked gently, "How are you holding up?"

"I am okay," Lisa lied, quickly wiping away the tears clinging to her cheeks. She hesitated, then added, "I do have a question, though."

91

"Okay, what is it?" Regina said, her voice brightening.

Lisa took a breath. "Earlier, you said you could do my spell if you understood how my magic works. What did you mean by that?"

Regina's face lit up. "Oh! I'm a Nexus Mage," she said proudly. "Unlike most people, I'm not naturally attuned to any one magic system. Nexus Mages like me can tap into any system, but we have to learn how each one works and train ourselves to manipulate our mana properly for each."

Lisa blinked, struggling to grasp the concept. "But how would you even—" She trailed off, the words slipping away.

Regina waved it off with a grin. "Don't worry. Most mages and sorcerers struggle to understand Nexus Mages because they're introduced to their specific system so early. My mom used to say, 'Learner magic is a marathon, not a race.'" She smiled wistfully. "You could spend years on the basics of a dozen systems and still never master a single spell."

Lisa frowned and shook her head. "But magic is more than just spells," she argued. "It connects us to the world. It is a constant balance of give and take. You can't just boil it down to twisting mana and doing tricks."

"I don't do tricks," Regina shot back, her tone turning defensive. "It took me months just to learn Verboisance, and even longer to cast my first spell."

Lisa crossed her arms. "Well, it took me years to cast my first Earthbloom spell." She arched an eyebrow, pride creeping into her voice. "I would love to see how long it takes you to learn my magic."

Regina missed the edge in her voice. "Do you have a reference book?" she asked eagerly. "It sounds challenging...I'd love to try."

Lisa's eyes narrowed, offended by the casualness of Regina's curiosity. Without another word, she quickened her pace, moving closer to Annabelle and leaving Regina behind.

Regina faltered, confusion flickering across her face. She hadn't meant to upset Lisa, but it was clear she had. Her shoulders slumped, and she looked down, disappointed at the missed chance to connect.

Sophie, watching from behind, gave her a small, reassuring nudge. "Don't worry about it," she said. "She's just having a rough time right now."

Regina nodded weakly but couldn't shake the sting of Lisa's reaction. She fell into step beside Sophie, quieter than before.

Up ahead, Annabelle glanced over her shoulder, her sharp eyes catching Regina's dejected expression. She leaned in and whispered to Lisa, "Hard on her, don't ye think?"

Lisa's jaw dropped. "Me? You say hurtful things to her all the time, and I am the one being hard on her?" she shot back in a hushed tone.

Annabelle shrugged, unconcerned. "I'm just having a bit of fun. She doesn't seem to mind." Her gaze softened slightly. "But hey, just thought it was worth mentioning."

Lisa huffed but said nothing, chewing on Annabelle's words as they walked down the pier, the *Stormfang* still a distant speck on the horizon.

The quartet of young women continued on, passing shuttered shops and silent ships, their footsteps echoing against the worn wooden planks. Dim lanterns swayed in the night breeze, casting long shadows that danced across the hulls of docked vessels.

As they approached, a sailor stood before a line of short, round pillars rising from the pier, thick ropes strung between them to form a makeshift aisle. Beyond the barrier stood a large ship with a lowered ramp, part of the deck and hull folded down to allow for unloading. Faint noises of restless animals drifted from within.

"Sorry, girls," the sailor said, raising a hand to stop them. "Unloading livestock." He gestured toward the ship, where a few deckhands wrangled a stubborn goat down the ramp.

Annabelle leaned in, lowering her voice to a whisper. "Come on, ye can let us through," she coaxed with a sly smile.

The sailor shook his head, jerking it toward the guards flanking the aisle. Both stood stiffly, rifles at the ready, expressions sour and weary, clearly not thrilled to be working this late. "Can't do it. The guards."

Annabelle sighed, casting a calculating glance at them. "Aye, they don't look like the accommodating type," she mused, flashing the sailor a playful wink. Then she turned to Sophie, a spark of mischief in her eyes. "Oi, Copper, think ye could ask 'em to let us through?"

Sophie scowled and straightened. "My name is Sophie. Sophie Griffin. Not *Copper*." she said sharply. "And no, I won't. We're a group of young girls, some of us covered in blood, sneaking around in the middle of the night." She folded her arms. "I'd rather not draw extra attention to ourselves."

Annabelle considered that, then nodded. "Aye, good point."

Regina, ever curious, tilted her head. "Why do you always call her *Copper*? Is it because the metal of her badge?"

Annabelle smirked. "No, Regina. Us pirates and privateers call Aurorium folks Coppers cause they always find a reason to arrest us with copper cuffs, even when we ain't done nothin'."

Sophie shot her a hard look. "We don't just arrest people for nothing. A kingdom has to swear out a warrant for a mission to even be commissioned."

Annabelle waved a hand dismissively. "Sure, missy. Whatever ye say."

Before Sophie could retort, Regina chimed in, tapping her chin thoughtfully. "Actually, the Aurorium Clan doesn't have the power to make arrests unless a kingdom grants it, except when they witness a crime firsthand." She brightened, her scholarly tone taking over. "That was established in the Aurorium Treaty of the Year of the Goddess, 1715. For example, the Kingdom of Verdantia never signed the treaty and doesn't acknowledge the Aurorium. So no Aurorium agents can investigate or arrest anyone on their soil."

Sophie grinned triumphantly, gesturing to Regina with an open palm. "See? Told you so."

Annabelle rolled her eyes. "Aye, aye, Regina. Let's figure out how to get past *this* problem first."

As the girls waited, the ship's crew began guiding cows down the ramp and through the makeshift aisle, past the guards, and into the city. Hooves clattered on the wooden planks, and the cows' lowing echoed across the quiet pier.

Lisa watched the strange procession, a puzzled frown on her face. "Why would they do this in the middle of the night?" she wondered aloud.

Annabelle glanced at her and waved toward the slow-moving livestock. "Too big an operation, aye? During the day, the port's too busy to stall for something this long. Some ships don't stay overnight, they dock, unload, load up, and sail off. Can't waste time. Too many business folks losing coin."

Lisa nodded, her eyes scanning the scene with newfound appreciation. "I never thought about it that way."

"That's probably why they have the armed guards," Sophie added, nodding toward the rifle-wielding men flanking the aisle. "If someone hit this place, they could steal a merchant's entire fortune, and no earnings means no taxes for the kingdom. The guards make sure the crown gets its cut."

Regina's eyes lit up. "It's like an ecosystem," she answered, thinking aloud. "The plants feed the rabbits, the rabbits feed the fox, the fox feeds the wolf… and when the wolf dies, he feeds the plants again." She paused, then added, "If the wolf realized something was threatening the plants or the rabbits, it'd be in his best interest to stop it, because his own survival depends on it."

Annabelle smirked. "Aye, missy. Never thought about it that way."

But as the words left her mouth, Annabelle's expression darkened. She stiffened, eyes narrowing. "No," she muttered, her voice clipped and cold. "Ladies… we're being watched."

The others froze, eyes darting across the crowd.

"What do you see?" Sophie asked, her hand instinctively moving to the pistol at her side. "What are we looking for?"

Annabelle's voice was tense. "Red eyes. That Mage wench." She swallowed, scanning the crowd again, but the eyes were gone. "We should go. Now."

Regina craned her neck, searching. "Where did you see her?"

"I don't wanna point," Annabelle murmured. "Straight ahead. Just a bit bow-starboard."

"Uh... what?" Regina blinked.

Annabelle sighed, realizing she wasn't talking to a ship's crew. "In front... a little to the right."

Sophie squinted in the direction Annabelle indicated. "I don't see anything."

Lisa shielded her eyes with one hand, squinting into the dim lantern light. "Nor do I."

Annabelle's jaw tightened. "Oi, I know what I saw!"

"Calm down," Sophie said evenly. "We're all tired. Even if she was there, she's not going to attack in a crowd. We should stay cool and not draw attention."

Reluctantly, Annabelle nodded, though her hand hovered near the hilt of her cutlass. They continued scanning their surroundings. Tension hung thick in the air, but the red-eyed figure was nowhere to be seen.

Meanwhile, the crew pressed on, methodically unloading their cargo, oblivious to the unease brewing among the girls.

Annabelle's eyes darted through the crowd, tracing every face, every shifting shadow. That black figure with glowing red eyes, she knows she'd seen it. Maybe Sophie was right. Maybe she was tired... No. She shook the thought from her mind. *I know what I saw.* She just had to find her again.

Lisa glanced over at Annabelle, watching her tense, frantic movements. Exhaustion pressed on her shoulders, frustration bubbling under the surface. Her beauty coach always preached the importance of a full night's sleep, and she was certain she'd barely gotten an hour. A sharp voice in her head urged her to shake Annabelle, to insist there was no shadow. But instead, she took a breath and remembered her father's words: *Sometimes you have to be soft.*

"I want to help, Annabelle," Lisa said gently. "Can you describe her? Give us more details?"

Annabelle exhaled slowly, closing her eyes to focus. "Aye... she's taller than me. Her hair, it looked like black smoke, shifting and moving. Her skin was dark when she attacked me, but when sunlight hit her... it turned milky white." She opened her eyes and glanced at Regina. "It was like she was wearin' shadows for clothes." A sudden thought

94

struck her, and she turned sharply to Regina. "Missy, can you do that sunlight spell again?"

Regina hesitated, shifting uneasily. "I only have enough liquid for one more casting," she said. "I'm not sure I should use it."

"I *am* sure you shouldn't," Sophie cut in firmly. "If that Mage is out there, the spell could miss." Her sharp eyes swept the area. "Right now, she doesn't know if we've seen her. If we use a magic attack, she'll know we're onto her... and she might make a move on us."

Sophie paused, thinking fast. A plan surfaced. Misinformation could buy them time. She forced her voice into something calm and casual. "We'll be safe once we get to the Aurorium village."

Her voice faltered slightly on the word *village*, and for a moment, her thoughts flicked to the frozen horrors she'd seen there. She blinked hard, wiping a tear before it could fall. "We'll be safe there," she repeated, more steadily.

Annabelle, catching on, tilted her head and grinned. "Aye, I can't wait to see it myself." She winked at Sophie. "I'll show you coppers how to fight the right way."

Regina and Lisa exchanged confused glances. Regina, replaying the last few chaotic hours in her mind, began to wonder if Sophie and Annabelle had taken one too many hits to the head and were hallucinating. Lisa, meanwhile, felt her stomach twist, when had the group decided to go to her ruined village?

Before Regina could voice her confusion, Sophie pulled her into a hug, whispering, "We're lying. If that Mage woman is listening, she won't know we're heading back to the Stormfang. Just play along." She paused. "If you understand, talk about muffins."

Regina pulled back with a beaming smile. "I've heard so much about your muffins, Sophie. I can't wait to try the lemon chocolate ones."

Lisa stared at her, completely lost. Annabelle seized the moment, wrapping Lisa in a warm hug. "Listen, missy," she whispered. "We're puttin' up a front aye. If that Mage wench is listenin', she'll think we're headin' to the village and lose us in the crowd. We're still goin' to the *Fang*."

Lisa sighed and looked down at her colorful outfit. "How are we supposed to lose anyone dressed like this?" she muttered. But the exhaustion pulled at her, and she didn't have the energy to argue. "Okay."

Behind them, the last of the cattle trudged down the ramp. A crewman walked alongside, flicking a rope against their flanks and shouting, "Get on!" The animals plodded forward, disappearing into the alleyways beyond the pier.

As the final cow passed, two men grabbed the thick ropes strung between the pier's short pillars. Working in tandem, they looped the ropes around their arms, coiling them tightly. Midway through their task, another crewman emerged from the ship and shouted, "Take it up!"

Machinery clanked and whirred just out of view, and slowly, the ramp began to rise, folding back into the hull and sealing shut once more.

The last crewman strode to the nearest pier pillar. With a grunt, he gripped it, lifted slightly, then rotated it into a locked position. He let go, and the pillar dropped with a heavy thud, now flush with the wooden planks, almost invisible to anyone who hadn't seen it extended.

Annabelle's gaze flicked away from the ship and back to the crowd. Those red eyes... where did they go? Her grip tightened on the hilt of her cutlass, just in case.

The girls stood quietly, tension lingering in the air as the dock bustled around them.

Once the path cleared, the pairs pressed forward. Sophie's eyes scanned the slip numbers as they passed. Her heart sank when she spotted "*65*" painted on the nearest post.

They still had a long way to go.

Annabelle led the way, her eyes slicing through the crowd, openly searching for the shadowy figure with red eyes. She wasn't subtle, her shoulders were taut, and her fingers twitched near the hilt of her cutlass.

Regina, walking hand in hand with Sophie, glanced up at her. "Sophie, if you don't mind me asking... what kind of magic do you use?"

Sophie adjusted the rifle slung across her back and gave Regina a sidelong glance. "My magic's called *Kiroku-Mbili*. My momma was teaching me," she said, her voice shifting into a practiced tone. "It means 'the balance of the mind, body, and soul.' Using it, I can strengthen my strikes, run faster, jump higher, stuff like that."

Annabelle, never one to pass up a jab, chuckled. "Aye, I can punch and kick without magic," she teased. "You Coppers sure know how to make simple things complicated."

Sophie scowled at Annabelle's back, already calculating how many paces she'd need for a clean HARDKNUCKLE strike. "Any time you want to test that," she shot back, "I'd be happy to show you."

Annabelle grinned, but didn't get the chance to answer.

A chilling laugh sliced through the crowd, curling around them like smoke. She froze mid-step, blood running cold. That laugh.

"She's here," Annabelle whispered, her hand tightening on the cutlass hilt. Her heartbeat roared in her ears. "Did ye hear that?"

"I did," Sophie murmured, her fingers wrapping around her pistol grip, sharp eyes scanning. "I don't see her, though."

Regina swallowed hard and drew her wand from her pocket. "It sounds like she's everywhere," she said, her voice barely steady.

Sophie's mind raced. *If I were the bodyguard here, what would I do?* She exhaled slowly. Mage wasn't attacking, just toying with them, letting fear pin them in place.

"Annabelle," she said, voice calm but firm, "we need to keep moving."

Lisa's voice trembled. "But... what if we walk right into her?"

"We can't stay here," Sophie replied. "She wants us frozen. That's when people make mistakes."

Annabelle's eyes darted left, right, behind. No sign of Mage. The laughter wrapped around them, a suffocating taunt. Sophie's voice barely registered.

"ANNABELLE!" Sophie barked. "**Move! Now!**"

Annabelle snapped out of her daze, blinking fast. Her eyes flicked to Lisa still gripping her hand tight, then to Regina, clutching her wand, eyes wide with fear.

"HEY!" Sophie snapped again, sharp and commanding. "*Forward!*"

Annabelle swallowed hard, forcing the dread down. "Aye, Copper. To the village," she said, still keeping up the ruse. She turned sharply and pushed forward, dragging Lisa with her. Sophie and Regina followed close behind.

The laughter followed them, a phantom whisper that coiled around their ears and vanished just as they thought they'd pinned it down.

They pushed through the bustling pier, weaving past sailors, hauling crates and escorting passengers. Crew members from nearby ships moved with brisk purpose, heads down, too busy to notice the four girls. Annabelle figured her own crew aboard the *Stormfang* were doing the same—loading supplies, prepping for departure, lost in the tide of dockside labor.

Sophie kept her eyes moving, scanning every shadow as the eerie laughter gradually faded. Her grip on her pistol remained tight, ready for Mage to strike at any moment.

Regina walked in silence, mentally flipping through spells. *Tracking spell? No, I'd need something with her essence... Celestial Bloodhounds?* She bit her lip. *Still need to finish reading that spellbook.* Summoning something that powerful was far beyond her.

Lisa, meanwhile, was barely holding on. Exhaustion gnawed at the edges of her focus, her entire body crying out for rest. All she wanted was to curl up in a warm bed and sleep for days.

They passed "Slip 50," drawing near a wide gate to their right where a sea of people flowed through into the Granmark district. Sophie's shoulders tensed as she realized how few people remained ahead. Beyond "Slip 49," the pier stretched almost empty. Fewer distractions. Fewer places to blend in. Each step made them more exposed.

She swallowed the rising anxiety and called out over the din, keeping up the ruse. "This is where we turn to head to the Aurorium village."

Annabelle didn't break stride but shot Sophie a knowing glance. *Keep 'em guessing.*

The crowd thinned even further, and Sophie's gut twisted. They were running out of cover but all they could do now was keep pushing forward.

Toward Slip 17.

Toward the *Stormfang.*

Toward safety ... if they were lucky.

The girls pushed through the thinning crowd, weaving between travelers and merchants spilling off the pier into the bustling streets of Granmark. They were bumped and jostled as they crossed the central walkway that led deeper into the city.

As they passed Slip 49, the crowd thinned drastically. An Opulentian naval vessel sat docked, its polished hull proudly flying the flag of Opulentia. A soldier stood guard at the gangplank, rifle in hand, similar to Sophie's, but held tightly with the muzzle pointed skyward, ready for action. Sophie took note but didn't slow her pace, a flicker of relief blooming in her chest as they moved past without incident.

With fewer people around, their pace quickened. Traffic in the lower half of the pier was noticeably lighter. They breezed past Slip 40, and Sophie allowed herself a quiet smile. Her ruse had worked. Mage must have followed the larger crowd toward Granmark.

Annabelle, still leading, felt Lisa falter behind her, almost dragging her now. The weight in her grip was sluggish, heavy with exhaustion. Annabelle's eyes scanned the thinning crowd, constantly searching. For the first time in what felt like forever, there was nothing. No shadows, no red eyes. *I must've worked,* she thought, passing Slip 35.

Then she saw her.

A figure cloaked in darkness. Red eyes glowing in the void of her face.

"Dammit," Annabelle muttered before calling out. "can't ye take a hint, Wench!"

Mage grinned, her voice smooth and laced with amusement. "Well, hello there," she purred. "I'm ready to laugh now."

From the shadows at her feet, four wolves slithered into being, shifting, writhing forms that flanked her on either side.

Annabelle's heart kicked into overdrive. "We got to go back!" she hissed, yanking Lisa's hand.

"Not going to happen," Sophie called from behind, already dragging Regina in the opposite direction, until she spotted more wolves emerging from the shadows near Slip 50.

Mage tilted her head with a knowing smirk. "Did you really think I'd fall for that little village trick?"

Sophie's grip tightened around Regina's hand. Her mind raced. Too many civilians were still on the pier, passersby, dockhands, merchants, unaware of the approaching danger. If Regina cast a spell here, the crowd might block it... or worse, get caught in the crossfire.

She made a snap decision.

Ripping her pistol from its holster, Sophie raised it high and fired.

The gunshot cracked across the pier like thunder.

"Anyone still here is going to get shot!" Sophie shouted.

The reaction was instant, panic erupted. Screams tore through the air as sailors and merchants dropped everything and fled. Within seconds, the pier was nearly empty, leaving only Mage and her shadow wolves standing in eerie stillness, completely unfazed.

"You girls are in—" Mage began.

But Regina was already moving. She raised her wand high, her voice ringing with perfect clarity: **"Zyl'ethis lumindralis, cindraera dremisso!"**

A brilliant flash burst from her wand, flooding the pier with light like midday sun. The searing radiance swept over Mage and her wolves, dissolving them into nothingness.

Lisa gasped, eyes wide. "By the harvest... you killed her!"

"No," Annabelle said grimly, drawing her cutlass in one smooth motion. "Last time, it only burned away her shadows and wolves. She can make more."

The sunlight flickered out, plunging them back into the dim early morning.

Then came the laughter.

Mage's haunting cackle echoed across the pier as more wolves emerged from the dark, their glowing red eyes locking hungrily onto the girls.

Sophie turned, scanning both sides as the wolves closed in. Her mind raced. She released Regina's hand and thumbed the release on her pistol stopping just short of pulling it all the way down. Instead, she rotated the chamber to slot four and locked it in place.

"Girls, listen," she said sharply, her voice commanding. "When I start shooting, run. Head for the ship. I'll be right behind you."

Annabelle hesitated only a second before nodding, tightening her grip on Lisa's hand.

Sophie spun on her heel and opened fire on the wolves blocking their path to the *Stormfang*.

"GO!" she barked between shots.

Annabelle didn't wait. She surged forward, dragging Lisa with her, Regina right behind. Gunfire cracked through the air as Sophie covered their retreat, her eyes locked on the writhing shadows surging closer.

She fired round after round, each bullet igniting into bursts of flame as it struck. The shadow wolves howled in agony, their dark forms erupting in fire and dissolving into smoke.

The girls raced toward Slip 17, their shoes hammering against the wooden pier.

But their escape screeched to a halt at Slip 27.

A massive figure loomed ahead, shadowy and monstrous. A bear, easily twice the size of any normal creature, formed entirely of inky darkness. Its glowing red eyes locked onto them, and its guttural growl vibrated in their chests.

From far behind, Mage's voice echoed down the pier, thick with amusement.

"Oh, don't look now," she purred, her grin almost visible in her tone, "but my pet looks hungry."

The bear reared up on its hind legs and roared, the sound reverberating through the pier like a crack of thunder.

Annabelle didn't hesitate, she lunged forward, swinging her cutlass in a wide arc. The bear swatted her aside with a powerful backhand, knocking her off her feet. She crashed into Sophie, and both of them hit the ground hard.

"Oh, my dear," Mage chuckled, shaking her head. "You don't fight a bear with a sword."

Regina skidded to a stop and helped Sophie and Annabelle up, while Lisa stood frozen, her eyes darting between the massive shadow beast and the churning water beside the pier. Swallowing hard, she thrust her hands forward, summoning a shimmering blue spell circle etched with blue glowing runes.

A column of water shot up from the harbor, snaking through the air before slamming into the shadow bear with tremendous force. The beast stumbled back, crashing into the wall of a nearby warehouse—but with a low snarl, it shook off the blow and lumbered forward again.

Lisa's breathing quickened. She raised her hands again, a second spell forming beneath the pier. The wooden planks groaned and splintered as a powerful geyser exploded upward, launching the bear into the air. It roared, flailing, before crashing through the hole and vanishing into the dark water below. The surface rippled violently, then stilled—nothing but fading shadows beneath the waves.

Panting, Lisa turned, only to see Regina, Sophie, and Annabelle surrounded by three snarling shadow wolves.

She raised her hands to cast another spell, but the moment her mana flared, exhaustion clamped down like a vice. The spell circle flickered weakly—then vanished.

"No!" Lisa whimpered, tears welling in her eyes. She was drained. She had nothing left.

Sophie gritted her teeth, struggling to rise as she fired her last two bullets into the wolf lunging from the left, making it dissolve in a puff of black mist. The remaining two pounced, one pinning Annabelle while the other sank its teeth into Sophie's arm.

Annabelle, remembering her last encounter, twisted her blade just in time to catch the wolf's bite. Steel met fangs with a clang, and she held the creature at bay.

Regina froze, frantically cycling through spells in her mind, but none of them felt right.

"I don't know what to do!" she cried, panic cracking through her usual composure. In a burst of desperation, she kicked the wolf atop Annabelle, knocking it off balance.

Annabelle didn't waste the opening. She drove her cutlass into the beast again and again until it dissolved into darkness.

Nearby, Sophie grits her teeth through the searing pain in her arm, so happy that she sewed that rawhide into the sleeves of suit so the bite hurt but it didn't tear into her skin. Her pistol slipped from her hand as she let out a grunt, grabbing the wolf's leg. With a sharp yank, she rolled them both over. Now on top, she pinned the thrashing creature beneath her and brought her fists down again and again, pounding its skull until it faded to smoke.

When the last echo of violence faded, Regina, Annabelle, and Lisa stood frozen, staring in stunned silence.

Sophie retrieved her pistol and rose to her feet, shaking off the pain. "What?" she snapped, breathing hard.

No one answered.

She narrowed her eyes. "We've got to move. Now!"

That snapped them out of it. Sophie grabbed her things, and the group broke into a sprint, racing toward the Stormfang.

Slip 25. Slip 24. Slip 23. Almost there.

Then—they stopped cold.

At Slip 22, Mage stood waiting, her grin wicked and knowing. "Enough playing with your food," she cooed. "Say goodbye, girls."

From the shadows, three massive gorillas emerged, towering, inky forms flanked by four wolves, two on each side. The monsters stalked forward, eyes gleaming with hunger.

Annabelle hissed through her teeth. "Oi! Silver girl! Do that bomb thing!"

"I can't!" Regina shouted. "It takes a few seconds, and I need fire!"

"I've got fire," Sophie said, jamming a flame cartridge into her pistol with a click.

Lisa's hands trembled. "They are getting closer," she whimpered, eyes flicking between the advancing monsters and her friends.

Annabelle's voice turned sharp. "A few seconds start working." Then, to Lisa: "Girlie, can't ye do that water thing again?"

Lisa swallowed hard, dropping her bag and stretching out her hands. A faint blue spell circle flickered into view, its runes pulsing weakly, like dying embers.

"I do not think it will work." she said, voice tight with strain. "But I will try."

The shadow creatures paused, bracing for the expected attack.

Lisa pushed harder. The circle flared once... then fizzled out completely.

Mage's laugh rang out across the pier. "Ha! That's it? Dinner time."

The creatures resumed their slow, deliberate advance.

Sophie's eyes locked with Regina's. Asking *You ready? silently*

Regina nodded sharply, her hands trembling.

"DOWN!" Sophie barked.

Annabelle and Lisa dropped instantly.

In perfect sync, Sophie fired her flaming bullet just as Regina launched her air cannon. The two projectiles arced through the air and collided at the heart of the approaching monsters—

BOOM.

A fiery explosion ripped across the pier, the shockwave blasting outward with a thunderous roar.

Smoke billowed. Heat surged. The monsters were engulfed in flame and force, flung back in tatters.

The blast sent the girls sprawling.

Annabelle recovered first, staggering upright. She grabbed Lisa and hauled her up. "Come on, girlie!"

She turned to Sophie and Regina, who were rising shakily to their feet. "Coppers, you two good?"

Sophie gave a sharp thumb-up, brushing dust off her coat. "We're good." She reloaded her pistol with practiced speed, every chamber now full.

Annabelle's gaze darted ahead. "Six slips, we're almost there!"

"Your lips to the ancestors' ears," Sophie muttered, rolling her shoulders and steadying her stance. "Mad dash?"

Annabelle grinned wide. "Yeah." She tightened her grip on Lisa's hand. "**MAD DASH!**"

Lisa barely had time to snatch her bag before Annabelle took off, yanking her into motion.

Sophie holstered her pistol, grabbed Regina's forearm with a smirk. "Hold on to your glasses."

Regina barely managed a yelp before Sophie surged forward, dragging her into a full sprint.

The four of them bolted down the pier, boots and shoes hammering against the wooden planks. Ships and crates blurred past as they tore through the thinning shadows.

Dark shapes stirred at the edges of their vision, but Regina noticed something. "They're not forming in front of us anymore," she gasped. "She's losing her reach! I don't think she can conjure them too far from herself!"

"Let's hope you're right!" Sophie called back, pushing harder.

Ahead, Annabelle and Lisa were already at a breakneck pace. Annabelle's grip on Lisa's wrist was iron-tight, practically dragging her forward with startling speed.

They sped past Slip 20.

Slip 19.

Almost there.

Lisa glanced sideways, breath ragged. Annabelle moved with effortless confidence. *She's done this before,* Lisa realized. *She knows exactly how to run for her life.*

As they neared Slip 17, Annabelle didn't slow. She hit the gangplank at full speed, boots pounding up the narrow incline to the Stormfang's deck. Lisa stumbled slightly behind her but didn't stop, adrenaline lending strength to her aching legs.

Sophie and Regina followed seconds later, lungs burning, every step pure survival. Then...

Annabelle skidded to a halt just as her foot touched the deck. She threw up a hand. "Stop here!" she barked.

The girls lurched to a breathless stop behind her, chests heaving.

Annabelle cupped her hands to her mouth and bellowed, "Permission to come aboard!"

For a heartbeat, silence.

Only the sound of wind, water, and their pounding hearts.

The *Stormfang* loomed around them, its dark sails rustling in the morning breeze. Behind them, the pier had fallen eerily silent. For now.

"Get up here!" Captain Kidd's gruff voice cut through the tension. "Raise anchor! Head out to sea!" His sharp eyes swept the dock, scanning for any sign of pursuit.

The crew sprang into action, hauling up the gangplank with thick ropes, muscles straining as they worked in perfect unison. Others crowded the massive capstan wheel, gripping the handles and cranking steadily. The heavy chain clanked and rattled from below as the anchor rose, and the ship gave a low groan, shifting as it pulled free from the seabed.

The girls followed Annabelle's lead, stepping onto the deck at last, hearts thundering in their chests.

Just as they thought they were safe, that laugh started all over again.

Mage's laughter echoed across the ship like a curse.

The crew froze, eyes wide, heads turning.

A dark ripple ran across the deck, the shadows warping and moving under an unnatural force. Shadows pooled and twisted, gathering into the shape of a figure at the center of the storm.

"If you want something done right," the voice said, low and venomous, "you have to do it yourself."

Twin red eyes flared to life from within the shadowed face. Its left arm elongated, reshaping into a long, wicked blade that gleamed with dark energy.

Before anyone could react, Annabelle was already moving

Damned heifer dared attack me on me own ship, I'll give 'er a lesson.

With a metallic clatter, her cutlass hit the deck—abandoned. She sprinted forward, jaw clenched tight, and leapt into the air. Hands outstretched, she grabbed a swinging pulley and let the momentum hurl her across the deck like a slingshot.

The shadow's eyes snapped toward her—but too late.

With a fierce cry, Annabelle slammed both boots into the forming figure's chest. The impact sent the shadow woman flying, Mage's body hit the railing and tumbled overboard.

A massive *splash* followed.

The shadow vanished beneath the waves.

Annabelle clung to the pulley, swinging back to the deck with effortless control. She landed cleanly on the deck, boots hitting the wood with a thud, and sprinted straight to the railing.

Leaning over the edge, she cupped her hands to her mouth and shouted: **"OI! STILL NOT LAUGHING!!!"**

Mage surfaced, sputtering in the dark water below, treading furiously as her red eyes blazed burning with rage.

Annabelle grinned, pointing toward the horizon where the first glimmers of sunlight crept over the sea. "And look—the sun's coming out." Her voice dripped with satisfaction.

Mage hissed in frustration, the rising light searing the edges of the shadows that clung to her. With a final glare, she turned and slipped beneath the waves, vanishing into the depths.

A satisfied chuckle escaped Annabelle as she turned back toward the others.

"Belle!" Captain Kidd's stern voice snapped through the moment. From the raised bridge, he shot her a disapproving look, arms crossed over his chest. "Bring your friends to me Ops room—when ye're ready." Without waiting for a reply, he turned on his heel and strode inside, the heavy door slamming shut behind him.

The deck fell into uneasy silence as the ship moved steadily out to sea. The girls exchanged glances, the weight of what had just happened settling on their exhausted shoulders.

Annabelle smirked and dusted herself off. "Well," she said, picking up her cutlass from the deck, "that was fun."

Sophie groaned. "Fun is not the word I'd use."

Lisa exhaled shakily, clutching her bag to her chest. "Can we just get inside? Please?"

Sophie nodded. "Yeah. Let's go see what the captain wants."

The four of them headed for the captain's Ops room behind the bridge, leaving behind the slowly brightening horizon and the dark waters where their shadowy pursuer had vanished … for now.

Chapter 8

Captain Kidd's operations room was a spacious, rectangular chamber, every surface meticulously arranged to prevent chaos at sea. A sturdy desk, cluttered with scattered papers, sat beneath a sprawling map of the Seven Kingdoms pinned to the right wall. Colored markers dotted the various port towns, outlining a complex pattern known only to the captain. Against the opposite wall, a tattered old couch was bolted in place, a testament to the ship's constant motion. Along the left side, a towering bookshelf stretched from floor to ceiling, its compartments neatly divided and sealed behind thin glass panes, likely to keep the books from tumbling loose during rough waters.

Regina gazed around in awe. Everything in the room was secured, lashed down, or bolted tight. *They've thought of everything*, she mused. Her eyes drifted to Captain James "Kidd" Lowe, who regarded them with intense scrutiny, thoughtfully stroking his chin. He looked like a man trying to solve a puzzle without knowing where to begin.

"So, you four girls," he said at last, his voice gruff but curious, "are all goddesses? Part of The Order's grand design?" His piercing eyes settled on Annabelle, as if recalling what she had told him earlier.

Sophie, Lisa, and Regina exchanged bewildered glances before turning in unison to Annabelle, who only shrugged apologetically.

"That's what Brother Albert said," she admitted, her tone uncertain.

Regina furrowed her brow. "That's not exactly what he said," she corrected, folding her arms. "He told us the goddesses *blessed* us, not that we *are* goddesses."

Captain Kidd grunted. "Why would he say something like that, then?" His gaze sharpened. "What exactly did he tell you?"

Regina took a steadying breath. "Brother Albert said that before we were born, the goddesses blessed us with a portion of their power... because a great threat is rising in the world."

Sophie's voice quivered. "A threat we have to face." She wiped her eyes, a fresh wave of grief washing over her. "I think... I think it already reached my village."

Kidd's brow furrowed. "Your village?"

Sophie swallowed. "After I left Brother Albert and the others," she began.

"After you stormed off," Annabelle interjected then quickly fell silent under Kidd's disapproving glare.

Sophie clenched her fists. "Whatever," she muttered. "I went back home... but everyone was gone. Either killed by machines or..." her voice cracked "or frozen in place like..." Her breath hitched.

Lisa leaned closer, placing a comforting hand on her shoulder.

"Like my momma," Sophie whispered, her purple eyes dark with anguish. "I found her in the front room... frozen solid." Fire burned behind her tears, grief transforming into something far more dangerous.

Kidd leaned forward, his expression softening. "I'm sorry, my dear," he said gently, extending a hand across the table.

Sophie nodded stiffly. "Thank you." But her mind remained trapped in the memory the frozen figure of her mother, mouth open in a silent scream, forever calling out for a daughter who hadn't been there.

Kidd cleared his throat. "And what about this Brother Albert? Where is he now?"

Lisa sobbed, burying her face in Sophie's shoulder. Sophie held her tightly, murmuring soft reassurances.

Annabelle wiped her eyes and said, "Brother Albert... sacrificed himself so we could escape." Her voice wavered, but she continued. "That blue hussy..."

"Isabella," Regina corrected, adjusting her foggy glasses. "Isabella Morales. She must have been blessed too. She was too powerful... too strong. We barely held her off."

Kidd's eyes narrowed. "Isabella, huh? And she's the one who took your Order Brother?"

Annabelle shook her head. "No," she said firmly. "He took her." She hesitated. "He... he detonated himself. Used two of the Copper's fire grenades to make sure the blast was big enough." She swallowed. "If she's still alive, she's at least badly hurt."

Kidd's eyes widened. "Wait a minute, you have grenades?" His attention locked onto Sophie.

Without a word, Sophie unbuttoned her suit jacket, revealing neatly organized pockets sewn into the lining, each filled with bullets and small explosive devices.

"By the sea!" Kidd exclaimed. "What were you planning, girlie? A one-woman war?"

Annabelle's eyes widened. "She can't keep those! We have rules aboard the good ship *Stormfang*," she snapped. "Passengers aren't allowed to be armed!"

Sophie smirked. "What's the matter? You scared?" finally getting a chance to give Annabelle a taste of her own medicine.

Captain Kidd raised a hand, cutting through the tension. "She's right," he said. "Only the crew carries weapons aboard me ship." He paused, then shifted the conversation. "So... what now? Where do your girls go from here?"

"We're supposed to go to Order Island," Regina said firmly. "The monks there will help us."

Captain Kidd leaned back against his desk, arms crossed. "That might not be as easy as you think," he said, voice edged with skepticism. "No one can just sail up to Order Island you need an invite, or even better, a monk onboard."

Annabelle reached into her jacket pocket and pulled out Brother Albert's watch, its silver casing glinting faintly in the light. "Brother Al gave us this," she said, holding it up. "He said they'd let us in if we showed them."

Kidd studied the watch for a moment, then gave a slow nod. "Guess we'll find out soon enough," he said. "We'll play it by ear when we get there." He glanced over the group, noting their exhausted expressions. "You lot look like ye've been dragged through hell and back. Let's get you to your bunks, you girlies need your sleep."

He stood, motioning for the girls to follow as he led them through the door and into the ship's bridge. The ship's wheel stood at the center, manned by Smitty, first mate or the second-in-command. Regina's eyes drifted upward, noting the sails furled tightly against the masts, yet they continued to glide swiftly across the sea.

"The sails are rolled up," Regina said, puzzled. "How are we moving?"

Annabelle grinned. "We've got engines from Magitekopolis," she said, pride in her voice. "Cost us a small fortune, but they make the ship faster than most."

The group descended a narrow staircase to the first landing, leading into the galley. Two crewmen, Quinn and Phelps, sat at a bolted-down table, their chairs secured to tracks so they could be slid beneath when not in use. They ate breakfast quietly, offering the newcomers only a passing glance.

"This here's the galley," Captain Kidd said, gesturing around the space. "We take our meals here, morning, noon, and night." He glanced at the girls. "I'm guessing you'd rather clean up before eating."

Sophie and Lisa exchanged a look and nodded in silent agreement.

Kidd led them farther down the stairs, stopping at the next landing. "This is our operations deck," he said, opening a door to reveal a narrow hallway lined with doors on either side. "Down here we've got the training room, map room, pantry, sickbay, and the armory." His gaze shifted to Sophie. "Let's mosey to the armory first."

He reached into his coat and pulled out a metal cylinder, giving it a firm shake. A soft green glow rose from within, casting an eerie light along the corridor.

"What's that?" Regina asked, eyes wide.

"One of my man Sparks' inventions," Kidd said with a smirk. "These rocks inside glow when you shake 'em up, handy little things."

They walked down the dim hallway, passing doors labeled with carved wooden signs. Each one bore a small illustration: the map room with a hand-drawn map, the training room with a dumbbell, the pantry marked by a chicken leg, and sickbay by a cross with a coiled serpent. At last, they reached the armory, marked by a crossed sword and flintlock pistol.

Kidd tossed the glowing cylinder to Annabelle, who caught it easily and held it high. Pulling a key from his jacket pocket, he unlocked the armory door and swung it open, revealing rows of weapons neatly secured in racks. Rifles of various makes lined the back wall, each strapped tightly in place. A large rectangular shelf stood in the center of the room, its compartments enclosed behind glass and filled with pistols and daggers. Shelves along the sidewalls held rows of uniquely designed cutlasses.

"Alright, missy," Kidd said, turning to Sophie. "Let's have those weapons."

Sophie scowled but stepped into the room. She unslung her rifle and handed it to him. He secured it into a rack, then pulled a thick rope over the barrel to keep it steady. Sophie removed her backpack and set it on the floor, then shrugged off her suit jacket to reveal the vest and white shirt beneath. She handed the jacket over, and Kidd nearly dropped it, surprised by its weight.

Muttering under his breath, he stowed it in a larger compartment at the bottom of the shelf and closed the glass door with a firm click.

"Now the pistol," he said, holding out his hand.

Sophie hesitated. "I'd... I'd like to keep it," she said quietly, her fingers tightening around the weapon's grip.

"No deal, missy," Kidd replied, curling and uncurling his fingers expectantly.

Sophie took a step back, gripping the pistol tighter. "I... I really need to keep it," she pleaded, memories of Isabella flashing through her mind. *If only she'd had her pistol ready back at West's tavern—maybe things would have gone differently.*

Kidd's eyes darkened. "I don't allow passengers to be armed on me ship," he said firmly.

"Yeah, and for good reason," Annabelle added, folding her arms.

Sophie's shoulders trembled. "I just... I can't," she whispered, her eyes shining with tears.

Kidd exhaled slowly, running a hand over his stubbled chin. "Alright," he said at last. "You can keep yer pistol." He raised a finger. "*But hear me, girlie...* if that gun leaves the holster on yer hip without permission, you're off my ship. Goddess or no."

"What?!" Annabelle protested. "Cap'n, you can't just..."

Kidd silenced her with a raised hand. His gaze locked onto Sophie. "Do ye understand?" His voice was like stone.

Sophie nodded quickly.

"I need to hear ye say it."

"I understand," she said, swallowing hard. "I won't take my pistol out on this ship unless I have permission from you or your crew."

"Good," Kidd said with a curt nod. "And just so we're clear," he added, pointing upward with his index finger, "first time you break that rule, yer gone. No second chances."

Sophie wiped her eyes and nodded resolutely. "Understood."

Captain Kidd led the way out of the armory, passing the girls, while Annabelle lingered behind, locking the door with a key from her own pocket. The group moved back toward the stairs, descending deeper into the ship's belly.

"This here is the stateroom deck," Kidd explained, pushing open a door to reveal a narrow hallway lined with more doors, each marked with a unique symbol. He walked halfway down before stopping at a door bearing a single star. Turning to Lisa, who stood closest behind him, he gestured.

"Green lass, you get the star room."

Lisa blinked in surprise, then offered a shy smile. "Thank you," she said softly, stepping inside.

As the door shut behind her, she slid the latch closed with a satisfying click, securing herself inside. The scent of salt and wood filled the small cabin, and sunlight streamed through a propped-open window, carrying the crisp tang of sea air.

She turned slowly, taking in the space, the berth, as it was called aboard a ship. A folded hammock hung against one wall; its ropes fastened securely about three-quarters of the way across to the opposite side.

Lisa crossed to the wardrobe near the door, opened it carefully, and placed her shopping bag inside. Stripping down, she shivered slightly, then pulled on a loose shirt.

She grasped the looped rope attached to the hammock's pulley system and gave it a gentle tug, watching as it stretched across the room and locked into place. With a tired sigh, she climbed in, sinking into the built-in pillow and closing her eyes.

It's okay, my dear.

Brother Albert's voice echoed in her mind, his face bloodied and bruised. The guilt clawed at her, tightening her chest. *If only I had worked harder... If only I were better...*

Silent sobs wracked her frame as regret spilled from her eyes in quiet tears.

[-----✿-----]

Meanwhile, Captain Kidd led the others to a door marked with a sun. He glanced at Regina with a small, knowing smile. "I believe this one's for you, grey lass."

Regina adjusted her glasses nervously, then nodded. "Thank you."

She stepped inside, and Kidd closed the door behind her with a solid thud. Sliding the latch into place, she turned to examine the room. Even through the blur of her vision without glasses, she could appreciate the clever use of space.

The wardrobe by the door caught her attention first. She opened it, gently placed her glasses into her dress pocket, and hung the dress on a hook at the back. As she shut the wardrobe, a small metal latch slid into place with a quiet click, keeping it secure.

She approached the folded hammock against the wall and found a crank mounted beside it. Turning it steadily, she watched as the hammock stretched across the room, its fabric pulled tight and secure.

Climbing in, she rested her head against the sewn-in pillow and closed her eyes.

Her thoughts drifted unwillingly back to the alley beside West's tavern, the memory of Brother Albert leaning on Sophie for support, urging them to learn how to work together. Regina's throat tightened as she accepted, perhaps for the first time, that she would never hear his voice again.

A single tear slipped down her cheek.

[----- ⬇ -----]

The captain led Sophie and Annabelle farther down the hallway to a door adorned with a pair of sharp, animalistic teeth. Kidd swung it open and gestured inside. "Here ye go."

Sophie nodded and stepped in. "Thanks, Captain."

She locked the door behind her and leaned against it for a moment, breathing in the salty air. Her eyes swept across the room, quietly admiring the ingenious craftsmanship.

Opening the wardrobe by the door, she placed her backpack carefully inside, setting her pistol belt on the shelf with deliberate caution. She undressed, hanging her clothes on the hooks within, and shut the door, listening to the soft click as it latched closed.

She turned to the hammock; its metal ring hooked securely to the wall. Pulling it across to the opposite side, she latched it in place and took a deep breath before climbing in.

Closing her eyes, she focused on her breathing, deep inhales, long exhales. But as she tried to coax herself into sleep, the image of her mother surged into her thoughts: frozen solid, sword and shield locked in place, that fierce look of defiance etched onto her face. *Screaming for me...*

The guilt crashed down like a tidal wave. Sophie clutched the hammock's fabric, her shoulders trembling.

"I'm so sorry, Momma," she whispered, her voice breaking into sobs.

But there was no one there to forgive her.

[----- ⚓ -----]

Back in the hallway, Annabelle stopped at her stateroom the door marked with an anchor. She opened it, then turned to Captain Kidd and spoke in a hushed voice.

"Cap'n... what gives?" she asked, brow furrowed. "Why'd you let her keep her gun?"

Kidd crossed his arms, fixing her with a steely gaze. After a moment, he spoke. "You know that necklace o' yers?"

Annabelle instinctively touched the pendant resting against her chest and nodded.

"Anyone who knew what ye could do with that trinket would try to take it from ye, right?" he said. "And you wouldn't let it go, would you?"

Annabelle hesitated, then sighed, conceding his point. "Nay... I wouldn't."

"That's why," Kidd said firmly. "And mark my words, Belle. First time she crosses me, she can swim to Order Island for all I care."

Annabelle chewed her lip, then gave a reluctant nod. "Aye, Cap'n."

Kidd turned to leave. "Get some sleep."

She closed the door and let out a long breath, turning to take in her small quarters. Opening the wardrobe, she pulled off her anchor belt and hung it from a hook inside. Then she removed the belt holding her cutlass, setting it carefully against the back wall.

Annabelle stripped out of her clothes and slipped on an oversized nightshirt before shutting the wardrobe door.

Sliding into the hammock, her hand instinctively found her amulet, fingers tracing its familiar shape. She let out a shuddering breath, her eyes closing.

Her thoughts drifted to Brother Albert—his warm but weary smile, his unwavering belief in them.

What more could he have told us about the goddesses?

But then all she could see was him lying broken in that alley next to West's. Tears slipped down her cheeks as sorrow settled heavy in her chest.

I wish we had more time...

The gentle rocking of the ship eventually lulled her into uneasy sleep.

[----- ⚓ -----]

Annabelle awoke to the rhythmic creaking of the ship and the distant call of seagulls beyond her porthole. A salty breeze drifted through, carrying the scent of the open sea and stirring her senses awake.

Sitting up in her hammock, she stretched her arms overhead, the gentle sway of the ship rocking her slightly. With a contented sigh, she swung her legs over the side and hopped down onto the wooden floor.

Crossing to her wardrobe, she opened it and rummaged through her clothes, pulling out a skirt and shirt. A quick sniff confirmed they were still wearable. Satisfied, she changed out of her nightclothes and into the fresh outfit, then tied a rope around the wardrobe handle to keep it from swinging open with the ship's motion.

Once ready, she stepped out into the bustling corridor and made her way up to the main deck. The crew was already hard at work, adjusting rigging, hauling ropes, and turning cranks to fine-tune the sails. Though the engines had powered them out of port, relying on them too heavily would drain their fuel, and those tanks didn't refill themselves.

Annabelle climbed the short set of stairs to the bridge, where First Mate Smitty stood at the helm, his sharp eyes scanning the deck below.

"Mornin', First Mate," she said with a friendly nod. "How goes the day?"

"Mornin', Ops O," Smitty replied in his usual gruff but steady tone, eyes never leaving the horizon. "Smooth sailing, for now."

"Any special orders from the captain?"

Smitty shrugged. "Just to keep an eye on our new passengers." He paused, then added with a knowing glance, "We ran hot out of Granmark, so the engines will need refueling soon."

Annabelle sighed inwardly. Of course they do. She knew exactly what that meant, either burn through their precious Ember Root, Void Pepper, and Serpent's Kiss fuel mixture... or fall back on good old-fashioned sweat in the training room.

Sparks, the ship's eccentric but brilliant engineer, had rigged up a clever system: the engines could run off rechargeable batteries, but those only charged if the crew put in physical work. That meant pedaling exercise bikes or grinding the heavy bars bolted into the training room walls. And it was her job to make sure everyone pulled their weight.

"I'll get to work on a schedule," she muttered, more to herself than to Smitty. "Did we manage to pick up any fuel in Granmark?"

Smitty shook his head. "It was on the list, but we had to leave sooner than planned." His tone was apologetic, but the look in his eyes said it wasn't up for debate. "We're stuck with the hard way."

Annabelle grimaced. "Right... better get to it."

With a quick wave to the First Mate, she turned and headed below deck.

Back in her quarters, she changed into her training clothes, loose-fitting pants and a matching shirt emblazoned with the *Stormfang*'s signature flag across the chest. Tying her hair back, she made her way to the operations deck and pushed open the training room door.

What she saw stopped her in her tracks.

Sophie was already there, drenched in sweat and pedaling furiously on one of the exercise bikes. The rhythmic creak of the pedals echoed through the small space. Her purple hair clung to her face as she stared straight ahead, locked in unwavering focus.

Annabelle crossed her arms. "Copper, what are ye doing here?" she asked, suspicion creeping into her voice.

"Morning training," Sophie huffed, her legs pumping furiously.

Annabelle frowned and walked over to the wall-mounted control panel. She flipped open the leather flap covering the screen. Behind the glass, three glowing green pie charts displayed the engine's battery levels, nearly full. That didn't make sense.

She glanced at the girl. "How long have ye been at this?"

"I don't know... an hour maybe?" Sophie replied without looking up.

Annabelle narrowed her eyes. *That's a lie.* She'd seen this before…what Smitty called the "Curse of the Living." Survivors of wrecks and raids often reacted the same way: pushing themselves to exhaustion, refusing rest, afraid to be alone with their thoughts. They moved constantly, as if motion could silence memory. And if they couldn't snap out of it, they'd be dropped at the next port with a share of coin and a quiet goodbye.

But something about Sophie, her pain, her fire, made Annabelle want to try.

"That can't be true, Copper," she said, stepping closer. "It takes hours to charge the batteries this much."

Sophie's legs kept churning, sweat streaking down her face, but Annabelle's words broke through her tunnel focus.

"What batteries? What are you talking about?" she snapped, her irritation sharpening every pedal stroke.

Annabelle crossed her arms and nodded toward the leather flap. "These bikes charge our engine batteries," she explained. "We burned through fuel getting out of Granmark, so now we're running on empty. But look at that." She flipped the flap back and pointed. "Three batteries, all nearly full. And you look like you've been here a long while."

Sophie shrugged, glib and defensive. "So?"

Annabelle didn't let it go. "So," she said, stepping forward, "I'm guessing ye woke up from a short nap, came straight here, and started punishing yourself. Me? I'd at least have taken a second to look at the beautiful sea."

Sophie's grip tightened. "What do you know?" she snapped, jumping off the bike and yanking her towel from the bench.

Annabelle's patience cracked. "What do I know?" she repeated, her voice rising. "Lass, you act like you're the only one who's lost a parent." Her eyes locked with Sophie's. "When ye found yer momma... I felt it. Like I was standing there in the room with ye. Looking at me own."

Sophie's heart slammed against her ribs. She felt exposed. Violated. "How could you?" she whispered, voice trembling.

Annabelle held up her hands. "I didn't ask for it," she said gently. "It was forced on me." She saw the tension in Sophie's body, the stiffness of someone about to lash out. Annabelle had seen that look before. And she knew how dangerous grief could be when cornered.

Before Sophie could react, Annabelle stepped forward and wrapped her arms around her.

Sophie froze, fists pressing against Annabelle's sides. But Annabelle didn't let go.

"It's okay, Sophie," she whispered, voice soft in her ear. "Ye did everything ye could."

Sophie struggled at first, trying to pull away. But something cracked wide open inside her. She sagged forward, her body shaking as grief overtook her. Her sobs came in broken gasps, and she buried her face in Annabelle's shoulder.

Annabelle rubbed small circles on her back. "Cry all you want, lass," she murmured. "It's alright."

After a while, Sophie pulled back slightly, her tear-streaked face searching Annabelle's. "You... you called me Sophie."

Annabelle smiled through the tension. "Yeah, well... ye'll always be me, Copper." She gave Sophie's shoulder a reassuring squeeze. "Come on. Let's get ye to yer bunk."

She led her down the stairs to the door with the sharp-toothed emblem. Sophie climbed into her hammock without a word, curling up in the fabric.

Annabelle pulled down the folding chair and sat at the foot of the hammock, arms crossed. "I'm staying," she said. "Yer gettin' some sleep missy."

Sophie turned her head, eyes still red. "I can't sleep," she mumbled. "Every time I do, I just... wake up."

She started to sit up, but Annabelle raised a hand coaxing her to stay.

"Just try," she said gently. "I'll be right here. Yer not alone."

Sophie scowled. "It's awkward if you just sit there watching me. Sing or something."

Annabelle rolled her eyes and muttered under her breath, "The tings I do fer this here ship."

After a beat, she sighed. "Alright... me mum used to sing me this lullaby before..." Her voice faded, the memory too heavy to finish. She took a deep breath, then began to sing:

"Hush now, my darling, the stars are gleaming bright,
In dreams we'll sail the seas, on ships of pure delight.
For you're the child of courage, with a spirit brave and bold,
A pirate queen's own daughter, a treasure to behold."

Her voice softened as Sophie's eyelids fluttered. Encouraged, she continued, letting the melody carry her words:

"So, close your eyes, my little one, and dream of golden shores,
With sails unfurled, we'll conquer all, as the ocean gently roars.
We'll seek adventure, seek the gold, with hearts that will not sway,
And through the storms and darkest nights, we'll find our own sweet way."

Sophie's breathing slowed, her body relaxing. Annabelle gave the hammock a gentle push, letting the ship's rhythm take over, gently rocking the girl like a baby's crib.

She continued more softly now, her voice weaving through the cabin like a warm breeze:

"The winds may howl, the waves may crash, but we'll never be afraid,
With courage as our compass, our fears shall be allayed.
We'll sever every shackle that tries to hold us back,
And dance upon the deck, my love, along this pirate track."

Her words faded into stillness. Sophie's chest rose and fell in slow, even breaths.

With a quiet sigh of relief, Annabelle stood and tiptoed to the door, easing it shut with practiced care.

Out in the hallway, she leaned against the wall and shook her head, smiling tiredly.

"If that Copper ever tells anyone about this..." she muttered, "I'll beat her within an inch of her life."

Still smiling, she padded off toward her quarters, swapping her training gear for her usual clothes.

With luck, their new cook Jeffie had something warm in the galley. After all, she'd more than earned it.

[-----⬤-----]

Lisa Nozaki woke to the gentle creaking of the ship and the distant crash of waves beyond her porthole. She stretched in her hammock, the fabric cradling her like a cocoon, before swinging her legs over the side and landing lightly on the wooden floor.

Crossing to her wall locker, she opened it and surveyed her limited options. A frown tugged at her lips. Great. Two choices: her plain white sundress, streaked with sweat and dirt, or the elegant dress from Islewind, stained with Brother Albert's blood. Her fingers hovered over the latter. The memory was still too raw. Too painful. With a sigh, she reached for the sundress.

As she pulled it over her head, Lisa caught a glimpse of herself in the small mirror mounted on the wardrobe door. Her eyes were red and puffy, and the absence of her usual beauty routine was starting to show. She frowned, fussing with her hair. *Hopefully, no one pays too much attention.*

After freshening up in the communal bathroom at the end of the hall, Lisa made her way to the galley, hoping for something warm to eat.

She arrived to find Annabelle lounging at a table, cup in hand, looking like she'd been waiting.

"Good morning, missy," Annabelle greeted with a smirk, raising her mug in a mock toast. "How'd ye sleep?"

Lisa hesitated. "Good, I guess." She glanced around. "When is the lunch service?"

Annabelle nearly choked on her drink, bursting into laughter. "Service?" she repeated, eyes twinkling with amusement. "Aw, princess, we don't do service on the *Stormfang.*" She leaned back and propped her boots on the table with a grin.

Lisa's cheeks flushed as she smoothed her dress, realizing Annabelle was teasing her. Scowling, she sat across from the orange-haired pirate and folded her hands in her lap.

Annabelle hollered toward the kitchen. "Oi Jeffie, one more soup out here, mate!"

From behind the kitchen window, a voice called back, "One more soup coming up!"

Lisa bit her lip, unsure of what to expect, as crew members began trickling in, calling out for their own bowls. Moments later, Jeffie, the ship's new cook, placed several steaming bowls on the counter.

"Ops O!" he called, dropping two bowls with a heavy clatter.

Annabelle winked at Lisa before sauntering over to collect them. She returned with two bowls and slid one across the table. "Dig in while it's hot," she said, already halfway through her own.

Lisa hesitantly picked up her spoon, stirring the contents. Chunks of vegetables floated in a dark broth. She sniffed, beef stock, clearly, but, thankfully, hers seemed to lack actual meat.

She took a tentative sip.

The taste hit her like a slap.

Her face twisted in horror, and she barely managed to swallow. Carefully setting the spoon down, she stared in disbelief as Annabelle and the others ate without a second thought.

"How can you eat this?" Lisa demanded, appalled.

Annabelle grinned mid-bite. "Told you to eat it while it's hot," she said with her signature smirk. "Come on, Jeffie's still learning'. Give 'em a chance."

Lisa sighed, guilt prickling at her for complaining. But as she stared back into the bowl, the thought of another spoonful made her stomach churn. *I may be wearing dirty clothes and sleeping in a dingy hammock on this smelly ship,* she thought grimly, *but I draw the line at eating ...this!*

Steeling herself, she carried the bowl to the kitchen counter. "Um, excuse me," she said, trying to sound polite. "I do not think you made this soup... right."

Jeffie, a wiry young man with wild blond hair, whirled around, glaring. "Oi! If ye don't like it, get yerself behind the counter and cook it yerself!" he barked, slamming a ladle against the pot.

Lisa blinked in shock, taking a step back. She glanced toward Annabelle, who simply raised her brows and tilted her head toward the ceiling, a silent *you are on your own.*

Lisa squared her shoulders. "You know what? I will."

Before Jeffie could stop her, she vaulted over the counter with surprising grace, landing lightly without letting her sundress flare.

The galley went still. Jeffie gaped. "Lass, ye can't just..."

Ignoring him, Lisa grabbed a dish towel and wrapped it around her head to keep her long hair back. She shooed him aside and crouched to inspect the fire beneath the stove.

Annabelle chuckled from her seat, thoroughly enjoying the show.

Lisa studied the flames for a moment before standing. She extended her hands, and an orange spell circle flickered to life before her. Runes spun as a warm glow filled the kitchen, feeding magical energy into the fire. The flames roared higher, crackling with renewed life.

Jeffie took a wary step back. "Oi, what're ye..."

Lisa shut the compartment door and dusted off her hands. "Good soup needs a good fire," she said confidently, turning to the pot.

She grabbed a spoon and tasted the broth. Her face twisted. "No spices?" she muttered, appalled.

Turning to Jeffie, she asked sweetly, "Where do you keep your spices?"

Jeffie looked to Annabelle for backup. "Ops O?"

Annabelle shrugged, feet still on the table. "Hey, *ye* told her to cook it. Might learn a ting or two."

Lisa crossed her arms, tapping her foot expectantly. "Come on, Jeffie. Spices?"

He groaned, rubbing his face. "Left-side cabinet."

Lisa grinned and retrieved a line of spice jars, arranging them neatly. "Alright. Let's fix this mess."

As Lisa set to work, Annabelle watched with an amused grin. *Maybe this princess has more fire in her belly than I thought.*

Jeffie sighed and opened a different cabinet behind him, revealing a neatly organized shelf of spice jars. He stepped aside reluctantly as Lisa's face lit up.

"Okay," she said, clapping her hands together. "Let's get cooking."

She grabbed a few jars and set them beside the stove. Picking up one labeled *cumin*, she removed the cork and sprinkled a dash into the bubbling pot.

Just then, the ship lurched beneath their feet. The jars on the counter slid dangerously toward the edge.

"Whoa!" Jeffie lunged forward, catching them before they tumbled. "Listen, missy," he said sternly, glaring at her, "the ship moves. If these break, we're out of luck till the next port."

He returned the jars to the cabinet with a pointed look. "So don't go wrecking' me kitchen tryin' to *fix* me soup."

Lisa frowned. "You think I do not know ships move?" she said, tilting her head.

Jeffie smirked. "Just making sure, *Princess.*"

The galley burst into laughter at the jab.

Lisa rolled her eyes but didn't miss a beat. "Sure. I have been on ships plenty. I am just trying to figure out how you had the nerve to call this stuff *soup.*"

The laughter doubled, and Jeffie's smirk faltered. He grumbled under his breath and slammed the jars back with more force than necessary. "Yeah, yeah. Just go one at a time, alright?"

Lisa grinned and handed him the cumin. "Okay. Now, pass me the garlic essence?"

For the next ten minutes, Lisa and Jeffie worked side by side, tasting, seasoning, and occasionally bumping elbows. Lisa adjusted the broth's flavor carefully, casting another orange rune to reduce the flame to a gentle simmer.

"Alright," Lisa said, wiping sweat from her brow. "Let it cook ten to fifteen minutes, then we'll taste it."

Jeffie sniffed the air and nodded reluctantly. "Might actually be decent," he muttered. "But we should clean up while we wait."

Lisa blinked. *Clean up?*

She looked around at the cluttered counters and stacks of dirty pots. "Uh... right," she said uncertainly, suddenly realizing she had no idea how cleanup worked aboard the *Stormfang*.

Jeffie walked to a closet, pulled out an iron pot and a bottle of cleanser, and to her surprise, handed *her* the pot...keeping the cleanser for himself.

[----- ❁ -----]

Regina nearly hit the floor.

She stood there, clad only in her undershirt and underwear, silver hair falling loosely around her face, shifting like water with the ship's movements. Her bare feet shuffled awkwardly on the wooden floor as she squinted around the room.

Annabelle ran from her chair, rushing to Regina's side. "What in the seven seas are ye doing, missy?" she hissed, grabbing her arm. "**In yer knickers?!?**"

Regina's cheeks flushed crimson. "I couldn't see," she mumbled, looking down. "It was too dark... I fell and hit my head when I got out of bed." her words cracking as she was on the verge of tears.

Annabelle glanced around the galley and caught several crew members staring, their eyes lingering far too long. "What are ye scallywags looking' at?!" she barked, her voice like a whip. The crew snapped their attention back to their food, heads down, spoons clattering against bowls.

"That's what I thought," Annabelle muttered, scowling as she pulled Regina toward the stairs. "C'mon, missy. Let's get ye sorted before you give someone a heart attack."

"I'm sorry," Regina whispered, voice trembling. "I couldn't see anything... then I fell."

Annabelle's heart softened at the crack in her voice. She gave Regina's hand a reassuring squeeze. "It's okay, lass," she said, hurrying her down to the stateroom deck.

They stopped at Annabelle's room first. She flung the door open and crossed to her locker. Rummaging inside, she pulled out a small metal cylinder filled with tiny glowing rocks.

She gave it a firm shake. The rocks began to glow with a soft greenish light, filling the room with a warm shimmer.

Annabelle pressed the device into Regina's hands. "Keep this wit' ye. Just give it a shake when ye need light."

Regina stared down at the glowing cylinder. "Thank you," she murmured, still avoiding Annabelle's gaze.

Annabelle gently tugged Regina's hand, leading her to her stateroom and shutting the door with a firm click. "Make sure the door stays closed," she said.

Regina turned and pushed the door shut, then turned back, looking utterly deflated. "I'm sorry. I didn't mean to..."

"Don't be sorry," Annabelle snapped, hands on her hips. "Ye don't just wander the crew decks in your knickers!" She marched over to the wooden slat covering the porthole beside Regina's hammock and pushed it open, letting in a soft breeze and streams of morning light.

"If ye can't see, open the porthole or use the light shaker," she said, pointing at the device still clutched in Regina's hands.

Regina wiped at her tear-filled eyes. "I didn't mean to..."

"Stop yer apologizing!" Annabelle barked, her voice cracking. She paused, then added more gently, "We could've lost you, girlie."

Regina froze, wide-eyed, as Annabelle's tough exterior finally cracked. "Ye could've fallen all the way down to the hold," Annabelle said, her own eyes brimming with unshed tears. "Ye could've been... on the other side of the veil before anyone found you." She swallowed hard and quickly wiped her face, trying to regain her composure. "Come on, then. Let's get ye dressed."

Regina nodded, sniffling, and turned to her wardrobe. Now that the room was properly lit, she could see as well as she ever did without her glasses. She pulled out a dress and slipped it on, taking her time with the buttons.

Annabelle crossed her arms and turned to face the window, giving her some privacy. "Tell me when your decent," Annabelle said.

"Almost... okay, I'm decent," Regina replied, tugging the dress into place.

Annabelle turned back around, giving her a small, approving nod. "Aye, much better."

Regina retrieved her glasses from her dress pocket and slid them onto her nose. "I'm really sorry," she muttered. "I just didn't know."

Annabelle placed her hands firmly on Regina's shoulders. "Stop saying sorry, girlie," she said more gently. "Just take care of yerself, alright? Yer goddess wouldn't be too happy if we let you go and get yourself killed."

Regina gave a small smile. "Okay." She glanced down at the light shaker in her hand. "I'll keep it with me."

Annabelle grinned. "Good. And if I catch you walking' the decks like that again, I'll personally tie ye down to yer bunk."

Regina laughed lightly, wiping away the last of her tears. "Did I smell food in the kitchen?"

"Galley, missy. On ships, it's called a galley," Annabelle corrected as they stepped out of the Sun stateroom into the hallway. "Show me the shaker."

Regina held it up with a shy smile. "Right here."

"Good girlie." Annabelle said, offering a nod of approval.

As they walked down the dim corridor, Annabelle found herself glancing at shaky little Regina, clutching the glowing shaker like a lifeline. She smirked, remembering how Sophie and Lisa had once navigated the same hall in total darkness without a hitch. *Maybe there's hope for them yet,* she thought.

"Let's see what our green princess has cooked up," Annabelle said aloud.

"In the galley," Regina teased.

Annabelle chuckled, and together they climbed the stairs.

Inside, the crew sat idly at their tables. Jeffie stood behind the counter, all eyes waiting expectantly. Lisa had taken over his spot, looking quite pleased with herself.

Annabelle didn't miss a beat. "Oi! When's the soup going to be ready?" she called, her voice ringing out. Regina trailed behind and slipped the shaker into her dress pocket.

Lisa scowled, green eyes narrowing. "Just a little longer," she huffed.

Annabelle raised her hands in mock surrender, her orange eyes wide and playful.

Lisa softened. "Is Sophie joining us?"

"Don't think so," Annabelle replied. "She finally went back to sleep."

Lisa nodded thoughtfully. "Then I will save her some."

She hopped down from the stool and lifted the pot lid, inhaling deeply. A satisfied smile spread across her face. She grabbed a spoon, took a small taste, and nodded.

"Yes," she whispered to herself, pumping her fist. The flavors were rich and balanced—just as she'd hoped.

She turned to Jeffie. "You have to try this," she said, offering him a spoonful. Jeffie took the taste reluctantly, chewing for a moment before shrugging. "It's... a little better, I guess," he muttered, looking away.

Lisa's shoulders drooped, disappointment flickering across her face.

She turned to the crew. "Lunch is ready!" she announced.

No one moved. The galley remained eerily quiet, and Lisa's confidence faltered.

"Can I have some?" Regina asked timidly.

Lisa brightened instantly. "Of course you can."

She grabbed a bowl from the shelf, ladled the hot soup into it, and handed it over. Regina carried her bowl to the table, where Annabelle was already seated. She took a tentative bite, and her eyes widened in delight.

"This is really good!" she exclaimed.

Annabelle looked at her, skeptical. "Lemme have a taste," she said, reaching for Regina's spoon.

Regina handed it over. Annabelle took a mouthful.

The moment the soup hit her tongue, her expression shifted—eyes wide, mouth hanging open. She handed the spoon back to Regina and shot to her feet, grabbing a bowl and striding to the counter. Clearing her throat dramatically, she said, "I would like some soup, please," using her *proper voice*.

Lisa smirked, seizing the opportunity. "What, no 'princess' or 'missy' this time?" she teased, tilting her head. "Do you even know my name?"

Annabelle faltered for half a second, then quickly recovered. "'Course I do," she said confidently, though inside she scrambled. "Those are just terms of endearment."

Lisa arched a brow. "Hmm-hmm. Then what is my name?"

Annabelle cleared her throat and crossed her arms. "Lisa Nozaki," she said with a triumphant grin. "Now, can I please have some more soup, princess?"

Lisa's smirk faltered, and she handed over the bowl with a reluctant smile. "Here you go. Do enjoy."

Annabelle returned to her seat and dug into her soup eagerly. The rest of the crew watched closely. Blaze, the man who manned the cannons and powder stores, leaned in. "Well? How is it?"

Annabelle set her bowl down and wiped her mouth with the back of her hand. "Good," she said with a nostalgic smile. "Like when Ruben was with us."

The name drew a murmur from the crew, their gazes shifting toward Lisa with newfound interest. Suddenly, chairs scraped back as hungry privateers rushed the counter.

Lisa blinked in surprise, overwhelmed as she hurried to serve bowl after bowl.

Regina leaned toward Annabelle. "Who's Ruben?"

Annabelle leaned back in her chair, a wistful look on her face. "Oh, he was our cook a year or two ago. That man could cook, let me tell you."

Regina smiled. "What happened to him? Did he open a restaurant?"

Annabelle barked a laugh. "Nope. Got caught robbing some rich folk of their art." She shook her head with amusement. "He's locked up in Stoneridge now."

Regina's eyes widened. "You didn't try to get him out?"

Annabelle waved a hand. "Nah. No one breaks in or out of a Stoneridge prison. The captain even tried to pay his way out, but the guards weren't having it." She finished off her soup, drinking straight from the bowl. "Man, those rich folk were really mad about their art."

Regina frowned. "Do you think he actually did it?"

Annabelle smirked, leaning back. "Oh yeah, no doubt. The way he'd go on about those 'rich bastards in Stoneridge,' he had it out for them." She picked her teeth with a toothpick. "Said he'd rob them blind, maybe even burn their mansions down."

She noticed Regina's worried look and softened her tone. "I'm sure he stole it all right, but the coppers never found it. Probably burned it for warmth while he was on the run in the mountains."

Regina shook her head in disbelief. "Wow... they must've wronged him so badly."

Annabelle shrugged. "Nope. Far as we know, he'd never even been to Stoneridge before."

Regina blinked, speechless, and returned to her soup, stirring it thoughtfully.

Annabelle sighed dramatically. "I really miss those crêpes," she said, propping her feet on the table. "That man really could cook."

Chapter 9

Marcus Igbinedion, a dedicated brother monk in the Order of Saint Lorraine, served double duty: first, as an investigator for the College of Sages sect; and second, as the first assistant to Brother Albert Thompson, the man entrusted with guiding the four known avatars blessed by the Twelve Goddesses.

Brother Albert took his duty with unwavering seriousness. Marcus had once known him as a man who indulged in the pleasures of fine spirits and charming company, but in recent years, Albert's focus had shifted entirely to his self-proclaimed responsibility of "keeping up with his girls."

As his assistant, Marcus was responsible for meticulously documenting the information Albert sent back from his various surveying assignments.

At first, Marcus dismissed many of Albert's theories as far-fetched, mere conjecture strung together by coincidence. A noble's mysterious death in one kingdom, a vanished ship in another—seemingly unrelated events that Albert insisted were connected. Marcus was constantly amazed by the threads Albert managed to weave between them. When Marcus applied his own investigative methods, he often struggled to see the patterns his mentor found so easily.

He vividly recalled one particular evening when he'd challenged Albert on the credibility of his connections. "You can't possibly know these things," Marcus had argued.

Unfazed, Albert arranged an offsite surveying mission and confidently predicted they would witness the infamous blue-haired Isabella Morales break a group of men out of jail, and escape before they could be recaptured.

Marcus had been skeptical, but that day shattered his doubts. As if following a script, Isabella Morales strode into the jail with confident purpose. With little effort, she tore open the cell doors and unleashed her terrifying metal constructs, which laid waste to the guards and soldiers who tried to stop her. Before anyone could comprehend what had happened, Morales and her band of freed prisoners vanished without a trace.

That moment taught Marcus never to doubt Albert's instincts again.

Upon their return to Order Island, Albert finally revealed his investigative approach. "Find something that doesn't fit," he explained. "Because odds are, there's something else that won't fit in that same place and time. Piece those together, and you've got yourself a view of the bigger picture."

Albert's technique fascinated Marcus. It wasn't about knowing every piece of the puzzle, it was about identifying the missing fragments and understanding how they connected.

Together, they began referring to the mysterious network of individuals and incidents as *The Conspiracy*, a name Marcus himself had suggested. He reasoned that such well-coordinated actions had to be part of a larger, unseen force working toward an unknown goal.

Despite all they had uncovered, there were still more questions than answers, and Marcus couldn't shake the feeling that their work had only just begun.

He pulled the watch from his pocket, its surface gleaming with the insignia of the Order. Pressing the button on top, the watch face flipped open: 08:30 AM. Still no word from Albert.

A familiar pang of worry settled in his chest.

Had something happened after Albert made first contact with the girls? He had warned Marcus about their strong personalities and the delicate balance he needed to maintain to prevent conflicts from spiraling out of control. Perhaps Albert had failed to establish the cohesion he'd hoped for and had decided to drown his frustrations in a mug…or five of ale.

Not knowing should mean not worrying. Marcus reminded himself as he stepped into the Order's cafeteria. Though Albert had left him with an extensive list of tasks, he figured they could wait until after breakfast. *Coffee first, duty later.*

The cafeteria buzzed with the quiet energy of his fellow monks, each absorbed in their tasks. Some were assigned to teams that gathered intelligence or investigated strange phenomena, while others pored over reports detailing the intricacies of their world. The large room was divided into a seating area filled with long tables arranged lengthwise, leaving convenient gaps so people could find seats without navigating all the way to the ends.

Marcus made his way to the front where food was being served. Grabbing a bowl, he ladled a generous helping of oatmeal, twice, watching the thick, steaming grains settle. With practiced ease, he sprinkled in a handful of cut-up strawberries, their red contrasting vividly against the neutral tones of the porridge.

Sister Ester, dressed in crisp kitchen whites, greeted him with a warm smile. Everyone in the Order took their turn at cafeteria duty for a month each year, typically the younger monks before they received permanent assignments. While the Order employed a few full-time cooks, tasks like boiling eggs, chopping vegetables, and washing dishes fell to those on rotation.

"Coffee?" she offered, lifting a pot in one hand.

Marcus returned her smile. "Yes, I'd love a cup."

The rich, dark liquid poured into his mug, releasing a comforting aroma that Marcus privately considered a divine gift from the Goddesses themselves.

"Milk or sugar?" Ester asked.

"No, thank you," he replied. "I like it black." Experience had taught him that indulging in comforts while on the island made it harder to adjust during field assignments, where luxuries could be scarce.

With breakfast in hand, Marcus made his way to the first empty table he could find. He set down his tray and grabbed a spoon from the communal cup in the center. As he dug into his oatmeal, he fell into a familiar rhythm: scoop, sip of coffee, repeat, barely registering the murmured conversations around him.

"Marcus, have you heard the rumors?"

The voice cut through his focus, and Marcus looked up to see Sister Sallie Young approaching. They had grown up in the Order together, often swapping notes and gossip during their early years. Now, she worked in the Earth Studies office under the College of Sages sect.

Marcus shook his head, chewing quickly to avoid talking with his mouth full.

Sallie leaned in, lowering her voice. "Word is, one of the investigation brothers detonated his journal."

Marcus raised an eyebrow. "Last night?"

She nodded, sliding onto the bench across from him. "Yeah. Burned the whole thing to ash before anyone could get to it. People are saying it must've had something big inside."

A frown crept across Marcus' face as he stirred his oatmeal absently. The Order took great care to preserve information; destroying a journal is the last resort, only used when the knowledge inside was too dangerous to fall into the wrong hands.

"Did anyone say who it was?" he asked, his appetite fading.

Sallie shrugged. "Not yet. But the administration sect is being really tight-lipped about it."

Marcus swallowed another spoonful and glanced at her. "Really? Who told you that?"

She shifted in her seat, scanning the room with a conspiratorial glance. "You know how it is, I heard it around," she murmured. "One of the younger brothers was working the locator board yesterday and saw the journal light up."

Marcus continued eating, occasionally casting skeptical looks her way. Sallie's expression shifted to mild irritation, clearly annoyed by his doubt.

"You're just being difficult," she said. "You know how these things go. The rumor tree always blooms before the official announcement."

He sighed, conceding with a small nod. "You've got a point. But where are the details?" He leaned in slightly, investigator's instinct kicking in. "Where did the journal detonate? Whose was it?"

Sallie tapped a finger against her chin, eyes drifting toward the ceiling. "Yeah... they didn't say," she admitted. "But I heard it from more than one person."

Marcus nodded, stirring the last remnants of his oatmeal. "Alright. Hopefully, we didn't lose anyone."

Before Sallie could respond, a group of three brothers approached their table. The leader, whom Marcus didn't recognize, stood at the front with a composed but commanding presence. His jet-black hair was tied in a neat bun atop his head, and his light brown face was framed by a well-groomed beard and mustache that connected at the corners of his mouth.

"Brother Marcus Igbinedion," the man said, his dark eyes locking onto Marcus with quiet authority. "You need to come with me."

Marcus set his cup down carefully. "What's this about?"

The man's gaze flicked briefly to Sallie before returning to Marcus. "I'll answer all your questions once you come with me, Brother. This is important."

Sallie gave Marcus a quick wave, sensing the tension. "Good luck," she said before excusing herself, walking past the group with a subtle glance of curiosity.

Marcus took one last sip of his coffee and stood. "As you wish, Brother...?" he prompted, waiting for an introduction.

"Brother James Hasegawa," the man replied crisply. "This way."

Without another word, Brother James turned and led the way out of the cafeteria, with Marcus falling into step behind him. The two other brothers, silent and stoic, flanked Marcus from the rear.

As they walked down the bustling hallway, Marcus observed his fellow monks carrying out their daily routines. Their expressions ranged from serene focus to mild curiosity at the unusual escort.

After a short walk, they turned into a quieter corridor. Brother James reached into his pocket, produced a small key, and unlocked a heavy wooden door.

Marcus inhaled deeply, steeling himself for whatever awaited on the other side.

"Please follow me," Brother James said, pushing the door open.

Marcus nodded and stepped inside. The door clicked shut behind him as the two other brothers remained outside, their backs to the entrance...*standing guard?*

The hallway stretched ahead, lined with open windows that carried the scent of the sea—a constant reminder of Order Island's coastal location. As Marcus followed Brother James, curiosity gnawed at him.

"I have a lot to do today," he said. "If you could just tell me what this is about..."

James raised a finger to his lips, silencing him. "Discretion is required," he said softly.

Marcus frowned but fell silent as they arrived at a door. James knocked three times in a precise rhythm.

"Come," a woman's voice called from within.

James pushed the door open and gestured for Marcus to enter first.

Stepping inside, Marcus took in the grand office. A large wooden desk stood near a balcony that overlooked the bay, and the scent of salt and parchment hung in the air. To the left of the door, a massive map of the Seven Kingdoms glowed with softly lit circles, some clustered, others isolated. To the right, a full-length mirror reflected the room, its surface subtly distorting the details.

Behind the desk, a woman studied a sheet of paper with calm intensity. She looked up as he entered.

"Brother Marcus," she said, setting the paper down. "Welcome."

"Thank you," Marcus replied cautiously.

Brother James followed him in, closing the door with a quiet click.

"I am Sister Ingrid," the woman said, folding her hands atop the desk. "We have important matters to discuss."

Marcus remained standing, glancing toward Brother James, who stood quietly at his side.

"You're Brother Albert Thompson's first assistant in his guiding duties, correct?" Ingrid asked.

"That's correct," Marcus said. "He left me a long list of tasks to complete before his return tomorrow."

"Please, have a seat." She gestured to the two chairs in front of her desk.

Marcus and James sat. The latter pulled a journal from the strap on his back.

"Brother James is from our Overseer Sect," Ingrid explained. "Brother James, if you would."

James nodded and flipped open the journal. "At 3:00 a.m. last night, the Overlookers received an alert: *Brother Albert Thompson's journal was destroyed using the erasure ritual.*" He paused to study Marcus's reaction. "Standard protocol dictates that when a journal is destroyed in this manner, we assume the brother is deceased or lost. However, we've detected his watch end route to Order Island."

Marcus stiffened. "His journal was destroyed?"

Every monk of the Order of Saint Lorraine knew that their journals were their most vital possession and tool, used to record knowledge, preserve insights, and, above all, return to the Order's library. The erasure ritual was only used when escape was impossible and the knowledge too dangerous to risk falling into enemy hands.

"That means..." Marcus trailed off, the weight of the situation settling on his shoulders. Albert had believed he wouldn't make it out.

"Brother Albert was making first contact with the avatars last night, was he not?" Sister Ingrid asked, her gaze sharp.

"Yes," Marcus confirmed. "He insisted it was necessary, given the threats coming their way." He kept his tone cautious, unwilling to reveal too much of Albert's suspicions without knowing how much Ingrid already understood.

"The Conspiracy is closing in on them," she said, finishing the thought.

Marcus blinked in surprise. He had always thought Albert overly cautious in guarding his theories. For Ingrid to mention the Conspiracy so openly meant she knew far more than he'd guessed.

"In your opinion, Brother Marcus," Ingrid continued, watching him closely, "do you believe the girls have been recruited by the Conspiracy? Perhaps by Salazar or Fournier?"

Marcus hesitated. "I don't think so," he said after a moment. "From what I know of them; they wouldn't be receptive to the Conspiracy's influence."

"There is still the matter of Brother Albert's watch," James interjected, his voice measured. "It is currently moving toward Order Island as we speak."

"Yes," Ingrid said, tapping her finger thoughtfully on the desk. "Marcus, have you received any messages from Brother Albert this morning?"

Marcus paused, choosing his words carefully. "No, Sister."

In truth, Albert had created a spell similar to the spell used by monks on scribe duty to report in to the Order, that allowed them to communicate via their writing pens, something he had sworn Marcus to keep secret. *How much did this Ingrid sister really know?*

She nodded. "Nor have I." A pause. "We must consider the possibility that Brother Albert is deceased."

The weight of her words settled heavily in the room.

"Brother James, how far is the watch from us now?" Ingrid asked.

"At its current speed and course, it should arrive within a day," James replied. "We suspect it's aboard a ship."

"Most likely Salazar's ship, *The Stormfang*," Ingrid answered. "Brother James, please make preparations to receive whoever arrives with the watch."

"At your command, Sister," James said, rising. He gave Marcus a brief nod before exiting the room.

Marcus remained seated, his thoughts spinning. Brother Albert's journal was gone, erased. Whatever had happened last night was beyond recovery. And yet, the watch was still making its way back.

Could Albert still be alive?

There had been rare cases in which Order members returned under dire circumstances, delivering verbal reports when written ones were impossible. If anyone could manage such a feat, it was Albert.

Sister Ingrid studied Marcus in silence.

The questions swirled in Marcus's mind. *What had happened to Brother Albert? And more importantly, what was coming next?*

Sister Ingrid leaned forward over her desk; her sharp gaze fixed on him. "How much did Brother Albert tell you about his duties?"

Marcus straightened in his chair. "Brother Albert told me everything," he said. "He was tasked with watching over the avatars until they were ready to make contact with the Order. He also monitored the world to identify the threat they were born under."

"Did he ever mention me?" she asked, tilting her head slightly.

Marcus hesitated. "No, Sister. He didn't."

A faint smile touched Ingrid's lips. "As the guide, Brother Albert reported to me daily," she said. "We are part of the Scribes of the Lands Sect. Our mission", she paused to let the words settle, "is to provide guidance and assistance to the avatars of the twelve."

Marcus nodded. That much he already knew.

"Did Brother Albert ever tell you why he chose you as his first assistant?"

Marcus frowned, searching his memory. "He always said I was assigned to him by the council." He paused. "He chose me?"

Ingrid's smile widened. "He did. He spoke very highly of you in his reports."

Marcus felt a flicker of disbelief. "Why would he lie about that?"

She shrugged. "He had his own way of doing things. But one thing was certain, he understood people."

Marcus considered this for a moment before another thought struck him. "Wait, he was away from the island a lot. How did he report to you every day?"

"You're familiar with the magic writing pen spell?" Ingrid asked, arching an eyebrow. "I was the one who taught it to him." She reached into a drawer and pulled out a round crystal orb, holding it up for him to see. "Brother Marcus Igbinedion, I am appointing you as the guide to the avatars of the Goddesses, effective immediately. Close your current journal and begin a new one, your duties to the College of Sages Sect are hereby concluded. You'll serve in this role full-time."

Marcus's eyes widened, and he sat up straighter. "We don't know that Brother Albert is dead," he objected, his voice firm. "He could be on that ship heading for the island right now."

Ingrid's expression hardened. "Let's say he is alive," she said, her tone edged with incredulity. "Why hasn't he sent us a message?" She paused, letting the silence carry her point. "And if he wasn't near death when he erased his journal, what possible reason would he have to stay silent?"

Marcus pursed his lips and rested a hand on his chin, thinking. "If Brother Albert is alive but incapacitated, he's likely badly injured, too weak to send messages." He exhaled slowly. "Second possibility: he was captured by the Conspiracy, and they're using his watch to draw us into a trap."

Sister Ingrid leaned back in her chair and nodded. "Go on."

"Third, he's dead, and his body is on the ship. If that's the case, the Conspiracy may not be involved, and the avatars could be aboard." He paused, his brow furrowing. "And fourth... if he's dead and his body isn't on that ship, then something far worse has happened."

"Very astute," Ingrid said, her expression unreadable. "In your opinion, what should our response be in each scenario?"

Marcus took a breath. "If Brother Albert is alive but injured, we assume the avatars are with him and bring them in. We treat his wounds and extract as much intelligence as we can." He hesitated. "If he's alive and uninjured but hasn't contacted us, we must consider he's been turned by the Conspiracy. In that case, we detain him immediately and proceed with extreme caution. If the girls are not with him... we must assume the Conspiracy will try to manipulate them the same way they did Isabella Morales and Greta Blomqvist."

He paused, drawing in a slow breath before continuing. "If he's dead and his body Is on the ship, we can trust the Conspiracy wasn't involved. We should extend an invitation to the girls and offer them sanctuary." He hesitated before addressing the final scenario. "If his body isn't aboard, then we need to treat everyone on that ship as a potential threat, and conduct a full investigation before making any decisions."

Sister Ingrid studied him for a long moment, then gave a nod of approval. "In every scenario, Brother Albert must be replaced. If he is dead, that's obvious. If he's alive but injured, he cannot fulfill his duties." Her gaze sharpened. "And if he has been recruited by the Conspiracy... we'll have no choice but to lock him away."

The weight of her words pressed heavily on Marcus, but he said nothing.

"There's much to do," Ingrid continued, rising from her chair and walking to the ornate mirror on the wall. She lifted the crystal ball and turned to Marcus. "Do you know what this is?"

"I can't say that I do," Marcus replied, eyeing the object in her hand. "What is it?"

"This," she said, holding it up, "is a Miracam crystal. It records moving pictures and sound. The magic behind it is complex, which is why the Order has so few." She gestured toward the large mirror behind her desk. "That, however, is a viewing mirror."

With a practiced motion, she touched the crystal to the glass. Instantly, the surface shimmered—then resolved into a vivid image of Brother Albert sitting in the very chair Marcus now occupied. The picture filled the mirror like a living, life-sized portrait.

Sister Ingrid returned to her seat and commanded, "Recitation emIncipe."

Marcus watched in awe as the image of Brother Albert stirred to life. He fidgeted in his seat, adjusting his clothes and glancing around the room with his usual restless energy.

"When do I start?" Albert asked, his voice echoing through the chamber.

"You already have," came Sister Ingrid's recorded voice—not from the present, but embedded in the memory.

Albert chuckled, caught off guard. "Well, alright then." He closed his eyes briefly, collecting himself. When he opened them again, his tone had shifted.

"Brother Marcus, I'm making this message for you because... there's a chance I won't come back." His voice grew quieter, heavier. "I leave today to make first contact with my girls, and things could go very wrong."

He glanced off-screen and frowned. "What?"

Sister Ingrid's recorded voice cut in, stern: "Your girls?"

Albert grinned at the gentle rebuke. "He knows what I mean." Then, turning back toward the crystal, his expression turned solemn. "Marcus, if I don't make it back, I want you to take over for me. The girls are younger than I'd hoped, but it can't be helped. The Conspiracy is closing in on them, and we must keep them safe so they can fulfill the Goddesses' purpose."

He paused to sip from a cup, then let out a long, weary breath. "Use that brilliant investigator's mind of yours to figure out what the Conspiracy is doing and help my girls stop it."

He leaned forward, voice thick with emotion. "You'll have to help them understand the world... and each other. They'll argue, they'll clash...probably with you, too; but be patient. Each of them is extraordinary in her own way. I can't wait to see what glorious things they'll accomplish together."

His eyes shimmered. He wiped a tear away and swallowed hard. "Whatever you do, Marcus...Please don't let them end up like Isabella and Greta." His voice cracked. "Not my girls."

He took one final breath, steadied himself, and smiled. "Take care of them, Marcus. I know you're the right one for this."

After a brief pause, Albert glanced off-screen again and asked, "How was that?"

The recording ended. Sister Ingrid waved a hand over the mirror. "Speculum revocatory, omnia delete." The image vanished, leaving only Marcus' reflection staring back at him.

He sat frozen, throat tight, tears brimming despite himself. Slowly, he wiped his face and swallowed the growing lump in his throat. "What happened?" he whispered, barely audible.

Sister Ingrid sighed, dabbing at her eyes with a handkerchief. "I wish I knew," she said gently. "Hopefully, when his watch arrives, we'll get the answers we need." She paused, composing herself. "In the meantime, there's much to do. You must select your first assistant and record a message, just as Brother Albert did."

Marcus frowned, the weight of the task pressing down. "How do I choose a first assistant?" he asked, uncertainty clear in his voice.

"There are no strict criteria," Ingrid replied, her tone shifting to pragmatic. "Brother Albert set a high bar, but he worked hard after his predecessor failed the girls and lost them to the Conspiracy."

"Isabella and Greta," Marcus murmured, the names heavy on his tongue.

Ingrid nodded. "Yes. You'll need someone who can fill your shoes... and Brother Albert's."

Marcus exhaled slowly, feeling the burden settle across his shoulders. "Those are some big shoes to fill."

"If you haven't chosen someone by the end of today," Ingrid added, her voice edged with quiet authority, "I'll be forced to choose for you."

Marcus heard the warning behind the words. He stood, his expression steady despite the storm inside. "At your command, Sister."

He turned to the door, mind already racing with names.

"Brother Marcus," Ingrid called after him.

He paused and looked back.

"My door is always open," she said, her voice gentler now.

Marcus gave a small nod. "Thank you, Sister." And with that, he stepped out, closing the door behind him.

[-----✝-----]

Brother Marcus sat in what was now Brother Albert's former office a large, rectangular space cluttered with maps pinned to every wall. Strings crisscrossed between them, connecting names and locations to small paper tags. The tables had been pushed together to form one massive workspace, now littered with scattered papers, half-unrolled scrolls, and assorted boxes. The chaos made Marcus uneasy, he preferred order, but this space had only become his responsibility this morning. And with it came an overwhelming list of tasks he had to complete before he could even think about making it his own.

He flipped through the leather-bound book Sister Ingrid had sent, a compiled list of Order members and potential candidates. Her subtle way of pressing him to choose a first assistant. His eyes lingered on a photo of Brother Andrew Zhao, a fourth-year member of the Elementalisms' Sect. According to the profile, Andrew excelled at understanding ecosystems and the cascading effects of seemingly small actions.

"Would Brother Albert approve?" Marcus wondered, tapping his fingers against the edge of the page. *Who knows*, he thought, shaking his head. *Albert had always been his own man, meticulous, insightful, with a knack for spotting patterns others missed. Could Andrew's analytical mindset help unravel the threads of the Conspiracy? More importantly, would he want to?*

Marcus mentally placed Andrew on the maybe list and turned the page.

A new face greeted him, Sister Alameda Ortega. He didn't know her personally, but her profile stood out. She had begun her training in the Scribes of Saint Lorraine, the Order's backbone, tasked with gathering information across the Seven Kingdoms. But after just two years, she had transferred to the Cartographers' Conclave, where she assisted in refining and correcting the Order's extensive geographic records.

Marcus frowned, tapping the page thoughtfully. It was an unusual transition. Typically, recruits began in one of those two rigorous sects before moving into less demanding roles. But why had she moved laterally between them?

A quick knock interrupted his thoughts. The door behind him creaked as Sister Ingrid slipped inside with practiced ease, navigating the clutter without hesitation, evidence that she'd spent considerable time in this office before.

"Good evening, Brother Marcus. How goes the search?"

Marcus stood to greet her, closing the book. "Good evening, Sister Ingrid. What can I do for you?"

"We've received another request for an update from the Overseer Sect," she said, remaining by the door. "I'd like you to accompany me."

Marcus nodded and reached for his newly started journal, but Ingrid raised a hand.

"Hold on," she said, her eyes narrowing slightly. "Have you chosen your first assistant?"

The question caught him off guard. He realized quickly that there was only one acceptable answer. "I have, actually," he said, standing straighter. "Sister Alameda Ortega."

Ingrid arched an eyebrow. "Interesting choice. Why her?"

Marcus gestured toward the book on the desk. "Her record stood out. She started with the Scribes of Saint Lorraine, like many of us, but then moved to the Cartographers' Conclave. It reminded me of what you said about Brother Albert, how he bounced around before finding his place here."

"Good point," Ingrid said with a thoughtful nod. "But you didn't."

Marcus blinked. "I... hadn't thought about that."

Ingrid studied him for a moment, then pressed further. "Do you stand by your choice, or do you need more time?"

Marcus recalled the image of Alameda in the book, Order uniform sharp, eyes focused as she examined a capture stone. There was something in her stance, a quiet confidence. He met Ingrid's gaze. "No, I'm sure. She'll be a good replacement."

"Alright," Ingrid said. "She's likely on assignment with the Conclave. I'll have her brought back to the island."

"Thank you, Sister," Marcus said, gesturing toward the half-blocked door. "Shall we?"

Ingrid gave a small smirk before slipping effortlessly through the narrow opening.

Marcus followed, grumbling slightly as he had to shove the door open wider to accommodate his larger frame.

The hallway outside buzzed with the usual hum of Order members tending to their duties. Sister Ingrid led the way, weaving through the crowd with an ease Marcus found almost unnatural. Watching her, he realized it wasn't just familiarity, it is a skill. She moves like someone accustomed to blending into the background, letting others take center stage while she observed unnoticed.

Typical of the Scribes, Marcus mused. Though the role of a Guide was well-known and respected within the Order, the Scribes thrived in going unseen. It made sense, if Ingrid moved unnoticed, it allowed her subordinates to attract attention while she gathered insight from the shadows.

Another detail caught his attention, she never spoke as they walked.

Most monks exchanged idle chatter in the hallways; the running joke was that if you cast a recording spell here, you'd know every secret the Order had to offer. Yet Ingrid remained silent. Proof, perhaps, that not everyone in the Order was so careless.

Marcus followed in her wake, the weight of his new responsibilities pressing down on him with every step.

They took two sharp turns, climbed two flights of stairs, and finally stopped at a sturdy wooden door. A brother stood outside, dressed in a simple shirt and pants, no uniform, marking him as support staff rather than a field agent.

The brother nodded politely. "Good evening," he said, pulling the door open with practiced ease. "Please, go in."

"Thank you," Sister Ingrid replied, her voice carrying a warmth that felt almost at odds with the urgency of their errand. She stepped inside without hesitation.

Marcus gave the brother a small nod as he followed, the tension in his chest tightening with every step.

Inside, the room buzzed with activity. Groups of Order members worked at large, cabinet-like machines affixed to the walls, the base of the magic writing pen spell Brother Albert had once taught Marcus. Each machine featured a mechanical arm suspended over a recessed workspace, where rolls of paper fed between two metal slats, allowing for smooth, automatic movement.

Marcus watched as the arms wrote with startling precision, ink flowing in crisp lines across the parchment. Attending monks stood ready to tear off the freshly printed reports, transcribing them swiftly into their journals with practiced ease.

At the front of the room stood a circular table. The monk in charge, an older man with graying hair and a stern but kind expression, motioned for Sister Ingrid and Marcus to join him.

"Sister Ingrid, thank you for coming," the head monk said, his voice steady and professional.

"Always a pleasure, Brother Timothy," Ingrid replied, taking her seat with practiced ease. She gestured toward Marcus. "Allow me to introduce Brother Marcus Igbinedion, the new guide to the avatars."

"A pleasure, Brother Marcus," Timothy said, offering a firm nod. "Time is short, and I have urgent information to share."

He flipped open his journal, scanning the page. "At 8 o'clock this morning, we confirmed a massacre in Aurorium Granmark. Casualties are high."

Marcus felt his chest seize. "Oh Goddess… Sophie Griffin," he murmured. "That's her village."

Timothy raised a hand, calm but serious. "We cannot yet confirm the list of the dead. Reports from the Aurorium Clan indicate that the village was attacked group controlling machine shaped like animals and insects, and others wielding snow and ice magic."

Sister Ingrid exchanged a knowing glance with him. "We have a strong idea who might be involved," she said softly.

Timothy nodded. "At this moment, those are the only confirmed details. We'll relay updates as they come."

Marcus leaned forward, rubbing his chin. "May I ask a question?"

"Please, Brother Marcus," Timothy said, gesturing openly.

"You said the massacre was confirmed at eight this morning," Marcus began. "But do we know when it actually happened?"

Timothy's brows lifted slightly, clearly impressed. "An excellent question. The initial report arrived sometime late last night, but it took time to verify. We believe the attack occurred early yesterday evening."

Marcus's stomach sank. The timing lined up *exactly* with Brother Albert's disappearance. His journal hadn't been destroyed by coincidence.

"What's the time gap between the destruction of Brother Albert's journal and the confirmed attack?" Marcus asked, his investigator instincts kicking in.

Sister Ingrid leaned back in her chair, allowing Timothy to respond.

"The journal's destruction was detected at 3 a.m.," Timothy said, flipping through a few more pages. "Roughly five hours before the massacre was officially confirmed."

Marcus tapped his fingers against the table. Five hours... *enough time for an escape? A cover-up?* His thoughts churned.

Ingrid's voice snapped him back to the present. "Marcus, what are you thinking?"

He looked up, his expression resolute. "If the massacre and Brother Albert's disappearance are connected, then whoever's behind this is moving fast. And if the Conspiracy is involved, they're escalating their plans."

Sister Ingrid nodded grimly. "Then we don't have time to waste."

"Unfortunately, the Aurorium Clan was unable to provide those details," Brother Timothy said, his tone even. "But their investigation is ongoing. They'll share more as soon as they have it."

Sister Ingrid gave a polite nod. "Understood. Thank you, Brother Timothy," she said, rising with a faint smile. "We'll leave you to your work."

Marcus rose as well and extended his hand. "Thanks, brother."

Timothy shook it firmly. "You're welcome. We'll update you both the moment we learn more."

With that, Marcus and Sister Ingrid stepped back into the hallway.

"I've been thinking about what we just heard," Marcus began, his brow furrowed.

Before he could go on, Ingrid raised a finger to silence him. "We don't talk in the hallway," she said, voice quiet but firm. "When you walk these halls, project confidence, show that everything is under control."

Marcus bit back his questions and nodded, falling into step behind her.

As they moved through the hallways, he focused on his expression, settling into his signature half-smile and willing his thoughts to quiet. It reminded him of his time in the Scribes of Saint Lorraine, where no matter how earth-shattering the discovery, you kept your face neutral. There was always time to process revelations in private. For now, composure is key.

They passed clusters of brothers and sisters engaged in hushed conversations, outside the cafeteria, near the supply room, and idling by the bathrooms. No one paid them much attention, but Marcus knew any hint of unease could spark rumors faster than the pen machines transcribed their reports.

At last, they reached the turn leading to Marcus' new office. Sister Ingrid bypassed the main entrance, slipping effortlessly through the narrow, half-blocked side door. Marcus, unwilling to wrestle with it again, opted for the main door and entered the front half of his office.

Stacks of boxes, some haphazardly piled, served as an impromptu divider between the front and back sections of the room. Chalkboards fastened to their sides were scrawled with notes and theories. Marcus retrieved his old journal from the desk in front and made his way to the back, arriving just as Sister Ingrid stepped in, gliding through the clutter like she belonged there.

Marcus watched her, once again marveling at how easily she moved through the space without disturbing so much as a paper.

"Alright," Ingrid said, breaking the silence. "That was an unexpected piece of information. What do you make of the attack in Granmark?"

Marcus handed over his old journal. "I'm not sure how it fits yet," he admitted. "But it depends on when the village was attacked."

She accepted the journal and glanced at him. "Meaning?"

Marcus folded his arms in thought. "If the attack happened before Brother Albert's disappearance, then the Conspiracy might have turned Griffin to their cause or at least tried to. If they failed, wiping out the village could have been a cover-up."

Ingrid frowned. "That doesn't track," she said, flipping through the journal absentmindedly. "If they wanted to get rid of her, they could've just made her disappear. The Conspiracy avoids drawing attention to itself." She tapped the journal lightly. "And if Griffin did turn, why attack the village at all? They would've just spirited her away."

Marcus nodded slowly. "Good point." He furrowed his brow. "Maybe... the attack and Brother Albert's disappearance are completely unrelated."

Suddenly, his eyes widened. "Wait!"

He rushed to the front of the room, shoving boxes aside in his haste. Reaching the chalkboard on the right wall, he traced a string of papers with his finger until he found what he was looking for. "Here," he said, pointing to a small slip of parchment attached to a thread. A date from a few days ago was scrawled across it.

Marcus turned to Ingrid. "We received an alert that Greta, Mage, and Isabella booked travel to Granmark."

Ingrid stepped closer, scanning the web of notes. "Alright," she said cautiously. "What does that tell us?"

Marcus exhaled, gathering his thoughts. "Let's assume the Conspiracy didn't know Brother Albert was making first contact with the girls yesterday. They must've had something significant planned in Granmark for three of their top enforcers to be there at once."

Ingrid pursed her lips. "That's logical." She narrowed her eyes at the board. "We know Greta and Isabella worked together in the past... but what about Mage? Was she working with them, or was she there for something else?"

Marcus stared at the board, his mind racing. "That's what we need to find out."

"We don't have enough information to confirm whether Mage was involved in the Aurorium Massacre," Marcus said thoughtfully. "Aurorium villages are fortified and well-protected. If destroying Granmark was the Conspiracy's plan, they would've deployed all four of their top enforcers to ensure success." He leaned back slightly, tapping his fingers on the desk. "And as a rule, I don't make two assumptions in a row. We stop here until we get more information, whether about the massacre or Brother Albert's meeting with the Avatars."

"We're definitely facing a deficit of information," Sister Ingrid agreed, crossing her arms. "Making firm decisions now would be premature." She sighed. "Hopefully, when Brother Albert's watch arrives, we'll finally get some answers."

A heavy pause settled between them. Ingrid glanced at the floor, clearly gathering herself. Marcus instinctively braced.

"We need to discuss your duties as the Guide of the Avatars," she said, motioning for Marcus to sit.

He nodded and sat behind his desk, flipping open his new journal, ready to take notes.

Ingrid smiled slightly, softening her tone. "As their Guide, you'll be the Avatars' link to the Order and to the world." She sat across from him, folding her hands in her lap. "We often talk about them as names on parchment, Annabelle Salazar, Regina Fournier, but we mustn't forget that they're just girls. Young, barely stepping into adulthood."

She studied him before asking, "Do you remember yourself at fourteen?"

Marcus smirked, momentarily lost in memory. "At fourteen, I was training for my first assignments with the Scribes of Saint Lorraine," he said, recalling the long hours of study and field exercises.

Ingrid leaned forward. "Now imagine waking up tomorrow as an Aurorium Sentinel, thrown into a mission with no idea how to wear the uniform, maintain your weapons, or understand the inner workings of your clan." She paused. "It would be overwhelming, wouldn't it?"

Marcus rubbed his chin, considering.

"At fourteen," Ingrid continued, "you wouldn't have had the maturity to handle it. The Avatars will be facing challenges far beyond anything someone their age encountered."

Marcus nodded slowly.

"Your duty," Ingrid said, her voice steady, "is to guide them. Help them understand the world they've been born into. But remember, **you** are their servant. The Goddesses chose them for a reason." She stood and placed a hand on his desk. "Once first contact is made, all the Order's resources will be at your disposal. You need only ask."

Marcus absorbed her words and nodded. "Thank you, Sister."

Her eyes hardened slightly. "You also need to think of yourself differently, Marcus."

He raised an eyebrow.

"The Order is like wind through the mountains, rumors spread quickly," she said. "You must control what information others gather about you."

Marcus thought of how open Brother Albert had always seemed, at least to him. But now, in hindsight, the last day had proven otherwise.

As if reading his thoughts, Ingrid gave a knowing smile. "Brother Albert was a master at letting people think they knew him while only revealing what he wanted them to know." She met his gaze. "The fact that you knew nothing about me until today proves that."

Marcus let that sink in.

"You need to learn how to control the flow of information," Ingrid said, smoothing her robes. "Do you have any questions?"

Marcus hesitated. "Concerning my first assistant, how much should I tell her?"

Ingrid considered this. "That depends entirely on what arrives on that ship," she said carefully. "If we make first contact with the Avatars, I'll take a more active role in training your assistant to ensure you have everything you need. She should know everything you know, so she can step in for you seamlessly."

Marcus pondered the idea and let it go with a blink.

"Speaking of Sister Alameda Ortega," Ingrid said, turning to leave, "I'll arrange to have her brought back to Order Island. Hopefully, she's not too far away."

Marcus stood as she made her way to the door. "Have a good day, Sister."

"You as well, Brother," she returned with a small wave before slipping out.

The office fell into silence. Marcus sank into his chair, staring at the scattered notes, maps, and artifacts surrounding him. His mind churned through the possibilities of what might be aboard the approaching ship. Each scenario played out in his head, some hopeful, others far darker.

After a few rounds of what-ifs, his gaze settled on the thick book resting on the edge of his desk: *The Guide's Manual*, passed down through generations of Guides before him.

He sighed, knowing he had a long night ahead. With a resigned breath, he opened the hardcover and turned to the first page.

"The Tenets of the Guide to the Avatars..."

Chapter 10

Annabelle Salazar walked through the dimly lit hallway on a lower deck of the *Stormfang*, where rows of cannons pointed outward just inside the bulkhead. She was accompanied by Regina and Lisa Nozaki, while Sophie Griffin had opted to stay on deck, assisting the crew with the sails. Sophie's routine had been erratic, after returning to sleep yesterday, she'd wake sporadically to work out, grab a bite to eat, and then drift back into slumber for a few more hours.

As Annabelle, Lisa, and Regina strolled, their conversation turned to the issue of lighting the hallways below deck. Currently, the crew relied on shakers, small, handheld light sources but Regina was eager to find a more permanent solution. Lisa chimed in, mentioning a plant called Nightshade that grew in the dark and emitted a soft, ambient glow. However, it required a constant supply of fresh water to thrive. Annabelle sighed and shook her head; fresh water at sea was a precious commodity. They were already pushing their water diffuser, a machine Sparks, the ship's engineer, had ingeniously designed to convert seawater into drinking water to its limits just to sustain the crew and keep the galley running.

She wasn't sure they'd come up with a workable solution, but Annabelle believed it was better to keep guests like Regina and Lisa busy rather than letting them sit idle and potentially stir up trouble. Working with them was refreshing, unlike her interactions with the regular crew, she didn't have to test their loyalty or worry about being conned. At least, she hoped she didn't.

"This is a tough one," Regina said, furrowing her brow. "I guess the real challenge is finding a solution that works for the ship while still providing continuous light." She paused, tapping her chin thoughtfully. "We could try a solar mirror, capture sunlight and send it below deck through a series of tubes. Or maybe a magical conduit that loops a sunrise effect... but keeping that going might be tricky. Hmm... maybe fireflies?" She sighed. "This really is a tough one."

Annabelle smiled, glad to see Regina back to her usual self.

Lisa ran a hand through her green hair. "What about glowing water? Some types of fungus glow in the dark, they could work while suspended in water."

Annabelle raised an eyebrow. "Don't funguses need something to eat? What exactly do they eat?"

"Fungi." Lisa corrected automatically. "They usually feed on whatever is around them mostly dead things."

Annabelle wrinkled her nose. "Yeah, that doesn't sound like a good idea. Can't exactly keep a bunch of dead things lying around the ship."

As the trio continued down the hallway, the sound of hurried footsteps echoed behind them. Annabelle instinctively turned, raising her shaker to illuminate the passage.

The light revealed Gimble, the ship's runner, sprinting toward them with a sense of urgency.

"What ye got, Gimble?" Annabelle asked as he skidded to a halt in front of them.

"Cap'n wants to see ye." Gimble panted. "Says we're l' close to Order Island, and he needs to talk to ye—posthaste."

"Aye," Annabelle nodded. "We'll be right up." She glanced at Lisa and Regina before addressing Gimble again. "Go on, let the Cap'n know we're on our way."

"Aye!" Gimble called over his shoulder, already dashing back up the stairs.

Annabelle turned to the others. "Come on, lasses, best not keep the Cap'n waiting."

As they reached the stairwell, Regina hesitated before asking, "Um, Annabelle... what kind of magic do you use?"

Annabelle paused at the thick wooden hatch leading to the stairs. "Me magic's called Maelstrom Mastery," she said, then pushed the hatch open and stepped through.

Regina followed close behind, curiosity lighting up her face. "How does it work?"

As they climbed the narrow steps, Annabelle replied, "It's the magic of the sea. I can manipulate water, summon storms, and even call sea monsters if I wants."

"Really?" Regina's eyes widened. "How does it all work for you?"

They reached the platform leading to the berthing levels, where most of the crew was resting. Annabelle sighed. "It's kind of complicated... hard to explain." She continued upward, tossing a wink over her shoulder.

Regina pressed on, determined. "Can you try? I'll pay real close attention."

"I'll tell ye later," Annabelle said, picking up her pace as she climbed.

Lisa, trailing behind, huffed in frustration. "Why do you always do that?"

Regina blinked. "Always do what?"

Lisa rolled her eyes. "Every person you meet, it's always, 'What's your magic? What's your magic?'" She mimicked Regina's voice mockingly. Then her expression turned stern. "Magic is a person's connection to the world. It's solemn and sacred, and you insult that by trying to make a crass copy of it."

Regina's expression hardened. "I'm a Nexus Mage," she said firmly. "My magic is about learning different systems and understanding how to apply them. I'm not copying anything or being crass."

Sensing the rising tension, Annabelle stepped in. "Seems to me there's room for a little *live and let live* here." She glanced at Regina with a grin. "The missy's just being who she is. Kinda cute when you think about it."

Regina blushed and smiled. "Thanks, Annabelle."

Lisa scowled and muttered, "if you say so."

As they stepped onto the main deck, the sudden sunlight blinded them momentarily. Squinting against the glare, they made their way toward the bridge where Captain James "Kidd" Lowe stood at the helm, one hand on the wheel, barking commands to the crew below.

"Morning, ladies," Captain Kidd greeted them, his voice carrying the usual mix of warmth and authority. "How'd the brainstorming go?"

"Very stormy," Annabelle quipped with a smirk.

Regina chuckled. "It was... okay. We tossed around ideas, glowing flowers, magic portals, maybe even glowing fungi." She sighed. "But there are a lot of restrictions, you know? This is a working ship. We didn't land on a solid solution, just bounced ideas around." She paused. "It's not as easy as I thought it'd be."

Captain Kidd blinked slowly as he absorbed the flood of information.

"Like I said, Cap'n," Annabelle added with a grin, "stormy."

He finally nodded. "I see, Belle." Then, glancing across the deck, he called out in a steady, deliberate tone, "Oi, Sophie Griffin! Come to the Captain's OPS room."

The command echoed across the ship as the crew repeated it in unison. Sophie, tying down a rope, quickly secured it before heading toward the bridge, wiping her brow.

"Shall we?" Captain Kidd gestured toward the operations room behind the wheel. "Smitty, keep us steady and maintain speed."

"Aye, Cap'n," Smitty replied, gripping the wheel firmly as Kidd released it.

As they entered the operations room, Regina turned to Annabelle. "Do you ever get to... drive the ship?"

"Steer, missy," Captain Kidd corrected with a grin. "And aye, Belle's taken the wheel before."

"That's right," Annabelle said, beaming with pride.

"But I got tired of ending up in strange places," Kidd teased, flashing her a mischievous smile.

Annabelle scowled playfully as she took a seat.

Sophie hurried in, sweat clinging to her purple hair, strands plastered to her forehead. She looked exhausted but alert.

"Sophie Griffin," Captain Kidd said with a nod. "Thanks for joining us. Have a seat." He gestured to an empty chair between Regina and Lisa.

Once Sophie sat down, Kidd leaned back in his chair, folding his arms. "Alright, girlies. We need to talk about what we're going to do when we reach Order Island."

Annabelle leaned forward eagerly. "We'll show them the watch Brother Al gave us and tell them we're the goddesses they've been waiting for." She grinned confidently.

Captain Kidd's expression darkened. His disapproving gaze cut through her excitement. "And what will you say when they ask what happened to him?" His eyes bore into hers. "Tell them he was taken by a goddess?"

Annabelle's grin faltered. She looked away, realizing how ridiculous her plan sounded when said aloud.

Sophie wiped sweat from her face with her sleeve. "We tell them the truth," she said simply. "Something tells me they'll know if we lie."

"Yeah," Regina agreed. "Brother Albert knew almost everything about us. He must've kept notes or records."

Annabelle shifted uncomfortably. "He did blow up his book," she admitted. "He wrote in that thing a lot... but now it's gone."

Lisa sniffled, tears welling in her eyes at the mention of Brother Albert.

Annabelle rolled her eyes. "So, what's the plan, Cap'n?"

"To get to Order Island, we'll have to sail past a checkpoint station," Captain Kidd said, mimicking the Stormfang's path with his hand, guiding it toward a cup in a special holder on the table. "First sign of trouble, we hit full engines, quick as we can, and get out of their gun range. After that..." He trailed off for a moment. "Then we get you girlies home." His gaze lingered on Regina and Lisa before shifting to Sophie. "Or..."

Sophie's face crumpled as tears slipped down her cheeks. Images of her mother and friends lying dead in the streets of her ruined village flashed through her mind. "I guess... I'll just go to another Aurorium village," she whispered, her voice cracking.

Captain Kidd rubbed his chin thoughtfully. "Sorry, love. I know those wounds are still fresh." His tone softened before he cleared his throat and refocused. "Back to the plan; when we land at the checkpoint, stay close to the ship."

"Ten-minute rule?" Annabelle asked, tilting her head.

"Aye," Kidd confirmed with a nod. "We've got a standing rule for places like Verdantia, where they arrest first and ask questions later."

"What the Cap'n means," Annabelle explained to Regina and Lisa, "is don't go any further than you can run back to the ship in ten minutes." She exchanged a knowing look with him.

Kidd leaned back with a sigh. "A little blunt, but yes." He glanced out the window, his eyes narrowing. "Those guys around Order Island have shredded ships bigger and fiercer than the Fang without breaking a sweat. Ten minutes will be pushing it."

Annabelle studied Kidd carefully. She'd seen him worried before, when they *found* things that didn't sit right or when passengers smelled like trouble but he rarely mapped things out this meticulously unless he was truly concerned. The realization gnawed at her, unease creeping in.

Lisa sniffled and dabbed her eyes with a handkerchief from her purse. "We should trust them," she said softly. "Just like we trusted Brother Albert... He said they wouldn't hurt us."

"Your lips to the Goddess' ears, love," Kidd said with a wry smile. He straightened up and cracked his knuckles. "We'll be at the checkpoint in a few hours. You lasses should freshen up, look your best."

A sharp knock on the door made them all turn.

"Come in," the captain called.

The door creaked open, and Jeffie, the ship's cook, stuck his head in. "excuse me, Cap'n," he said, eyes darting nervously around the room. "I was wonderin' if your meetin's about done?"

Kidd's eyes narrowed. "What is it to ye, Jeffie? Spit it out."

Jeffie fidgeted. "Cap'n... I was hopin' the green ma'am could help with lunch." He gave Lisa a sheepish look. "The crew loves her cookin'."

Kidd's scowl deepened. "Maybe I should give 'er your cut for this sail, since she's doin' all the cookin'." His voice slipped into his deep pirate patois, a clear sign his patience was wearing thin.

Annabelle stiffened. She knew that tone well. When Kidd slipped into patois, someone was about to get chewed out.

Jeffie paled and stammered, "Aye, Cap'n," before retreating and closing the door behind him with a soft click.

Lisa bit her lip, feeling bad for Jeffie; then remembered the dishwater soup from the day before. "If it is alright, I think I will go help him with lunch."

Kidd's expression softened slightly. "Careful what you give away for free, missy. Some folks... they like to take advantage."

Lisa smiled. "Purely self-interest, Captain." She stood, smoothing her dress before following Jeffie out.

Kidd chuckled, shaking his head. "Go on, lasses. Get ready, you should look your best when you meet with the Order."

[-----✝-----]

Marcus had finished reading *The Guide's Manual* the night before, just before sleep finally claimed him. Though the book held a wealth of knowledge, it was the Ten Tenets that truly defined the role of a Guide, each one a cornerstone of his duty to the Avatars.

- **"You are their servant, but not their slave."**

This tenet drew a crucial boundary: while the guide was meant to serve the avatars, there would be times when their requests could not, or should not, be fulfilled. His role was not to grant every desire.

- **"You are to nurture their purpose, even when you do not understand it."**
The manual urged Marcus to provide the avatars with knowledge, tools, and support, even when their purpose seemed unclear or beyond his understanding. He was to prepare them for what lay ahead, whether they asked for it or not.

- **"Yours is to observe, silently."**
This one came easily to Marcus. He was to remain vigilant but unobtrusive, learning all he could to better support the Avatars without interference. Silence was not only encouraged, but it is also expected.

- **"Your aid is to be unwavering."**
At first, this tenet seemed to contradict the first. How could his help be unwavering without becoming a slave? But the manual clarified: his assistance was to be absolute when the Avatars *needed* something, not when they merely *wanted* it. The difference was critical. He was to give what was essential, regardless of personal cost, to himself, the Order, or even the world.

- **"It is yours to seek their balance."**
This tenet served as a warning. The Avatars would wield immense power after communing with their goddess. Marcus was not just their support; he was their anchor. His task was to guide them, to keep them from falling into corruption.

- **"It is yours to provide clarity."**
Honesty was essential. He was never to lie or withhold the truth, even when it hurt. Clarity, the manual said, is the root of trust.

- **"It is yours to become of them."**
This tenet struck Marcus deeply. He was to adapt himself to the Avatars, not force them to change for him. Whatever they need, he is to become.

- **"It is yours to serve in silence."**
Recognition was never to be his. Praise was to be deflected; glory, refused. His work would remain unseen and unsung.

- **"It is yours to represent true faith and allegiance."**
At first glance, this felt redundant; his loyalty was already assumed. But the manual explained: he must serve the avatars' best interests at all times, even when his own desires or ambitions tried to interfere. His faith and service are absolute.

- **"In the face of evil, it is yours to sacrifice."**
This final tenet unsettled him the most. If one, or all, of the Avatars strayed from their path, consumed by power or darkness, it would be his responsibility to stop them. Even if it meant killing them. The weight of that burden pressed heavily on his chest, haunting him through the sleepless hours of the night.

[-----✝-----]

Marcus sat in the Order's cafeteria, stirring his oatmeal, blueberries dotting the bowl, while nibbling on two slices of toast and sipping from a much-needed cup of coffee. Under normal circumstances, he would have made sure to get a full eight hours of rest before an assignment as crucial as guiding the avatars. But last night didn't allow it. Too much reading, too many details to absorb before the ship carrying Brother Albert's watch arrived at the receiving house near Order Island. *Four hours of sleep will have to do.*

If he couldn't recharge with rest, he'd settle for food and strong coffee.

Just as he took another spoonful of oatmeal, a sharp flick on his ear made him flinch. He turned to find Sister Sallie standing behind him, balancing a tray that held a bowl of fruit salad and a steaming cup of jasmine tea, her morning ritual. She'd made it clear, more than once, that her day didn't officially begin until she had her jasmine tea.

"Sister Sallie," Marcus greeted after swallowing.

Sallie slid into the seat beside him and fixed him with a sharp look. "Don't *Sister Sallie* me," she huffed. "Why didn't you tell me you were going to be the new guide for the avatars?"

"I didn't know," Marcus replied. "I found out after we spoke at breakfast yesterday." He shook his head, surprised at how far away that morning already felt after everything that had happened since.

Sallie took a thoughtful sip of her tea. "Did you hear who they picked as your first assistant?"

Marcus hesitated, deciding to test the accuracy of the Order's gossip mill. "No, not yet," he lied casually.

Sallie leaned in, lowering her voice. "Some map maker from the Conclave," she whispered, clearly unimpressed. "Why wouldn't they pick someone with actual experience?"

Marcus gave a noncommittal shrug, though inwardly, he questioned the choice himself. "We have to trust the Council," he said, repeating the words as if trying to convince himself. "They always make the right decisions for the Order."

"I guess," Sallie muttered, stirring her fruit salad. "You're going to have your work cut out for you, that's for sure."

Marcus smiled, falling back on a familiar phrase. "I live to serve the Order."

Sallie snorted at his recitation of the code.

Marcus leaned back. "What's going on with you, anyway? What's the College of Sages up to?"

"Boring things," Sallie said flatly. "We're evaluating a new collection of magical tools to see if they can be used for anything beyond their intended purpose." She popped a piece of watermelon into her mouth.

"That sounds interesting," Marcus said, leaning in. "What are you working on today?"

Sallie smirked. "A hand shovel that supposedly breaks up tough ground. I'm going to see if it can chop down trees... maybe even try it on water."

Marcus grinned at her enthusiasm. Part of him longed for the simplicity of his old research work with the Astral Observers. But those days were gone, and fate had led him to a far greater task.

"What?" Sallie asked, narrowing her eyes. "Why are you looking at me like that?"

"No reason," Marcus said with a chuckle. "Just jealous of your shovel work."

Sallie shook her head with a smile. "Brother Marcus, you are a strange bird sometimes."

"You wound me, Sister." Marcus stood, gathering his tray. "Do your best today."

"You too, Brother," Sallie replied, turning back to her breakfast.

Marcus carried his tray to the counter, handing it off to one of the kitchen brothers before heading into the hallway. He decided to get an update on the ship's location before returning to the cluttered mess of his new office.

Walking briskly, Marcus turned right past the storage closet and auditorium, then climbed the stairs leading to the observatory. At the top, he expected to explain himself to the brother guarding the door, but to his surprise, the man simply opened it and said, "Welcome, Brother Marcus. Please go in."

Stepping inside, Marcus took in the familiar sight: younger brothers and sisters hunched over machines and magical maps, furiously scribbling notes into their journals. What he hadn't expected was Sister Ingrid seated at the large meeting table, her eyes fixed on a small map board, with Brother Timothy beside her.

"Brother Marcus," Timothy greeted warmly. "Please, have a seat."

Marcus glanced at Ingrid, who offered him an approving smile. Taking the cue, he sat down and pulled his journal from its sling, ready to take notes.

"I was just explaining to Sister Ingrid that the ship carrying the watch is only a few hours from the receiving house," Timothy said, pointing to the map. A small black dot marked the ship's position, inching closer to another black mark, the Order's designated docking point.

Marcus studied the map briefly before asking, "Have we received any updates from the Aurorium Clan about Granmark?"

Brother Timothy shook his head. "Not yet. I don't expect any news for quite some time."

"I imagine they're busy sorting through what happened," Sister Ingrid said, her voice calm but thoughtful. "Have you learned anything more about the ship itself?"

"Yes, Sister. We've confirmed it is in fact the *Stormfang*, as you suspected." Brother Timothy replied. "But at this range, we can't verify who's aboard."

"Of course, Brother," Ingrid said, making a quick note in her journal. She looked up. "One more question, if you have time?"

Brother Timothy nodded.

"Can you tell me where Salazar's ship, the *Stormfang*, was before it docked in Granmark?"

Timothy frowned in thought. "I don't have that information readily available, but let me check something." He stood and walked over to a tall bookshelf lined with worn journals. His fingers skimmed the spines until he found what he needed, flipping through the pages. Satisfied, he returned it and pulled down another, repeating the process until he finally nodded and brought the last journal back to the table.

Sliding into his seat, Timothy glanced between Ingrid and Marcus. "I can confirm that the *Stormfang* traveled from Granmark to the Stoneridge port of Steelhaven before returning to Granmark."

"Thank you, Brother," Ingrid said with a polite nod. She stood, gathering her things.

Marcus followed suit, and the two left the observatory, passing the brother stationed at the door. As they walked down the hallway toward the stairs, Marcus mulled over the new information. He could feel Ingrid's eyes on him; a subtle reminder of the warning she'd given him yesterday. He cleared his mind, careful not to reveal anything through an unguarded expression or careless word in the Order's public corridors.

Descending the stairs, his thoughts drifted to Sister Sallie's enchanted hand shovel. *I wonder what kind of magic it actually uses;* he mused. As they passed the cafeteria, he spotted Sallie stepping out, finishing her morning routine. They exchanged a silent wave, an unspoken ritual, before continuing on their respective paths.

Arriving at Marcus's new, cluttered office, they entered through separate doors, Marcus from the front, Ingrid from the rear. They met in the middle of the room, surrounded by scattered reports and half-unpacked boxes.

"So," Ingrid began, folding her arms, "Salazar's ship is bringing the watch to the island." She gave Marcus a pointed look. "What does that say to you?"

Marcus leaned against the desk, weighing his response. "The only thing it confirms is that Salazar and Brother Albert crossed paths." He paused. "It suggests Albert made first contact with Salazar, and we can assume he reached all four of the girls." He exhaled slowly. "What we don't know is how deeply the Conspiracy factored into the events that led to him destroying his journal."

"That's the big question," Ingrid agreed.

Marcus straightened, rubbing his chin. "I should prepare to meet the *Stormfang* when it arrives at the receiving house."

Ingrid nodded. "If the girls are on board, I'll leave it to your judgment whether to make first contact."

"We need a signal in case there's trouble," Marcus added, already working through contingencies.

"Agreed," Ingrid said firmly.

[----- ⚓ -----]

After a quick shower, Annabelle dressed in her best tights, paired with sturdy boots and a crisp white shirt. She tied a red bandana behind her head, covering her forehead and the top of her hair. Confident she'd be leaving the ship; she slipped into her favorite blue jacket, the comfortable fabric hugging her like an old friend. Smiling to herself, she made her way toward the bridge.

On the way, she passed the galley, where Lisa and Jeffie were cleaning up after lunch service. Lisa glanced up, and Annabelle gave her a quick wave before continuing on.

Arriving on the bridge, she spotted Sophie working with the deckhands, dressed in her purple pants and undershirt. *Her shirt and vest are probably stashed somewhere nearby,* Annabelle mused. Turning toward the helm, she greeted Captain Kidd.

"Afternoon, Cap'n."

"Afternoon," he replied, giving her a quick once-over. "Ye look nice."

Annabelle grinned. "Where's Regina?" she asked, already wondering if she'd have to help the girl get ready.

The captain squinted at her, then smirked. "Regina, huh?" he said, shaking his head. "I put her with Sparks. She had some idea about the engines… or storms… or sunlight, honestly, I don't know."

Annabelle chuckled. "That girl sure can talk." As she spoke, her gaze drifted toward the approaching landmass; Order Island loomed large in the distance.

Despite its name, Order Island wasn't a single island but an archipelago, hemmed in by towering mountains that formed a protective semicircle, like a mother's arms cradling her children. On the largest island, a massive gray fortress jutted into the sky, its imposing square silhouette rising from green-draped forests like a gauntlet clenched around the land. Just beyond the mountain border, an artificial island held a pier with seven slips, standing like guards at the gateway to the archipelago.

Every pirate and privateer knew to fear Order Island.

Occasionally, some foolish ship would attempt a raid, lured by rumors of the riches hidden within. But the fortress cannons, and the artillery stationed along the mountainsides, would tear them to splinters. Anyone who didn't drown would be dragged off to the coppers and locked in a jail cell.

Annabelle cast a glance at the captain. He was so tense. She had seen him uneasy before, but he rarely took the helm himself. Steering was usually left to Smitty, or the runner, or even Annabelle. When Kidd insisted on taking the wheel personally, it meant he was worried.

Her gaze swept the deck until it landed on Smitty, overseeing the crew as they secured tools and assembled the wooden planks for the gangway. He brings a steady presence, directing everything with his usual calm efficiency.

"Runner!" Captain Kidd's voice rang out.

Gimble appeared at the foot of the stairs leading to the bridge, eyes locked attentively on the captain.

"Go and tell the silver lass in the workshop and the green lass in the galley to come to the bridge," Kidd ordered, never looking away from the helm. "In that order, silver first, then green."

"Aye, Captain!" Gimble said, sprinting down the stairs toward the workshop.

[----- ✿ -----]

In Sparks' workshop, Regina sat at a table, frustration etched across her face.

"There has to be a way," she muttered.

Sparks leaned back in his chair, arms crossed. "Aye, missy, there's always a way," he said with a grin. "The question is, can we do it with what we've got?"

Regina sighed, scanning the workshop again. Along the far wall, she spotted shelves packed with labeled containers, screws, nuts, nails. At the bottom, a larger drawer held wires and cables, though she still wasn't sure what the difference was.

"Ye just need to train yer eyes," Sparks said, tapping his temple. "Then ye won't need so much light to see."

Regina shook her head stubbornly. "I know there's a way."

A knock at the door cut her off. Gimble poked his head in. "excuse me, silver miss. The captain has called ye to the bridge."

"Okay, thanks!" Regina said, flashing him a smile.

As Gimble retreated, she pulled her shaker from her pocket and gave it a quick shake to make the rocks inside glow. "Bye, Mr. Sparks," she called.

"Goodbye, silver missy," Sparks replied with a wave. "Good luck."

[----- ✿ -----]

Meanwhile, in the galley, Lisa and Jeffie were cleaning up. Jeffie scrubbed the dishes while Lisa dried them, both working over a special water pot with engraved runes on the lid. Jeffie activated it with a swipe of his finger, keeping the water hot inside and contained.

"And another one," Jeffie teased, handing Lisa another bowl.

"Oh no," Lisa replied with a playful smile, drying it and placing it in the cabinet.

After a moment, Jeffie glanced over at her curiously. "If I can ask, Ma'am... how'd ye learn to cook so well?"

Lisa chuckled. "Well, in Verdantia it is a woman's duty to take care of the home," she said, accepting another bowl from him. "So, from the time I was eight, my father had me working in the kitchen with the staff."

"Really?" Jeffie asked, handing over another dish.

Lisa nodded. "Oh yes. The staff were wonderful, but my father made sure they did not cut me any slack." She smiled at the memory. "I did everything, chopping vegetables, making bread, prepping for dinner service."

"Wow," Jeffie said, clearly impressed.

Just then, Gimble's voice echoed from the seating area. "Miss green lass! The captain wants ye on the bridge."

Lisa called back, "Alright, I am on my way." She turned to Jeffie with a grin. "Goodbye, Mr. Jeffie."

She hung her towel neatly over a metal bar, tying it in a knot before heading toward the bridge.

[-----⊕-----]

Sophie worked alongside the deck crew, helping to assemble the gangplank. She found it impressive how seamlessly the pieces fit together, each component roughly a king's reach. She had tested it earlier, stretching her arm from the center of her chest to the tips of her fingers.

Though wooden, the gangplank sections were crafted with clear purpose. Each one snapped securely into the next, extending the structure bit by bit. Once fully assembled, a rope was threaded through holes along the bottom, knotted at the end to keep it from slipping through. The crew then pulled the pieces tight, feeding the rope through holes at the top of a sturdy pillion and leaving enough slack to tie it off to an interior cleat.

"Sophie Griffin!" Captain Kidd's voice boomed from the helm. "Time to get yer clothes on."

"Yes, Captain!" she called back, nodding to Smitty as she stepped away from the crew and made her way up to the bridge.

Along the way, she passed Annabelle and offered a nod. "Annabelle."

"Copper." Annabelle replied with a smirk, nodding back.

Sophie entered Captain Kidd's operations room and quickly slipped on her white collared shirt, straightened her purple tie, and adjusted her purple vest. Finally, she placed her purple hat atop her head and glanced in the mirror for a final check.

It's all your fault.

The whisper crawled through her mind like an insidious shadow. She squeezed her eyes shut and shook her head, forcing the voice away. Then she took a steadying breath and stepped out of the room.

On the bridge, Captain Lowe stood at the helm, expertly guiding the Stormfang into the slip. A man on the pier signaled with white and red flags, each marked by a red lengthwise triangle, guiding the ship with precise movements.

"Cut sails!" Kidd commanded.

The deck crew responded swiftly, pulling the ropes to drop the sails and slow the ship's approach to the pier.

"Alright," the captain muttered, eyes locked on their destination. "Now comes the hard part."

[-----✝-----]

Marcus stood on the pier, watching as a brother from the administration sect expertly guided the *Stormfang* into place. He recognized the ship instantly, Brother Albert had once shown him so many snapshots and pictures of it, he must have spent nearly his entire allowance to obtain these shots. Now, seeing it in person, Marcus felt a creeping unease settle in his chest.

On deck of the ship, a flurry of activity unfolded as the crew worked to lower the sails and assemble the gangplank. Each movement was practiced, efficient. As Marcus observed, another brother from the Overseer's sect approached and stepped up beside him.

"Almost time for answers," the overseer commented.

Marcus glanced at him, trying to recall his name. They had traveled together from the main island, and introductions had been made, but the name slipped his mind. Marcus knew he was responsible for the island's safety and the investigation into Brother Albert's fate. His close-cropped hair barely covered his scalp, a style common among Overseer.

"Yes," Marcus replied, eyes fixed on the approaching ship. "I'm looking forward to seeing what we find."

The brother turned slightly. "How does one become the guide for the goddesses' avatars, anyway?"

Marcus exhaled, folding his arms. "First, you have to be chosen as the First Assistant," he explained, then hesitated. He was always cautious about what information circulated within the Order. "I was appointed by the Council, but when I asked why they chose me... they never gave me an answer."

"Oh," the brother mused. "And which sect did you serve before?"

Marcus shrugged. "Most recently, the Astral Observers. Before that, I worked with the Ethnographers' Union." He glanced over. "But, as I said, I was never told why they picked me."

"The wisdom of Saint Lorraine," the brother intoned solemnly.

The ship eased into the slip, and the gangplank extended smoothly onto the pier. The directing brother set down his flags and secured the gangplank to the metal rings embedded in the dock.

Marcus took a calming breath. "May the goddesses grant me grace," he muttered before stepping forward. The Overseer Sect brother kept pace beside him, leaning in as they approached the ship.

"You should let me speak first," he said in a low voice. "I know how to deal with these *pirate* types."

"As you wish," Marcus agreed, still trying to recall the man's name.

Stepping onto the deck, Marcus took in the bustling scene, crew members tying down ropes, securing equipment, and organizing supplies. But it was the figures near the helm that truly caught his attention.

There they are.

To the right, behind the wheel, stood Annabelle Salazar, her fiery orange hair hanging down to her shoulders, a red bandana tied across her forehead. She wore her signature oversized blue jacket and carried herself with unmistakable confidence. To her left, Sophie Griffin stood in her violet Aurorium plain clothes uniform, her rank badge gleaming, and a long-billed fedora perched neatly atop her head.

At the foot of the stairs leading to the bridge stood Regina Fournier, dressed in a black dress and white shirt, round glasses perched on her nose, and shoulder length curly silver hair cascading down. Beside her stood Lisa Nozaki, her green hair pulled into a ponytail, wearing a well-worn white sundress smudged with travel dirt.

All four looked exhausted, their expressions bearing the weight of whatever trials they'd endured.

The Overseer Sect brother stepped forward. "Good morning, everyone," he announced. "I am Brother Todd of the Order of Saint Lorraine."

Marcus committed the name to memory. *Brother Todd.*

Brother Todd continued, "What business do you have with the Order today?"

"Oi!" Annabelle's voice rang out across the deck. "yer doin' it wrong!" she called, exasperated. "You always ask permission to come aboard first!"

Todd flushed slightly. "I apologize," he said, clearing his throat. "May we come aboard your... boat—?"

"*Boat?!*" Annabelle's voice cut through the air like a whip.

Before she could launch into a full tirade, Captain James "Kidd" Lowe stepped in, gently tapping her shoulder. "Please," he said in a calm but firm tone, "the two of you, come up to my operations room so we can speak." Motioning to the set of double doors behind the bridge.

Annabelle's irritation simmered beneath the surface, but she knew better than to challenge the captain, her adoptive father, when he was in a mood. With a sigh, she turned and made her way inside, followed closely by Regina, Lisa, and Sophie.

From the helm, Kidd called out, "Smitty, you have the bridge."

"Aye, Cap'n," Smitty replied, already directing the crew with practiced precision.

Marcus watched Todd closely as they made their way across the deck and up the stairs to the bridge. The man still seemed rattled by Annabelle's sharp tongue. Marcus couldn't help but recall Brother Albert's words: *Salazar's got teeth. She grew up among pirates and privateers.*

"Are you alright, brother?" Marcus asked quietly.

Todd hesitated. "Yes, oh yes, I'm fine," he said, though his voice betrayed lingering unease.

Inside the captain's operations room, the four girls were already seated, with Captain Kidd at the head of the table. The room smelled of sea breeze, rum, and old inked papers, its atmosphere thick with anticipation. Two empty chairs awaited Marcus and Todd, positioned between Sophie Griffin and the captain himself.

"Welcome, welcome," Lowe said with an easy smile. "Please, gentlemen, have a seat."

Marcus and Todd sat down, both pulling their journals from their slings. As expected, Todd chose the seat closest to the captain, while Marcus settled in beside Sophie.

Once seated, Todd leaned forward. "As I asked before," he said, trying to regain his composure, "what brings you to Order Island?"

Sophie hesitated, unsure where to begin.

Regina fidgeted with her hands, uncertain how to explain their story.

Lisa, filled with worry, doubted whether their tale would even sound believable. How much should they share? Where should they start?

"We, sir, are the goddesses ye've been lookin' fer," Annabelle declared suddenly, breaking the silence. "Brother Al got us together and told us we were goddesses, and that the Order would help us stop that Isabella hussy."

The room fell into stunned silence. Eyes widened in disbelief, some in horror.

"He never said we were goddesses," Regina corrected quickly, her voice firm. "He said we were blessed by the goddesses."

Sophie let out an exasperated sigh, shaking her head and covering her face with one hand. "Seriously, what is wrong with you, Annabelle?"

Annabelle crossed her arms defensively. "What do ye know? Ye left, remember?"

"I know he didn't tell us we were goddesses," Sophie snapped back.

Across the table, Brother Todd leaned in. "Brother Al... who is that?"

Marcus watched him closely. Was Todd genuinely unaware, or just pretending? It was hard to tell. Marcus stayed silent, giving Todd space to ask his questions without interference.

"Ye know, Brother Al," Annabelle said casually. "Old guy, gray hair, liked to drink ale."

Lisa wiped at her eyes. "His name was Brother Albert," she whispered, voice cracking. "Brother Albert Thompson." Tears welled up again as the painful memories returned. She buried her face in her hands, shoulders shaking with quiet sobs.

Regina placed a comforting hand on Lisa's shoulder and gave it a gentle rub.

Captain Lowe, sensing the unraveling emotions, cleared his throat. "Maybe we should start over," he suggested. His sharp gaze landed on Annabelle, a silent message: *Not you.*

Regina tapped Lisa's back reassuringly, then took a deep breath and began. "About a week ago, I received a letter from Brother Albert at the Main Library of the Scholars, where my family is on maintenance duty. The letter asked me to travel to Granmark with a sunlight spell and deliver a message to Annabelle." She paused, gathering her thoughts. "The day before yesterday, I went to Granmark and found Annabelle about to be killed by the Witch named Mage."

"Oi!" Annabelle protested. "I wasn't *about* to die."

Sophie let out a soft laugh, despite her lingering tears. "I don't know, you showed up bloody and beat up. If Lisa hadn't been there, you'd probably be with the goddesses right now."

Annabelle waved a dismissive hand. "Bah, what do you know?"

Captain Lowe tapped the table twice, his fingers drumming with quiet authority. Annabelle fell silent beneath his stern glare.

"Please, missy," he said, turning back to Regina. "Continue."

Regina touched her finger to her lips, thinking. "Right…where was I? Oh. So, I had a letter for Annabelle from Brother Albert. It told us to go to West's Tavern. When we got there, he said we were blessed by the goddesses. He even proved it with some delicious tea." She paused, smiling faintly at the memory. "Then Sophie and Annabelle got into a fight. Sophie stormed off, said she had to get home and that her clan would handle any problems."

Sophie stared down at the table. That felt like a lifetime ago. She'd gone home expecting comfort, but instead found only icy death and destruction. Her mother and friends, gone. Her village, in ruins. Tears spilled down her cheeks, and she wiped them away quickly.

Regina's voice softened. "After that, Brother Albert sent Annabelle to book our passage on this ship. While she was gone, Sophie found her village destroyed by someone using freezing magic. And Isabella... that Mechana-Mage... they killed everyone."

Regina reached out and placed a gentle hand on Sophie's trembling shoulder. "I'm so sorry, Sophie."

Sophie nodded, unable to speak, hiding her face in her hands.

Regina pressed on. "That night, Brother Albert woke Lisa and me. Isabella attacked us with a group of men Granmark. At first, it looked like we were winning... but then Isabella's metal monster..." She stopped, took a breath. "It hurt Brother Albert so badly that Lisa... Lisa couldn't heal him with her magic."

Lisa's quiet sobs intensified as the weight of her failure crashed down again. "I'm sorry," she whispered.

Regina rubbed her back gently. "You did everything you could," she said softly. Then, continuing: "After that, Brother Albert made us promise to hurry to the Stormfang. He

143

gave Annabelle his watch so we could enter Order Island and find Brother Marcus Igbinedion." She glanced at Marcus. "Then... he created a diversion for Isabella. Used himself as bait. He took two of Sophie's firebombs and... detonated them, sacrificing himself to stop her."

A heavy silence filled the room.

Regina finally finished. "After that, we ran from that shadow witch Mage and made it to the ship. We set sail for Order Island... and now we're here."

Marcus sat back in his chair, dazed by the weight of it all. The puzzle pieces were falling into place...but there were still so many gaps. He was grateful Brother Todd had taken the lead in questioning; it gave him time to absorb everything... and compare it to the reports the Order had already gathered.

"You mentioned he gave you a watch too..." Brother Todd said, his eyes settling on Annabelle. "Anna?"

"*Aye, Annabelle,*" she corrected, pulling the watch from her pocket and sliding it across the table.

Marcus recognized it immediately, *Brother Albert's watch.* Stained with blood. He had seen it countless times before. It was an older model; Marcus had often asked why he never replaced it, and Albert would always brush him off, saying he was too busy for such menial things. Besides, the old watch worked just fine, even if he had to wrestle with the button to open it and wind it daily to keep it accurate.

Brother Todd picked it up and examined the worn surface. He pressed the button at the top...nothing. He frowned and tried again. Still, the watch refused to open, almost as if rejecting unfamiliar hands.

Unable to watch him struggle, Marcus offered a quiet suggestion. "The catch is a bit tricky. Try winding it a little first."

Todd glanced at him, unsure, but with everyone watching, he gave it a small turn and pressed the button again. This time, the face popped open with a soft click. The hands on the face were frozen at 3:45.

Marcus frowned. Was it AM or PM? There was no way to tell. Newer models, like the one in his pocket, had tiny sun-and-moon dials to indicate day or night. Alberts didn't.

Captain Lowe, leaning back in his chair, broke the silence. "So, gentlemen... where do we go from here?"

Brother Todd scribbled in his journal for a moment before glancing up. "Well... that would be up to Brother Marcus." He gestured toward him.

Regina blinked. "*Oh You're Brother Marcus?*"

"I am," Marcus said evenly. "Brother Albert was my mentor."

"Aye, that was easy," Annabelle quipped, leaning back in her chair.

Sharp glances from Captain Lowe and the others quickly shut her up.

Marcus cleared his throat. "I have some questions of my own, if you are finished, Brother Todd?"

"Just one more," Todd replied, finishing his notes. "Do you know what happened to Brother Albert's body?"

A heavy silence fell over the room. The girls looked down, the question settling over them like a weight.

Finally, Sophie spoke, her voice soft and strained. "We can't be sure... His plan was to detonate his journal using a magic ritual. That would trigger the two fire grenades I gave him, creating a much larger explosion." She wiped at her tears. "Since the plan was for us to run to the ship immediately, there was no chance to recover his body."

"So... he could still be alive?" Todd asked carefully.

Sophie shook her head. "Doubt it. The explosion was massive. I'd be surprised if the wall we propped him against is even still standing."

Marcus listened carefully. He recalled Albert's reports on Sophie, a prodigy of the Aurorium Clan who had achieved the rank of Sentinel in just one year. Most initiates took two or three. Albert had speculated that her connection to the violet goddess gave her an edge, though the Order never had access to the clan's exact testing methods.

Her knowledge of explosives likely came from her father, a legendary Eclipse named Oscar Griffin known as *The Seeker* famous for using any means necessary to complete his missions. If Sophie said the explosion destroyed everything in its path, Marcus had every reason to trust her.

Todd's voice cut into his thoughts. "What did you mean when you said you *propped up* his body?"

Lisa, still fighting tears, managed to speak. "Isabella's mechanical monster... it grabbed him. Mangled him so badly." Her throat caught. "I... I tried to save him, but I didn't have enough mana to heal all his wounds."

Annabelle nodded solemnly. "Aye, he was in rough shape looked like he'd danced with a shark." She wiped a tear from the corner of her orange eyes.

"So yeah," Sophie murmured, her voice hollow. "I'm sure he isn't alive."

Brother Todd leaned back, rubbing his chin in thought. "He *got involved?*" His brow furrowed. "Members of the Order of Saint Lorraine are sworn to passively observe and record. Interfering directly... that's highly irregular."

Marcus absorbed the words in silence. It was true, the Order operated in neutrality. They were record keepers and historians, not warriors. But Albert had run afoul of rules and conducts standards more often than he'd like to admit. He did what he believed was right, not just what doctrine allowed.

"It makes sense to me," Marcus said, breaking the tension. "One of the tenets of the guide speaks to giving everything for the avatars."

Todd jotted more notes, then looked up. "Captain, where was the *Stormfang* before it docked at Granmark a few days ago?"

"We had a run to Stoneridge," Captain Kidd replied. "Cargo to transport. The client only paid half up front, so we had to sail back immediately to collect the rest."

"Can you tell me who your customer was?" Marcus asked.

"Aye," Annabelle chimed in without hesitation. "A shop owner named Aaron."

Marcus made a mental note of their transparency. *They are being honest,* he thought.

He turned his gaze to Sophie. "Miss Griffin, what were you doing before you met with Brother Albert?"

Sophie hesitated. "I had a bodyguard mission for Viceroy Lonergan," she said carefully. "I was attacked by a group led by that same ugly old man who showed up at the tavern that night."

Marcus leaned forward, eyes narrowing as he studied the group. "Ladies, indulge me for a moment," he said, his tone shifting. His gaze swept across each of them—Sophie, in her violet Aurorium colors; Annabelle, vibrant in orange and blue; Lisa, green ponytail neat despite her travel-worn dress; and Regina, the silver-haired scholar with quiet resolve.

"Sophie," he asked, "what do you think of Annabelle?"

Sophie glanced at Annabelle, lips curling slightly. "She's... a bit much. And kind of a bully." She paused, then added, "But she's also... kind ... sometimes."

"Oi," Annabelle huffed, raising a fist in mock threat. "I'll show ye a bully."

Marcus ignored the exchange and turned to Annabelle. "Miss Salazar, what are your thoughts on Lisa?"

Annabelle leaned back with a smirk. "Oh, the princess?" she said, crossing her arms. "Well, she thinks the sun shines outta her backside... but I gotta admit, she can cook."

"Hey!" Lisa snapped, glaring at her.

Annabelle shrugged with a playful grin.

Marcus shifted his focus. "Lisa, what do you think of Regina?"

Lisa glanced at the silver-haired girl. "She talks a lot," she said with a sigh. "Always asking about people's magic. Constantly."

Regina blinked, clearly confused. "I...I just like learning," she murmured, lowering her gaze.

Marcus nodded, then turned to Regina. "Regina, what are your thoughts on Sophie?"

Regina shifted uncomfortably. "She's... really scary," she admitted. "I always worry I'll say something that makes her punch me. Or shoot me. Or something." She paused, thinking. "But she's amazing in a fight. She kept us safe after Brother Albert... I think she works too much. To avoid thinking about her village."

Sophie, touched but amused, adjusted her hat with a grin. "I would never shoot you," she said with a smirk, leaving the other possibility open.

Marcus watched the exchange with a faint smile. *This is exactly what he was looking for.* If these girls were part of a conspiracy, planted in the Order like hidden weapons, they would've been too perfect, with no friction, no real personalities. But these four were different people, clashing, connecting, and somehow managing to survive together.

"Thank you for indulging me, ladies," Marcus said finally. "I needed to be sure you were safe."

Captain Kidd frowned. "*They* were safe?" he echoed, eyes narrowing.

"Yes," Marcus replied. "There's much going on, and much we must do." He turned to Brother Todd. "My apologies, Brother Todd, but this is where I leave you."

Todd's eyes widened. "What? Why do you have to leave me here?"

Marcus remained calm. "The avatars and I have much to discuss." He gestured toward the docks. "You still need to file your report at the receiving house, and time is of the essence."

Todd hesitated, clearly unsettled. After a pause, he closed his journal and stood. "Thank you all for sharing with me," he said, reciting the Order's formal farewell. He then turned to Marcus and nodded. "May all be well, Brother."

Marcus nodded back. "May all be well, Brother."

As Todd exited the operations room, Marcus became acutely aware of the four girls watching him. Their expressions were a blend of curiosity, suspicion, and expectation. Captain Lowe, too, was studying him, weighing his every move.

Marcus hadn't been under this much scrutiny in years.

He silently recalled the contingency plans he and Sister Ingrid had prepared in case the *Stormfang* was compromised. If the ship posed a threat, he would dive overboard, drawing enemy attention while Ingrid turned the fortress cannons on it, destroying the vessel and eliminating everyone aboard.

But if he found no threat... he would remain on the ship and ride it safely into the docks.

He turned to face the waiting crew.

"Captain," Marcus said, addressing Kidd, "you may proceed to the main pier. Dock at spot three please."

"Aye," Kidd replied, pushing back his chair and heading for the bridge.

Once the door shut behind him, Marcus looked at the girls. "How much did Brother Albert share with you before…" he paused, carefully choosing his words. "Before everything happened?"

"Well," Annabelle began, "he told us—"

"Please don't," Sophie cut in, glaring at Annabelle. "He didn't tell us we were goddesses."

"He *did* tell us," Lisa added hesitantly, "that the Order has been watching us for a long time."

Marcus nodded. "We have. Or rather, Brother Albert was," he admitted. "The Order deals in information, and Albert was a master at using it." He leaned back, thoughtful. "He once said there had to be a great danger coming…something big. Normally, there's one, maybe two avatars chosen. But four?" He shook his head. "That's the highest number ever recorded."

The girls exchanged uneasy glances, the weight of the moment settling heavily over them. Until now, none of them had considered that their number might reflect the scale of the looming threat.

"Oh!" Annabelle perked up as a memory surfaced. "I remember Brother Al saying he was our servant."

Marcus smiled. "Yes, girls. You can think of me as your servant too. I'm here to assist you in any way I can."

Annabelle grinned mischievously. "Aye, good. In that case, I've got a list of ship chores that need doing—"

"I'll have to respectfully decline," Marcus said, smiling.

Sophie smirked at Annabelle, enjoying the moment of mild payback.

Marcus steered the conversation back to business. "The first thing you must do is commune with your goddess," he said, recalling the instructions he had read. "Your goddess will complete your blessing and give you guidance."

"I thought we were already blessed?" Lisa asked, frowning in confusion.

Marcus shook his head. "From what I understand, the goddesses granted you part of their blessing at birth. The communion will complete the process while helping you understand your purpose."

The door opened, and Captain Lowe reentered, settling back into his chair. "So, Mr. Marcus," he said, leaning forward, "what does all this goddess business mean for our Belle?"

"Honestly? I wish I knew," Marcus admitted. "We're at the mercy of the goddesses' plans." He sighed. "But I do know the conspiracy is tied to the threat…especially with Isabella and Gretta attacking the Aurorium village."

The mention of the village made Sophie flinch. The memories surged, walking through the ruins, the lifeless bodies of friends, the ice-covered corpses left behind by Isabella's magic. Tears slid down her cheeks before she could stop them.

Marcus immediately regretted the words. *Of course.* She had lived in Aurorium Granmark. She had been the first to witness the massacre.

"Oh, Miss Griffin, I'm so sorry," he said gently.

Sophie wiped her tears away with one hand, lifting the other to stop him. "No. It's fine," she said, voice trembling but firm.

Marcus made a silent note: don't bring it up again unless absolutely necessary. "Even so," he added softly, "you have my deepest condolences. I can't imagine what you've endured these past few days."

"I said it's fine!" Sophie snapped, her voice sharper this time.

147

Annabelle leaned over casually. "She gets like that," she said. "Sometimes it's best to let her be."

Sophie shot her a scowl but didn't respond, choosing instead to look away.

Lowe cleared his throat, breaking the tension. "I hate to bring this up now," he said, "but there's the matter of payment for transporting these fine young lasses."

Marcus straightened in his chair. "Typically, when we book passage, the Order pays half upfront, with the remainder upon arrival. Did Brother Albert manage to cover the deposit?"

Lowe grinned. "He did."

Marcus nodded. "Once I get the girls settled, I'll ensure you're paid in full." He paused, then turned to Annabelle. "Regarding your ship, Miss Salazar, since you'll be a guest of the Order for an indefinite period, what are your plans? Will the *Stormfang* remain docked, or do you intend to rejoin her later?"

Annabelle blinked, the thought hitting her like a rogue wave. *The Stormfang leaving without her?* It hadn't crossed her mind. She glanced at Captain Lowe…the closest thing she had to a father and felt an uneasy knot form in her stomach.

She saw it in his eyes, he is already calculating. A privateer couldn't afford to sit idle; the ship had to work to stay afloat. The coin from Brother Albert would only last so long.

Kidd, sensing her worry, gave her a reassuring smile. "We'll play it by ear," he said gently.

Annabelle let out a breath she hadn't realized she was holding and nodded with a small, grateful smile.

[-----✝-----]

The main pier sat on a smaller island, not too far from the fortress on Order Island proper. Ten slips lined the dock, with a large boathouse standing watch near the entrance. Beyond it, a narrow road passed by the boathouse, curved sharply around the base of the wall, and widened into a sweeping path that led to the towering fortress gates. The entire structure loomed in the distance, silent and imposing, a watchful guardian of the Order's secrets.

Marcus stood on the *Stormfang's* deck as the crew lowered the gangplank again, his thoughts heavy. Brother Albert had likely imagined this moment for years. He'd probably rehearsed his speech to the girls a dozen times, perfecting every word. Now, the burden had shifted to Marcus, and he found himself wondering how he'd keep them focused, without constant bickering.

"Brother Marcus," came Regina's voice behind him. "I'm all ready to go."

He turned to find Regina Fournier standing expectantly, without a single bag in sight. Her round glasses perched on her nose, silver hair spilling to her shoulders, and her black dress worn over a slightly dirty white shirt.

"No baggage?" Marcus asked, raising an eyebrow. "You realize you may not return to the *Stormfang* for some time."

"Oh, I know," she replied brightly. "But I don't have any baggage. I thought I'd be back home the same day I went to Granmark."

Marcus frowned slightly. "So... you've been wearing that dress for the last two days?"

"Yeah," Regina said with a nod. "They only do laundry on the ship every two weeks. I was gonna wait, but then I thought, *what would I wear while it was being washed?*" She tapped a finger thoughtfully against her lips. "Does the Order have laundry? And spare clothes?

I don't have any money, I spent it all on the ticket to Granmark." Her smile faded into concern. "Oh no. Are you going to tell my parents I'm here? Brother Albert's letter said to keep it a secret, but I've been gone for days. My dad's probably worried sick... I bet he'll put me on punishment forever."

Marcus blinked, letting the flood of concerns wash over him before answering with a reassuring smile. "Yes, we have laundry and spare clothes, I'll see to that first thing." Then, considering her family, he added, "And I'll have a message sent to your parents, letting them know you're safe and assisting the Order with an important task."

Regina sighed in relief. "Thanks!" she beamed.

Marcus glanced toward the stairs as Sophie Griffin emerged onto the deck, her rifle slung across her back and a backpack over her shoulder. The dark circles under her eyes betrayed the exhaustion dragging her down. He suspected sleep had been elusive, understandable, given all she had endured. He made a quiet mental note to arrange for her to speak with someone trained to help process such mental trauma.

"Miss Griffin, may I carry something for you?" he offered, extending his arms.

Sophie shook her head. "No, thank you. I'm pretty self-sufficient."

"I see," Marcus said, respecting her space.

Peering over the ship's railing, Marcus spotted the waiting carriage at the pier, just as he had requested: no driver. He'd chosen to take the reins himself, partly for control, partly because the solitude might offer a brief reprieve from their inevitable squabbles.

Lisa Nozaki soon arrived, stepping onto the deck with a cheerful smile. She wore a brown dress adorned with dark blue leaf patterns and carried a white dress in a shopping bag. Her long green hair was tied in a neat ponytail, and a white sunhat shielded her face from the sun.

"Okay, I'm ready to go!" Lisa announced brightly, waving.

"Glad to hear it," Marcus replied warmly. He looked up to the bridge, where Annabelle stood beside Captain Lowe. "As soon as Miss Salazar is ready, we can embark."

From the bridge Annabelle nodded, grabbing her bag and descending the stairs to the main deck. To her surprise, Captain Lowe walked beside her. She assumed he'd simply come to see her off, *he's always been protective like that*. But when they reached the group, Lowe didn't turn to her. Instead, he faced Marcus.

"I hate to do this to you, mate," Captain Lowe said, resting a hand on Annabelle's shoulder, "but I think I have to go with you all. Gotta looks out for me Belle here."

Marcus raised his hands in a placating gesture. "Captain, I assure you the Order has only the best intentions for Miss Salazar." He nodded to the others. "For all the avatars."

Lowe crossed his arms, his gaze drifting toward the fortress. "Oh, I'm sure you do," he said, his voice laced with skepticism. "But she's family. And looking at that place..." He let the sentence trail off before turning back, his expression sharpening. "If something goes wrong, me and the crew wouldn't be able to break in and save her." His eyes locked on Marcus. "So, I'm going to have to insist."

Annabelle shifted, a little embarrassed. She could take care of herself. Still, she couldn't help but feel touched.

Marcus sighed, preparing to argue, but Annabelle cut him off with a grin. "Didn't ye say ye were our servant?"

Marcus blinked. "I did. But I'm not sure how that applies here."

Regina caught on with a sly smile. "Brother Marcus," she said sweetly, "I'd like to request that Captain Kidd accompany us to Order Island."

Marcus stared at her, then exhaled in reluctant acceptance. "As you wish." He straightened and added, "But I assure you, that you are in no danger from the Order."

Turning to Lowe, he extended a hand. "Captain Lowe, it would be my pleasure to host you on Order Island."

Lowe shook his hand with a smirk. "Aye, thanks. Won't be needing a thing we can go now."

The six of them made their way down the gangplank to the pier where the carriage waited. Marcus efficiently loaded Sophie's backpack and Lisa's shopping bag into the roof compartment. Sophie, however, kept her rifle close, gripping it firmly as she climbed into the passenger cabin with the other three girls.

Marcus and Captain Lowe took their seats up front in the driver's box.

"If everyone's ready, we can be off," Marcus called over his shoulder.

"Aye, we're good," came Annabelle's voice from inside.

Marcus glanced at Lowe, who gave him an approving nod. With a flick of the reins, the horses trotted forward, wheels creaking as they began down the road toward the fortress.

For a moment, Marcus debated starting a conversation. Aside from his connection to Annabelle, he realized he knew little about James "Kidd" Lowe. Not wanting to seem cold, he decided to break the silence with a simple question.

"Captain," Marcus began, "how did you get your start as a... pirate?"

Lowe gave him a sharp look. "Privateer, mate," he corrected. "Pirate means criminal to everyone else. We just like working for ourselves, same as a shopkeeper or a farmer." He leaned back slightly, running a hand through his hair. "I reckon my story's the same as most who take to sea."

Marcus listened closely as Lowe continued.

"I grew up poor, and there weren't many opportunities where I came from," Lowe said. "Started out hauling crates for a shopkeeper, just to scrape by. Then one day, I saw a group of men roll into port off a ship. They were laughing, carefree looked freer and happier than anyone I'd ever seen." He chuckled. "I slipped away from the stall and asked what they did. Told me they were privateers."

Lowe sat up straighter and glanced at Marcus. "When I got back, the shopkeeper was so mad I'd disappeared for five minutes, he fired me on the spot. Told me to find my own way home…two hours by carriage from me village." He smirked, shaking his head. "So, I went back to those free men and asked to join their crew." He smiled wistfully. "Never looked back."

Marcus noted Lowe's emphasis on *freedom*. It was clear that it meant everything to him.

"That's an interesting beginning," Marcus said thoughtfully.

Kidd tilted his head. "And you? How did you get started with the Order?"

Marcus's answer came without hesitation. "Like everyone else, I was given to the Order as a baby."

Kidd blinked. "What? You're telling me every member of the Order was just... donated as a baby?"

"Yes," Marcus said plainly. "Every one of us."

Lowe shook his head in amazement. "Why would anyone do that?"

Marcus kept his tone even, he'd answered this question more times than he could count. "Think about it from their perspective. Most families have more children than they can care for. Donating a child to the Order means securing some form of capital, whether that's money, opportunity, or simply relief from another mouth to feed."

"So they sell their children?" Lowe's voice carried a note of restrained outrage.

"It's not that simple," Marcus replied, eyes still on the road.

Lowe frowned, clearly unsettled. "Do you ever get to see your family?"

"The Order *is* my family," Marcus said firm, but smooth. "We break all ties with the family that gave us up. That's how it works for both sides."

Lowe exhaled slowly, letting the information sink in. "That's... a unique situation."

Marcus gave him a sidelong glance. "Is it really so different from being a privateer?" he asked. "Take Annabelle, for example. She was born to Captain Salazar, but she's never met any other family. Captain Salazar must've had brothers, sisters, cousins, even but she'll never meet them." He steered the carriage smoothly along the winding road. "Privateers have their own code. Their own family."

Lowe was quiet for a moment, then nodded slowly. "You may have a point there, Brother Marcus."

[----- ⊕ -----]

Inside the passenger compartment, Annabelle, Regina, Sophie, and Lisa sat quietly, gazing out at the breathtaking scenery of Order Island. Towering mountain walls enclosed the lush landscape, a view they'd never experienced from this perspective before.

"This place is very beautiful," Lisa said, admiring the vista through the window. "I have sailed past here plenty of times, but I never imagined how stunning it would be from the inside."

"Aye," Annabelle agreed, a rare note of appreciation in her voice. "'Tis quite a lovely place."

Sophie, lost in thought, was startled when Regina's voice broke the silence.

"Sophie, can I ask you a question? About your magic?"

Snapping out of a daydream about her mother, Sophie turned to Regina. "Sure, Regina. What's on your mind?"

Regina adjusted her glasses, curiosity lighting up her face. "You said your magic helps you punch, kick, and move faster... but how does that work with shooting fire bullets?"

Lisa groaned and rolled her eyes. "Here we go again," she muttered, turning back to the window.

Sophie shot Lisa a glare, then focused on Regina. "Oh, that." She reached into her jacket and pulled out a single bullet, holding it between her fingers. "Kiroku-Mbili, that's my mom's magic," she explained. "But this," she handed the bullet to Regina, "this is my dad's magic Alrunia."

Regina examined the cartridge closely, noting a symbol etched into the side.

"When I fire the bullet," Sophie continued, "my mana ignites the rune, casting a fire spell that engulfs the bullet in flames."

Intrigued, Regina traced the rune with her fingers, instinctively channeling a small pulse of mana into it. Nothing happened. "How does it work?" she asked, frowning at the unresponsive bullet.

"It's a two-step process," Sophie said. "The rune alone doesn't activate without a special kind of metal. My rifle's and pistol's trigger, are made from that metal. When I pull the trigger, it activates the rune. Boom. Instant fire bullets." She gave her rifle, resting between her legs, a small pat.

Regina's eyes lit up. "Oh, can I see your rifle?"

Sophie smirked. "I'll show you later. It's a bit tight in here."

"So," Regina said, leaning in, "what other runes do you know?"

Sophie's expression dimmed. "Just the fire rune. My dad... he died not long after teaching it to me. And my mom doesn't use this kind of magic, so I didn't get the chance to learn any others."

Annabelle, sensing an opportunity, grinned mischievously. "Sounds like ye got a lot more magic to learn."

"At least I can use magic," Sophie shot back with a glare, crossing her arms.

"Oi, I can do magic!" Annabelle snapped, her orange eyes flashing with annoyance.

Regina tilted her head. "You know... now that I think about it, I haven't actually *seen* you do any magic."

"**I SWEAR TO THE SEA I CAN DO MAGIC!**" Annabelle bellowed, fists clenched.

Lisa smirked. "Well, you *are* yelling pretty loud. You could just, I don't know... do some magic and prove it."

A deep, simmering frustration bubbled inside Annabelle. The teasing, the doubt, it all crashed over her like a wave about to break. *I'll show them,* she thought.

Clapping her hands together, Annabelle closed her eyes, envisioning the ocean swelling inside her. She channeled her mana into her hands, her breathing slow and deliberate.

The other three girls tensed. Sophie and Lisa exchanged uneasy glances, realizing they might have pushed her too far. Regina, meanwhile, watched with bright, eager curiosity, eyes locked on Annabelle.

"Uh... Annabelle," Sophie said carefully. "We're in a carriage."

Lisa, still unconvinced, leaned back in her seat. "It is a trick," she challenged loudly. "She is going to stop any second now and say something like, *I did not feel like it.*"

Annabelle opened her eyes, her lips curling into a wicked grin. "Nay... *I feels like it now.*"

She pulled her hands apart, and a single droplet of water appeared in midair, falling harmlessly to the carriage floor.

Lisa snorted. "All that for a single drop of water?"

Sophie rolled her eyes. "You must not pract..."

Before she could finish, a torrent of water burst from Annabelle's hands, flooding the carriage in an instant.

[-----✝-----]

As the carriage rolled steadily along the winding road, Marcus glanced at Captain Lowe, curiosity finally getting the better of him.

"So, why do you go by the name Kidd?" he asked.

Captain Lowe chuckled. "Ahh, that's a bit of a story," he said, adjusting himself in the chair. "My first Cap'n, Javier Salazar, he never bothered learnin' proper names. He'd just give you a nickname like Hood or Boots, and that's what you'd be forever." Lowe leaned back slightly, the memory bringing a grin to his face. "So, me first day on the *Espada Sovereign*, I'm workin' the deck, tryin' to keep the sails full, but I've got no idea what I'm doin'. Course, the mate who *does* know what he's doin' steps away to, eh... relieve himself."

Lowe chuckled, shaking his head. "Then the wind picks up. Rope starts pullin' harder than a buckin' horse, and me? I panic. Hold on for dear life, thinkin' I can control it." He gestured dramatically. "and oh I was so wrong. Next thing I know, I'm flyin' through the air, danglin' from the mast, holdin' on like my life depends on it 'cause, ye know, it *does*."

Marcus smiled, picturing the scene.

Lowe continued, "Now, Cap'n Salazar, he's steerin' the ship himself. Sees me up there, locks eyes with me, and just says, 'Get him down and bring him to me.'" Lowe smirked. "Turns out, the fellas who signed me on ran a scam. See, *ye don't pay* to crew a ship, *ye get paid*. But they took every coin I had and didn't tell the Cap'n a thing."

Marcus raised an eyebrow. "And what happened next?"

Kidd's smile softened. "Well, the first mate drags me to his cabin. Salazar's sittin' there, bouncin' his little orange-haired daughter on his knee." His expression turned distant. "He looks me over and says, *Yer just a kid, barely older than me own Bella here.* And from that moment on, *Kidd* was my name." He chuckled. "Annabelle must've called me *Kidd* a thousand times a day after that, and when the *Espada Sovereign* was sunk... well, I ended up with Belle, and the name stuck. Cause ye know, I mostly always had a kid wit' me." He glanced at Marcus. "Belle can be a handful sometimes... but bein' wit' Her's been a blessin'. I wouldn't change it fer anything."

Before Marcus could respond, a sudden torrent of water burst from the passenger compartment, spraying from the carriage windows in massive streams.

Marcus immediately pulled the reins, bringing the carriage to a lurching stop. He and Lowe jumped down, rushing to either side of the coach and flinging the doors open.

Sophie and Regina tumbled out the left side, coughing and gasping for breath, while Annabelle and Lisa spilled out the right, landing at Lowe's feet in a sopping heap.

The girls lay on the ground, drenched and panting, as Marcus and Lowe helped them to their feet.

"What in the name of the harvest is wrong with you?!?" Lisa sputtered, wringing out the hem of her soaked dress. She screams "**You could have drowned us, Annabelle!**"

Annabelle, dripping wet and grinning sheepishly, rubbed the back of her head and shruged. "Aye... sorry about that," she said, flashing an apologetic smile. "Guess I don't know me own strength."

"Belle!" Captain Lowe called in a warning tone, arms crossed. "What in the name of sanity were ye doin' now?"

"They kept tellin' me I couldn't do magic!" Annabelle said defensively, pointing at Sophie and Lisa as if she knows Kidd is going to take her side: *How could he not.*

Lowe arched an eyebrow and scowled. "So ye decided to drown 'em to prove ye can? That'll show 'em, aye?"

Annabelle squirmed under his gaze. "No, but..."

"Sorry," Kidd cut in sternly.

Annabelle lowered her head. "Sorry, Cap'n," she echoed.

"Don't apologize to me, Belle," Kidd said, gesturing toward the other girls. "They're the ones ye nearly drowned."

The group moved behind the carriage to escape the growing puddle beneath the coach. Kidd gave Annabelle a gentle nudge forward.

Annabelle took a deep breath, stepping up in front of the others. "Aye I'm sorry, girls."

Sophie and Lisa stared at her, unimpressed, while Regina, dripping wet and grinning ear to ear, clapped her hands excitedly. "That was amazing!" she exclaimed. "How did you do that?"

"Amazing?!?" Lisa snapped, glaring at Regina. "She could have killed us!"

Annabelle folded her arms. "Oi, ye can control water. Why didn't *ye* do yer magic?"

Before Lisa could respond, Lowe gave Annabelle another light kick. She sighed. "Yer right, Lisa. I should've been more careful."

Marcus cleared his throat. "If everyone's okay... and the water conjuring is complete, shall we continue to the main complex?" He shot Annabelle a pointed look. "If everything is alright now."

Annabelle fidgeted where she stood, looking sheepish again.

"All should be fine now, Brother Marcus," Lowe assured him, resting a hand on Annabelle's shoulder. "Belle here won't be no more trouble." He grinned down at her. "Ain't that right, Belle?"

"Aye, Cap'n," Annabelle mumbled, avoiding his gaze.

Marcus motioned to the carriage. "let's go and get you ladies some dry clothes?"

Lowe and Marcus held the doors open as the girls climbed back inside. Sophie and Regina entered on Marcus' side, while Lisa and Annabelle took their seats on Lowe's.

As Annabelle passed Kidd, he leaned in slightly, fixing her with a firm, silent *be good, Belle* look. Annabelle avoided his gaze, sliding into her seat beside Regina without another word.

Once everyone was settled, Marcus and Lowe climbed back onto the driver's bench. Marcus gave the reins a flick, and the horses trotted down the road once more.

After a long pause, Lowe sighed and announced, "I'd like to make a correction, mate."

Marcus glanced at him. "Oh?"

Lowe smirked. "Sometimes... it's a blessing."

[-----✝-----]

After arriving at the complex, and finding some dry clothes for the girls, Marcus led the girls and Captain Lowe to the gardens at the heart of the grounds. Each of the four girls sat on a curved stone bench forming a semi-circle, while Captain Lowe took a seat beside Annabelle. The garden was lush and serene, the soft rustling of leaves and scent of fresh earth creating a peaceful atmosphere.

Marcus wheeled a cart of tea into the garden, the clinking of porcelain cups breaking the stillness. A metal pitcher of ice water rested beside the teapot, for himself and Lowe who unable to partake.

"My apologies for the wait," Marcus said as he stopped in front of the semi-circle. "I had to brew a fresh pot."

He looked around. "Brother Albert explained the tea to you ladies, right?"

Lisa, her green hair wrapped in a towel and now dressed in a fresh green dress marked with a white insignia of Saint Lorraine, nodded. "Yes, he said it somehow makes us closer together."

Captain Lowe leaned back on the bench, skeptical. "How can a cup of tea make four girls closer?" he asked, one brow raised. "I mean…it's just tea."

Marcus smiled. "It's not that simple, Captain." He began pouring the tea into four porcelain cups. "The Order used to be the Church of the Pantheon. Back then, this place was called the Tabernacle. Priests and priestesses came here to meditate and commune with the Goddesses."

He handed the first cup to Regina, who accepted it with bright curiosity.

"Like we're going to do?" she asked.

"Exactly," Marcus said, offering a second cup to Sophie. "This is the only place where the Goddesses can be directly contacted. Some scholars believe the barrier between our world and theirs is thinnest here."

Sophie accepted her tea with a thoughtful nod. Her violet hair was still damp from earlier, and she now wore black training pants and a loose shirt adorned with the golden sigil of the Order.

"When the church collapsed and Saint Lorraine founded the Order," Marcus continued, "we lost the ability to speak directly to the Goddesses. Some believe only the chosen avatars, like yourselves have ever truly communed with them."

He passed a third cup to Lisa, who cradled it in both hands.

"So, the tea doesn't really bring you closer to each other," Marcus clarified. "It strengthens your connection to your Goddess and that connection, in turn, brings *you* closer to one another."

Finally, he offered the last cup to Annabelle, who took it with a grin.

Captain Lowe raised an eyebrow. "Can I get a cup, my good man? I'd like a word with the Goddesses myself." He smirked playfully.

Marcus chuckled. "Sadly, Captain, the tea is for avatars only. Anyone else who drinks it... becomes violently ill." He gestured toward the pitcher. "But I do have some excellent ice water."

"Aye, let's have some water then," Lowe said, still eyeing the tea with interest.

Marcus poured him a cup of water, then another for himself. He turned back to face the girls, nerves setting in.

He is sure that Brother Albert had practiced this speech to the point of perfection. But this is just one more of the guide's duties that had fallen to Marcus, and he could only hope he'd do it and Albert justice. As the girls sipped their tea, Marcus took a breath and began.

"You are the chosen avatars of your Goddesses," he said. "They selected you before you were born to act upon their will in this world." He paused to choose his next words carefully. "It is their will that you commune with them, to learn their purpose and share in their power."

Sophie, never one for long speeches, frowned. "You've said that a dozen times. How do we actually *do* that? Just sit here drinking tea?"

Annabelle nodded. "Aye, the copper's got a point fer once."

Marcus smiled, undeterred. "A fair question. Beneath us lie the Chambers of the Goddess, what we in the Order refer to the Goddess Clock room. Tomorrow morning, you'll enter and meditate seeking the core of your being. There, you'll find your connection to your Goddess."

Lisa set her cup down. "What do you mean, *the core of our being?*"

Marcus shifted slightly. "From what we understand, it's like channeling your mana but deeper. Beyond magic itself." He hesitated. "That's... all we know."

Annabelle wrinkled her nose. "Channelin' mana?"

"You know," Sophie said with a smirk. "Like when you first learned how to use magic as a kid."

Annabelle blinked. "I never had to learn anything. My magic just... comes to me."

Lisa smiled and looked teasingly at Annabelle. "That explains so much."

Regina's eyes sparkled. "I can show you how to channel mana," she offered eagerly. "Then maybe you can teach me that water conjuring spell."

Sophie groaned. "May the ancestors protect us." She and Lisa exchanged a quiet giggle.

As Marcus turned back to the cart, Captain Kidd shot Annabelle a conspiratorial glance and subtly motioned for a sip of her tea.

Annabelle hesitated, with a quick shake of her head then mouthing silently, *it'll make ye sick!*

Kidd scowled, clearly unimpressed. With a sigh, she shrugged and handed him the cup. Kidd took a quick sip, passing it back just as Marcus turned around.

The four girls watched intently as Kidd swallowed. He looked left, then right, patting his chest and shrugging.

Marcus, oblivious, continued. "Let's talk about your sleeping arrangements."

Almost on cue, Kidd's face twisted in discomfort, and he erupted into a violent coughing fit. His wide-eyed look at Annabelle screamed, *what have I done?*

Marcus frowned. "Captain Lowe? Are you alright?"

Kidd waved him off weakly, his stomach visibly rebelling.

Suddenly, Annabelle blurted out, "Oi—he drank the tea!"

Marcus's eyes widened. *He knew exactly what was coming.* The Order's younger members sometimes dared each other to drink the tea, testing how long they could last before vomiting. A foolish tradition before their first scribe assignments, and now Kidd was about to learn why.

Marcus grabbed the water pitcher, dumped its contents, and rushed forward. "Hold this!" he said, but he was just a few steps too slow.

Kidd's eyes bulged, and a forceful wave of vomit exploded from his mouth, right onto Marcus's chest.

Marcus stood frozen, eyes clenched shut, the warm, sour mess soaking into his uniform.

Kidd dropped to his knees, still retching. Annabelle knelt beside him, patting his back. "Get him some water," she said quickly.

Marcus wiped his face with his sleeve and sighed. "It won't help. I've been through this before. Anything he eats or drinks for the next half hour... will come right back up."

Kidd groaned.

Returning to the cart, Marcus set down the empty pitcher with a grimace. "I've arranged rooms for each of you," he said, voice weary but composed.

Annabelle tried not to laugh. Regina sipped her tea, wide-eyed with fascination.

"What about me crew?" Annabelle asked, folding her arms. "Where do they sleep?"

Marcus blinked. "I... hadn't considered that. I assumed they'd stay aboard the *Stormfang.*"

Annabelle shook her head. "Then take me back to the *Fang.* I won't sleep in comfort while me crew's stuck on the ship."

Marcus exhaled, trying to remain calm. "Miss Salazar, please understand, your time may be in high demand. It may take days, even weeks, to decipher the Goddess's will, let alone commune with her. Traveling back and forth daily... it isn't practical."

Annabelle chewed her lip, then nodded. "Aye, ye've got a point. Then find rooms for me crew here on Order Island."

Marcus considered it. Weighing his options, he realized he'd rather deal with Sister Ingrid's inevitable fury than haul Annabelle to and from the pier every day. He sighed. "How many crew members are we talking about?"

"We're sailin' wit' thirteen strong," Annabelle replied proudly, her voice lifting with pride.

Marcus nodded slowly, doing the math in his head. "Alright. Once you're all settled, I'll arrange quarters for your crew."

Annabelle grinned in triumph. Even Kidd, still hunched and pale, managed a shaky thumb-up.

Marcus rubbed his temples. "Well... let's get you ladies settled?" he said, gesturing for them to follow.

Chapter 11

Journal Entry: April 12, 1910
Yesterday, I met the four Avatars: Sophie Griffin, Annabelle Salazar, Lisa Nozaki, and Regina Fournier. They arrived aboard the Stormfang, accompanied by Annabelle's guardian and captain of her ship, James "Kidd" Lowe. They answered many questions about Brother Albert's final hours and fate, but sadly the motives of The Conspiracy remain a mystery that hopefully we can solve with the help of the avatars after they commune with their goddesses.

I delivered the best introduction I could, outlining their divine purpose and the importance of communing with their respective goddesses. As expected, the message was met with varying degrees of acceptance. Miss Griffin remains particularly guarded, her grief over the destruction of Aurorium Granmark still heavy upon her. Miss Salazar, by contrast, seems to embrace her role with a kind of bravado. Nozaki and Fournier appear more trusting of the Order, though their youthful curiosity may yet prove to be both a strength and a weakness.

To be expected Captain Lowe, despite his initial resistance, chose to remain with us, citing his responsibility for Miss Salazar's safety. His ill-advised sip of goddess tea an unfortunate yet inevitable consequence of his skepticism, served as an unexpected icebreaker, though I doubt he would describe it that way.

After settling the avatars into their accommodations within the main complex, I turned my attention to the crew of the Stormfang. Addressing Miss Salazar's refusal to enjoy comfort while her crew remained aboard their vessel, I coordinated with the Overseers Guild to open Building 607 on the islet nearest the pier. First Mate Yancy "Smitty" Smith was informed that his men could use the building for the duration of their stay. He expressed his gratitude for the accommodations.

I intended to report to Sister Ingrid regarding our progress, but she was absent from her office when I arrived. This concerns me. I will have to seek her out later today to provide a full debrief and determine if there have been developments I have not been made aware of.

[-----✝-----]

Sitting alone at a table in the Order cafeteria, Marcus finished his journal entry and tucked the new journal securely into his book strap. With a sigh, he pulled his breakfast tray closer, oatmeal topped with strawberries and blueberries, alongside a steaming cup of coffee. He planned to brief Sister Ingrid after breakfast, before escorting the girls to the Temple of the Goddesses. He'd missed his chance to speak with her last night after everything that had transpired.

Just as he took his first sip of coffee, Sister Sallie slid into the seat across from him, balancing a tray carrying a fruit salad and a stack of three pancakes.

"Good morning, mister guide to the avatars." She teased, her eyes glinting with mischief as Marcus swallowed his coffee. "Is it true? You've actually met them?"

Marcus nodded, scooping a spoonful of oatmeal. "Yes, it's true. I've met all four."

Sallie leaned forward eagerly. "And?" she pressed. "Don't hold out on me."

Marcus smiled, amused by her curiosity. "And... they're four young women who've just been told that the goddesses who created the universe have a plan for them," he said with a shrug. "They're handling it... well."

Sallie rolled her eyes. "Oh, Marcus, you're so analytical and dispassionate. You've met the avatars of the twelve goddesses, and you're not even a little excited?"

Marcus hesitated, stirring his oatmeal absentmindedly. In truth, he had been so busy that he hadn't taken the time to truly process the weight of it all. As he thought about it, he realized he didn't feel excitement, he felt fear. The goddesses had seen fit to raise four avatars, and through Albert's planning and influence, they had found each other and begun forming bonds. *But what awaited them on their journey?* It was that thought that unsettled him.

"I wouldn't say I'm excited," he admitted after a pause, recalling Sister Ingrid's advice about discretion, especially with Sallie. She meant well, but Marcus was certain she couldn't keep a secret if the Seven Kingdoms depended on it. "I feel... challenged, and honored, of course, that the Council selected me to lend my abilities to the girls in their divine quest."

Sallie smirked. "Ever the exemplary Order monk," she teased. "Do you think I could meet them?"

Marcus blinked, caught off guard. "What? Why would you want to meet them?"

"Are you serious?" she asked, incredulous. "These girls are manifestations of the Goddesses! Just imagine what we could learn from them."

Marcus frowned. "I don't think they have much to teach you, honestly. At the end of the day, they're still just fourteen-year-old girls."

"But think about it!" Sallie's eyes shone with excitement. "If we could study them, maybe we could figure out how to channel the Goddesses' power without needing avatars."

A chill ran down Marcus's spine. He remembered the mystic man from Umbrathorn...someone who had pursued knowledge he was sure was there but couldn't understand, seeking a power he believed lay just beneath the surface. It had been monstrous...driven by ignorance and a cold disregard for life and decency.

"We will not be studying the avatars like that," he said, his voice suddenly cold and commanding.

Sallie quickly backtracked, waving a hand dismissively. "Alright, alright. I still want to meet them, though." She flashed a bright smile, clearly still hoping to enlist his help.

Marcus leaned back in his chair, his appetite fading. He no longer wanted his coffee. "I don't see why it would be a problem," he said at last, standing and checking his pocket watch. 6:17. The weight of the day ahead pressed heavily on his mind. "But I can't guarantee they'll have time for social calls anytime soon."

He pushed in his chair abruptly. "My apologies, Sister, but I have to go."

Sallie nodded, taking a sip of her tea. "Of course."

"Good day, Sister," Marcus said, offering a friendly but distracted wave as he strode out of the cafeteria.

Marcus made his way down the long, quiet hallway toward Sister Ingrid's office, his footsteps echoing off the polished stone floors. He knocked on the heavy wooden door, silently hoping she had started her day early. Time was slipping away, and he wasn't sure he'd have another chance to check in with her amid the demands of guiding the girls through their communion with the Goddesses.

"Come in," came Sister Ingrid's familiar voice from within.

Marcus opened the door and stepped inside, immediately noticing that Sister Ingrid was not alone. A woman with her hair pulled into a tight bun sat across from Ingrid, dressed in the standard amber and grey Order uniform; the colors marking her as a member of the Cartographers' Conclave.

"Brother Marcus, good morning" Ingrid greeted warmly, motioning to the empty chair in front of her desk. "Please, have a seat." She offered a small smile. "Apologies for missing you last night, I was down at the port welcoming Sister Alameda."

As Marcus walked to his seat, he stole a glance at the woman. Her face matched the photograph from her file in the Order's records. *She must have taken that picture just before her last assignment,* he mused. A brief thought flickered; *How did Ingrid know I'd come by last night?* But he set it aside. Pleasantries first of course.

"Good morning, Sister Ingrid. Sister Alameda." He nodded politely as he took his seat. "It's a pleasure to finally meet you."

Sister Alameda adjusted herself in her chair, turning to face both Marcus and Ingrid. "Likewise, Brother Marcus," she said, though there was a hint of uncertainty in her tone. "I have to admit, I'm not entirely sure why I'm here." She glanced between them. "I never applied to join the Scribes of Saint Lorraine."

"That's true," Sister Ingrid acknowledged with a calm nod. "However, the Council has selected you to serve as Brother Marcus's First Assistant." She gestured toward Marcus. "As you may already know, he has recently been appointed the Guide to the Avatars of the Twelve Goddesses."

Alameda blinked, clearly caught off guard. "I have to ask why me?" she asked reflexively, the question slipping out before she could stop it.

Marcus offered a knowing smile. "I asked the same question when I was chosen." He leaned back slightly. "All my guide could tell me was that the council selects us based on our records and skills."

"There's much more to the selection process than meets the eye," Sister Ingrid reassured her. "The council weighs many factors before making their decisions." She folded her hands on the desk. "Did you have a chance to review the manual I provided last night?"

"I did, Sister," Alameda replied, though her voice carried a note of hesitation. "I haven't finished it yet, but I plan to do so today."

"Please make that a priority," Ingrid said, kindly, but firmly. "Brother Marcus will be relying on you sooner than you may think."

"At your command, Sister." Alameda nodded respectfully before standing. Turning to Marcus, she asked, "Where will I be able to find you later today?"

Marcus thought for a moment. "Most likely, we'll be in the Temple of the Goddesses, in the Observation room."

"Good to know." She inclined her head slightly. "Good day to you both."

Marcus and Ingrid nodded in farewell as Sister Alameda exited the office, closing the door softly behind her.

Sister Ingrid leaned back in her chair, her expression thoughtful. "So, Brother Marcus," she said, steepling her fingers, "what is your opinion of the girls so far?"

160

Marcus took a moment to consider his response. "I believe they're telling the truth: *Brother Albert sacrificed himself to save them from the conspiracy.*" He exhaled. "And I'm convinced they weren't recruited into it. Based on Salazar and Fournier's accounts, the conspiracy was actively targeting Salazar for elimination."

"That's reassuring to hear," Ingrid said, tapping a finger against her chin. "But what evidence do you have to support your belief?"

Marcus folded his arms. "It's mostly circumstantial," he admitted. "Griffin isn't sleeping, which is understandable, given that she found her village, and her mother, massacred by Gretta and Isabella. Nozaki is grieving because she couldn't save Brother Albert." He paused. "Salazar... she's affected, but living the life of a privateer has taught her how to mask it well." He hesitated before continuing. "Fournier, on the other hand, she seems relatively unaffected, or perhaps she's moved on quickly. Likely because she lost her mother to sickness a few years ago."

Ingrid regarded him carefully. "It could all be an act," she countered. "The conspiracy has already shown it has the means to corrupt avatars. It stands to reason they'd train them to avoid raising suspicion."

"I considered that," Marcus said. "But the way they interact with each other... it's genuine. They're still figuring out how to get along. One wrong word, and their relationships spiral into petty squabbles." He allowed himself a small smirk. "If they were part of a well-coordinated deception, I'd expect them to be more... harmonious."

Sister Ingrid's lips twitched in approval. "A fair point," she conceded. "So, you're convinced?"

Marcus nodded. "I am."

"Good," Ingrid said, exhaling softly, relief evident in her tone. She leaned forward and opened the bottom drawer of her desk. From it, she retrieved a wooden box, light in color and sealed with a metal hasp. The symbol of the Order of Saint Lorraine was etched onto the top. She placed it gently on the desk between them.

"You've read the Manual for the Guide, correct?" Ingrid asked, watching him closely.

"I have," Marcus confirmed, eyeing the box with curiosity. "The duties it outlines... they're quite challenging."

"Yes, they are," Sister Ingrid said with a smile, her tone shifting into what was clearly a well-rehearsed speech. "As the Guide to the Avatars of the Twelve Goddesses, you must understand that all the resources of the Order are at your disposal." She paused before continuing. "Once the Avatars commune with their Goddesses, they will begin acting upon their will, and it is your duty to support them in every way possible. Just as they are avatars of the Goddesses, you are to think of yourself as an avatar of the Order ever in their service."

Marcus nodded solemnly. "I will, Sister."

Without another word, Sister Ingrid slid the wooden box across the desk toward him. "This is for you," she said simply.

Curious, Marcus unfastened the metal hasp and lifted the lid. What he saw inside left him momentarily speechless. A six-shooter pistol rested withing, its grip adorned with the symbol of the Order of Saint Lorraine. Intricate runes were etched carefully into the cylinder and barrel. Beside it lay a finely crafted leather holster strap and twelve bullets.

Marcus stared at the weapon, stunned. He looked up at Sister Ingrid, searching for an explanation. "Sister...?" he asked, his voice tinged with uncertainty. *Was he to be their protector and guide maybe?*

161

Sister Ingrid met his gaze with unwavering resolve. "Think about the final tenet of the Guide," she said softly, but firmly. "It will all fall into place then."

A chill ran down Marcus's spine as realization took hold. "By the Goddesses..." he whispered, leaning back in his chair. "I never imagined..." He was not to be their protector if necessary, he was to be their executioner.

"We serve by the will of the Goddesses, Brother Marcus," Ingrid said, her eyes sharp as they gauged his reaction. "As you yourself admitted, the tenets of the guide are... challenging."

Swallowing the weight of the implication, Marcus nodded, pushing his thoughts into order. "Of course, Sister. You are right."

"That pistol stays with you at all times," she instructed, pointing to the weapon still nestled inside the box. "Do not tell anyone you have it."

Marcus nodded again. "Understood."

She leaned back in her chair, her expression measured. "As a member of the Order, you will never be searched, so there's no risk of it being discovered through routine security."

"Yes, Sister," Marcus affirmed, closing the box with deliberate care.

Seemingly satisfied, Ingrid shifted the conversation. "Regarding Sister Alameda, since the girls are now active, I will personally ensure she's prepared to support you and the avatars. You may assign her any tasks you deem appropriate, but one of you must remain on Order Island at all times, unless you are given explicit permission for the both of you to leave the island."

"Understood," Marcus said, glancing at his watch. The hands pointed to 7:02.

Sister Ingrid caught his glance. "What time are you meeting with the avatars?"

"We agreed to meet at the cafeteria at 7:30." He replied.

"That gives you just enough time to strap on your pistol and get there," she observed with a knowing smirk.

Marcus sighed internally but maintained his composure. "Yes, of course. You are correct." He rose from his seat and inclined his head respectfully. "Good day, Sister."

"Good day, Brother Marcus," Ingrid replied, offering the traditional blessing. "May the goddesses lead your path."

With the wooden box held securely in his hands, Marcus turned and walked out of the room, his mind racing with the weight of his new, complicated responsibility.

[----- ✿ -----]

Regina checked herself in the mirror, making sure she looked presentable in the new dress Brother Marcus had got for her; a black skirt paired with a crisp white shirt. On the top left of the shirt, just above her heart, was a small, embroidered symbol of the Order of Saint Lorraine, about the size of her hand.

Brother Marcus had even been thoughtful enough to include a brush, a comb, and a bag of black hair ties. They weren't fancy or anything, but against her silver hair, they looked cute in a simple way. Regina wondered whether he'd picked them out on purpose or if it was just dumb luck, like when her dad used to choose outfits for her.

Dad... A pang of longing crept in as she thought of him. *How was he doing? And Mommy June? And little Matthew—Mattie, as she always called him. Was he still starting his mornings the same way, crashing into her room to stealing her precious sleep away?*

Shaking off the thoughts, Regina gave herself one last glance in the mirror before turning away. She opened the door but paused to double-check her purse for the key.

The wooden tag attached to it had the number "7" stamped on it. Satisfied, she let the door click shut behind her and stepped into the hallway of dormitory rooms.

Brother Marcus's directions echoed in her mind: To get to the cafeteria turn right and walk straight. To reach the temple turn left, walk to the statue of Saint Lorraine, then take the second hallway on the left.

Breakfast first. Definitely breakfast.

She turned right, walking down the hallway, passing other members of the Order along the way. Some of them stared at her with curiosity, some ignored her entirely, and others quickly averted their gazes when she greeted them with a cheerful, "Hi!" Those ones hurried past as if they hadn't heard her.

As she neared a large corridor branching off to the right, leading to who-knows-where, her eyes caught sight of a familiar figure: _Sophie_. Dressed in her signature purple vest and pants, with a matching bow tie draped in two neat tails over her white shirt, Sophie looked exhausted. She glanced back and forth, clearly unsure of where to go.

Regina's face lit up. "Sophie!" she called, waving enthusiastically.

Sophie spotted her and made her way over, forcing a smile to mask her exhaustion. "Hey, girl. How are you?"

"I'm good," Regina said brightly. "I was just heading to grab a little breakfast before we meet with Brother Marcus."

"Yeah, I was trying to do the same thing, but I got lost in the hallways," Sophie admitted with a sheepish grin. "Now I don't even know where I am."

Regina pointed confidently down the corridor. "Brother Marcus said the cafeteria should be this way." Her stomach rumbled at the thought. "I really want to try the pancakes. I hope they have strawberry toppings, like my Mommy June makes."

Sophie gestured for Regina to take the lead. "Sounds good. Lead the way."

Regina started walking, glancing over at Sophie. "So, what did you do last night?"

Sophie hesitated before replying, "After Brother Marcus dropped me off, I just went to sleep." She gave a small smile, not wanting to admit she'd cried most of the night, barely sleeping at all. "What about you?"

"Annabelle stopped by, and I showed her how to channel mana," Regina said with pride. "She even taught me that conjuring spell she does."

Sophie raised her eyebrows in mild surprise. "How did that go?"

Regina grinned as they weaved through the morning crowd of Order brothers and sisters some hurrying to their duties, others moving at a relaxed pace. "She picked it up really quickly," she said. "But explaining her magic to me? That took a while."

Sophie smirked. "You don't say."

Regina nodded. "It's really difficult for mages and magic users with a natural affinity to teach their magic to us learner mages," she explained, echoing her mother's wisdom. "It's like trying to explain to someone how to grow hair."

Sophie glanced at Regina thoughtfully. "But we all learn magic, right? My mom... she taught me how to use mine."

"We learn spells," Regina clarified. "But spells are just ways to shape mana using a specific magic system. Without understanding the system, manipulating mana is almost useless." She paused, recalling her mother's analogy. "You can style hair, but you have to grow it first."

Sophie considered that. "Your magic system sounds really complicated."

Regina beamed. "I like it, though. Some magic can be tough to learn, but I can't wait to try Earthbloom magic!"

Sophie rolled her eyes playfully. "Oh, I'm sure Lisa's going to love that."

As the girls continued down the hallway, they passed corridors marked by wooden signs with names like The College of Sages and The Oracles of Time. Brothers and Sisters of the Order bustled in and out of rooms, moving with a purpose that reminded Regina of ants in a colony. Their uniforms varied in color, deep crimson, vibrant orange, muted green, and grey each hue signifying a different sect within the Order.

She couldn't help but wonder: *if they were this busy just after seven in the morning, what time did they even wake up?* The thought made her feel very sorry for them.

Eventually, they reached the cafeteria, blending into the steady stream of Order members entering the large space. They each grabbed a metal tray from a stacked pile and made their way to the food counter, where an assortment of dishes awaited. Sophie picked up a bowl of fruit salad and a plate of crispy bacon, while Regina skipped the bacon in favor of sausage links and a stack of golden griddle cakes.

As they moved along, they passed trays of oatmeal, scrambled eggs, and other tempting options before reaching the end, where a woman in a simple dress, like Regina's, stood behind the counter. Her outfit was covered by a clean apron, and her hair was tucked neatly under a bonnet.

"Would you ladies like some juice or coffee?" the woman asked, gesturing to the neatly lined pitchers behind her.

Regina hesitated, considering. "Coffee?" she mused aloud. "My dad doesn't let me have coffee at home."

Sophie glanced at her, then at the woman, and quickly decided. "I think we should just get juice." She had a feeling Regina on coffee would be... a lot.

"Yeah, maybe you're right," Regina sighed. "Can I have some apple juice, please?"

"Orange juice for me," Sophie added.

The woman handed them each a cool metal cup and smiled warmly. "I have to say, it's an honor to meet you girls."

Regina beamed. "Thank you!" she said in her usual perky way.

Sophie, however, shifted awkwardly. "Uh... thanks," she muttered, unsure why the woman seemed so excited.

Carrying their trays, they moved into the seating area, scanning the room for a spot. Their *friends*, Annabelle, Lisa, and Captain Kidd, were gathered at a table in the center. Annabelle spotted them first, waving with exaggerated enthusiasm.

"Over here!" she called, flapping her arm dramatically.

Regina grinned and took the seat across from Annabelle, while Sophie sat opposite Lisa.

"Good morning, Regina!" Annabelle greeted cheerfully, then smirked at Sophie. "Copper."

"Good morning," Regina chirped, grabbing a fork and knife from the cup in the center of the table.

Sophie gave a small nod as she picked up her silverware.

"Top of the morning, girlies," Captain Kidd said with a wide grin. "How's the day treating you?"

"Great!" Regina replied before popping a sausage into her mouth.

"I'm doing well, thanks, Captain," Sophie said between bites of bacon. "How about you all?"

"I'm enjoying the soft bed," Captain Kidd said with a satisfied smile. "And the good food."

"I'm just wondering when they're going to ask us to pay," Annabelle said, sipping her juice thoughtfully.

"Pay?!" Lisa blurted, incredulously. "I am pretty sure they are not going to charge us."

"What?" Annabelle gaped. "They just give us all of this food... **_for free_**?!"

"Why would they charge us?" Sophie asked, raising an eyebrow. "Besides, how would they even keep track of a bill?" She popped a bite of fruit into her mouth.

Captain Kidd chuckled. "You'll have to forgive Belle," he said to the group. "She's lived the life of a privateer since she was in diapers. For us? Everything has a price."

Lisa giggled, shooting Annabelle an amused look. "That explains so much."

Annabelle wasn't paying attention to the conversation around her anymore. Her thoughts were stuck on all the delicious food she'd left behind at the counter. Without a word, she pushed back from the table and made a set course for the food line, her eyes zeroing in on the cake she'd seen earlier, the one with a perfect slice of pineapple on top.

She slipped past a pair of Order members, a man and a woman, and leaned eagerly over the counter, flashing the server a wide grin. "I want cake. Like four, nay, five pieces," she declared.

The woman behind the counter smiled patiently and slid a small saucer toward her. A single square of pineapple-topped cake sat neatly on the plate. "We ask that you take just one piece at a time, ma'am," she said with practiced diplomacy. "But you're welcome to come back for more as often as you like."

Annabelle frowned slightly but took the plate. "Only one?" she repeated, then shrugged. "Fine. Save me a few, I'll be right back."

She returned to the table like a champion returning from battle, proudly setting down her prize and digging in.

"Belle, you, okay?" Captain Kidd asked, eyeing her.

Annabelle gave a thumb-up, her mouth full of cake.

"Good morning, everyone," Marcus said as he approached, his tone warm but measured. "I trust you all slept well?"

"Good morning, Brother Marcus!" Regina chirped, waving her fork before returning to her pancakes.

Lisa gave a polite nod. "And a good morning to you, Brother Marcus."

"Morning," Sophie added, finishing off her fruit salad.

Annabelle, mid-bite, waved lazily, then stood again, already eyeing the counter for round two.

Captain Kidd chuckled. "Top of the morning to you, Brother Marcus. How goes the day?"

"The day goes quite well," Marcus replied, offering a faint smile. "I trust you ladies are prepared for what's ahead?"

"Yes!" Regina said brightly. "I can't wait to speak to the Goddess. There's so much she can tell me!"

Lisa nodded solemnly. "I am ready. Serving the Goddess is a great honor."

Annabelle returned with her second piece of cake and noticed everyone staring at her. She blinked. "What?"

Marcus glanced around the table, noting that most had finished eating. Turning to the captain, he asked, "Captain Lowe, will you be joining us today?"

"Nay," the captain replied, leaning back in his chair. "I'll be checkin' on the crew, makin' sure they're well." He drained his coffee and set the mug down with a satisfied sigh. "I'll find ye lot later."

"We will likely be in the Temple of the Goddesses all day," Marcus said. "Just ask one of the brothers or sisters to escort you, they will bring you straight to us."

"Aye, thanks, mate," Captain Kidd said with a nod.

Marcus clapped his hands lightly. "Well, shall we get going?"

Annabelle, halfway through slice number two, raised a finger. "Let me grab one more piece," she said brightly. "Then I'll be ready."

Everyone turned to look at her with disapproval.

"Oi! Belle, that's enough!" Captain Kidd said with a firm stare.

Annabelle pouted, setting her fork down with a sigh. "Aye, Cap'n."

With breakfast finished, the group gathered their trays and left the cafeteria together.

Marcus led the four girls, Regina, Sophie, Annabelle, and Lisa, through the large double doors of the Temple of the Twelve Goddesses. The wood was carved with an intricate symbol, a silent testament to the history contained within. Their footsteps echoed as they entered the long, rectangular hall.

At the far end, a plush couch sat against the wall with a sturdy coffee table in front of it. Two chairs flanked the table, one on either side. Across from the couch, another set of double doors bore the same carved symbol, beside which stood a smaller, simpler door.

Regina's eyes lingered on the carvings. "Brother Marcus," she asked, curiosity lighting her voice, "what's that symbol on the doors?"

Marcus gestured for them to sit. "Before the Order of Saint Lorraine was founded, this island and complex served as the seat of the Twelve Goddesses' Pantheon, the headquarters of the religion, from what I understand it was found all across the world."

The girls took their seats, Lisa near the door, Regina and Annabelle on the couch, and Sophie settling into the far chair. Marcus remained standing before the table.

"The symbol you see is the insignia of that ancient Pantheon," he explained. "When the goddesses spoke to Saint Lorraine, as the Pantheon was disbanding itself, and the Order took its place." He clapped his hands lightly. "But enough history. Today, you begin communion with your goddesses."

Sophie leaned back, arms crossed. "Why do we have to do that? If they already chose us and gave us powers, why talk to them?"

Marcus smiled patiently. "As I understand the goddesses have yet to give you any significant portion of their power. Before bestowing their full blessings, they require a communion. Past avatars say the goddesses provide guidance and purpose during this communion."

Lisa sat up straighter, eyes bright. "I cannot wait," she said with excitement.

Annabelle rolled her eyes. "Oi, princess, relax. We don't even know if your goddess has boots for you to lick."

Lisa scowled. "Just for that, I will ask my goddess to kick you out!"

"Try it," Annabelle shot back, sticking out her tongue and pulling down the skin under her eye, a rude gesture Lisa didn't seem to recognize.

Marcus sighed and lifted his hands in a calming motion. "Ladies, let's keep things civil."

"She started it!" Lisa said, pointing at Annabelle. "I am just trying to be a loyal servant."

"I was simply informing *Lisa* that goddesses don't wear boots," Annabelle replied, slipping into her refined *proper voice* the captain insisted she practice often.

Regina chuckled, only to stifle it quickly when Lisa glared at her.

Sophie rubbed her temple. "Can you two not? It's too early for this nonsense."

Lisa turned away with a dramatic huff and crossed arms. Annabelle grinned in victory and relaxed into the cushions.

Marcus sighed again, the weariness creeping into his voice. "Ladies, please. The goddesses chose you to act on their behalf in this world."

Sophie tilted her head. "Why don't they just do it themselves?"

"A fair question, Miss Griffin," Marcus said. "As far as we know, the goddesses cannot intervene in our world directly, that's why they need avatars." He looked at the large double doors. "Beyond those is the Goddess Clock Chamber, where your communion will take place."

Sophie frowned. "Then why are we out here talking? Why not just take us in?"

Marcus shook his head. "Because I'm not allowed to enter. Once you arrived on the island, only you can open those doors. Not even I, as your guide, may enter until you exit."

Regina's eyes sparkled. "What kind of mechanism does that? A sensor? A spell? An invisible guardian spirit? Ooh—maybe an invisible golem!"

Sophie rolled her eyes. "Maybe your goddess will tell you."

Marcus chuckled. "If you'll excuse me, I'll prepare some goddess tea before we begin." He walked toward the smaller door near the back.

"Got any of that pineapple cake back there?" Annabelle called after him with a grin.

"Sadly, no," Marcus replied, vanishing through the door.

As soon as it clicked shut, Annabelle popped to her feet. "I'll be right back."

Sophie frowned. "Seriously? How much cake can you eat?"

Annabelle wagged a finger. "Copper, copper, that's the wrong question. The right question is: *how much free cake can I eat*?" And with that, she dashed out, heading for the cafeteria.

Lisa scowled. "Freeloader," she muttered. "How could a goddess pick her?"

After a few moments Marcus returned from the utility room, carrying a gleaming silver tray with a metal tea kettle and four delicate cups. "Ladies, tea is served," he said with a pleasant smile. But as he looked up, he noticed the empty seat on the couch. "Oh… where is Miss Salazar?"

Lisa didn't even glance up from her cup. "Where do you think?"

Marcus sighed. "She really enjoys pineapple cake, doesn't she?"

"She really enjoys freeloading," Lisa corrected, casting a sharp glance toward the door.

Regina tilted her head. "I don't get it," she said sincerely. "How is it freeloading if the food's free?"

Lisa looked to Sophie for backup, but she is fast asleep, head tilted back in her chair. Resigned, Lisa sighed and said in a practiced tone, "You shouldn't feast at the table of generosity: Law number seven."

Regina tapped her chin. "Isn't that from the Alchemists' Laws of Prosperity?"

Lisa's lips curled smugly. "Yes it is."

Before Regina could respond, Annabelle swept back through the double doors and flopped onto the couch with a dramatic sigh.

"No more cake?" Lisa asked, raising an eyebrow. "Did they finally run out?"

"Nay," Annabelle grumbled. "Turns out they don't want ye taking food from the cafeteria." She crossed her arms, clearly offended.

Suppressing a chuckle, Marcus poured the tea and handed the first cup to Lisa.

Lisa accepted it with a polite nod. "Thank you, Brother Marcus."

167

He continued, offering cups to Annabelle and Regina.

"Thank you!" Regina beamed, voice bright with gratitude.

"Aye, thanks." Annabelle said, sipping with a contented sigh.

Their eyes turned to Sophie, still peacefully asleep. Marcus hesitated. He knew they had to begin soon, but exhaustion was clearly catching up with her.

Suddenly, Sophie's eyes snapped open. She bolted upright as if something had jolted her awake, startling the others.

"Sorry," she mumbled, rubbing her eyes. "Guess I nodded off."

"It's quite alright," Marcus said gently, pouring the last cup and handing it to her. He set the tray aside and took his place in front of them. "Before we begin, do you have any questions?"

Regina raised her hand. "How do we actually reach out to our goddess? You said it's like channeling mana, but… that can't be it, right?"

Marcus nodded. "Good question, Miss Fournier. From what past avatars have written, they had to search within themselves; just like when learning to channel mana. During that process, they found their connection." He paused. "Unfortunately, that's all I can tell you."

Annabelle smirked and raised her hand, palms up. "Sounds easy enough. Just like Regina showed a lass."

Lisa and Sophie leaned in slightly, eyes narrowing.

"Wait," Sophie said, holding out a hand. "Hold up."

Annabelle's grin widened. "What, Copper? Afraid you'll get soaked again?"

"Yes!" Lisa blurted. "There is no drain in here!"

Annabelle laughed. "Relax, Princess. I'm not summoning the sea, just channeling mana through me fingertips."

Regina extended her hand, palm forward. With a flick of concentration, she summoned a small, shimmering sphere of seawater into the air. "See? A little focus, and the sea doesn't rush out of control like before in the carriage."

Lisa and Sophie exchanged wary glances, clearly unconvinced.

Marcus cleared his throat. "If there are no further questions," he said pointedly, "I believe it's time for you to begin."

"Okay," Regina said, nodding. She closed her fingers to dispel the water, but lost focus, and the sphere burst with a quiet pop, splashing both her and Annabelle with seawater.

The two girls stared at each other for a beat, then burst into giggles.

Sophie and Lisa, dry and unscathed this time, exchanged exasperated glances and rolled their eyes in perfect unison.

"You learned Miss Salazar's magic system overnight?" Marcus asked, raising an eyebrow.

"She's already better at it than Annabelle," Sophie added with a smirk.

"Oi!" Annabelle huffed, crossing her arms. "I can do that, watch!"

"NO!" Lisa shouted, throwing out a hand. "We're supposed to be communing with the goddesses! No time for distractions, right, Brother Marcus?"

Marcus, noting the urgency in Lisa's voice, nodded. "Miss Nozaki is quite correct. Time is of the essence."

"Bah," Annabelle muttered with a wave, though a mischievous glint still sparkled in her eye.

They finished their tea and neatly placed their cups on the table before rising. Together, they stepped toward the looming double doors. Sophie and Lisa reached them first, their hands hovering over the handles. The green and purple hued girls exchanged a look, anticipation flickering in their eyes.

"Well," Sophie said, inhaling, "away we go."

She pushed, surprised by how easily the massive door opened. Lisa followed, bracing for resistance, but the other door gave way just as smoothly as if it was made of paper.

As the quartet stepped inside, awe spread across their faces. A vast chamber stretched before them, bathed in soft, ethereal light. At its heart stood twelve statues arranged in a perfect circle, like the hours on a clock, each figure facing inward. Carved from shimmering stone, they radiated hues that matched the goddesses they represented.

Directly ahead, ts back to the entrance, stood a statue of radiant white, gleaming beneath sunlight from high-arched windows. To its left stood a figure of deep green; to its right, one of soft pink. Both glimmered with light like divine energy in their respective goddess colors.

As Annabelle crossed the threshold, the doors creaked shut behind them of their own accord, sealing with a low, final thud. Instinctively, the girls turned—but there was no handle, no latch. Only smooth stone.

"Too late to turn back now," Sophie murmured with a grin.

Together, they approached the center of the chamber, stepping into the circle of statues. Heads tilted back, they studied each towering presence. Before every goddess stood an animal companion, carved from the same luminous stone, each radiating an aura that shimmered just beyond the veil of the ordinary.

Lisa's gaze locked on the green statue. The goddess stood tall, hands clasped over her chest, her carved face calm and commanding. At her feet rested an elephant, trunk raised proudly.

Without hesitation, Lisa stepped forward and pressed her palm gently to the smooth stone. It was cold, but then warmth bloomed beneath her fingertips. Subtle. Surprising. Alive. Something stirred in her chest. A name she couldn't quite remember hovered just out of reach.

She recalled Brother Marcus's guidance. Quieting her thoughts, Lisa sat cross-legged before the statue. She folded her hands together, took a long, centering breath, and closed her eyes.

Then she searched.

Inward, deeper.

Beyond mana.

Toward the presence waiting in the quiet.

[----- ⚓ -----]

Annabelle, meanwhile, felt drawn to the orange statue of a striking goddess with long, flowing hair tied back in a ponytail. The figure wore a draped robe, cinched at the waist by an elaborate chain belt adorned with a large, jeweled buckle. Her right hand extended outward, fingers pressed together as if awaiting an offering, while her left cradled a blazing fireball. The goddess's expression was unreadable calm, calculating.

At her feet crouched an orange lion monkey, its low posture and hands planted firmly on the ground. Its intense, unblinking gaze was fixed forward, as if sizing up a threat or plotting something.

Annabelle reached out and touched the monkey's stone mane. Her mind told her it was cool, smooth stone, but her hand insisted otherwise—it felt warm, soft, like real fur. She grinned.

"Channel me mana and look inside meself, right?" she muttered. "How hard can it be?"

Sitting down cross-legged, she placed her hands on her knees, fingers curling slightly. Taking a deep breath, she began to hum softly; a pirate shanty she often sang to help herself focus. As the melody took shape, her mana responded, stirring to life withing her.

[-----✿-----]

Regina, watching Annabelle settle in, turned her attention to the silver statue standing between the orange and golden goddesses. The goddess had short, swept-up hair with playful bangs framing her face and a mischievous looking grin frozen in stone. In one hand, she held a mirror; in the other, a delicate feathered quill.

In front of her, a silver fox sat gracefully, its narrow eyes glinting with hidden wisdom. Regina knelt and placed her hand gently atop the fox's head. She blinked. Though clearly carved from shimmering stone, it felt warm, soft, like real fur.

Fascinated, she lifted her hand, rolling her fingers slowly. No residual mana clung to her skin. Still uncertain, she pressed her palm back down. The warmth remained.

Her mind raced through possibilities: *illusion magic? Some kind of possession enchantment?*

Crouching lower, she adjusted her glasses and examined the statue closely. The floor beneath it was the same glossy silver stone, but when she touched it, it was cold and lifeless—just ordinary stone.

Shaking her head, Regina recalled Brother Marcus's words and sat down cross-legged, facing the fox. She rested her hands palms-up, fingers relaxed, and began channeling mana through her limbs, seeking the connection.

[-----✛-----]

Like the others, Sophie was drawn to her statue, the violet goddess. The figure stood strong, one foot forward, spear in hand, pointing toward the ceiling. Her left hand rested atop an ornate shield. Her expression was fierce, focused, with a jeweled circlet holding her hair in a tight braid that rested over her shoulder and across her chest.

In front of the goddess crouched a badger statue, low in an attack stance. It radiated tension, as though moments away from pouncing. Sophie stared at it, her chest tightening.

Choosing to follow Marcus's instructions, she sat on the violet floor, crossed her legs, and placed her hands on her knees. She turned her palms upward, bringing her pointer, middle, and thumbs together in the formation her mother had once called a mana point. Drawing a deep, steadying breath, she held it, then slowly exhaled. Her muscles loosened. Her body settled into stillness.

Then, it came again.

It's all your fault.

The whispered words slithered through her thoughts. Her eyes flew open.

Her hands clenched into fists. She wiped a tear from her cheek with her sleeve.

"Come on, Sophie. Stay focused," she whispered, shaking her head before taking another breath and trying again.

[-----✠-----]

As the heavy doors closed behind the four girls, Marcus couldn't resist testing them once more. He pressed his hand to the handle and pushed, just as he had the day before their arrival. As expected, the door didn't budge—it had seamlessly fused into the wall, denying him entry.

Satisfied, Marcus turned away and returned to the utility room, carrying the metallic grey tray with the girls' empty cups.

The utility room was a long, narrow space, meticulously organized. To his left, nearest the entrance, stood a storage cabinet where he neatly returned the tea set and tray. Next to it is a worn but sturdy sink, complete with a spigot for washing dishes. A wood-fueled stove sat just beyond, the kettle still resting atop it. Like most things in the room, it was rarely used, only when the goddesses' chosen avatars were present.

Opposite the stove, a food preparation counter stretched along the wall. Beside it stood a lidded trash bin, which Marcus emptied daily to keep pests away. Farther down, a solid wooden table waited for meal prep, and next to it, a tall cabinet held the kitchen essentials.

The bottom drawers stored plates and silverware; the middle shelves, concealed behind glass doors, held simple spices, salt, pepper, sugar. The top shelves housed neatly folded placemats and tablecloths, untouched for years. The room's quiet sanctity reminded Marcus that this part of the compound was only used when avatars were present. It always made him feel like a guest in a place steeped in sacred tradition.

He washed the dishes and kettle, then brewed a fresh pot of coffee. The rich aroma filled the room, offering a fleeting sense of comfort. With a steaming cup in hand, Marcus stepped into the adjacent observation room.

This smaller room had a single long window offering a clear view into the Goddess Clock chamber. Marcus leaned against the frame, eyes fixed on the four girls as they sat in silent meditation, attempting communion with their goddesses.

At last, he allowed himself to relax, savoring the warmth of the coffee. The past two days had been a whirlwind, meeting the girls, preparing their schedules, ensuring every detail was in place, but now, for the first time, he had a moment to breathe. He took a deep breath, held it, and released it slowly, the tension easing from his shoulders.

His gaze returned to the girls. Regina, Annabelle, and Lisa appeared fully immersed, their expressions serene and focused. But then he saw Sophie.

She shifted abruptly, breaking her concentration. Marcus watched as she shook her head and wiped her face with her sleeve before trying again. A flicker of concern tightened in his chest.

Has she been through too much?

The weight Sophie carried was clear, her trauma, her struggles. *Would it prevent her from connecting with her Violet Goddess?*

Marcus frowned, tapping his fingers against the ceramic cup. *If Sophie couldn't complete the communion, how would they get her out?* The goddesses' will is clear: only the avatars could open the doors once inside.

If she fails...

He shook his head, pushing the thought away. He took another slow sip of coffee and closed his eyes. *No contingency plans, not yet.*

Instead, he chose to believe in her. He believed in the goddess who had chosen her. Whatever Sophie was facing inside, she would find a way through it.

She had to.

So, he waited.

An hour passed. Marcus stretched and returned to the utility room for another cup. As he took his first sip, the sound of the main foyer door opening drew his attention. He stepped out with his mug in hand and saw Captain Lowe being escorted inside by a brother from the Overseer's Sect, likely the one stationed at the entrance when the captain had returned from visiting his crew at building 607.

"Captain Lowe," Marcus greeted with a polite nod. "Welcome to the Temple of the Twelve Goddesses." He turned to the escorting monk. "Thank you, brother."

The monk gave a respectful nod. "Have a good day," he said before exiting.

"How goes it, mate?" Captain Lowe called, raising a hand as his sharp eyes scanned the room. "Where's Belle?"

Marcus gestured toward the Goddess Clock room with his free hand. "Communing with her goddess."

Curious, Captain Lowe approached the massive double doors and pressed a hand against one, trying to sneak a peek inside. The door didn't budge. Frowning, he pressed harder, but it remained immovable, solid as stone.

He glanced back at Marcus. "Alright... how do ye unlock this thing?"

"We can't," Marcus replied simply. "Once they're inside, the doors somehow seal themselves. Only the girls can open them now."

Captain Lowe gave Marcus a skeptical look. "You're serious?"

Marcus offered a knowing smile and waved a hand. "Ours is not to question the will of the goddesses."

The captain considered that for a moment, then shrugged. "This goddess stuff is odd, mate."

Marcus chuckled and motioned toward the utility room. "Come, have some coffee. Freshly brewed."

Captain Lowe eyed him with mock suspicion as they entered. "Nay, mate, I'm good," he said, raising a hand in polite refusal.

Marcus smirked. "Relax. It's just coffee. I wouldn't do that to you."

Lowe chuckled, grabbed a mug from the cabinet, and poured himself a cup. He took a cautious sip, his expression shifting to pleasant surprise. "Oh, this here is good coffee."

"I'm glad you like it," Marcus said, leading him into the observation room.

They took their seats, gazing through the long viewing window into the meditation chamber. Annabelle sat in the center, diligently channeling her mana, her expression unusually serene.

"How long they been in there?" Captain Lowe asked, taking another sip.

Marcus pulled his watch from his shirt pocket and checked the time. "About an hour and a half."

Lowe blinked. "An hour and a half?!?" He looked from Marcus to Annabelle, then back again. "Ye got to tell me how ye got her to sit still that long."

Marcus smiled, taking a slow sip of his coffee. "All credit goes to the goddesses. I just explained to her, like I did to all of them, that the goddesses wished to commune."

He paused, thinking. "Actually... now that I recall, Miss Salazar asked Miss Fournier to help her learn how to properly channel her mana."

Lowe nodded slowly. "That's right... I remember Belle asking to spend time alone with the silver girlie." He scratched his chin thoughtfully. "Guess she really wanted to learn how to do magic right."

Marcus tilted his head. "How did her magic training go when she was younger?" he asked, curious.

Lowe let out a short laugh. "Well, when she was little, her papa taught her a bit of sea magic. And her mum gave her..." He hesitated, shifting uncomfortably before continuing. "Let's just say Belle gets her fire from her mum."

He cleared his throat. "I tried to teach her meself, but, well... I'm not magical. Not even a little." He chuckled and took another sip. "I mean, I tried. Bought a book and everything. But she can't sit still long enough for lessons."

Marcus nodded. "That explains a lot about her approach to magic." He glanced through the window at Annabelle, still in deep concentration. Settling back into his chair, he asked, "So, Captain Lowe, how's your crew settling in?"

Lowe grinned. "Mate, ye cleaned me sick off ye, we're close enough now you can just call me *Kidd*." He chuckled. "The crew's loving the new digs, and the fact they can eat in the cafeteria? A boon straight from these here goddesses."

Marcus nearly choked on his coffee. He hadn't considered the logistical impact of Kidd's entire crew using the cafeteria. His eyes widened. "I'm, uh, glad to hear they're adjusting well," he said, collecting himself. "I'm sure it'll put Miss Salazar at ease knowing they're being taken care of."

Kidd smirked over the rim of his cup. "Aye, it sure will."

Chapter 12

Regina closed her eyes, turning her focus inward as she channeled mana through her hands and feet. She envisioned the silver energy flowing outward, then traced it in reverse, through her fingertips, past her wrists, up her arms, and into her core. Within, she observed the raw, shifting currents of her power: some moved like water, smooth and steady, while others swirled like air, separating and reforming. At times it was rigid and unyielding, then suddenly soft and malleable, like melted wax.

With a deep breath, she pushed deeper, navigating the turbulent streams toward the very source of her strength.

A sudden sound, *a sharp yip,* snapped her out of focus. She startled, eyes darting around, but saw nothing. Shaking it off, she forged ahead, wading through the swirling energies like a swimmer cutting against the tide.

Finally, she arrived.

Before her stood a vast workshop, the air thick with the scent of oil, ink, and old books. A large chalkboard dominated the room, covered in intricate sketches, one depicting a sphere surrounded by smaller orbs, encircled by script she couldn't read. Some symbols resembled numbers or equations; others appeared to be a language she had never seen, yet almost remembered.

Scattered throughout the space were tools and machines, some familiar, like a manual drill press, while others defied understanding. One contraption caught her eye: a four-legged machine with a flat, rotating surface and a basin-like top. An articulated arm hovered above it, poised with what looked like a cutting tool.

Another yip echoed through the room.

Regina looked down and found a silver fox gazing up at her, its silver eyes bright with playful curiosity. She knelt, running her fingers through its silky fur. "Well, hello there," she greeted, scratching behind its ears. "What's your name?"

The fox leaned into her touch, clearly enjoying the attention, then pulled away and trotted toward the far end of the workshop. It paused, looking back expectantly.

Regina stood, brushing off her hands. "Oh? Where are we going?" she asked, following it with cautious excitement.

Regina followed the silver fox as it wove effortlessly through the cluttered workshop, dodging piles of strange and wondrous objects. She passed jars filled with swirling galaxies, glittering jewels, and what looked like miniature planets suspended in liquid. The fox moved with purpose, guiding her to the far end of the room where a woman with long, silver-grey hair sat perched on a workbench.

Dressed in a well-worn denim outfit, the woman worked with quiet precision, a pair of tongs in her gloved hands. Regina watched in silent awe as she carefully lifted what appeared to be a miniature sun from a container. Its surface pulsed with molten brilliance, casting flickering golden light across her face as she nestled it into an intricate contraption.

The fox let out a soft yip, its eyes flicking between Regina and the woman. But the woman merely waved it off with a distracted hand, still focused on her work.

Regina hesitated, unsure what to do. *Should I introduce myself? Speak?* Instead, she remained still, observing with quiet fascination. The fox, however, had other plans. With a sudden, piercing scream, it demanded attention.

The woman flinched, nearly dropping her tongs. "What, Tiktik?! What is it?" she snapped, turning to glare at the fox. But when her gaze landed on Regina, her expression shifted to surprise, *and then warmth.*

"Regina?" Her voice softened. "You made it here already?"

"I...um, yes," Regina stammered, her mind spinning. *Where was here?* She tried to retrace her steps, channeling her mana, exploring its flow, and then somehow arriving in this surreal workshop.

"Where is here?" she asked, her thoughts spilling out in rapid succession. "Did I go through a portal? Was I kidnapped? Is this a trance? Or time travel? Or maybe... a separate universe?" She paused, eyes narrowing. "Can I teleport back? How will I return to the Order? To my family? Am I in danger? I don't *feel* in danger..."

As she rattled off each question, she noticed the woman watching her, not confused or annoyed, as many people were when Regina spiraled, but with an adoring smile. She seemed to enjoy every word.

"Oh, you're done?" the woman asked with a laugh. "You're safe, I promise." Her voice held a knowing calm. "Welcome to my workshop." She paused, tapping a finger against her chin. "Or should I say... welcome back?"

Regina frowned. She had a almost-photographic memory, she would *remember* being here before, wouldn't she? Yet something about the place *felt* so familiar. And then one question leapt to the front of her mind. "Why do you have silver hair and eyes like me?"

The woman blinked, caught off guard. With a gentle smile, she pulled a strand of silver hair forward, examined it, then let it fall.

"That, my dear Regina" she said, "is such a good question." She set her gloves aside and clasped her hands, her smile playful. "The last time we met, I gave you a gift and that's what changed your hair and eyes."

Before Regina could process that, the woman clapped her hands.

The workshop vanished.

Regina blinked. She now sat in a cozy parlor, across from the woman in a plush armchair. Between them rested a table set with a delicate tea set and a tray of pastries. Above, the ceiling shimmered with tiny suns and galaxies, their soft glow bathing the room in ethereal light.

"Ahh, much better," the woman said, biting into a pastry. She now wore a striped shirt beneath her denim vest, her goggles still resting atop her head.

Regina glanced around, noting the sharp contrast between this room and the chaotic workshop. Where the workshop had been full of tools and odd contraptions, the parlor was refined and serene. Paintings adorned the walls, and elegant statues stood in the corners.

After a brief pause, Regina reached for a pastry. The first bite flooded her senses with a delightful blend of apple and banana—flavors somehow richer, more vivid than she'd ever tasted. She smiled and reached for another.

"I knew you'd like those," the woman said, looking pleased. "I made them special, just for you."

"Thank you," Regina replied in her signature cheerful tone, savoring the taste. But the warmth of the moment gave way to lingering curiosity. "Wait... what did you mean by *welcome back* to your workshop? I don't remember ever being here before."

The woman takes a slow sip from her teacup, her silver eyes twinkling. "You may not remember the last time you were here," she says gently. "I know your memory is remarkable, but this was before you could remember anything."

Regina blinks. "Before I could remember?"

The woman nods. "Yes. We met before you were born, right here, in this very room."

Regina stares, struggling to grasp the idea. "Before I was born?"

The woman chuckles softly. "The first time we spoke was when your soul was first formed, before you found your way into your mother's arms." She pauses, taking another sip. "We had a talk much like this one... well, minus the pastries. You weren't quite ready for these gifts back then."

Regina tries to recall something, anything, but it's like reaching for fog. Her brow furrows. "I just... I just can't remember."

The woman sets her cup down with care. "Your memory began the moment you entered your body, so it's not your fault," she says with a warm smile. Then, with a playful tilt of her head: "Do you know who I am?"

Regina presses a finger to her chin, piecing things together, the familiarity, the silver hair, the strange sense of knowing. Slowly, she ventures a guess.

"You... you're the goddess," she says, though a trace of uncertainty lingers.

The woman beams. "That's my Regina, got it on the first try!" She raises her hand over the table, palm out towards Regina.

Regina tilts her head, puzzled. "Um... what are you doing?"

"It's called a high-five," the woman grins. "I just invented it, clap your hand into mine."

"I... I don't know if I'm supposed to touch a goddess."

The woman's eyes soften. "You, my dear, are my avatar." With a flick of the goddess' fingers, Regina's hand rises involuntarily to meet hers. Their palms touch in a gentle clap, and the woman's delighted smile lights up the room. Regina can't help but smile back.

The goddess lowers her hand and leans in slightly. "You see, my avatar, my sisters and I can't enter your world ourselves, it's part of how we made it. So, every now and then, we choose someone very special like yourself, to carry out our will."

Regina nibbles another apple-banana pastry, thinking. "How will I know your will?" she asks. "Will you tell me what to do?" She brightens suddenly. "I know this great whisper spell my mom taught me! I could show it to you."

The goddess laughs, a sound like wind chimes in spring, and claps her hands. "That's my Regina, always eager to help and share her knowledge." Her eyes twinkle. "I already know that whisper spell, my sweet avatar, but I'm a little too far away to use it myself."

She sips from her teacup, Regina notices it looks different from before.

"If I give you the rest of my gifts," the goddess continues, setting the cup down with a knowing smile, "we will be much closer. You'll feel my will as if it were your own... at times."

Regina nods, though a flicker of disappointment crosses her face. "Okay."

"Oh, it isn't so bad," the goddess says gently. "Three of my sisters have chosen avatars as well. You'll have them beside you for your journey through life." Her smile softens. "I wouldn't trade anything in the universe for my sisters."

She pauses, lost in thought, then shakes it off with another bite of pastry.

Regina wrinkles her nose. "I like Annabelle, and Sophie's okay... but kind of scary. And Lisa..." she sighs "Lisa's always mean to me when I talk about my magic."

The goddess chuckles, reaching across the table to squeeze Regina's hand. "Relationships rarely stay the same, my avatar. Friends can become enemies, and enemies can become friends." She gives her hand a comforting pat. "Those girls are as special as you are. Just give them time."

Regina frowns slightly but doesn't argue. She takes a sip of tea and asks, "Why did you pick me?"

The goddess smiles, a smile bright like sunlight. "Because you are tenacious, sweet, clever, and dauntless. Everything I want in my avatar."

Regina glances down. "But... I get scared all the time. I wouldn't call myself dauntless."

The goddess tilts her head, silver hair shimmering in the light. "Then you are selling yourself far too short," she says with a wink. "One day, you'll see what I see."

Before Regina can answer, the goddess snaps her fingers with a playful flourish.

In an instant, the parlor disappears.

Regina now stands on a lush, manicured lawn. The grass is impossibly green; the air scented with blooming flowers. Above, the sky stretches wide and golden, streaked with violet hues.

The goddess's attire has changed. She wears a flowing black sundress that shimmers with stars and galaxies, as if the entire cosmos were stitched into the fabric. A silver sash wraps around her waist, gleaming like moonlight.

Beside Regina, Tiktik yips impatiently, his silver tail wagging with anticipation.

"He wants you to throw the ball," the goddess says with a knowing smile.

Regina blinks, just about to ask *What ball?* ...when she realizes she's already holding one. A small cloth sphere of red and blue rests in her palm, soft to the touch and jingling faintly with a bell inside.

Tiktik yips again, bouncing up and down eyes bright with excitement.

With a laugh, Regina tosses the ball across the yard. The silver fox dashes after it, his movements fluid and swift. He returns moments later, but drops a different ball at her feet, this one solid gray, yet it jingles just the same.

Regina picks it up, examining the texture before throwing it again.

"He loves that game," the goddess muses, watching Tiktik dart through the grass.

Regina turns her attention back to the goddess, now wearing a black bowler hat with a silver trim, as if it had always been there. Tilting her head, she taps a finger to her chin.

"Brother Marcus said I'm supposed to commune with you," Regina says hesitantly. "But... I don't really know how. Is there a prayer I should say? Or..." she fidgets "...some kind of dance? I mean, I don't *really* know how to dance, but I can learn if it'll help."

The goddess bursts into laughter, covering her mouth with a delicate hand. "No, my dear avatar, you don't need to dance for me." She pauses, eyes gleaming with mischief. "Although... next time we meet, I *would* like to see you dance."

Regina groans, her cheeks flushing as the goddess chuckles.

"To commune with a goddess," the goddess continues, her tone soft and reassuring, "is simply to speak. To listen. To understand what I plan I place upon your heart."

Regina blinks. "You have a plan for me?"

"Oh, I do," the goddess replies, sipping once more from her ever-changing teacup that floats near her. Then she leans forward, voice bright with mischief. "But first, what is my domain?"

Regina thinks. She taps her chin with a knuckle. Then, slowly, a smile spreads across her face. "Oh, that's easy," she says with growing confidence. "You are the goddess of Change."

The goddess beams. "My avatar," she says, delighted. "I knew you'd see it."

Regina grins and picks up a green-and-yellow ball Tiktik drops at her feet. "It was tricky at first," she admits, tossing it across the lawn, "but playing with Tiktik made it obvious."

"As clever as ever," the goddess says warmly, watching her with affection.

She turns away, her silver hair now short, soft curls resting above her shoulders. Her gaze sweeps across the vast meadow, her voice heavy with quiet wisdom. "Change, my dear avatar, is everywhere and in everything."

She lifts her hand.

With a flick of her wrist, the tranquil meadow vanishes, replaced by a scorched wasteland. Rivers of lava wind between jagged black stone, casting a fiery glow over the broken earth. "Even the most unforgiving places ..." she says.

Then another motion—gentler this time—and the lava plains shift into paradise. Palm trees sway in a balmy breeze, jewel-bright birds' flit through the canopy, and the air hums with life and the scent of blossoms. "...can become beauty, with the subtlest shift."

Regina stares in wonder, eyes wide. "Whoa," she breathes.

The goddess glances over her shoulder, smiling. "I am the only constant in the universe. Each tick of the clock is my voice. I am the Catalyst...the turning of tides, the whisper that urges caterpillars to become butterflies."

In her palm, a silver caterpillar coils and glows. She closes her fist gently, then opens it to reveal a radiant silver butterfly. It flutters free into the transformed world.

Regina giggles but quickly covers her mouth, unsure if laughter is allowed.

The goddess chuckles and turns to face her, then winks.

Regina gasps, then breaks into a wide smile.

The goddess's face is no longer her own. It's Regina's. Her own curious eyes, her silver hair, her own wonder reflected back at her.

"You see," says the goddess in Regina's voice, "a part of your lives within me, just as a piece of me dwells within you."

She gestures toward her chest, and for a moment, Regina feels warmth blooming deep inside. "We are bound, you and I, in ways deeper than you know."

Regina stares, uncertain whether to feel awe or fear. "But... how?" she whispers.

The goddess smiles gently. "If I am the Catalyst, then you are my Impulse."

At those words, something clicks inside her. A pulse of heat. A thrum of something old, something *hers*. She touches her chest, eyes wide. "I feel it."

"As my Impulse," the goddess says, her face shifting back to her own, "you will bring my will into the world." Her silver eyes gleam—mischievous, eternal.

Regina swallows hard and nods, a small smile creeping onto her lips. "I think... I think I understand."

The goddess smiles fondly. "But understanding, my dear, is only the first step."

Her expression shifts, silver eyes darkening as she gazes across the meadow. "There's something you must watch for, my dear Impulse," she says, her tone soft but weighted. She lifts her hand, and with a slow, deliberate motion, the landscape changes. The meadow vanishes, replaced by a vast garden, rows upon rows of identical flowers, each petal perfectly shaped, every blade of grass standing at the exact same height. Even the breeze moves in systematic, calculated intervals.

Regina looks around uneasily. "It's... nice, I guess," she says, though something about it feels wrong. Too neat. Too perfect.

The goddess watches her closely, a small, knowing smile at her lips. "Uniformity has its charm," she muses, plucking a flawless rose from a bush, its petals spiraling in mechanical symmetry. "It's predictable. Safe. But beware, my dear." She tightens her fingers, and the rose crumbles to dust in her palm. The garden begins to fade, vibrant colors drain into muted grays, soft curves harden into rigid lines, until only a barren stone courtyard remains. "When conformity grows too strong, it becomes the prison of tyranny."

Regina shivers, hugging her arms. "What... what is this?"

"The danger," the goddess says, her silver hair catching the pale light. Her words settle heavily in the air. "It whispers promises of stability, of safety, of peace. But true peace, real harmony—doesn't come from stillness, Regina. It comes from motion, from growth."

Regina frowns, unease crawling up her spine. "But... if it's so bad, why would anyone listen?"

The goddess steps closer, tucking a stray strand of Regina's hair behind her ear. "Because conformity feels good. It feels right. It offers certainty, in a world full of doubt. And that is why it is so very dangerous."

Regina glances down at her hands, fear rising in her chest. "How do I..." She trails off, her voice caught in that fear.

The goddess kneels and looks into her eyes, seriousness overtaking her playful demeanor. "You adapt," she says flatly. "Remember, change is constant, even inside you." She playfully flicks Regina's nose, making her hair and eyes glow silver. A small golden light, the size of a coin, begins glowing inside the goddess near her heart.

Regina's eyes widen. "What's that?"

"That, my dear avatar, is the piece of you within me," the goddess says, her smile returning, though it doesn't quite reach her eyes. "When the world starts feeling too perfect, when questions are not allowed, when choices begin to disappear... that is when you'll know." She leans in, whispering, "Beware the control of uniformity."

Regina nods slowly, the weight of the words settling in her chest like stone.

With a snap of the goddess's fingers, the meadow returns, wild, vibrant, alive, as if the barren courtyard had never existed. The strange glowing feeling inside her is gone.

The goddess grins and nudges Regina's shoulder. "But enough of that. You have a whole world to change, my Impulse."

Regina forces a smile, but the chill in her heart lingers.

"I have important things to tell you before our time is over." the goddess says gently. As she approaches, the galaxies swirling in her dress shift, stars and nebulae flowing with every step. She stops before Regina and places a hand on each of her shoulders, her eyes bright with warmth and wisdom.

"First," she says, her voice soft yet firm, "you must follow Brother Albert's lead. He was close to the truth, and he left you everything you'll need to stop all this, before it spirals out of control."

Before Regina can speak, the goddess leans in and kisses her cheek, a tender, familiar gesture that echoes her mother's love. "And," she adds, resting her forehead against Regina's, "go see your family when you can. They will need you soon." She kisses

Regina's other cheek, different from the first, yet somehow even deeper. The meaning behind it lingers like a promise unspoken. Then, without warning, the goddess wraps her in a strong, unwavering embrace. Regina feels everything, the burden, the love, the quiet strength encircling her like armor.

"Go forth, my avatar," the goddess whispers. "And bring a great change to the world."

In her arms, Regina feels a spark ignite an inferno inside her soul. She draws a breath, steady and sure. Inspired. Determined. Unshakable.

She will change this world.

For the better.

[----------]

Marcus and Captain Kidd sat in the observation room, their coffee nearly gone. Kidd's eyes stayed locked on Annabelle, still amazed that Marcus had managed to get her to sit still for so long.

After a moment, Kidd leaned back in his chair. "Brother Marcus, how long does this usually take? Three, four hours?"

Marcus rubbed his chin, thinking back to what he'd read in the guidebook. "We're at the mercy of the goddess," he said. "One girl took three whole days before she could commune."

Kidd nearly choked on his coffee. "Three days? How'd she eat? Or sleep?"

"I had the same questions," Marcus admitted with a sigh. "The book didn't say." He paused, then added, "We'll have to put our faith in the goddesses... and of course, their avatars."

Kidd smirked, raising his cup in a mock toast. "Your lips to their ears, mate." He turned his eyes back to the girls, all sitting in deep meditation, each in her own style.

Marcus pulled his journal from its sling, preparing to write, when suddenly a brilliant silver light flooded the observation room. Both men looked up as the silver section of the goddess clock blazed with a glow unlike anything they'd seen before.

Their attention snapped to Regina, still seated beside Annabelle, but now silver light poured from her body. Her curly hair lifted in every direction, as if caught in an invisible whirlwind.

Marcus sat frozen as Regina rose to her feet. The energy swirled around her like a storm, her dress billowing in the current, the fabric resisting as though it moved against a tide. Then, without hesitation, she walked to the great doors, those only avatars could open. She raised her right hand, and with a soft hum, the doors parted.

Marcus snapped out of his daze and rushed from the observation room, arriving in the foyer just as Regina entered. The swirling energy faded, her hair and dress slowly settling. Marcus swallowed, staring into her glowing silver eyes. "Miss Regina?" he asked, unsure if the same girl he'd met yesterday still stood before him.

"Yes, Brother Marcus?" Regina said calmly, the glow in her eyes gradually dimming. "What can I do for you?"

He blinked, still processing. "Are you... are you okay?"

Regina's face lit with a bright, familiar smile. "Yes, I feel fine! Actually, I feel great!"

Kidd chuckled from behind Marcus, tipping his hat. "Well, missy, you're absolutely radiant."

Regina giggled in that sweet, unmistakable tone. "Thank you!"

Marcus and Kidd watched as the last traces of silver light faded from her skin, leaving her once again unmistakably herself.

Then Regina swayed, bringing a hand to her forehead. "Oh... I'm kind of tired all of a sudden."

"Please, have a seat." Marcus stepped forward, gently guiding her to the nearby couch.

Regina sank into the cushions with a soft sigh. "I met my goddess... she is so fun..." she murmured dreamily, drifting off mid-sentence.

Marcus watched as her breathing evened out, then eased her into a more comfortable position. Looking around the room, he realized with concern that there weren't nearly enough couches if all four girls came out this exhausted.

Frowning, he glanced toward the double doors of the goddess clock room. "I need to get her back to her bed. If the others come out like this, we'll run out of space all too fast."

"I'll keep an eye on the others while you get the little miss settled," Captain Kidd offered with a nod.

Marcus gave him a grateful look. "Thank you, Captain. I'll be back as soon as I can."

"No worries, mate," Kidd said with a casual wave.

Carefully, Marcus reached under Regina's sleeping form. "Up we go," he said to her, lifting her effortlessly. Regina stirred only slightly, leaning into his arms as she slipped deeper into sleep.

Marcus carried her from the temple, moving swiftly toward the dormitory to return Miss Fournier to her bed, his mind racing with the implications of what he had just witnessed.

Chapter 13

Annabelle hummed her favorite shanty, letting its rhythm guide her as she relaxed. With each note, she channeled mana through her hands in a steady, measured flow, the melody weaving through her thoughts like an old companion. She mouthed the words silently, using them to keep time as she worked her magic:

We work the ship with all our might,
To keep her sailing through day and night.
We work the deck, and we work the hold,
Keep our pockets full of gold.
Hey ho, let me go, I got none left to even show,
Check me pockets, check me bed…

As the tune filled her mind, Annabelle envisioned her mana as a vast ocean the glassy surface concealing powerful currents beneath. Below that calm exterior, her energy churned restlessly, splitting into intricate channels that wove and merged like a living map. Some currents spiraled into whirlpools, pulling the surface layers into unseen depths where forgotten things waited.

Ghostly remnants drifted below, wreckage from shattered ships and skeletal sailors, their hollow eyes watching from the dark. As her focus deepened, Annabelle traced the mana's flow through her grip, her fingers curling on instinct. Then she paused. Something is … odd… different.

In the swirling tide of bones and debris, a shadowed shape caught her eye. She reached for it, brushing aside a weathered skull to reveal a dark orange hook nestled in the current. It felt heavier, denser, solid like nothing else here. A strange weight settled in her chest as her hand closed around it.

Curious, Annabelle pulled. The hook resisted at first, then tore free, dragging with it a thick, ancient-looking chain from the depths. The moment it emerged, a gust of wind rushed through her senses, carrying the tang of salt and the distant creak of timber.

When she blinked, she was no longer in the realm within herself.

She stood on the deck of a ship sailing across an unfamiliar sea. The water shimmered with a rich orange hue, contrasting against the bright blue sky overhead, where fluffy white clouds drifted undisturbed. Around her, the crew bustled with purpose, securing lines, adjusting sails, and hauling gear into storage.

Annabelle took a cautious step forward, her boots thudding against the wooden planks. She turned toward the bridge, but before she could take another step, a wiry young man darted across the deck toward her. His uniform, though worn from years at sea, was neatly kept, and his sharp eyes scanned her with a blend of curiosity and urgency.

"Good day, ma'am," the runner said, tipping his cap. "The esteemed passenger requests your presence in her suite."

Annabelle nodded, shifting her stance. "Aye, lead the way then."

With a quick wave, the runner turned. "Aye, follow me, miss."

Annabelle trailed behind him, descending a narrow staircase that led to a set of imposing double doors. An unknown, yet strangely familiar, symbol was carved into the wood, its curves and edges stirring something long-buried in her memory.

The runner gave a slight bow. "Here you go, ma'am. Good day."

"Aye, good day to ye," Annabelle replied, watching him retreat up the stairs, no doubt off to deliver another message.

She approached the doors and knocked three times in slow succession, ship protocol demanded courtesy, after all.

"Come in, girlie," called a woman's voice from within.

Girlie? It had been a long time since anyone had called her that. A faint frown tugged at her lips as she pushed the heavy door open and stepped inside.

The stateroom was larger than expected, cluttered with weapons, dice, and odd trinkets scattered across shelves and tabletops. The air carried the scent of salt and exotic spices, a mix that reminded Annabelle of old port towns full of secrets.

At the center of the room, lounging in an oversized chair big enough to be a royal throne, sat a striking woman. Her black bodice hugged her figure, trimmed with white panels laced by vivid orange threads, cut to accentuate her shapely bosom. The sleeves draped off her shoulders, exposing flawless tanned skin that gleamed in the lantern light. A welcoming smile played on her lips, but it didn't quite reach her sharp orange eyes, eyes that mirrored Annabelle's own.

Her hair, long and full of natural curls, cascaded down her back, a sharp contrast to Annabelle's tightly braided and dreaded curls. Both women wore bandanas tied across their heads; Annabelle's was red, while the women were white with orange stripes and intricate lettering sewn into the fabric.

Perched comfortably on the woman's lap was an orange-furred lion monkey. Its beady eyes fixated on Annabelle as it clutched a small ball, seemingly mid-game.

The woman glanced at Annabelle, arching a brow. "Well, girlie?" she said, her voice carrying a sharp edge. "What do ye want? As ye can see, I'm busy playin' with me Simba here."

The monkey screeched at Annabelle, making it abundantly clear she wasn't welcome.

Annabelle hesitated, momentarily thrown by the woman's tone. "I... I think I'm here to see the goddess," she said carefully.

The woman barely looked up. "Well, I'm busy, girlie," she said with a smirk, then clapping her hands. The monkey flung the ball into the air, and on her second clap, she missed it. Simba caught it with a chirp, his tiny fingers curling triumphantly around the prize.

Annabelle swallowed her frustration. "Excuse me," she said, quieter now. "I was told I needed to speak with ye."

The woman gave an exaggerated sigh. "No one told me ye were comin', so why don't ye wait somewhere else? As ye can see, I'm very busy... doin' somethin' important, *girlie*." The final word dripped with pointed disrespect.

Simba screeched in agreement, tossing the ball again.

Annabelle's heart sank. The rejection stung more than she cared to admit, she'd hoped for understanding, for guidance. Feeling dejected, she turned to leave, her hand resting on the door handle.

"Why don't ye come back tomorrow?" the woman called behind her, then added with a smirk, "Or better yet...next week."

Annabelle froze. **That** was one insult too many.

"Nay," she said coldly, her grip tightening before she let go and turned back. "I won't be back tomorrow, next week, or next month." Her eyes burned with fire. "Yer going to see me right now."

She strode forward, boots thudding hard against the wooden floor.

Simba let out a shriek and hurled the ball at her. Annabelle snatched it mid-air and hurled it right back, striking him square on the head. The monkey recoiled, eyes wide with offense.

"That's enough out of ye," she said, then settled into the chair across from the woman. "Ye see, I've been through a lot to get here."

The woman's smile widened. "Oh? Well, why didn't ye say so?" She lifted Simba off her lap and placed him gently on the floor.

With a chitter, Simba scampered up the wall to a perch piled high with toys and scraps of cloth. He rummaged through the collection before curling up, his sharp gaze still locked on Annabelle.

The goddess studied her for a long moment. Then, a slow smile spread across her face. With a flick of her wrist, a deck of cards appeared, the edges glinting in the low light.

"I know...let's play a game o' Crew, girlie."

Annabelle blinked. "*Crew*?" she echoed, suspicion rising. The sudden shift unsettled her. "We usually play for coin. What are we bettin'?"

The goddess leaned forward, orange eyes gleaming. "How about this...if you win, I grant ye my gifts." She let the silence grow heavy. "But if ye lose... I'll get meself a new avatar."

Annabelle's breath caught. The stakes were higher than she'd imagined. Losing meant severing her connection forever. But Crew is her game. Not even Kidd could best her on most days. A confident grin curved her lips.

"Aye," she said. "Deal the cards."

The goddess held the deck above the table and snapped her fingers. The cards sprang to life, shuffling themselves mid-air before landing in front of Annabelle.

She split the deck, placing the bottom half on top with practiced ease, then slid them forward.

Another snap, and the cards dealt themselves into perfect arcs across the table. Seven landed in her hand. She fanned them out—queen of spades, 2, 7, jack, and king of diamonds, 3 of clubs, and queen of hearts.

She placed the queen of hearts beside the queen of spades and silently hoped for a third. Across the table, the goddess's cards hovered mid-air, glowing with a soft orange light as they arranged themselves.

Out of courtesy, Annabelle waited until the goddess looked up before making her first move. She laid down the three of clubs and the king of diamonds with a flourish.

"After a short fight in an alley, I found a treasure map," she recited, discarding a useless low card and a risky high one. Drawing a new card, she smiled, it was the jack of hearts.

"Yer turn."

The goddess grinned. "Three queen payday."

The cards floated down onto the table in perfect formation, the queen of hearts, the queen of clubs, and...

Annabelle's eyes widened. That was *her* card. *What the hell just happened?*

184

"Oi!" she snapped, staring at her hand. The queen of hearts she had placed earlier was gone, replaced by the ten of diamonds. "Ye took me card!"

The goddess feigned innocence, a playful smirk on her lips. "I don't know what ye are blabin' 'bout." With a flick of her fingers, two more cards floated down before her, the five of diamonds and the ten of hearts. "While lookin' for a bit of coin, I found the treasure of love."

Annabelle barely had time to protest before the goddess casually plucked a card from the draw pile. Three more cards landed on the table: the seven of clubs, the seven of spades, and the seven of diamonds.

"Three seven payday!" the goddess declared, leaning back with a satisfied grin. "Good game."

Annabelle's stomach sank. Her hand felt off, lighter, and when she looked down, her seven of diamonds was gone, replaced by the eight of clubs. Her heart pounded. She'd never been beaten this quickly, not even by Kidd, and they played Crew nearly every night.

She clenched her jaw. "Best of three," she challenged, voice tight.

The goddess chuckled. "Well, I *did* beat ye rather quickly," she teased, smile turning smug.

The cards gathered themselves from the table and floated neatly in front of Annabelle.

"Ye lost. Ye deal," the goddess said, folding her arms.

Annabelle scowled. "But ye can make the cards shuffle and deal themselves."

"Aye, so what?" The goddess shrugged, tilting her head. "I won, which means I don't have to deal."

Annabelle stared at the deck, gears turning. Then she straightened her posture, softened her tone, and said in the most refined, *proper voice* she could muster, "It looks so wonderful when you make the cards dance with your magic."

The goddess perked up immediately, placing a hand to her chest. "It *does* look wonderful, doesn't it?"

With another snap of her fingers, the cards danced again swirling into two perfect halves before stacking neatly in front of Annabelle.

"Oh, I really liked the way you dealt the cards earlier," Annabelle added, in her *proper voice*, sweet as honey, playing to the goddess's vanity again.

But the goddess's sharp eyes narrowed. "Nice try, girlie," she said, unimpressed. "Ye lost. Ye deal."

Annabelle sighed, picked up the deck, and dealt seven cards to both of them. Then, without pause, she flipped the top card from the deck and placed it face-up beside the pile, the eight of hearts.

She picked up her hand, fanned the cards briefly, then closed them again without so much as a glance.

Across the table, the goddess's cards floated in the air, shifting and rearranging themselves with an elegant orange glow. Annabelle could tell she was organizing them for easy plays. The goddess's gaze flicked up to Annabelle, a smirk tugging at her lips.

"Ye nay going to look at yer cards?" the goddess asked, amusement lacing her tone. Then, her voice sharpened. "Are ye nay taking this seriously?"

Annabelle leaned back in her chair, lips curling into a cocksure grin. "Aye," she said confidently. "But I'll trust in me luck to see me through."

The goddess narrowed her eyes. "Oh, we'll see." With a flick of her fingers, three cards floated down onto the table, the five, six, and seven of clubs. "Walking five to

185

seven, fighting all the way," she declared, drawing a card from the deck. A moment later, she flicked it toward the discard pile, the two of spades. "Yer turn, girlie" she said, her voice dripping with mockery.

Annabelle inhaled deeply, tapping her face-down cards twice on the table before lifting them, hitting them with a bit of luck. Fanning them out, she couldn't suppress a grin. *Jackpot.*

Her hand held the jack of clubs, jack of spades, and jack of hearts, a perfect payday. Alongside them were the four and three of clubs, the two of hearts, and the two of clubs. She knew she wouldn't have long before the goddess took the cards she wanted from her hand, so she had to act fast.

With a sharp motion, she laid down the three jacks. "Jack payday."

Then, without missing a beat, she placed the four of clubs onto the goddess's five, six, and seven. "Dragging ye back into the fight."

Next, the three of clubs joined the chain. "One more step, aye."

Her hand hovered over the two of clubs, playing it now would leave her with a single card, and a single card meant a loss, because the goddess would shift her cards again. Her eyes darted to the discard pile, locking onto the two of spades.

"And a small…" she said, laying down the pair of twos before swiping the card from the discard pile. "Twos payday."

The goddess arched an eyebrow, her floating cards settling on the table. "Well, how about that," she mused, watching Annabelle's flawless victory.

With a snap of her fingers, the cards gathered themselves in mid-air, shuffling and dancing before landing in front of Annabelle once more.

Annabelle allowed herself a triumphant smile. *One down, one to go.* She tapped the top of the deck with her pointer and middle fingers, signaling she wouldn't cut the cards.

They shuffled again, dealing out a fresh set of seven to each of them, with the first card flipped face-up, a six of diamonds.

This time, Annabelle examined her cards more carefully. They weren't as generous as before: the four and five of hearts, the five and six of spades, the eight of spades, the nine and ten of clubs, and the jack of hearts. *No immediate paydays, but some potential.*

She drew the top card from the deck, the seven of spades.

A grin tugged at her lips. *Aye, not bad.*

She laid down the five, six, seven, and eight of spades in a smooth motion. However, instead of passing her turn, Annabelle considered her next move carefully. She knew the goddess wouldn't hesitate to *cheat* if given the chance.

"Oi, **I don't cheat, girlie**," the goddess corrected her. "*The cards just like me better…* because I am so beautiful."

Thinking fast, Annabelle laid down the four of hearts. "I once had a love…" Then the nine of clubs. "That would fight her way out of most situations." Finally, the ten of clubs. "But I had to break up with her after a big bar fight, where I lost a tooth."

With a final flourish, she discarded the five of hearts, leaving herself with an empty hand. She leaned back with a satisfied smirk. "Good game."

The goddess stared at the cards in disbelief. "Since when can ye tell a three-part story?"

Annabelle shrugged, shifting back to her *polite voice* "Three-part stories although rare," she said sweetly, "are allowed by the rules of me ship."

The goddess huffed, eyeing Annabelle with both irritation and amusement. "Aye, ye don't say."

With a wave of her hand, the entire scene shifted. The walls of the stateroom shimmered and dissolved, revealing the sweeping view from the ship's observation deck beneath a sky swirling with orange and deep blue.

Annabelle steadied herself as the new environment settled around her. Whatever came next, she hoped she was ready.

She found herself sitting at a grand table across from the goddess, who absentmindedly scratched the back of Simba's head. The little lion monkey leaned into the touch, eyes closed in pure contentment, a soft chirping escaping him.

The table was laden with an assortment of pastries, candies, and fresh fruit, their vibrant colors standing out against the gleaming wooden surface. Empty plates sat before both Annabelle and the goddess, waiting to be filled.

Glancing around, Annabelle realized they were on a large observation deck near the stern of the ship. The gentle pull of the water confirmed it. The sprawling deck was enclosed, but only partially, on her left stood a solid wooden wall with a pair of sliding double doors leading inside the ship. The other three sides were bordered by waist-high wooden walls topped with thick, polished railings.

The pristine condition of the railings caught Annabelle's eye. Not a speck of mold or grime in sight. The crew must spend hours scrubbing them clean, she thought with a wince, imagining the endless chores it would take to keep a ship this immaculate.

"It's not that bad," the goddess said, continuing to stroke Simba's fur without looking up. "Me crew worships the very ground I walk on. They fight to drink the water I bathe in."

Annabelle stiffened, eyes widening in shock. "What?!?" she blurted, realizing with horror: *the goddess had read her thoughts as easily as if she'd spoken them aloud.*

The goddess smiled slyly. "Me dear Annabelle, we have been connected since the first time we met."

Annabelle frowned. "I don't remember meeting ye," she said, folding her arms. "And trust a lass, I would remember meeting someone as grand as yerself."

The goddess placed a hand over her chest in mock offense. "Ye've forgotten me? Why do ye wound me so?" She paused, a sullen look on her beautiful face, letting the words linger before adding with a dramatic sigh, "I thought I meant more to ye."

Annabelle felt heat rise in her cheeks. "Oh... I'm sorry," she muttered, feeling a pang of embarrassment.

The goddess looked scornfully at Annabelle. "I know ye didn't yet have a memory, but..." she sat up, preening in her chair, "How could ye forget me, this beauty, me beauty once tamed, gods' little avatar of mine?" Her gaze pierced Annabelle's bravado.

Annabelle was mortified. She could tell the goddess was beside herself with a bruised ego. She knew she had to say *something* or this would only get worse. In her proper voice, she said, "Great goddess, I do apologize. My own tiny mind was not strong enough to contain even a visage of your mountainous beauty. If you would grant me your forgiveness, I swear on my very soul to honor and venerate your very name."

The goddess smiled and batted her eyes, receiving the complimentary devotion. "I guess I can forgive ye... this time" With that, she gently lifted Simba from her lap and placed him on the ground. He immediately screeched in protest, jumping up and down in a tantrum.

"I have to do this," the goddess said, giving him a pointed look. "Just wait."

Simba let out one final screech before scampering off to his play area near the double doors, sulking among a pile of toys and trinkets.

"He isn't happy," Annabelle remarked with a smirk.

The goddess sighed. "He enjoys me attention, and now he has to share it with ye," she said, shaking her head. "He's just acting like me spoiled little baby."

Taking a calming breath, the goddess reached for an orange fruit speckled with tiny red dots, rolling it between her fingers. She studied Annabelle for a moment before speaking.

"So, Annabelle Salazar," she said, her voice rich with authority. "Ye are me Avatar, acting on me will in the mortal realm." She locked eyes with Annabelle, their matching orange hues burning with unspoken power. "What questions do ye have for me?"

Annabelle leaned forward, nerves creeping into her voice. "Does this goddess thing mean I'll have to leave the *Fang*?" she asked quickly, eyes soft with concern. "Because ye know the Cap'n would be lost without me. I gots to give him time to find a suitable replacement."

The goddess's lips curled into a knowing smile. "I will not dictate the small details of yer life," she said, popping the small fruit into her mouth and chewing thoughtfully. A brief pause followed as she savored the flavor. "But know this..." her tone turning serious... "the life of an avatar, especially me avatar, can be a dangerous one. You may find those close to ye... will pay the price for yer actions."

Annabelle swallowed hard, unsure how to respond. The weight of the goddess' words settled heavily on her chest. To distract herself, she reached for a pastry and took a tentative bite.

The flavor exploded in her mouth, sweet like strawberries with a tang of pineapple, the texture as soft as the finest pillow. Before she realized it, she had finished the first and reached for another, rolling it between her fingers as she pondered the goddess's warning.

"I knew ye would like those," the goddess said, popping another grape-like fruit into her mouth with a satisfied hum. "But you should try the ones with the cherries on top...those are really good."

Annabelle finished the pastry in her hand, licking a stray crumb from her finger before reaching for the cherry-topped treat the goddess recommended. She placed it on her plate instead, deciding to savor it later. Right now, there were more pressing questions on her mind.

Once she swallowed the last bite of her strawberry-pineapple pastry, she leaned back in her chair and asked, "What exactly am I supposed to do as yer avatar?" Her gaze flicked to the pastry waiting on her plate, but she forced herself to stay focused.

"Ye are meant to act upon me will," the goddess said with a casual shrug.

Annabelle raised an eyebrow. "And how will I know when it's the right situation? Are ye going to tell me?"

The goddess shook her head, an almost wistful look in her eyes. "Sadly, me voice doesn't reach into yer world," she said. "But ye'll feel it, trust a lass. When the time comes, you won't miss it."

Annabelle thought back to what Brother Marcus had told her. She smirked knowingly. "Right... and yer supposed to give me a gift," she added, arching an eyebrow.

"Aye, ye a clever girlie, ain't ye."

Annabelle leaned in with a sly grin. "So, if I were to use me gift to make a bit o' coin... would that offend ye?"

The goddess gave her a thoughtful look, tapping a finger against her chin. "Depends," she said playfully. "If ye bring home a good heap a coin, then it's fine by me. But if ye only bring back a coin or two..." She paused, leaning in judgmentally. "That would just be unforgivable."

Annabelle chuckled, making a mental note: *never return empty-handed.*

Still pondering her situation, Annabelle frowned and asked, "Do I really have to work with the copper?"

The goddess tilted her head. "Copper? Who's that?"

Annabelle rolled her eyes. "Ye know... the purple girl. Sophie. She's one of them Aurorium coppers. I don't have to work with her, do I?"

The goddess rolled her eyes and sighed, giving Annabelle a pointed look. "Annabelle, I would do anything fer me sisters, and ye should feel the same about they Avatars."

Annabelle groaned. "But she's so uptight."

The goddess smirked knowingly. "Aye, well... me sister is uptight too," she admitted with a sigh. "But if I ever needed her, especially in a fight, I know she'd be right there, sword and shield at the ready. No questions asked."

Annabelle huffed, clearly unconvinced.

The goddess' eyes twinkled mischievously. "Besides, having her close makes it so much easier to make fun of her. If she isn't around, she won't hear ye."

Annabelle smiled acknowledging the opportunity granted to her by this beautiful goddess. "Aye! Ye are the best goddess of 'em all."

The goddess smirked, tilting her head with an exalted air. "Tell me, me wee avatar, do ye even know the goddess you admire so?"

Annabelle searched her mind, thinking through everything she'd seen of the goddess so far. After a moment's hesitation, she wagered, "The goddess of beauty?" She leaned on flattery, hoping to soften the blow if she was wrong.

"Beauty?!?" The goddess's expression darkened, and the air around Annabelle grew thick with tension. "Beauty, ye say?"

The goddess took a slow breath, her lips curling into a devilishly evil smile. "Aye... the goddess before ye be beautiful but..."

With a snap of her fingers, the world around them shifted violently.

Annabelle gasped as she found herself hovering high above a raging sea, trapped in the heart of an enormous storm. The wind howled in her ears, and colossal waves crashed below, each threatening to swallow her whole. She remained frozen, terrified that the slightest movement would send her tumbling into the watery abyss.

The goddess, however, floated effortlessly within the storm, untouched by the howling winds or driving rain. The elements bent to her will, the rain parted before reaching her, and even her hair stayed still, as if the fury itself feared to touch her. "I am the storm," she proclaimed, her voice booming over the Storm's wrath. "Me whims can create kingdoms... or tear mountains from their very roots."

She strode across the empty air as if it were solid ground, circling Annabelle with predatory grace. "With but a snap of my beautiful... little... fingers, I've birthed entire species, and snuffed out galaxies that dared block me view of me favorite nebula."

Annabelle's breath came quick and shallow as she drifted closer, her presence both suffocating and mesmerizing. The goddess reached out, gently cupping Annabelle's chin, drawing her forward until their noses nearly touched.

Then, in a voice barely above a whisper, she spoke, her tone rich and seductive. "Aye, I am the most beautiful of the twelve," she purred, lips curling into a wicked grin. "But make no mistake, me dear avatar..."

She paused, letting the moment stretch unbearably long. Then, with a flash of lightning and a deafening clap of thunder that seemed to shake the heavens themselves, she declared, "I am the great... and glorious... goddess of CHAOS."

The storm itself bowed in reverence, lightning streaking across the sky in wild, chaotic patterns while thunder rolled like applause.

Annabelle swallowed hard, eyes wide with awe. "Aye," she whispered, barely audible over the storm.

Chaos held her gaze, orange eyes locking onto Annabelle's own. "And ye are me tempest."

Annabelle no longer trembled. The fear that had gripped her moments ago was gone, replaced by something else entirely; thrall, awe, and a desire to be something greater. Her lips curled into a small grin as she asked, "Can ye do that again?"

Without moving or breaking eye contact, Chaos responded smoothly, "Nay, we have business to discuss." She snapped her fingers, never breaking eye contact, and Annabelle found herself aboard Chaos' ship again. This time, they were on the bridge, where Annabelle could see just how massive the ship was, *large enough to qualify as an island*.

"Me ship is big enough to qualify as a continent," Chaos corrected, watching Annabelle with a wink and sly smile. "Ye see, me Annabelle, the way of chaos is marked by grandeur." She spread her arms wide, as if embracing the vastness of the sea.

Annabelle chuckled. "Aye, 'tis grand alright. But what's this business ye wanted to discuss?" She leaned on the railing, expecting the goddess to finally give her some magical gift to make her fortune.

Chaos sighed, plucking an orange-speckled fruit from a nearby tray and rolling it between her fingers. "Ah, business... yer right tis time to be serious." She took a slow bite, chewing thoughtfully. "You ever notice, love, how some folk spend their whole lives tryin' to keep things... tidy?"

Annabelle's thoughts drifted to Lisa, lips quirking in a smirk. "I know a biddy like that."

Chaos smirked back. "Not her. She'll come around." She waved the idea off. "I'm talkin' 'bout someone who can't let themselves learn and grow. They say things like, 'everything has a proper place,' but deep down, they're always, lookin' for ways to create a mess for everyone else." She leaned on the railing beside Annabelle, gazing out at the endless waves. "Some folk, they can't stand the ebb and flow of life. They cling to their little rules and plans like a sailor cling to driftwood in a storm."

Annabelle raised an eyebrow. "Sounds exhaustin'." Her mind returned to Lisa, and she added with a grin, "Are ye sure you know who I'm thinkin' about?"

Chaos chuckled. "Tempest, the one ye are thinkin' 'bout of just has standards. She believes in fairness for everyone. What I'm talkin' about is far worse." She tossed the fruit core into the wind, where it burst into a puff of orange sparks. "I'm talkin' 'bout a biddy who makes plans fer other folk's lives, then uses force to make 'em follow 'em. People like that? They aren't just dangerous—they're downright _ruinous_."

"Ruinous?" Annabelle's curiosity was piqued.

"Aye," Chaos said, summoning another fruit to her hand. The orange-speckled orb floated lazily before landing in her palm. "Folk like that is always seekin' power, always tryin' to force their way onto the world. They don't stop till someone's got the guts to punch 'em in the nose."

Annabelle grinned. "Ohh, you want a lass to punch 'em in the nose."

Chaos took a bite of the fruit, speaking as she chewed. "Annabelle, remember this: *timin' is everythin'*. Show up to a con too early, an' the mark will sniff ye out. Show up too late, an' someone's already fleeced 'em." She swallowed, fixing Annabelle with a knowing look. "Ye got to act at the right time, Tempest."

Annabelle tilted her head. "Ohh, I tink I gets it," she lied, eager to move the conversation along.

Chaos smirked knowingly. "Ye will, me wee avatar. Ye will." She winked and snapped her fingers.

The air around them crackled, and in an instant, the world shifted. Annabelle found herself back on the observation deck, standing beside Chaos. The horizon stretched endlessly before them, the sea calm yet vast. Annabelle gripped the railing, but her thoughts lingered on Chaos's cryptic words.

Chaos, meanwhile, smiled as if savoring a secret only she could see.

She glanced around at the ship, the endless sky above, and the sprawling sea below. A faint smile played on her lips, but her gaze carried a trace of finality. "Our time is comin' to an end," she said softly, holding out her hand. "Take me hand, Tempest."

Annabelle hesitated only a moment before reaching out, her fingers wrapping around Chaos's hand. A pang of sadness welled in her chest, she didn't want this moment to end. There was something about this goddess, about her very presence, that made Annabelle feel alive in a way she never had before.

Chaos gave her a knowing smile. "Don't ye feel sad, love," she said, her voice warm and reassuring. "I'll be with ye the whole time, through all your grand adventures."

Before Annabelle could respond, Chaos pulled her into a tight embrace, squeezing her close.

Annabelle squeezed back, burying her face in the goddess's shoulder, fighting back the sting of tears.

"Now listen," Chaos said, her voice low and steady. "This is important." She didn't release Annabelle from the hug, instead she pulled back just a little locking orange eyes to orange eyes she speaks as if she wanted her words to sink deep into her avatar's soul. "Ye got to learn yer magic, all yer magic. Not just the magic in your necklace."

Chaos pulled back slightly, still holding Annabelle close, her hands firm on her shoulders. "Follow Brother Albert's investigation," she urged. "He almost had it all figured out."

Annabelle nodded, her voice quiet but resolute. "Okay, I promise."

Chaos's grip softened as she released her, stepping back just enough to look into Annabelle's eyes. "Use me gifts well, Annabelle Salazar," she said, her tone both serious and proud. "The others will need ye."

Then, with surprising gentleness, Chaos leaned in and pressed a kiss to Annabelle's forehead.

The world began to shift around Annabelle. Chaos, the ship, and even the crew started to dissolve into orange sparks, as if melting back into the wind and sea. The goddess remained serene, her radiant presence fading as if she were becoming one with the air itself.

As the last traces of Chaos disappeared, Annabelle's mana surged. She gasped, feeling it expands and grow within her like waves crashing against her very being. The intensity was overwhelming, pushing against her physical body as if she had eaten far too much, but instead of discomfort, there was raw untamed power. It filled every corner of her, roaring like a storm beneath her skin.

[-----✚-----]

In the observation room, Brother Marcus and Captain Kidd sat across from one another, discussing the girls and reflecting on their progress.

"I'd wager Griffin'll be the next one to finish with her goddess," Captain Kidd said, leaning back in his chair. "She's a hard worker, that one. Always pushin' herself."

Marcus frowned, hands folded neatly in front of him. "As their servant, I don't think it's proper to wager on their success," he replied evenly. "Besides, what about Annabelle? She was impressive with that water conjuring spell earlier."

"Aye, but that's her only reliable spell," Captain Kidd countered, shrugging. "She's got spirit, I'll give her that, and she's clever, but…"

A sudden burst of orange light flooded the goddess clock room, cutting him off mid-sentence. The orange section of the clock glowed brightly, casting its light into the observation room.

Both men turned toward the glow, their conversation forgotten as the air seemed to hum with energy. In the next room, Annabelle stood at the center of the orange goddess section, her body radiating mana in wild, uncontrollable waves. Her hair, normally bound in braids and dreadlocks, whipped around her as if caught in a fierce wind. The force of the mana had blown her bandana clear off her head.

The two men exchanged a wide-eyed glance before rushing out of the observation room and into the foyer.

As they reached the doors to the goddess clock room, the doors opened just in time for Annabelle to step through the threshold. She was a vision of power, orange light flowing from her body in brilliant waves. The light was blinding at first, illuminating the entire foyer, but with each step Annabelle took, the glow began to fade. Her hair gradually settled around her shoulders as the mana calmed, the energy slowly dissipating until only faint wisps of light remained.

"Belle!" Captain Kidd called to her, his voice filled with concern.

Annabelle lifted her head to look at him, her orange eyes unfocused and dazed. Her voice was soft, distant. "I met me goddess, Cap'n," she said, her accent heavy with exhaustion. "She said I can stay with the Fang…"

She took another step toward him before her knees buckled.

Captain Kidd surged forward, catching her just as she fell into his arms.

Marcus stood nearby, observing quietly. He was certain the captain remembered what had happened with Regina…the same exhaustion, the same sudden collapse after an encounter with the divine. Captain Kidd had been ready.

The captain adjusted Annabelle in his arms, her head resting against his shoulder. He glanced back at Marcus with a small smile. "Don't worry, mate. I got this one." He stopped on the way to the door and said, "Oi, Brother Marcus, don't tell Belle I bet against her."

As he turned to carry Annabelle to her room, he paused, looking over his shoulder. "Two down, two to go."

Marcus gave him a smile and watched him leave. His thoughts drifted to Miss Nozaki and Miss Griffin. He wondered how much longer it would take for the remaining girls to reach their own goddesses, and what revelations awaited them when they did.

Chapter 14

Today marked a significant milestone for Regina Fournier and Annabelle Salazar as they communed with their respective goddess. Regina achieved contact in ninety minutes, a remarkable feat, though still an hour longer than Fiona Murphy's legendary thirty-minute record. Annabelle, showing equal determination, followed Regina and successfully communed within two hours and fifteen minutes. Both girls are now resting, having received their blessings. I anticipate they will awaken by breakfast, their spirits renewed and their connection strengthened.

Meanwhile, Lisa Nozaki and Sophie Griffin labored through the night, striving to reach their goddess. Their perseverance is commendable, though the exact time needed for their breakthrough remains uncertain. My faith in their abilities is unwavering; I am sure they will succeed in their own time.

Captain Lowe and his crew have retired to Building 607. He mentioned undertaking "reset maintenance" on the Stormfang, a task I am sure is meant to keep his crew occupied and, I suspect, prepare the ship for its inevitable upcoming journeys. His leadership methods never cease to intrigue me, particularly how he balances pragmatism with a subtle undercurrent of optimism.

Lastly, I met with the new first assistant yesterday. Sister Ingrid was nice enough to lead her through orientation yesterday, though I have yet to decide which tasks she'll be assigned. Given the myriad personalities under the Order's roof, I am confident she will find no shortage of challenges to tackle.

For now, the air here hums with a blend of anticipation and exhaustion.

[-----✠-----]

Frustrated by her lack of progress, Sophie adjusted her approach. The settled tree method, once her dependable go-to, no longer produced the desired results. This time, she pressed her fingertips together, channeling a focused stream of mana upward, feeling it moves with precision and intent. Rising to her feet, she stretched her stiff limbs, muscles aching from hours of unbroken concentration. Not since her days as an initiate had she pushed herself this hard.

She eased into a series of stretching movements, fluid motions from combat skills training meant to release tension and loosen her frame. The familiarity of the routine brought a measure of comfort, though her thoughts remained unsettled.

"How do I overcome this?" she muttered, frustration sharpening her voice.

Lowering herself to the floor once more, Sophie crossed her legs and brought her hands together, palm to palm, settling into the balanced goddess form. She resumed channeling, infusing expended mana into her hands. It was the first technique she'd mastered as an Aurorium Initiate, a foundational practice drilled into her by the Den Mother. The memory surfaced unbidden: she and her fellow initiates sitting in disciplined rows, the Den Mother's steady presence guiding them.

But those faces, her companions, her mentors, were all gone. Frozen or slaughtered by some mechanical monstrosity. The weight of that loss pressed against her chest like a physical burden. Sophie didn't know how to change any of it, but she was certain of one thing: her path led to the goddess, and she would follow it to the end.

"Come on, girl," she whispered. Closing her eyes, she drew a deep, steadying breath and turned her focus inward. She urged her muscles to release the tension she hadn't realized she was holding.

In her mind's eye, she saw her body as a temple, a sacred vessel for the mana flowing within. She imagined rivers of glowing purple water streaming through her hands, crossing from right to left and left to right. But the current wasn't calm. It churned, surging upward in chaotic spouts before crashing down again, thrashing like a storm trapped within her.

"It's all your fault," a voice hissed in her mind; faint but denying to be ignored.

Sophie froze, her breath catching.

Jaw clenched, she forced herself to continue, peering into the turbulent currents of mana. Amid the bursts and wild surges, she narrowed her focus. And then, suddenly, the world shifted.

She was no longer seated on the floor but standing in her childhood living room. Her mother was there, screaming her name. Sophie's heart lurched as she saw the shield in her mother's hands, the sword poised beneath it, a stance of defiance, of desperation.

But it wasn't enough.

Her eyes widened as the memory overtook her. Her mother, strong, fierce, was frozen solid, encased in a block of ice.

Sophie's eyes snapped open, tears spilling down her cheeks. The vision tore at her, raw and relentless. Her posture crumpled as she collapsed into herself, sobbing into trembling hands.

"I'm sorry, Momma," she whispered, voice cracking. "I'm so sorry…"

[-----⦿-----]

Lisa sat with her palms facing upward, fingers slightly curled as she pushed mana from her hands. A soft, steady glow radiated from her skin, drifting upward like mist before merging with the unseen energy of the earth. She tried to maintain her focus, but her gaze slid toward Sophie.

Her new friend was clearly waging her own emotional battle, her determination evident even through the strain. Watching Sophie fight through her pain stirred a quiet ache in Lisa's chest. She couldn't fully grasp what Sophie had endured, but the weight of her sorrow was unmistakable.

"You can do it, Sophie." Lisa said softly over her shoulder, her voice threaded with quiet encouragement.

Sophie didn't respond, lost in her own struggle, but Lisa still felt compelled to offer her support. Refocusing, she closed her eyes and steadied her breathing. She envisioned the mana pouring from her palms, heavy and dense like fog, spreading outward until it mingled with the earth's energy beneath her.

Despite her resolve, frustration simmered beneath the surface. *Why hadn't the goddess spoken to her yet? What was she doing wrong?*

Lisa clenched her jaw and forced the doubts aside. This wasn't the time to falter. Drawing in a slow breath, Lisa reaffirmed her focus. Her mana flowed steadily as she vowed to remain vigilant. When her goddess chose to speak, Lisa would be ready.

[-----✝-----]

Marcus sat in the observation room; his weary eyes fixed on the girls below. Sophie wrestled with her inner turmoil, every movement a testament to her struggle. Beside her, Lisa fought her own quiet battle, seeking a connection to their goddess. The room was silent except for the faint creak of Marcus shifting in his chair.

He sipped from a glass of ice water, the cold bite jolting him awake. Coffee had been his crutch throughout the last day, but even he had his limits. The bitter yet tasty brew no longer helped, and the icy water offered a welcome alternative.

Exhaustion pressed down on him, he hadn't slept all night. He'd remained to watch over the avatars, just in case they needed him, though they never had. Still, the responsibility weighed heavily on his shoulders, leaving him unwilling to abandon his post.

A soft knock broke the stillness. The door opened, and Sister Alameda entered, composed and graceful. Her hair was swept into a neat bun, her demeanor calm and collected.

"Good morning, Brother Marcus," she said softly, her eyes scanning his disheveled appearance.

Marcus looked up and offered a faint smile.

"I'm guessing you didn't sleep at all last night," she observed, her tone gentle but pointed.

"The girls might have needed me," Marcus replied, a trace of stubbornness in his voice. He set the glass down and stretched, feeling the stiffness in his back. "Can you watch over them while I freshen up?"

"Of course, Brother," Alameda replied with a reassuring nod. "Take your time."

"Thank you," Marcus said, pausing to glance out the observation window one last time. His gaze lingered on Sophie and Lisa. "I may take a little nap as well."

"It would be well deserved," Alameda replied, smiling kindly.

Marcus nodded, grateful for her understanding. He drained the last of his water and rose, his movements slow but deliberate. As he left the room, a faint sense of relief settled over him. For now, someone else could bear the burden of vigilance.

"Thanks again, Sister," Marcus said over his shoulder as he left the temple of the goddesses, heading in search of a shower and, eventually, his own bed.

In the central hallway, his eyes were drawn to the towering statue of Saint Lorraine. Lantern light flickered across the sculpture's serene face, casting shifting shadows across its features. Marcus paused, letting the silence enfold him. He studied the intricate details, wondering what kind of strength it had taken to build the Order from the ashes of a failed religion, while bearing the voices of twelve goddesses in her heart.

"Sister Ingrid," he called out, remembering his neglected morning duties. He hadn't checked in with her. The temptation to skip it tugged at him, but he knew himself too well, a shower would likely be followed by a stretch of unconsciousness. With a resigned sigh, Marcus turned on his heel and headed for Sister Ingrid's office.

As he passed the cafeteria, he spotted Sister Sallie sitting at their usual table. A steaming cup of tea rested in her hands, a small bowl of fruit in front of her. She didn't look up; her focus fixed on the curling wisps of steam above the cup. Marcus lingered a moment, then moved on, climbing the stairs toward Ingrid's office.

At her door, he knocked quickly and stepped inside. "My apologies, Sister Ingrid. I lost track of time."

Sister Ingrid looked up from the papers in her hand, offering a sharp but forgiving smile. "Good morning to you as well, Brother Marcus."

Marcus's attention shifted to Brother Alex, who stood in front of her desk, his back turned. He turned at Marcus's arrival, surprise flickering across his face before it vanished behind a composed mask. Marcus noted the papers in Ingrid's hand, likely documents from Alex's Overseers sect.

She turned to Alex with a curt nod. "Thank you, Brother. You may go."

"Of course, Sister," Alex replied, voice clipped. He left without sparing Marcus a glance.

"Come, have a seat, Brother Marcus," Ingrid said, gesturing to the chair across from her desk. Her tone softened slightly. "Tell me about communing with the goddesses."

Marcus sat down, pulling his journal from the strap across his back and flipping to the day's entry. "Well, Sister," he began, scanning the page, "Regina Fournier made contact with her goddess yesterday after ninety minutes of channeling. She was followed shortly by Annabelle Salazar."

"And Lisa Nozaki or Sophie Griffin?" Ingrid asked, folding her hands neatly atop the documents.

"They're still working at it," Marcus admitted. His expression darkened as he closed the journal and rested his hands on it. "I'm particularly concerned about Miss Griffin. The trauma she's endured seems to be causing her significant difficulties."

Ingrid nodded thoughtfully. "They are at the whim of the goddesses. It may take time, Brother Marcus."

Marcus nodded as well, leaning back slightly in his chair. "If there's one thing I've learned over these past few days, it's that serving the goddesses requires patience."

That earned an approving look from Ingrid. "Indeed, Brother. And it seems you're learning that lesson well." She continued. "We've received communications from the Aurorium Clan, Verdantia, and the main library in Laminae," Ingrid added, waving the papers she'd taken from Alex.

"Oh?" Marcus asked, tilting his head. "What do they say?"

She glanced down, flipping through the pages. "Verdantia is pressing us to return young Miss Nozaki as quickly as possible. The main library in Laminae is displeased, apparently, they're not thrilled with how Regina Fournier ended up with us. And following the massacre at Granmark, the Aurorium Clan sent thanks for keeping Sophie safe. They've promised to send further instructions soon."

Marcus frowned slightly, his hand brushing his chin as he absorbed the news.

Sister Ingrid's sharp eyes lifted to him. "So, Brother Marcus, guide to the avatars, what will you do?"

He hesitated, brow furrowed as he considered the weight of the question. Finally, he said, "I serve the avatars, Sister. I'll do what's right for them."

A hint of a smile touched her lips. "It's good to see you taking your new duties so seriously," she said. Then, with a tilt of her head, she asked, "Did Regina or Annabelle give you any indication of what the goddesses want them to do?"

Marcus sighed and leaned back slightly in his chair. "Miss Regina fell into a deep sleep after communing with the Goddess of Change, so I can't be sure whether anything she said afterward came from the goddess or her dreams. Miss Salazar was much the same. She communed with the Goddess of Chaos and fell asleep almost immediately. Captain Lowe took her to her dorm before I could speak to her directly."

"It seems you're still in a holding pattern," Sister Ingrid observed. "Have you given any thought to what you're going to leave in your message for Sister Alameda?"

"I have a few ideas," Marcus admitted, shifting in his seat. "But I haven't written a proper draft yet."

Sister Ingrid's gaze flicked briefly to a framed picture of Brother Albert on her desk. "I suspect the goddesses' will is going to take the girls from this island before long. I wouldn't let that message wait, especially considering what happened to Brother Albert."

Marcus's expression tightened as he glanced toward the photo. "You make a good point, Sister," he said, voice quieter. "I'll make it a priority."

"After some sleep, Brother Marcus," Sister Ingrid said pointedly. "You'll be of no use to the avatars if you're too exhausted to think straight."

He chuckled wearily and rubbed his temple. "Point well taken, Sister. I'll rest first."

"Good," she said, rising and extending the papers toward him. "Well, let me not keep you."

"Thank you, Sister," Marcus replied, accepting the stack of messages. He stood and inclined his head politely. "If that's all?"

"That's all," she confirmed.

Marcus turned and stepped toward the door, his hand on the knob when her voice stopped him.

"Oh, and Marcus," Sister Ingrid added, her tone softer now. "We'll be holding a memorial service for Brother Albert tomorrow afternoon in the statue garden. I'll understand if your duties prevent you from attending."

Marcus paused and looked back over his shoulder. "Thank you, Sister. I'll try to make it," he said sincerely, then stepped out of the office.

The weight of the day followed him as he descended the stairs toward his quarters. For now, the pull of sleep was undeniable.

[-----◉-----]

As Lisa channeled mana from her hands, she pictured it in her mind, flowing and shaping itself. First, the energy became lush, vibrant plants, their leaves reaching toward an unseen sun. Then it transformed into fire, flickering, crackling, alive. Mountains rose next, jagged and immense, their peaks crowned in clouds.

She pictured herself soaring through those clouds, arms outstretched like a bird gliding effortlessly through the sky. The sensation thrilled her. A pale green cloud brushed her cheek, leaving behind a cool, dewy mist. She smiled, a deep contentment blooming in her chest.

Feeling bold, Lisa dove through the clouds, descending toward a shimmering green lake. She plunged into its surface, the cool embrace of the water enveloping her. Her body moved without resistance, as if she belonged there. She didn't kick or swim; the lake carried her, weightless and free.

A school of fish darted past, their silvery bodies glinting. They paid her no mind. Grinning playfully, Lisa reached out and poked one at the edge of the group. It startled and the others scattered, vanishing into the depths. Her laughter rippled through the water like a melody.

Breaking the surface, Lisa leapt from the lake and landed gracefully in a meadow blanketed with flowers. The colors dazzled, vivid greens, yellows, purples stretching endlessly around her. She lay down in the grass and gazed at the sky above, an enchanting dark green, with pale clouds drifting lazily across it.

As her breathing slowed, her eyes caught on a single flower that stood apart. Its green was deeper, richer than the others, almost glowing. Curious, Lisa reached for it. The petals felt unlike any other, smooth, warm, almost alive. She leaned in and inhaled. The scent was radiant and intoxicating, like sunlight and spring woven into one perfect breath.

The world shifted.

Lisa now stood in a vast, immaculate flower garden belonging to a grand estate. Her heart quickened as she took in the sight, rows of blooms cascading in waves of color. Carefully, she moved toward a stone path, ensuring she didn't disturb the blossoms.

Cool stone met her bare feet as she followed the path toward a towering house with tall glass-paneled doors. Inside, the rooms were sunlit and empty. She paused, then heard it, a woman's laughter, light and melodic, mingling with the sound of splashing water.

Lisa turned, following the sound around the side of the house.

There she is.

A beautiful woman stood in an open space; long green hair swept into an elegant bun. With magic alone, she guided scrub brushes across the wrinkled hide of a baby elephant. The tiny creature squealed in delight, spraying water into the air. Droplets caught the sunlight like diamonds.

The woman laughed, her joy warm and infectious, filling the space with peace.

As Lisa approached, the woman glanced over her shoulder, emerald eyes alight with curiosity.

"Well, hello," she called, her voice gentle and inviting.

Lisa froze. Her heart pounded. She knows *this is the goddess.*

Dropping to her knees, Lisa bowed deeply, forehead nearly to the ground. "Goddess, you honor me with your presence," she said, her voice trembling with reverence.

The goddess turned fully, smiling. "Please, my Lisa, rise." she said, her tone both kind and commanding.

Lisa stood but kept her gaze on the ground. "What is your will, Goddess?"

The goddess tilted her head. "My will?" she repeated, thoughtful.

"Yes, my goddess," Lisa said earnestly. "I live to serve your very will."

The goddess's brows knit. "Why are you not looking at me?"

Lisa stiffened. "I would not dream of offending you with my unwashed mortal gaze."

The goddess sighed, sadness softening her voice. "Oh, my Lisa. It is my will for you to look at me."

Lisa's head jerked slightly. Her training battled with the goddess' command. She hesitated, searching for a solution: *then found one.*

In a quick motion, she lifted her gaze, locking eyes with the goddess just long enough to see her fully: the curve of her hair, the depth of her emerald eyes, the hum of life in her presence. Then, just as quickly, she looked away again, hoping the compromise would satisfy both her goddess and her faith. Hoping the compromise would satisfy both the goddess and her deeply ingrained sense of decorum, Lisa lowered her eyes once more.

"Erisol," the goddess called out suddenly.

Before Lisa could react to the name, a sharp arc of water struck her squarely in the chest, dousing her from head to toe. The baby elephant's trunk had been the mischievous culprit, its aim precise and unrelenting.

The water wasn't painful, but it soaked her thoroughly, leaving her hair plastered to her face and her clothes clinging to her skin. Lisa gasped, stunned by the drenching. Her shock swiftly gave way to indignation.

"Why did you do that?!?" she demanded, looking up at the goddess with wide eyes and flushed cheeks.

The goddess folded her arms, her expression serene yet amused. "Because I wanted you to look at me," she replied with a glib smile. "Why would you think you shouldn't?"

Lisa blinked, completely baffled. "What?" she asked, shaking her head. "Because it is disrespectful for a woman to cast her unclean gaze upon the goddess of the harvest." Her voice still carried a touch of anger, *why didn't the goddess know this?*

The goddess raised a brow, visibly unimpressed. "There's so much wrong with what you just said," she said, her tone firm but not cruel. "First, I am not the goddess of the harvest."

Lisa's brow furrowed. "You are not?"

"No," the woman replied evenly. "I am the goddess, Unity."

Lisa's breath caught. "Unity?" she echoed, disbelief tightening her voice. The name wasn't part of any scripture she'd ever studied. "I do not understand."

"Oh, my Lisa," Unity said with weary tenderness. "Let's start over."

With a snap of her fingers, the world shifted.

Lisa found herself seated at a round picnic table on a shaded veranda overlooking the same flower garden. The table was elegantly set with a porcelain tea set trimmed in green, matching cups, and an array of fresh fruit and pastries. The air was thick with the fragrance of blooming flowers, touched with a hint of honey and warm spice.

"Have some tea," Unity offered warmly. A teacup floated gently to the place before Lisa. The teapot followed, pouring a steady stream of amber liquid. A golden ring of honey lifted from a nearby dish, melting into the tea, followed by a spoon that stirred with graceful, mechanical precision.

Unity prepared her own cup in the same way, adding two rings of honey. She smiled as she lifted the teacup with effortless poise.

Still stunned, Lisa blew gently over her cup and took a cautious sip. The flavor was extraordinary, richer and more layered than any tea she'd had, even at the Order. Without thinking, she murmured, "Mmm... that is tasty."

Unity's smile brightened. "I knew you'd like it."

Lisa flushed. "The tea is quite delicious, Goddess," she said, stiffening her posture.

Unity sipped hers without bothering to blow. Her expression turned serious, emerald eyes locked with Lisa's. "As my avatar, you will carry out my will on Earth."

"It will be my honor, Goddess," Lisa said, the words automatic, though her voice trembled.

Unity leaned back, her tone calm but heavy. "I've found that the best path to unity is through domination. After this, you will use the Order's power to destabilize the world. When the time is right, you will lead the Verdantia military in a war of extermination to topple the Seven Kingdoms. From the ashes, true unity will rise."

She sipped her tea as if discussing the weather.

Lisa's stomach twisted. Her hands shook slightly as she set the cup down. "Goddess," she said carefully, "I do not think I can do all that."

199

Unity's face didn't change, but her voice sharpened. "Don't worry. Once I give you my blessings, you'll be capable of truly amazing things."

Lisa hesitated. "Goddess… I do not think it is right."

Unity's eyes narrowed. "How dare you presume your morals outweigh mine?" she snapped. "I am one of the twelve who shaped the known universe. I hold truths that your children's grandchildren will never begin to grasp."

Lisa's throat tightened, but she held her ground. "But goddess, the world you describe would be soaked in blood. It would bring only death and suffering. That cannot be the path to unity."

"To be my avatar is to fulfill my will," Unity said, her voice hard as stone. "If you lack the vision to understand greatness, you are useless to me." She waved her hand, eyes cold and distant.

Lisa took a slow breath, sipping her tea to steady herself. Her father's voice echoed in her mind: *Always finds the angle.* But no angle here could justify what the goddess had asked. There was no winning move.

Setting the teacup down, she spoke softly but firmly. "Goddess, I beg you to reconsider. Your plan would turn the Seven Kingdoms into a barren, blood-soaked wasteland."

Unity's smile returned, but it was bitter. "I refuse," she said coldly.

With a flick of her hand, a glowing doorway appeared behind Lisa.

"Please," Lisa whispered, desperation breaking through. "Please reconsider."

Unity stood slowly, her back to Lisa now. Sunlight caught in her green hair as she turned her gaze toward her elephant companion. Over her shoulder, she said, voice frosted with disdain: "Have a joyful, mediocre life, Lisa. I was so wrong about you."

Tears streamed down Lisa's cheeks as she rose from the table, her heart breaking under the weight of divine rejection. "Goddess," she whispered, her voice cracking.

"Your tears mean nothing to me," Unity said dismissively, her back still turned. "If you'd be so kind as to hurry on your way, I have no time for fools who refuse to do what's right."

Lisa cast one final glance at Unity, her tears falling in silence. With no other choice, she stepped toward the glowing doorway, her heart shattered by the exchange. Upset and humiliated, she wiped her tears with trembling hands. Her heart ached, but she forced herself forward. Just before stepping through, she paused on the threshold. Turning back, she saw the goddess still standing at the table, her back to Lisa, a silent dismissal that cut deeper than words.

In that moment, Lisa made a quiet vow: *I will stop her avatar from destroying the world.* She had no idea how, but she clung to the certainty that time was still on her side. With one last look, she stepped through the glowing doorway.

As Lisa crossed the threshold, blinding light engulfed her. She expected to awaken in the Goddess Clock Room, her trial failed, but when her vision cleared, she found herself right back where she had started.

The veranda stretched out before her, unchanged. The flower garden still shimmered in vibrant hues beneath the green-tinted sky. Unity sat calmly at the picnic table, sipping tea as though nothing had transpired. A fruit-covered pastry rested on the plate before her.

Lisa froze, breath catching in her throat. She couldn't make sense of what was happening. Tears still blurred her vision.

"Welcome back," Unity said, her tone calm, almost amused.

"What…" Lisa stammered. "What is going on?"

Unity gave a small, enigmatic smile. "I'm sorry, my Lisa, but I had to be sure." With a wave of her hand, a handkerchief appeared, floating gently toward her. "The way you thought about me revealed a dangerous understanding of power and the world. You see, just because a being is powerful doesn't mean their decisions are just. And those in their service must possess the strength of character to resist them, to thwart them, if necessary."

Lisa stood rooted in place, confusion swirling with the remnants of sorrow and fury. After a moment, she approached the table and took the handkerchief offered. Slowly, she dried her tear-streaked face and smoothed her hair before sitting down.

Unity gestured to the teapot, which poured fresh tea into Lisa's cup. "You must use your conscience to determine what is right," she said, her voice firm but gentle. "The danger you face is insidious. It will tempt you with promises of power and righteousness. But without a conscience to guide you, you risk becoming a monster in the name of peace and stability."

Lisa's gaze dropped to her cup. Her fingers tightened around the saucer. "Like... Isabella?"

Unity tilted her head. "Who?"

Lisa hesitated. "The woman with blue hair. The one with the machine arm."

Recognition flickered in Unity's eyes. She nodded. "Ah. My sister's avatar," she said, glancing briefly to her right, as if seeing something unseen by Lisa. Then her gaze returned. "My sister has waited a long time to speak to her."

"She was so powerful," Lisa said softly, her voice tinged with awe and unease. "How did she do that without communing with her goddess?"

Unity's expression darkened, her earlier calm overtaken by sorrow. "The danger," she began, her tone heavy with regret, "found a way to draw out my sister's power and give it to her avatar. It twisted the gift, exploiting it for its own ends." She paused. "It's a tragedy, what happened to that girl."

Lisa's chest tightened. "What can I do?" she whispered, the weight of the question pressing down on her.

Unity met her eyes, gaze unwavering. "You can stop her." She gestured to the vibrant garden around them. "Do you see this garden, Lisa?" she asked softly.

Lisa nodded, her eyes tracing rows of flowers, each one unique in shape, size, and color, yet thriving together in perfect harmony.

"This garden represents my domain," Unity said, her voice gentle but brimming with conviction. "Each flower represents something unique, a culture, a person, a belief. Alone, each one is beautiful. But together, they create something far greater than the sum of their parts."

Lisa glanced at the flowers, her brow furrowing slightly. "But it takes work to keep a garden like this," she said hesitantly.

"Precisely," Unity replied, her eyes lighting with approval. "Unity isn't about forcing everything to be the same. It's not about domination or conformity. It's about nurturing diversity while ensuring all things coexist in balance." She knelt beside a bed of flowers, her hand hovering over a patch where a few unruly vines crept toward the blooms. "When one element grows unchecked, it threatens the harmony of the whole. These vines, for example, are like ambition or greed. Left untended, they choke the life from everything around them."

With a graceful wave of her hand, the vines recoiled, curling back into the soil.

Lisa watched in silence, the metaphor settling within her. "So your role is to keep the garden balanced," she said, her voice quiet with understanding.

Unity nodded, rising and brushing her hands clean. "Exactly. But balance is delicate, Lisa. It can't be achieved by force alone. It requires care, attention, and the wisdom to know when to act, and when to let things grow freely." She turned to Lisa, her emerald eyes   piercing.
"That's why I chose you. You understand that power without restraint destroys everything it touches. And you know how to listen, to the garden, to the world, to your own conscience."

Lisa hesitated, her gaze returning to the vibrant flowers. "But what about the vines?" she asked softly. "Sometimes they're so strong that no matter how much you pull, they keep coming back."

Unity gave a faint smile. "That is the greatest challenge of unity," she said. "Some vines can't simply be removed. They must be understood, guided to grow in a new direction. Or, if necessary, pruned to protect the greater whole. True unity demands constant vigilance, compassion, and strength in equal measure."

Lisa let the words sink in, feeling both their weight and the hope, they carried. She looked once more at the garden, seeing it anew, and nodded. "I think I understand, Goddess."

Unity's expression darkened. The lightness in her demeanor faded as her gaze shifted to the horizon. For a long moment, she said nothing, her eyes distant, as if watching something only she could see. "There is a danger in the world, Lisa," she said at last, her voice quiet but heavy. "A force that seeks to bring everything and everyone under its control. That's why I chose you to be my avatar."

Lisa nodded silently, her full attention fixed on Unity.

The goddess turned to her, emerald eyes sharp. "Imagine a hand so powerful it could reshape the world. A hand that promises safety, stability, and peace, but in truth, brings only chains. Chains disguised as unity. Shackles disguised as salvation."

Lisa's brow furrowed. "But safety is a good thing, is it not? Why should we not want stability and peace?"

Unity regarded her as a mentor guiding a student through a difficult lesson, her smile patient and loving. "I once served a god, the god of Conquest," she said, her voice steady, tinged with disdain. "He was always thirsty for more, always seeking to expand his dominion. His favorite promise was safety. And he was persuasive. So, persuasive that many didn't realize he was only offering to protect them from himself."

Lisa's breath caught.

"Conquest used me and my domain to fabricate a false peace and false freedom for those he conquered," Unity continued, her voice growing colder. "Tyranny often dresses itself in the garb of freedom and safety. It whispers sweet promises but shackles true liberty. And when it's challenged, it becomes the most destructive force of all, killing unity in the name of power and domination."

Lisa's chest tightened. She could feel Unity's lingering disgust for her former master, and it chilled her. "Do you mean… the god of Conquest has returned for you?"

Unity shook her head, a sad smile ghosting her lips. "No. The way we built this universe prevents the gods from pursuing us here. That's why I cannot act directly in your world."

Erisol, the baby elephant, reached out with his trunk, brushing it gently against Unity's neck. She smiled and stroked his trunk affectionately.

"Aww, thank you, Erisol. I love you too."

Lisa hesitated. "Is the danger the one who… did that to Isabella?"

"Yes," Unity said curtly, her expression hardening. She stepped forward, placing a hand gently on Lisa's shoulder. "Trust your conscience, Lisa. And remember: the greatest danger often comes wrapped in benevolence. When someone offers peace, ask yourself: who truly benefits, and who will suffer?"

Lisa nodded, her mind spinning from the weight of Unity's revelation. Her chest felt heavy, filled with both fear and resolve.

Unity stepped back, her expression softening slightly. "You have the strength to face this, my Lisa. The world will test you, and you'll doubt yourself. But remember this: true unity isn't born from domination, but from the courage to let others thrive as they are."

Lisa felt helpless. The magnitude of her circumstances pressed down on her. She had no idea how to move forward, *how to meet the expectations now placed upon her?*

"Don't worry so much," Unity said gently, her voice a soothing balm. "You're not alone in this. You have my sisters' avatars to help you."

"Oh... them," Lisa muttered, hesitation clear in her voice.

Unity's lips curved into an amused smile. "Them? And what, exactly, is wrong with *them?*"

Lisa hesitated, then blurted, "Well, Regina is... annoying. She wants to copy every magic she sees like she is desperate to prove something. Annabelle is a criminal, I mean, who knows what she's capable of? And Sophie? She is always on edge I am in constant fear she is going to hurt me." She sighed, shaking her head. "I do not think the other goddesses chose very well."

Unity chuckled softly, her green eyes warm and knowing. "Oh, my Lisa. Those girls are as dear to their goddesses as you are to me."

She waved her hand toward the meadow below, where Erisol played with a white wolf, an orange monkey, a silver fox, a blue hawk, a brown leopard, and a purple badger. The animals ran and tumbled through the grass, mock-fighting and chasing one another with infectious joy.

"Unity," the goddess continued, "is not about making everyone the same. It's about embracing differences and drawing strength from them. Look at Erisol. Some of those animals nip at him, others chase him, but he knows they're not trying to hurt him. He plays with them as they are, accepting their quirks."

Lisa watched the meadow thoughtfully, sipping her tea. She tried applying Unity's lesson to Regina, Annabelle, and Sophie. Each had their flaws, *or what Lisa saw as flaws,* but maybe there was more to them than she'd allowed herself to see.

Her thoughts drifted to Brother Marcus, and then, painfully, to Brother Albert. The memory of Albert's lifeless body struck her like a blow to the chest, and guilt rushed in. She had tried so hard to save him, but it hadn't been enough. *She had not been enough.*

"Oh," Unity said softly, as if reading her heart. She placed a hand over her chest, mirroring Lisa's pain. "You're thinking about Brother Albert, aren't you?"

"I..." Lisa's voice cracked, tears rising again. "I failed him, Goddess. I was not strong enough to save him. If I had practiced more, if I'd been better... I could have saved him."

Unity's expression softened, a tear slipping down her emerald eye. "That's my Lisa," she said tenderly. "A heart as vast as the universe." She leaned closer, voice full of quiet reassurance. "But my dear, you did not fail him. Meeting you girls brought him so much joy."

Lisa looked up, uncertainty in her tear-streaked face. "It did?"

"Oh yes," Unity replied with a gentle smile. "Let me show you." She waved her hand, and a smoky circle formed in the air. Within its swirling depths, an image slowly appeared.

Brother Albert sat on a stool in a bustling tavern, a mug of ale in hand, telling a story to an enraptured crowd.

Lisa leaned forward, unable to hear the words but captivated by his animated gestures and bright expression. She didn't need to hear the tale to know, it was about her, Regina, Annabelle, and Sophie. His joy was written in every movement. A soft smile broke through Lisa's tears. He had been happy. She wiped her cheeks with the back of her hand, a flicker of peace softening her grief.

Unity looked around, her expression bittersweet. "It seems our time together is drawing to a close," she said gently.

"But it feels like I just arrived." Lisa protested, her voice tinged with reluctance.

Unity smiled knowingly. "Yes, my dear. But we're all slaves to time." She rose gracefully from her seat and walked to the edge of the veranda, where the garden stretched endlessly before them. Holding out her hands, she said, "Come, my Lisa. Stand with me."

Lisa hesitated only briefly before rising to her feet. She stepped beside Unity, placing her hands in the goddess's, feeling their warmth and quiet strength.

"My Lisa," Unity said softly, her emerald eyes filled with love and gravity. "Above all, you must believe in yourself. Trust that you'll do the right thing, even when the path is unclear. Brother Albert led the way, retrace his footsteps, and you'll find the strength to protect this world." Her voice carried a weight that settled deeply into Lisa's heart. "And more than that, you must be the glue that holds the avatars together. The times ahead will test you all. But if you falter, the bonds between you may break."

"I will," Lisa said, her voice steady despite the ache of departure.

Unity smiled, gently squeezing her hands. "Oh, do not be sad," she said, her tone light yet reassuring. "We will meet again, once your journey is complete. Until then, do all you can to make the world a better place."

Before Lisa could respond, Unity pulled her into a warm embrace. She held her tightly for a long moment, then kissed Lisa's cheek, whispering, "Until I see you again, my Lisa."

A surge of mana rushed through Lisa's body, powerful and profound, leaving her trembling. Her Earthbloom sense expanded outward, filling her with an intimate awareness of every plant, rock, tree, body of water, and even the animals moving across the island. The sensation was overwhelming yet harmonious, as if the world itself was breathing with her.

Rising from her meditative position, a calm certainty settled within her. She walks toward the door, passing Sophie, who remained deep in her own search for her goddess. Lisa cast a quiet glance her way, silently wishing her success, then continued forward.

As she neared the towering double doors, a deep, commanding voice echoed through her mind like distant thunder. **"Only the worthy shall pass. Announce yourself."**

Lisa paused, her heart pounding. When she opened her mouth, the voice that emerged wasn't from her mouth it was from her magical core. *"I am Lisa Nozaki, the Avatar of Unity."* she declared. The words rang with power.

"You are the worthy," the voice replied.

The great doors creaked open, their immense weight shifting with effortless grace.

Lisa stepped forward, mana spilling from her like an overflowing river. In the chamber beyond, plants bloomed in her wake. Vines unfurled, flowers burst into radiant color, and the air shimmered with life.

Crossing the threshold, she felt the surge slowly ebb. The energy receded, leaving her body heavy with exhaustion, but filled with deep fulfillment.

"Lisa," someone called, their voice faint beneath the lingering hum of the world's magic.

She turned. A woman from the Order stood nearby, her expression curious and concerned.

Lisa's legs wobbled, and she made her way to a nearby couch, collapsing into the cushions with a grateful sigh.

"I met my goddess," she said softly, joy glowing behind her words. "She told me... we made Brother Albert so happy." A peaceful smile bloomed across her lips as she leaned back, eyes fluttering closed.

Before the woman could respond, Lisa drifted into a deep, restful sleep.

Chapter 15

egina awoke in her dorm room, morning sunlight filtering through the window and bathing the space in a warm glow. She lay under the covers for a moment, disoriented, trying to remember how she'd gotten there. A faint sense of disconnection gnawed at her. She glanced down, realizing she was still fully dressed, except for her shoes. *I never sleep in my clothes,* she thought, frowning. Yet the memory of crawling into bed remained stubbornly absent.

Sitting up, she swung her legs over the edge of the mattress and stretched, her movements slow and deliberate as she shook off the lingering haze of sleep. Her eyes drifted toward the wardrobe. With a small smile, she crossed the room, pulled out the dress she'd brought from home, and laid it across the bed. Outside the window, birds chirped in harmony with the gentle breeze. The world had fully awakened.

"Well," she said to herself, "guess I should get cleaned up." She grabbed the bag of toiletries Brother Marcus had kindly given her from the Order's stores and headed to the communal bathroom.

After a refreshing shower, Regina brushed her teeth and worked through her morning routine, carefully moisturizing her skin with the lotion in her bag. Back home, these simple rituals had often felt like chores, squeezed between obligations. But here, on Order Island, they felt almost indulgent. By the time she returned to her room, she felt grounded, ready to meet the day.

She slipped into her freshly laundered dress, grateful for the island's laundry service, a far cry from scrubbing clothes by hand as she'd done at home. Pausing at the mirror, she smoothed the fabric over her waist and checked her reflection. Satisfied, she stepped into the hallway, her shoes tapping softly on the polished floor as she made her way toward the circular hub where all the dormitory halls converged.

Her stomach growled, a sharp reminder she hadn't eaten since the previous morning. Food quickly became her highest priority. The scent of sizzling bacon greeted her before she reached the cafeteria door. Inside, she grabbed a tray and served herself a generous breakfast: sausage links, scrambled eggs, creamy grits, and a towering stack of pancakes. At the drinks station, her gaze lingered on the coffee. "Could I have a cup of coffee with milk and sugar, please?" she asked, voice polite but tentative.

The woman behind the counter raised an eyebrow, momentarily surprised. Then, with a nod, she poured the coffee, added milk and sugar, and placed the mug on Regina's tray with a faint smile. "Can I get you anything else, young miss?"

"No, thank you," Regina replied with her signature bright smile. Balancing her tray, she stepped into the seating area and scanned the rows of tables. None quite called to her. She wandered a bit, indecision tugging at her steps. Then, halfway down the room, she spotted Brother Marcus seated beside a woman Regina didn't recognize. The two were deep in conversation over breakfast. Regina approached the table. "Brother Marcus, may I sit with you?"

"Miss Fournier," Marcus greeted warmly, gesturing to the empty seat. "It would be an honor if you joined us."

She set her tray down and slid into the chair. The woman beside her, dressed in a distinctive blue-and-white dress with the Order's insignia sewn onto the bodice, extended a hand and offered a kind smile. "Hello, Miss Fournier. I'm Sister Sallie. It's a pleasure to meet you."

"Hello," Regina said, shaking her hand.

"Miss Regina," Brother Marcus asked gently, "did you just wake up?"

"Yeah," she admitted, poking at her scrambled eggs with her fork. "I must've been really tired, I don't even remember going to bed."

Marcus chuckled, then relayed "After communing with your goddess, you passed out in the temple. I carried you back to your room. I figured you'd rest better in a bed than curled up on the couch."

Regina paused, warmth blooming in her chest at his thoughtfulness. "Oh. Thank you," she said softly, her voice sincere. She gave him a grateful smile and took a bite of sausage.

"You spoke to a goddess?" Sister Sallie's eyes widened. "You have to tell me, what was it like?"

"She was really fun and happy," Regina replied, her voice glowing with the memory. "And her fox was so adorable."

"You actually spoke to her?" Sallie leaned in, curiosity gleaming in her eyes. "What did you talk about?"

"A lot of things," Regina said, twirling her fork through her pancakes. "She told me to follow Brother Albert's work, and... oh! She said I should visit my family at the Luminous."

Marcus, who had been quietly sipping his coffee, raised an eyebrow. He recognized "the Luminous" as the colloquial name for the main library of Laminae—a vast archive Regina's family maintained in rotating shifts. He knew they lived there for months at a time, though he wasn't exactly sure what they did.

"We can arrange that," Marcus said thoughtfully. "But the Luminous is a few days' sail from here, even on the Stormfang, and that ship is faster than most."

"You could use one of the message ships," Sister Sallie suggested. "With the right pilot, you could be there in just a days travel."

"Message ship?" Regina asked, intrigued.

"Well, Miss Regina," Sallie began, "we've got a fleet of small boats donated by Magitekopolis. They're powered by the mana of the passengers aboard. And they're fast, really fast. We usually use them to send urgent messages, but they can carry small groups and light cargo too."

"Could I leave today?" Regina asked, cutting into her pancakes and popping a bite into her mouth.

"In theory, yes," Sallie said with a mischievous smile. Then she turned to Marcus. "What do you think, Brother Marcus?"

Marcus set down his coffee. "I don't see a problem with it," he said after a pause.

Sallie's eyes lit up. "I've never been to the Luminous! Do you think I could go with her?"

Marcus frowned slightly. "I'm not sure, Sallie. You've got responsibilities at the College of Sages."

"Oh, come on, Marcus," Sallie groaned dramatically. "I'm just testing a shovel on fruit."

"It's not my place to interfere with another branch of the Order," Marcus replied diplomatically. "But I'll check if they can spare you for the trip." He smiled faintly, though his tone suggested he didn't want to raise her hopes too much.

"I get to travel to the Luminous!" Sallie nearly bounced in her seat. "I can't wait!"

As Regina ate, a thought struck her, and she paused mid-bite. "What kind of magic do you two use?"

Marcus drained the last of his coffee before answering. "Well, Miss Regina, I'm not magical. Like every member of the Order, I can manipulate my mana, but I lack the ability to use it for spellcasting." He gestured toward Sallie.

"I use a system called *Smoke and Mirrors*," Sallie said, a hint of pride in her voice. "it lets me hide from most people who don't have magical senses. In the right circumstances, I can even turn invisible." She tilted her head. "Odd question, though."

"Miss Regina here is a Nexus Mage," Marcus said in her defense. "She was born without a magical affinity, which gives her the ability to learn as many magical systems as she can remember."

"Oh," Sallie blinked. "I didn't know that was even possible. How does that work?"

"Learner Mages aren't very common," Regina explained. "My mom's the only other one I've ever met. We have to figure out how to shape our mana just to get started and then learn how to manipulate it to cast spells. For most mages, their affinity handles that first part automatically. But for us? It's a lot trickier."

She paused, then added, "We usually need a magical sourcebook to teach us the basics. After that, experienced mages can help refine our techniques, especially by sharing the mistakes they've made. Those aren't usually written down."

She held out her hand, palm open, and cast the Sea Bubble summoning spell Annabelle had taught her. A massive sphere of rushing water burst into form, far larger than she intended, nearly the size of a grown man.

Conversation across the cafeteria screeched to a halt. Marcus, Sallie, and everyone nearby stared at the towering bubble.

"Whoa!" Marcus exclaimed.

"By the goddess!" Sallie breathed.

Regina winced. Realizing her mistake, she focused on desummoning the bubble. To her surprise, it was easier than ever. She opened a dismissal point at the bubble's center and closed it with precision like she had practiced the spell many times before. The water vanished without spilling a single drop.

"Wow," she whispered, marveling. "That worked perfectly."

"That was quite the display, Miss Regina," Marcus said, his voice caught between awe and concern. "But maybe save that much power for somewhere less... crowded."

"I used the same amount of power as yesterday," Regina said, frowning. "I don't know why it came out so big."

"Wait," Sallie said, brow furrowed. "Yesterday, when you cast that spell, wasn't the water a lot smaller?"

Regina nodded, a little embarrassed. "Yeah... I don't know what happened. I'm sorry."

"Oh no, dear," Sallie said gently, placing a hand on Regina's shoulder. "Did you cast that spell *before* you communed with the goddess?"

Regina hesitated, then nodded. "Yeah."

"Well, that might explain it." Sallie's eyes lit up like someone solving a puzzle. "The goddess may have altered your mana, maybe an enhancement or expansion. Your spells would naturally adjust to match your new mana capacity."

"It's more than that," Regina said slowly. "It was so much easier this time. Yesterday, it was messy. I couldn't desummon the spell right and ended up splashing water all over myself and Annabelle."

"Incredible," Sallie breathed. "I'd love to study these effects more, if you're willing."

Across the table, Marcus's expression darkened. His eyes narrowed, and his tone turned cold. "I don't think studying the avatars is a good idea."

Sallie blinked at his sudden shift. "What? I don't understand," she said, her voice confused and unsure. "I just meant, there's so much we could learn from studying their physiology. Especially after the goddesses' modifications."

"To what end, Sister?" Marcus's tone was sharp but controlled. "Would you try to replicate these changes in people who haven't been selected by a goddess?"

"Why not?" Sallie countered, her voice edged with defiance. "Think of the good that kind of power could do in the world."

Marcus paused. He closed his eyes and took a slow, steady breath before speaking. When he did, his voice was calm but firm. "There's so much we don't understand about the goddesses or their connection to their avatars. I've seen what happens when well-meaning people overreach when they tamper with things they barely comprehend. Good intentions don't prevent devastation."

Sallie opened her mouth to argue, but Marcus cut her off by standing and gesturing to Regina. "If you'll excuse us, Sister, I believe I have something that may interest Miss Fournier."

"Of course, Brother," Sallie replied, her voice filled with mellow surprise and slight afront. Her eyes sparkled with mischief, but Marcus ignored her as he turned to Regina.

"Miss Regina," he said, his tone softening, "I have something I think you'll enjoy while I arrange transportation to the Luminous."

Regina drained the last of her coffee, a small smile tugging at her lips. Back home, she wasn't allowed to drink coffee, but here, no one said a word. Feeling slightly rebellious, she grinned. "Okay, let's go!"

Oblivious to the tension between Marcus and Sallie, Regina followed him out of the cafeteria. They stacked their trays onto a rolling cart for dirty dishes, then continued through the circular hallway. Soon, Marcus led her down a corridor she hadn't yet explored.

This hallway buzzed with the usual activity of Order members, the rustle of clothes, murmured conversations, purposeful steps. At the far end stood a large wooden door bearing an ornate plaque:

Magical Archives – Maintained by the College of Sages

Marcus opened the door and stepped aside with a slight bow. "After you, Miss Fournier," he said, gesturing for her to enter.

Regina stepped inside, and froze, wide-eyed. Endless rows of towering bookshelves stretched across the room, each labeled with elegant signs. The air was thick with the scent of parchment and ink, and a tranquil stillness hung in the air.

"Wow," she whispered, her voice nearly reverent.

Marcus smiled, pleased. In their short time together, he had come to understand that Regina's quiet awe spoke volumes. "This," he said, "is the Mystical Archives. As the sign says, these books detail every known type of magic studied by the Order." He closed the door behind them. "As a Nexus Mage, I imagine you'll make good use of them."

Regina's face lit up. "This is so awesome!" she blurted, running toward the nearest shelf. Her silver hair bounced as she skidded to a stop in front of the section labeled *Elemental Magic.*

Her fingers hovered over the spines of books: *"Water Elemental 1,"* she read aloud. She scanned lower shelves. *"Hydrodynamo."* Her eyes danced over *Fire Tamer, Lava Elemental...*

She craned her neck upward at the towering shelves. "Brother Marcus!" she called, pointing. "How do I reach the books up there?"

Marcus chuckled and gestured toward a rolling ladder tucked behind the attendant's desk. "That ladder should help you reach all the way to the top."

"Got it!" she said, already darting toward the next shelf labeled *Earth Magic.* Her fingertips brushed over titles like *Harvest Magic, Spells of the Forest, Geomancy, Terrakinetics,* and *Crystalmancy.*

Marcus watched her a moment, a faint smile tugging at his lips. "If you're alright here, I'll go make arrangements for your transport to the Luminous," he said.

Regina peeked out from behind the shelves, beaming. "I'll be fine," she said, then vanished back into the stacks.

"Very well. I'll see you later, Miss Fournier." Marcus gave her one last glance, watching her vibrate with excitement, before quietly stepping out and closing the door behind himself.

"Oh, right," Regina said aloud, recalling Lisa's request to see how quickly she could learn Earthbloom Magic. She made her way to the attendant's desk to grab the ladder but paused when a book titled *Reference Guide* caught her eye.

Curious, she flipped it open and was relieved to find it worked just like the reference books in Laminae's libraries. The first section contained an alphabetical index of all the books in the archives, each entry accompanied by a tower, shelf, and location code. Turning to the "E" section, she scanned the list until she found *Earthbloom.*

Her eyebrows rose. *Five volumes?* She thought. Most magical systems only had one. She noted the location of the first volume, grabbed the ladder, and wheeled it to the tower labeled *Earth Magic.* The ladder glided smoothly as she positioned it beneath the shelf.

Climbing up, she retrieved *Earthbloom Guidebook, Volume I* and carried it to one of four large reading tables. Settling into a chair, she flipped to the introduction, eager to begin.

The opening described Earthbloom Magic as a versatile system of spells that influenced the natural world. Regina skimmed through examples; many she had already seen Lisa perform, like healing wounds or commanding plants to bloom and grow. But others surprised her: *manipulating the earth to raise mounds, split the ground, and even control fire although an Earthbloom mage cannot create fire.*

The guide explained that Earthbloom mana flowed in stream-like patterns, expanding like tree branches or condensing into solid forms. Mages used spell circles to direct this mana into the earth's energy. The runes surrounding each circle acted like commands: *grow taller, bloom,* or *harden.*

Regina tapped her fingers against the book's edge as she absorbed the information. She began designing a practice exercise: shape her mana into streams, form a spell circle connecting to the earth's energy, then practice breaking the connection cleanly.

On the next page, she found a section detailing types of spell circles. The simplest was a single circle with up to eight surrounding runes, the one Lisa had used. Then came more advanced configurations.

One was the double-joined circle: two spell circles connected at a single point, each with independent runes. One could manipulate the ground while the other summoned water, together forming a lake.

Then came two types of three-circle formations. The first, called a fusion circle, showed overlapping rings that formed a central triangle surrounded by ovals. When runes were placed strategically, the synergy allowed powerful effects, like transforming arid land into lush forest.

The second configuration added a third circle to extend or layer spells, like growing grass by a newly formed lake. The guide speculated that four- and five-circle arrays might be possible, though no mage in the Order had ever achieved them.

Regina's mind lit up. *How many combinations could she create?* She made a mental note to test the limits through hands-on practice.

The final section covered the system's limitations: *practical, sometimes sobering*. Some were obvious: *creating a lake required water nearby, and moving large amounts of earth could destabilize terrain*. Others were subtler. Plants forced to grow unnaturally fast required proportional resources like water and soil nutrients. Without enough, they'd wither just as quickly. Likewise, creating an ecosystem in a dry climate without proper support would eventually cause collapse, draining nearby resources.

Closing the book, Regina leaned back in her chair. The intricate balance between magic and nature fascinated her.

Eager to try it herself, she moved to an open spot in the archive. Sitting cross-legged, she assumed her mana-channeling pose and closed her eyes. She visualized streams of light coursing through her body, flowing like gentle brooks.

Gradually, she guided the mana toward her hands, letting it ripple and pool before extending it into the air. Her brow furrowed in concentration. One by one, she shaped the streams, aligning them with care. With steady breath and growing focus, she began to grasp the subtle complexities of Earthbloom Magic.

[----- ⚓ -----]

Annabelle strode briskly up the gangplank of the *Stormfang*, her footsteps echoing across the sturdy planks. The crew was scattered around the deck, busy rewrapping sail guide ropes and removing hooks and gear. She reached the top and called out, "Permission to come aboard!"

"Permission granted," came Smitty's gruff sleepy voice from the bridge. He stood behind the helm, a spread of tools laid out across the deck as he worked on resetting the ship's wheel.

Annabelle crossed the deck quickly, a bright smile on her face. "Good mornin', First Mate!"

"Mornin'?" Smitty muttered. He pulled a gold pocket watch from his vest, flipped it open, and shot her a dismissive look. "Belle, it's two-thirty. Hardly morning."

"Well, it's mornin' somewhere," she said with a grin, brushing off his correction. "Anyway, Smitty, I gots me a favor to ask."

"I don't have any extra coin, Belle," Smitty said automatically, pausing over the wheel to squint at her.

Annabelle laughed and waved a hand. "No, no, it's not about coin."

211

"Then what's it about?" he asked warily.

"I want ye to help me learn me Maelstrom Mastery Magic," she said earnestly, her smile widening. "Yer so good at it, and I want to get better!"

"No."

The reply came fast and flat. Smitty turned back to his tools without looking at her.

"Oh, come on, Smitty!" Annabelle begged. "I know I wasn't the best student before, but I swear I'll work hard this time."

"No Belle!" he said, firmer now, glancing up with a sharp look. "Absolutely not. Last time all ye did was argue and pick fights. Ye didn't do any of the self-work, and I'm still pretty sure you were the reason we sprang that leak in the hold."

Annabelle's smile faltered. She stared at the heavyset old man, her usual confidence slipping. Then she dropped her gaze. "I'm sorry, Smitty," she said softly. "I really was the worst. I should've done better by ye... It's just, sometimes I get so nervous I'll mess up then I do, and then I joke about it to hide how I'm feeling; and ye didn't deserve that."

Smitty froze mid-turn of a screwdriver. He looked at her, unreadable. For a moment, it seemed her words had reached him. Then his scowl deepened. "Nice try, Belle. But the answer's still no."

She blinked, stunned. She hadn't expected him to brush her off so quickly. Out of options, she played her final, most desperate card. "Name yer price," she said, folding her arms.

Smitty's head snapped up. "What foolishness are ye on about now?"

"I'm serious," Annabelle said, meeting his gaze. "Name yer price. I needs to learn, and ye've got the know-how. Or" she lifted a brow "are ye not interested in coin no more?"

Smitty set down his tools and stood to his full height. He stepped closer, squinting at her like he was trying to see through a trick.

"No games," he said at last, his voice low. "Ye pay up front. Ye do as yer told. First time you talk back, I'm done. I keep the coin, and yer out."

"Deal," Annabelle said instantly, thrusting out her hand.

Smitty shook it firmly, his rough fingers gripping tight. "Fifteen coins," he said, a sly smile tugging at his lips. "Per lesson."

Annabelle's jaw dropped. *Fifteen coins?!* That was more than she could afford for a few lessons, tops. But she didn't hesitate, things like this had a way of working out for her.

She was going to learn this magic, no matter what.

"Like I said, *deal*." she replied, tightening her grip.

"Good," Smitty said with a satisfied nod. "Now go change into something ye don't mind ruining. And don't forget … me coin."

Instead of running off, Annabelle threw her arms around him, catching him off guard.

"Thank ye, Smitty!" she said, voice full of genuine gratitude.

He stiffened in the hug, his face turning red. "Alright, alright," he grumbled, gently prying her off. "Get on, before I change me mind!"

Grinning, Annabelle darted off, already running numbers in her head. The price stung, but she was sure it would work itself out.

About an hour, and fifteen gold coins, later, Annabelle stood knee-deep in the surf, waves lazily lapping around her legs. Across from her, Smitty stood with his hands on his hips, his red-and-white striped pants rolled to the knees, a dirt-streaked white shirt clinging to his frame. Behind him, an old wooden folding chair acting like a shelf for a tattered book.

"All right, Belle," Smitty called, his voice cutting through the steady rush of the tide. "Let's see ye summon a bubble o' the sea."

Annabelle clapped her hands together and tried to focus her mana. She glanced at Smitty *that was mistake*. His expression was had full of disapproval. She sighed, closed her eyes, and began humming her shanty under her breath. The melody steadied her nerves as she shaped her mana, picturing the ocean in her mind. She raised her right hand, molding the magic into a sphere. Slowly, a shimmering bubble of water formed, larger than she'd meant it to be, but breathtaking. Tiny waves churned inside like a miniature sea, alive in her palm.

When she opened her eyes, Smitty was staring at her, mouth slightly agape. For a heartbeat, he said nothing. Belle, how did ye…" He stopped, cleared his throat, and crossed his arms. "Looks like ye've got this one down. Go ahead and get rid of' that bubble so we can move on."

Pride bloomed in her chest. She nearly gloated…then stopped herself. *Ye are paying for this lesson, Annabelle; save the bragging for later.* She tossed the bubble back towards the sea and the Stormfang, where it burst on impact, sending ripples spreading toward shore.

"I noticed ye still need to work too hard to channel yer mana," Smitty said, his voice back to its usual sleepy gruff tone. "If yer ever in a tight spot, no one's going to wait for ye to hum a tune just to get yer spell ready." He gestured toward the sea. "Next up is a spell called *current*. Ye'll need to channel mana through both hands, steady-like, and keep your connection to the sea. Got it?"

Annabelle crossed her arms and tapped her chin. "Doesn't sound too bad."

"Good. Watch me first." Smitty lifted both hands toward the ocean. Without warning, two torrents of seawater blasted from his palms, crashing into the waves. The spell lasted nearly two minutes before he finally let it go, then casually wiped his hands on his pants.

"What'd ye see?" he asked, turning to her.

"Ye shot seawater from yer hands," Annabelle said, resting her knuckles against her chin, replaying it in her head.

"How long did it take me to start?"

"A few seconds?"

"Aye, and what else?"

"The water was strong," she said slowly. "And constant."

"Exactly. Quick start. Strong force. Steady flow. Now—let's see it."

Annabelle squared her stance, facing the sea. The *Stormfang's* silhouette loomed in the distance. She closed her eyes briefly, letting her shanty guide her as she drew mana into her palms. A small stream sputtered from her left hand. Nothing from the right. Panic flared. She shoved more mana into the spell…and twin jets of seawater exploded from her hands, launching her backward into the surf. Flat on her back, Annabelle blinked at the sky, mouth full of seawater, clothes clinging to her skin.

"What did ye do wrong?" Smitty called, just barely holding back a laugh.

Annabelle groaned and sat up, soaked and sandy, hair in her face. She ran through the spell in her mind and muttered, "Didn't channel me mana right."

Smitty raised a brow. "Very good," he said, surprisingly pleased. He picked up the book and sat in the folding chair. "Keep practicing."

Annabelle got to her feet, brushing off wet sand and seaweed. "That all ye're going to say? What if a lass needs a bit of help?"

"I'm here if ye've got questions," Smitty replied without looking up. He turned a page. "Again, please."

Annabelle huffed and faced the waves again. She circled her palms, channeled her mana, and this time, two steady streams flowed. Encouraged, she pushed harder… and once more, the streams exploded, flinging her into the surf.

She rose again, drenched and scowling, seaweed tangled in her hair.

"Again, please," came Smitty's calm voice from behind his book.

Annabelle glared, teeth clenched. *Next time,* she promised herself, *I'm gonna get meself a better deal.* But for now, she raised her hands again, more determined than ever to get it right.

[----- ⊕ -----]

Sophie sat alone in the Goddess' Clock Chamber, her body aching from hours spent in various meditation poses. Her mana felt low. Her legs were stiff, her back sore, and though frustration simmered beneath the surface, exhaustion dulled it into quiet resignation. With a heavy sigh, she pushed herself to her feet. Stretching her legs and arching her back, she welcomed the faint relief of movement.

To clear her mind, she began pacing, her steps carrying her from the warm, violet-hued slice of the clock into the neighboring goddess' domain, its stone floor a dull brown. As she crossed the threshold, an icy chill slipped into her bones, like someone had snuffed out a fire. The warmth she hadn't realized she'd been basking in vanished, replaced by a stark emptiness that made her skin prickle.

Curious, she stepped back into the violet goddess' slice, and warmth rushed to greet her like an embrace. Sophie closed her eyes, drawing a long, centering breath. She turned inward, searching for the source of that warmth. When she found it, she etched the feeling into memory. Then, with renewed resolve, she returned to her seated position, legs crossed, hands pressed to together poised before her chest.

She began channeling mana, letting it flow steadily through her hands as she mentally retraced the path to that internal warmth. She pushed deeper, moving beyond the familiar current of her magic. For a moment, she hesitated, navigating this new terrain felt like walking an unknown trail, but she pressed on, guided by the warmth of the connection.

Deeper still, Sophie encountered something solid and foreign, heavy with presence. She moved toward it in her mind's eye, lifting it with imagined hands. It was a small wooden door, smooth and handleless. She frowned, uncertain. With a tentative shrug, she knocked three times.

The sound echoed faintly into the void. A moment later, three knocks responded, sharp and deliberate. But the door remained closed. Sophie hesitated, unease prickling at her skin. *Was that wrong?* Unsure what else to do, she pressed a finger to the door, and forced it to break.

Suddenly, she was standing in a dimly lit room. Brick walls closed around her, damp and cool to the touch. The door she'd entered through was gone. Weapons and shields lined the walls, their metal glinting faintly in flickering torchlight. Heart pounding, Sophie stepped through an open arch into a long, narrow corridor. The torches sputtered as she passed, their flames casting erratic shadows.

A low, menacing growl rooted her in place. From the darkness ahead emerged a badger, its fur streaked with intricate violet patterns. Its claws clicked on the stone floor as it lowered into a defensive stance, eyes locked on Sophie. The growl deepened, *it is a warning*.

Sophie's breath caught. Beyond the badger, through the doorway it guarded, came a rhythmic scrape of stone against metal, repeating like clockwork. Someone, or something, was working. Her gaze returned to the badger, its claws digging into the floor as it held its ground. *That's where I need to go*, Sophie realized. "I have to get past you," she told him, her voice calm but firm. She stepped forward. The badger tensed but didn't lunge. Instead, it took a step back, never breaking eye contact.

Sophie pressed on, slowly. Her heart pounded. She met the creature's eyes, refusing to look away. The growl rumbled on, low and steady, but the badger continued to retreat. "Don't you attack me," Sophie warned, her voice tight with resolve. Step by step, she edged past. Every muscle in her body braced for movement. But the badger held its ground, growling until she was clear.

She exhaled, shaky but composed, her back prickling with the fear of unseen movement. But the badger remained behind. Her focus returned to the rhythmic scraping beyond the door. Sophie continued forward, each step deliberates. At the corridor's end stood a large wooden door reinforced with steel. The badger's growl echoed faintly behind her. She paused, glancing back. It watched her still, its gaze sharp and unwavering. Drawing a breath to steady herself, Sophie pressed her hand to the door and stepped inside.

The room was dimly lit; Its stone walls lined with weapon racks and faintly shimmering shields. At the center, a woman sat at a workbench, sharpening a large sword with slow, deliberate strokes. The blade gleamed with a vibrant violet hue, pulsing faintly with energy.

She wore a striking dress with an armored bodice, an ensemble that spoke of both beauty and battle. Her violet hair was pulled into a sleek braided ponytail, and her piercing eyes, violet…identical to Sophie's, seemed to study her without even lifting her gaze.

"Welcome, Sophie," the woman said, finally looking up.

Sophie froze. "Hello," she replied hesitantly, her voice soft. She had never seen anyone else with hair and eyes like hers, and the sight left her momentarily speechless.

Behind her, the badger chittered and rushed past, scampering toward the woman. Setting the sword aside, the woman extended her arms, her stern expression softening with a warm smile.

"Hello, Titus," she said as the badger leaped into her lap. She kissed the top of his head and stroked his fur. The once-ferocious creature now curled up against her, utterly content.

"So… he can be nice," Sophie said, her voice tinged with amusement and surprise.

The woman smiled faintly. "He just wants to protect his mama."

Before Sophie could answer, a whisper echoed faintly through the room, chilling and unmistakable: *It's all your fault.*

The words pierced through her like a dagger. She staggered slightly, a wave of sorrow washing over her. The violet haze in the room shimmered, fading into streaks of white light. Sophie squeezed her eyes shut and took a steadying breath.

Keep it together girl, focus. she told herself.

When she opened her eyes, the haze was gone. The woman sat as before, calmly stroking the badger in her lap, as if nothing had changed.

"Oh, my Sophie," the goddess said gently. "You couldn't have protected your mother. Release yourself from that guilt."

Sophie's chest tightened. She forced herself to nod. "I will," she lied, though her voice wavered.

The woman narrowed her eyes slightly. After a long sigh, she snapped her fingers.

The room shifted instantly.

Sophie now stood at the foot of a grand dais, dwarfed by a towering throne. The goddess sat upon it, regal and commanding. Titus remained curled on her lap. Her presence filled the chamber, her voice echoing off the walls.

"Sophie," she said, "your guilt will blunt your growth and dull your wit. The path ahead will demand your full strength."

"I understand," Sophie replied, trying to sound steady. "I'll strive to find peace."

The goddess tilted her head, gaze cutting through her. "You should not lie about such things," she said firmly. "I am the Goddess of War, and you are my avatar. We are as one, Sophie. I feel your sadness, your misplaced blame, the weight of your guilt, it is suffocating."

Sophie's defenses crumbled.

"But if I had been there," she tearfully protested, "I could've helped. If I hadn't read that letter—" Her voice broke. "She wouldn't have…"

She covered her face with her hands as sobs wracked her body. "I failed her."

The goddess said nothing at first. She gently lifted Titus from her lap and set him on the floor. With a small gesture, she sent him toward a fur-lined bed near the wall. Obediently, he padded over and curled up.

"Sophie," the goddess said, her voice calm but unshakable. "You could not be more wrong."

She raised her hand and snapped her fingers.

Light flared behind Sophie, bathing the chamber in a gentle glow.

She turned…and then froze.

A familiar silhouette stepped through the light.

"Sophie-bear," said a voice, soft and unmistakable.

Only one person had ever called her that. Without hesitation, Sophie ran forward and threw her arms around the figure. "Momma," she sobbed. "I'm so sorry."

Her mother, Arisa, wrapped her arms around her, one hand settling on the back of Sophie's head the way she always had. The touch unraveled her completely.

"Sorry for what?" Arisa asked gently. She paused, her expression shifting as understanding dawned. She pulled back slightly, her hands on Sophie's shoulders. "Sophie… what happened to Benjamin?"

"I don't know," Sophie admitted. "I looked everywhere, but he was gone."

Arisa closed her eyes, and a small smile touched her lips. "Then he made it out."

"What?" Sophie blinked. "How do you know?"

"Don't you remember?" Arisa's voice was gentle, patient. "When you were little, I taught you, if your home isn't safe, you run to the safe place and wait." She gave Sophie the familiar look she used when pointing out something obvious.

"I'm so sorry, Momma," Sophie whispered. "I should've been there to help you. We could have…"

"We would have what?" Arisa interrupted, her tone sharpening. "We would both have died. That witch's power was more than even an Apex could handle."

"But…" Sophie trailed off, her words swallowed by fresh sobs.

Arisa turned her gaze to the Goddess of War, still holding Sophie's shoulders. For a moment, the two women seemed to communicate without speaking. The silent exchange was so intense it sent a shiver down Sophie's spine.

Finally, Arisa looked back at her daughter, her eyes fierce. "Sophie," she said firmly, "it is the duty of every Aurorium mother to lay down her life to protect her children. Why would you think I'd want you to die with me?"

"You were yelling for me," Sophie whispered, her mind drifting back to the haunting image of her mother frozen in their living room. The memory wrapped around her like a vice, squeezing the breath from her lungs…until Arisa's voice snapped her back.

"I wasn't screaming for you!" Arisa said, shaking her head. "I was screaming for Benjamin to get him running."

Before Sophie could respond, Arisa pulled her into another embrace. Her warmth stood in stark contrast to the cold void Sophie had carried for so long. "Oh, Sophie-bear," she said soft and warm, holding her tightly.

Sophie clung to her, burying her face in her momma's shoulder. Her sobs quieted but remained raw.

"It's not fair," Arisa said softly, her voice laced with sorrow. "Losing your dad and now me." She kissed the top of Sophie's head and tightened her embrace. "But you have to let go, sweetheart. You're needed."

"I can't." Sophie said, her voice breaking.

"You can't?!?" Arisa snapped, her tone sharp with the familiar disappointment Sophie knew all too well from training. She wrenched Sophie's arms away, forcing her to break the embrace. "The clan needs you, hell the world needs you!" Her voice rose, fierce and unrelenting. "You are Aurorium. We don't solve our problems with tears!"

Sophie staggered back, her face crumpling. She wiped her tears with trembling hands; eyes fixed on the floor. She couldn't meet her mother's gaze.

"Look at me." Arisa commanded, voice firm.

Sophie hesitated, then wiped her face again and lifted her eyes. Her mother's brown eyes burned with determination.

"You were where you were supposed to be, I would **NEVER** want you to die at my side." He looked into Sophie's eyes her brown eyes burning with determination and will. "Now go show that ice witch what I taught you," Arisa said, voice steady. She pressed a firm kiss to Sophie's forehead. "Promise me, you will not shed one more tear."

Sophie swallowed hard and nodded, feeling the shame of weakness.

Arisa turned to the Goddess of War and inclined her head. "I'm ready to return, goddess."

With a snap of the goddess' fingers, the doorway of light reappeared. Arisa walked toward it, her steps sure and deliberate. At the threshold, she stopped and turned back, her face softening. She gave Sophie one last look, a smile that said everything without a word. Her familiar *do your best* smile.

Then Arisa stepped into the glow and disappeared.

Sophie wiped her face with the back of her hand and straightened. She turned to face the goddess, lifting her chin. "I am ready, Goddess." she said, her voice steady despite the ache in her very soul.

War studied her for a moment, her gaze softening. "I am glad," she said, nodding once. Then she snapped her fingers. The room shifted in an instant.

Sophie blinked and found herself in a modest dining room. A square table stood at the center, set with a plentiful but not excessive spread of meats, fruits, breads, and cheeses.

The goddess was already seated and gestured to the chair across from her. "Please, sit. Have something to eat."

Sophie hesitated briefly, then complied. Her stomach growled, and she reached for a turkey leg and a warm roll.

With a flick of her fingers, War levitated slices of meat and fruit to her own plate. Her movements were deliberate, her manner calm but commanding. "There is much we must discuss," War said, cutting into a piece of meat. "As my avatar, you will act upon my will. In return, I will grant you access to my power."

Sophie paused, hand hovering. "What exactly will I have to do? Fight wars?" she asked cautiously, then bit into the turkey leg, eyes locked on the goddess.

"If it comes to that," War replied, setting down her utensils. "But first, you must understand, there is a great danger rising in the world."

Sophie swallowed, brow furrowing. "So... you want me to fight this danger?" she asked, leaning forward, doubt edging her tone.

"Sophie," War said, "you must understand what my domain truly is."

With a resounding clap, War changed their surroundings. Sophie blinked as smoke and blood thickened the air. They now stood on a battlefield scarred by a brutal conflict. Fallen soldiers lay scattered, their weapons abandoned, armor battered. Tattered flags fluttered in the wind, relics of a forgotten cause.

"War is the language of the battlefield," War declared, her voice sharp and clear. "A man's testament to an ideal...and his willingness to fight for it."

As she spoke, two groups of armored warriors materialized on the battlefield, their weapons gleaming as they marched into formation.

"It is during battle," War continued, her reverence warming to Sophie, "that you see men at their truest selves. No need for *diplomacy* or *decorum*." The way she spat those words made Sophie flinch, though their bond made it clear, War has little patience for such things.

The two groups charged, clashing in a chaotic symphony of swords, shields, and battle cries. Sophie felt War's exhilaration radiating through their connection, not just from the violence, but from the intricate dance of tactics, coordination, and survival unfolding before them.

"Look there," War said, pointing toward two warriors near the front lines.

Sophie followed her gesture. One man carried only a large rectangular shield, the other wielded a heavy battle axe. Their mismatched armor left them partially exposed, but their eyes met briefly, a silent exchange, a shared understanding.

"They speak the purest language of all," War explained, her voice rising with anticipation. "The language of battle." The intensity in her tone made Sophie's chest tighten. Her skin prickled with heat, as if War's excitement were her own.

The battle unfolded with ruthless precision. The axe-wielder struck first, carving a path through the chaos. The shield-bearer followed, intercepting counterattacks and opening space for his partner to strike. Together, they dismantled their enemies, blow by blow, until the last soldier fell at their feet.

War's violet eyes gleamed with satisfaction. "The battlefield is thrilling," she said calmly, "but it is far from the edge of my power."

Another clap of her hands—and the scene shifted.

Sophie now stood in a strategy room, thick with the tension of calculation and consequence. A large table dominated the space; its surface covered with a detailed map of the battlefield. Painted miniatures marked troop positions and fortifications. Men in crisp military uniforms circled the table, debating tactics and moving pieces with grim focus.

"Scholars and generals alike obsess over strategy," War said, her tone nearly mocking, "as if the perfect plan will coax me into granting them an easy victory. But they ignore the truth." She turned to Sophie, a mischievous glint in her eye. "The only easy thing on the battlefield is defeat."

Sophie couldn't help but smile. There was something contagious about War's dark humor, the way her voice wrapped wisdom in warning.

"I do appreciate their effort, though," War added with a shrug. Her grin widened, her violet features glowing faintly against her deep skin.

With another clap, the scene dissolved.

Now Sophie stood in a sleek, modern chamber. High windows framed the outside world, and a long conference table stretched through the center of the room. Men and women in tailored suits sat rigidly, their faces tense, their voices hushed.

"This," War said, her voice edged with amusement, "is the truest demonstration of my power. They fear me too much to speak my name aloud, lest they end up paying tribute to me in blood and sinew."

Sophie scanned the table. Fear flickered in the leaders' eyes as they whispered and avoided each other's gaze.

"They cede land, forge alliances, offer concessions," War continued, her smile sly. "All to keep my hunger at bay."

Then she looked down at Sophie, her expression hardening. "And now, Sophie, this power, my power, is yours to wield."

With a final resounding clap, they returned to the dining table. Sophie blinked, still disoriented by the rapid transitions.

"Do you understand now, Sophie?" War asked, her tone firm yet patient. "Fighting is only a fraction of our strength."

As she spoke, warmth bloomed in Sophie's chest. A violet glow flickered inside her, faint at first, then steadily brighter. She turned toward a nearby mirror and gasped.

Her afro-puffed hair shimmered with light. Her eyes burned violet, like twin fires held barely in check.

"What the...?" Sophie breathed, brushing her fingers against her glowing curls.

"This," War said, placing a hand over the glowing circle on her chest, "is the piece of you within me." She gestured toward Sophie's reflection. "And that is the piece of me within you."

Sophie tilted her head, puzzled. "But the piece of me in you is so much smaller than the piece of you in me. Why aren't they the same size?"

"Oh, but they are," War replied, a note of humor in her voice. "You, my avatar, are one person." She held up a single finger. "But I am a goddess." She spread her arms wide, her own violet glow intensifying as Sophie's fragment blazed bright near her heart. "I am vast. You are small. Any more of me in you, and you'd pop like a balloon."

Sophie blinked. "That... sounds very complicated."

"Life is complicated," War said with a knowing smile. "But you are not alone. My sisters—Change, Unity, and Chaos—have chosen avatars of their own."

"Oh, them," Sophie muttered, her tone darkening at the thought of Lisa, Regina, and Annabelle. A note of frustration crept into her voice.

War chuckled softly, then her tone turned firm as steel "Without my sisters, I would be lost. And without me, they would be lost." She picked up a piece of fruit from the table, studying it thoughtfully.

219

Sophie fell silent, thinking about her own relationship with the other avatars.

"There isn't a being in this reality or any other I would put above my sisters," War continued, her voice softening. "Our relationships are trying, sometimes downright frustrating." Her violet eyes drifted to her right, as though gazing at someone just out of view. "But make no mistake, I would face any battle for them."

"I guess I understand," Sophie murmured, though her mind still swirled with doubts. Her thoughts drifted to the wild-haired pirate girl. "But they're so... hard to deal with."

War smiled. "Ahh, I know what you mean." She placed her hand under her chin thoughtfully, then said, "I'll give you a special gift. Although you are NOT to fight my sisters' avatars, I will allow you to strike my sister Chaos' avatar", she raised a finger then says "once. One free hit, with my approval." She grinned mischievously. "Life is long, my dear Sophie. Don't waste it."

Empowered by the thought of finally shutting Annabelle's big mouth, Sophie gave a dutiful nod with a fulfilled smile. "Yes, thank you, Goddess."

"The next time we speak, tell me about your relationship with my sisters' avatars," War said, her gaze locking on Sophie with piercing intensity.

"We'll talk again?" Sophie asked, nibbling on a warm, delicious roll.

"We will speak one more time," War promised. "After your journey is complete."

"But how will I know what you want me to do?" Sophie asked, her voice rising in frustration. "What if I have questions? What if I need clarification?" The enormity of her task pressed down on her chest.

War's smile was calm and reassuring. "Life, my dear Sophie, is complicated. But I trust you will make the right decisions when the time comes."

Before Sophie could say more, War snapped her fingers. The dining room dissolved, returning them to the weapons chamber where Sophie had first arrived.

"What's going on?" Sophie asked, her body tensing. "Are we going to fight now?"

War tilted her head, a sly smile curling her lips. "Do you want to fight me?" she asked, almost teasing. Before Sophie could answer, War snapped her fingers. Every weapon and shield along the walls lifted into the air, hovering in place as if awaiting command.

Intimidated, Sophie raised her hands in surrender. "No!" she said firmly.

"What a shame," War chuckled. "Maybe next time." She snapped her fingers again, and the weapons returned gently to their racks.

"Our time together is ending," War said, stepping forward and opening her arms. Her violet eyes softened.

Sophie hesitated only a moment before stepping into the goddess' embrace. She felt the cold press of armor against her, a stark contrast to the warmth of War's arms. She closed her eyes, allowing herself to enjoy a rare moment of peace and affection.

"Thank you, goddess," she whispered. "For my momma."

"No thanks are required," War replied, her voice steady and kind. She held Sophie a moment longer, then stepped back. Her gaze intensified. "I have two things for you to remember."

Sophie nodded, holding her breath.

"Keep the other girls safe," War said, kissing Sophie on the left cheek. "And follow Brother Albert's trail. They'll show you how to stop the danger." She kissed her on the right cheek, the gesture solemn and final.

A sudden warmth surged through Sophie's body. Her mana flared outward, rushing like a flood from deep within. She gasped, her clothes vibrating and fluttering with the force of it. Her legs trembled. Exhaustion crashed over her like a wave. She staggered toward the double doors leading to the temple's reception hall. The air shimmered around her, her vision distorted by waves of raw energy.

Just as she reached the doors, a powerful voice rang out, disembodied and absolute. **"Only the worthy shall pass. State your name."**

Sophie didn't speak aloud. The answer came from within. "I am Sophie Griffin, the Avatar of War."

"You are the worthy," the voice declared. **"You shall pass."**

The massive doors creaked open.

Sophie stepped through, lightheaded and wavering from the physical drain. A woman she didn't recognize hurried from the storage room, rushing to her side. "Sophie," the woman said, her voice laced with concern.

"I met my goddess," Sophie mumbled, slurring slightly. Her limbs felt like lead. "I'm so tired…"

She collapsed into the woman's arms before she could say another word, as darkness claimed her.

Interlude 1 – The Sovereign

The Sovereign sat in her planning room, a grand chamber dominated by a large round table with high-backed chairs. She occupied the central, throne-like seat, her commanding presence radiating authority.

Across from her, a man she hired almost a year ago, stood nervously, clutching a device made of smooth, polished stone. He wore black denim pants and a tan shirt, his discomfort obvious in the way he shifted his weight.

"Your Majesty," he began, voice strained. "There's an issue with the Codex."

The Sovereign narrowed her eyes, irritation flickering across her face. "An issue? Please … *be specific.*"

"When we tested it in Islewind, it functioned perfectly," the man stammered, tightening his grip on the device. "But now it doesn't work. Every test phrase returns... nonsense. Gibberish."

"So," she said, leaning forward, her voice cold, "you're suggesting it broke in transit?"

"No, Your Majesty." he replied quickly. "I packed it myself. The container could withstand bullets or a horse's hooves with ease."

"Then explain the failure," she snapped. "and more importantly...can you fix it?"

The man hesitated, sweat beading on his brow. "If I had to guess, Your Majesty, the Codex was either tampered with or enchanted somehow. I know how to use it, but I don't understand its full construction. I...I am not sure I repair it."

Her annoyance deepened. She steepled her fingers in front of her lips. "So, you're saying it's unfixable?"

The unspoken threat hung in the air.

"If there's a way, I will find it," he said quickly, his voice trembling. "I'll study the texts again, dig deeper maybe the answer is there."

"How long?" she asked, her gaze, cutting like a blade.

"I can't say yet, Your Majesty," he admitted. "But I will inform you the moment I have answers."

"See that you do," she said curtly, flicking her hand. "Go."

He bowed deeply. "Good day, Your Majesty." Then he turned and hurried from the room.

As the door closed behind him, the Sovereign leaned back, exhaling slowly attempting to calm her growing frustration. A knock broke her focus. Before she could respond, the door opened, and Beaumont, her chief advisor and administrator, stepped inside with a respectful incline of his head.

"Yes, Beaumont?" she asked, feigning patience.

"Your witches are ready to see you," he said, his voice low and deferential.

She sighed, straightened, and gave a crisp order. "Send them in."

Beaumont stepped aside, bowing as four women entered. Each carried her own aura of power and quiet tension.

Gretta, the brown-haired ice witch and chosen avatar of the goddess Justice, moved with stiff precision. She wore a thick leather overcoat to stave off the perpetual cold her magic exuded.

Mage, the shadow witch, seemed to glide, her form shrouded in ever-shifting darkness that molded itself into the shape of a dress.

Isabella, the blue-haired mechana-mage, bore visible signs of their journey together: a mechanical right arm and left leg that glowed faintly her blue enchantment. Her coveralls were pristine despite their utility, a testament to her discipline. She is wearing a new patch over her eye, a *trophy* of her failed encounter with Albert Thompson from the Order of Saint Lorraine.

Last came *Hema*, the blood witch, her crimson gown soaked with weaponized blood. Her axe-headed staff was slung across her back, the head blunted but ready at a moment's notice.

Beaumont gave the Sovereign a subtle nod before quietly exiting, the door clicking shut behind him.

The Sovereign's sharp gaze swept over her four witches, each powerful, yet each marred by recent failures.

"Tell me, my witches," she commanded, reclining and elegantly crossing one leg over the other. Her eyes pierced them one by one. "What happened?"

"Your Majesty," Hema began, voice steady, "I successfully retrieved the Codex from the Aurorium evidence holding room after Killian's man was arrested."

"Yes, Hema you did," the Sovereign replied coolly, a faint smile tugging at her lips. "You, of course, set the standard."

The insult rang clear. The others stiffened.

"I have failed you, Your Majesty," Mage said. Her voice reverberated like whispers in a cavern, an eerie echo of her shadow magic. "The orange pirate escaped me twice. I didn't anticipate the silver girl would intervene. Next time, I'll strike without hesitation. The pirate will not escape again."

"See that you do," the Sovereign said, her tone icy.

Isabella's blue hair gleamed in the light as she spoke next, her voice cold and devoid of emotion. "I failed to retrieve Brother Albert's journal. I walked into a trap. The avatar girls were captured by the Order. I was overpowered and deceived."

"And why," the Sovereign asked, her tone like a drawn blade, "did you not leave the castle with enough material to create ten familiars, only to have so few left when you needed them?"

Gretta stepped forward, her brown overcoat sweeping the floor. "My queen," she interjected, "we were discovered in the Aurorium inside their village before we could escape. We had no choice but to fight our way out."

The Sovereign's eyes narrowed as she fixed Gretta with a piercing gaze. The ice witch stiffened, but her resolve buckled. "Isabella," the queen said sharply, "is that true?"

"No," Isabella replied flatly, her gaze fixed on the floor.

The Sovereign's tone chilled. "What is true, Isabella?"

Without lifting her head, Isabella answered. "Gretta said *she had a score to settle*. She walked into the courtyard and started killing Aurorium members. You ordered me to protect her, so I deployed my familiars to stop them. When we reached the front gate, she told me she was behind me but somehow, we were separated."

The Sovereign's face hardened, fury simmering beneath the surface. Her hand clenched, and a glowing, mana-formed hand erupted into existence, wrapping around Gretta's body and lifting her into the air. Only her head and legs dangled below the shimmering grip.

Gretta gasped as her ice magic drained upward into the Sovereign's Makio-stone crown through her construct hand.

"You forgot," the queen said softly, venom curling in her voice, "that Isabella cannot lie."

Gretta gasped again. "Please, my queen…"

"Silence!" The Sovereign's voice cracked like a whip. "You jeopardized everything for petty revenge. I ordered you to remain unseen. A stolen codex from their stores would have drawn suspicion but your senseless slaughter guarantees it. The Laminae prince's death? They'll connect the dots very soon." Her gaze swept over the remaining witches, her expression dark as thunderclouds. "One of you," she said coldly, "remind me how the prince died."

"His heart was frozen while he slept," Hema offered calmly.

"Hema, *you* are truly an asset," the Sovereign said, her praise sharp as a blade. Her grip on Gretta tightened, the magical hand constricting further.

Gretta squirmed against the spell, clawing at the translucent construct wrapped around her midsection. She lacked the power or experience necessary to break free.

"Your reckless actions," the queen spat, "have left a trail the Aurorium will follow straight to us. Do you not understand what you've done?" Her tone turned lethal. "The Aurorium Clan will not rest. They will hunt down every lead to avenge their dead." The Sovereign's fingers curled deeper into her fist. The trap spell responded, squeezing Gretta until a sharp crack echoed through the chamber. Gretta coughed violently, blood spattering her lips as she tried in vain to speak.

Satisfied with her pain but not yet ready to release her, the Sovereign loosened her grip just enough for the Ice Witch to breathe. "We must erase every trace of this one's foolishness before it brings the dogs to our doorstep." She turned to Mage, voice clipped and imperious. "Mage, return to Granmark. Deal with the local contact. Make certain he can never speak of us *to anyone.*"

Mage bowed low, her voice reverberating through her shadowed form. "As you command, my queen."

"My queen," Hema interjected quickly, tone eager. "I established those contacts and managed our resources in Granmark. Please, allow me to handle it."

The Sovereign's expression did not waver. "No, Hema. You will go to Laminae and retrieve a resource. We can no longer wait for the codex to be repaired. We will do this the hard way." She turned her gaze to Isabella. "Isabella, see the healer. I'll have work for you soon."

The mechana mange nodded. "Yes, my queen."

Still suspended in the crushing grip, Gretta gasped. "You punish only mem but we all failed!" she cried, voice hoarse and breaking.

The Sovereign's fury reignited. Her first closed tighter.

Gretta screamed.

"Failure is inevitable," the Sovereign hissed, her voice colder than ice. "Failure, is a teacher a trainer of the powerful. I can forgive failure. But disobedience? Lying to me in my own court?" She leaned forward; eyes locked on Gretta's. "Those, I will not tolerate."

She inhaled deeply, composing herself as she straightened. "Your inability to understand this is *my* failure, as your ruler, to lead you effectively." Then, to the others: "You have your orders. Go. Gretta and I have much to discuss."

Mage, Hema, and Isabella bowed and turned to leave. Gretta's panicked cries rang out as she pleaded, "No! Please don't leave me! Don't leave me alone with her!"

The witches paused, just for a moment. They exchanged a glance. But duty outweighed sympathy, and they continued to the door. Only Isabella hesitated, casting one final glance back before stepping out.

The chamber doors closed with a heavy, foreboding thud, muffling Gretta's screams as electricity surged through her. The Sovereign remained still, watching impassively as the spell did its work.

Chapter 16

Sister Ingrid leaned back and said "Absolutely not," sharply, sitting rigidly behind her desk, her gaze fixed on Marcus with thinly veiled irritation. "Either you or Sister Alameda must accompany one of the girls. That's final."

"I understand," Marcus replied, his voice calm despite her tone. "My concern, however, is that with four avatars, Sister Alameda and I are stretched thin."

"Challenging, is it?" Ingrid mocked, arching an eyebrow. "Two of the four have already communed with their goddesses, one will be unconscious for most of the day, and who knows when the other will finish. For now, the two of you are more than sufficient."

Marcus sighed inwardly but kept his expression neutral. "I apologize, Sister," he said, bowing his head slightly. "I only thought Regina could learn a great deal from Sister Sallie. She's highly knowledgeable about magical tools and their applications. Given that Miss Fournier is a Nexus Mage, time with her would greatly expand Regina's understanding."

Sister Ingrid's lips tightened. "I thought *absolutely not* was clear enough, Brother Marcus."

"I wasn't suggesting Sister Sallie go alone," Marcus countered, carefully choosing his words. "Either I or Sister Alameda would accompany them, of course."

"Brother Marcus," Sister Ingrid said, her frustration rising, "this subject is closed."

"Please, hear me out," Marcus pressed. "If Regina spent a day or two with Sister Sallie here on the island, while the others are otherwise occupied, would that be acceptable?"

Sister Ingrid's demeanor softened slightly. "It would," she admitted.

"In my view, the only difference is the location," Marcus said. "Whether they're here or traveling together, the value of that time remains the same."

She leaned back in her chair, folding her hands. "You make a fair point, Brother Marcus. Now allow me to make mine." Her tone sharpened. "The goddesses chose avatars four of them, because something very dangerous is coming. Order Island is **safe**. A small mana-powered boat, crossing open waters on what any reasonable person would call a long journey, is not." She paused, letting the weight of her words settle. "You are the avatars' guide. You know the risks as Brother Albert's death so vividly reminded us. Sister Sallie, however, does not."

Marcus clenched his jaw, absorbing the truth in her words.

"If you told her now that the journey could be dangerous, she'd insist she understands. But in her heart, she still sees Regina as the goddess of Change. When she lies dying on the floor of that boat, because the conspiracy waited for the avatars to be vulnerable, your assurance that she *understood the risks* will offer you no comfort."

Marcus swallowed hard, picturing Sallie lying motionless, her eyes dull and lifeless. He forced himself to sit with the image, feeling the pain. He thought of the brothers and sisters who had died in service to the Order. He'd known their names. Their faces.

"I understand, Sister," he said at last. "My first instinct is to tell Sallie she cannot accompany Miss Fournier and I to the Luminous." He paused. "But I think that would be a mistake. Treating her like a child in an environment we pretend is safe does her no favors. Sallie could die tomorrow testing a magical fire axe on the beach outside this window."

Sister Ingrid turned to glance out the window, her expression unreadable. When she looked back, a flicker of respect lit her eyes. "You make a compelling argument, Brother." She leaned forward, her voice quieter but firm. "Let's suppose you are right, then you owe it to your friend to explain the risks in excruciating detail and make sure she listens. She deserves to understand the danger she's walking into."

"I will," Marcus promised.

"See that you do," she said curtly. "My advice stands: tell her she's not allowed to go. But ultimately, I'll leave the decision to your discretion." She leaned back, signaling the conversation was drawing to a close. "If there's nothing else?"

Marcus hesitated, then nodded. "Since I'll be leaving the island, I still need to prepare a message for Sister Alameda."

Sister Ingrid smiled faintly and opened her desk drawer, withdrawing the familiar crystal cube. "Yes, you do," she said, handing it to him with a knowing look.

[-----✟-----]

After recording his message for Sister Alameda using Sister Ingrid's crystal cube, Marcus packed a day's worth of clothes and toiletries into his bag. He figured Regina wouldn't need much time to prepare, after all, she hadn't brought anything with her to Order Island and the Luminous was essentially her home.

Marcus made a quick stop by Sister Sallie's working area in the College of Sages wing. A nearby brother informed him that Sallie had already left, claiming she was on a mission for an avatar. Marcus left her supervisor a message, noting that she might be tied up with the avatars for the next few days but should return shortly after. Not wanting to delay further, he collected Regina, and the two headed to the islet near the main pier where the Stormfang was docked.

The boathouse was a large structure housing twelve vessels of varying sizes and types: four medium-sized sailboats, three simple rowboats with makeshift sails, and five newer messenger boats with vinyl-covered passenger areas. Marcus spotted Sister Sallie by one of the newer boats, loading an overnight bag into the cargo compartment. She saw them and waved cheerfully. "Hey, you two!" she called. "We should take this one, it's one of the newer models. It has an updated mana-leeching system that's much more efficient."

Marcus and Regina waved back and approached.

"Sister Sallie," Marcus said with mild amusement, "you beat us here." His tone carried a hint of unspoken meaning.

"Of course," Sallie replied brightly. "Why waste time testing spoons and fire axes when I could get everything ready for our trip?" She gestured toward the boat with enthusiasm. "I even stopped by the cafeteria and had them make us box lunches, just in case we get hungry on the way."

"Wow, that's very thoughtful," Regina said warmly. "What kind of lunches?"

"Sandwiches, salads, and some fruit," Sallie replied. "Oh, and I grabbed a few extra slices of today's cake."

"Impressive," Marcus said dryly, giving her a pointed look. "*It's like you thought of everything.*"

"As I've been saying, Marcus," Sallie quipped, "*I should be the first assistant.*"

"That's not up to me," Marcus lied smoothly, placing his bag in the boat's storage. He turned to Regina. "Miss Regina, I need to speak with Sister Sallie for a moment. Can you wait for us on the boat?"

"Sure," Regina said, picking up the lunches. She stepped aboard and settled into the front passenger seat, placing the food neatly beside her.

Marcus led Sallie a few paces away, lowering his voice. "Sister, there's something important we need to discuss."

"Oh my," Sallie teased, placing a hand to her chest theatrically. "*Sister?* This must be serious."

"It is," Marcus said firmly, suppressing a flicker of irritation. "You need to understand, it could be dangerous for you to come with us to the Luminous."

"*Danger?!?*" Sallie gasped in mock alarm, eyes wide with exaggerated fear. "Marcus, you're so melodramatic! What kind of danger, exactly? A rogue wave? A particularly aggressive librarian?"

"Sallie, can you please take this seriously?" Marcus said, his voice rising.

"*Take what seriously?* My duties are far more dangerous than **yours**. Need I remind you of the time I broke my arm testing a prototype mana coil?"

"That isn't the same! Sallie." Marcus said, struggling to stay calm, and keep his voice low enough to keep Regina from listening in on their conversation.

"*Oh really?*" she shot back. "*What kind of danger am I supposed to encounter at a library? Paper cuts? Starving in a labyrinth of bookshelves? Or, oh, I know a killer termite feasting on some ancient tome?*"

Frustrated, Marcus rubbed his face with both hands. "Do you remember the brother who died a few days ago?" he asked sharply.

"Of course I do. *I told you about it, remember?*" Sallie said, now visibly annoyed.

"That was Brother Albert Thompson," Marcus said grimly. "He was the avatars' original guide. He and the avatars were attacked by an unknown group." Marcus paused working through his own grief and said "He sacrificed himself to keep the avatars from being captured."

Sallie snorted and shook her head. "*And you tell me I'm the one who believes wild stories.*"

Seeing the conversation was going nowhere, Marcus turned to the boat and called out. "Miss Regina, can you come here for a moment?"

"Sure," Regina said, closing the lunch bag and hopping out. She approached with a playful mix of walking and skipping.

"*You asked what kind of danger.*" Marcus said to Sallie, his voice tightening. He placed a hand gently on Regina's shoulder. "Miss Regina, can you tell Sister Sallie everything that happened the day you met Brother Albert? Start from the beginning. Share as much as you remember."

"Okay." Regina replied with a warm smile, her near-perfect memory making the task effortless. She began recounting the events in vivid detail, how she arrived in Granmark, discovered the alley drowned in inky shadow blackness, and met Brother Albert in West's Tavern. She described their frantic escape to the Stormfang and how they barely evaded capture by sailing away at sunrise.

Her story unfolded with her usual blend of innocence and curiosity. She wandered into tangents, marveling at Isabella's mechanical constructs and Mage's shadow magic. At one point, she paused, wondering aloud if anyone else in the tavern had been hurt when Brother Albert detonated his journal to stop Isabella.

Marcus listened quietly, though he had heard it before. Hearing it retold through Regina's lens, full of wonder and innocence, made the events feel even more harrowing. When she finally finished, he nodded solemnly.

"Thank you, Miss Regina," Marcus said. "Can you give us just a little more time?"

"Okay," she replied, glancing at the sky. "But we should get going soon. It's getting late."

"We're almost done, I promise" Marcus promised. Regina returned to the boat, settling into the back seat and stretching out comfortably.

Marcus turned back to Sallie, his expression serious. **"That,"** he said firmly, **"is the kind of danger I'm talking about.** *A little more severe than paper cuts.*"

Sister Sallie's tan face had gone pale. She stared at Marcus, wide-eyed, her earlier mockery replaced by shock. "How could all of that happen in one night?" she whispered.

Marcus saw her apprehension and gave her an out. "If you want to stay behind," he said gently, "I won't hold it against you."

Sallie hesitated; eyes fixed on him. "But you're still going, aren't you?"

"I am," Marcus said without pause. "I'm the guide to the avatars. It's my duty to accompany them."

Sallie took a deep breath, her resolve returning. "Then I'm still going too," she said firmly, though her voice held a trace of disbelief. "Seriously, all of that happened in just one night?"

"Yes," Marcus said grimly.

Sallie shook her head and muttered to herself as she climbed into the boat.

Marcus shrugged and followed, settling into the front passenger seat. Sallie took the helm.

Resting her hand on the console, Sallie activated the boat's systems. A crystal embedded in the panel glowed softly, then brightened as she spoke. "This boat has two mana-leeching modes," she explained. "The first only draws mana from the driver, which limits range. The second draws mana equally from everyone on board."

As she spoke, Marcus glanced around the vessel. Similar glowing crystals were embedded in the columns supporting the vinyl canopy. He guessed these worked in tandem with the console to draw mana from passengers and power the boat. He was fairly certain more crystals were hidden within the hull.

"The propulsion system draws water into a front intake and expels it from the rear for movement," Sallie continued, her enthusiasm returning. "Smaller output vents and a rudder help with steering." She set the leeching mode to "shared" and launched the journey to the Luminous in Laminae.

First Hour: Picking Up Speed

After thirty minutes of smooth sailing, Sallie shouted over the wind, "We're making good time!" She glanced at the glowing console crystal, now a vibrant blue. "The faster we go, the more mana the boat pulls from us. It's a balance between speed and endurance."

"How fast can it go?" Regina asked, leaning forward, eyes locked on the console.

"Let's find out," Sallie said with a grin. She pulled a lever, and the boat surged forward, skimming the water.

"Woohoo!" Regina shouted, arms raised as the wind whipped past.

Marcus smiled at her excitement, but his attention drifted to Sallie, who was laughing and handling the controls with ease.

After fifteen minutes at top speed, Sallie eased the lever back. "Let's slow down a bit," she said, catching her breath. "It gets a little too hard to steer at high speeds."

Second Hour: Magic and Curiosity

During the second hour, conversation turned to magic. Sallie and Regina took the lead, with Marcus quietly observing. He was surprised by how much Regina had already learned.

She spoke of the magical systems she'd studied: *Child's Play*, every Nexus Mage's first magic system taught to her by her mother; she then learned *Verbolsance*; and *forge de l'espace aérien*. Though not a master, her understanding was sharp, and she described several spells in detail.

Sallie, clearly intrigued, offered to teach her Smoke and Mirrors magic. Regina declined politely, saying she was focused on <u>Earthbloom,</u> a system recommended by Lisa Nozaki. She spoke of the challenge in balancing personal mana with the energy of earth and element.

Curious, Marcus asked, "Is there a limit to how many systems a mage can learn?"

Regina tilted her head. "I don't think so. I guess it depends on a mage's memory and mental endurance."

Third Hour: Magical Tools and Mana Fatigue

As they passed the halfway point, talk shifted to magical tools. Sallie described a magical spoon designed to dig through tough frozen food. Her research had inspired tactical shovels used by Stoneridge's military to set up camps in the kingdom's frozen terrain.

Regina listened with interest, asking sharp questions about testing methods. Sallie explained her process: start with the tool's intended use and test it on target material, then experiment with others like stone or sand and adjust from there.

As the third hour wore on, no mana fatigue set in. Even in shared mode, the drain should have caused mild symptoms: *headaches, sore muscles, and mental fog.* Nothing severe, but that should be noticeable.

Marcus monitored the console's crystal and map, watching for signs of trouble while keeping an eye on Regina and Sallie.

Toward the end of the trip, Sallie frowned, glancing between the glowing crystal and the console display. "That's odd," she said. "How are you two feeling?"

"I feel fine," Marcus replied, though he shifted uncomfortably in his seat. "Just want to stretch my legs."

"I'm good," Regina said from the back, her head resting against the seat. "Just ready to get home."

"Huh," Sallie murmured, studying the crystal more closely. She turned to Marcus with a furrowed brow. "How far are we from the Luminous?"

"If we maintain our speed, just over thirty minutes," Marcus said. "Why? Did you find something wrong?"

"We've been traveling at a very high speed," Sallie explained, her tone concerned. "I expected us to be running low by now. At this pace, the leeching system should've drained half our mana reserves."

She tapped the crystal, expecting its color to shift, but it remained a deep blue. Curious, she stopped the boat and switched the leeching system from *shared* to *driver-only.* The crystal turned green immediately.

"Oh, that feels better," Regina said with a relieved sigh, stretching her arms.

Sallie's eyes widened. She turned in her seat. "Wait, Regina, did you feel the mana drain the whole time?"

"Yeah," Regina said sheepishly. "...Did I do something to the boat? Is it broken?"

"No," Sallie said slowly, her mind racing.

"I don't understand," Marcus said. "What's happening?"

Sallie tapped the crystal again. "So... apparently, the mana leeching system doesn't actually split the drain evenly. It targets whoever has the highest reserves and draws from them first, it must then normalize over time." She looked at Regina, smiling. "And your mana pool must be enormous. You've been powering the boat almost entirely by yourself, even at full speed, and you're still up and talking like nothing's happened." She turned to Marcus. "According to every technical manual I've read, that much leeching would knock most mages out cold within an hour, like casting spells nonstop."

Marcus looked at Regina, who gave a nervous, lopsided smile. "Are you absolutely sure you're okay, Miss Fournier?"

"Yes," Regina said quickly. "Did I mess up the boat somehow?"

"No, my dear," Sallie said warmly, looking back at her she gives her a wink and says. "We're just realizing how amazing you are."

She switched the leeching mode back to *shared* and restarted the engine. The boat surged forward with a burst of water and speed, the hum of mana filling the air once more.

Entering Laminae

"Regina." Sallie called over the wind. "Can you tell me how to find the Luminous once we're in Laminae?"

"It's pretty easy" Regina shouted back, digging through the lunch bag. "It's kind of hard to miss!"

"Have you been there before, Brother?" Sallie asked Marcus.

"I haven't," Marcus said. "I've been to the other kingdom libraries in Laminae, but never the Luminous itself."

Regina glanced up, a piece of cake in hand. "a lot of people visit to see my dad."

Sallie blinked. "Wait, your dad? Who's your father?"

"Jules Fournier," Regina said casually. "He's one of Laminae's ritual scholars."

Sallie turned wide eyes toward Marcus and mouthed, *did you know that?*

Marcus chuckled and nodded. "Mr. Fournier is one of the most respected ritual scholars in the Seven Kingdoms."

Regina grinned. "My mom used to say he only learned all those rituals to keep up with her."

They passed under a weather-worn floating sign reading: **Kingdom of Laminae – Welcome to the Land of Libraries.**

The sign stood proud despite years of wind and salt spray.

Sallie eased back on the throttle as they entered Laminae's waters. "Which way now?"

"Maintain this course," Marcus replied, checking the map. "We've just crossed into the border province of Goudeux. If we keep heading west, we'll reach Arcanum."

He paused. "The Luminous is near a mountain, right?"

"Not exactly," Regina corrected. "It's inside Kipler Mountain. Just past Arcanum."

"Got it," Sallie said, adjusting course.

Approaching the Luminous

Crossing into Arcanum, they passed beneath Laminae's flag, a golden border surrounding a royal blue field. At its center, an open book sat between a feathered quill and a key: symbols of the kingdom's devotion to knowledge and its preservation.

In Laminae, the pursuit of knowledge was so revered that families were conscripted to maintain libraries, just as Stoneridge conscripted soldiers into its military.

The sea stretched wide before them until a jagged silhouette pierced the horizon. Kipler Mountain rose like a standing sentinel, and from its peak extended a breathtaking spire: a glass and stone tower that shimmered in the sunlight.

"So that's why they call it the Luminous," Sallie said, guiding the boat toward a pier that extended from a building seamlessly carved into the mountain's side.

"How was this built?" Marcus asked, awe coloring his voice.

Regina answered automatically, reciting from memory, she had given this explanation so many times. "The kingdom of Laminae partnered with a firm from Stoneridge. Their architects and mages hollowed out the mountain and crafted the structure to last for generations. It's a blend of magical and engineering excellence." She smiled faintly.

The boat slid smoothly into the first slip, and Marcus wasted no time hopping out. He tied the retaining rope to a sturdy column on the pier, both the dock and the vessel followed the standardized design used throughout the Seven Kingdoms.

Regina leapt from the back of the boat onto the pier, her excitement bubbling over. "I'm going in now!" she called to Marcus.

"Very well, Miss Fournier," Marcus replied with a nod. "We'll be right behind you."

"Okay," she said, flashing a smile as she set off down the pier. Her eyes scanned the area, looking for the man with the red hat Brother Albert had mentioned, but he was nowhere to be seen.

She reached the base of the grand two-tiered staircase leading up to the Luminous. The building loomed ahead, both magnificent and imposing. Halfway up the steps, she glanced back toward the boat and saw Marcus speaking with Sister Sallie. Shrugging, she continued her climb, anticipation rising with each step.

At the top, she paused to take a deep breath. The massive double doors of the legendary library stood before her. She couldn't wait to see her family again, *to tell her father and Mommy June everything*. Smiling to herself, she pushed open the doors of the Luminous.

[-----✝-----]

"All tied up," Marcus informed Sister Sallie, who remained seated in the boat, diligently writing in her journal. Stretching stiff limbs after the three-hour journey, he glanced at her and asked, "What are you working on?"

"I'm recording my observations about the mana leeching system," she replied, eyes on the page as her pen scratched steadily. "Specifically, how it targeted the passenger with the highest mana reserves. And how vast Miss Fournier's reserves must be to power the boat at full speed with almost no visible strain."

Marcus nodded, watching as she continued to write. His gaze drifted across the pier. The area was eerily quiet.

Ships moved across the distant water, their sails stark against the horizon, but the dock beside the Luminous was empty. Not a soul in sight, only him, Sallie, and Regina. His brow furrowed.

"Isn't it odd," Marcus said, breaking the silence, "that we're the only ones here?"

Sallie held up her finger as she finished the last line in her journal with a flourish. Closing the book, she looked around, frowning at the deserted pier. "It is odd," she agreed, setting the journal aside. "This is Laminae. The Luminous is a supposed to be a hub, scholars, travelers, students. There should be people coming and going."

Marcus scanned the surroundings again, unease prickling at the back of his neck. The stillness didn't belong, not here, not in a kingdom that prized the exchange of knowledge. Folding his arms, he continued to study the dock and the towering library above, instincts sharpening into alertness.

[-----✿-----]

Regina pushed open the heavy door of the Luminous, her voice echoing through the grand library's entryway. "Dad! Mommy June! I have so much to tell you!"

She stepped inside, closed the door gently behind her, and hurried through the entrance hall. Her excitement quickened her steps as she entered the familiar foyer, where Mommy June always waited, ready to greet her with a warm smile.

But Mommy June wasn't there.

Regina froze. Her heart dropped as her eyes locked on a chilling figure standing over Mommy June's lifeless body in the middle of the floor in front of the resting couch.

The woman had deep red hair spilling from beneath a tattered crimson witch's hat soaked with red … *Blood.* Her dress also soaked through with *blood* was frayed and battle-worn, clinging to her frame like smoke. In her hands, she gripped a battle axe with a long shaft the blade is circular and gleamed faintly with a red hue.

"I can't wait to hear it," the woman said, her voice curling into mock sweetness, her smile edged with cruelty.

Regina's eyes widened. Her breath caught. "Get away from my Mommy June!" she screamed, voice cracking with panic and fury.

The woman tilted her head. Her damp hair clung to her face, and that terrible smile widened. "No," she drawled, voice dripping with contempt. "I don't think I will." She raised the axe and pointed it at Regina. The blade hummed with quiet menace. "Why don't you come and make me?"

Rage surged through Regina. Her hand clenched around the wand in her pocket. She yanked it free and cast her spell: "**Envoûtement des Cercles Éternels!**"

Four glowing rings snapped into existence, encircling the woman's ankles, knees, waist, left arm, and neck. The air trembled with magical pressure as the bindings locked into place. For one breathless moment, the woman stood frozen, *immobilized.*

A shaky sigh escaped Regina. *Yes! The spell worked.*

Then

"What?" the woman hissed, real surprise flashing in her eyes. She strained against the glowing circles but couldn't move.

The triumph didn't last.

Her smile returned…wider now, savage. Blood began to churn and ooze from her hair and gown, slithering free like sentient rope. The crimson strands coiled, then cracked outward with a whip-like snap.

In a flash of red light, the blood shattered all four magic rings.

The woman cackled, sharp and merciless. "What was that?" she sneered.

She lunged forward, axe arcing through the air in a deadly swing.

Time slowed. Regina did not have the time to move.

Fear rooted her to the spot, her thoughts spinning too fast to summon a new spell. The blood which closed the distance, weapon gleaming with fatal intent.

What would Annabelle do? Regina thought desperately.

Then it came to here: the ***sea bubble spell***. Annabelle had shown her just days ago.

Regina's grip tightened around her wand. No hesitation. She poured mana into it, more than the spell required, channeling every ounce of fear, desperation, and determination. She pictured the sea: vast, surging, unstoppable.

A roiling orb of seawater erupted from her wand, expanding rapidly.

The sphere burst outward, filling the space between her and the charging witch. The woman, mid-leap, couldn't stop. She slammed into the sphere of rushing water.

[-----✞-----]

Marcus and Sister Sallie made their way down the pier, overnight bags in hand, toward the grand entrance of the Luminous. The rhythmic thud of their footsteps echoed in the quiet air, but Marcus noticed something odd, Sallie was unusually silent.

Normally, he'd ask what was on her mind. But fatigue from their three-hour boat ride tugged at his focus, and he let it go.

As they climbed the stairs, Marcus caught a sudden flash of light from one of the entrance-level windows. He frowned, his instincts sharpening.

"What's going on?" Sallie asked, her voice uneasy. She glanced at him, clearly expecting answers he didn't have.

Before Marcus could reply, a thunderous crash erupted water exploded through the Luminous's windows, spraying shards of glass and torrents of seawater across the entryway. The roar of shattering glass and rushing water filled the air.

Marcus's heart lurched.

Without hesitation, he dropped his bag and ran up the stairs, his shoes pounding the stone steps. Reaching the top, he threw open the doors, just as a wave of seawater surged out.

The blast nearly knocked him over.

He caught the doorframe, clinging tight as cold water slammed into his legs, soaking him from the knees down.

"Watch the water, Sallie!" he shouted over the chaos.

Bracing himself, Marcus pushed forward into the Luminous, forcing his way through the rush of water. He waded deeper, soaked and breathless, eyes scanning the soaked hall for the source of the eruption.

[-----✿-----]

Regina found herself slumped against the counter, dazed by the backlash of her overcharged sea bubble spell. Her back throbbed, her head swam, but she forced herself upright, water dripping from her clothes and hair.

Across the room, Mommy June lay in a crumpled heap beside the couch, coughing weakly, clearly thrown by the blast.

"Mommy June!" Regina cried, rushing to her side. She dropped to her knees and gently shook her.

"Regina..." Mommy June rasped. "What happened?"

Before Regina could answer, the grating sound of metal dragging across stone echoed from beyond the foyer.

Regina's blood ran cold.

The axe.

"Mommy June, we have to go," she urged, trying to pull her stepmother upright. But Mommy June was too weak to stand.

"Where do you think you're going?" came that voice like cracked ice.

Regina turned to face her.

The blood witch stood in the doorway, her tattered crimson dress soaked and dripping with writhing blood. Rage twisted her face, and she dragged the murder axe behind her, its blade scraping the floor with a shriek-like nails on a chalkboard.

Panic surged through Regina.

She looked from the witch to Mommy June, then made a decision.

She couldn't carry her to safety., but she could draw the witch away.

Regina stood, heart hammering, and sprinted toward the staircase that led to the reading level.

"Don't run!" the witch called after her, voice laced with mocking delight. "I've got something to share with you!"

As she hit the stairs with familiar speed, a blade of blood shot past Regina, slicing through the air just above her head and embedding into the stone wall with a violent crack.

She didn't look back.

Her feet pounded the stairs as fast as they could take her. Her breath came in short, panicked gasps. She didn't know if the blade would have killed her, but she wasn't going to find out.

Behind her came a thud, the witch had leapt down after her.

Regina could feel it, the pressure of danger closing fast.

She's going to strike! Her mind screamed.

On instinct, she dove to the left.

She hit the ground hard, skidding next to a large reading table just as the axe came crashing down, slamming into the stone where she'd been a heartbeat earlier.

Regina scrambled beneath the table, her hands trembling, breath ragged.

The witch wrenched the axe free with a furious growl, muttering a sharp curse in Ashani, a language of Islewind. Then, snarling, she brought the axe down on the table with a roar.

The thick wood shattered above Regina's head.

"Hide all you like, little worm," the witch snarled. "Sooner or later, I'll cut you down."

She jumped onto the table.

It groaned under her weight.

Another brutal swing smashed into the wood, and the axe's jagged head punched through like it was a hook. Regina's breath caught.

The axe looked different now, sharper, more vicious. It was changing... *Somehow*

Laughing coldly, the witch slammed it down again, cracking the table's frame.

"I'm going to chop you into pieces," she hissed, voice calm and cruel. "Drain every last drop of blood from your body..."

Another sickening crack made Regina flinch.

"...and then," the witch called to her, grinning wickedly, "I'll chop up your mother."

[-----✝-----]

Marcus stepped into the waterlogged foyer of the Luminous, his shoes splashing through shallow puddles. The room was in chaos, furniture overturned, water dripping from every surface. Against a couch on the far side lay a lone, unconscious woman.

His instincts took over.

He rushed toward her.

As he crossed the flooded floor, a flicker of motion caught his eye. He turned, and his stomach dropped.

Hema, The blood witch of The Conspiracy

The blood witch was perched on a table at the far end of the stairwell, swinging her massive axe in a frenzy. Each strike shattered thick wood, her voice shrieking with glee about chopping insects to pieces.

Marcus swallowed hard, bile rising. But he reminded himself: *I am not here to interfere in the Avatars' battles. I am here to support them.*

He forced his attention back to the unconscious woman. Dropping to his knees, he quickly checked her for injuries, no visible wounds, no broken bones. Gently, he pressed his ear to her chest.

Her breathing was ragged but steady. Likely water in her lungs.

She was alive.

"By the goddess..." came a voice behind him.

Sister Sallie stood frozen in the hallway, her wide eyes locked on the witch and her devastating blows.

"Sallie!" Marcus snapped. **"Over here—now!"**

She flinched, then hurried to his side, kneeling beside him. Her face was pale.

"We have to help her," she said, glancing toward Regina and the Blood witch.

"We *are* helping," Marcus said firmly. "I guide the Avatar by trusting her. But *this...*" he nodded to the woman, "...this is where we're needed."

Sallie stared at him a beat longer, surprised by his calm. Then she nodded. "Give me a moment." She rose to her feet and clapped her hands. Her fingers danced in fluid circles, tracing glowing patterns in the air. Then she pressed her palms together, paused, and swept her arms wide.

In an instant, the world shifted.

Color drained from the room like ink in water. The walls, the furniture, the air itself turned gray and desaturated, except for Marcus, Sallie, and the unconscious woman, who still glowed with natural hue.

Marcus blinked. His lips parted to ask a question, but Sallie held up her hand to silence him.

She pointed toward Hema and Regina, then to her eyes—shaking her head. *They can't see us.* Then to her ear—nodding. *But they can still hear us.*

Marcus gave a thumb-up. Then he pointed to the woman, to the door, and made a sweeping motion: *We get her out.*

Sallie nodded. She moved to the woman's legs while Marcus positioned himself behind her, sliding his arms beneath her shoulders and chest. Together, they lifted her, careful but swift.

The woman hung limp between them, but their grip was strong.

Without speaking, they moved toward the entryway. Behind them, the crashing of magic and the shriek of steel echoed like thunder. The table was breaking apart. The witch was still hunting.

Marcus didn't look back.

He carried the woman forward, every step a silent prayer—for Regina, for the goddess, and for what came next.

[----- ✿ -----]

Under the battered reading table, Regina gripped her wand tightly, heart pounding as her mind scrambled through every spell she knew.

None of them felt like enough.

Above her, the murder woman's axe slammed into the wood again, splintering it with a deafening crack. Regina flinched as a jagged chunk broke away, leaving her face-to-face with the blood witch.

"There you are," the woman said, grinning with sick delight. "Time to squash the worm."

She raised one hand. Blood slithered from her hair and dress, coalescing into a pulsing orb in her palm.

Regina's breath caught.

She didn't know what kind of spell this was, but she wasn't waiting to find out. Her wand was already pointed at the right leg of the table. An idea sparked.

She shoved mana into the spell and cast: **"Compression Space Cannon!"**

The blast struck the joint where the leg met the table, shattering it instantly. The structure toppled backward with a violent crash, tipping the witch off balance.

The blood orb shot harmlessly into the ceiling.

Regina didn't wait.

She scrambled out from under the collapsing table and looked toward the couch. **Mommy June's gone.** Relief hit her like a wave, followed by panic. *Where had she gone?*

No time to wonder. The murder woman was already rising; face twisted with fury.

Regina ran for the stairs leading down to the library's lower levels.

"**Don't run away!**" the woman bellowed. "**I told you I have something to share with you!**"

Regina dove forward, landing on the banister and sliding down just as a razor-sharp blood blade sliced the air above her head, gouging a deep wound into the stone wall.

Her heart slammed in her chest.

The blood which cursed above, then laughed.

Why is she laughing? Regina thought only for a moment until she looked down at the landing, then it hit her like a slap: *She knows where I'll land.*

Regina's mind raced. She needed something, anything. One spell surfaced. Simple, almost too childish. But it just might work.

"**Child's Play – Hide and Seek!**" she cast the spell mid-slide.

Back before she communed with Change, she could create two or three projections, four if she really pushed herself. This time, nearly twenty identical versions of her shimmered into existence with a flash the moment she hit the floor.

The illusions scattered at her command, darting into shelves and shadows.

The blood which roared in frustration, then fired blades of blood into the crowd, slicing through three projections at once. But Regina had more to spare.

She ran with them, weaving through shelves toward the magic books section. Slipping behind a tall case, she crouched, pressing her back to the cool wood.

I need time, she thought, scanning the spines of books in front of her: mystical mapping, geomancy, stone shaping…nothing helpful.

Another illusion fell. She could feel it. The witch was getting calmer. More precise. *She's not smashing everything anymore. She's hunting.*

Regina bit her lip. *I have to make her mad again.*

An idea hit.

Quickly, she traced a glowing ritual circle in the air, one her father taught her from his own magic. A voice projection spell. She'd used it once to play pranks on Mattie. Now it is a lifeline.

She pressed her palm to the sigil. At that moment it locked into place, her voice would echo from every projection.

The blood which struck down another one.

Regina smiled. Time to try a page from Annabelle's playbook.

She covered her mouth and laughed softly.

The sound rippled across the library—every illusion laughing with her.

"Nope, not me!" Regina called playfully.

The blood which spun, furious.

"You're really bad at this," Regina taunted again, her voice echoing through all her doubles.

That did it.

The woman screamed and vaulted to the next shelf, smashing it with her axe. Books spilled in every direction.

She was in a frenzy.

Regina took a deep breath and moved quietly. *That should buy me some time... but how much.*

From her hiding spot, her voice echoed through her projected doubles: **"Hey! Be kind to the books! Their priceless knowledge lights our lives!"**

At her command her illusions darted around, drawing the witch farther into chaos. Regina crept through two more aisles, arriving at the ritual section.

She scanned fast.

Wall-breaking spells. Summoning circles. Familiar bonds...

Her eyes lit on one: **Portal Transportation Rituals.** She quickly pulled the book down and flipped through it, she finds just the ritual she needed: A human-sized gate to anywhere, if the caster could calculate the target's relative location.

At the far end of the library, the blood witch had stopped moving.

Regina peeked from behind the shelves while ordering her doubles to move around the floor more and more, she notices the blood soaked witch perched on a shelf, her eyes were shut. Blood trickled from her hands, stretching to the floor, branching out like crimson veins. *What is she doing?* Still, Regina couldn't help herself. She smirked and let the projections speak once more. **"You're bleeding! There's a first aid kit at the desk you should go get a bandage!"**

But this time, the witch didn't respond.

She turned back to the ritual and a warning beneath the spell caught her eye: **"The mana cost of the portal increases proportionally with distance and the mass passing through."**

Regina hesitated. That could be dangerous.

But she shoved the doubt aside. *I have bigger reserves. It'll be enough.*

She tapped her pockets for chalk. Nothing, her frustration surged. The ritual was too intricate to trace with wand-light, she needed chalk. And she needed it now.

"There you are," came the murder woman's voice, low, menacing, and cold.

Regina's head snapped up. A blood tentacle, ending in a grotesque eyeball, peeked over the top of a nearby shelf, staring straight at her.

Her heart dropped.

She used her magic to scout me out, she's learned to tell me from the illusions.

A shadow leapt. The blood witch hurled herself from her position towards Regina.

Regina ran as fast as she could, clutching the ritual book to her chest.

The witch landed on the shelf Regina had just fled, snarling. A blood blade lashed out, slicing deep into Regina's leg.

Pain flared. She hit the ground hard, the ritual book tumbling from her hands.

"Ooooh, that looks bad," the blood which cooed, dropping down. Her eyes glittered with cruelty. "What was it you said? That I am bad at this?"

She rested her axe lazily on one shoulder, striding forward.

Regina's leg burned, but she crawled backward, refusing to stop.

"This is where you belong," the witch sneered. "Crawling on the floor like the worm you are."

Regina's mind spun. *I need a plan.* She reflexively called her projections to her.

She rounded a corner, dragging herself faster, and summoned every remaining projection to her location.

The blood which scoffed. "You think I'll fall for that again?" Her tone dropped into something colder. "No. I think I'll put you out of your misery."

She swung around the corner, axe raised, and brought it down hard onto Regina's chest.

The girl's projection vanished in a flash of light.

The axe slammed into the wood with a crack, sending splinters flying.

The blood witch screamed in rage, yanking the blade free and collapsing the bookshelf in her fury.

She turned, only to find Regina standing, wand in hand.

"Compression Space Cannon!" Regina roared as she cast the spell. The focused blast of warped space slammed into the blood witch's chest, hurling her back. She crashed into a smaller shelf, which toppled over, burying her in a storm of books.

Regina didn't wait to see if it had finished her.

Wincing, she limped toward the front service desk, blood dripping from her gashed leg. She ducked behind the counter, yanking open drawers and searching blind her hand closed on a stick of chalk.

"It's supposed to be in the first drawer!" she yelled, cursing her little brother Mattie under her breath.

Finally.

She snatched it and turned to the old globe on the desk.

Spinning it, her eyes fixed on Mount Bisouveiak, the tallest peak in Stoneridge. Using the coordinates to do some quick math and calculate the distance from where she was standing to the middle of that square. She'd meant to escape to Order Island. But a sick thought hit her. *If I run there... she'll go after Mommy June. After Sister Sallie. Marcus. She'll kill them all.* Her jaw clenched. *I can't allow that.*

She dropped to the floor doing her best to ignore the pain in her leg and began drawing. The ritual circle had to be right *no room for error, no second chances on this assignment.* Her chalk scratched against stone, painstakingly recreating every glyph.

Then she limped ten paces away, calculated the offset from where she was standing to a spot outside, and drew the second circle.

Her hand trembled. Her vision blurred. But she kept going.

When it was done, she hobbled back to the first circle and raised her wand.

Mana surged as she activate it. A shimmering portal flared open, revealing snow-whipped cliffs and a pale sky. There it was right through the wavy window: **Mount Bisouveiak.**

"And where do you think you're going?"

239

Regina froze.

The blood which stood behind her, axe resting on her shoulder, her voice was full of venomous calm.

"You really thought you'd portal away? Leave your precious Order monks and mommy dearest to die? You're worse than me, that little bookworm is real evil."

She raised her hand. Blood gathered again, forming something deadly.

Regina didn't hesitate.

She pointed her wand, not at the witch, but at the **second** circle.

Mana surged again as it activated.

From the ocean outside the window, a surge of sea water exploded through the second portal, rushing into the library like a tidal wave. The freezing deluge slammed into the witch, sweeping her off her feet and hurling her forward.

Right into the **first** portal.

Regina watched, chest heaving, as the blood which flew through and landed hard in the snow the water covering her bloody dress and hair league after league. Over the witch's distant scream, Regina closed the first portal, then collapsed the second.

Silence…Then the **pain**.

Her leg throbbed. Her head hurt like someone was hammering nails into it.

She slumped to the wet floor in front of the desk, she had to close her eyes to decrease the pain whatever little bit she could. The world faded as Regina passed out, her body finally surrendering to its mortality.

[-----✝-----]

After settling Sister Sallie and the unconscious woman who he recognized as Regina's Stepmother June Fournier in the boat, Marcus made Sallie promise to watch over June while he returned to the Luminous to check on Regina. He trusted in Regina as the Avatar of Change, but trust wasn't naivety, he knew Hema could tear Regina apart if the girl made even a small mistake.

He hurried into the waterlogged foyer, following the trail of destruction through the main library floor. Shattered bookshelves and scattered volumes painted a grim picture. Finally, he spotted Regina on the floor, clutching her leg, tears streaming down her face.

"Miss Regina!" Marcus shouted, rushing to her side. "Where is Hema?"

Regina laid on the floor squeezing her eyes shut, pain etched across her face. "Who's that?" she gasped between sobs.

"The woman with the axe," Marcus clarified, crouching beside her. His eyes dropped to her leg, and he winced. "Oh, that's deep."

"It hurts!" Regina snapped, her voice trembling with pain and frustration.

Marcus shook his head, forcing himself to stay focused. "Where is the blood witch?"

"I sent her to Stoneridge," Regina said, pointing to the fading ritual circles on the floor. The glowing symbols were vanishing, their purpose spent.

Relief flickered in Marcus's chest, but he didn't relax. "Is there an infirmary here?"

"By the living quarters… fourth floor," she replied, her voice barely above her painful sobs.

Marcus's gaze swept the area. They were in the basement. A five-story climb with an injured girl in his arms. He reassured himself. "My aid is to be unwavering."

He slid his arms under Regina and lifted her. She cried out as his arm brushed her wound. "I'm so sorry, Miss Regina," he said, wincing.

Regina gritted her teeth but didn't argue. Marcus climbed the stairs, carrying her past the wrecked reading level and into the foyer, but paused, unsure which way to go.

Through her pounding head, Regina noticed and pointed weakly to the door behind the couch in the waiting area. "Stairs... that way," she muttered.

"Thank you," Marcus said, carefully navigating through the soaked entry and onto the stone staircase. The climb was grueling, Regina's weight, his soaked clothes, and frayed nerves all bearing down. Regina whimpered from the pain, but he pressed on.

At last, they reached the fourth floor. Marcus paused, chest heaving.

"I can walk," Regina said, clutching her head. The pressure of being carried made her leg throb worse.

"Are you sure?" Marcus asked, panting, arms trembling.

"Yes," she said, trying to sound tougher than she felt.

He hesitated but set her gently on her feet. She winced but limped forward, heading for the dormitory entrance.

She turned the dials—8-6-3-5. The lock clicked. The door opened.

"This way," she said.

Marcus silently followed her, vowing to restart his exercise routine.

The infirmary was just inside, first door on the left. Regina sighed in relief.

The room was plain but well-equipped: one raised bed in the center, cabinets flanking a large mirror on the far wall, a deep sink nestled in a counter to the right.

Marcus got to work, pulling out supplies: a metal pan, cotton, ointment, silver iodine. He searched for a needle and thread but found none. Whoever stocked the room hadn't expected the kind of deep wounds Hema could inflict.

Meanwhile, Regina untied the ribbon at her waist and eased the dress down. It stuck to her wound, and she let out a cry, peeling it away. Her breath caught as she saw the cut—running from just above her knee to mid-thigh. Blood oozed steadily into her sock.

"Ugh," she muttered, gently touching the torn skin.

Marcus turned, arms full, then quickly turned away when he saw her undressed. His face full of embarrassment. He cleared his throat. "Miss Regina, please lie face down on the bed so we can treat the cut."

"Okay," she murmured, stepping out of the dress entirely. She limped to the bed and lay across it.

Marcus pulled up a chair and surveyed the wound. Despite her childishness, this girl had faced Hema the blood witch and survived. That alone was remarkable, but Miss Regina had **Won** the encounter. Hema had killed trained warriors be they court guards, criminal enforcers, or soldiers. *Regina had done the impossible.*

He dipped cotton into the ointment. "This will hurt."

"Okay," Regina whispered through the multiple painful things drilling into her.

Marcus began carefully spreading the ointment. Regina flinched and pounded the bed with her fists.

"It hurts!" she sobbed, voice cracking with pain and helpless anger.

"I'm so sorry, Miss Regina," Marcus said softly, his tone heavy with regret. He worked as gently as he could, but without a needle and thread, stitching the wound was impossible. He improvised, pressing the wound's edges together, applying adhesive ointment liberally to seal it, then wrapping it tightly with cotton and cloth bandages. It wasn't perfect, especially with Regina squirming and protesting the whole time, but it would hold until proper care could be arranged.

By the time he finished, more than half the tin of adhesive ointment was gone. He secured the bandage with a final dab to keep it from unraveling. "All done," Marcus said gently, his voice reassuring.

Regina rolled onto her back, wiping her tears. She tested the bandage with cautious fingers and winced, but nodded. With Marcus's help, she eased off the bed and stood, carefully putting weight on her injured leg. It still hurt, but it was bearable now.

"It still hurts," she said, touching the bandage's edge, "but it's better."

Marcus turned away to give her privacy. "Please put your dress back on."

"Oh! Right." Regina picked up her silhouette dress and slipped it back on, adjusting the waist ribbon with care.

As she tied the final bow, the distant echo of the front door opening reached them, followed by a voice.

"Hello? Who's here?"

Marcus and Regina turned as a man entered the infirmary, lantern in hand. Flickering light danced along the walls. He wore a vest marked with an Aurorium Shadow badge and a pistol holstered at his hip. His eyes swept the room, landing first on Regina, then on Marcus beside a bloodied metal pan.

"Good evening," Marcus said calmly, inside he wondered and worried *What must this have looked like to this man?*

The Shadow's gaze narrowed as he took in the scene: Regina fixing her dress, Marcus stained with blood and ointment, the general disarray. "What's going on here?" he asked sharply.

Marcus froze, choosing his words with care. "I was escorting Miss Fournier back to her parents, who are on caretaking duty at the Luminous," he began, steadying his voice. "When we arrived, she was attacked by a dangerous woman, someone I believe is named Hema the blood witch."

"I call her the murder woman," Regina added, her voice shaking. "She hurt my Mommy June."

The Shadow's expression hardened. "Where is Jules Fournier now?" he asked, hand steady on the but of his pistol.

Regina blinked. The question struck her hard, she hadn't even thought about her father or little brother. Her shoulders sagged. "I don't know," she replied tears welling up with this new reason to cry.

Marcus stepped in. "I haven't seen him either. So far, we seem to be the only ones here."

"That's the problem," said another voice behind the Shadow, this one lower, rougher, marked by a Laminaen accent.

The Shadow stepped aside. Another man entered, clad in a leather jacket with an Aurorium Eclipse badge. His presence shifted the room. Sharp eyes flicked between them, expression unreadable.

"Do you know what happened here?" the Eclipse asked coolly.

"I've already told you everything I know," Marcus said, standing straighter despite his weariness.

"And who are you?"

"Brother Marcus Igbinedion of the Order of Saint Lorraine," he replied, starting to extend his hand before realizing it was bloodied. He let it fall awkwardly.

"Hi, I'm Regina Fournier," she said instinctively. She hesitated but didn't mention her avatar status.

The Eclipse raised a brow. "And where have you been, Miss Fournier? Your father's been worried."

Marcus answered. "Through a series of events, Miss Fournier found herself on Order Island, helping us with an important matter."

The Eclipse looked between them, his thoughts and expressions unreadable. "And this *murder woman* Hema, was it?" He tilted his head. "Where is she now?"

"I sent her to Stoneridge with a portal ritual," Regina said.

The Eclipse's eyes sharpened. "So, you helped her escape?"

"No!" Regina protested. "She was trying to kill me, I forced her through the portal with blast of seawater. I sent her to Mount Bisouveiak."

The Eclipse studied her for a moment, then shifted and looked at the Shadow.

"Did you find my Mommy June?" Regina asked, hope flickering in her voice.

"Yes. And the other woman from the Order. They're both safe." He said, then added with official weight: "We'll need you both to come with us for further questioning."

Marcus stepped forward. "Might I request the questioning take place at a hospital?" he asked calmly, yet firmly. "Miss Fournier and her stepmother are both in dire need medical attention."

The Eclipse held his gaze a moment, then nodded. "That we can do." He signaled to the Shadow. "Let's get them to a facility."

Chapter 17

The Aurorium team arrived in a vessel nearly identical to the mana boat Marcus, Regina, and Sister Sallie had used. It comprised four members: an Eclipse, ranked fourth-tier; a Shadow, ranked third-tier; and two Sentinels, second-tier operatives equivalent in rank to Sophie Griffin.

Following the attack on Granmark, all Aurorium villages had increased their security measures. In Laminae, patrols were assigned to protect national libraries and their staff. The team's presence there reflected this renewed commitment to safeguarding their institutions.

During a routine patrol, the Aurorium team encountered the mana boat carrying Sister Sallie and June Fournier. When they found June unresponsive, the Eclipse made the decision to leave the Sentinels behind to protect the women, while the more experienced Eclipse and Shadow moved toward a nearby building to investigate the source of the disturbance.

The Aurorium members worked with quiet precision, addressing each other only by rank. They chose to divide themselves between the two boats: the Eclipse and one Sentinel transferred Marcus and Sister Sallie into the Aurorium's boat, while the Shadow and the remaining Sentinel took control of the Order's mana boat, the same one Marcus, Sister Sallie, and Regina had originally arrived in.

Departing the pier at the Luminous, the team directed both boats toward a secondary dock near Arcanum, a thirty-minute ride from their original location. Upon arrival, the Shadow and Sentinel escorted Regina and her stepmother into a sleek, white coach marked with a red shield. Meanwhile, the Eclipse hailed a standard coach to transport Marcus and Sister Sallie to the same destination.

During the ride, Marcus observed a charged silence between the Eclipse and the Sentinel. The tension was unmistakable. It was clear their story hadn't fully convinced the Eclipse. While the relationship between the Order and the Aurorium was usually defined by cooperation and trust, this encounter brimmed with unspoken suspicion, leaving both Marcus and Sister Sallie in unfamiliar territory.

Twenty minutes later, the coaches pulled up to Arcanum Hospital. The Eclipse led Marcus and Sister Sallie inside, with the Sentinel close behind, ensuring they didn't stray. Upon entry, they were separated and placed in small, private offices within the facility.

Marcus surveyed his assigned room. A desk sat squarely in the center, but he chose not to sit behind it, it felt like a presumptuous mistake, given the circumstances. He was certain the Aurorium expected answers, and he was ready to comply, so long as Regina and June Fournier received the medical care they so desperately needed.

Alone in the room, Marcus decided to pass the time with a journal entry. From his many travels, he had learned that waiting was inevitable in situations like this, and in times like this it is a real opportunity to record important details that may be useful later.

Journal Entry, April 14, 1910

While escorting Regina Fournier back to her family at the Luminous, we were ambushed by Hema. In my opinion, this attack confirms that the conspiracy is deliberately targeting the Avatars with lethal intent. Despite the odds, Regina managed to defeat her, though not without consequence. She sustained a deep laceration on the back of her left leg, just above the knee. With limited supplies, I did my best to disinfect and seal the wound, but the injury remains severe.

A side observation: during the journey aboard the mana boat, Sister Sallie gained further insight into the scope of Regina's blessings. It appears her mana reserves have increased significantly, far beyond anything we'd previously observed. That said, her battle with Hema made it clear that her mana is not infinite. Regina is now suffering from mana depletion in addition to her physical injuries.

Following the confrontation, we discovered that Jules and Matthew Fournier were missing. There was no sign of them, no trace, no indication of where they might have gone. Given Hema's presence, I suspect the conspiracy is also responsible for their disappearance.

We are currently in the custody of Aurorium Laminae. They've brought us to what I believe is the main hospital in Arcanum. The Eclipse in charge, who has yet to give his name, appears skeptical of our account. His caution is understandable, though no less unsettling. For now, our only option is to cooperate and hope that Regina and her stepmother receive the care they urgently need.

Marcus heard a knock at the door just before it opened, revealing the Eclipse from earlier. The man entered with calm precision, sat behind the desk, and retrieved a sheet of paper and an ink pen from the drawer. He fixed Marcus with a steady gaze. "So, Brother Marcus, let's review."

Before the Eclipse could continue, Marcus raised his voice, cutting him off. "Before I answer any questions, I need to know the status of Regina Fournier and her stepmother."

The Eclipse's expression sharpened as he leaned back in his chair. He tapped his index finger against the wooden desk, the sound deliberate, almost calculating, before asking, "What is your interest in young Miss Fournier?"

"My duty is to serve Miss Fournier and ensure she has everything she needs," Marcus replied carefully, knowing that giving the full truth would make him sound like an unhinged lunatic.

"And this duty," the Eclipse pressed, "was assigned to you by the Order?"

Marcus closed his journal with deliberate composure. "I can assure you that it was."

The Eclipse tilted his head slightly, his skepticism apparent. "I have to say, in all my dealings with members of the Order, I've never heard of such an assignment."

"It's a very specific one," Marcus admitted, maintaining his calm. "I am the guide to the avatars of the goddesses."

The Eclipse frowned and jotted something down. "The guide to what, exactly?"

"The guide to the avatars," Marcus repeated, though he sensed the question was more rhetorical than sincere. "Now, about the Fournier women?"

The Eclipse finished writing and looked up, meeting Marcus's gaze. "Of course, Brother Marcus. Young Miss Fournier is receiving stitches for the deep laceration on her leg. The doctor has also ordered her a pot of ember root tea to help replenish her mana reserves." He shifted in his chair, the window light catching the badge pinned to his chest. "The elder Mrs. Fournier is a more complex matter. Her doctor believes she has been poisoned by something magical and has sent for a specialist healer to confirm and treat it."

Relief washed over Marcus. While the elder Fournier's condition was concerning, knowing that Regina was receiving care lifted a weight from his shoulders. "Thank you for the update, Eclipse," he said sincerely.

The Eclipse inclined his head. "Now, if you'll indulge me, I'd like to go over the events at the Luminous this evening."

Marcus nodded, though he noted the man still hadn't given his name. "This afternoon, Sister Sallie, Regina Fournier, and I traveled to the Luminous to retrieve some of Miss Fournier's belongings and to speak with her family. When we arrived, Hema ambushed Regina. I don't know the exact reason for the attack. Sister Sallie and I took the elder Mrs. Fournier and evacuated her from the area to keep her safe. By the time I returned to the library, Regina had already defeated Hema and sent her to Stoneridge. I then moved Regina to the medical room and treated her injuries as best I could."

The Eclipse leaned forward slightly. "Just to clarify," he said, his voice measured, "what time did you leave Order Island?"

"A little after two o'clock," Marcus replied.

"And the boat you used at the Luminous, was it the same one you departed in?"

"Yes," Marcus said, beginning to see where the questioning was headed. He quickly added, "The mana-leeching system on that boat has passenger settings. It allowed the craft to draw mana from all of us, enabling it to maintain a higher speed than normal."

The Eclipse opened his mouth, seemingly ready to ask another question, when a knock came at the door. He glanced at Marcus. "Thank you for your time, Brother." Rising smoothly, he pushed his chair back, the legs scraping faintly against the floor.

"It was my pleasure," Marcus replied as the Eclipse stepped out, closing the door behind him.

He barely had time to collect his thoughts before the door opened again. This time, two figures entered.

The first was a man in a white shirt similar to Marcus's, though his bore a blue and black insignia—marking him as a member of the Ethnographer's Union, a sect within the Order. He moved directly to the desk and took the seat the Eclipse had just vacated.

Behind him came a woman who carried herself with quiet authority. She wore a long blue skirt and a crisp white shirt, but what truly caught Marcus's attention was her badge: a piece of white crystal engraved with the Aurorium "A," set against a black background flecked with white specks like stars scattered across the night sky. It marked her as an Apex, the highest rank within the Aurorium clan.

The Apex didn't sit. Instead, she leaned against the door behind Marcus, arms crossed, watching him with an intensity that made every movement, every breath, feel like a silent test.

"Good evening, Brother," the Order member greeted, placing his journal neatly on the desk.

"Good evening, Brother," Marcus replied, meeting his gaze with steady composure. He extended a hand. "Brother Marcus Igbinedion, Guide to the Avatars."

"A pleasure, Brother Marcus," the monk said, shaking his hand briefly. "Brother Theodore Macy." He offered no mention of his sect, skipping formalities, his focus already honed on the conversation ahead.

"How can I assist you, Brother?" Marcus asked, leaning back in his seat. He deliberately avoided glancing at the Apex still stationed behind him. If she wanted his attention, she'd take it.

"You're the guide?" Brother Theodore asked, his tone curious but measured. "Because the last report I read listed Brother Alfred Thomas in the role."

"Albert Thompson," Marcus corrected gently, his voice softening at the memory. "Unfortunately, Brother Albert has crossed into the land of the dead."

"That is a shame," Brother Theodore said, bowing his head slightly in respect before continuing. "And Miss Fournier, she's the avatar of a goddess?"

"She is one of the Four," Marcus confirmed simply.

"Four," Brother Theodore echoed, his brow furrowing. He glanced briefly at the Apex. "Are you certain? That's rare, typically only one or two appear in a generation."

Marcus allowed himself a faint, knowing smile. "As I understand it, I'm something of a record holder with four. I suspect, with so many avatars to serve, I'll be relying on my assistant's talents far more than Brother Albert ever needed mine."

"The guide is part of the Oracles of Time sect, isn't that right?" Brother Theodore asked, his tone sharpening with a subtle challenge.

"Actually, you've got that wrong, Brother," Marcus replied smoothly, recognizing the test. "We belong to the Scribes of Saint Lorraine."

"Ah, so you are," Brother Theodore murmured, the faintest flicker of a smirk touching his lips. "Would you mind, Brother, if I read your journal?"

Marcus hesitated.

He understood the weight behind the request and the risk. Refusing might raise suspicion, but giving full access posed dangers, especially where sacred knowledge of the avatars and goddesses was involved. After a pause, he answered carefully.

"Because my journal contains sensitive information about the avatars and by extension, the goddesses I must ask that if you read it, you keep its contents to yourself. It should not appear in your journal or be shared beyond this room."

From behind him, the Apex let out a sigh sharp and deliberate, cutting through the tension like a blade.

Brother Theodore glanced toward the Apex, his expression unreadable, before nodding back at Marcus. "I can agree to that, Brother."

Marcus reached into his lap, where his journal was tucked close, and handed it to him.

The monk opened it without hesitation, flipping through the pages with practiced efficiency. His eyes skimmed quickly entry to entry. The journal was still new, containing only a handful of notes, and Brother Theodore finished within moments. Closing it gently, he looked up.

"Do you mind if my associate reads your journal?" he asked, gesturing subtly toward the Apex.

Marcus didn't flinch. "I'm afraid I must refuse, Brother," he said, calm but resolute. Allowing anyone outside the Order to read a journal, especially one still in use was strictly forbidden. More importantly, he knew this was another test.

Brother Theodore gave a slight nod, as though Marcus's response confirmed something. He turned to the Apex, exchanged a glance, then returned the journal.

"Please forgive the intrusion, Brother. But we've had more than a few people arrive with fantastic stories, hoping to trade on the Order's reputation in pursuit of ill-gotten gains."

Marcus accepted the journal with a respectful dip of his head. "Completely understandable, Brother."

The two figures traded places. The Apex moved behind the desk while Brother Theodore leaned casually against the doorframe, arms folded.

In a composed, measured voice, the Apex began, "I am Apex Sanderlin. Why are you in Laminae, Brother Marcus?"

He kept his tone polite, but deliberate. "I'm here to escort and assist Miss Fournier as she visits her family and retrieves some of her belongings."

She arched a brow, gaze narrowing. "Would it surprise you to know that her family reported her missing? That she vanished from Granmark?"

"It would not," Marcus said. "My predecessor, Brother Albert, arranged to meet her in Granmark to explain her situation. Unfortunately, he died saving her and the other avatars."

The Apex leaned in slightly. "Saving them from what, exactly?"

Marcus hesitated. *How much should he say?* He knew the full truth would sound unbelievable possibly dangerous.

The Apex leaned back, exchanging a glance with Brother Theodore. Though calm, her voice held an unmistakable edge. "The Aurorium and the Order share a relationship built on trust and cooperation, Brother Marcus. But right now, you're withholding information. I have citizens missing. I have others hospitalized. I need you to trust me."

This is something that Marcus was uniquely qualified to understand given his own history during scribe duty in the Umbrathorn Empire. He decided to keep that to himself, figuring it would only serve to antagonize the situation.

"I agree," Brother Theodore added. "Apex Sanderlin has proven herself trustworthy time and again."

The Apex acknowledged this with a nod, but continued. "Here's my perspective, Brother Marcus. A girl was lured away from her home where she was safe with her parents by a verified member of your Order. She disappeared for nearly a week. When she returned, it was with the man replacing the one who took her. Her father and younger stepbrother are missing. Her stepmother was found poisoned by some unknown substance."

She paused, took a steadying breath.

"Now I'm speaking with someone who clearly has answers that could resolve this but chooses to stay silent, citing the rules of a secretive organization."

Marcus weighed her words carefully. He also considered that Sophie Griffin was from the Aurorium, albeit a different village. At last, he exhaled.

"There is much I don't know," he said. "But what I do share must remain in this room."

"I'm listening," said the Apex, leaning forward.

"The woman at the Luminous today was named Hema," Marcus began. "She wields magic tied to blood. She's part of an organization we believe is operating throughout the Seven Kingdoms. Hema is one of four witches we have knowledge of though we know far too little to predict their movements."

The Apex straightened in her chair, expression hardening as he spoke.

"The others are Gretta, a corrupted Avatar who wields ice and snow magic; Isabella, another corrupted Avatar, whose power lies in the mechanica-magic of Magitekopolis;

and Mage, whose real name I do not know who uses shadow magic. Her abilities resemble those of the Umbrathorn Empire's shadow wielders, but far more powerful and deadly."

Apex Sanderlin's expression hardened, her focus unwavering. "Ice and mechanica-magic, you say?"

Marcus nodded quickly. "We had no knowledge of an attack on Aurorium Granmark. I assure you of that."

"Did you know these individuals would be in Granmark?" she pressed.

"I didn't," Marcus said firmly. "And I sincerely doubt my predecessor did either. Brother Albert was murdered for his journal, and the avatars were nearly captured. I assure you, he would never knowingly risk their safety."

"So you claim, Brother Marcus," Apex Sanderlin replied, skepticism tinting her voice. "But I've seen ambition lead to tragedy before."

"Apex Sanderlin, if I may," Brother Theodore interjected. "The role of Guide to the Avatars is among the most honored and sacred duties in the Order. No Guide would knowingly endanger the Avatars, who embody the goddesses' will on earth."

The Apex cast a sharp look at Theodore, lips pressed thin. Taking a deep, cleansing breath, she turned back to Marcus. "You'll have to forgive me, but I cannot understand how you could know such dangerous people are active and yet fail to alert the Aurorium Clan."

Marcus steadied himself, setting aside the implied insult. "We lacked solid information sufficient to act on. Had we possessed it, we would have informed you."

"You could at least have told us these four witches are active within our domains," Sanderlin countered, her tone unrelenting.

Brother Theodore nodded thoughtfully. "Apex Sanderlin makes a strong point, Brother Marcus. Your predecessor's information, though incomplete, might have been critical. While it may not have prevented the assault on Granmark, it could still prove mutually beneficial."

"What are you suggesting, Brother Theodore?" Apex Sanderlin asked, eyes narrowing.

"A pact between us," he proposed. "If Brother Marcus provides all the information he has about this organization and its members," he emphasized, "then Apex Sanderlin would allow him to take both Fournier women back to Order Island."

"No," Sanderlin said flatly, cutting him off. "I could agree to Regina Fournier's return to Order Island, but June Fournier will remain under Aurorium Laminae's protection."

"Apex Sanderlin" Brother Theodore began, but she raised a hand to silence him.

"In the interest of cooperation, however, I will offer something else." Reaching into her purse, she retrieved a slip of paper. "Brother Marcus, you mentioned you are responsible for four of the goddesses' Avatars?"

"I did," Marcus confirmed, though uncertain where she was leading.

"Who are they?" Sanderlin asked, calm but firm.

"Regina Fournier of the Kingdom of Laminae, Annabelle Salazar of the good ship Stormfang, Lisa Nozaki from the Kingdom of Verdantia, and … Sophie Griffin of the Aurorium Clan, in Granmark." Marcus listed evenly, savoring the mention of Sophie's name.

At the mention, Apex Sanderlin's eyes narrowed. "Sophie Griffin is a Sentinel," she said firmly. "You may not realize this, Brother Marcus, but the Aurorium does not allow our Sentinels to operate independently except on short, simple missions."

She slid a paper across the desk a communication Marcus had sent after first contact with the girls.

"My part of the pact," Apex Sanderlin continued, "is that I will not demand Sophie Griffin's immediate return to the Aurorium. Understand, Brother Marcus, that we value our children highly, and this concession is no small thing."

Marcus sat back, weighing her words and the stakes. He glanced at Brother Theodore, then back to the Apex. "I have conditions," he said finally. "First, Miss Regina must agree to this arrangement, leaving her stepmother in your protection. Second, the Aurorium Clan must guarantee free passage for the Stormfang's crew."

Brother Theodore frowned slightly and leaned forward. "Brother, that is a lot to ask. We don't know what crimes the crew of a pirate ship might face."

"I also have conditions," Apex Sanderlin interjected, measured as ever. "If Apex Molina demands Sophie Griffin's return, I will not impede him in any way; and this entire pact depends on June Fournier waking. If she dies, the pact dies."

Marcus noted the flicker of surprise on Theodore's face.

After a pause, Marcus nodded firmly. "I accept." He extended his hand across the desk.

Apex Sanderlin clasped it in a firm grip. "I accept," she echoed, resolute.

[-----✿-----]

After receiving stitches in the back of her leg, Regina sat on the hospital bed, her mind heavy with worry for her mommy June, her father, and Mattie. A dull, throbbing mana-drain headache pulsed in her temples, clouding her thoughts.

A nurse entered the room, pushing a cart with a tea set. At the sight of it, Regina perked up, hoping it was the goddess tea from the Order.

The nurse smiled warmly and poured the tea into a cup, placing it on a saucer before handing it to Regina.

"Thank you," Regina said with a small, hopeful smile. She blew on the tea and took a sip then immediately grimaced. The tea was bitter, with a foul taste like old socks. Scoffing, she handed the cup back to the nurse.

"You have to drink the tea," the nurse said firmly. "It will help with your mana headache."

"But it's nasty," Regina complained, sticking out her tongue in disapproval.

"No excuses, little miss," the nurse replied, her tone leaving no room for debate. "Do yourself a favor and drink it quickly."

Resigned, Regina took another reluctant sip under the nurse's watchful eye. "Do you have any honey?" she asked hopefully, glancing at the cart.

"Sorry," the nurse said with a sympathetic shrug. "No such luck."

Frowning, Regina continued drinking the bitter tea. After a few sips, she asked, "How is my mommy June?"

"I'm sorry, miss, I don't know," the nurse replied, raising her hand and miming a *drink up* motion.

Regina sighed and took another sip just as a knock sounded at the door. A woman entered, dressed in a blue skirt and white shirt, her black hair cut short to the nape of her neck. Regina's attention was immediately drawn to the badge pinned to her chest ;a circular design with the Aurorium "A" made of crystal. The badge's background shimmered like a starry night sky, similar to Sophie's badge but far more intricate.

The woman smiled at Regina. "Hello, Regina." Her voice was calm and confident. She glanced at the nurse.

The nurse gave Regina a pointed look, gestured to the tea, and left the room.

"Hello," Regina replied cautiously, clutching the cup as she took another reluctant sip of the foot-flavored tea.

"I am Apex Sanderlin of the Aurorium Clan," the woman introduced herself, settling into a chair near Regina's bed. "Can you tell me what happened to you earlier today?"

Regina hesitated, wanting to be thorough. She started from the beginning, recounting everything: waking up in her dormitory bed on Order Island after speaking to the goddess; learning about Earth-Bloom Magic; taking the boat ride to the Luminous with Brother Marcus and Sister Sallie; Sister Sallie's discovery about the mana leeching system and Regina's unusually deep mana reserves; and finally, her battle with the "murder lady." She described using portal ritual spells to send Hema to Mount Bisouveiak in Stoneridge and how Brother Marcus tried to treat her leg before they were discovered by the Aurorium patrol.

Throughout the story, Apex Sanderlin scribbled furiously in her notepad, occasionally glancing at Regina to show she was listening. When Regina finished, Apex raised a finger. "One moment, please." She completed her notes, set the pad down, and looked up with a faint smile. "That's quite the story."

"Do you know where my dad and little brother are?" Regina asked bluntly, cutting through the polite exchange.

Apex Sanderlin's smile faded. "I'm sorry to say I don't. I do know your father was at the Luminous, yesterday our patrol spoke to him. I have a team of investigators combing through the Luminous as we speak. If there's anything to find, they'll find it."

Regina's face tightened with concern. "Is my mommy June going to be okay?"

"Well, you don't mess around, do you?" Sanderlin said with a small chuckle, though her tone quickly turned serious. "Your mother has been poisoned. The doctors have called for a healer to help diagnose and treat her."

"Can I see her?" Regina asked, taking another sip of the foul tea.

"When you finish your tea, I'll take you," Apex Sanderlin said.

Regina smiled faintly, looking down at her almost-empty cup.

"Not just the cup the pot," Sanderlin added, her voice firm, as if reading Regina's mind.

"The pot?" Regina protested.

"Yes, the pot," Sanderlin confirmed. "Right now, you're in a state we call 'mana extreme low.' That's why you have the headache. Below that is 'mana zero,' which you want to avoid at all costs. Your body can't replenish your reserves at a normal pace, so this tea will help fill your reserves and get you back to 'mana normal.'" She gave Regina an encouraging look. "So yes, the whole pot. It's not that big you'll survive."

Regina sighed heavily but acquiesced, finishing her first cup of tea with a dramatic frown.

Sanderlin poured her another cup and asked, "Can you tell me about the Avatar from the Aurorium Clan?"

"Sophie?" Regina perked up slightly. "She's really good at fighting. She saved us from the shadow witch." She paused, her tone softening. "She's really sad, though. Her family and friends died."

Apex Sanderlin closed her eyes briefly, the weight of the words settling over her. When she opened them again, her expression was grim. "A lot of people in the Granmark

Aurorium Village were murdered," she said quietly. "I had some very good friends there."

"I'm sorry," Regina offered, her voice sincere as she sipped more of the bitter tea.

"Yes, me too." Sanderlin said, her tone heavy with sorrow. She straightened in her chair. "We need to discuss your mother's situation."

Regina blinked, then said matter-of-factly, "My mother died. Mommy June is Dad's new wife."

The revelation caught Apex Sanderlin off guard, and her composure wavered for a moment. "I see," she said softly, before composing herself once more.

"My mistake," Apex Sanderlin said gently. "Your friend, Brother Marcus from the Order, wants you to go with him. Meanwhile, I want to ensure your stepmother stays safe."

"Okay..." Regina replied cautiously, unsure where the conversation was headed.

"If it's agreeable to you," Apex Sanderlin continued, "I will place your stepmother under the direct protection of the Aurorium Clan, while you continue your work with Brother Marcus." She slipped her notepad into her purse and added, "Of course, that depends on what your Mommy June wants as well."

Regina frowned, her uncertainty evident. "I don't know what to do. Why would you do all that? Is it just because I'm an avatar?"

"Partially," Apex Sanderlin admitted. "But it's also because the people who took your father and little brother are incredibly dangerous. From what I've learned, they may be the same people who murdered everyone in Granmark, including Sophie's friends and family." She gave Regina a reassuring smile. "And I suspect they intended to kill your Mommy June because she has information that could lead us to them."

"Lead you to them?" Regina asked, tilting her head.

Apex Sanderlin nodded. "The people who attacked Aurorium Granmark disappeared without a trace, and I suspect the same would have happened with the ones who struck at the Luminous. They left behind the blood witch to deal with her, while they made their escape; however, they never planned for your stepmother to survive. That means she saw something or someone that could lead us to them." She leaned forward slightly. "If they realize she's alive, they'll come after her again. And next time, she may not be so lucky."

Regina stared into her cup of tea, processing the weight of what Sanderlin was saying. A thought flickered in her mind: *Is this what it feels like when I explain things to people?* She took another sip of the bitter drink and considered the situation. "So... it benefits both you and me if Mommy June is under Aurorium protection?"

"It does." Sanderlin said simply, her tone even.

Regina mulled it over for a moment longer before asking, "Can I talk to Brother Marcus? I want to hear what he thinks about all this."

"He's busy right now," Apex Sanderlin said, "but he should be with us when we go check on your stepmother." She gave Regina a knowing look. "As soon as you finish your tea."

With a frown, Regina took another sip of the bad-tasting tea.

[-----+-----]

Marcus, Sister Sallie, and Brother Theodore sat around a table in a quiet area across from the room where June Fournier was being treated. Each had a cup before them coffee for Marcus and Brother Theodore, tea for Sister Sallie as they silently observed the healer's intricate work inside the treatment room.

Through the glass window, Marcus watched June lying on the hospital bed, a bottle of shimmering sapphire liquid inverted and feeding into a tube connected to her arm. The healer, wearing magically enhanced glasses, had carefully examined June earlier and left written instructions for the hospital staff. Now, she was focused on a more elaborate task.

Marcus noted the six ritual circles she had drawn one on each wall, one on the floor, and one on the ceiling. The symbols shimmered faintly, indicating that whatever she used wasn't ordinary chalk. As the blue liquid was administered by nurses, the healer activated the ritual magic.

The process was intricate. Each circle glowed softly as the healer chanted a series of complex spells. Her familiar a medium-length white snake with black patterns turned ghostlike, phasing into June's body. The familiar seemed to be extracting the poison, which emerged as dark red bubbles floating from June's arms, chest, and legs. The healer used her wand to gather each bubble and carefully deposit it into a jar resting on the bedside table.

Marcus couldn't help but marvel at the precision of the work. "What magic is she using?" he asked Brother Theodore without looking away.

"It's called Guérisoncharmé," Brother Theodore explained. "Ms. Fleurette is especially skilled with it, one of the best. She's even managed to incorporate her familiar, Daniel, into advanced spells. The poison must've been horrendous if they called her first." He took a slow sip of coffee before turning to Marcus. "What exactly are you mixed up in, Brother?"

"I wish I knew," Marcus replied, sipping his coffee.

Sister Sallie, watching the bubbles intently, asked, "Are those bubbles the poison?"

"You'll have to ask her once she's finished," Brother Theodore replied.

Sister Sallie tilted her head, her analytical mind turning. "I wonder what the circles on the walls are for. They're active, but don't seem to interact directly with the healer or patient."

Before anyone could speculate further, Brother Theodore shifted in his seat, his tone sharp. "I have to ask, Brother, how much did you know about the blood witch's organization before today?"

"The organization is incredibly secretive," Marcus began, setting down his cup. "We've only been able to observe them from a distance. Investigating them has been nearly impossible." He paused, choosing his words carefully. "I've never seen the blood witch up close like today. But I have seen the blue-haired mechanica-witch Isabella. She smashed her way through a jail in Islewind, killing and maiming royal guards as though it were nothing."

Brother Theodore's brow furrowed, frustration building. "I'm sorry, Brother, but I don't understand why you didn't warn the Aurorium Clan about people like this." His tone carried a quiet accusation, aimed not just at Marcus but also his predecessor, Brother Albert.

"That information would've endangered even more people," Marcus explained, calm but firm. "Especially Aurorium members and royal guards. Most of what we've seen are just sightings. They appear, enter a place, or board a ship, then vanish. Imagine trying to arrest Hema or Isabella on incomplete info. It would only get them and potentially innocent bystanders killed."

Brother Theodore's frustration boiled over. "I believe your decision to withhold information helped this organization operate with an impenetrable shroud of secrecy, working toward their goals without resistance!"

Sister Sallie interjected. "We control information all the time," she said neutrally but thoughtfully. "We don't tell neighboring kingdoms about future tyrants' schemes, hoping someone will stop them quietly before they act."

Brother Theodore sipped his coffee loudly, ignoring her point. Setting the empty cup down, he asked Marcus, "Is that why you agreed to share all your information with Apex Sanderlin when I suggested it?"

"Like you, I see this organization has been using our habit of controlling information against us," Marcus said. "Today proves they have a plan, and targeting the avatars is part of it."

Brother Theodore's eyes narrowed. "So aren't you risking Aurorium lives by giving them this information?"

Marcus sighed. "The attack on Aurorium Granmark shows Aurorium lives are already at risk. I'm giving them the means to prepare and defend themselves. We don't know enough to predict the organization's actions, but we all need to be ready."

Brother Theodore stood abruptly, frustration evident. "It shouldn't take something like this to realize that, Brother." He walked away, presumably to refill his coffee, punctuating the conversation with his departure.

"That was harsh," Sister Sallie remarked, watching him leave. "Doesn't he realize you've only been the guide for a few days?"

"I understand why he's angry," Marcus said quietly, offering nothing more.

Brother Theodore returned to the table with a fresh cup of coffee, settling into his seat without a word. The trio sat in silence, watching the healer work.

Inside the room, the dark red bubbles floating from June's body had shrunk from the size of grapefruits to small marbles. With precise movements, the healer moved the spheres into a glass jar with the lid open. After she moves the last of the spheres into the jar the healer snapped a metal clasp over the jar closed, then drew glowing sigils across its surface on the sides, top, and bottom begin to glow as what appears to be the containment spell activates.

Her familiar, the white snake Daniel, emerged from beneath June's gown, slithering out through her sleeve. Without looking down, the healer extended her hand, and Daniel coiled up her arm before disappearing beneath her clothing. With a simple wave, she dispelled the ritual circles on the walls, floor, and ceiling, returning the room to normal.

The healer stepped out of the room, holding the now-sealed jar. "Well, that's done," she announced, exhaling as if she had just completed an exhausting task. "That was a really nasty poison, it was like it was alive or something."

"Mrs. Baudin, this is Brother Marcus Igbinedion and Sister Sallie Young," Brother Theodore introduced, motioning toward the two Order monks.

"Hello," the healer said, offering a tired smile before walking toward the nurse's desk. "Could I get a cup of ember root tea, please?"

"Yes ma'am, of course," the nurse replied, picking up the telephone.

Fleurette Baudin sank into the empty seat at their table, clearly drained from the complex spellwork she had performed.

Marcus took the opportunity to ask, "If you don't mind me asking, what kind of poison was that?" He gestured toward the jar in her hand.

"I'm not sure," Fleurette admitted, turning the jar slightly to examine the swirling, dark substance inside. "But it was a really nasty one."

Sister Sallie leaned forward. "What spell did you use to extract it?"

"It's called Guérir de l'intérieur," Fleurette explained. "Loosely translated, it means *healing from the inside*. My familiar, Daniel, enters a spirit state and phases into the patient's body, pushing the affliction out while simultaneously healing the damage."

As if on cue, Daniel peeked his head out from Fleurette's blouse. She gently stroked his head, whispering something to him in an affectionate tone.

"But how did the ritual circles work with the spell?" Sister Sallie pressed, clearly fascinated.

"That explanation will have to wait for Apex Sanderlin," Fleurette replied with a knowing smile. "Daniel will explain it."

The snake turned his head toward Sister Sallie and let out a small, rhythmic hiss. Fleurette sighed. "No, she doesn't have any mice for you."

An attendant approached, setting a steaming cup in front of Fleurette. "Ma'am."

"Thank you," she said, lifting the cup. "Could I have a bit of honey?"

The attendant obliged, drizzling honey into the tea. Fleurette nodded when it was enough, stirring the mixture as the attendant walked away passing by Apex Sanderlin and Regina as they entered the hallway.

Marcus's eyes flicked to Regina, noting the playful smile on her face despite the limp in her step.

"Good evening, everyone," Apex Sanderlin greeted as she approached, Regina in tow.

"Apex Sanderlin," Fleurette said with a smirk. "You always bring me the most interesting challenges." She sipped her tea, then glanced at Regina. "Well, hello there. Long time no see, little Miss Button."

Regina's expression shifted to confusion. She didn't recognize this woman, yet the nickname was one only her family used. "Umm... who are you?" she asked skeptically.

Fleurette chuckled. "You don't remember me? I was close with your mother a long time ago. Addie used to bring you to my father's farm when you were a little silver-haired girl."

Regina's face fell. "My mom is gone now," she said quietly.

Fleurette's expression softened. "Yes, I know. I miss her, too. I tried everything I could to heal her." She sighed before taking another sip of her tea.

Regina's frown deepened. "How can you drink that? It tastes like feet."

The group chuckled at her bluntness.

"It's not so bad with a bit of honey," Fleurette offered.

Regina's eyes widened in betrayal as she turned to Apex Sanderlin. "I could have had honey?"

Apex Sanderlin simply shrugged.

Marcus smiled at Regina's dramatic reaction before asking, "How's your headache, Miss Regina?"

"Better," Regina replied, though her attention quickly shifted. "How's my Mommy June?"

"She should be fine by morning," Fleurette assured her. "Right now, she's resting."

Apex Sanderlin leaned in slightly. "What was it?"

Fleurette sighed, swirling her tea. "I've never seen anything like it before," she admitted. "The poison was attacking her internal organs, but that's not the worst part it was connected to something outside the room."

Apex Sanderlin tensed, immediately pulling out her notepad. "What?"

255

Fleurette nodded grimly. "It was responding to commands. From someone. Or something." She placed the jar on the table, staring at it as if willing it to reveal its secrets. "The poison was already deadly on its own. But I had to seal off the entire room with barrier rituals before I could even attempt to remove it. And even then, I had to use our most advanced healing technique just to drive it out of her system."

Apex Sanderlin's grip tightened on her pen. "What else can you tell me?" she asked, eyes locked on Fleurette.

Fleurette exhaled and glanced down at Daniel. "I'll have to let him explain it to you," she answered before quickly finishing the rest of her tea.

Then, she closed her eyes and began muttering an incantation under her breath.

A few moments later, she opened them again but now her irises glowed with an eerie greenish-white light.

Daniel, speaking through Fleurette, turned his glowing eyes toward Apex Sanderlin. "The poison was transformative in nature. By the time I entered the subject's body, it was attacking her heart, lungs, and appendix simultaneously but it wasn't the same in each organ. Its structure shifted depending on where it had taken hold."

"So, it was multiple poisons mixed together?" Apex Sanderlin asked, not looking up from her notepad as she scribbled notes.

"No," Daniel replied. "It was all made of blood."

Apex Sanderlin's pen paused mid-stroke. She looked up. "Blood? Are you sure?"

Daniel inclined Fleurette's head slightly. "I can assure you, Sanderlin I am very familiar with blood."

Apex Sanderlin's grip on her pen tightened. "Was it her blood?"

"No," Daniel said firmly. "It belonged to someone else. I've never encountered anything like it before."

Apex Sanderlin exhaled through her nose, tapping the end of her pen against her pad thoughtfully. "Thank you, Daniel."

"Just doing my duty," Daniel replied. His eyes flicked to Regina. "It's good to see you again, little one." Then, he closed Fleurette's eyes. When she reopened them, the eerie glow had vanished.

Apex Sanderlin wasted no time. "When can we speak to June?"

"When she wakes," Fleurette answered. "But keep it brief she needs to rest."

Apex Sanderlin peered into the treatment room, watching the rise and fall of June's steady but unconscious breaths. Then, she turned back to the group. "I've spoken with Regina about our agreement," she said. "But she wanted to speak with you, Brother Marcus, before making her final decision."

Marcus stood and approached Regina; he bends down slightly before her to meet her at eye level. He gave her his full attention. "What are your concerns, Miss Fournier?"

Regina hesitated. "I don't know what to do," she admitted. "Can't you decide?"

Marcus paused, considering his words carefully. Then, he shook his head. "My duty is to serve you, not to govern you. I must respectfully decline." His voice was steady but kind. "I will give you the best counsel I can, but this decision must be yours."

Apex Sanderlin scoffed and shook her head, clearly unimpressed by his response.

Regina chewed on her lip, considering the situation. "What are the advantages of taking the deal?" she asked.

"You wouldn't have to worry about your stepmother's safety," Marcus explained. "And we would have the Aurorium Clan's resources to aid us against the conspiracy. They may even help us find your father and younger brother."

Regina pressed her finger against her lower lip, thinking. "And what are the disadvantages if I don't accept?"

Marcus exhaled. "First, Sophie Griffin would have to return to the Aurorium Clan she isn't ranked high enough to continue working with us on her own. We would also lose the Clan's support, which could be invaluable in our efforts."

Apex Sanderlin folded her arms. "Not to mention," she added, "as a member of a family in service, I am responsible for your family's safety. If you decline, you will be required to stay in Laminae under Aurorium protection, because whether you accept it or not, you and your family are targets."

Marcus glanced at Sanderlin, noting that this condition had not been mentioned before.

Regina felt the weight of the choice settle over her. She looked up at Marcus. "My Mommy June will be safe?"

Apex Sanderlin met Regina's eyes. "I personally guarantee her safety. Anyone who tries to harm her will have to go through me."

Marcus nodded. "It is said that an Aurorium Apex could defeat an entire army."

"Here, here," Fleurette agreed from the table, stirring her tea. "I've seen the Crystal Fairy Queen in action I'd feel safer in her care than I would in my mother's arms."

Regina closed her eyes, searching for the quiet certainty Change had told her to trust. She focused, feeling for her will, waiting for the answer to settle inside her.

When she opened her eyes again, she spoke with certainty. "We'll take the deal."

"Very well," Marcus said with a nod.

"Good," Apex Sanderlin said simply. Without further ceremony, she turned and walked toward the nurse's station. As she passed, she called over her shoulder, "Contact me the moment she wakes."

"Yes, ma'am," the nurse replied without looking up from her paperwork.

Fleurette turned to Regina. "Miss Button," she called out warmly, "would you like to join me for a cup of tea?"

Regina hesitated, then asked, "Can we get honey with it?"

Fleurette grinned. "Is there any other way?" She stood and walked toward Regina, pausing as she passed Marcus before extending her elbow.

Regina accepted, slipping her arm through Fleurette's, moving slower because of her limp. "Let's go," she said with a small smile.

Together, they walked toward the stairwell, following signs that led to the cafeteria.

As they descended, Fleurette glanced down at Regina. "So, little Button... what do you do now?"

"For now, my family takes care of the Luminous," Regina explained. "So I do all the chores and watch my little brother, Mattie."

"Little brother?" Fleurette asked, tilting her head. "Your mom had another child before she passed?"

"No," Regina replied. "Mattie is Mommy June's son."

"Oh," Fleurette said with a nod. "Most kids would call each other stepbrother or stepsister."

"Yeah, Dad didn't like that," Regina said, smiling faintly. "He said Mommy June and Mattie took all the steps, so they're just family, plain and simple."

Fleurette chuckled. "Yes, that sounds like Jules."

They arrived at the cafeteria and made their way to the counter, each getting a cup of ember root tea, with honey this time. They carried their drinks to a quiet corner, settling at a square table with four chairs in the mostly empty seating area.

After taking a sip, Regina asked, "What type of magic do you use?"

Fleurette raised an eyebrow. "Why is that important?"

"As a learner mage, I can study multiple types of magic," Regina explained. "So I like to ask people what they use."

Fleurette leaned back in her chair, taking a thoughtful sip of tea before asking, "Have you ever asked anyone what they do for fun?"

Regina blinked at the unexpected question. "No…"

Fleurette smirked. "Don't you like to have fun?"

"Yeah, of course," Regina said, confused. "Who doesn't like fun?"

"Only stupid people," Fleurette replied playfully. "I love having fun. Back in Maryville, I grew up with a girl who turned out to be a learner mage, just like you. When we were little, we'd fly kites, pick flowers, sneak cookies, oh, we had so much fun." She smiled at the memory. "But then she started learning magic. She got so obsessed with learning new magic that she stopped hanging out with me. She never said she didn't want to be my friend anymore, but she locked herself up in the library, reading about cryomancy, geomancy, water manipulation always something new. And when she did come out to play, all she wanted to talk about was magic."

Regina frowned, stirring her tea. "What happened to her?"

Fleurette sighed. "One day, I found her sitting in the park outside our school, crying." Her voice softened. "She had a crush on a boy, and finally worked up the courage to ask him on a date. But he said something really cruel to her. The other kids joined in, teasing her, and she ran off to the park."

Regina huffed, crossing her arms. "Boys are terrible."

Fleurette chuckled. "They can be, sweetie. But she wasn't crying because of him. She looked at me and asked, *Why don't people like me?*" Fleurette's expression grew wistful. "She asked why we didn't have fun anymore. And I had to tell her the truth she was so busy learning magic that she never wanted to just play and have fun. I spent enough time in magic class talking about spells, I wanted to do other things when we were together. She had never even thought about that before."

Regina listened intently as Fleurette continued.

"After that, we made a no-magic rule when we played together," Fleurette said with a fond smile. "She'd backslide every now and then, but I got my friend back."

Regina tilted her head. "What happened to her? Do you still talk to her?"

Fleurette's smile turned sad. "She moved to the capital. Learner mages are in high demand here. She met a handsome young man from a family of ritualists, got married, and had a daughter with silver hair and gray eyes." She paused, exhaling. "We saw each other whenever we could. Until she got sick."

Regina suddenly felt very small. A knot formed in her stomach as she realized Fleurette was talking about her mother. "So… you're saying I shouldn't ask people about their magic?" she asked quietly, suddenly unsure.

"Not exactly," Fleurette said gently. "I'm saying that if you only focus on magic, you'll miss out on life." She set her tea down, watching Regina carefully. "I know so many interesting people who aren't magical. My first husband couldn't cast a single spell but he could conjure an incredible meal out of whatever we had in the kitchen." She laughed softly. "Magic is one part of who you are, Button. Don't let it be all you are."

Regina looked down at her tea, the honey making it taste like foot-flavored candy. She wasn't sure how to feel but she knew she'd remember this conversation for a long time.

Regina thought for a moment before asking, "What do you do for fun, Miss Fleurette?"

Fleurette smiled. "I like tending my garden, painting, and traveling to new places. What about you?"

Regina perked up. "Can I see one of your paintings?"

"Oh, Gods, no," Fleurette laughed. "My second husband used to make fun of them said they looked like a toddler's scribbles."

Regina smirked. "See? Terrible."

"You may have a point." Fleurette chuckled. "You should find yourself a hobby, something you love, outside of magic. You might be surprised how much it helps you as a mage."

"Learning magic is my hobby," Regina admitted. "I don't do much else."

"Have you ever flown a kite?" Fleurette asked.

Regina shook her head. "No."

"Well, you should try it," Fleurette suggested. "I'm sure your manservant can get you a nice one. Or that talkative woman could probably teach you how to make one." She grinned, taking another sip of tea.

Regina made a mental note to ask Brother Marcus for a kite, still marveling at how much this woman knew about her.

Then, Fleurette's expression shifted. "So… you're the avatar of the goddesses?" she asked bluntly.

"Huh?" Regina blinked, caught off guard. "How did you find that out?"

Fleurette leaned back. "I was friends with your mother." Her voice softened. "When she had a baby with silver hair and gray eyes, she started researching. When she realized no one in either her or your father's family had those traits, she started asking around. Eventually, a monk from the Order visited her and explained everything. And, well… your mom wasn't great at keeping secrets, at least, not from me."

Regina stared at her tea, stirring it absently. "Yeah…"

Fleurette hesitated before asking, "So… what's it like? Being the avatar?"

Regina lifted her eyes. "I'm not the avatar. There are four of us."

Fleurette looked surprised. "Four?"

"Yep," Regina confirmed. "Me, Annabelle, Sophie, and Lisa."

"You don't say…" Fleurette murmured, finishing the last of her tea. "Did you actually speak to the Goddesses?"

"I spoke to my Goddess," Regina said, a small smile forming. "She's really pretty. And smart."

"What did you talk about?"

Regina hesitated. She felt like she should keep her conversation with Change private. "A lot of things," she said vaguely. "The planet. Magic." Then, hoping to shift the conversation, she asked, "Are you friends with Apex Sanderlin?"

Fleurette smirked. "Professional friends, I'd say. She can be intense sometimes."

"Sophie is like that," Regina agreed. "I'm always afraid she's going to punch me."

Fleurette laughed. "That's how Aurorium Clan folks tend to be. When you consider their history, it makes sense." She leaned in slightly. "I meant what I said about Sanderlin, though. I've seen her in action. Once, a group of pirates tried to kidnap an aristocrat girl. By the time the royal guards caught up, Sanderlin had them all knocked out, and was calmly sipping tea."

Regina's eyes widened. "So… Aurorium people are really good at fighting?" she asked, suddenly worried Sophie might punch her for real someday.

"We're good at a lot of things," came a voice from behind her.

Regina stiffened as Apex Sanderlin approached the table. "May I sit?"

"Of course," Fleurette said, gesturing to the empty seat.

Sanderlin settled in, placing a cup of coffee in front of her.

"No foot tea?" Regina asked, raising an eyebrow playfully.

Sanderlin smirked. "I didn't drain my mana too low today, so I don't need ember root tea. I do, however, need to stay awake for the next few hours. So... coffee."

Then, she turned her full attention to Regina. "So, what's your situation, Regina Fournier?"

Regina blinked. "What do you mean?"

"I mean," Sanderlin said, leaning forward slightly, "you have two monks from the Order following you around, asking for your permission to act. I looked into your background your father is a high-tier ritualist, but he's not royalty. So... what am I missing?"

Fleurette smiled slightly. "Funny you should ask, Apex. Young Button here is an avatar of the Goddesses."

Sanderlin's expression remained unreadable.

"Just one goddess." Regina corrected with a bright smile. "She's really nice. And fun."

"One of the Twelve Goddesses?" Sanderlin asked skeptically. "Like from that old Pantheon of goddesses religion with the clock?"

"Yep." Regina hesitated, suddenly unsure how much to reveal.

Sanderlin studied her for a moment before saying, "You know... there's no gray Goddess."

"Not gray, silver," Regina corrected. "I'm the avatar of the silver goddess of Change."

Sanderlin's fingers drummed against the table. "I see..."

Regina suddenly felt uneasy. She had said too much.

Sanderlin's gaze sharpened. "And what does that mean, exactly?"

Regina hesitated. "I... don't really know yet," she said, keeping Change's instructions to herself.

Sanderlin gave her a long, assessing look before taking a sip of her coffee. "When you figure it out, do let me know." Apex Sanderlin said in a lightly mocking tone before taking another sip.

Regina made a mental note to send Apex Sanderlin a message when she finally understood her purpose as the avatar of Change. Then, a thought struck her. "Apex Sanderlin... what do you do for fun?"

"Sadly, nothing," Sanderlin sighed dramatically. "Aurorium members aren't allowed to have fun. No vacations, no free time, not even a kiss from a handsome boy."

Regina's eyes widened in horror. "What? That's terrible!"

Fleurette and Sanderlin burst into laughter.

"You are too much," Fleurette said, shaking her head at Sanderlin. "Yes, of course, she's allowed to have fun."

Regina scowled, feeling ridiculous for falling for the joke.

Sanderlin's smirk softened. "Though our lives are dedicated to service, we do have personal time. Balance is very important."

"Button and I were just talking about that," Fleurette said. "The importance of having a life beyond work and magic."

"Oh, absolutely," Sanderlin agreed. "Even in the Aurorium Clan, we struggle to get our Sentinels and Shadows to understand that. I personally like to go fishing with my husband. My daughter used to come with us, but ever since she became an initiate, she can't seem to find the time."

"You know how they are," Fleurette teased. "Mothers don't exist until they need something."

Sanderlin chuckled. "Emily isn't that bad. She visits twice a year, ever since she moved away. I still can't get her on a fishing boat, though."

Regina, fascinated by this new side of Sanderlin, leaned forward. "If you don't mind me asking... why did Miss Fleurette call you the Crystal Fairy Queen?"

Sanderlin exchanged a glance with Fleurette and smirked. "Like some children with two magical parents, I was born with a dual affinity. My father had fairy magic, and my mother had crystalmancy. In my training, I learned how to fuse both magic systems into something entirely new."

"You should see her wings," Fleurette teased, standing up from the table.

"That sounds amazing," Regina said, her eyes shining with curiosity.

"It really isn't," Sanderlin countered. "My magic will most likely die with me. There's no one to pass it on to." She took another sip of coffee. "My daughter was born with my crystal magic and her father's lava magic, so she can't inherit my fusion magic."

Regina frowned. "That's kinda sad." She thought about it, then said, "That is really sad. If you don't pass it down to someone, then it could disappear forever. Maybe you can work with the Order and have them write a source book. Or maybe you could write one yourself. Does the Aurorium Clan have anything like magical archives like the Order does? I guess you'd call it something different, like magical training libraries or something like that. Maybe I should start one just for myself."

Sanderlin paused, blinking absently, then shrugged and set her cup down. "I was thinking about what you told me about your fight with the blood witch. And I have some advice for you."

Regina immediately perked up. "What is it?"

"You were extremely lucky today," Sanderlin said, her tone turning serious. "But luck is a fickle mistress. I think you should learn at least one magic system with both offensive and defensive spells. And you should start training physically, too."

Before Regina could respond, an Aurorium Sentinel approached, standing behind her with his hands clasped behind his back, waiting patiently.

Sanderlin glanced at him, then at Regina. "I'd suggest Crystalmancy. It has both offensive and defensive applications and would serve you well against someone like that blood witch." Then, with barely a shift in her posture, she turned to the Sentinel. "What is it?" she asked, her tone sharp and commanding.

"Ma'am," the Sentinel said, "Mrs. Fournier is awake."

Sanderlin gave a curt nod. "Very well. Return to your post."

"Yes, ma'am," the Sentinel acknowledged before leaving the cafeteria.

Sanderlin turned back to Regina. "Shall we?"

Regina drained the last of her 'honey-flavored foot tea' with a grimace and stood. "Yes, we shall."

As they made their way out, they passed Fleurette, who was returning to her table with a croissant and a fresh cup of tea.

"Oh? What's this?" Fleurette asked, noticing their approach.

"My Mommy June is awake!" Regina said, her excitement barely contained. "Do you want to come up and talk to her?"

Fleurette smiled but shook her head. "Not tonight, Button. I'm going to enjoy my tea and croissant, then head home." She gave Regina a warm look. "It was very good seeing you again."

Regina hesitated for only a second before stepping forward and wrapping Fleurette in a tight hug. "It was nice meeting you... again."

Fleurette chuckled, managing to return the hug as best she could while balancing her food. "You too, sweetness. Come see me when you find time between your adventures."

"I will," Regina promised, releasing her.

With that, she turned and rejoined Apex Sanderlin, the two continuing their slow but steady walk toward June's hospital room.

[-----✝-----]

After an hour and multiple cups of coffee, June Fournier awoke with a scream, calling desperately for her husband and son.

The nurse, startled, nearly dropped the telephone she had just picked up. She quickly placed it back on the wall and rushed into the room, closely followed by the doctor.

"Mrs. Fournier, please you need to stay calm," the doctor urged gently but firmly. "You were poisoned. Your body is still weak. You mustn't overexert yourself."

But June's panic overwhelmed reason. Tears streamed down her face as she sobbed, her cries raw and desperate. "Please! Gods, bring them home! Bring them back to me!"

Outside the room, Marcus watched silently, his expression unreadable. As a monk of the Order, he was trained to be an impartial witness, a recorder of the world's events, whether joyful, tragic, monumental, or mundane. Yet this time, detachment felt wrong. This wasn't just another entry in his journal. This is Miss Regina's family. His charge's family. And that made it feel more personal.

Inside, the doctor gave the nurse a quick directive. She hurried to her desk, pulled open a drawer, and retrieved a stack of paperwork before making another call on the wall telephone. Moments later, an orderly arrived carrying a syringe on a tray. The nurse handed him a form she had just completed, then carefully took the tray from him and rushed back toward the room.

Marcus, Sister Sallie, and Brother Theodore stepped aside as she passed, moving with practiced urgency.

By now, the doctor had managed to soothe June slightly she no longer thrashed, but tears still ran freely down her face as she lay curled up in the hospital bed.

The nurse entered and handed the doctor the syringe. "This will help," he reassured June as he gently took her trembling hand. She flinched slightly as the needle pierced her skin, but the sedative worked quickly. Within moments, her sobs quieted, her breathing evened out as she sagged back against the pillow, exhausted.

The nurse collected the empty syringe, carefully placing it back onto the tray before leaving. The doctor followed shortly after, glancing back to ensure June was resting.

Just as he stepped out, Apex Sanderlin and Regina arrived from the stairwell. Regina trailed slightly behind, slowed by her limp.

"Doctor," Sanderlin called as she reached the nurses' station. "How is she?"

The doctor looked up from his paperwork, rubbing a tired hand over his face. "She's shaken pretty badly," he admitted. "The poison appears to be completely gone, a testament to Miss Fleurette's skill but she just lost her husband and son, not long after her daughter went missing."

"A stressful situation, to say the least," Apex Sanderlin agreed. She gestured toward Regina. "Luckily, her daughter is here. We need to speak with her about her husband and son."

The doctor exhaled heavily. "She needs rest, Apex."

"Time is of the essence, Doctor," Sanderlin countered.

He sighed, clearly reluctant. "Please... just make it quick."

Sanderlin studied Regina for a moment, then nodded. "Let's go talk to your Mommy June."

Regina swallowed hard, then nodded. "Okay."

The two entered the hospital room alone. June lay in bed, her face blotchy and red from crying.

"Mommy June," Regina said, the name slipping from her lips without thought.

June's head turned sharply toward the sound of her voice. Her eyes widened in disbelief. "Button?" Her voice was hoarse, raw from screaming.

Regina limped to her bedside and knelt down. "Yes, Mommy June. I'm here."

June's face crumpled, fresh tears spilling down her cheeks. She gripped Regina's hand like a lifeline. "Button, they took them your dad and Mattie. They just took them."

"I know, Mommy," Regina whispered, squeezing her hand. "It'll be okay." She wasn't sure if she was telling the truth.

"How many people were there?"

June flinched at the sound of her voice, as if only now realizing someone else was in the room. She blinked at Sanderlin in confusion before shaking her head. "I... I don't know. There were a lot of them."

"Please, anything you remember could be helpful," Sanderlin encouraged gently.

June took a shaky breath, resting her head against the pillow as she struggled to recall. "We were working in the library. Mattie was at the welcome desk while I was straightening up the reading area. A woman came in with a group of royal guards. She asked for my husband, said it was urgent."

June's grip on Regina's hand tightened. "I knew Jules was most likely surveying the upper levels, so I asked them to wait while I went to get him. But when we came back..." Her voice wavered, her free hand clenching the blanket. "She..."

She stopped, eyes squeezed shut as the memory overwhelmed her.

"Take your time," Sanderlin said softly, pausing her note-taking.

Regina held June's trembling hand, her own heart twisting. "It's okay, Mommy June," she whispered gently.

June wiped at her face, forcing herself to continue. "When we got back... the woman looked different. Her dress was dark red like blood. And she had an axe... pressed against Mattie's neck."

Regina's breath caught.

June swallowed hard. "She forced Jules to come with them or else. I begged her to let Mattie go, and she promised she would if Jules complied. But after they took him... I yelled at her. Told her to keep her word." Her voice cracked. "She laughed. Told me to make her. I tried to fight her, but... I don't know, she she kicked me or something."

June's voice broke completely, and she dissolved into sobs.

Sanderlin closed her notepad. "Thank you, Mrs. Fournier. I'll follow up after you've had more rest." She cast Regina a glance, silently signaling her not to take too long, then left the room.

June turned her swollen eyes back to Regina. "Oh, Button," she whispered brokenly. "They just... took them."

"I know, Mommy," Regina said, trying to sound strong. "We're going to get them back."

June's breath hitched. "What?" She searched Regina's face. "How are we supposed to…?" Her words trailed off, as if her mind couldn't grasp the thought. Then, her expression shifted as she took in Regina's silver hair, her presence, her confidence. "Where have you been?"

Regina took a deep breath. "I've been with the Order," she explained. "I… I'm an avatar of a goddess."

June frowned. "What are you talking about?"

"The reason my hair and eyes look like this… it's the goddess's touch," Regina said softly. She saw the exhaustion pulling at June's face, the sedative making it harder for her to stay awake. She reached up and smoothed a strand of hair from her stepmother's damp forehead. "I'll explain everything later. I promise. But I have to go back to the Order to find Dad and Mattie."

June fought to keep her eyes open. "But you just got back," she murmured.

Regina swallowed against the lump in her throat. "Don't worry, Mommy June. You'll be safe here. Just focus on getting better."

June exhaled a heavy, uneven breath. "If you have to go…" she whispered, barely audible, "then take Galahad. It'll protect you." Her eyes fluttered closed, her grip on Regina's hand loosening as sleep finally overtook her.

Regina sat still for a moment, watching her stepmother breathe.

Galahad.

Her father had created the protection spell for June, knowing she wasn't magical. It was a summoned spirit of a knight, bound to a ritual that cast protective magic on the wearer in times of danger. He had tied it to a simple leather strap, making it easy for June to wear every day.

Regina's gaze drifted to June's belongings. Quietly, she stood and sifted through them, finding the familiar leather strap among her stepmother's clothes. She held it in her hand, running her fingers over the worn surface.

She'd have to figure out how to attune it to herself before wearing it. No point in putting it on just yet.

Regina took a final look at June, sleeping peacefully for the first time in days.

She stepped back and whispered, "Goodnight, Mommy June."

Then, slipping the leather strap into her pocket, she turned and stepped softly into the hallway.

Chapter 18

Journal Entry – April 20, 1910

Sister Sallie Young, Miss Regina, and I remain under the hospitality of Apex Sanderlin of Aurorium Laminae. She has arranged accommodations for us at Arcanum Main Hospital, ensuring Regina can remain close to her stepmother, June Fournier, during her recovery.

Following our conversation with Mrs. Fournier, Apex Sanderlin issued orders to her subordinates the specifics of which were not disclosed to me before confirming that we would be staying overnight at the hospital. This arrangement allows Regina and June the opportunity to meet with Apex Sanderlin to discuss June's continued protection under the Aurorium Clan.

Once that meeting concludes, Sister Sallie, Regina, and I will return to the main Laminae library to collect Regina's belongings, including clothing and books from her family's quarters, before making our journey back to Order Island.

[-----✿-----]

Regina sat in a chair beside June's bed, her eyelids heavy from lack of sleep. She hadn't gotten as much rest as she'd hoped, but something urged her to begin the day early there was too much to do.

Apex Sanderlin stood by the door, arms crossed over her chest, her long dark green dress flowing to the floor. Her badge, a symbol of her rank, gleamed over her left breast.

Meanwhile, Mommy June sat up in her hospital bed, hands wrapped around a warm cup of coffee.

"Wait, wait, wait Button, you're telling me you stopped that axe-wielding monster woman?" June asked, her voice edged with disbelief.

Regina grinned proudly. "Yeah. Sure did."

"But how?"

"I sent her to Mount Bisouveiak through a portal," Regina replied.

June blinked. "Wait what about your dad? Mattie?" She paused. "And when did you learn portal magic?"

Regina's smile faltered. "They were gone before I got home." Her fingers tightened around the hem of her dress. "But we're going to find them."

June studied her carefully. "How?"

"With the Order."

June's brows furrowed. "Why is the Order even helping you?"

"Because I'm an Avatar of Change," Regina said simply.

June exhaled, sharp and disbelieving. "Since when?"

"Since before I was born."

June pressed a hand to her forehead. "This makes no sense. Last week we were studying for a debate, and now you're what? Some kind of angel?"

"If we could focus on the issue at hand," Apex Sanderlin interjected smoothly.

June turned to her, incredulous. "Focus? My daughter just told me she's a goddess on Earth!"

Apex Sanderlin's expression softened. "As a mother, I understand this is a lot to take in. But Mrs. Fournier, your safety is my top priority. Regina is following a path laid out by the divine, and that path saved your life I'm certain of it." She gave Regina a nod of approval. "Considering those facts, the Clan, Regina, and the Order can find your family before it's too late."

Regina met her gaze with a grateful smile. The Apex returned a small, reassuring one.

"This is just nuts," June muttered, shaking her head. Then, after a long breath, she asked, "Okay. So where do we go from here?"

"I'm going back to the Order," Regina said. "They know about the people who took Dad and Mattie. We'll use their resources and the Aurorium to track them down."

"And you, Mrs. Fournier, will be under my direct protection," Apex Sanderlin added. "I won't always be physically with you, but you'll be as safe as if I were. We'll use a water bowl spell to stay in contact."

June sighed and gave an exaggerated shrug. "I guess that'll have to work."

Regina hesitated, then pulled a leather strap from her pocket. "Mommy June… do you really want me to take Galahad?"

June frowned. "What are you talking about?"

"Last night, you told me to take it. To keep me safe."

June stared at the strap for a long moment before lifting her hand slowly. "No, that makes sense. If the Apex is going to keep me safe, then you should have it."

Regina turned the strap over in her hands. "Do you remember what ritual Dad used to bind it to you?"

June shook her head. "He didn't do a ritual. He just gave it to me."

Regina nodded, slipping the strap into her dress pocket next to her wand. Her dad *had* done a ritual to bind the spirit to the strap and Mommy June's mana; she must not remember or something like that.

After meeting with Mommy June and Apex Sanderlin, Regina, Marcus, and Sister Sallie set off together. They made a quick stop at the Luminous to collect a few changes of clothes and Regina's spare wand before heading back to Order Island.

During the trip, Regina attempted to bring up the conspiracy again, eager to piece together the situation. But Marcus gently redirected the conversation, clearly unwilling to discuss sensitive details in front of Sister Sallie. Instead, he suggested that all four avatars should review the information together in his new office.

With that topic off-limits, the conversation shifted to lighter fare. Regina and Sister Sallie fell into an animated discussion about hobbies a subject that seemed to genuinely surprise Marcus. He had always known that Sister Sallie had interests outside her clerical duties, but he hadn't realized just how many. She built ships in bottles, painted miniatures, practiced various styles of sewing and knitting, and most recently dedicated an hour each day to learning the lute.

Regina's eyes lit up with delight. "Sister Sallie, could you help me make a kite?"

Sister Sallie tilted her head thoughtfully. "I used to fly kites, but I found it a bit boring after a while."

"That's okay, I just want to make one," Regina replied, undeterred.

A small smile tugged at Sister Sallie's lips. "I could make one for you."

Before Regina could accept, Marcus interjected. "Sister, I know you're talented, but don't neglect your duties to the Order just to make a kite." His tone was gentle but firm. Then he turned to Regina. "How about you two build it together?"

Regina beamed. "That sounds even better!"

Eventually, the conversation circled back to Marcus. Regina turned the question on him. "What about you? What do you do for fun?"

Marcus hesitated, then sighed. "I don't really have hobbies. I just... spend more time serving the Order."

Regina frowned. "That's kind of sad."

Sister Sallie nodded in agreement. "You should have something just for yourself, Marcus. Everyone needs an outlet."

Marcus didn't argue, but he didn't promise anything either. Instead, he stared quietly out the window as Order Island came into view.

[-----⛊-----]

Sophie arrived at the cafeteria around noon, well-rested after a much-needed sleep following her conversations with War and her mother. She grabbed a breakfast of oatmeal, bacon, and fruit, along with a cup of orange juice. As she made her way to the seating area, she admitted to herself that she'd probably go back for seconds.

Scanning the room, she spotted a familiar head of green hair across from an unruly mane of orange dreadlocks and braids Annabelle and Lisa, deep in conversation with a woman in a black and white uniform. Without hesitation, Sophie slid into the seat beside them.

"Good morning, Sophie," the Order monk greeted warmly.

"Good morning..." Sophie paused, studying the woman's face. "I'm sorry, I don't think we've met."

"Sister Alameda Ortega," the monk introduced herself. "I'm the first assistant to your guide, Marcus Igbinedion. How did you sleep?"

"Really well," Sophie admitted. "I think it was the first good night's sleep I've had since..." She trailed off.

"Aurorium Granmark," Sister Alameda finished gently. Her tone held quiet understanding. "How are you holding up?"

Sophie hesitated, the memory of her fallen friends and clanmates flashing through her mind. "I'm... okay, I guess." She quickly changed the subject. "So, what do we do now?"

"That's entirely up to you, ladies," Sister Alameda replied. "We are but your humble servants."

Sophie leaned forward, more determined now. "I think I want to retrace Brother Albert's steps. Someone sent Isabella to kidnap him and steal his journal sounds like he was onto something."

"Aye" Annabelle agreed.

"That makes sense to me," Lisa added.

"After breakfast, I'll take you girls over to the office," Sister Alameda said, cutting into her pancakes. "Luckily, Brother Albert kept a lot of notes."

267

As Sophie ate her oatmeal, another thought struck her. "Where's Regina?" She paused. "And for that matter, where's Brother Marcus?"

"Brother Marcus accompanied Regina back to Laminae to gather some of her things," Sister Alameda explained. "But after an altercation, they're on their way back to Order Island as we speak."

Annabelle smirked. "She was talkin' about how she wanted her things."

Lisa scoffed. "How could you even tell? She never stops talking."

Annabelle and Sophie both shot Lisa a sharp look.

Lisa glanced away in mock innocence, then sipped her juice smugly.

"You aren't perfect there, princess." Annabelle muttered, spearing a strawberry and popping it into her mouth.

Lisa, satisfied with her jab, continued drinking.

The group finished their breakfast in relative quiet before rising from the table. As they made their way out of the cafeteria, Sophie couldn't help but notice the Order monks watching them subtly, but watching, nonetheless. It was as if they were trying not to be noticed while keeping track of the avatars' every move.

Sister Alameda led the trio down the hall past the dorms. But instead of turning toward their rooms, she took a sharp turn down an unfamiliar corridor. Midway through, she stopped at a narrow doorway and gave it a push. The door opened only partially, forcing her to edge her way through the gap. Without hesitation, the avatars followed.

The room beyond was a large double office, cluttered from floor to ceiling with boxes and stacks of paper. A desk sat at the front, half-buried under scattered documents. Beside it stood a chalkboard on wooden legs, a world map pinned next to it. Colored string connected various points across the map, forming a tangled web of leads and locations.

In the center of the room stood a square table though it was difficult to tell at first, as boxes and loose papers covered nearly every inch of it. The floor was no better: a narrow path led from the door to the desk, and another forked off toward the back of the room, where a mountain of boxes loomed like an archive avalanche.

Lisa took one look and threw up her hands. "What in the name of the Harvest?!? How are we supposed to follow Brother Albert's steps in this disaster?"

"It's just like being buried under six feet of dirt," Sophie said, walking up to a stack of papers. She picked up the topmost box and hefted it into her arms. "You just have to dig your way out."

"Aye, the copper here's got the right idea," Annabelle agreed, grabbing a box of her own. "No point complainin'. Best to get to work."

Lisa let out an exaggerated sigh but followed suit, picking up a box and trudging toward the hallway. Sister Alameda joined in, and soon all four of them were hauling stacks of papers and boxes out of the office, clearing enough space to work.

As they shifted things around, they discovered that the large square table in the center was actually two smaller tables pushed together beneath a single cloth.

After about an hour, Annabelle glanced out the window and suddenly remembered something. Her expression shifted, and she turned to Sister Alameda.

"Sister Al!" she called. "What time is it?"

Sister Alameda pulled a pocket watch from her breast pocket, flipped it open, and checked. "Two thirty-five."

Annabelle's eyes widened. "Oh, I gots to go!"

Sophie frowned. "Go where?"

268

"I've got something to do fer the Fang," Annabelle said, already dusting off her hands. "'Tis important."

Lisa arched an eyebrow as she set another box down in the growing pile. "What is this now?"

"Privateer business," Annabelle replied vaguely. "I'll be back soon."

"That girl," Sophie muttered, shaking her head as she carried another box into the hallway.

Lisa rolled her eyes. "You know how those pirates are." She said, disappearing back into the office for another load.

[----- ⚓ -----]

After quickly changing into her training clothes, Annabelle rushed down to the beach for her expensive Maelstrom Mastery lesson. As she arrived, she spotted Smitty seated in his usual chair, book in hand, facing the waves.

She jogged up beside him. "Sorry, First Mate."

Without looking up, Smitty extended a hand. Annabelle sighed and dropped three five-coins into his palm before stepping in front of him, standing at attention.

"Yer late," he remarked, still not looking up.

"I was working on something," she offered.

Smitty shrugged. "No problem. 'Tis yer coin."

Annabelle tensed. She'd already wasted precious minutes getting here now she had less than an hour to train. "But..."

She froze. Smitty was peering over his book, clearly waiting for her to argue. If she pushed, he'd leave with her coin.

"Sorry," she muttered, swallowing her frustration. "I'll do better."

Smitty smirked. "Let's see the current."

Annabelle nodded and stepped into the shallows, the cool water rushing past her ankles. She stretched out her hands, channeling mana through her palms. She visualized the flow, forming two invisible circles at her hands and pushing energy through them.

The left-hand spout surged into the ocean steady and strong. But the right nothing.

Frowning, she funneled more mana into her right palm.

BOOM!

Water exploded from her hands, blasting her backward. She hit the surface hard, landing flat on her back.

The sky swirled above clouds drifting lazily, birds gliding on unseen currents. Frustration bubbled in her chest, and to her horror, tears pricked her eyes. She had worked on this spell all night. She almost had it. She *should* have had it.

But she still couldn't do it.

Annabelle sat up, fists clenched, then punched the water in frustration. "Why?!?" she shouted, striking it again.

Smitty stood, marked his place in the book, and strolled to the shore. "It's okay, Belle," he said gently.

"NO!" she snapped, blinking back tears. "I worked on this all bloody night! Why can't I do it?!"

Smitty sighed, crossing his arms. "Are ye done?" His tone was calm, but his stance made it clear *keep sulking, and he'd leave.*

Annabelle drew a shaky breath, forcing herself to calm down, though the frustration still simmered beneath the surface.

"Ye understand Maelstrom Mastery is about the sea, right?" Smitty asked.

"Aye," she muttered.

"Then tell me about the sea."

"It flows," she said. "It's made o' water, and it's full of danger."

Smitty pinched the bridge of his nose. "The sea," he said, his voice steady, "is a living thing. We all share an unbreakable bond with it."

Annabelle blinked, caught off guard by the reverence in his tone.

"At the surface, she shimmers like jewels in the sun, concealing the secrets of kingdoms lost, shipwrecks, and treasures buried deep." He gestured toward the horizon. "Her rhythms, gentle lullabies and violent skirmishes, touch the very essence of who and what we be. That's where we draw power. The sea isn't just water. Tis life."

Annabelle looked down, watching the tide swirl around her ankles. Slowly, she closed her eyes.

She imagined the water not as a force to command, but as something alive untamed, yet willing to dance with her. She pictured it weaving a path around the Fang, rushing into the open sea, an eternal pulse that had existed long before her and would endure long after she was gone.

She inhaled slowly, feeling the sea not just the water flow around her feet, through her body, rising from her core and pouring into her hands.

A steady stream flowed from both palms.

Her eyes snapped open. *Yes! She has it!* "See, I go…"

BOOM!

A surge erupted from her hands, launching her backward once more. She landed flat on her back, staring up at the sky just like before.

Defeated. But this time determined.

She sat up, spitting out seawater as Smitty calmly returned to his chair. He sat, opened his book, and without looking up, said, "That was a good try."

Then, with a wave of his hand, he gave a single command: "Again."

Annabelle frowned, shook her head, and climbed to her feet. She squared her shoulders, aimed her open palms, and muttered, "Come on, Belle. Ye can do this."

[----- ✿ -----]

Marcus, Regina, and Sister Sallie arrived at Order Island, passing the Stormfang as they glided toward the boathouse. Strangely, this three-hour trip felt longer than the one to the Luminous yesterday.

Leaning over the edge of the boat, Regina caught a flash of familiar orange hair by the shore. Annabelle stood ankle-deep in the water, while the old man, Smitty, lounged in his chair, nose buried in a book.

"What are they doing?" Regina wondered aloud.

"Hm?" Marcus blinked, pulled from thoughts of their next move once they disembarked.

"Annabelle and Smitty," she said, pointing toward the beach.

Marcus followed her gaze and squinted. "That's a good question, Miss Fournier." He made a mental note to check in with both Annabelle and Mr. Smith after meeting with Sister Alameda and Sister Ingrid.

Sister Sallie steered the boat into its slip and tied it off with practiced ease. Once docked, the trio retrieved their bags from the cargo hold and stepped onto the pier. They exited the docking house and entered the broader Order complex, arriving at the first of the smaller statue circles.

"So, what's the plan?" Sister Sallie asked, glancing between Marcus and Regina.

"I think you should check in with your sect while Regina and I catch up with the other avatars," Marcus said.

Sister Sallie frowned. "I'd be more useful helping you and the avatars."

Marcus hesitated. "Honestly, I don't know what our next move is yet," he lied.

But Regina had her own idea. "Did Brother Albert keep notes?" she asked. "We should look through them maybe there's something in there that could help us find my dad and Mattie."

"He kept plenty of notes," Marcus replied, turning his attention to her. "That's actually a solid idea."

"I can help with that," Sister Sallie offered.

Marcus shot her a look. "Your time is better spent with the College of Sages."

Sister Sallie narrowed her eyes at him, clearly offended by it. After a pause, she relented. "I guess you're right," she said, though her tone was tinged with reluctance. Turning to Regina, she softened. "I'll see you later, Regina."

"Okay," Regina said with a nod. "See you later." She shifted her bag and limped off toward the dorms.

Marcus smiled. "See you later, Sister."

"Yes. Later," she replied coolly before heading to her own dormitory.

Marcus sighed. She's definitely annoyed with him but that is a problem for another time. Right now, he has other things to handle.

He caught up with Regina as she made her way toward the dormitory. Thankfully, he'd had the foresight to move his room to the same hallway as the avatars. After quickly dropping off their bags, he escorted her to his new office.

As they approached the double doors, they spotted Lisa, Sophie, and Sister Alameda stacking boxes in the hallway.

"Well, hello," Marcus greeted.

"Hi, girls!" Regina called, stepping forward.

Lisa barely spared them a glance. "Hi," she said flatly before disappearing back into the office for another box.

Marcus turned to Sister Alameda. "What's all this?"

"Sophie, Lisa, and Annabelle wanted to retrace Brother Albert's steps," Sister Alameda explained, setting down a box. "Though Annabelle had something else to take care of."

"We saw her on the beach," Regina added.

Sister Alameda turned to her with a warm smile. "Oh, you must be Regina Fournier." She extended a hand. "I'm Sister Alameda. A pleasure to meet you."

Regina limped forward and shook her hand. "Nice to meet you, too."

Sister Alameda's gaze dropped to Regina's leg. "Are you okay? What happened?"

Regina shrugged. "Got into a fight with Hema, the Blood Witch. She messed up my leg pretty bad."

Sophie, who had just dropped another box onto the growing pile, snapped her head up. "Who did you fight?"

"Hema, the Blood Witch," Regina repeated.

Lisa, setting down her own box, frowned. "Who is that?"

Marcus crossed his arms. "She's with the same organization as Mage and Isabella." He looked at the avatars. "There's a lot we need to go over now that you've all communed with your goddesses. If you don't mind, I'll go find Miss Salazar."

Lisa scoffed. "If she's done sunning herself on the beach." With that, she grabbed another box and disappeared into the office.

"Fine by me," Sophie said before following Lisa inside.

"Then I'm off," Marcus said, turning on his heel and heading toward the beach where he had last seen Annabelle.

Regina limped into the room, determined to help the other avatars. She bent down, picked up a box from the floor, and carefully placed it in the hallway atop a small stack of two others.

Lisa stopped beside her. "I can take a look at your leg if you want," she offered.

Regina let out a breath of relief. "That would be great. It really hurts when I walk."

Without missing a beat, Lisa turned to Sister Alameda. "Regina and I are going to the washroom," she said, heading down the hall.

Regina hesitated, glanced at Sister Alameda, then quickly limped after Lisa, realizing she wasn't going to wait for permission.

Sophie watched them go, shrugged, and returned to the office for another box. Sister Alameda followed, stepping over to a nearby stack and lifting another crate into the hallway.

Standing beside the growing wall of boxes and papers, Sister Alameda sighed. "Feels like we're going to be doing this forever."

Sophie grinned. "Maybe not forever," she said with a shrug. "When I was an initiate, we had to clean out dorms, storage rooms, warehouses... We just chipped away at it until it was done." She glanced at the long line of boxes and shook her head. "The hard part won't be moving them, it'll be sorting through everything and figuring out what to do next."

[-----❂-----]

Lisa pushed open the washroom door and held it for Regina, who limped inside behind her. Once they were in, the door swung shut, enclosing them in the quiet space. She motioned for Regina to step into the open area between the stalls. "Is anyone in here?" she called out, pausing for a moment. When no reply came, she turned back to Regina. "Alright, can I take a look."

Regina nodded and reached for the bow at her waist, untying it so her dress silhouette slipped down and pooled around her ankles. She carefully unwound the bandage from her leg, holding the fabric gently in her hand.

Lisa crouched, eyes narrowing as she examined the stitched wound. A deep scar ran across Regina's leg, the skin still raw and angry-looking.

"That must hurt a lot," Lisa murmured.

"Yeah," Regina admitted. "It hurts every time I take a step."

"I am going to heal it now. Please stay still," Lisa said firmly.

Regina nodded. "Okay."

Lisa raised her hand, weaving a red glowing spell circle between her palm and Regina's injured leg. Six intricate runes shimmered in the air, forming a delicate healing array around the wound. As she focused, her Earthbloom sense probed deeper, revealing the full extent of the damage.

Lisa's eyes widened. "By the Harvest—she nearly lost her leg!" The words slipped out before she could stop them.

Regina swallowed hard, surprised by the severity.

Lisa quickly refocused and began channeling her magic, spinning the runes to heal from the inside out.

Regina gasped as her muscles started knitting back together. Sharp, aching pain flared as tissue reconnected, then softened into soothing warmth as the healing took hold.

Trying to distract herself, Regina asked, "Lisa, how do you choose the runes for your healing spells?"

"What?" Lisa replied, still concentrating.

"I was reading about Earthbloom magic," Regina explained, wincing through another wave of pain. "I want to learn it, like you suggested but I haven't gotten to the book that explains which runes to use in spell circles."

Lisa let out a small huff. "Earthbloom magic is tough. You might not get it." Despite the dismissive tone, she was surprised by how quickly Regina's leg was healing usually wounds this deep took longer.

Regina let out a relieved sigh as the pain faded. Lisa's magic dimmed, the glowing runes dissolving as the wound fully closed. She touched the spot where the injury had been, feeling smooth skin beneath her fingertips. The sutures remained, but when she took a test step, there was no pain or soreness.

She looked up at Lisa with a grateful smile. "Thank you, Lisa."

Lisa returned the smile warmly. "You are welcome, I am happy to help."

Standing, Lisa turned to the mirror to check her reflection while Regina pulled her dress silhouette back up and tied the bow at her waist.

Regina moved to the sink, glanced at herself in the mirror, and washed her hands. As she dried them, she turned toward Lisa, still near the door. "So, what exactly are we doing in Brother Marcus' office?"

Lisa pulled the door open. "Cleaning. The place was packed with so much junk we could barely move inside."

Regina hurried into the hallway. "We've got to get back."

Lisa rolled her eyes. "Oh, don't worry. People like Sophie enjoy the physical work it's what they do best."

Regina stopped and frowned. "That's messed up." Without waiting for a response, she headed down the hall toward Brother Marcus' office.

Lisa shrugged and followed at a slower pace.

[-----✝-----]

Marcus arrived at the beach, approaching Yancy Smith from behind. From this angle, he could see Annabelle standing shin-deep in the water, her boots abandoned in the sand beside Smith's chair. "Hello there, Mr. Smith," Marcus called as he drew nearer.

Smith looked up from his book, glancing over his shoulder. "Ahoy there, Brother Marcus," he replied.

Marcus stepped up beside the old privateer's chair, his gaze shifting to Annabelle. She faced the sea, arms outstretched, streams of water flowing steadily from her hands. For a moment, it looked controlled—then, without warning, a powerful blast erupted from her palms, knocking her off balance and sending her sprawling into the water.

She floated for a few seconds before sitting up and pushing herself to her feet, preparing to try again.

"What is she doing?" Marcus asked, watching her struggle.

"Magic training," Smith said casually. "Usually, she gives up by now, but for some reason, she's stickin' with it today. Shame, really. If she'd started this years ago, it wouldn't be so hard for her now."

Marcus nodded. "From what I've seen, Miss Salazar is a fan of doing things the hard way."

Smith chuckled. "Brother Marcus, ye are a truly perceptive man."

With a flick of his wrist, he pulled out a pocket watch, checked the time, and called out, "Five minutes!"

Annabelle, still knee-deep in the water, frowned. "Are ye sure? It doesn't feel like I've been out here that long."

"Aye, Belle I'm sure" Smith answered firmly.

Taking a deep breath, Annabelle steadied herself and made another attempt. This time, a small stream of water left her palms, before exploding into another massive surge that knocked her back into the surf.

She sat up, fists clenched, and smacked the water in frustration. "Stupid damn spell! Why won't it work?!?"

Smith stood and wandered to the water's edge, watching her calmly as she fumed.

Annabelle turned to him, shoulders sagging in defeat. "I don't understand what I'm doing wrong."

Smith stroked his chin thoughtfully. "Honestly? Ye aren't too far from figurin' it out. Ye just got to stick with' it."

Annabelle hesitated, then asked tentatively, "Do ye think... ye could show me again?"

A small smile tugged at Smith's lips. "Aye. Pay close attention now."

He raised his hands, positioning them slightly apart. A moment later, a controlled spout of water surged from his palms, arcing gently to either side of Annabelle. She studied him carefully, memorizing the set of his shoulders, the placement of his hands, the steady, deliberate way he directed the sea.

After a few moments, he let the spell fade, lowering his arms. "That's it for today," he said, turning back toward his chair. "See ye on the morrow."

As he reached his seat, he gave Marcus a nod. "Brother Marcus."

"Have a good day sir." Marcus replied.

Smith grabbed his book, then, in a single fluid motion, flipped his chair closed with his foot and hand. Marcus had to admit it was an impressive bit of coordination. Whistling a tune, Smith slung the chair under his arm and walked off down the beach toward the Stormfang.

With Smith gone, Marcus took the opportunity to approach Annabelle without interrupting her training. He watched as she attempted the spell once more only for the same explosive result to send her crashing into the water again.

By the time he reached her, she was sitting up, the sea lapping around her waist.

"Looks like a tricky spell," Marcus said, hoping to establish some common ground.

"It shouldn't be this hard," Annabelle muttered, eyes locked on the water. He wasn't sure if she was talking to him or just voicing her own frustration.

"If you have time, there are things we need to discuss," Marcus said. "All six of us."

Annabelle let out a breath. "Aye. I think I needs me a break anyway."

Marcus extended a hand, and she took it, letting him help her to her feet. Together, they started walking back toward the complex. Along the way, Annabelle bent down to grab her boots, slipping them back on as they neared the entrance.

Just before they reached the stairs, she turned to Marcus with a serious expression. "Yer me servant, right?"

"I am," Marcus confirmed.

Annabelle smirked. "Then ye don't be tellin' the others nothin' ye seen here." With that, she turned and strode up the steps, leaving Marcus to follow.

Marcus reached his office ahead of Annabelle, who had stopped by her room to change clothes. Wasting no time, he joined the effort to clear out the remaining boxes, lining them up neatly along the hallway while leaving enough space for people to pass.

With six people working together, they managed to empty the two-room office in just under three hours. Though the temptation to start digging through the contents was strong, the group agreed to hold off until they had a proper discussion.

Once the last box was placed outside, Marcus turned to the group. "Thank you for cleaning out our office," he said, glancing around the now open space. "Who knew there was this much stuff in here?"

The girls and Sister Alameda exchanged amused glances, chuckling softly at the sight of their hard-earned progress.

Marcus' expression grew serious. "I don't know how much Brother Albert told you about the people targeting you, but one of the biggest things he was investigating was something we call the Conspiracy a group working toward a goal we still know next to nothing about."

The room fell quiet.

"Brother Albert had a knack for tracking them," Marcus continued. "Whether through rumor or pure instinct, he had a way of finding traces of their influence, sometimes before they even acted."

"He mentioned it." Regina said. "He told us there were people watching us like the man outside my house in the red sweater."

Marcus nodded. "To be honest, Brother Albert and I didn't always see eye to eye on his methods. He made connections that I thought were... leaps of logic. Some of them didn't seem to lead anywhere, but somehow he still managed to predict their movements and maybe even disrupt some of their plans."

Sophie crossed her arms, pressing a finger to her nose. "What exactly do they do?"

"As far as actions go, we rarely catch sight of them beforehand," Marcus admitted. "It's only after an event that we start noticing things details that seem off or directly link back to known members of the Conspiracy."

"Who are the known members?" Sophie pressed.

Marcus gestured grimly toward a collection of pinned-up photos and sketches on the office wall.

He pointed first to an image of a blue-haired woman. "Isabella Morales. Mechanawitch from Magitekopolis. She is also the avatar of the goddess Resilience who was somehow corrupted."

Next, he indicated a woman with sharp features and brown hair. "Gretta Blomqvist. A witch of snow and ice. We don't fully understand her history because most of her village was arrested by the Stoneridge Aurorium for counterfeiting and selling fraudulent Verdantian harvest crowns across the Seven Kingdoms. Her brown hair and eyes marks her as the Avatar of Justice also corrupted by the Conspiracy."

Moving his hand, Marcus pointed to a drawing of a hooded figure. "This woman is known as Mage. Her shadow magic marks her as a citizen of the Umbrathorn Empire, or at least a descendant of one. We do know she isn't an Avatar, but she's a very powerful shadow witch. One important note: she can't stand direct sunlight. It physically harms her."

Annabelle smirked. "Aye, I can vouch for that," she said, throwing a knowing glance at Regina.

Finally, Marcus pointed to the last drawing a woman with piercing eyes and a cruel expression. "And this is Hema, the Blood Witch," he said. "We don't have much information on her. We know she uses blood in her magic, but we aren't certain if it's her own or taken from others."

Regina's stomach twisted at the memory. "She takes it from others," she said firmly. "She told me she was going to add my blood to her supply."

Marcus exhaled sharply. "That's new information." He folded his arms. "And she poisoned your stepmother using her own blood as well."

Regina's jaw tightened, but she said nothing.

Sophie narrowed her eyes. "Where are they based?"

Marcus shook his head. "We don't know. So far, we've only caught glimpses of them small appearances here and there, always linked to something unusual. But nothing that leads us to a specific location."

Regina clenched her fists. "That's not very helpful." She took a steadying breath before meeting Marcus's gaze. "How are we supposed to find my dad and Mattie?"

Marcus sighed. "I'm sorry to say I don't know." He met her eyes. "But we'll use every resource The Order has to find Jules and Matthew."

"And let me tell you, ladies," Sister Alameda added with a warm smile, "that's a lot of resources."

Marcus smirked at her remark, but Sophie wasn't satisfied.

"How is my village involved?" Sophie asked, crossing her arms. "Why did the ice and blue-haired witches attack my home?"

"Another question we need to answer, Miss Griffin," Marcus admitted.

Lisa scoffed. "It sounds like all you have are questions."

"You're absolutely right, Miss Nozaki," Marcus said, unfazed.

Regina frowned. "Did the Conspiracy take my dad and Mattie to use against me?"

Marcus considered this. "That may be their goal. They clearly know who each of you are."

"That doesn't quite add up," Sophie interjected. "If they just wanted leverage over Regina, they wouldn't have poisoned her stepmother. Hema tried to kill Mrs. Fournier, but she took Jules and Mattie alive. That suggests they need them for something specific."

"How did ye figure, Copper?" Annabelle asked.

Sophie raised a finger. "First, when Regina arrived, Hema was still poisoning her stepmother." She raised another. "Second, there was no sign of her dad or little brother, meaning they were already gone before Regina arrived with Brother Marcus. If they wanted hostages, they would've taken everyone."

The room fell silent, thoughtful.

"All this speculation is great," Lisa said, "but my question is what are we supposed to do now?"

"I think we need to follow Brother Albert's work," Regina suggested. "Something he found made Isabella come after him."

"Aye, makes sense to me." Annabelle agreed.

Marcus nodded. "That brings me to an agreement I made on your behalf with Miss Fournier's approval with the Aurorium Clan. All the information we have about the Conspiracy will be given to Apex Sanderlin of Aurorium Laminae," Marcus explained.

Lisa raised an eyebrow. "That does not sound like a good deal." Her bargaining instincts kicked in. "What did we get in return?"

Marcus met her gaze steadily. "We get to keep Sophie Griffin and Regina Fournier with us."

Lisa frowned. "Explain, please."

"Miss Sophie is ranked Sentinel and a Sentinel isn't usually allowed to be independent this long without a superior officer," Marcus said, nodding toward Sophie. "Apex Sanderlin could have required Sophie to return to duty." He glanced at Regina. "She also made it clear Regina could have been required to stay in Laminae under her protection if we didn't agree to share all our information."

Annabelle grinned, turning to Sophie with mock horror. "I canna believe it. Ye had a chance to give the Copper back, and ye didn't take it!" She shook her head dramatically. "Yer a terrible servant."

Sophie glared. "Ha ha ha," she said flatly.

Lisa wasn't ready to let it go. "So, we did not actually gain anything new from this deal." She said, folding her arms. "What if we just... do not give them anything?"

Marcus sighed. "I don't think that's a viable option."

"No, it's not," Sophie said firmly. "My clan has the resources to sort through these files way faster than we ever could, and the investigators of Laminae are *legendary*."

"Except," Lisa said, "we need to go through them ourselves first to figure out what Brother Albert found before he..." She hesitated, "...before he reached out to us."

Regina nodded. "We should read through everything before handing it over to Apex Sanderlin. Right, Brother Marcus?"

"Yes, Miss Fournier," Marcus confirmed. "Brother Albert was very organized there must be a method to how these files are sorted."

Lisa eyed the towering stacks of boxes outside. "There's a lot of papers out there," she said. "Can we not just get some monks to help sort through them?"

Sister Alameda shook her head. "Due to the sensitivity of matters that concerns you avatars, we can't involve Order members from other sects. The risks are too high." She exchanged a knowing look with Marcus.

"In that case, we should get started," Sophie said, rolling up her sleeves. "A million-mile journey is just a collection of footsteps."

Lisa groaned. "Of course you would say that."

Sophie blinked. "What's that supposed to mean?"

Lisa shrugged. "You know. Your people were made for work."

The room went silent.

"What?!?" Sophie demanded, eyes narrowing.

Before tension snapped, Annabelle threw an arm around Sophie's shoulders and grinned. "Can't ye hear, Copper?" she teased. "She just told ye she's lazy."

Sophie and Regina burst into laughter. Lisa, however, scowled.

Marcus had to admit; he found the exchange amusing. But he kept his thoughts to himself, inhaling through his nose, catching the faint scent of stale air and old books.

"Ladies," he said evenly, "if we could focus."

The six of them got to work, pulling boxes into the room one by one and sorting through their contents. The first box they opened was filled with shipping invoices from

Laminae's port city, Scholar's Reach, to an island on the outskirts of the Kingdom of Islewind San Raphels.

Sophie frowned as she flipped through the records. "This could be something. If there's this much movement between Scholar's Reach and San Raphels, it might be a base of operations."

The others exchanged glances but said nothing. *It was too early to tell.*

The next box, however, hit much closer to home.

It was filled with files on Sophie Griffin.

Inside was a photograph from her promotion ceremony to Sentinel, alongside detailed notes about her missions with Eclipse Baker. Most were training assignments patrolling rural areas in Opulentia, investigating reported crimes, and gathering intelligence under Baker's guidance.

One report detailed a significant mission: a gang of bandits had preyed on villages near the forests of Oswego, in Farmington province. Sophie had helped uncover their hideout, leading to a large-scale operation involving both the Aurorium Clan and Opulentia's local guards. Though she had been too young to participate in the final raid, her contributions earned her recognition.

Tucked beneath that report was another photograph, this one attached to a funeral report.

Sophie's expression hardened as she pulled it out.

Oscar Griffin, her father.

The report detailed his final mission, an Aurorium operation to capture a corrupt businessman who had twice escaped custody in the Umbrathorn Empire during his trial. Oscar was renowned for tracking down those who didn't want to be found, earning him the title *The Seeker.*

He succeeded in locating his target and called for backup from local law enforcement. But the businessman, tipped off about his impending arrest, attempted to flee. Undeterred, Oscar tried to subdue him alone, only to be shot by one of the target's hired bodyguards. Despite his wounds, he managed to hold his target until reinforcements arrived.

He succumbed to his injuries the next day in an Islewind hospital.

Sophie barely glanced at the report before setting it aside. "I miss him," she said simply.

No one responded. No one really knew what to say.

As the group continued sorting, Regina noticed a faint violet splotch on the corner of one of the boxes. Scribbled notes covered the side, with one word standing out Griffin.

She glanced at the box of shipping invoices. It had a different marking light blue with red stripes.

Her eyes drifted down the long hallway, where stacks of boxes lined the walls. As she inspected them more closely, she realized every box was marked with a color and sometimes additional notes. Some colors matched the avatars' respective colors, while others were different solid blue, solid red, white with red stripes, white with blue stripes.

"These colors must mean something," Regina said.

The others gathered around, confirming that each of their files had been placed in boxes matching their Avatar colors.

After a brief discussion, they agreed not to go through their own boxes after all, they already knew their own stories.

Instead, they pulled a solid blue box into the room.

Inside were reports from Order monks detailing sightings of Isabella Morales in Islewind, in the coastal town of Kikouwa. The reports confirmed it was her sapphire blue hair made her hard to mistake, but she hadn't been seen doing anything suspicious. She visited a few shops, stayed at an inn, and moved on without incident.

Another report described a similar sighting this time of Gretta Blomqvist. Unlike Isabella, Gretta had drawn attention by wearing a thick winter coat despite the warm weather. She was spotted in Gainsport, a town in Opulentia, speaking with local farmers and even attending a political rally for a candidate named Graham Shaw, who was campaigning for provincial governor.

Hours passed as they sifted through more files, more reports, more pictures. The deeper they dug, the more frustrating it became.

There were so much information pieces of something big but no clear path forward. Fatigue settled over them.

"We are not getting anywhere." Lisa finally said, rubbing her eyes.

"Aye." Annabelle added, stretching her arms overhead.

Marcus nodded. "Let's call it for today. I'll go through Brother Albert's journals, see if I can find any kind of pattern in his notes. There has to be some kind of system to all this."

No one argued.

They were all too mentally exhausted to continue.

Chapter 19

Later that night, Sophie stood at the shoreline, holding a small lantern boat crafted from thin wood and delicate paper.

Back in her village, it was tradition to craft these boats for the dead to send them out to sea as a way of wishing their spirits well on their journey to the ancestors. Normally, Sophie didn't put much stock in such rituals. She doubted a spirit would care about a burning boat drifting across the waves, no matter how beautiful it looked.

But tonight, she hoped.

She hoped for her mother, Arisa. Her patrol commander Eclipse Baker. All her fallen friends and comrades.

She hoped they knew she was still here.

Still thinking of them.

Still wishing them peace as they crossed through the veil.

Striking a small piece of flint against a handheld wooden block fitted with a steel plate, she caught a spark and lit the candle inside the lantern. The soft glow flickered against the night. Carefully, she secured the cover over the base and lifted the illuminated boat.

Stepping into the water, she walked forward until the waves reached her shins. Slowly, she knelt and placed the boat on the surface. It bobbed gently, its light reflecting in shimmering ribbons across the dark sea.

Clasping her hands, she whispered a quiet prayer not to War, but to the ancestors so they might watch over her family and friends and welcome them to the afterlife.

She stayed there, standing in the cool water, watching the lantern drift farther from shore.

She had promised her mother she wouldn't shed another tear.

She intended to keep that promise.

Once certain the little boat would make its way out to sea, Sophie turned back toward the beach and retrieved her boots from where she had left them in the sand. Instead of putting them on immediately, she let herself enjoy the sensation of warm, dry sand beneath her feet, deciding to walk back barefoot.

As she passed the docked Stormfang, she noticed two crew members working on deck Harmon and Popper. She recognized them from the trip that brought her to Order Island, probably servicing the deck machinery. The Stormfang hadn't moved since it arrived days ago.

Reaching the paved walkway, she sat on the edge, brushed sand from her feet, and slipped on her socks and boots. Just as she rose to continue toward the complex, a sudden noise caught her attention, water splashing, followed by a string of frustrated swearing.

She hesitated, then turned toward the sound instead of heading back.

Following the noise down the path, she crossed onto the next islet. The splashes were rhythmic, almost like... an explosion? As she drew closer, she spotted a figure in the shallows, arms raised, attempting some kind of magic spell.

Another burst of water erupted followed by the person losing their balance and crashing into the waves.

Sophie quickened her pace, concern pushing her forward. If someone was struggling, she needed to help.

As she neared, the figure became clearer.

Orange hair, soaked and tangled.

Annabelle.

Sitting in the water, looking very much like someone who had just lost a fight with the sea.

Seeing that Annabelle wasn't in any real danger, Sophie slowed her approach. Once close enough, she crossed her arms and smirked. "What do we have here?"

Annabelle scoffed, standing up and brushing water from her arms. "Nothin'. Just playin' in the water," she said casually. Then, with a sneer, she added, "Not for dumb coppers to watch."

Sophie raised an eyebrow. "Yeah, you have a point. *If I couldn't do magic right, I wouldn't want anyone to watch either.*"

Annabelle's expression darkened. "Shows what ye know. I'm just practicin' me magic."

Sophie let out a laugh. "Oh, right. And what do you call that one? Super 'Sploder?"

Annabelle clenched her fists. "Shows what ye know, Copper," she repeated, irritation creeping into her voice. "Me goddess gave me super mana." She sneered again. "Yer goddess must've left ye short."

The remark stung more than Sophie expected. She frowned, suddenly realizing something she hadn't used any magic since communing with War. "Hold on," she said, thinking through her options. If she wanted to test herself, she needed something simple yet effective.

Then, an idea struck her: *The Astral Vault.*

Gathering mana into her legs, Sophie visualized two glowing spell circles forming beneath her feet. She bent her knees slightly, then, in one swift motion, jumped simultaneously releasing the stored energy through the circles.

The result was far more powerful than she had anticipated. Instead of a controlled hop, she launched into the air three, maybe four times higher than intended. Her stomach lurched.

Oh. Shit.

Panic flooded her as she realized she had no control over her descent. The ground rushed up at an alarming speed. Acting on instinct, she tucked her arms in to protect her midsection and funneled mana into her hands, forming another spell circle just before impact.

She barely had time to activate it before she hit the sand.

Even with the cushioning effect of her spell, the force of the landing rattled her bones. Pain radiated through her chest and arms, and for a long moment, she just lay there, catching her breath.

A burst of laughter echoed from the water.

"Wow, Copper, that was some good magicin'. " Annabelle called, covering her mouth. "Can ye do that again?" She kept laughing.

Sophie gritted her teeth, pushing herself to her knees. Embarrassment flared red-hot in her chest. "At least I can do my magic." she shot back.

Annabelle smirked. "Oh, ye want to see me magic?"

She raised her hands at Sophie, channeling mana into her palms, envisioning the spell circles forming over them. Confident this time, she sneered, "Have a taste of the sea."

A thin stream of water trickled from her palms.

Her smirk faltered.

Determined to push through, she channeled more mana

BOOM!

The water exploded from her hands, sending her flying backward into the sea.

Sophie doubled over, laughing so hard she had to clutch her sides. Annabelle resurfaced, sputtering, her once-smug expression replaced by sheer disbelief.

"Yeah, you really showed me," Sophie teased, walking toward the waterline.

Annabelle sat up, looking defeated. Her fists clenched at her sides.

Then, she swore loudly.

"Why, dammit?!" she yelled, pounding her fist into the water. "What's wrong with me magic?!"

The frustration in her voice made Sophie pause. She had heard people struggle with their magic before. She had never heard anyone blame the magic itself.

Annabelle must have caught the look on her face, because she glared. "What're ye lookin' at, huh?"

Sophie hesitated. Then, with a small shrug, she muttered, "Nothin'."

Turning away, she started back toward the complex, but something nagged at her.

Guilt.

She sighed and stopped. Without turning around, she said, "You know, I do know why your spell isn't working."

Annabelle looked up sharply. "What...?" Then her eyes narrowed. "Tis a trick," she accused, standing up. "Ye just want to make fun of me!"

Sophie turned back to face her. "No, really. I've seen this before."

Annabelle crossed her arms, still skeptical. "Oh aye? Then what is it?"

"In the Aurorium, we do fundamentals in Initiate training," Sophie explained. "It helps us understand how magic works on a basic level."

Annabelle eyed her warily. "Uh huh."

Sophie held up a hand, palm out. "Throw a punch."

Annabelle frowned but did as she was told, swinging hard, much harder than Sophie expected.

Her first slammed into Sophie's palm, sending a shock of pain through her hand. Sophie shook it out, grimacing. "Damn! Usually, people don't punch someone's hand with all their strength."

Annabelle just smirked. "Ye asked for it."

Ignoring her, Sophie continued, "Okay how did you throw that punch?"

Annabelle shrugged. "Gathered me strength, then released it all at once."

"Exactly. That's how your magic should work, too." Sophie flexed her fingers before pointing at Annabelle's hands. "Right now, you're starting with a little bit of mana to establish a path, but then you're forcing too much at once. That's why it explodes and knocks you over."

Annabelle's brows furrowed.

"Try again," Sophie instructed. "But this time, push out all your mana at once don't hold back."

Annabelle turned to face the sea. Raising her hands, she gathered her mana, focused her breath then released it all at once.

For the first time, she felt it, a steady unbroken flow.

When she opened her eyes, two powerful streams of water surged from her hands, arcing into the ocean.

She is doing it!

Annabelle grinned wildly, clenching her fists and thrusting them into the air in victory. "Ha!"

She turned back to Sophie, took a deep breath, and in her most formal voice said, "Thank ye, Copper."

Then, without warning, she raised her palm toward Sophie.

Sophie's stomach dropped. "Wait! Don't you…"

A torrent of water blasted into her, drenching her from head to toe.

Annabelle burst into laughter as Sophie stood there, soaked, her purple vest, pants, and white shirt completely drenched.

Sophie wiped water from her face and scowled.

Annabelle laughed. "Ye should see yer face!"

Sophie stood there, drenched, her clothes heavy with seawater, her hair matted down. Her fists clenched at her sides as Annabelle's laughter rang through the night air.

She squeezed her eyes shut.

Don't fight with the other Avatars. That's what War had told her. She was not going to waste her 'free hit' from her goddess.

Gathering mana into her thigh, she formed a large spell circle just in front of her foot. The moment she opened her eyes, she kicked forward, releasing the stored energy through the circle. A massive wave of sand erupted from the ground, surging forward like a miniature landslide. Sophie had not anticipated just how strong she was.

The blast buried Annabelle completely, coating her wet hair, clothes, and skin in a thick layer of sand. She stood there, stunned, small mounds of sand piled on her shoulders and head. Slowly, she opened her eyes. More sand tumbled from her face, falling into the water below.

It became Sophie's turn to burst into laughter.

Annabelle sputtered, spitting sand from her mouth. "Oh aye?" she growled.

Without warning, she charged, tackling Sophie to the ground.

The two of them wrestled, rolling through the wet sand, each struggling to gain the upper hand. For several minutes, neither relented until exhaustion finally set in. Both collapsed onto their backs, panting, staring up at the starry sky.

Annabelle let out a wheezing chuckle. "I knew" she panted, "ye coppers weren't tough."

Sophie, equally breathless, scoffed. "I just didn't want to hurt you, pirate girlie."

Annabelle snorted. "Likely story, Copper," she teased, pushing herself up onto her elbows.

Sophie groaned as she sat up. Glancing down at herself, she sighed at the state of her clothes. The once-wet fabric was now caked in a mixture of sand and mud. She wiped at her arms, only to realize she was just smearing the mess around. "You're lucky I'm feeling generous," she teased, knocking clumps of sand from her pants. She ran a hand through her hair only to pull back a handful of thick, gritty mud.

Her face sank.

"You can't be serious," she said, voice tight. She checked again. More sand. More mud. "You got sand in my hair!"

Annabelle blinked. "There's sand in me hair too, ye know."

Sophie inhaled sharply, forcing herself to stay calm. Then, after a pause, she exhaled. "Do you know how hard it is to get sand out of black hair?"

Annabelle frowned. "Missy, ye got purple hair."

Sophie shot her with a scowl. "You know what I mean."

Without another word, she turned on her heel and stormed off toward the complex.

Annabelle stared after her, confused. Then, shaking off the moment, she called out, "Oh, don't be like that, Copper! We were just havin' a bit a fun!"

Sophie didn't turn around.

Annabelle grinned to herself, brushing sand from her arms. "Aye, that was fun."

[-----❀-----]

Marcus escorted Regina into Sister Sallie's workshop, where the monk stood waiting beside a completed kite, its string coiled neatly on the table. As soon as she saw them, she rose briskly from her chair and approached.

"Good evening, Regina," she greeted the silver-haired girl with warmth. Then, with a sudden chill in her tone, she added curtly, "Brother."

Marcus immediately sensed the tension. She was still upset with him for reminding her to mind her duties earlier. Hoping to keep the peace, he answered in a calm voice, "Sister Sallie. It's good to see you."

Regina noticed the shift in Sallie's tone and hesitated before murmuring, "Hello, Sister Sallie."

Sallie gently took Regina's hand and led her to the workbench. With a smile that rekindled her earlier warmth, she picked up the kite. "I made this for you," she said, placing it carefully in Regina's hands. "Do you like it?"

Regina examined the kite. Its simple wooden cross frame featured a sturdy vertical spine with a cylindrical horizontal beam secured across it. A green canvas had been stretched and tied tightly over the structure, and three trailing ribbons red, blue, and yellow hung from a sewn loop at the base.

She turned it over slowly in her hands. "It's okay, I guess," she said after a moment. Then, pausing thoughtfully, she added, "But... I think it's kind of plain. I bet I could make it better."

Sallie blinked, her smile dimming. "What?"

"If I changed the base design," Regina said, tilting her head, "and maybe used different colors I think I could make it really fun."

"You... don't like it?" Sallie asked, her voice barely above a whisper. But the hurt in her expression was unmistakable.

"Sister" Marcus began, sensing where this was headed and trying to soften the blow.

Sallie's eyes snapped to him, sharp and burning with frustration. Her glare was colder than before furious, almost accusatory, as if she blamed him for this, too. Then, without another word, she turned and rushed out of the workshop, her shoulders trembling as she vanished out the door.

Regina stared after her, then turned to Marcus, her brows knitting in concern. "Did I do something wrong?"

Marcus sighed, his gaze lingering on the empty doorway. "No, Miss Regina," he said gently. "I think Sister Sallie just misunderstood something."

284

He scanned the room and spotted a chalkboard. "Tell you what," he said, offering a small smile. "I'll go talk to her. In the meantime, why don't you sketch out your new kite design? That way, when she comes back, you two can work on it together."

Regina hesitated. "Are you sure that's okay? She seemed really mad, and she was already upset with you after we got back from the Luminous."

Marcus chuckled. "If I'm not back in ten minutes, you might have to come rescue me like you saved your Mommy June from Hema."

Regina giggled, some of the tension easing from her posture. "I don't know if I have enough magic to stop her."

"You may have a point," Marcus said, still smiling.

With that, he left the workroom, walking past rows of now-empty stations. The workday had ended, and a hushed stillness had settled over the College of Sages. As he stepped through the double-door glass panes etched with the college's insignia he paused and glanced both ways down the hallway. Sallie was nowhere in sight.

He exhaled through his nose, thinking. Then it clicked. Snapping his fingers, he turned right and headed toward the restrooms.

Pushing open the women's door, he immediately heard muffled sobs echoing from one of the stalls.

"Sister Sallie?" he called gently.

"Go AWAY!" she shouted between sobs. "I don't want to talk to you!" She was using her magic to echo her voice around the room making it impossible for Marcus to pinpoint where the screams were coming from.

Marcus frowned. "I can't do that," he said, raising his voice just enough to be heard over her crying. "You're my friend, and I want to make sure you're okay."

"Just go back to the Goddess!" she yelled, her voice raw. "She needs you!"

"She's not the Goddess," Marcus replied softly, stepping forward and opening the first stall on the right. *Empty.* "Please, Sallie. Let's just talk."

He heard only more sobbing in response. He moved to the second stall. *Also empty.*

"Come on, Sallie. It's me," he coaxed, reaching for the third stall door, there, he saw her: slumped on the toilet, dabbing her eyes with shaking fingers. *He could always see through her projections.*

The projection looked up at him, sheepish. "I'm fine, okay? You can go now."

Marcus sighed. He knew better. Wordlessly, he turned, closed the door and opened the third stall on the left.

There sat the real Sallie.

Her makeup was smeared beneath bloodshot eyes, with fresh tears still slipping down her cheeks. She scowled at him, her voice thick with both anger and embarrassment. "What are you doing in the ladies' room?! Does being the Guide to the Goddesses mean you can barge in here too?!"

"No," Marcus said, his voice softer than ever as he crouched to meet her tear-streaked gaze. "I'm here because I'm worried about my friend someone I value very much."

Sallie scoffed and waved a hand. "Wrong stall," she muttered. "Go talk to her over there." Another weak attempt at deflection.

"I don't want to talk to a projection of you," he said gently. "I want to talk to you."

She clenched her fists. "NO!" she screamed. "GO AWAY!"

Marcus closed his eyes and exhaled slowly. He wasn't getting through. At last, he resigned, "Okay. Sister, I'm sorry about all of this." He rose to his feet and stepped back, letting the stall door close between them. Defeated, he turned toward the exit.

But before he could reach it, another projection of Sallie materialized in front of him, holding out a hand to stop him.

He turned.

The real Sallie had stepped out of the stall, wiping her cheeks with trembling fingers. Her voice was barely a whisper. "Why… didn't she like my gift?"

Without hesitation, Marcus crossed the space between them and wrapped her in a warm, steadying embrace. He had never seen her like this. Sallie who defied titles, who clashed regularly with her superiors in the many sects of the Order had always been a paragon of stubborn strength. Now, she was unraveling over something *as simple as a kite*.

But Marcus suspected it wasn't just about the gift. It was something deeper. Something about who Sallie was or what she wasn't. Something about the avatars and what they represented.

"Sallie," he said, voice quiet but firm. "I know you put your heart into that kite."

"Then why didn't she like it?" she asked, her voice fragile and uncertain.

Marcus sighed. "Sallie… she's fourteen. Do you remember what you were like at fourteen?"

"But," Sallie insisted, "she's a goddess on earth."

He frowned. *That wasn't right not really.* "I wouldn't call them goddesses," he said carefully. "They're avatars."

He loosened his arms and stepped back, watching her closely to be sure she was steady.

Sallie sniffled and wiped her nose with a tissue. "You're lucky," she muttered, tossing the tissue into the trash. "You get to be with them all the time. You get to be part of something bigger. Meanwhile, I'm stuck here, testing enchanted forks on trees and seeing what a healing blanket does to a rotten apple." She turned toward the mirror, gazing at her own reflection. Her voice was low, weighted with frustration. "The last day or so it was exhilarating. We were actually doing something. Helping the god…" she caught herself, "helping Regina save her family. I just… I want more of that."

Her makeup was smeared, her eyes red-rimmed and swollen, fresh tears still slipping down her cheeks.

Marcus exhaled. "Sallie, we *almost died*. If Hema had turned her attention on us, she would've torn us apart."

"But …"

"And we didn't save her family," he added, more gently. "Her father and brother are still missing. We don't know if they're alive."

Sallie fell silent.

Marcus softened. "Regina's incredible but she's still just a girl. She's facing a world she doesn't understand. She doesn't need reverence. She needs people who will *stand beside* her."

He thought of her silence after Apex Sanderlin. The way Fleurette Baudin's words had shaped her so easily. The way she'd held herself afterward. "She needs support, not followers who will put her on a pedestal."

Sallie stared into the mirror, her expression tight. Then she let out a long sigh. "I really messed this up, didn't I?"

Marcus smirked. "Nooo," he drawled sarcastically.

She shot him a look, but a tired smile tugged at her lips.

"Give me a minute," she said, straightening. "I just need to fix my face."

Marcus nodded and exited only to come face to face with a sister from the Cartographers' Conclave. Her brows lifted as she registered his presence.

"Sister," Marcus greeted, offering a polite nod before continuing out of the ladies restroom.

He returned to the workshop and found Regina standing in front of a chalkboard, deep in conversation with Sister Ingrid. The board now displayed a new kite design circular center, open core, skeletal frame connecting at four key points. Notes littered the margins.

"Brother Marcus!" Regina beamed, turning to him. "I was just talking to your friend, Sister Ingrid!"

"Yes, I see," Marcus replied, nodding to the other monk. "Sister, how are you?"

"Well, thank you. I was actually looking for you. But I was lucky enough to meet Miss Regina here." She gestured to the board. "She was just explaining her kite design. It's fascinating."

Marcus looked at the diagram, then at Regina who practically glowed with enthusiasm.

"It does look promising," he said.

Regina nodded eagerly. "The open center should reduce drag and help it catch updrafts better. I was thinking of a dual-string setup for extra control, but maybe I'll keep it simple..."

"Why not build both?" Marcus suggested. "You could test them side-by-side."

Regina lit up. "Yes! That's a perfect idea!" She turned toward the supply shelves. "I'll have to ask Sister Sallie if she has enough materials for two more kites..."

Sister Ingrid gave her a fond glance, then turned back to Marcus. "Brother Marcus, could we speak privately?"

He nodded. "Of course." He turned to Regina. "Miss Fournier, I'll step away a moment. You all, right?"

"Yes," she said, rummaging through the bins next to the chalkboards. "I'm fine."

Marcus and Sister Ingrid walked through the halls of the complex, making their way to her office. The room was familiar spacious, with a large window behind her desk offering a breathtaking view of Order Island at night. Beyond the glass, the mountainous wall encircling the island loomed, a silent guardian of their sanctuary.

Sister Ingrid took her seat behind the desk and gestured for Marcus to sit in the chair opposite her the one he'd grown used to during past meetings.

"Welcome back to Order Island," she said with a smile. "I read your report on your visit to the Laminaen main library." Her expression shifted. "And I wanted to discuss a few things."

Marcus nodded. "Yes, of course."

She leaned forward slightly. "I have to ask, what were you thinking, promising all the information we gathered about the conspiracy to the Aurorium Clan?"

Marcus exhaled. "I was caught between three impossible problems."

"Why don't you list them for me?" she said, her tone measured.

He pushed down the irritation that came with being questioned by a superior, especially a new one and complied.

"The first major problem was Sophie Griffin. As a Sentinel, she's not permitted to operate independently for long periods. If I hadn't come to an agreement with Apex Sanderlin, she would have demanded her return through formal channels." He paused. "Then there's Regina Fournier. Because her family was in service at the Luminous, they fall under the direct protection of Aurorium Laminae. That meant Apex Sanderlin could have taken Regina out of our custody completely, placing her within the Aurorium village."

He let the point settle before continuing.

"The final problem," he said, "is that the conspiracy is ahead of us. They already committed a massacre in Aurorium Granmark, most likely targeting Sophie Griffin a second time after their first attempt failed. Then there's Jules Fournier's kidnapping, which happened shortly after Regina came under our protection. And let's not forget the attempt on Annabelle Salazar's life when she arrived at Granmark." Marcus folded his hands. "With the Aurorium Clan's help, we might just gain the upper hand. Without them, we'll be at the conspiracy's mercy."

Sister Ingrid's expression darkened. "Like Brother Albert."

"Exactly." Marcus nodded grimly. "He thought he was watching them, but his death proves they were watching him first."

"A harsh assessment," she murmured.

"But a true one," Marcus said. He hesitated, then admitted, "I didn't realize how much I looked up to Brother Albert until he was gone. He should have seen the trap coming. Based on the accounts we received from Regina Fournier and Annabelle Salazar, he knew about the attack on Salazar early enough to send a letter to Miss Fournier a full week in advance, prompting her into action. But they still snuck up behind him."

Sister Ingrid tapped her fingers against the desk. "Duly noted," she said. "But I do have objections to your deal with Apex Sanderlin."

Marcus sighed but said nothing.

"First," she went on, "you made the agreement and then presented it to Fournier all wrapped up in a neat little bow. I understand that you didn't have the opportunity to consult the other three Avatars at the time, but I'd wager a week of kitchen duty that you never once *considered* asking for their input before making such a major decision."

Marcus remained silent, and that silence said enough.

She frowned. "Second, what assurance do you have that Apex Sanderlin won't release all our findings to the public? If the conspiracy realizes how close we are, they'll have time to prepare a trap for you and the Avatars." She folded her hands. "Or worse how do you know the Laminae Aurorium isn't involved in the conspiracy?"

Marcus tilted his head.

"I know we think of the Aurorium Clan as incorruptible," she continued. "And that may be true of the organization. But individuals? Individuals can be very different."

"The fact that they accepted the deal including the pass for the Stormfang crew is proof they aren't directly involved with the conspiracy," Marcus countered. "If they were part of it, they wouldn't need our information. Apex Sanderlin may have approved of us keeping Fournier and Griffin, but I can't imagine she would've allowed free passage for the Stormfang crew unless she truly wanted what we had."

"I remember reading that in your report," Sister Ingrid mused. "So that part of your deal it was a test of her true motives?"

"Not entirely," Marcus admitted. "Considering how quickly things escalated after we left Order Island, I think we're going to need better protection than anonymity can provide."

She arched a brow. "You're planning to use the Stormfang for transportation?"

"I plan to suggest it to the Avatars," Marcus corrected. "If we can determine our next move. There's still too much information to sort through before they can form any kind of strategy." He leaned back in his chair. "I'm going to read through Brother Albert's last journal. Maybe it'll help me figure out how to sift through everything he left behind."

Sister Ingrid was quiet for a moment. Then she asked, "Have you ever considered why he kept so much information?"

Marcus shrugged. "He was thorough. He collected anything he thought might be useful."

She gave him a knowing look. "What if I told you there was another reason?"

Marcus narrowed his eyes. "And what reason would that be?"

Sister Ingrid studied him for a beat before replying, "I'll leave that for you to figure out when you're ready. I'll only say this there is a reason."

She leaned back, smoothly shifting the subject. "Now, what exactly was that situation with your friend, Sister Sallie?"

Marcus hesitated. "Sister Sallie was…" He trailed off, reluctant to say anything that might damage her reputation.

"Let me guess," Sister Ingrid interjected. "She thought that if she gained the approval of an avatar a person she sees as a goddess on earth she could escape her mundane duties and find something more exciting?" A smirk touched her lips. "How close am I?"

Marcus sighed. "Oddly accurate." He narrowed his eyes. "How did you know?"

"I did my homework on your friend when you became the Guide. You two are very close," Sister Ingrid said simply. "She put herself in the position she finds herself in. And before you ask, I will not bring her into our fold."

Marcus frowned, choosing his next words carefully. "What if I chose her as my first assistant?"

"I'd try to talk you out of it," she said without hesitation. "And if that didn't work, I'd overrule you."

Marcus blinked, caught off guard by her swift, unwavering response.

"You care about her," Sister Ingrid went on. "Which is why you likely don't see what I see. Sallie is brilliant, one of the best minds in the Order of Saint Lorraine. But she takes shortcuts. She refuses to acknowledge her mistakes, and that's too dangerous a flaw."

Marcus thought back to Sallie's stories her failed assignments, her clashes with authority. He had always dismissed them as signs of being strong-willed, unwilling to back down when she believed she was right. "It's true she can be intimidating, and many of her former managers have struggled with her. But doesn't that say more about their leadership than about her?"

"If it were just one manager or even two, I might agree," Sister Ingrid said evenly. "But when every superior says the same thing, the problem isn't with the leadership. The problem is with the monk."

She opened a drawer and pulled out a stack of papers, placing them on the desk between them. "These are formal complaints I've received from her current supervisor." She picked up the first sheet and scanned it. "Brother Thaddeus reports: '*Sister Sallie claimed that she was tasked by the Guide Marcus*,'" she glanced up, "he spelled your last name wrong, but you're the only Guide, so I know he meant you, *to stop her assigned work and prepare for an immediate trip to the Luminous in Laminae. When asked when she would return, she reportedly said something along the lines of I'll be back when the Avatar is done with me.*"

Sister Ingrid lowered the paper and met Marcus's gaze. "Is that how it happened?"

Marcus remained silent, sifting through his memories.

"Allow me to continue." She picked up the second sheet. "Another complaint states: *The Guide instructed Sister Sallie to craft a kite for the avatar instead of completing her assigned research.*" She set the paper down and folded her hands. "Brother Thaddeus specified he wouldn't have objected, except that she had already been absent for two days after traveling to the Luminous." She gave Marcus a pointed look. "Did you ask her to make Regina a kite?"

Marcus exhaled. "I did not."

Sister Ingrid nodded, unsurprised. "Sallie is too clever for her own good. She may grow into a renowned member of the Order, but she's lost sight of her purpose. Our duty is to serve the Order first."

She returned the papers to the drawer and shut it with a decisive click. "That being said, your report makes it clear that Sister Sallie's contributions were invaluable to the success of your mission. Because of that, I will take responsibility for her transgressions…*this time.*" She leaned back, lacing her fingers together. "But from now on, you are not to assign her any tasks that interfere with her official duties under her supervising monks."

Marcus nodded. "I understand. I'll speak with her."

Sister Ingrid studied him for a moment. "Would you like me to handle it?"

"No," Marcus said firmly. "I will handle it."

[-----◉-----]

After dinner in the cafeteria, Lisa wandered toward the gardens on one of Order Island's smaller islets. This particular islet hosted a massive greenhouse, which covered most of the land. She half-expected to be shooed away upon entering, but instead, the monks finishing their evening tasks greeted her with inviting yet quiet nods and welcomed her inside.

One of them, Brother Dennis, lingered to show her around.

The greenhouse was divided into four sections. The front held their tools pitchforks, shovels, hand spades, watering cans, and pruning shears all neatly arranged for easy access. The second section featured a horseshoe-shaped collection of pots, each nurturing a different fruit tree. The third section, filling half the open space inside the horseshoe, was dedicated to tomato and cucumber plants. The fourth mirrored the third but focused on lettuce and potatoes.

"We use ceiling baskets to transport tools and collect harvested produce," Brother Dennis explained, pointing to the woven baskets suspended overhead. They glided along tracks stretching from the entrance to the far wall a simple but remarkably efficient system.

"Wow," Lisa murmured, her eyes tracing the ceiling tracks. "That is ingenious. I have never seen anything like it."

"Surely Verdantia has greenhouses?" Brother Dennis asked with a smile.

"We do," Lisa said, "but nothing this size or this efficient." She glanced around again, clearly impressed. "How did you manage all this?"

"Our biggest expense is food," Brother Dennis said, sweeping his hand toward the crops. "To offset it, we built multiple greenhouses like this to grow our own fruits and vegetables." He paused. "We also keep livestock, though not as much as we'd like. If we could be fully self-sufficient, we wouldn't need to buy anything from other kingdoms."

Lisa's mind clicked into business mode. "I am sure Verdantia would offer you a discount if you signed an exclusive trade agreement with us."

Brother Dennis chuckled. "We used to have a deal like that with Verdantia. But when your kingdom changed its currency exchange laws, we had to renegotiate. Now, we source food and livestock from Stoneridge, Magitekopolis, and the Umbrathorn Empire instead."

Lisa furrowed her brow, recalling when her father had explained Verdantia's recent economic shift. The kingdom had begun accepting only Harvest Crowns as legal tender, finding it too burdensome to convert transactions into the universal Seven Kingdom Coin. "I remember that," she said. "but how did that change affect your trade with us?"

Brother Dennis hesitated. "I'm not entirely sure… something about additional fees, I think."

Lisa didn't press further. Instead, she turned her attention to the neat rows of crops, stopping beside the tomato plants and gently inspecting their large, vibrant fruits.

"What kind of magic do you use to get them this big?" she asked.

"We actually don't use magic to enhance our plants," Brother Dennis replied. "We don't have enough mages to sustain magical agriculture at this scale. But some of our monks in Magitekopolis and the Umbrathorn Empire discovered new fertilization techniques that don't rely on magic. After some trial and error, we developed our own methods to boost crop yields. With any luck, we'll perfect the process and share it with the Seven Kingdoms."

Lisa's eyes widened. "You are growing these without magic?" she asked, stunned. "I would love to bring your techniques back to Verdantia. Our farmers could really use this."

Brother Dennis shook his head gently. "I'm afraid I have to refuse."

Lisa blinked. "Why?"

"Our policy is to distribute knowledge equally among the Seven Kingdoms," Brother Dennis explained. "If we gave this technique exclusively to Verdantia, it could create an imbalance one kingdom gaining an advantage over the others."

Lisa frowned. "I do not see how better farming methods would be an *imbalance*. Would it not just make food more accessible for everyone?"

Brother Dennis stopped and turned to face her. "Think of it this way," he said. "Let's say we share this technology with a kingdom like Islewind, which has never been a major agricultural producer." He gestured toward the rows of plants as he spoke. "If they suddenly became self-sufficient or better yet, exporters they could disrupt the entire agricultural economy."

Lisa followed his reasoning but still didn't quite see the problem. "So Islewind becomes a new competitor," she said. "How is that a bad thing?"

"It could shift the balance of power," Brother Dennis explained. "Verdantia is currently the leading producer of crops and livestock. If Islewind were to dethrone them, Verdantia might retaliate by cutting off access to other forms of knowledge. The Order depends on cooperation from all Seven Kingdoms for our historical records, scientific research, and mystical discoveries. If we were seen as favoring one kingdom over the others, it could have far-reaching consequences."

Lisa thought about that for a long moment. It was a different way of looking at things one her father had never taught her.

"So… you are saying knowledge has to be managed as carefully as trade information," she said slowly.

Brother Dennis nodded. "Exactly. We ensure progress doesn't come at the cost of stability."

Lisa glanced at the thriving plants once more, the weight of the conversation settling over her.

For the first time, she began to understand just how much the Order influenced the world, not just through history and magic, but through the choices they made about what knowledge to share… and what to withhold.

"I had not considered that," Lisa admitted as she followed Brother Dennis down the path. "So the Order must maintain good relationships with all Seven Kingdoms?"

"We do," he confirmed. "It's a two-way relationship. The Order wouldn't share the knowledge we gather with a kingdom that refuses to share its own discoveries with us, or one that fails to provide our monks with safety and freedom of movement."

Lisa glanced at a banana tree as they passed, admiring the large, ripening fruit. "Why would a kingdom agree to those terms?" she asked.

Brother Dennis smiled. "Because the Order is a fount of knowledge," he explained. "If a kingdom were to reject our accords, we would withhold all our findings from them, mystical, scientific, historical. Meanwhile, the other six kingdoms would continue receiving that knowledge, advancing while the outlier stagnates." He gestured toward the greenhouse around them. "No kingdom wants to be left behind in the race for knowledge."

Lisa considered his words, beginning to understand just how much influence the Order truly wielded, not through force, but through the careful control of information.

Chapter 20

After finishing his morning journal entry, Marcus made his way to the cafeteria. He collected his breakfast oatmeal with fruit, two slices of buttered toast, and a cup of coffee before scanning the seating area for Sister Sallie, and she was nowhere in sight. Frowning slightly, he took his usual seat in the middle of the row of tables along the right side of the room. He glanced around once more, but still, she was absent. *Maybe she's just running late,* he thought, turning his attention to his meal.

As he ate, he rehearsed how he would approach their conversation. He needed to make sure she understood the importance of stepping back from the avatars, of regaining perspective on her service to the Order. More importantly, he promised himself he wouldn't let her take control of the conversation, *as she so often did.*

Halfway through his meal, just as he took a bite of toast, Sister Sallie appeared.

She sat down across from him, carrying a tray with a small bowl of fruit salad and a cup of tea. She looked tired.

"Good morning, Brother Marcus," she greeted.

"Good morning, Sister Sallie," Marcus replied warmly, offering a smile. "How was kite-making with Miss Regina?"

Sallie sighed, stirring her tea. "That girl can talk, she has so many ideas. By the time we actually finished a kite, it was midnight." She shook her head. "I don't know how you're going to handle four of her."

Marcus chuckled. "Each avatar has their own unique challenges. I just have to find a way to balance them all."

Sallie took a sip of her tea, then set it down and looked at him. "Marcus, can you apologize to Regina for me?"

Marcus raised an eyebrow. "Apologize for what?"

"I have a lot of backed-up work," she admitted. "I don't think I'll have time to work on her projects anytime soon."

Marcus blinked.

Just yesterday, she had been determined to embed herself in the avatars' work. Now, she is... *walking away?* The abrupt change didn't track in his mind. But he wasn't about to question it, not when this was exactly the outcome he had wanted.

"That's understandable," he said carefully. "I'm sure your shop has been missing you."

She smirked. "They were so lost without me."

Marcus smirked back. "What are you working on today?"

"Not sure yet," she replied, poking at a piece of fruit with her fork. "Probably need to finish my report on that shovel I was testing. Then maybe move on to something else from that tool kit."

Marcus nodded as he finished his toast, washing it down with the last of his coffee.

"What about you, Mr. Guide?" Sallie teased. "What's on your agenda?"

"Well," Marcus said, "I'll be spending the morning reading my predecessor's journal, hoping it holds some key to sorting through the mountain of papers he left behind. Meanwhile, the avatars and first assistant are blindly sifting through said mountain, trying to figure out our next move."

Sallie smirked. "Sounds so fun."

Marcus dabbed his mouth with his napkin, then checked his watch. 7:30 AM. He stood, picking up his tray. "Have a good day, Sister."

Just as he turned to leave, she spoke again.

"One thing …" she said

Marcus paused, glancing back. "Hmm?"

"Do you know a Sister Thomas?"

He frowned, thinking. He had met many monks over the years, but the name didn't ring a bell.

"Sorry," he said. "Can't say I do. Why do you ask?"

Sallie hesitated, then shrugged. "She said she knew you, that's all."

Marcus studied her for a moment, but she offered no further explanation.

"Have a good day, Brother," she said before casually popping a piece of cantaloupe into her mouth.

Marcus gave a small nod before heading out, thoughts of a *Sister Thomas* lingering in the back of his mind.

He left the cafeteria, placing his tray on the cleaning shelf before making his way toward the central circle. From there, he turned down the first hallway to the right, passing the magic archive room the same place he had shown Regina before their journey to Laminae.

Just beyond it, Marcus arrived at a door labeled *Journal Archives*. He pushed it open and stepped into a modest office. Chairs lined both sides of the room, all facing inward, while a tall counter rising halfway to the ceiling separated the public area from the archive storage. Behind the counter stood an older monk dressed in a white shirt emblazoned with a blue insignia, marking him as a member of the Guardians of Lore the sect responsible for maintaining the Order's records, including personal journals.

Marcus approached the counter and greeted the monk. "Good morning, Brother."

The monk smiled warmly. "Good morning, Brother. What can I do for you?"

"I'd like to read the last recorded journal of Brother Albert Thompson," Marcus requested with a polite nod.

The older man hummed in acknowledgment and flipped open a ledger, running his finger down a list of names. Then, suddenly, he stopped.

"Oh."

The shift in the monk's expression caught Marcus's attention.

The older man looked up. "What is your name, Brother?"

Marcus hesitated. He had read other monks' journals before, and it had always been as simple as asking. He tells him "Brother Marcus Igbinedon."

The monk reached into his desk, pulling out a separate sheet of paper and scanning another list. After a moment, he nodded.

"Ah, there you are." He met Marcus's gaze. "I'll bring it to you in the reading room, Brother."

Marcus nodded. "Thank you, Brother."

As the monk disappeared through a door at the back of the office, Marcus stepped out into the hallway and entered the adjacent room marked *Reading Room*.

Inside, he took a seat at one of four large tables, the silence settled around him like a heavy cloak.

His thoughts drifted. *Why had Sister Sallie asked about <u>Sister Thomas</u>? Could this enigmatic figure be the reason for her sudden change of heart?* It was unlike Sallie to shift gears so drastically, especially after how determined she had been just a day ago.

And then there was that name *Thomas*. A woman named Thomas was rare, uncommon enough that it stood out in his mind.

Ten minutes later, the back door of the reading room opened, and the older monk returned, carrying Brother Albert's journal in his hands.

Something about it was... different.

Marcus's eyes immediately locked onto the strange device securing the journal shut. He hadn't seen many sealed journals before, but the few he had encountered were only tied shut with simple strings. This was something else entirely.

"What is that?" Marcus asked.

The attendant placed the journal on the table. "As you know, this journal is on the restricted list," he explained. "This device ensures that only authorized individuals can access its contents, lest its information find its way into circulation where it shouldn't be."

With practiced ease, the monk unlocked the device, removing it from the journal's cover. Then, he slid the book across the table.

"When you're finished, return it directly to the attendant," he instructed.

Marcus nodded. "Understood, Brother." That is... a change in procedure. Normally, journals were simply left in the reading room, and an attendant would collect them periodically.

The monk gave a final nod before disappearing through the back door, leaving Marcus alone with the book.

The silence of the room pressed in around him.

Slowly, deliberately, he placed his hands on the worn cover of Brother Albert's journal. Then he opened it and began to read.

[-----❀-----]

After a brief morning study session on Earthbloom magic, Regina made her way to Brother Marcus's office.

She stepped through the double doors to find Sophie and Sister Alameda bent over a box with a striped blue and red mark on the corner of the box, sorting through its contents.

"Good morning!" Regina called out cheerfully.

"Morning," Sophie muttered without looking up.

Sister Alameda offered a warm smile. "Good morning, Miss Regina. How's your morning going?"

"Good," Regina replied brightly. "I think I learned a new Earthbloom spell. It mixes earth and water magic I can create a pond, maybe even a lake if I concentrate really hard."

295

"That's amazing!" Sister Alameda said with genuine admiration. "You only started Earthbloom studies a few days ago, right?"

"Yup," Regina said thoughtfully, tapping her chin. "The Order's library books are really well-written, so the harder parts were easier to grasp." She added, "Do you think Lisa could teach me Earthbloom sense?"

"It's worth asking," Sister Alameda shrugged. "Worst she can say is no."

"She can say a lot worse than no," Sophie said dryly, still focused on her papers.

Regina giggled while Sophie flipped to the next document, scanning intently.

It was a travel record showing Gretta leaving Islewind's port town of Pendleton for the Umbrathorn Empire a year ago, on June 13, 1909. The next document showed her staying three weeks at an inn in Umoja-Yama, a town in the province called Enmu no Tani, the Valley of Shadows, before booking passage on the ship *The Millennium*, bound for Verdantia.

After that, the trail went cold. Sophie frowned in frustration. She knew she had seen something else related to Gretta from that time but couldn't recall it. She realized she needed to map these findings out.

"Sister Alameda," she said suddenly, "can we get some chalkboards? It's hard to keep track of all this."

"I'm sure we can find some," Sister Alameda replied. "Let's go see."

They left the room, leaving Regina alone with the files.

Curious, Regina pulled out an overflowing folder and carried it to a nearby table. She flipped it open.

The first page was a black-and-white photograph of Machana-witch Isabella, standing alone on a ship's deck, wrapped in a heavy cloak.

The next document was a travel receipt for a woman named Jane Anderson.

At the bottom was a handwritten note: *Jane Anderson = Isabella Morales.*

Regina raised an eyebrow, so Isabella had been traveling under an alias.

The record showed she boarded the *Moonbeam Dancer* in Verdantia on June 20, 1909, arriving in Islewind's port city of Cretia nine days later.

The next document was a transport log a coach driver's statement given to a monk of the Order. The driver claimed a blue-haired woman named *Jalice Simmons* hired him, requesting transport to Ardnot.

Regina skimmed ahead.

Several pages contained reports detailing sightings of Isabella in Ardnot. Regina immediately recognized the handwriting it matched the letter Brother Albert had sent her. These were *his* notes.

According to Brother Albert's reports, Isabella had been seen at a local tavern multiple times over three weeks. She never stayed overnight, suggesting she lodged elsewhere possibly with co-conspirators.

Albert noted nothing unusual had occurred in Ardnot no major political or criminal activity leading him to wonder if Isabella was simply on vacation or sabbatical.

However, later in his investigation, he had spotted Isabella himself.

She hadn't noticed him. She ate her meals in silence, barely interacting with anyone. A few sailors approached her likely seeking company but a few sharp words, or perhaps the sight of her mechanical forearm and hand, were enough to drive them off.

Albert followed her.

He was certain Isabella could end his life if she noticed him so he ensured to keep from being noticed following her.

Regina swallowed, gripping the paper's edges as she read on.

Albert trailed Isabella out of the city into Islewind's forests.

She traveled to an ancient temple belonging to a dead faith: the Cult of the Fallen Star.

Albert watched as Isabella used her mechanical constructs to restore the temple's decayed architecture. The walls were covered with hieroglyphs and writings in an ancient Centegrin dialect, a language Albert didn't understand. He recorded as many symbols as possible in his journal for later study.

For two days, he observed her, until he was discovered. The shadow witch Mage arrived to assist Isabella. The moment Albert realized he'd been spotted; he fled only to be pursued by a horde of bloodthirsty shadow beasts.

He barely escaped with his life. According to his notes, sunlight dispelled the beasts on contact. As he ran, he heard a little girl's voice calling after him, urging him to return. Albert knew it was a trap. He did not turn back. Shortly after he took the first ship back to Order Island.

Regina slowly closed the folder, exhaling.

"Maybe it has something to do with that temple in Islewind," she muttered.

A voice interrupted her thoughts.

"What temple?"

Regina nearly jumped.

She turned to see Annabelle sitting across the table, flipping through her own papers.

"Annabelle! When did you get here?" Regina asked, startled.

"Ten minutes ago. I spoke to ye when I gots here," Annabelle replied, surprised.

Regina blinked. "Wait what?"

"Ye even asked me how me evening was," Annabelle said, raising an eyebrow.

Regina frowned. "I did?"

Annabelle nodded.

"Oh... sorry," Regina admitted sheepishly. "I guess I was too focused on reading. Sometimes I respond without really listening. My dad hates when I do that." She asked, "Can you tell me again?"

Annabelle smirked. "Aye, well, I'm only telling me story once." She returned to her documents, scanning shipping receipts related to a large, heavy crate sent to Stoneridge.

Regina placed her folder on the "Maybe" pile they had started yesterday.

Then, reaching into the box again, she pulled out the last folder.

As she turned to walk back to the table, the double doors creaked open behind her.

"Helloooo!" Lisa sang as she strolled into the room, her voice lilting like a melody. She beamed at the two avatar girls already buried in their work. "How many crops are we going to reap today?" she added, quoting a well-known Verdantian poem.

"Hi!" Regina responded cheerfully.

Annabelle, barely glancing up from her pile of papers, snorted. "No crops, princess. Just paperwork." She flipped to the next document a formal announcement stating that Prince Thaddaeus of the Umbrathorn Empire had died at sea when his diplomatic vessel sank before reaching Stoneridge.

Lisa set her purse on the table. "It is a saying, Annabelle," she clarified, rolling her eyes as she peered into the now empty document box. Without hesitation, she grabbed the discarded box and tossed it onto the growing pile near the door. Scanning the hallway, she selected a new box this one marked with a solid red stripe on the corner. It was small, but as soon as she lifted it, she nearly buckled under its weight.

"By the harvest!" she muttered, shifting her grip to cradle it like an oversized, very heavy baby. With a grunt, she heaved it onto the main table, where it landed with a thud.

Regina eagerly stepped closer, curious about the new box.

As Lisa openned the lid, Regina seized the opportunity to ask, "Lisa, can you teach me how to use Earthbloom sense?"

Lisa, focused on opening the box, barely registered the question. "What?"

"I can already form Earthbloom spells, but I can't get them to interact with plants, earth, and water," Regina explained. "But the book says I need to use Earthbloom sense to get them to execute."

Lisa finally looked up. "Oh."

A beat of silence.

Then Lisa's expression hardened. "You should not be messing around with Earthbloom magic. It's harder to master than those books make it seem."

Regina shook her head. "I almost have it figured out," she insisted. "This morning, I even created a spell that fuses earth and water magic."

To demonstrate, she lifted a hand and channeled mana through her fingertip. Carefully, she traced two joined circles in the air one brown, one blue.

Around the brown circle, she inscribed runes: Pit, Dig, Hollow, Open, Smooth.

Around the blue circle, she added: Lake, Fill, Rush, Water, Sparkling.

Holding her finger at the center point, she stabilized the spell, keeping it from executing.

"See?" she said proudly. "I've got this much figured out."

Lisa's eyes widened, a cold wave of anger surged through her.

The sight of Regina forming an Earthbloom spell a magic that wasn't meant for her made Lisa's stomach turn. A deep, visceral outrage exploded inside her, stronger than she could control. Without thinking she struck.

Her hand, charged with mana, slapped Regina's hand away from the spell. The sudden disruption caused a sharp backlash, shattering the spell circles into flickering fragments of energy.

With her other hand, she shoved Regina hard in the chest.

Regina gasped as a searing bolt of pain shot through her hands and ran down her forearms from the mana backlash. She barely had time to register it before her back slammed against the floor with a heavy thud.

Her glasses tumbled from her face, landing just out of reach.

Dazed, she blinked up at Lisa her vision blurred, but the intensity of Lisa's rage was erupting.

Lisa was furious. "YOU STAY AWAY FROM MY MAGIC! IT IS NOT FOR YO…"

She could not finish her admonition. A fist crashed into her nose like a stone hurled from a catapult. The impact sent Lisa reeling backward onto the floor.

Stunned, she clutched her face, her nose throbbing with pain.

Through the haze, she saw Annabelle standing over her, furious, orange hair wild, fists clenched tight. The pirate's voice was low and dangerous.

"Say whatever ye want, princess," Annabelle growled. "But ye keep yer hands to yerself."

Lisa touched her upper lip warm and wet with blood. Fury surged inside her. "What do you know?!" Lisa snapped, glaring up. "You cannot even use magic!"

Annabelle's fingers tightened around the pirate coin amulet at her neck. "Ye wanna to see me magic?" she whispered darkly.

Lisa's stomach twisted. The eyes of the skull glowed faintly between Annabelle's fingers, Lisa could not be sure, but it looks like her eyes turned as black as coal.

For the first time since that night with Brother Albert, Lisa felt fear washing over her. Her gaze darted around the room, searching for a way out only to land on Regina, still on the ground, tears streamed down the silver-haired girl's face. Lisa's breath caught in her throat. A deep sickness churned inside her, like she'd swallowed something rotten.

Annabelle noticed Lisa's change. She exhaled slowly and loosened her grip on the amulet and closed her eyes. Then, she turned her back "Nay," she muttered to herself. "Yer not worth the effort." Her eyes turned back to normal but now burned daggers at Lisa.

The double doors swung open.

Sophie entered, struggling under the weight of a large wooden chalkboard.

"Alright, I got ..." She stopped mid-step, taking in the scene.

Lisa lay on the floor, blood on her lip.

Regina sat dazed, eyes full of hurt.

Annabelle stood tense, fists still clenched.

Sophie dropped her end of the chalkboard with a thud.

"...What happened here?" she demanded.

No one answered.

Regina grabbed her glasses from the floor, shoved them onto her face, and ran out the back door.

"Regina!" Annabelle called after her, rushing to follow.

Lisa sat frozen, staring at the empty space Regina left behind. Her stomach twisted tighter than ever.

Annabelle jogged down the hallway, her boots echoing sharply against the stone floor as she searched for Regina. The hurried footsteps behind her had faded, leaving only silence in their wake.

[----- ⚓ -----]

"Regina, girlie, where'd ye go?!?" she called, glancing into open doorways and peering cautiously around corners.

She halted when she spotted a man in black trousers and a white shirt bearing the insignia of the Order. Without hesitation, she stepped directly in front of him.

"Oi, monk! Ye seen a girl with silver hair run past here?"

The man blinked, startled, shifting uneasily. "A... silver girl?"

Annabelle huffed. "Aye, a girl with silver hair," she repeated, raising her hand to Regina's height. "'bout this tall. Wearin' glasses."

The monk hesitated. "Sorry, miss, I don't know what you're talking about," he mumbled, then hurried away.

Annabelle scoffed. "Aye, you go that way and report back to me." She called after him, shaking her head. "Regina, girl! I'm sendin' out a search party! We are going to find ye!"

She pressed on, scanning every corner until a faint, muffled crying caught her attention. Following the sound, she turned a corner and froze.

Regina curled up against the wall, arms wrapped tightly around her knees, her shoulders trembling.

Annabelle crouched beside her. "Why're ye crying? She hit ye, missy?"

Regina sniffled, shaking her head. "I... I always mess everything up." Her voice cracked as fresh tears spilled down her cheeks.

Annabelle frowned, struggling to understand why it mattered so much to Regina that Lisa, the princess, liked her. That kind of need for approval was foreign to Annabelle, like a language without words for water or the sea, but to Regina, it meant everything.

With an awkward pat, Annabelle placed a hand on her shoulder. "Ye don't need no one's approval. Especially not the princess'."

Regina hesitated, wiping her nose. "What?"

"Come on," Annabelle scoffed. "She's probably just mad yer better at her magic than her."

"You think so?"

"Obviously." Annabelle plopped down beside her. "Hell, you even managed to learn me magic, and that isn't easy, let me tell you."

Regina giggled, wisely keeping silent about Annabelle's struggles with her own Maelstrom Mastery.

"I bet ye could learn the copper's magic in, what? A day? Two at most?" Annabelle nudged her shoulder playfully. "If ye take yer time."

Regina chuckled, pulling off her glasses to wipe her tears with a worn handkerchief. She glanced down at it, fingers tracing the fabric. "This was Brother Albert's. He really liked all of us."

"Aye" Annabelle agreed. "He was a good one."

Regina's expression softened. "I think Marcus really misses him."

Annabelle tilted her head. "What makes ye say that?"

"When he talks about him, he stops mid-sentence and closes his eyes like he's apologizing to him." Regina let out a shaky breath. "My dad used to do the same when he talked about my mom, after she died."

Annabelle was quiet for a moment. She hadn't noticed that about Marcus. It made her wonder how much Regina saw but never says aloud. She made a mental note to play cards with her silver-haired friend later to see just how sharp she really was.

Regina took a deep breath and straightened her posture. "We should probably get back to work."

"Nay" Annabelle waved her off. "Let's sit here and talk about how much we don't like the Copper now."

Regina smiled. "I like Sophie."

"What? Why?" Annabelle looked appalled. "She always acts like a plank o' wood. It's like those coppers aren't allowed to have fun or nothin'!"

Regina shrugged. "They are. I met Apex Sanderlin, and she told me she likes to have fun, she goes fishing every week with her husband."

Annabelle scoffed. "Bah! Fishin' is a job. That's like sayin' She cleared her throat and switched to her *proper voice*. "I like to sweep for fun, and sometimes even mop."

Regina burst into laughter. Annabelle made her feel so happy her shoulders relaxed.

Chapter 21

As Marcus read through Brother Albert's final journal, he uncovered secrets his late mentor had never shared. Among them was a network of guard sentries Albert had cultivated across nearly all the Seven Kingdoms, paid with food, drink, and sometimes coin. One particular guard commander from Opulentia received direct payments, which puzzled Marcus, monks of the Order rarely used their own money. That meant Brother Albert must have been filing those expenses with Sister Ingrid. The thought of Albert justifying these transactions to her made Marcus smirk.

One entry stood out. Brother Albert wrote about a guard named Blanco Harris, whose reports were consistently vague or misleading seemingly designed to confuse rather than inform. What struck Marcus as odd was that Harris sent reports from multiple kingdoms. While immigration was common, Marcus had never heard of a crown-appointed guard serving in more than one kingdom. That alone raised his suspicions.

As he continued reading, Marcus came across an entry from two years prior, detailing Brother Albert's trip to Verdantia to gather information on Lisa. Since she was away at boarding school in Laminae, Albert had used his time to explore the countryside. He described discovering a hidden gully, untouched and unseen by passersby a small valley with a babbling brook, ringed by trees, its banks covered in clusters of blue flowers with scattered red blossoms.

Brother Albert's descriptions painted the scene vividly: he had sat beneath a tree, resting from the long journey, when a leopard emerged from the foliage, drank from the brook, and slipped away without noticing him. Moments later, a hawk swooped down, snatching a small creature perhaps a chipmunk or squirrel. Unlike the leopard, the hawk locked eyes with Albert, let out a cry, and ascended into the canopy with its prey. Uneasy at the encounter, Albert left soon after, unwilling to risk another predator crossing his path.

The following day's entry recounted a meeting with Commerce Minister David Azules In the Verdantian capital of Vendura. The minister had been surprisingly cooperative, providing Albert with invoices that revealed off-schedule shipments of livestock and produce to various kingdoms, always to different, seemingly unrelated locations. With Azules' help, Albert began mapping what he believed to be the conspiracy's base camps.

Then, unexpectedly, the journal ended.

Marcus stared at the last entry, confused. The book was only two-thirds full. Normally, a monk would write until the last page, unless, as Marcus himself had recently experienced, they were reassigned to another sect. Otherwise, their journal would be packed with knowledge and observations. Yet Brother Albert had chosen to close it early, without explanation.

Flipping through the blank pages, Marcus found nothing. No hidden notes, no unfinished thoughts—just the standard closing entry every monk wrote when retiring a journal:

Journal Entry: August 9th, 1908

I, Brother Albert Thompson, hereby close this journal and commit it to the archives of the Order of Saint Lorraine, to be preserved for all time.

Marcus frowned. Why had Albert ended his journal so abruptly? Had Sister Ingrid instructed him to do so? Was there something in these pages he wanted to ensure his successor, *Marcus* found quickly? Or had he simply switched to a different type of journal?

No matter how he looked at it, Marcus couldn't shake the feeling that he was missing something. It was as if Albert were trying to tell him something important, but the words were just out of reach.

Leaning back in his chair, Marcus let out a slow breath and ran a hand through his hair. He flipped through random pages again, hoping for some overlooked clue, but nothing stood out.

A sharp knock at the door pulled him from his thoughts.

Sister Alameda stepped inside the reading room. "Brother Marcus, there has been an incident with the avatars."

Marcus immediately shut the journal. "What happened?"

"There was some kind of fight involving the Ladies Nozaki, Fournier, and Salazar," she explained. "I wasn't there, and I can't find any of them for an explanation."

Marcus stood, rolling his shoulders. "Well then, Sister," he said, "let's go figure this one out."

After returning the journal to the attendant, Marcus and Sister Alameda made their way back to his office, only to find Sophie Griffin standing at the chalkboard, writing with swift, deliberate strokes. The boxes that had once cluttered the space were gone, replaced by the board now covered in a structured timeline.

At the top, a capital "G" sat enclosed in a circle, with a horizontal line extending from it across the left side of the board. Several vertical lines intersected the timeline, each labeled with month and year combinations starting with Jan 08, followed by Feb 08, continuing all the way to Apr 10, the present month.

"Miss Griffin," Marcus greeted, stepping closer to examine the board. "Have you seen the other three Avatars?" He paused, then nodded at her work. "Nice job, by the way. This makes tracking the conspiracy's movements a lot clearer."

"Thanks," Sophie replied, tapping the chalk against the board. "It's called a time and agent map. I learned it in investigator training."

"If we could focus on the situation at hand," Sister Alameda interjected, folding her arms.

"Yes, Sister, you're right," Marcus said with a nod. Turning back to Sophie, he repeated, "Have you seen the others?"

"Not since they ran out."

Marcus frowned, rubbing his chin. "Where could they have gone?" He glanced at Sister Alameda. "Would you mind waiting here in case they return? I have an idea where to find at least one of them."

"Of course, Brother," Sister Alameda agreed.

Leaving the office, Marcus strode down the hall, heading toward the center of the complex. If the Avatars had scattered, there was one place they were all familiar with— the temple of the goddesses.

[-----✝-----]

Upon reaching the main foyer, he scanned the area but saw no sign of them. He opened the double doors to the Goddess Clock, but the room was empty. Frowning, he moved to the adjacent utility room, checking inside. Empty. He continued into the observation room. Still no one.

He exhaled through his nose, frustrated. He had been certain he'd find at least one of them here.

Then another thought struck him.

He retraced his steps to the utility room but, instead of heading back inside, he slipped through the side door leading to an outdoor stairway. The stairs ascended to the garden above the temple one of the first places he had spoken with the avatars before they had communed with their goddesses.

At the top, Marcus found her

Lisa Nozaki.

She stood at the stone railing, leaning forward slightly, her gaze fixed on the vast seascape beyond the mountain walls of Order Island. The sky was a brilliant blue, streaked with wispy clouds. Below, ships moved across the water, some sailing left to right, others in opposite directions, a few at diagonal paths that overlapped before diverging again.

Lisa's long green hair rippled in the wind, a few strands breaking away from the rest, following their own course.

"Beautiful view, isn't it?" Marcus said, approaching gently.

Lisa glanced over her shoulder at him but didn't straighten up. Instead, she turned back to the horizon.

"Is this where you tell me I messed up?" she asked flatly.

Marcus considered his response before answering. "I don't think that's my place." He stepped beside her at the railing. "I came to check if you're okay. I'd like to know what happened, but if you don't think it's my place to know, I'll accept that."

Lisa blinked. She wasn't used to this. Adults usually told her what was right and wrong lectured her, corrected her. But Marcus wasn't doing that. Testing him, she asked, "What if I told you the pirate girl punched me, and she should be punished?"

Marcus remained calm. "As I am your servant, I am also Miss Salazar's servant," he explained. "It isn't my place to punish her just as it isn't my place to punish you." He looked at her, his voice steady. "I do, however, feel responsible for helping the two of you resolve your differences. If that isn't possible, I would consider it a failure on my part. Nothing more."

Lisa studied him, searching his expression for any sign of favoritism. Finding none, she asked, "So what if I punched her back?"

"I would counsel against it," Marcus said, "but my response wouldn't change."

Lisa sighed. She had wanted him to take her side, and when he didn't, disappointment flickered in her eyes. Turning fully toward him, she leaned her back against the railing, arms crossed. She watched Marcus for a long moment. His face was composed, calm, dedicated to his role. That kind of certainty unsettled her. She felt a swirling discomfort in her stomach from earlier and frowned.

"Do you want to know what the Goddess told me to do?" she asked suddenly.

Marcus smiled. "Only if you want to tell me. Your conversation with the goddess was yours alone to know and share."

Lisa hesitated, then exhaled. "She told me to make the world a better place," she admitted, shaking her head. "How am I supposed to do that?"

Marcus thought for a moment before answering. "I don't know how you should do it," he admitted, "but I do believe you can."

Lisa scoffed, rolling her eyes. "You have to say that. It's probably in your job description or something."

"I can assure you, Miss Nozaki, that it is not one of my duties to lie to you," Marcus replied evenly. He studied her for a moment before adding, "But I do feel obligated to ask why did Miss Salazar punch you?"

Lisa huffed. "That stupid Regina," she muttered. "She was messing around with my Earthbloom magic and drew an advanced circle that I know she wasn't ready for." She hesitated, carefully omitting how she had pushed Regina down and screamed at her. "So, I used a mana surge to break her circle, and the next thing I knew, that… pirate girl punched me in the face."

Marcus listened carefully, noting what she wasn't saying. Annabelle Salazar was no angel, but he had never known her to strike someone unprovoked. Without pressing too hard, he asked, "Did Miss Salazar say anything before or after she hit you?"

Lisa shrugged, looking away. "She did, but you know how she talks in that pirate nonsense. I couldn't understand a word."

Marcus raised an eyebrow. "Patois," he corrected. "The privateers' language is called Patois."

Lisa waved him off. "Yes, so it is," she said dismissively, her gaze shifting downward.

Marcus decided to take a different approach. "And what about Miss Fournier?" he asked. "What has she done to earn your ire?"

Lisa's lip curled. "Her magic," she said with venom. "It's just wrong. Why can't she just pick one magic system and stick with it?"

"Because that isn't how her magic works," Marcus explained patiently. "Asking her to stop shifting her magic would be like someone telling you to only use the plant manipulation aspect of Earthbloom and nothing else."

Lisa scoffed. "Whatever," she muttered, crossing her arms and looking away.

Marcus sighed. "I'm sorry, Miss Lisa," he said. "Brother Albert would have known exactly what to say to help you understand your situation. But sadly, I feel like I lack his wisdom."

Lisa looked at him, smirking. "It is okay," she said, her tone deceptively sweet. "I am sure you are doing your best."

Marcus felt the sting of her words like a slap. He might not have Brother Albert's gift for persuasion, but this needed to be said.

"Miss Nozaki," he said, his voice steady, "I fear your behavior will isolate you from the other avatars something I'm sure would disappoint the Green Goddess of Unity." He raised a hand before she could protest. "I don't know what it's like to be chosen by a goddess to represent her will on earth. But I do understand what it means to bear a great duty that is thrust upon you. And if you continue down this path, I worry you may become vulnerable to the conspiracy's designs."

Lisa considered his words but struggled to grasp what he meant by *continuing the way she is*. "You forget, Brother Marcus," she said, straightening her posture, "the goddess chose me."

"Yes, Miss Lisa, that is true," Marcus acknowledged. Then he tilted his head thoughtfully. "But have you considered that the goddesses also chose Annabelle, Regina, and Sophie?" He let the question hang between them. "How does your disapproval of Annabelle's behavior or Regina's magic fit with that course of logic?"

Lisa opened her mouth to respond but found no argument. Cornered by logic, she muttered in frustration, "It does not matter."

Marcus exhaled softly. "To be honest, Miss Lisa, I am worried about you," he admitted. "The goddesses also chose Gretta and Isabella who have now become servants of the conspiracy. That alone proves that even the chosen are not beyond corruption. You could be in danger."

Lisa tensed at the warning.

Before turning to leave, Marcus added, "I suggest you find a way to clear the air with the other avatars for no reason other than your own safety."

As he walked away, Lisa stared after him, chewing on his words. Then she called out, "Do not worry, Brother Marcus. I am as solid as an elephant."

Marcus glanced back, a slight smile tugging at his lips. "I'm sure you are, Miss Lisa," he said before descending the stairs.

As Marcus made his way back through the temple, her words lingered.

An elephant...

He entered the Goddess Clock room, his eyes sweeping over the sacred statues. His gaze landed on the Silver Goddess and her fox, then the Violet Goddess and her badger, and finally, the Orange Goddess and her lion monkey. Then he stopped in front of the Green Goddess her sacred animal, *the elephant*, a symbol of unity and strength. Marcus turned, scanning the room again. His eyes locked onto the Blue Goddess and her sacred hawk. The statue stood tall, the bird poised as if surveying him. Nearby, the Brown Goddess loomed, her leopard crouched low, muscles tense, ready to pounce at the slightest wrong move.

He closed his eyes.

And suddenly, he saw it. Albert's journal. The gully. The hawk and the leopard. It hit him with the clarity of a spoken message over morning coffee.

"That's it," Marcus whispered aloud.

He spun on his heel and hurried out of the temple, back toward Albert's old office.

[----- ⬙ -----]

Lisa remained on the terrace, letting the cool breeze wash over her as she took in the vast, ever-moving sea. Ships drifted steadily across the horizon, their sails billowing as they followed unseen currents. Overhead, birds swooped gracefully above the waves, occasionally diving into the water to snatch unsuspecting fish. Below them, creatures great and small leapt from the surface, suspended for a fleeting moment before vanishing back into the depths.

Then, she felt something.

A familiar presence.

Lisa turned happy to see Unity again.

Standing before her, instead, was the elephant Erisol, wrapped in a faint green glow.

Her gaze flicked around, searching the terrace for another figure. Unity would understand what Lisa was trying to say, she would *take her side*. So where is she?

"She isn't here," Erisol's voice told her. But it didn't come in sound. Instead, it resonated inside her mind, just like the guardian of the Goddess's chamber had spoken.

Lisa narrowed her eyes, and asked "Why are you here?"

Erisol's reply wasn't spoken aloud, but she felt the weight of his words settle deep in her bones. *"You are failing the Goddess."*

Lisa stiffened. "What?!?" she snapped, her voice sharp in the still air. "Listen, the Goddess chose me, and you need to accept that."

"The Goddess chose you because the avatars will need to unify to face the threat coming for you all." Erisol interrupted, his voice steady, unwavering. "But instead of fostering unity, you are sowing division."

Lisa clenched her fists. "You do not know what you are talking about," she argued, refusing to respond in magical speech. "I am only holding things to the proper standard how they are supposed to be."

Erisol was silent for a moment. Then, in the Goddess's own voice, he repeated her words:

Unity is about accepting everyone as they are, not how you want them to be.

Lisa's breath caught. Hearing her Goddess's voice turned the words into something undeniable. The sharp criticism cut deeper than she wanted to admit.

She squared her shoulders, unwilling to concede so easily. "I had to do something," she insisted. "Regina was going to lose control of that spell. She could have caused havoc in the building!"

"You know that is not true," Erisol said simply. "And your attack on her left her more afraid of you than she already was."

Lisa scoffed. "She is not afraid of me," she dismissed, though her voice lacked conviction.

A flicker of movement caught her eye. A sleek silver fox danced around Erisol's feet, its luminous fur shimmering in the light. The elephant extended his trunk in greeting, then gently lifted the fox onto his back.

"Allow me to show you," Erisol said.

And with those words, the world around Lisa began to shift.

Without warning, Lisa's surroundings shifted.

She opened her eyes, disoriented, and found herself standing in Brother Marcus's office. Boxes were stacked around the room, and across from her stood... herself.

Her green hair cascaded down her back, the image so vivid it sent a chill through her, she knows from what she is seeing she must be inside Regina's body. **Regina** excitedly traced a combination spell circle in the air, eager to show what she had learned. With a single, fluid motion, she carefully drew two interlocking circles, their centers joining seamlessly. Around the Earth circle, she inscribed the runes: *Pit, Dig, Hollow, Open,* and *Smooth.* The Water circle bore the symbols *Lake, Fill, Rush, Water,* and *Sparkling.*

She held her finger at the midpoint of the spell, ready to dispel it once she finished explaining.

"See?" **Regina's** voice was bright with enthusiasm. "I've figured out this much!"

Lisa, her other self, turned slowly to face **Regina**, anger flaring in all her features. Without hesitation, she unleashed a surge of mana, disrupting the spell circles entirely. Before Regina could react, Lisa shoved her to the ground, screaming:

"YOU STAY AWAY FROM MY MAGIC! IT IS NOT FOR YO…"

306

Before she could finish, Annabelle vaulted over the table. Her first connected cleanly with Lisa's nose in a brutal punch.

The privateer glared down at her, voice cold and warning. "Say what ye want, princess, but ye keep yer hands to yerself."

Lisa felt the scene hit her like a blow to the chest. A wave of sorrow crashed over her, deeper than she expected. She had been so furious, but now, watching it unfold from the other side, all she could feel was **Regina's** shock and hurt.

Then the pain struck.

Her hands and forearms burned as if seared by lightning. A sharp, electric agony pulsed through her fingers and up her arms. She recognized it immediately mana backlash. The cost of violently disrupting a delicate spell.

Regina scrambled to her feet, eyes shining with unshed tears. Without another word, she turned and bolted through the office's back door, running through winding hallways.

"Regina!" Annabelle called after her, taking a step forward.

But **Regina** didn't stop.

One tought played in her mind *I always mess everything up.*

The scene dissolved into nothingness.

Lisa's eyes fluttered open as the trance shattered like ripples across still water.

The experience was unlike anything she had ever felt before. She hadn't merely seen through Regina's silver eyes, she had felt everything the girl experienced. Every thought and emotion lay exposed, the fear that she would never find her father or her little brother, anxiety that she had caused Lisa to *Hate* her, it was all pressing heavily against her chest.

She blinked and turned to Erisol, his emerald form calm and steady. The silver fox perched on his back stirred, shaking as though wet. It let out a series of chittering sounds before Erisol gently lowered it to the ground.

The fox glanced once more at both, chittered again this time at Lisa then vanished.

Erisol's deep voice echoed inside her mind. "You have seen how your actions fracture the unity of your group." His knowing eyes met hers. "I wonder is that why the Goddess of Unity chose you?"

Lisa felt a sting behind her eyes as the weight of his words settled. A tear slid down her cheek, and she wiped it away. "I see," she whispered, voice tight.

Erisol stepped closer, towering yet calm. When he spoke again, it was in the Goddess's voice.

"You are the glue that will hold the avatars together in the trying times to come."

Lisa swallowed hard and nodded silently, accepting both the truth and the burden.

Erisol held her gaze a moment longer, then began to fade. "There is work to be done."

And then he was gone.

Lisa took a deep breath, brushing away her last tears. A new resolve settled within her.

She had to make this right.

Not for herself.

For them.

For her new sisterhood.

Because she **is** the Avatar of Unity

Chapter 22

Annabelle sprinted onto the beach, sand kicking up behind her as she ran toward Smitty, who lounged in his usual chair with a book in one hand. Captain Kidd sat beside him, reclining with arms crossed.

"Sorry, first mate," Annabelle called out, slightly out of breath. "Had some difficulties to take care of."

Smitty didn't glance up. "No worries. Ye aren't that late." He held out an open hand.

Annabelle sighed and dropped her last ten-coin into his palm. "I'll get you that other five real quick-like."

Smitty glanced at the coins, unimpressed. "The price is fifteen, Belle."

"I know, I just" She huffed. "don't have the last five right now, but I'll get it to you soon."

"Then we'll pick up lessons soon." Smitty said, unfazed.

Captain Kidd interjected, "Come on, Smitty. Can't she owe ye the last five?"

Smitty shot the captain a disapproving look. "The deal was fifteen coin per session."

Kidd raised an eyebrow at Annabelle. "Fifteen? Belle, didn't I teach ye how to negotiate?"

"Cap'n," Annabelle protested, "that was the negotiation. He said no five or six times."

Kidd frowned at Smitty.

Smitty, unfazed, met the captain's stare. "Ever tried teachin' her magic? Fifteen coin is a steal."

Kidd laughed. "Smitty, she's an avatar. She's good for it. Can't she just pay you later?"

"Nope." Smitty said flatly. "Sets a bad precedent. But you can cover the five."

Kidd sighed, pulled a five-coin piece from his pocket, and flipped it to Smitty, who caught it midair with practiced ease.

"You drive a hard bargain, me First Mate."

"Aye, Cap'n." Smitty grinned as he pocketed the coin.

Annabelle beamed. "Thanks, Cap'n!"

"Thanks, hell!" Kidd shot back, pointing a stern finger. "Ye better get me that five coin back, Belle."

Annabelle straightened, hand on her chest, and said in her best *proper voice*, "I will gladly repay your kindness as soon as I can."

"Oi, see that ye do," Kidd grumbled.

Smitty checked his pocket watch. "I don't mind ye two chattin' but ye wastin' me time now."

Annabelle turned to Kidd, curiosity sparking. "Cap'n, why are ye here?"

"Smitty told me ye were workin' hard to learn magic. Had to see it for meself." He grinned sharply, clapping his hands. "Oi, get out there and get to magicin'!"

"Aye, Cap'n!" Annabelle kicked off her boots and ran toward the shoreline. The cool seawater lapped at her ankles as she glanced back. "I figured out the current spell!"

"Oh aye? Let's see." Smitty said, leaning forward.

Annabelle smirked mischievously.

"If ye spray me, I'm leaving," Smitty warned.

Annabelle scowled. "I wouldn't dream of it, teacher," she said in her best proper voice before switching back to her usual tone. "Now watch this."

With one smooth motion just as the Copper had shown her, she fired twin jets of seawater from her hands in opposite directions, strong and steady.

Smitty's eyes widened slightly, impressed despite himself. He lifted a hand, signaling her to stop.

Annabelle cut the spell and planted her hands on her hips, standing triumphantly in the water, chest puffed out.

"That spell was too strong, Belle," Smitty said. "Have ye not learned how to scale yer mana release?"

"I have!" Annabelle insisted. "Regina told me all about it."

Smitty smirked. "Regina, ye say? Alright then why don't ye tell me what *Regina* told ye?"

Annabelle cleared her throat, putting on her best *proper voice*. "When you cast a spell, you channel mana from inside your body to a point in your body or space in the world, like a spell circle. Mana scaling is the practice of portioning your mana into a casting, so you don't give too much to a spell."

Smitty nodded approvingly. "If you had ten fingers of mana," he said, holding up both hands, "how many fingers did ye put into that spell just now?"

Annabelle frowned, tapping her chin. "Half a finger, I think." She paused, reconsidering. "aye, half a finger."

Smitty stared at her like she'd just claimed the sky was green. "Ye can't be serious," he said, incredulous.

He turned toward the water and raised his open palm. A surge of mana pulsed through him as a powerful jet erupted from his hand, shooting straight out over the ocean, unbroken, for a solid five or six paces before it finally arced down. When the spell ended, he exhaled, clearly showing the strain.

"That," he said after a beat, "was me spell at five fingers." He turned back to Annabelle, his gaze sharp. "Now ye do it. Five fingers."

Annabelle considered the instruction carefully. Taking a deep breath, she extended her hands parallel to the shoreline, fingers spread wide. She pictured her mana as ten fingers and deliberately funneled five of them into the spell, releasing it all at once.

A surge of energy rushed through her, and twin jets of water erupted from her palms, each nearly as tall as she was. The spouts shot forward, carving through the air for what she guessed was twelve paces before arcing down into the sea. She held the spell steady, pushing through the resistance, forcing out every last drop of water until it naturally dissipated.

As she finished, she clenched her fists, breathing heavily. Her hands ached, muscles stiff, as if she'd been holding onto something unbearably heavy for too long. She turned back to Smitty, eyes wide with excitement and was met with an expression of pure disbelief.

"Bugger," Smitty muttered, rubbing the back of his head. "That was five fingers?!? Ye sure?"

"Aye" Annabelle said proudly, though fatigue from the mana drain crept in.

Smitty exhaled sharply, shaking his head. "Well, that changes things a bit."

Annabelle grinned. "So, I have gots me a lot of mana! Why's that such a bad thing?"

"Tis a bad thing," Smitty said flatly, "because ye got a lot of mana but no control." He folded his arms. "Which means we're going to have to focus on your mana control."

Annabelle groaned. "Ugh, why? That stuff is so boring."

Smitty's eyes narrowed. "Look, missy," he said, his tone sharp, "ye got too much power at your disposal to be lackin' control. The sea is a powerful mistress. If ye don't learn to tame her, she'll sweep ye and the entire crew away."

Annabelle shrank slightly under his scrutiny.

Smitty crossed his arms. "And I, personally, don't want to die just cause ye were playin' around with your magic and not listening."

"...Okay," Annabelle muttered, looking down.

Smitty wasn't having it. "Good. Now, ye are going to do the wave spell," he said, jabbing a finger toward the water. "And I don't want to hear another word out ye 'bout it."

[-----✝-----]

As Marcus walked down the hallway leading to his office, he noticed a member of the Cartographers' Conclave rummaging through a box marked with a white symbol. Puzzled, Marcus approached the monk.

"Excuse me, brother," he said as he neared. "Can I offer you any assistance?"

The monk flinched at the unexpected voice and quickly turned around. "Oh!" He paused to compose himself before saying, "I saw these boxes blocking the hallway and wanted to figure out who to speak to about getting them moved."

"You're in luck brother," Marcus replied. "These boxes are part of my duties. I apologize for the obstruction I'll have them cleared out as soon as possible."

The monk gave Marcus an inquisitive look. "If I may ask, brother, what duties involve reports about marriage announcements and property transactions?"

Marcus smiled. "I am the guide to the avatars," he said, extending a hand. "Brother Marcus Igbinedion. And you are?"

The other monk took his hand in a firm shake. "Brother Barnabas Henry, Cartographers' Conclave," he introduced himself with a grin. "Everyone calls me Brother Barney."

"Nice to meet you, Brother Barney," Marcus said before releasing his grip. "And don't worry I'll have these boxes out of your way soon. My apologies for the inconvenience."

"No need to apologize," Brother Barney assured him. He gestured toward the half-filled hallway, the stacks of boxes reaching down toward the offices. "If you need help sifting through all of this, I'd be happy to allocate a few monks to assist."

Marcus took note of the office at the far end of the corridor the *Mapmakers' Union*, the conclave responsible for meticulously reproducing and updating maps. He had once considered applying there but ultimately decided it wouldn't be fulfilling enough for him.

"No need, brother," Marcus replied. "When the avatars put their minds to something, they often accomplish the miraculous."

Brother Barney chuckled. "I'd love to see that for myself."

310

Marcus felt the same unease creeping in that he had experienced with Sister Sallie. Instinctively, he chose to shut the conversation down. "Maybe some other time, brother," he said, offering a polite nod before heading through the double doors into his office.

Inside, Sophie was at the chalkboard, stepping back to examine her diagram. Sister Alameda sat nearby, sifting through the maybe pile, likely searching for useful details to feed to Miss Griffin.

"How goes the search?" Marcus asked.

"It's going," Sophie said, tapping the chalk against her palm. "It looks like the conspiracy's witches, traveled to Islewind and Verdantia at different times. Isabella and Mage were actually in Verdantia together two years ago."

Marcus moved to study the diagram. The board had been carefully arranged, with a timeline running horizontally across it. Each of the four witches was represented by an initial inside a circle:

G for Gretta

I for Isabella

M for Mage

H for Hema, the Blood Witch

Lines stretched from each name across the board, intersected by vertical markers representing months and years. At points where the witches had been sighted, a circle denoted the location.

Marcus followed the patterns, noting key movements:

Gretta first appeared in Cantubo, Islewind, in February 1908. She didn't resurface until August 1908 in Ferryville, Verdantia. Over the next year, she was spotted in various locations across Stoneridge, Hargrave (June 1909), Peakson (July 1909), and Nearoth (September 1909). In February 1910, she was confirmed in Granmark, Opulentia, and again in April 1910 during the massacre at Aurorium Granmark.

Isabella had been seen as early as January 1908 in Kuraihime Mura, a village in the Umbrathorn Empire. She wasn't spotted again until May 1908 in Misty Harbor, Islewind. From there, her movements became more frequent, Rivondale, Stoneridge (August 1908), Gastone, Stoneridge (October 1908), and Ferryville, Verdantia (December 1908). By March 1909, she had traveled to Cattlehurst, Verdantia, then Anderson (June 1909), where she boarded the Moonbeam Dancer—marked by an arrow—heading toward Islewind. In July 1909, she arrived in Ardnot. Her next confirmed appearance was the Aurorium Granmark massacre in April 1910.

Mage was more difficult to track. She surfaced in Bakersville, Laminae (April 1908), then in Serin, Opulentia (August 1908). After disappearing for several months, she was next seen in January 1909 in Spellforge, Magitekopolis. Her movements after that were sporadic, Ardnot (July 1909), Cudot, Islewind (January 1910), Granmark, Opulentia (February 1910), Karunda, Umbrathorn Empire, and Rivondale, Stoneridge (March 1910). She was confirmed in Granmark, Opulentia, during the April 1910 attacks on Salazar.

Hema, the Blood Witch, had fewer recorded appearances. She was first seen in Martindale, Verdantia, in March 1908. Her next sighting was in September 1908 at Tideport, Islewind. She remained hidden until April 1909, when she appeared in Kirisame, Umbrathorn Empire. By July 1909, she surfaced in Peakson, Stoneridge, followed by another sighting in Coralton, Islewind, in September 1909.

Marcus traced the lines on the timeline, absorbing the unsettling pattern. It was as if the witches' movements were pieces of a calculated plan falling into place.

The final piece clicked into position.

Hema had been confirmed in April 1910 in Laminae coinciding with the attack on The Luminous and the abduction of Regina Fournier's family.

Marcus stepped back and scanned the diagram again. "The witches have surfaced across multiple kingdoms over the past few years," he observed.

Sophie tapped the chalk against the board. "Yes, but we assume they all traveled for the same purpose." She frowned. "We still don't know what that purpose is."

Sister Alameda added, "That's our greatest problem. Without understanding their goal, it's difficult to connect their movements to their actions."

Marcus nodded. "Exactly. Assuming too much about their intentions risks costly mistakes."

A quiet weight settled in the room as they considered this.

Sister Alameda turned to Marcus. "Brother Marcus, were you able to resolve the altercation between Ladies Nozaki, Fournier, and Salazar?"

Marcus shook his head. "No. I found only Miss Nozaki. From what she said, there was an argument between her and Miss Fournier, and Miss Salazar intervened to defend Miss Fournier."

"That fits," Sophie said. "Regina doesn't realize she's annoying Lisa with all her … energy."

Sister Alameda frowned. "Isn't adapting different magic how Miss Fournier learns? Why would Lisa take offense?"

Sophie shrugged. "You'd have to ask her." She returned to her work, uninterested in the reasoning.

Sister Alameda looked at Marcus, hoping for more insight. He hesitated, then shifted the topic.

"I found something in Brother Albert's last journal." Marcus faced her. "The markings on the boxes are a color code. Blue and red indicate purchases linked to the conspiracy and the witches. Solid blue likely marks confirmed witch sightings. White boxes seem to hold unimportant records."

Sophie raised an eyebrow. "You believe?"

"Yes," Marcus admitted. "Brother Albert's journal was … puzzling."

Sister Alameda tilted her head. "How so? Journals are usually straightforward."

"For one, he stopped after using only two-thirds of the pages," Marcus explained. "His last entries weren't in his usual style. It was like he was burying a message, one only someone working with the avatars would recognize."

Sophie crossed her arms. "Why go through all that trouble to hide a message about boxes? Why not write it plainly?"

"Yes," Sister Alameda agreed. "Who was he hiding it from? Only Order monks read those journals."

Marcus sighed. "It's more complex. When I accessed the archives, Brother Albert's journal was restricted. I could only read it because I'm the current guide to the avatars. He must have known only select Order members would see it."

Sister Alameda folded her arms. "But why hide information already restricted? Why not use the Order's resources?"

Marcus stared at the timeline, pondering. The question echoed in his mind. *Why?*

Why keep this knowledge locked away in chaotic piles of unsorted documents? If he had help, he could have made something as clear as Sophie's diagram.

Why hoard the information like a hermit?

Marcus recalled Sister Ingrid's question from earlier. *"Have you ever considered why he kept so much information?"*

Suddenly, it clicked.

His heart pounded as realization crashed over him while staring at the board.

"By the Goddess," Marcus whispered. He snapped his head up. "We need to lock the doors."

Sister Alameda blinked. "Why Brother?"

Marcus pointed at the timeline. "Brother Albert kept those boxes in that chaotic mess because he realized the conspiracy was somehow siphoning information from the Order." His finger traced the dates. "Look here late 1908 into early 1909. Almost all their movements disappear. That must be when they realized he was tracking them. That's when they started watching him back."

Sophie's eyes widened.

Sister Alameda's expression darkened. "How could the conspiracy get information from the Order? We control everything that leaves these walls."

Marcus clenched his jaw. "Not tightly enough."

"That's easy," Sophie said, crossing her arms. "It's corruption. You see it in banks and cash organizations all the time. They have teams of trusted employees to count, store, and transport their coins. Most even have retention teams to prevent theft." She paused. "And yet, some still skim money no matter how well paid or harsh the punishment."

Sister Alameda frowned. "No disrespect, Miss Griffin, but we are not bank employees. We dedicate our lives to the Order."

"That's true," Marcus said, leaning forward, "but that doesn't make us immune to the same weaknesses. We work hard to earn comfortable positions only to eventually fall victim to the boredom of safety."

Sister Alameda considered this. "Even if true, how would the conspiracy reach an Order monk to recruit them? Few monks serve both in the world and on Order Island." She hesitated. "And those who do don't usually suffer from that *Boredom from safety.*"

"That's not how it works," Sophie said, shaking her head. "When a criminal group or a government turns someone into a spy, they don't go for those with direct access. They look for someone whose normal duties already involve passing information. Then that person finds someone else inside the Order to dig up exactly what's needed."

Marcus's gaze drifted toward the door as a thought struck him. His encounter with Brother Barney replayed sharply in his mind.

His expression darkened.

"Yes, Miss Griffin," he murmured. "You may be right."

[----- ✿ -----]

Regina sat alone in the cafeteria, cradling a warm cup of coffee and nibbling at a buttery croissant the taste of it reminded her of mommy June's breakfasts back home, before her father forbade her from drinking coffee.

The room was quiet, almost meditative, occupied by only a few Order monks. It wasn't a regular mealtime. These people must've come early for their own reasons.

She stared out through the glass windows into the hallway. Monks in flowing, colorful clothes drifted past like schools of fish gliding through clear water.

Then she saw her.

Lisa.

313

Her long green hair trailed behind her like strands of seaweed caught in a current. Regina's stomach clenched. She sank deeper into her seat, praying Lisa wasn't searching for her.

But Lisa stopped. Right outside the window. Her eyes scanned the room, a flicker of that familiar sensation sparking in her chest that strange, unexplainable awareness that one of the other avatar girls was close.

Oh no. She is looking for me. Regina thought as she held her breath.

Then their eyes met.

Lisa waved, smiling gently before hurrying toward the entrance.

Regina thought about running, but there was only one door unless she wanted to vault the service counter and flee through the kitchen, she was not exactly sure she could do that.

So, she stayed in her seat.

Took another sip of coffee. Swallowed the last bite of her croissant. And braced herself.

Lisa entered, her steps confident. "Hello Regina," she said softly. "I was looking everywhere for you."

Regina stared into her cup. "Sorry. I just wanted some coffee."

She hesitated, then she looked up and met Lisa's gaze. She decides to give Lisa what she wants "I'm sorry. I won't use Earthbloom magic anymore. I didn't know how much it meant to you and I don't want to fight."

Lisa blinked. That wasn't what she expected. A tightness rose in her throat. A tear threatened but she blinked it away. "No," she said gently. "That would not make me happy, it would actually make me so very sad." Her voice dropped. "I am sorry I yelled at you. I should not have done that."

Regina frowned. "You pushed me down. You're leaving that part out."

Lisa winced. "You are right. I should not have done that either. I was angry... and I did not treat you well. You deserved better." She admitted

Regina studied her carefully. "Why were you so mad? I was just doing what you told me."

Lisa blinked. "What I told you?"

Regina nodded. "You said, *I'd like to see how fast you can learn my Earthbloom magic.* Don't you remember?"

Lisa's expression grew distant. "No... when did I say that?"

"When we were walking on the docks in Granmark," Regina said quietly. "After Brother Albert..."

Lisa's chest tightened. That whole night was a blur. Pain, exhaustion, grief... so much she never dealt with. "You remembered that?"

Regina nodded. "I have a good memory. My father says it's like a camera crystal." Her voice softened. "I really want to find my father. Before something bad happens to him."

Lisa saw the fear flicker across Regina's face and decided to shift the conversation to something she could offer instead.

"I would be honored to help you with Earthbloom magic," she said, voice warm. "You said you had a question earlier?"

Regina perked up. "Yes! I was reading this Earthbloom spellbook, and it kept referencing something called *Earthbloom sense.* But it didn't explain what it was. Do you know?"

314

Lisa smirked. "I do; it was one of the first spells I learned when I began studying under Mistress Hestra."

Regina perked up. "So, what is it?"

"It is a passive spell that lets you detect life around you."

Regina's brow furrowed. "Passive spell?" She leaned forward. "How do you cast a passive spell?"

Lisa paused, searching her memory. "It has been so long... I've forgotten how it works. I just remember it working for me one day."

She closed her eyes, recalling her early training under Mistress Hestra the long hours planting flowers, sitting in dirt pits, trying to connect with the Earth before she was even allowed to draw spell circles. She remembered her mistress's frustration when she failed to grasp Earthbloom Sense. Once, she'd even made Lisa stuff dirt in her underwear, insisting she needed to feel her bond with Mother Earth in the most direct way possible.

Lisa let out a small sigh. "My mistress always told me to open myself up and connect my mana with the mana of the Earth."

"Like mana channeling?" Regina asked, finishing her coffee.

"Sort of," Lisa said, tilting her head. "But it's more like drawing in just a little of Mother Earth's energy and using that bond to sense the life around me." She closed her eyes, listening to her Earthbloom Sense, searching for the right words to explain it.

"It feels like I'm holding hands with Mother Earth," she explained. "And she's showing me the light of every living thing nearby."

Regina listened closely, then shut her own eyes. She shaped her mana into the Earthbloom configuration, following Lisa's guidance. But she struggled. She didn't know how to draw in the Earth's energy, only how to push hers outward. Pulling, not pushing, felt unnatural.

Lisa opened her eyes and frowned as she watched Regina's mana swirl chaotically.

"No, not like that," Lisa said, stepping closer. "If you keep doing that, you will get mana backlash." She placed a calming hand on Regina's shoulder.

Regina kept her eyes closed, trying to hold her mana steady. "I'm searching for the Earth's energy... trying to touch it with my mana. How are you moving yours?"

"I am not moving my mana," Lisa said simply.

Regina frowned. That didn't make sense. She tried different patterns, different flows, nothing worked. Frustration mounted until she finally groaned and opened her eyes. "This is so hard!"

Lisa chuckled, her voice gentler now. "I remember how long it took me too. My mistress was furious. She yelled at me, made me sit in mud, even buried me in dirt..." She trailed off, shaking her head at the memory. "She kept screaming at me to try harder, but I never understood what she meant."

"She sounds really mean," Regina muttered.

Lisa nodded. "She was. I hated magic lessons with her. But my father insisted I keep learning from her said she was the best in the kingdom."

She looked at Regina thoughtfully. "Earthbloom Sense might take time. If you push too hard, you will only frustrate and hurt yourself." She exhaled. "Maybe we should get back to Brother Marcus' office and keep going through boxes."

Regina sighed. "Yeah... There are so many boxes."

"And so much paper," Lisa added. She remembered Unity's words and straightened her shoulders. "But Unity said I must find my path by following Brother Albert's footsteps." She held out her hand.

Regina took it without hesitation. "Change told me the same thing."

To her surprise, sharing what Change had told her with Lisa didn't feel wrong not like it had when she tried to talk to Sister Sallie. That realization made her smile.

Lisa felt Regina's warm hand in hers, and something inside her softened. A memory not her own, but Regina's flashed through her mind. She felt the fear, the humiliation, the pain of being shoved down.

Her throat tightened.

"I am so sorry I hit you," she said, her voice trembling with sincerity.

Regina blinked, startled by the rawness in Lisa's voice. Then she grinned. "It's okay. If it'll make you feel better, I can knock you down."

Lisa laughed, surprised and for the first time since their fight, the tension between them melted away.

Hand in hand, they left the cafeteria, heading toward Brother Marcus' office.

Chapter 23

Annabelle is exhausted, Smitty had pushed her harder than ever today, drilling two new spells into her until her limbs ached and her mana reserves were nearly depleted.

The first spell, *Whirlpool*, required her to manipulate water into a spiraling vortex capable of dragging objects or people beneath the surface. The second spell *The wave spell* allowed her to generate towering waves in still water, commanding their height, strength, and direction with precision.

Unlike when she first learned the *current* spell, Smitty hadn't given her the luxury of figuring things out at her own pace. This time, he had pushed relentlessly correcting her form, making her cast repeatedly until the spells became instinctive. He hadn't even let her rest between attempts until she got them right.

Now, her muscles burned, her magic felt drained, and all she wanted was a hot meal.

After training, Captain Kidd offered to escort her back to Brother Marcus' office. He waited as she changed out of her soaked, ragged training clothes into something more presentable. She left her jacket an old one of Captain Kidd's hanging in the closet before the two of them set off through the Order complex.

Annabelle led the way, head held high despite her exhaustion. "Ye'll see, Cap'n," they'll be lost without me," she declared confidently as they passed monks in the hallway.

"Oh, I bet." Captain Kidd replied, following close behind.

They turned a corner and entered a hallway cluttered with stacked boxes. Annabelle's gaze sharpened when she spotted a monk rummaging through one of them, a box marked with a white symbol in the corner. She stepped closer, peering over his shoulder.

"Oi, mate," she called. "Find anything interesting?"

The monk jumped, startled. "What's that?" he blurted, spinning around.

"Ye were looking through the box," she said, tilting her head. "Find anything good?"

She assumed Marcus had recruited help to sort through the endless piles of maps, invoices, reports, and papers. It made sense.

But then she saw his face. Fear flickered across his expression when he recognized her.

Without hesitation, he stammered, "I have to go, sorry; I have... responsibilities."

Then he turned and hurried off, walking as fast as he could without breaking into a run.

Annabelle and Captain Kidd watched him disappear around the corner in silence.

"Well," Captain Kidd said finally, "that was ... odd."

"Wonder what his problem is." Annabelle muttered, still watching the empty hallway. She shook her head then pushed open the double doors to Brother Marcus' office.

Inside, Sophie stood at the chalkboard, scribbling notes while Sister Alameda flipped through a folder. Brother Marcus sat nearby, alternating glances between a scrap of paper and a larger document, deep in concentration.

"It looks like Gretta was spotted in Creatia, Verdantia, staying at an inn in March of 1908," Sister Alameda called out, scanning the stack of papers in her hands.

Annabelle smirked as she sauntered fully into the room.

"Ye can all relax," she declared with dramatic flair. "I have returned from me crucial privateer duties, and now I am here to lead you through these here trying times."

Sophie didn't even look up. "Yeah, whatever," she muttered, tapping her chalk against the board. "Grab a folder and lead some information out of it."

"Oi!" Annabelle barked. "Is that any way to speak to your leader?"

"Leader?!?" Sophie scoffed. "Since when did we make you the leader?"

Annabelle crossed her arms. "I mean, it wasn't formal or nothing," she admitted. "But me natural leadership just rose above the rest of ye inexperienced girls, all clearly in need of real-world guidance."

Sophie rolled her eyes. "If I need guidance, I'll grab a map," she said. "They don't even let you steer your own ship."

Captain Kidd burst out laughing. "She's got you there, Belle."

Annabelle scowled in defeat and snatched up a folder.

Still chuckling, Captain Kidd turned to Brother Marcus. "Hey, Brother Marcus. Weird thing happened when we got here. Some Order monk was rummaging through yer boxes outside, but the second Belle said hello, the guy ran away like he owed us coin."

Marcus set his papers down. His thoughts immediately flew to Brother Barney.

"Was he wearing an amber and blue shirt? Brown hair?" Marcus asked.

Annabelle shook her head. "Nope. Orange and white shirt. Blonde."

Marcus frowned. *Orange and white.* That was the color of the Explorer's Guild. This was *not* Brother Barney.

"Did he give you a name?" Marcus pressed.

Captain Kidd shook his head. "Didn't say a word. Belle said hi, and he started babbling about 'responsibilities' before running off."

Marcus exchanged a glance with Sister Alameda. Her expression confirmed what he was already thinking, whoever that was, it wasn't the man he'd spoken to earlier.

"Excuse me," Marcus said, rising swiftly and setting down his papers.

He left the room and made his way down the hallway cluttered with boxes, heading for the office at the far end. When he reached the door, he knocked and tried the handle. Locked.

"Just a minute," a voice called from inside.

Marcus heard a chair scrape back, followed by approaching footsteps. The door creaked open to reveal a heavyset older monk with olive skin. His amber-and-blue uniform sleeves were rolled up, and his ink-stained forearms hinted at cartographic work. His expression barely concealed his irritation.

"How can I help you?" he asked, tone clipped but courteous.

"Apologies for interrupting, Brother," Marcus said with a nod. "I was looking for Brother Barney. He said he would be here."

The monk frowned. "Brother who?"

"Brother Barnabas Henry," Marcus clarified.

The monk shook his head slowly. "We have no monk by that name."

Marcus hesitated. "He did mention that he wasn't stationed here only that he was visiting on official duties," he said, trying to piece things together. "I'm sorry, Brother,

318

but we have no Barnabas Henry in our entire sect," the monk replied. "You must be mistaken."

Marcus kept his expression neutral, though his thoughts were already racing. "Apologies for the disturbance," he said. "Thank you for your time."

"Yes, yes. Thank you," the monk muttered before shutting the door and returning to his duties. His footsteps faded behind the closed door.

Marcus turned and headed back toward his office, his mind spiraling. *Brother Barney didn't exist?*

Someone had infiltrated Order Island under a false identity freely moving through the complex, gathering information, perhaps even manipulating what others knew.

We are not safe here.

Brother Albert's carefully compiled collection of his reports, sightings, and patterns had been secret for a reason. The sheer number of prying eyes made it impossible to know how much had already been compromised.

We must leave Order Island.

Marcus knew now that the Avatars could not continue their work here. They would need to take Albert's files and leave Order Island.

When Marcus returned to his office, he quickly scanned the room. Captain Kidd, Annabelle Salazar, Sophie Griffin, and Sister Alameda Ortega were still there. But Lisa Nozaki and Regina Fournier were absent.

Turning to Annabelle, who was buried in a folder she had just pulled from the latest box, he asked, "Miss Salazar, do you know where Miss Nozaki or Miss Fournier are? There's something important we need to discuss."

Annabelle barely looked up. "Nay. I haven't seen the princess since I popped her in the nose." She shrugged. "And I left Regina in the cafeteria when I was off to do... privateer things."

Sophie, flipping through a document, suddenly looked up. "You hit Lisa?" she asked, incredulous. "What is wrong with you?"

"Oi, copper!" Annabelle huffed. "She knocked Regina down for showing off her magic, so I stepped in."

Sophie's brow furrowed. "Wait she knocked Regina down?" She pressed her lips together, her expression unreadable as she silently questioned what she'd gotten herself involved in.

Marcus sighed. "We need to find them," he said. "There's something important we must discuss."

He turned to Sister Alameda. "Can you check the cafeteria and bring back Miss Fournier if she's still there? I left Miss Nozaki at the Temple of the Goddesses I'll start looking for her there."

"Where should I search?" Sophie asked unexpectedly.

Marcus blinked. He hadn't considered involving Sophie or Annabelle in the task.

"My apologies," he said. "That didn't occur to me."

Sister Alameda stepped in. "Miss Griffin, why don't you check the dormitories?" she suggested. "And Miss Salazar, you and Captain Kidd should remain here in case they return."

"Aye," Annabelle agreed, only just realizing how drained she felt after training. Staying put sounded like a good idea.

Sophie nodded. "Alright. If we don't find them, let's meet back here in thirty minutes to regroup."

"Good idea, Miss Griffin," Marcus said. "Alright. Let's go find Miss Nozaki and Miss Fournier."

Before anyone could move, Lisa and Regina entered the office hand in hand, giggling. They halted when they noticed all eyes fixed on them.

"What's going on?" Lisa asked, glancing around at the stares.

Marcus exhaled. "We were just about to come looking for you two," he said. "There's something important we need to discuss."

Annabelle, however, was focused on something else entirely. She pointed at their joined hands. "And what's all this, then?" she asked, gesturing between them.

"Lisa apologized for knocking me down," Regina said simply. "and we're friends now."

Sophie blinked. "Lisa apologized?!?" she asked, clearly stunned.

"Hey!" Lisa protested.

"Oi, princess," Annabelle teased, tilting her head. "Are ye feelin' alright?"

"You are all acting like I am some kind of monster," Lisa huffed.

"Well..." Sophie shrugged.

Lisa scowled, folding her arms. It was infuriating how easily they assumed the worst of her.

Regina, sensing the frustration building, stepped in gently. "Lisa, I don't think you're a monster," she said.

Lisa turned to her, her expression softening. "Thank you, Regina," she said sincerely. A small smile touched her lips. "You are such a good friend."

"If we could focus," Marcus interjected, his tone firm as he turned to the avatars. "There's a dangerous situation at hand one that requires the four of you to make a decision."

Sophie narrowed her eyes. "A decision about what, exactly?"

"As I mentioned earlier," Marcus began, "I believe Brother Albert suspected someone within the Order was giving information about him and you to the conspiracy. Today, we encountered two Order monks who had clearly taken steps to conceal their identities when discovered. That tells us this search through the records has exposed us. And that puts all of you at risk."

Lisa pulled out a chair and sat beside Sister Alameda. "How does the conspiracy having this information put us in danger?"

"They'd know exactly where we're heading," Sophie answered before Marcus could. "They could track us while we follow Brother Albert's clues, then ambush us when we're most vulnerable." She tapped a finger against the table. "We should guard this information until we're ready then burn it all."

"Or," Marcus countered, "we leave immediately and take it to Apex Sanderlin in Aurorium, Laminae."

Lisa folded her hands. "And how do we know Apex Sanderlin is not part of the conspiracy?"

"The first tenet of the Aurorium is *All for the Clan*" Sophie replied without hesitation. "In the Aurorium, corruption is betrayal, and traitors are dealt with swiftly."

"What does that mean?" Regina asked, looking around.

"'Tis the same among privateers," Annabelle explained. "Betray the ship, and you walk the plank."

"Aye" Captain Kidd nodded. "Death to all traitors."

Lisa tapped her chin, thinking. "So, we wait in Laminae while Apex Sanderlin goes through the documents?"

"No," Marcus said firmly. "If Apex Sanderlin lays eyes on Miss Griffin, she will have to demand her return to the Aurorium Clan."

Sophie stiffened. "Could I refuse?" she asked, though she already knew the answer and it already weighed heavy in her chest.

Marcus shook his head. "Unfortunately, no. The Aurorium places high value on its young members. The Order wouldn't have the authority to keep you from them." His gaze shifted to the crates of documents. "What I'm proposing is this: we sail aboard the *Stormfang* to Laminae, deliver the boxes to the Aurorium, and then continue on to Verdantia."

Annabelle raised an eyebrow. "Why sail to the Sacred Acres?"

Marcus gestured to the diagram Sophie had drawn on the chalkboard. "Because all four witches were sighted in the same region of Verdantia. I believe there's something significant there."

Lisa's face lit up. "And I get to go home," she said, her voice unusually bright. "And sleep in my own bed."

Captain Kidd leaned against the table, arms crossed. "So, Brother Marcus, let me get this straight: you want to ship all these boxes to Laminae and then drop these girls off in Verdantia?"

"To be honest, Captain, I'm looking to hire the *Stormfang* indefinitely," Marcus clarified. "Rather than paying to ship the cargo, I believe it's wiser to hire the entire vessel, since we don't know what lies ahead."

Captain Kidd stroked his chin. "Well, Brother Marcus, you'd have to pay by the day," he mused. "I'd quote you a fair price... but it's still a costly request."

Marcus didn't flinch. "According to the administration sect, the standard rate for ship hire is one hundred and eighty coins per day." He met Kidd's eyes. "Would that be acceptable to you?"

Annabelle noticed Kidd restraining a reaction. He continued stroking his chin, lost in thought.

Finally, he grinned. "Aye," he said. "and in a show of good faith, I'll even throw in Belle's magic lessons fer free." He gave Annabelle that charming smile of his with a sly wink.

Lisa perked up. "You were taking magic lessons?" she asked, clearly thrilled to have something to tease Annabelle about.

"Oi, princess!" Annabelle protested. "We're trying to make an important decision here!"

Regina turned to Marcus. "What decision do we need to make?"

Marcus folded his hands. "The decision is whether to deliver all of Brother Albert's files to the Aurorium Clan in Laminae and then travel to Snyder in Verdantia to uncover what he and the conspiracy were searching for." He paused. "Or... we stay here and continue our research risking that the conspiracy already has access to the same information and could target us again."

Lisa narrowed her eyes. "And what if we give them everything and the Aurorium cannot connect the dots?"

Sophie scoffed and shook her head at the question.

Marcus motioned to the chalkboard. "Given how Miss Griffin organized the data into this grid," he said, gesturing to Sophie's diagram, "I'm confident the Aurorium will find connections we may have already missed."

"In my experience," Sister Alameda added, "the Aurorium Clan is highly skilled at investigations of this kind while exposing corruption and conspiracies."

"Laminae is home of *The Investigators*," Sophie explained. "They specialize in complex cases. They're the best investigators in the Aurorium...maybe even the best in the world." She crossed her arms. "I say we send the files to Laminae."

"Me too," Regina agreed. "Apex Sanderlin was very smart."

"I vote we pay the *Stormfang* the one-hundred-and-eighty-coin daily rate as well," Annabelle chimed in.

Lisa and Sophie both scowled at her.

"I am going home!" Lisa said smugly as the realization rested in her mind.

Captain Kidd leaned forward, resting his palms on the table with a grin. "Welcome aboard the *Stormfang*. We're happy to have the six of you."

"Not six," Marcus corrected. "Sister Alameda will remain here."

Regina blinked. "She will?"

Sister Alameda gave a sympathetic nod. "Yes, sorry, girls. Only one of us can leave Order Island at a time," she explained. "And since Brother Marcus is your actual guide, it makes more sense for him to take the initial voyage with you."

"Okay," Regina said, accepting the decision with a small nod.

Captain Kidd straightened. "Well then, let me say that the *Stormfang* and her crew would be honored to welcome the five of you to our family." He swept his arm with theatrical flair before letting his grin sharpen slightly. "Brother Marcus about that deposit."

Marcus arched a brow. "I assume you would prefer the thirty-day standard?"

Captain Kidd nodded, slipping seamlessly into his charming salesman persona. "That would be best."

Marcus gave a knowing smirk. "There are a few things I must take care of before we depart," he said. "But you avatars should begin packing your things and preparing to board the *Stormfang*."

[-----✝-----]

Marcus and Sister Alameda sat across from Sister Ingrid's desk, waiting as she entered the room carrying her personal journal.

"My apologies for keeping you waiting," Sister Ingrid said as she took her seat. "I had to meet with the Administration division to finalize the payment for the *Stormfang*. Brother Alex was very surprised you agreed to pay so much to conscript the ship."

Marcus raised an eyebrow. "The going rate was one hundred eighty coins a day," he replied evenly.

Sister Alameda folded her hands in her lap. "That is the standard rate, Brother, but when a ship is hired for a longer period, the price usually drops." She tilted her head slightly. "Did you notice how happy Captain Kidd was to accept the contract?"

Marcus exhaled, realizing his mistake. "I did," he admitted. "But I assumed it was because he was eager to get back to work after being docked for some time with no real prospects on Order Island."

Sister Ingrid leaned forward, a knowing smile playing at her lips. "Brother Marcus, let this be a lesson in deal-making. In Laminae, you secured an excellent agreement with the Aurorium Clan because they had a pressing need you fulfilled with minimal effort. But pirates, especially captains, negotiate for their lives. They are master deal-makers. You must always be careful not to give away too much."

Marcus nodded. "I will take that lesson to heart, Sister."

Sister Ingrid regarded him with approval. "When are you planning to depart?"

"I spoke with Captain Lowe," Marcus replied. "His crew will need the rest of the day to prepare the ship and stow all of Brother Albert's boxes. We agreed to set sail tomorrow morning."

"Then I look forward to your last in-person report for a while," Sister Ingrid said. She clasped her hands together. "Before you and the avatars depart to walk the path of the goddesses, there is just one more thing you need to do."

Marcus frowned slightly, running through the mental checklist she had given him earlier. "What is that?"

"In the Order, we have a tradition," Sister Ingrid explained. "Whenever a guide is assigned to avatars, we take a photograph of them together and place it on the wall near the Temple of the Goddesses."

"Oh," Marcus said, blinking at the unexpected task. He hesitated for a moment, then nodded. "Alright... I will gather them."

Sister Ingrid leaned back in her chair and removed her glasses, studying him carefully. "Is something wrong, Brother? You seem... hesitant."

Marcus hesitated again, then sighed. "To be honest, a part of me still feels like Brother Albert is the avatars' actual guide. I keep thinking that I am just holding things together until he returns." He glanced at Sister Alameda. "No offense, Sister."

"None taken," Sister Alameda said with a knowing smile. "Keeping up with all four Avatars is quite the challenge."

Sister Ingrid exhaled, folding her glasses in her hands. "I understand why you feel that way, Brother Marcus. But I can assure you Brother Albert is not coming back."

She paused, her expression softening as she gathered her thoughts.

"He was the standard for guides," she continued. "He knew everything about the Avatars studied them, adapted his communication style to fit each of them, made sure he was exactly the guide they needed." A rare flicker of emotion crossed her face. "But you are their guide now. And Brother Albert chose you for a reason. Knowing your record, I am certain you are the guide they need."

Sister Alameda's head snapped toward Sister Ingrid, eyes narrowing. "Excuse me, he chose you?"

Sister Ingrid placed her glasses back on. "We will discuss that after the avatars depart," she said smoothly.

Marcus held Sister Ingrid's gaze for a long moment before exhaling slowly. "I will take your words to heart, Sister." He straightened his posture. "Where shall we take the photograph?"

"In the regular studio," Sister Ingrid replied calmly. "I suggest you do it today."

"I agree." Marcus turned toward Sister Alameda. "Sister, can you gather the Avatars and bring them to the studio?"

"Of course," Sister Alameda said with a nod.

[-----⚕-----]

Sister Alameda had gathered the four avatars into the photo studio within the Order complex. The room was divided into two sections, the front area served as a waiting space, complete with a table likely used for organizing subjects before their photographs were taken.

The four Avatars sat in chairs, waiting somewhat impatiently, while Sister Alameda stood at the back of the room behind the camera. She held an instruction book in her hands, glancing back and forth between the manual and the device, carefully familiarizing herself with its workings.

"Oi, where is Brother Marcus?!?" Annabelle suddenly exclaimed, breaking the silence.

"He is taking care of something," Regina replied calmly. "Sister Alameda already told us he would be here soon."

"Bah, a good servant wouldn't make ye wait." Annabelle muttered dismissively, slumping back into her chair.

A moment later, the door opened, and Marcus entered, holding a photograph in his hands.

"I apologize for keeping you waiting," he said.

"Oi, ye kept us waiting," Annabelle huffed. "Yer a bad servant."

Marcus sighed in mock disappointment, then motioned toward the camera set up. "Shall we, ladies?"

The group moved to the back of the room, standing in formation for the photograph. The four Avatars lined up in front of Marcus, who towered behind them. Lisa stood on the far left, Regina next to her, then Annabelle, and finally Sophie on the right.

"Miss Fournier, Miss Salazar," Marcus said, holding out the photograph. "Would you two hold this between you?"

"Sure," Regina said, taking the picture from him. She positioned it at the center, ensuring it was equally between herself and Annabelle.

Annabelle took hold of the other side and smirked. "Servants ain't supposed to ask fer favors," she quipped.

Marcus merely raised an eyebrow but said nothing.

"Alright, everyone, please smile." Sister Alameda instructed, raising a rod topped with a glowing crystal.

The five of them straightened up, offering their best attempts at smiles. The crystal atop Sister Alameda's rod emitted a flash of bright light, illuminating the room. A second later, she pressed a button on the camera, which responded with a loud click.

"That is done," Sister Alameda announced, signaling they could relax.

She pulled a wide cartridge from the camera, its edges silver, its center black, and placed it on the table beside her. Opening a drawer, she retrieved a single sheet of paper, roughly the same size as the cartridge. Carefully, she laid the paper on top of the cartridge and tapped it three times.

A soft glow surrounded the cartridge before light passed through it, transferring an image onto the paper.

Once the process was complete, Sister Alameda lifted the developed photograph, examining it briefly before nodding in approval. "This is a good picture," she said, handing it to Marcus.

Marcus took the photo, glancing at it carefully.

The four Avatars stood in front of him, their smiles slightly forced, while he stood behind them, his own expression just as artificial. But what caught his attention most was the smaller photograph at the center the one Regina and Annabelle had held up for the camera.

It was an old picture of Brother Albert, sitting in the very same studio. He wore a sardonically powerless expression complete with a smirk, holding up one hand in a shrug, as if silently saying, *well, here we find ourselves.*

Marcus couldn't help but smile.

"Yes, Sister," he said, still looking at the image. "This is a very good picture."

To Be Continued in Book 2…

Epilogue 1 – Sallie Young

Sister Sallie Young's Journal Entry – April 15, 1910

In collaboration with the Avatar of Change, Regina Fournier, we have designed and constructed a new type of kite. While preserving the traditional diamond shape, our design incorporates a circular opening at its center, allowing it to harness airflow in a manner that differs significantly from conventional kites.

This innovation could have broader applications beyond simple recreation. If adapted correctly, the principles behind this design could lead to advancements in ship sails, enhancing maneuverability and efficiency. Furthermore, with proper refinement, it may even serve as the foundation for the development of airships.

I eagerly anticipate the blessings the Goddess may bestow through Avatar Fournier's future discoveries.

[-----S-----]

Sallie Young blew gently on the ink, ensuring her journal entry dried quickly. Hours of meticulous work had gone into designing and constructing the kite for Avatar Fournier, and now exhaustion was beginning to settle in. She longed for a cup of jasmine tea, a moment of quiet, and then sleep.

As she set her journal aside, her thoughts drifted. *What new ideas would Avatar Fournier dream up next? And how could Sallie help bring them to life?* Surely, Regina could have her reassigned to serve directly under the Guide to the Avatars. Perhaps the Order would even create a new position for her Second Assistant, or Special Assistant. If that wasn't possible, she could always replace Ortega, *the mapmaker.* After all, her brilliant mind and scientific expertise would make her far more valuable to the avatars and through them, the goddesses.

Marcus wouldn't like it, of course. He would complain, like he always did. He would resist. But eventually, he would accept the new order of things. And if not? Well, then Sallie would happily replace him as the guide, and he could be her first assistant.

She took a slow sip of tea, letting the honey-sweetened warmth spread through her. The heat seeped into her tired limbs, easing her into the comfort of her chair. Her eyelids grew heavy, the warmth lulling her toward rest

Knock, knock.

Her eyes snapped open.

Surprised by a visitor at such a late hour, she reached into her shirt pocket and pulled out her watch. *Just after midnight.*

Could it be Regina? The silver-haired embodiment of the goddess had said she was going to bed... *but perhaps she had changed her mind?*

Sallie stood, collecting her brown hair into a quick ponytail as she walked to the door. "One minute, please," she called out.

Opening the door, she found herself face-to-face with an older woman.

The visitor wore black pants and a white shirt, the emblem of Saint Lorraine displayed on her shirt identifying her as a member of the Scribes of Saint Lorraine. Her blonde hair was pulled into a tight bun, but loose bangs framed either side of her face. Behind round eyeglasses, sharp eyes studied Sallie in return.

Sallie straightened slightly, her curiosity piqued.

This was unexpected.

"Sister Sallie Young?" the woman asked, her sharp eyes settling on her.

"Yes?" Sallie answered cautiously, wondering why this stranger was at her door at such a late hour.

"May I come in?" the woman said before stepping inside without waiting for permission.

Sallie blinked, momentarily taken aback by the woman's presumption. Who just walks into someone's room uninvited?

"Excuse me," Sallie protested, closing the door behind her. "I don't even know who you are."

The woman ignored the remark, walking straight to the desk. She casually closed Sallie's journal, then turned her chair to face the bed. With a motion toward it, she said, "Please, have a seat."

Sallie folded her arms. She was exhausted, irritated, and increasingly suspicious. "Look, Sister, it's late. How about you come back tomorrow?"

"Trust me," the woman said, leaning back in the chair as she pulled off her glasses and blew on the lenses. "You don't want that."

Something about the way she said it made Sallie pause.

With an exaggerated sigh, she relented. "All right." She shut the door and crossed the room, flopping onto the bed with an air of forced patience. If she didn't like what this woman had to say, she'd ask Regina to help her deal with this new problem.

"And who are you, exactly?" Sallie asked, eyeing her visitor.

The woman smiled as she replaced her glasses. "Forgive me. You can call me Sister Thomas." She leaned forward slightly. "You have quite the reputation among the Order's leadership."

Sallie perked up at that, a small smirk forming. "Oh, thank you," she said, pleased by the insinuation. "I try my best."

Sister Thomas's expression remained unreadable. "It's late, so let's skip the pleasantries, shall we?" She reached into her robe pocket and pulled out a rolled-up parchment.

Sallie tilted her head. "Fine by me."

The woman's voice took on a sharper edge. "You're treading a dangerous path, Sister. I suggest you step back before you get in over your head."

Sallie raised an eyebrow. "I don't know what you're talking about." She folded her hands in her lap, her tone deliberately mild. "I only offer my assistance to the Avatar of the Goddess when she requests it, just as any loyal member of the Order would."

Sister Thomas tilted her head slightly, watching her. "The Avatars can be... intoxicating. But girls of that age can also be fickle." She let the words settle before continuing. "It's important to remember that your duties should come before any side projects you may foresee coming from the Avatars."

Sallie stiffened. "Is this about Brother Thaddeus complaining that I didn't finish testing the shovel?" she asked, her voice laced with annoyance. "Anyone can finish that research. I was working on something important for the Avatar. The kite we made could revolutionize ship design. That's far more valuable than testing whether a shovel can be used to cut through rocks."

Sister Thomas's expression remained neutral. "And what if it doesn't?"

Sallie blinked. "What?"

"What if your kite doesn't lead to a monumental shift in society?" the woman pressed. "Should Brother Thaddeus simply assume you're too important to be assigned any routine work?"

Sallie rolled her eyes. "That would be nice. Why don't you go ahead and tell him that?"

Sister Thomas let out a slow breath, clearly holding back frustration. "Sister," she said, her tone softer now, "we serve the Order in the way we are called to serve." She studied Sallie with something almost like concern. "I've met monks like you before brilliant, driven, smarter than their own good. I've also seen them become the architects of their own downfall. To be honest I don't want that for you."

Sallie narrowed her eyes. "You've seen all this before," she said skeptically. Then, with a knowing smirk, she asked, "But have you ever met an Avatar of a Goddess?" She leaned forward slightly. "Because I don't understand how you can sit there and tell me that testing a shovel is more important than assisting the goddess herself."

"I have," Sister Thomas said cooly.

Sallie blinked. "You have what?"

"I have met an avatar," Sister Thomas clarified. "Three, in fact—Fiona, the gold avatar of hope; Emily, the red avatar of creativity; and Contessa, the white avatar of order." A somber expression crossed her face. "Those girls were extraordinary. They could have changed the world. But they died serving their Goddesses... barely after becoming avatars."

She paused, wiping away the tears gathering at the corners of her eyes before continuing. "I've watched my brothers and sisters in the Order see the potential the avatars represent, see them as opportunities. And I've watched them try to trick those girls to serve their own petty purposes." Her lips pressed into a thin line. "It disgusted me. It still does." Bile dripping from her words.

"Well, I'm not doing that," Sallie retorted. "I just want to serve the goddesses."

Sister Thomas exhaled through her nose. "You did it again."

"Did what?"

"You referred to the avatars as the goddesses." She folded her hands in her lap. "They aren't the same, Sister Young. The avatars are teenage girls not the timeless twelve goddesses of the pantheon."

Sallie scoffed. "It was just a slip of the tongue."

Sister Thomas tilted her head, studying her. "No, it wasn't." A beat of silence passed before she continued. "You believe Regina and the goddess of Change are one and the same." Her voice softened just a fraction. "If you truly wish to serve the avatars, you must first learn to separate the girl from the goddess."

Sallie crossed her arms. "I'll keep that in mind next time I see Regina."

Sister Thomas sighed. "That's what I need to talk to you about. You shouldn't see the avatar at least for a while."

Sallie's arms tightened over her chest. "And who are you to tell me that?"

"I am someone who knows your history," Sister Thomas replied calmly. "Someone who has seen people like you, brilliant, ambitious, full of potential become consumed by the power and possibilities the avatars represent."

"I'm not consumed by anything," Sallie snapped. "I just enjoy spending time with godde…" She caught herself. "Regina. We made a kite together earlier. That's all."

Sister Thomas removed her glasses and pinched the bridge of her nose before sliding them back on. "I'd wager that, right now, in that intelligent mind of yours, you're already scheming a way to formalize your involvement with the Avatars." She met Sallie's gaze. "Most likely, you're planning to replace the First Assistant. *And if Marcus protests?* You're ready to replace him too." She paused, letting the weight of her words settle. "How close am I?"

Sallie hesitated for half a second just enough to betray herself.

"Would it be so wrong if I did spend all my time assisting Regina?" she challenged. "What does that *mapmaker* have that I don't?" she did not waste her time hiding her indignation towards Marcus' first assistant.

Sister Thomas gave her a flat look. "I'm not going to waste my time answering that."

Silence stretched between them before she continued. "Your reputation precedes you, Sister Sallie Young. You are intelligent very intelligent. But you are also stubborn, headstrong, and reckless. Your supervisors acknowledge your brilliance, yet every report I've read describes the same pattern, you take risks instead of building contingencies to ensure the success of your projects. You make your sect less effective, not more."

Sallie scoffed. "Let me guess Brother Thaddeus told you that?"

"It wasn't Brother Thaddeus," Sister Thomas corrected. "I read Brother Nathaniel's report when you left the College of Sages." She regarded Sallie carefully. "Have you ever wondered why you've changed sects so many times?"

Sallie frowned. "People change sects when they return to Order Island from scribe duty. It's all too normal."

Sister Thomas raised an eyebrow. "Not as many times as you have."

Sallie opened her mouth to argue but stopped herself. Instead, she asked, "…Honestly, why are you here, Sister?"

Sister Thomas's expression softened. "Because Brother Marcus values your friendship."

Sallie narrowed her eyes. "So, he sent you. Is that it?"

"No," Sister Thomas replied evenly. "In fact, if he knew I was here, he'd probably ask me not to interfere."

She handed Sallie the rolled-up paper she had been holding. "Believe it or not, I'm here to help you," she said. "Do me a favor and read this."

Sallie took the paper, unrolling it as she skimmed the contents. At first glance, it looked like an assignment order with her name on it. But as she read further, her stomach twisted.

It wasn't an assignment order.

It was an expulsion order.

She scanned the words again, hoping she had misread them. But no, it was clear as day. She was to be removed from the Order of Saint Lorraine. She would be given one hundred and fifty gold coins and transported to a port of her choice.

Her hands trembled.

Her vision blurred as tears welled up. "What… what is this?" she whispered, the words barely escaping her lips.

"It's an expulsion order," Sister Thomas confirmed. "With your name on it."

Sallie looked up, betrayal and confusion battling in her expression. "But… why? This doesn't make any sense."

Sister Thomas exhaled softly. "When I heard about it, I decided to step in and stop it." She met Sallie's gaze. "This time."

"But… why?" Sallie choked out, tears streaming down her face. "Did Thaddeus do this?"

"No," Sister Thomas said calmly. "He only asked for assistance in getting you to understand that your duties should come before your personal relationships." She folded her hands in her lap. "The council reviewed your record and saw a pattern neglected duties, frequent transfers between sects. In the end, they determined that you weren't serving the Order… you were looking for the Order to serve you."

Sallie's breath hitched as Sister Thomas continued. "They voted on your expulsion." She paused. "And you lost."

Sallie swallowed hard, barely able to breathe.

"But I chose to intervene on your behalf," Sister Thomas added, her tone softening. "I asked them to reconsider. After weighing your potential contributions, they agreed to give you a second chance."

Sallie wiped at her eyes. "Why would you do that?"

"Because I appreciate everything you did to assist Brother Marcus and Regina these past few days," Sister Thomas said. "And because I know how intoxicating being in an avatar's presence can be." She met Sallie's gaze her green eyes as hard as Stoneridge steel. "But let me be clear this is your opportunity to sober up. I won't intercede for you again."

Sister Thomas stood and held out her hand.

Sallie hesitated before handing back the expulsion order. "Thank you, Sister," she murmured, her voice subdued. "I'm sorry for any trouble I caused."

Sister Thomas offered a small smile. "No need to apologize." She turned toward the door. "If you'll excuse me, Sister I'm as tired as a *mapmaker*." The remark made it clear she'd heard the insult toward Marcus' first assistant.

With that, she walked out.

Sallie's gaze lingered on the door, watching as it clicked shut.

"…Good night, Sister," she whispered.

Slowly, she moved through her nightly routine: removing her uniform, placing it in the laundry bag, and changing into her sleeping clothes. She sat on the edge of her bed, staring at the floor.

For the first time, she truly considered what her life would have been like if she had been cast out of the Order. *Out in the world*, as the monks said. *What would she have done? Where would she have gone?*

She had been a breath away from exile. A single favor away from being dropped off at a port with nothing but one hundred and fifty gold coins to her name.

The thought was unbearable.

Her shoulders shook as fresh tears spilled down her cheeks.

She must let go of her plans involving Regina.

There is no choice.

With a quiet, resigned sob, Sallie buried her face in her hands.

She could not afford to make a mistake like this again.

Epilogue 2 – Jules Fournier

Jules Fournier was somewhere in the Seven Kingdoms a place he had never seen before.

Four days earlier, while his family was carrying out their duties as caretakers of The Luminous, a group led woman had arrived. She took his son, Matthew, hostage, forcing Jules to board a boat docked behind the Luminous. Now, he sat in a dimly lit bedroom, watching over his sleeping son.

Matthew suffered frequent crying fits, overwhelmed with guilt. He blamed himself for being caught by the Bloody Axe Woman, as he had started calling her. He believed his capture made it possible for Jules to be taken, never realizing she could have taken Jules by force anyway.

He tried to comfort his son, telling him there was nothing he could have done. But the words felt hollow. June had always been better at these things. For a fleeting moment, he wished his wife were with them then immediately reminded himself that her absence was a blessing. If June wasn't here, maybe she and Regina were safe. Maybe someone was coming for them.

The Order of Saint Lorraine had managed to send a message, confirming Regina was with them, doing something important. He could only hope the Order, along with the Aurorium Clan, would find them before it was too late.

The door creaked open with a deep, mechanical, heavy, too loud for an ordinary bedroom door. Though it appeared to be white-painted wood from the inside, the weight of the hinges and the metallic clang made one thing clear: the door was solid metal.

Jules turned just as she entered.

The Bloody Axe Woman.

She strode into the room, her crimson-stained dress still damp in places, her expression cold and unreadable. In her right hand, she held what appeared to be a metal ink pen, its surface carved with runes.

"Stand up," she ordered, impatience edging her tone.

Jules rose slowly, meeting her gaze. "Why are we here?" he demanded.

The woman ignored his question. "Hold out your hand."

Jules clenched his fists. "I will not comply until you give me an answer." Standing as strong as he could against this foe, she did not appear to have her large Axe with her maybe Jules could overpower her.

A smile ghosted across her lips. "Monsieur Fournier," she said, tilting her head, "how much do you love your son?"

Jules stiffened. The threat in her words was clear.

He instinctively moved between her and the sleeping Matthew, his body a shield. "I won't let you harm him."

The woman didn't move; the blood soaked into her dress however did. The liquid detached itself, swirling upward in a slow, unnatural motion. It gathered into a ball midair, pulsing like a living thing. Then, with a flick of her finger, the sphere shot forward morphing into a razor-sharp shard it rushed past Jules and stabbed into the wall just above Matthew's stomach.

Jules spun, breath catching in his throat.

Matthew hadn't stirred. He was unharmed. But the blood-made projectile was lodged deep in the wall mere inches from his son's sleeping form.

His body went cold, as it became so very clear that *he would not be overpowering anyone today.* Slowly, he turned back to the woman.

She raised an eyebrow. "I already told you what to do."

Jules hesitated only a moment before lifting his left hand, palm open in reluctant surrender.

Without warning, she drove the metal rod into his flesh.

Jules hissed in pain as the runes on the rod flared to life. His blood surged toward it, wrapping around the metal in twisting tendrils until every carved symbol was covered in red, they then began to glow with energy.

Satisfied, the woman yanked the rod from his hand. Without another word, she turned and walked toward the door.

Jules took a shaky breath. "Please," he said, his voice raw. "At least tell me why we're here."

The woman paused at the threshold. "You are here," she said her words cold as ice from the mountain tops of Stoneridge. "to do as you are told."

Then she stepped out. The heavy door slammed shut behind her, sealing them in once more.

[-----J-----]

"I can't open it," Jules said to Hema, the Blood-Axe Woman. His voice was steady, but inside, frustration gnawed at him.

He gestured toward the stone door embedded in the stone wall. Above it, a series of unfamiliar symbols were carved into the stone, and on the door itself, cube-shaped stone blocks with numbers etched into them fit into matching recesses.

"The symbols make no sense," he continued, running a hand through his disheveled hair. "They could be instructions to arrange the number blocks according to the size of the world, or they could be saying, *this isn't the door.*"

Hema stood motionless, her staff slung across her back. The tan ropes securing it contrasted starkly with the deep, dried red of her blood-soaked dress. Her eyes, however, held nothing but impatience.

"You're lying," she said flatly.

Jules took a breath, carefully choosing his words. "Mistress Hema," he wasn't sure how he knew her name. It had simply come to him one day, as if whispered into his mind. "I do know the size of the world, but when I arrange the blocks in the correct order, the door doesn't open." He hesitated. "There may be a gap in my understanding. If I knew where we were, that might help me solve this problem." He kept his voice measured. *Don't provoke her. Don't show frustration.* Mistress Hema had proven herself volatile over the past few days, and he had no desire to test her patience.

332

Hema regarded him for a long moment. Then she smiled.

Jules' stomach twisted, sure something terrible was coming.

"DADDY! DADDY! DADDY!"

The scream tore through the wooden enclosure.

Jules whirled around to gaze upon his son.

Matthew was behind him his small frame engulfed in a writhing mass of blood. The liquid slithered up from the ground, creeping over his legs, winding around his torso like a living cocoon. The boy frantically swiped at the encroaching red, but his struggle only spread it further, coating his hands, climbing up his arms.

Jules' breath caught in his throat as Matthew fell, thrashing against the viscous prison swallowing him.

A surge of instinct *pure, rage* propelled Jules forward. He spun back toward Hema, fists clenched. Only to find the massive axe point at his throat after a step.

The curved blades formed a perfect triangle, trapping him before he could so much as lunge.

Hema tilted her head. "Were you told to strike me?" she asked deadly ice in her voice.

Jules' pulse thundered in his ears. "…No, Mistress," he said through gritted teeth, forcing himself to remain still.

The axe withdrew, its blade gliding back from his neck with excruciating slowness.

Jules exhaled in relief, then gasped as Hema's foot crashed into his midsection.

The force of the kick sent him to the ground, pain ripping through his ribs. He curled inward, trying to draw breath, but the impact had stolen the air from his lungs.

Behind him, Matthew's wails filled the enclosure.

Jules tried to rise, but before he could move, the weight of Hema's battle axe settled against his spine, pinning him in place.

"Please, Mistress," he rasped, his forehead pressed against the dirty ground. His entire body trembled from the effort of speaking. "Please… spare my son. I will open the door."

"Why is that?" Hema asked.

Jules swallowed hard. "Because… I was told to open the door."

Hema's blade lifted. "Then get back to work," she ordered, sliding the axe back into its sling the blade retracting into the staff just as she finally releases it.

Jules lay there for a moment, panting through the pain. His ribs burned, his body protested, but he forced himself upright. Behind him, the blood binding Matthew receded, slithering back toward Hema's dress as if drawn to her.

Matthew sobbed, trembling as he crumpled to the ground.

Jules staggered toward him, gathering the boy into his arms. "It's okay, Mattie," he whispered, pressing his cheek to his son's hair. "It's okay." His lie the only comfort he can provide.

"It's not," Matthew whimpered. "I miss Mom."

Jules clenched his jaw, willing himself not to break. "Me too, son," he admitted.

A voice smashed the moment. "Get back to work." Her orders are quite clear.

Jules looked up.

Hema sat in a chair a few steps away, watching them with an unreadable expression.

He squeezed Matthew's shoulder one last time before gently letting him go. If he didn't… there would be more *lessons*.

"Yes, Mistress," Jules called back, turning toward the door once more.

Ignoring the pain clawing at his ribs, he grabbed his scratch book from the ground and flipped it open.

The symbols above the door. The number blocks. The surrounding walls.
He had missed something. *He must figure this out!*
Before Hema gave him another lesson.

Autor Bio

Jackson Owens has been creating stories since childhood, driven by a love of imaginative worlds and compelling characters. His goal is simple: to craft tales worthy of sharing shelf space with the books that inspired him. When he isn't writing, Jackson works in information technology and enjoys playing guitar, experimenting with 3D printing, and dreaming up new adventures.

www.ingramcontent.com/pod-product-compliance
Lightning Source LLC
Chambersburg PA
CBHW011514240626
47154CB00010B/3022